I0611726

Vienna

The Savage Brood: Book Three

Emyll O'Bryan

Copyright © 2017 by Emyll O'Bryan.

All rights reserved. Without limiting the rights under copyright reserved above, no part of this publication may be reproduced, stored in or introduced into a database or retrieval system, or transmitted, in any form or by any means (electronic, mechanical, photocopying, recording or otherwise), without permission of the copyright owner of this book except in cases of brief quotations embodied in critical articles and reviews. Please do not participate in or encourage piracy of copyrighted materials in violation of the author's rights. Purchase only authorized editions.

Cover design by Emyll O'Bryan, featuring *Theater an der Wien* by Jakob Alt, 1815.

This book is a work of fiction. Names, characters, places and incidents either are a product of the author's imagination or are used fictitiously. Any resemblance to actual persons, living or dead, events, or locales is entirely coincidental.

This edition published by Jade Publishing Company, P.O. Box 240, Austin, AR 72007.

NOTICE: This work may contain descriptions of adult situations, including language, nudity, sex, and violence, some readers may find objectionable. It is intended for mature audiences only, and reader discretion is advised.

ISBN:
978-1-944040-08-6

Acknowledgements

I want to continue to express my gratitude to all the researchers and historians without whom my work would be impossible. I would specifically like to thank the folks at the David Rumsey Map Collection, firstly. What can I say? Your site has been of inestimable help to me from book one. I'd also like to thank AEIOU, the Austrian Cultural Information System, and ANNO, Austrian Newspapers Online. For the wonderful information you provide to us poor souls without passports, free of charge, *danke*. Lastly, I would like to thank explographies.com. The information you provide on the catacombs of Paris was invaluable. *Merci*.

As always, I would like to thank Ann. You've been impatient for it, so here 'tis. Thanks for the Japanese translations I didn't get to use, but there's always next time. And the Russian…we can't forget the Russian. I couldn't get away without thanking Phil, too. Thanks for being my sounding board. Even if you don't want to hear it, I'm still going to thank you.

And finally, thank you, reader, for coming along again. Without you, the words are only ink splotches on a page.

Emyll O'Bryan
October 25, 2017

This one is for Darla, because you said I could.

Chapter One

Plink! Plink! Plink! Plink!

Persephone frowned with her eyes closed and rolled onto her stomach, putting a pillow over her head.

Plink! Plink…! Plink! Plink!

Persephone groaned and pulled the pillow even tighter against her ears. It was too early. She had been up late playing cards with some of the stable hands, and she really wanted to sleep. Just once…just *one* day, Persephone wished Eurydice would give it a rest. After several minutes of silence, she began to grow hopeful that was the case and started to drift off to sleep again.

Plink! Plink! Plink! Plink! Plink!

"Bloody hell!" groaned Persephone in aggravation.

She threw the pillow across the room and tossed the covers aside. She blearily tumbled out of the bed and stalked toward the door, muttering under her breath and cursing even more when she stubbed her pinkie toe on the raised edge of a rug near the exit. She went the short distance down the hall to the next room and entered without knocking. Then she went to her sister, snatched the offending item out of her hands, and dealt with the situation. She calmly handed it back and folded her arms across her chest expectantly.

Eurydice looked from one to the other.

"You broke my G string," she said dryly.

"Be glad I didn't break the whole bloody thing!" bit out Persephone. "Two hours. Either give me two hours or go elsewhere."

"Where am I supposed to go?"

"I don't care, Dicy. Try the solarium. Psyche has moved most of her stuff out, so she won't mind. Will you, *please,* just give me two more hours?"

Eurydice looked at her younger sister. It *was* early, and she did look tired. It was just the thought of climbing all those stairs, and Eurydice liked the acoustics of her bedroom. She liked the projection and reverberation that resulted from her careful arrangement of her belongings over the years. But this wasn't the first time Persephone had broken a string on her violin. She had been doing it a lot more often of late. Eurydice's replacements were dwindling.

"Oh, all right. I'll go to the solarium."

Persephone smiled with relief and gave her sister a kiss on the cheek. "Thank you. I'm sorry about the string."

"Mm-hmm," said Eurydice noncommittally. "If you break another one, *you'll* have to buy my new strings."

"I will buy you a dozen more if you will just let me sleep two more hours."

Eurydice shrugged and went to her desk to get another string for her violin. She put her instrument and the string in the case and closed it. Then, she went to her stand for the folio she was practicing and the stand itself. Once she had her things, she looked at Persephone with a grin.

"You know, your temper would improve remarkably if you weren't up playing cards until all hours."

"No, it would improve if you would wait till after breakfast to play."

"Humph," said Eurydice as Persephone opened the door for her. "You'll only have to suffer through it until August. Then you'll be missing it."

"Don't bet on it," said Persephone with a cheeky grin.

Persephone went down the hall to her bedroom, and Eurydice sighed resignedly as she turned in the opposite direction to go down the hall to the stairs for the tower. She made sure she had a firm hold on her things and began to climb. By the time she made it to the top of the stairs, she was slightly winded, and she paused for a moment on the landing to catch her breath. She supposed if she made the climb more often, it wouldn't be so tiring.

She pushed the door open with a shove of her shoulder and looked at the large room. It was bright from all the windows, and the sun that shined in also made the room warm enough she wouldn't need to light a fire. The solarium was mostly empty except for a few bare work-tables and three or four large wooden crates that held the remainder of her sister's belongings. They would very soon be sent to the Isle of Sheppey, probably the day after tomorrow when the family left for London. At the end of the Season, neither Psyche nor her things would be returning to Wilderland, their family's home in Wales.

The reason for that was nothing catastrophic; she was simply getting married. Eurydice thought it was rather bizarre that her sister was looking forward to it and was even impatient for it. Her future husband, the Earl of Sheerness, was a nice man, and it was obvious he cared a great deal for Psyche, but Eurydice had never imagined Psyche would be that excited about binding herself to a man for the rest of her life. Then again, Pandora, Psyche's identical twin, had been equally thrilled to get married almost two years ago. Not only that, but she was happy to have *children.*

It left Eurydice bumfuzzled because she and her four sisters weren't what she herself would have thought to be marriageable. Eurydice supposed she would get married as well...one day, but she couldn't see herself being as enthusiastic as Psyche or Pandora were. At least Persephone and Arachne still showed absolutely no interest in getting married. That made Eurydice relieved because she knew once they married...if they married, her own solitude would be considered a shortcoming...if only to people outside their family.

As she set her case on one of the work-tables, Eurydice realized she owed a debt of gratitude to Psyche and her fiancé. If Psyche hadn't gone with him to Greece the previous year, their parents would most likely still not have been willing to let Eurydice make her own trip to Vienna at the end of this Season in August. Not only that, but the newlyweds were going to be her chaperones—at least to Venice. She was very grateful for that because she had not been looking forward to making the entire journey over land. Going with them would allow her to go at least half the distance by ship. Going by sea wouldn't make the journey any shorter, but she was willing for it to take a little longer if it meant traveling comfortably.

Psyche's trip the previous year had been planned, but then again, not. It had been intended for her to go with Lord Sheerness, but their brother Myron was to have gone as well to be her chaperone. But he had been killed in a duel last June—a senseless tragedy that had left his family reeling. After it had happened, Psyche had thought she would no longer be going. Then Pandora had tricked her onto Lord Sheerness's ship, and she had gone after all. Eurydice's parents, the Duke and Duchess of Aberdare, had consented to let Eurydice go to Vienna under the terms of Psyche's original plans, but they hadn't changed their minds when those plans were drastically altered. They hadn't even called it to a halt when Psyche returned engaged to Sheerness.

Even still, Eurydice's trip was almost canceled...by her own choice. Their brother Gregory was killed in January in another senseless tragedy. He had been working for the War Office during the conflict with the United States, even if he hadn't been commissioned or enlisted in the Navy. He had been home at the beginning of December to bring his new wife, Annabelle, to stay with his family to await the birth of their first child. Just weeks after he returned to service, word of the Treaty of Ghent, ending the war, reached his family. They were elated the conflict was over, and that Gregory had survived without even a scratch had given them greater cause to celebrate. Word of the treaty didn't reach America in time. Gregory was killed in a skirmish with an American frigate that also claimed Harold Granger, Annabelle's father. Gregory was only twenty-two, and now his only child would be born never knowing its father.

The duke and duchess took the loss very hard, the duchess particularly so. Gregory was buried at sea, which was appropriate, but Julia, the duchess, had no body to mourn, no final look at her son, just a box of his belongings that had been rescued from his irreparably damaged ship before it was scuttled. The duchess had developed silver streaks at her temples, seemingly overnight, which stood out starkly against the black of the rest of her hair. To have lost two of her sons in less than a year was almost unbearable.

When Myron died, it had been unexpected, but it had been a foreseeable outcome. He had even written letters to his family and friends, delivered after his death, providing his farewells and final wishes. With Gregory, there had been nothing but his loss. There had not even been a will; he was so young, he had not anticipated he would need one. And so his family was left with nothing but an empty hole where he used to be.

Annabelle was stoically bearing the loss of her husband and father. Being the daughter of a ship's captain, from a family with a long history of military service, had seemingly bred stolidity into her character, but she and Gregory had truly been in love and married for less than a year. She was devastated. There was no question of her staying with the Aberdares. She was due to deliver the baby in May, and knowing at least part of Gregory would live on gave her the strength to survive. That his family had accepted her as one of their own was also of great comfort.

It had been Annabelle who convinced Eurydice that she still needed to go to Vienna. She was sure her husband wouldn't have wanted his family to lose themselves to their grief. The duke and duchess followed Annabelle's wishes on the matter, and they, too, voiced the opinion that Eurydice should still go. She had only made up her mind that she would almost a week ago.

Psyche, too, had almost altered her plans to marry Sheerness…as difficult as that had been for both of them. His home, Belle Glade, on Sheppey in Kent, was almost entirely on the other side of the country from Wilderland, which was near Glyncorrwg in Glamorgan. The two of them had seen each other rarely since their return from Greece. They were constantly sending letters back and forth to one another, and their desire to be close was one of the reasons the Aberdares would be going to London for the season, even though they would not be attending any social functions because of Gregory's death. Sheerness would have to be there for Parliament, so the affianced pair would be able to see each other every day, even if they couldn't get married yet.

As Eurydice tuned the new string on her violin, she puzzled over Psyche and Sheerness. The thing that caused her confusion was how the two of them had gone from barely tolerating one another to apparently being unable to live without each other. Psyche had begun to do what could only be considered *moping*. Sheerness had come to Wilderland for a brief stay shortly after the beginning of the year and again after they received news of Gregory's death. During the time in between and since, when Psyche wasn't burying herself in her work translating hieroglyphs and deciphering a map on the back of a necklace she had received as a gift the previous year, she walked around with a wan expression, emitting sighs of melodramatic woe. Eurydice had gotten to the point that she avoided Psyche at times because her mawkishness was trying. It was difficult enough tolerating Persephone's irrational behavior, but at least her younger sister's attitude was more understandable.

Persephone had been very close to both Myron and Gregory, and now they were gone. Her already unruly temperament had become edged with sarcasm and surliness of late. Eurydice understood it was her younger sister's way of dealing with the loss of her brothers, and she was hopeful Persephone's frolicsome cheer would eventually return. Since Annabelle had joined their family, the two of them had become very close friends, and the older girl's presence seemed to provide a calming influence. Perhaps by the time Eurydice returned from Vienna, Persephone would return to something of her former self. She did at least have a reprieve from being debuted into society until next year. For a girl like Persy, who preferred breeches and boots to gowns, the London season would be sheer torture. Eurydice wasn't so sure society was going to be able to tolerate her any more than she could tolerate it...not if she didn't become less of a termagant.

Once Eurydice had her strings tuned to her satisfaction, she set the folio onto her stand in the center of the room. It was large and cavernous from the open ceiling above exposing the rafters and mostly empty, but she had noticed as she walked across the floor that there wasn't a lot of unwanted echoing despite this. She settled the violin beneath her chin and drew the bow across the strings. She raised her head and looked around herself in surprise. The sound quality of the room was extraordinary. She played an arpeggio, and a wide grin spread across her face. The climb to the top of the stairs was worth every panting breath she had taken.

She began to practice the piece by Haydn, and the fun of the composition and the pleasure she received from listening to the sound of her instrument in the solarium soon made her lose track of time. She was so focused on what she was doing that she nearly dropped her violin when her maid, Agniezka, tapped her on the shoulder to get her attention. Eurydice squeaked and looked at her in round-eyed surprise.

"I brought you a tray with some breakfast," chortled Agniezka at her reaction.

"*Spasibo*. I didn't know it was that late."

"I suspected as much. It is already 10:00, and the rest of your family has finished eating."

Eurydice went to the work-table where Agniezka had set the tray and looked at what her maid had brought: eggs, bacon, fried potatoes, toast, sliced tomatoes, and a pot of coffee. It was unsurprising Agniezka would bring that. She had been Eurydice's maid since she was nine years old. After ten years, she knew exactly what her mistress would like to eat. What did surprise Eurydice was that Agniezka had known to find her in the solarium.

"How did you find me?" she asked as she began to nibble on a piece of bacon after carefully laying her violin into its case. She fully intended to resume practicing after she ate her breakfast. She couldn't believe she had never played in the solarium before.

"I could hear you playing, so I knew you had to be somewhere in the castle. When I found you weren't in your room, I had Oba rout your sister from bed long enough to tell where she had chased you off to." Agniezka shook her head. "That girl gets wilder every day. Your mother and father are going to have a very difficult time with her next year. I doubt they will be able to get her out of the house."

"She's just sad…and angry. She did everything with Myron and Gregory, and now she's lost them both…for no good reason." Eurydice shrugged. "I think they were the only ones in our family who really understood her. It's just going to take some time for her to move beyond it. I don't think she'll ever be the same as she was when they were here, but she needs time to accept it."

"Humph," said Agniezka doubtfully. "Someone needs to give her a good spank."

Eurydice chuckled. "Don't think Oba hasn't tried."

"Oh, I know," agreed Agniezka with a chuckle of her own. "I've started packing your things for London already. You'll be out of mourning when we leave in August."

"I know. I ordered some things made when Janet came up to see about Psyche's trousseau. She should have them ready and sent up to Town in plenty of time."

"Are you intending to take Amati?"

"No, I'm going to leave him here. I hardly ever ride him when we're in Town, and I especially won't be now. He'll be happier in the meadow. I'll ride one of the other horses should I need to, but I don't think I will."

Agniezka nodded approvingly. Last season, Eurydice had only gone to the park three times. The rest of the time, the horse had been ridden by Jim, one of the family's drivers, while he accompanied Psyche for her daily rides.

"Are you going to take all your instruments?" asked Agniezka. She would have to find another trunk if that were the case.

Eurydice frowned thoughtfully as she ate a piece of toast. "I'll definitely be taking *La Ragazza Dolce*." She shrugged. "I think I'll take the Stainer and possibly the Guadagnini. The Tecchler and the Amati can stay."

"Yes, I think three will be enough," said Agniezka, her lips twitching. "Exactly how many violins can one play at a time?"

"Oh, I don't know. I think I'll take my Quantz," said Eurydice as an afterthought.

"The flute?" asked Agniezka in surprise. Eurydice only practiced with it for a few hours once a week, and she played beautifully, but her violin was her passion and was her reason for going to Vienna in the first instance.

"I do need it to practice or to play if I write a composition for it. I'm not going to look for a teacher, but I don't want to become rusty. I hope Miss Mahone has a piano."

Agniezka's expression grew even more puzzled. The piano was also another instrument that Eurydice played extremely well—almost as well as the violin—but, like the flute, was one she only practiced for a few hours a week. Agniezka suspected once Eurydice found a maestro, her time to practice either would be reduced even more. Still, there was no knowing how long it would take her. The maid also idly wondered if her grace had prepared Miss Mahone for how incessant Eurydice was with her practice. Her family had grown accustomed to it, but even they were tried by it at times, as Persephone's evicting her sister from her bedroom that morning had demonstrated.

"You could ask your mother about that, I suppose."

"Yes, I'm sure she would know."

The two of them continued to talk about things that would need to be packed for the journey to London and things that would need to be brought along for their trip to Vienna in August while Eurydice continued to eat. As Lord Sheerness had his ship moored at the docks in London, they would be leaving from there, which simplified things. Eurydice supposed she could send someone back to Wilderland should she forget something, but it would be so much more convenient if she just remembered to take it from the beginning.

Just as Eurydice was finishing her breakfast, Psyche came into the room. She was just as startled to see her younger sister there with her maid as they were to see her come through the door.

"Oh," said Psyche dully.

"Why didn't you tell me the solarium had such a wonderful sound?" blurted Eurydice.

Psyche frowned. "It does? Pan and I don't play instruments, Dicy. How would we know?"

"Here we are leaving for London the day after tomorrow, and you have been hiding the best place in the house to play."

"I *did* ask if you wanted to practice up here more than a year ago, if you'll remember, but you said you weren't interested," said Psyche defensively. Her expression turned gloomy, and she shrugged dismissively. "In any event, now you can have it all to yourself when you come back from Vienna."

"You didn't come here to mope, did you?" asked Eurydice exasperatedly.

"Maybe," said Psyche noncommittally.

"Oh, for pity's sake! You'll be seeing him in four days…five at the most."

Psyche's eyes grew teary. "I know," she squeaked. "It's not just that. I *do* miss Sebastian, but I'm not going to be *here* anymore, and I miss Myron and Gregory, and I miss Pandora…and…and…oh!" she wailed strickenly.

Eurydice and Agniezka exchanged long-suffering glances. Agniezka silently held out a handkerchief to her mistress, and Eurydice went to her sister to give it to her and put a comforting arm around her shoulders. She guided her over to the window seat and sat beside her. She had the distinct feeling she would not be getting any practicing done for a while. Eurydice patted Psyche's shoulder while she wiped at her eyes with a shake of her head.

"I'm sorry," said Psyche on a hiccup. "I really *hate* being so maudlin, and I know you don't like it, Dicy."

"That's true," agreed Eurydice bluntly. "And I honestly don't understand it at all…not really." She clicked her teeth. "He's only a man, and you'll be seeing Dodo when we get to London, too."

Psyche's eyes widened. "Oh, Dicy, you really don't understand. Maybe one day you will."

"I certainly hope not," said Eurydice shortly.

"All right, then, Dicy. Let me try to put it into a perspective you *will* understand. Imagine how you would feel if you couldn't play your violin…at all…. What if you couldn't even *look* at your violin?"

"Which one?"

"None of them."

Eurydice blinked. She wouldn't like that a bit. It was unlikely it would ever happen, but still….

"How did it happen?" asked Eurydice with a puzzled frown. "How did you become so…I don't know…*addicted*?"

"I don't know, but I'm happy."

Eurydice chuckled amusedly. "Are you really? Is that why you walk around like Ophelia?"

"Well, I'm not right now…I suppose, but when I am *with* Sebastian, I'm very happy. I sleep better and longer. I feel at peace."

Eurydice looked at her sister in surprise. Everyone in their family knew Psyche suffered from insomnia. Not only that, but she also woke with the sun, sometimes before. For her to have a solution to her sleep difficulties was miraculous. Could it really be attributed to just Lord Sheerness? Eurydice didn't see how that was possible. As she had said, he was only a man. But she could understand passion…in a way, and she couldn't imagine what her life would be like if she could no longer play her violin. It was like breathing.

Before Psyche had gone to Greece, before she had become engaged to Sheerness, Eurydice would have thought antiquities and languages were her greatest passion. She still spent a lot of time with her work, and her future husband was willing to let her pursue it once they were married, even encouraged it. Pandora still worked with chemistry and her other pastimes since she married, too. But Eurydice didn't see how there could be room for two loves for her. Music was her life. It was the only thing that mattered.

At least Psyche's tears had stopped. Her expression was still wistful, but she wasn't leaking anymore, and for that, Eurydice was grateful. Her sister was usually very calm and practical, and to see her so unlike either of those was discomfiting. Eurydice looked forward to going to London if only to have a reprieve from her sister's recent histrionics. Of the twins, Pandora was the more dramatic, but one wouldn't know that from Psyche's present condition.

"Mamà was looking for you at breakfast," said Psyche dully after she blew her nose.

"Why?"

"I think it has something to do with who is to be your chaperone once you leave Venice. I think that's been settled."

"Hmm," said Eurydice thoughtfully. She looked back to her violin on the work-table longingly. "I suppose I should go see what she wanted."

8

"It will still be there when you come back, Dicy," said Psyche with a grin.

Eurydice walked up the stairs to the solarium with a thoughtful frown. She had gone to see her mother, finding Psyche's thoughts proved to be correct about why the duchess had wanted to speak with her. Eurydice knew she had to agree to what her parents had arranged or else not go, but she wasn't sure she was going to like it much.

The duchess told Eurydice her old friend, Mrs. Ellsworth, would be her chaperone. That by itself was not the problem. She liked Mrs. Ellsworth and had known her since she was a little girl. The problem lay in the fact that Mrs. Ellsworth would also be escorting her four grandchildren, one of whom would only be a year old. None of the other three were older than six. While Eurydice adored her younger brothers and her three nephews, the children of other people made her uncomfortable. If the truth be told, the reason she cared for her younger brothers and nephews as much as she did was because she saw them rarely. Her brothers, the eleven-year-old twins, Cosmo and Christopher, and the nine-year-old Damon were tended by Nanny Bixley or her mother. Her nephews, Pandora's twins, Alex and Myron, and Thomas, Dorian and his wife Selena's son, did not live in the castle at Wilderland; although, Dorian and Selena did live in a lodge on the property. She wasn't sure how well she would do traveling with strange, *young* children by coach for several days.

Eurydice was sympathetic to the reason the children would be going to live with their grandmother. It seemed heartache was visiting everywhere. The children had lost both their parents in a carriage accident in Dorset the previous June, just days before Myron had been killed in the duel. The youngest child, Corinna, had been born prematurely as a result of the accident. Mrs. Ellsworth had needed to wait this long to take them with her to Austria because they had been unsure whether the little girl would live. As it was, Corinna would be little more than a year old in August when they left. It wasn't going to be an easy journey, which was part of the reason Mrs. Ellsworth would be making much of it by sea and would be in Venice to provide Eurydice her chaperone.

With the death of Natalie Windham, Mrs. Ellsworth's daughter and the mother of her four grandchildren, Mrs. Ellsworth was left with one surviving son, Gareth. Eurydice had met him once, almost two years ago, when he came with his mother to a dinner party given in honor of her parents' anniversary. She wasn't sure what her opinion was of him. Her mother had told her that he was musically inclined, but Eurydice had been unable to engage him in conversation. He was polite, and he didn't seem arrogant—just offish. He had spoken briefly with her father, and when there were more people for him to talk to besides her, he would speak…somewhat. Going from that, Eurydice could only assume there was something about her personally that he found unappealing. Eurydice was unsurprised…and unbothered.

She wasn't sure if he would be traveling with his mother. Eurydice could only assume not. He was a grown man, so it wasn't as if he had to go wherever his mother went. The duchess hadn't mentioned whether he was even in England. He wasn't titled, so he wasn't in Parliament…as far as Eurydice knew. She didn't think he was in the Commons. She could be wrong. She knew nothing about him, other than what he looked like. Actually, since she had only seen him once, and his personality hadn't left a lasting impression, she couldn't be sure she would even know him if she saw him again.

She tried to remember what he looked like. The memory was very vague. He was tall like her brothers…even taller perhaps. She didn't remember him being thin or heavy, but she also didn't remember if he was well-built, either. His hair was some dark color. It might have been black, but it could have just as easily been some shade of brown. As for his eyes, she could not remember at all. She didn't recall whether or not he had actually made eye contact. She might be able to remember what color his eyes had been if he had actually *looked* at her. Mrs. Ellsworth's eyes were blue. Eurydice could only assume his were as well. In the end, she decided it didn't matter whether she could remember what he looked like because she wouldn't be seeing him.

Eurydice supposed she would be able to tolerate the children for the carriage ride. She wasn't sure what kind of vehicle it would be. It could be the continental equivalent of a mail coach, but the more she thought about it, the more she suspected Mrs. Ellsworth would hire a private one. With four children, herself, Eurydice, Agniezka, possibly (probably) a nanny, and Mrs. Ellsworth's lady's maid, it would make riding in a mail coach very crowded. Not only that, but there would be the luggage to consider. Eurydice would have three trunks of her own. She could only imagine how much everyone else would have. Because the children were going to live with their grandmother permanently, they would be carrying all of their belongings, including toys and other things they had wanted to keep. To her, it didn't seem beyond possibility that Mrs. Ellsworth would need a coach for everyone to ride in and a separate wagon for the luggage. It would make the journey from Venice to Vienna take that much longer, but it would be more comfortable for everyone that way.

When Eurydice pushed open the door to the solarium, she found that Psyche had fallen asleep in the window seat, her cheek resting on her folded arms on the window sill. Eurydice was hesitant to wake her. Psyche really did have a hard time sleeping. It may have grown even worse since Psyche had found a "cure" for it and didn't have it with her. Eurydice didn't know how he made her sleep better…unless Psyche had been sleeping *with* him. They had been together unchaperoned for several months, so Eurydice supposed it was possible. If Psyche had been sharing the same bed with him, Eurydice realized she had probably been doing more than just *sleep*. Eurydice might be innocent, but she wasn't naïve. She idly wondered if her parents knew. They had made no mention of it one way or the other, and since the two of them were getting married, the impropriety of it was moot.

Eurydice looked longingly to her violin. The solarium really was the best room in the house to practice. She could kick herself for not taking Psyche up on her offer the previous year. She could have been enjoying it all this time. Now she would only have today and tomorrow until she returned from Vienna. She had been to the opera many times. The acoustics of the solarium reminded her of that. It almost made her feel as if she were playing on a stage, and she thought rather wistfully that this was probably as close as she would ever get.

Even if she managed to find a maestro in Vienna—and she was hopeful, the possibility that she would ever perform for the general public was unlikely. She tried to console herself by thinking that she would at least learn to play better, if nothing else, once she found a teacher. Her performing in London, other than as an oddity at the occasional social function, was impossible. As the daughter of a duke, she couldn't do it without causing a scandal. Her parents didn't give a fig one way or the other if she was seen playing her fiddle in public, but the rest of society did. Even playing on the continent was pushing the boundaries of what was acceptable. It would be less likely someone from *London* society would be there to spread gossip of it among the *ton*, but it could happen. And then there was her anxiety at performing in front of people other than family to consider. Even if she found a maestro and was able to perform in public, she didn't know if she *could.*

Eurydice went to the work-table and picked up her violin. She couldn't practice the Haydn because it was too rambunctious. She started to play another piece, one she had composed herself. It was slow and mostly quiet, and she hoped it wouldn't wake Psyche. It used a lot of complicated progressions and arpeggios, soaring and dipping yet delicate. It was like a butterfly flittering through a meadow from flower to flower, which was appropriate because Eurydice had titled the work *Le Papillon.* She loved the way the song sounded in the solarium, and she was pleased to hear that it was a good composition. She had been unsure when she had written it.

"I like that one," said Psyche with a soft smile, blinking her eyes sleepily when Eurydice was finished.

"I'm sorry. I didn't mean to wake you."

Psyche waved a hand dismissively. "I needed to go back to my room anyhow. Chrissoula is making some things for me, and I have to try them on."

"Are you not getting enough from Janet?" asked Eurydice in surprise.

"Janet is only making my things to wear in Venice or somewhere else that might require *normal* clothes. Chrissoula is making my things for Greece and Egypt...well, she and Shailesh are making my things. I think Agniezka is helping."

"What is Agniezka making for you?" asked Eurydice curiously. How many clothes could her sister possibly need?

"She's making a few more ganseys. She is so very good at knitting. I wear those and my split skirts while we're on the ship. They're very comfortable and practical."

"Hmm," said Eurydice doubtfully.

11

"Believe me. I wouldn't have thought so either, but they really are. I threw seven fits when I saw them in my trunk last year, but you couldn't convince me *not* to wear them now."

Eurydice still didn't believe pants could possibly be more comfortable than a dress. To Eurydice, it just seemed the air circulation would be better than any freedom of movement that might be achieved by wearing pants. Psyche had taken to wearing her split skirts with a redingote when she went riding, and she had also had several pairs made up for Pandora. Persephone wore form-fitting men's breeches or trousers, but the split skirt would be a less unseemly thing for her to wear if she went riding in the Park in London. Eurydice preferred to ride aside, so a habit worked fine, especially since she didn't ride nearly as much as her sisters. As long as her sister was happy with it, Eurydice could only shrug.

Persephone always wore breeches. Even now, while they were at home, she was wearing *men's* mourning dress. When they left for London, at least for the times when someone other than family might see her, she would wear a dress. That wouldn't be very often, and Persephone was relieved. She had only ever worn an evening gown once before, and Eurydice knew Persephone found that even more constricting than a simple cotton day dress.

"Oh, well, maybe you can try a pair while you're on the *Medea*. You'll see what I mean."

"I'll think about it," said Eurydice slowly, "but I don't think I'll like it."

Chapter Two

Eurydice looked at herself in the mirror as Agniezka styled her hair. It wasn't a complicated coiffure; she had braided the length of it high on her head and coiled it around, pinning it in place. There were no decorative combs or ribbons, but the simplicity of it suited the auburn shade of Eurydice's hair much better than something more intricate. On someone else, it might have seemed severe, but it complimented the angular symmetry of her features.

The dull black of her dress, however, was not helpful. It was made of plain linen with simple embroidery and no lace. The sleeves were long and fitted to the elbow but became puffed beyond that point to the shoulder. The dullness of it made the flawless, golden shade of her complexion seem sallow…almost jaundiced. Her sisters, with possibly the exception of Persephone, could wear black clothing made of any fabric, but Eurydice could only carry the color as an accent in satin or velvet, embroidery, and lace. But then, Eurydice did not resemble her sisters much in coloring or any other fashion.

She was shorter than her sisters by two inches, three in the case of Arachne and Persephone. Their skin was a dusky beige, while Eurydice's was a golden olive color, but she had none of the freckles that usually accompanied red hair. She also had a slightly rounder figure, although she could in no way be considered fat or even stocky. Then there was the color of her eyes. They might have been called green or brown, but the only proper description would be amber. Persephone's were the same color, perhaps a little more brown, and comparison to the eyes of their cat, Archimedes, would not be inappropriate.

As for her personality, her sisters were far more outgoing, even Arachne. Eurydice was quiet and serious. She was in no way melancholy, but she wasn't given to silliness or practical jokes like Pandora. She wasn't given to speaking her mind like Psyche and Arachne; she usually kept her opinions to herself unless asked. No one was like Persephone. Eurydice could become irritated at times, but she never lost her temper. She also didn't laugh very often. She never raised her voice, but she spoke clearly and without hesitation. There was never any misunderstanding of what she was saying, either by tone or eloquence. She was similar to Psyche in that she did not lie, but she wasn't plagued by the hives Psyche developed if she had to tell the occasional half-truth. Eurydice simply didn't see the point of it, and she was rarely, if ever, placed into a position that required her to be dishonest.

Eurydice resembled her *Babushka* Alexa, her father's mother. There was a painting of her as a young woman hanging in the portrait gallery at Wilderland. It could have been a painting of her granddaughter, even the color of her eyes and the solemn expression. But Eurydice inherited more than her looks. It was Alexa who began to teach Eurydice the violin when she was old enough to hold it. Her favorite violin, a Stradivarius called *La Ragazza Dolce*, had been given to her by her *babushka*. Alexa had inherited it from her father's mother as well, so it was appropriate it had been handed down in the same fashion. Eurydice had been heartbroken when her grandmother died almost five years previously from a septic infection. Then there were the dreams.

All of Alexa's grandchildren had inherited something from her. They sometimes had dreams that came true. The ability was more pronounced in some of them than others. It was one of the reasons Psyche had trouble sleeping. If she didn't sleep, she couldn't dream. Pandora and Dorian had simply learned to ignore them. If Persephone had them, she never mentioned it. Gregory and Myron had been blessed (or cursed) to a lesser extent. Of the three younger boys, it seemed to be more developed in Damon than in Cosmo and Christopher. For Eurydice and Arachne, it was a constant source of irritation. They tried to ignore it as much as possible, but it was always there.

Their *babushka* had called it *pronicatel'nost'*, the Insight. Eurydice would have to agree the name was appropriate, but it was bothersome and worrisome. There were things she sometimes saw that she would rather not. The things she would just as soon forget were the things that were hurtful or painful. Yet not all the dreams were terrible; some were actually comforting…not always, but sometimes. Eurydice usually tried to forget them because it wasn't very fun to already know what was going to happen, especially if it was bad. That occasionally worked, but more often than not, something would happen and leave Eurydice with the disorienting sensation that it had already occurred before. She didn't like that, but she had become accustomed to it.

Agniezka finished putting up her hair, and Eurydice nodded approvingly as she looked in the mirror before standing up. She really had no preference on how she looked. Her maid decided what she was going to wear for the day and how her hair would be styled. When Janet was at Wilderland for Psyche's trousseau, the dressmaker and her sister had decided what things Eurydice should have made for Vienna. Eurydice could only assume what they had selected would be fine. She couldn't recall ever being accused of shabby dressing. Agniezka must be doing a sufficient job. Eurydice had more important things on her mind than what her dress looked like.

Eurydice grabbed her drawstring bag that contained only a handkerchief and a few coins and left her room to go to Psyche's. They were going to Pandora's for a while. Eurydice would have much rathered staying home to practice, but she had not been to her sister's house since they came to town. That was over a month ago. Psyche was going to sit for a portrait. Eurydice didn't know why she couldn't pose for it at Aberdare House, but Psyche didn't really need an excuse to go visit her twin. Even though she was in mourning, she went to see Pandora several times a week. Eurydice loved her sister, but they didn't have enough in common for endless hours of conversation.

When Eurydice reached Psyche's room, she was unsurprised to see that her sister was still in the process of getting ready to leave. Psyche was always late. Three days earlier, she had almost been late to attend her best friend Amalie's wedding. Amalie Nichols was married to Robert Cochran, the Earl of Westerkirk, and Amalie's brother was Psyche's fiancé, Lord Sheerness. Psyche had only managed to arrive in time for the ceremony, which was fortunate because Amalie had asked her to sign as a witness. Sheerness was the other. Because she was in mourning, Psyche had not been able to attend the breakfast afterward, but Amalie had insisted she had to be a witness. If Psyche hadn't talked to Sheerness, Amalie and Westerkirk might not have been married.

"I'm almost ready," said Psyche as she hurriedly rose from the dressing table to grab her gloves and reticule.

"I will never understand why you are always running behind," said Eurydice. "Especially these days. It's not as if you have to struggle over what to wear."

"I honestly don't know," sighed Psyche. "I'll be back before supper, Chrissoula," she called over her shoulder as she left the room with her sister. "I've tried to figure it out. I can't. I guess I dawdle." She stopped at the top of the back stairs, her eyes growing round. "Dicy, you've got to make sure I get to the church on time in August. Sheerness will never forgive me if I'm late for our wedding."

Eurydice chuckled and linked her arm through Psyche's as they walked down the stairs together. She shook her head.

"Don't worry. You'll be on time…barely, but you'll be there on time."

Psyche looked at her hopefully. "Are you sure?"

"As sure as I can be," said Eurydice wryly.

Psyche's expression turned relieved. "Thank you. I feel so much better!"

"It's not guaranteed, you do realize? Just because *I* say you'll be there on time does not make it so. You have to help."

"Oh, I know," said Psyche as they walked down the path through the garden to the gate to the mews. "I was just afraid I would be late no matter what I did. As long as I do my best, I guess that will be enough."

"Absolutely," soothed Eurydice.

Jim was waiting for them beside one of their family's coaches. Eurydice was unsurprised he was to be their driver. He always took Psyche anywhere she went. He had designated himself her personal driver and bodyguard. It had started last year at the request of the duke and duchess, but he had taken it as a permanent order. He took it so seriously, in fact, that he would be leaving the employ of the duke and duchess to work for the Earl of Sheerness after Psyche married him in August.

Jim's sister, Mary, would be leaving as well, to take a position as their new cook. That would be a promotion for her; she had been only a kitchen girl for the Aberdares. She might have eventually been promoted to cook, but their Irish cook, Mrs. O'Flaherty, was not quite sixty yet and had no intention of retiring at any point in the immediate future. The siblings were the only family each other had, and Mary could not let her older brother go all the way across the country without her. Luckily for Mary, Psyche had managed to convince Sheerness he needed to hire her.

Psyche's maid, Chrissoula, would be going as well. Of course, Psyche couldn't go on her honeymoon—let alone to her new residence—without her maid, but there was another reason, in addition to that, for the woman to be leaving. She was going to be married to the bosun of the *Medea*, William Stockbridge, next Thursday. That was something Psyche had managed to arrange without much difficulty. Sheerness had given them a cottage at Belle Glade, and they would live there once the *Medea* returned from the Mediterranean. They were well-suited to each other, for he was bossy and Chrissoula was no less so. As Stockbridge had no family, and Chrissoula's was all the way in Greece, living at Belle Glade seemed the perfect idea.

The two sisters talked idly about several different things on the short ride from Aberdare House on Bruton to the Bardseys' on Upper Grosvenor near the Park. They talked about their younger brothers, Cosmo and Christopher going to Harrow. Damon would not be able to attend because he was deaf, but Arachne was teaching him. Sheerness's oldest nephew, Jerome, would also be starting this term. The three boys were all good friends, and they were happy they would be attending the same school. Persephone had settled down somewhat since coming to the city. She was still temperamental, but the anger seemed to have lessened. Annabelle was due to deliver very soon, probably before the end of the month. Eurydice and Psyche tried to guess whether she would have a boy or a girl. When Eurydice said she thought it would be a boy, Psyche didn't try to argue. Eurydice was rarely wrong.

Psyche knew that was one of the reasons her sister always seemed so dispassionate and unsurprised by anything. It had to make life pretty dull to know what was going to happen. The only time Eurydice expressed more than a moderate amount of emotion was when she played her violin. Psyche knew it wasn't that she didn't care about anything else except her music; there were a few things that could rile her...but not many. She simply had an inner calm that was very difficult to disturb. Although Eurydice had been heartbroken by the deaths of their brothers, Psyche had not seen her sister shed one tear...at least, not in front of other people. Eurydice never cried.

When they reached Pandora's, Jim opened the door of the carriage for them with a tug at his cap and a grin.

"We'll be a few hours, Jim," said Psyche. "If you want to go back to the house and come back, say—"she looked at the watch on a chain around her neck—"six, we should be ready by then."

"Six?" blurted Eurydice concernedly.

"Well, yes. Monsieur Isabey will only be here for a short time, and I want to have this done for Sebastian as a wedding present," said Psyche simply. She saw Eurydice's disconcerted expression. "If you cannot bear the thought of being away from your violin for that long for just one day, then you can go home with Jim."

"No, no," said Eurydice calmly. "It's only a few hours." Psyche grinned.

The two of them walked up the front steps to the door. Psyche pulled the rope to ring the bell, and it was shortly answered by Waldon, the Bardseys' formal British butler. Psyche had noticed, however, that his temperament had lightened remarkably since Pandora had joined the household. He let the two young women walk past him into the entry hall and closed the door.

"Good afternoon, Lady Psyche, Lady Eurydice. If you'll come this way, the Ladies Bardsey are in the informal sitting room with the children."

Psyche and Eurydice followed Waldon down the hall to the family's private sitting room. Eurydice was reluctant to go because her young nephews would be there, but it wasn't as if she would be left alone with them. When Waldon opened the door, they found their sister on the floor on her hands and knees, her two sons perched on her back as she crawled around. Pandora looked up with a grin when she saw her sisters. Alex and Myron jumped off her back and toddled toward Psyche with happy giggles. She picked them up for hugs and kisses with a chuckle.

"Hallo, little ones," she cooed. She adjusted them on her hips and looked at her sister wryly. "Actually, they're starting to become rather heavy. What have you been feeding them, Pan?"

"Alex adores macaroni, but Myron seems to prefer peaches and bananas."

"That explains a lot," chortled Psyche. "Good afternoon, Lady Bardsey. How are you?"

"Absolutely marvelous," responded Pandora's mother-in-law with a smile and slight Scottish lilt. "And how are the two of you? Are you looking forward to going to Vienna in August, Lady Eurydice?"

Eurydice blinked, momentarily surprised at being addressed directly. "Yes, I am. Thank you for asking, Lady Bardsey."

She nodded. "I think you'll enjoy it. It's a very beautiful city."

"I'm sure I will like it, provided I can find a maestro."

"But why would you need one?" asked Lady Bardsey in surprise. "You play far better than anyone I've ever heard."

Eurydice blushed uncomfortably. "Thank you for saying so, but I think I have room for improvement."

Lady Bardsey gave her a doubtful look but chose not to refute it. She wasn't going to tell the girl she had heard some of the greatest violinists of Europe; Pandora had told her, and she had seen enough for herself, to know that Eurydice was her own worst critic. Some time in the greatest city for musicians would help to convince her that she really was a wonderful violinist, and what she needed was to be *heard*.

"So, Lady Psyche, I understand Monsieur Isabey is coming to paint your portrait," she said instead.

"Yes, he is. I'm so glad Pandora was able to arrange it for me. I suppose it pays to save the life of a prince every once in awhile," said Psyche, giving her twin a wink.

"It does have its occasional benefits," chortled Pandora.

Kwan arrived to take the babies back to the nursery, and Lady Bardsey left for her room to take an afternoon nap. Pandora sent for tea, and the three sisters sat talking as they waited for Isabey to arrive. It wasn't a very long wait.

He was charming and handsome, and it was obvious he was taken with the three sisters. Much to Psyche and Eurydice's dismay, he would not begin Psyche's portrait until he had made a sketch of Eurydice. It didn't matter that she wasn't the intended subject for his visit. He had never seen a woman of such extraordinary coloring and beauty. She was a golden goddess, he thought. He would paint both Psyche *and* Eurydice, or he would paint neither. When couched in those terms, the sisters were left with little choice.

He posed Eurydice in a chair by the window overlooking the garden. Once he had her positioned just so, he set up his equipment and began. It wasn't difficult for her to sit still; she simply let her mind wander to the latest piece of music she was studying, and she began to hear it in her head. He quickly made a sketch in pastels for himself, and then he made one that would be used for the painting. Eurydice had no notion of what she would do with the painting once it was completed. She supposed she could give it to her mother as a gift for her birthday; although, she already had presents for her mother's birthday and for her parents' anniversary, which would be the same day. She wasn't sure if it would be ready by the middle of July anyhow. She didn't know how long these things took.

Once he finished with the initial work for Eurydice's portrait, he went with Psyche out to the garden to begin work on hers. She wanted to be painted in the garden temple. Pandora and Eurydice would watch from the sitting room. There was a dual purpose behind Psyche wanting her portrait painted there. As she intended to give the painting to Sheerness as a wedding gift, the replica of a Greek temple in her sister's garden was a special place for both Psyche and Sheerness. It would also provide a somewhat secluded location for Isabey to work, and Psyche wanted that because he would be painting her nude.

Pandora knew that was how Psyche wanted to be painted. She thought it was an excellent idea for a wedding present. Once Isabey had completed a full-sized portrait, he would copy it in miniature onto a pocket watch Psyche also intended to give to Sheerness. Her plan to be painted in the buff was the reason she couldn't have it done at Aberdare House. Even though she intended to give it to her future husband, for a woman of the nobility to be painted that way was just not done without causing a scandal. A courtesan, a mistress, or an unknown model, perhaps, but definitely not the innocent daughter of a duke. Of course, Pandora knew Psyche wasn't innocent…not anymore. Their parents probably knew as well, but appearances had to be kept. Pandora suspected Eurydice and the rest of her siblings (with the exception of her younger brothers) knew, too, but none of them except Pandora knew about the painting.

While Psyche was in the garden (and Pandora could clearly see Isabey where he had set up his equipment just inside the temple), Eurydice and Pandora talked about the things Eurydice planned to do while she was in Vienna. Pandora tried to encourage her sister to see and do things while she was in Venice as well, but she suspected Eurydice would, as usual, spend a majority of her time in her room playing her violin. Pandora had never been to the continent herself, so she knew *she* certainly wouldn't be spending all her time in her room were she ever to go, no matter what diverting entertainment her husband might be able to provide.

Eurydice talked with her sister, but her eyes would occasionally go to the clock on the mantel as she waited for six to approach. She really shouldn't have agreed to come, especially now that she would have to return several more times for Isabey to finish her portrait. She had wanted to refuse, but he had made it obvious he wouldn't paint her sister if he couldn't paint Eurydice. She thought that was a bit arrogant for a painter who depended on his work for his income, but his painting either of them at all was being done as a favor to the comte d'Artois.

Just before six, Islington, Pandora's husband, came in with Sheerness. The Marquess of Bardsey went to his wife for a kiss, but Sheerness bore a decidedly puzzled expression. It was obvious he expected his fiancée to be there.

"Did she already go home?" he asked disappointedly.

"No, she's in the garden," said Pandora with a grin. "Do you really think Dicy would still be here otherwise?"

Eurydice narrowed her eyes at her sister but chose not to comment.

"Are the boys with her, then?" asked Islington mildly.

"No, Kwan took them to the nursery ages ago. Psyche's with Isabey," said Pandora.

"Who?" asked Islington blankly.

"Monsieur Jean Baptiste Isabey," said Pandora leadingly. Both her husband and future brother-in-law stared at her blankly, and she shook her head vexedly. "He's a painter Artois was kind enough to convince to come all the way here to paint Psyche's portrait."

"Oh, well, I'll just pop out to see her," said Sheerness.

"No, you may not," said Pandora flatly. Sheerness raised an eyebrow. "She went to the garden to not be disturbed."

Sheerness grinned. "I don't think she's going to mind seeing me."

Eurydice looked out the window to the garden temple. Isabey's canvas wasn't very large, and it was quite a distance away, but she could see the beginnings of the portrait clearly traced onto it in charcoal and places where he had begun to apply paint. Her eyes widened in alarm. Sheerness could not go to the garden, and she now understood why her sister could not have it painted at home. Her expression of surprise was fleeting, and she quickly composed her features to their usual placidity as she turned to look at Sheerness.

"I understand you and Islington are working with Father and Dorian regarding Napoleon," she said mildly, attempting to change the subject. She was sure her sister would be in shortly…she hoped. "Is he going to delay my going to Vienna?"

Sheerness raised an eyebrow. "As much as I hate to say it, he may," he finally said. He started to look out the window when Eurydice drew his attention again.

"How could he have escaped from Elba? I thought he was under guard," she accused.

"*I* wasn't guarding him," said Sheerness with a sardonic smile. "He still has a multitude of supporters, and he also still has the resources to place bribes where necessary. His attempt to regain power really was ill-conceived, though. He won't be able to stay in control for much longer, but whether we'll be rid of him by August is anyone's guess."

Islington happened to glance out the window then and saw the canvas just before the artist pulled down a flap of cloth to cover it. He looked at his wife with a raised eyebrow, and she gave him a brief, warning shake of her head. Pandora had told him a painter was coming to make a portrait of Psyche for Sheerness, but she had failed to mention what *kind* of portrait. He had to admit he wouldn't mind one of his wife made in the same fashion, but he wasn't sure how Sheerness would react to finding out his fiancée was in the garden naked with a male painter. He might appreciate the gift once it was done, but catching her in the middle of the process could upset him.

Eurydice sighed inwardly with relief when Isabey began putting away his things. She just wanted him to cover up the painting before Sheerness saw it.

"I'll just go out to the garden, then," said Sheerness, preparing to leave.

"Oh, but you can't," said Pandora hurriedly. Sheerness looked at her with a raised eyebrow, and Pandora groaned. "She'll kill me if she finds out I told you, so pretend it's a complete surprise when you see it, but she's having the portrait painted as a wedding present for you. It's bad enough you know that; try not to spoil it even more by looking at it before she gives it to you."

Sheerness did look out the window to the garden then, but luckily, Isabey had put away the canvas and was walking back to the house with a fully-clothed Psyche. She was talking animatedly, her arms waving through the air as she described something, and the painter threw his head back and laughed amusedly. Sheerness sighed inwardly as he recognized she had made yet another friend with which to exchange letters. He had yet to find anyone who didn't like his fiancée—man, woman, young, old, even animals—adored her. He adored her so much himself that he *had* to marry her, and he was happy to know the feeling was mutual.

Eurydice glanced to the clock on the mantel again. It was after six. She was sure Jim was waiting for them, but she was also sure their departure was going to be delayed—at least for a little while—because Sheerness had arrived. She sighed resignedly. There would be no practice for her that day. She could hope Psyche would only stay briefly, since she saw her fiancé at least every other day, but Eurydice was sure that was wishful thinking.

She was surprised Pandora had told Sheerness what her twin was doing in the garden. She did notice, however, that Pandora hadn't told him the *entire* truth. Eurydice supposed it was the best way to keep him out of the garden without letting him know *exactly* what his present would be. She didn't understand why Psyche would want to give him a picture of herself in the buff, but Psyche seemed to think he would like it.

When Psyche came into the room and saw Sheerness, she smiled happily and practically skipped toward him to give him a brief kiss. Eurydice rolled her eyes. She had noticed the two of them couldn't seem to keep their hands off each other when they were in the same room together. Maybe a portrait of Psyche naked would be something he would greatly enjoy after all.

"*Geiá sas, agape mou,*" said Psyche with a smile.

"Mm-hmm," said Sheerness as he put his arms around her waist.

Eurydice rolled her eyes again. Public displays of affection were not considered appropriate, not even for a husband and wife, but the two of them excusing themselves to be alone would be considered even more inappropriate. Her parents were freely affectionate with each other that way also, as were Pandora and Dorian with their spouses. Gregory had been the same way with Annabelle. Eurydice found nothing wrong with them loving their spouses—or future spouse in Psyche's case, but she couldn't imagine loving someone enough to ignore propriety. Isabey, a complete stranger, didn't seem to be bothered, but the French view was somewhat different.

Pandora tried to convince them to stay for supper, but Eurydice put her foot down. It would be too late to practice on her violin once she and Psyche returned home, but she did have a new composition she was writing for the piano. It was only half-finished, and she had been working on it for months, even before the beginning of the year. Most of the sonatas she composed were for the violin, but she did occasionally hear music in her head that was better-suited for other instruments or groups of instruments. This happened to be one of those times. It was constantly playing at the back of her mind, beneath everything else, and sometimes it gave her a headache from its insistence. She wanted to get it put onto paper and out of her head.

It was nearly eight before they were able to go home. Isabey had taken his leave shortly after he returned from the garden and had been introduced to

Sheerness and Islington. He would come the following day at two to work on both portraits. Eurydice resigned herself. She didn't want a picture, but she would do it for Psyche. She only hoped she wouldn't have to do this for weeks on end; otherwise, Isabey would find himself with a half-finished portrait. She couldn't imagine that the painter would be able to stay that long in any event.

Eurydice returned home with Psyche late enough that she was unable to do more than write a few measures of her composition, and of course it was too late for her to play them and actually hear whether or not she had transcribed them correctly. She felt now more than ever that she should be practicing as much as possible in preparation for going to Vienna. With Isabey wanting to paint her portrait, she would have less time. She was concerned it was going to affect her chances of finding a teacher.

She had decided she would give herself two months to find a maestro. If by the end of that time no one was willing to take her as a student, she would return home. She wouldn't put away her violin; she would practice more and try again and again if necessary until she found someone willing to teach her. There had to be someone. Perhaps Miss Mahone could offer a suggestion.

Agniezka drew Eurydice a bath after supper and saw that she was properly scrubbed and dressed for bed. Eurydice did like soaking in the hot water. It was one of the few occasions when she would let her mind focus on other things besides music, but because her other interests were limited, she usually started to doze off with nothing on her mind to keep her alert. Agniezka had to splash water in her face to get her attention when it was time for her to get out.

As she went to sleep, Eurydice wondered what she would dream of that night and whether or not it would be a dream or a vision. She could usually tell the difference, but sometimes she wasn't so sure simply because of what it showed her. She kept a dream diary, where she wrote down the ones she could remember. She would occasionally go back to look at it, just to see if any of them actually happened. The last time she looked, about three out of five had…more than half, but not enough to make it a certainty whatever she dreamed *would* come true. Sometimes she couldn't recall having any dreams at all, but that was unusual. She could usually remember at least one.

She'd been keeping the diary since she was able to write. She was on her fourth notebook, the writing eventually becoming neater, the descriptions more detailed. She would occasionally go back to the dreams she had written down when she was very small. Some of them had only recently come true. Some of them she hoped never came true, whether she was alive to see it or not.

She tried not to think about it. Psyche didn't like to sleep because of the dreams she might have. Eurydice had become accustomed to them. Regardless of whether or not she dreamt about it, whatever was going to happen would happen. Sometimes it was a good thing to know about it beforehand.

Eurydice was idly staring out the window of the coach as it traveled slowly through the busy streets of Southwark. She didn't know why she had agreed to come with Annabelle to the docks. It was one more thing to keep her away from practicing. She hadn't been able to practice as much the day before because she had again gone with Psyche to Pandora's for Isabey to paint her portrait. She would go again today after she returned from the docks with Annabelle. It did seem, however, that it would not take him long to complete it, which relieved Eurydice immensely.

Eurydice hadn't been able to play her violin as much since her family had come to London for the season, which was peculiar because they weren't attending any functions. She had been able to play much more the previous year when she *had* been socializing, going out to one event or another nearly every night because it had been her debut.

She did have to admit to herself that she played her violin *a lot*. She didn't think she practiced any more than someone else, but she sometimes got the impression from her family that she might. What else was she to do? It was the one thing that made her happy above all else. When she played, she could forget everything else. She didn't think she was *unhappy*, but perhaps she did sometimes feel lonely and disconnected. She didn't know why she should. In some ways, she was very different from her family, but they were all like that. They all had different interests, different personalities, but it seemed the rest of her family was able to relate amongst themselves better. Of all her siblings, Arachne was the only one who seemed to really understand her, but perhaps that was because they shared more frequent dreams than everyone else. Eurydice had no doubt that her family loved her, as she loved them, but she sometimes didn't really feel as if she *belonged* with her family.

Annabelle would have had Persephone go with her on this errand to the docks, and the younger girl had attempted to go regardless, but she had a fever and probably influenza. No one else was able to go with Annabelle, so Eurydice said she would go. Her sister-in-law was due to give birth very soon, and Eurydice had tried to persuade her not to go and send someone else, but Annabelle would have none of it. A ship had arrived from Bermuda carrying the remainder of her father's belongings. Annabelle felt she had to collect them herself. Eurydice could understand that, but she wasn't sure what things they could be; she had thought everything had already been sent to Wilderland.

Annabelle was very quiet as they traveled. There was a slight frown between her brows, and Eurydice wasn't sure if it was due to the purpose behind their errand or discomfort from the jostling she was receiving from the coach traveling over the uneven road. Eurydice had asked her if she was all right, and Annabelle had assured her she was fine, but Eurydice wasn't convinced. The further they went, the more she began to think her sister-in-law should have stayed home.

When they reached the docks, they located the ship with some difficulty. It was a small sloop called the *Gloria Dei*. It reminded both women of the *Julia*, and Eurydice swallowed an unexpected emotional lump in her throat as she looked at it. Despite how impassive she often seemed, she did have feelings, and she missed both of her brothers terribly. She simply realized there was little to be gained from crying. It wouldn't bring them back.

Eurydice and Ivan, their driver, helped Annabelle step down from the coach. She didn't release Eurydice's arm once she was standing on the ground, and she kept her other hand to the side of her stomach. If anything, her frown had grown deeper, and she may have even grown a little pale.

"Are you sure you're all right?" asked Eurydice concernedly.

"I'll be fine," assured Annabelle softly with a smile. "I think a little bit of a stroll will work wonders for me."

"We'll have Ivan come with us to carry whatever it is we've come for," said Eurydice decidedly. "I don't feel like carrying it, and I don't think you *should* carry it."

Annabelle nodded agreement, and they went aboard the ship. The captain, Captain Robbins, was an old friend of Annabelle's father. She spent some time talking with him in his cabin before he brought out a small sea chest. They bade their farewells, and Ivan hefted the chest onto his shoulder to carry to the coach. Like all the Aberdares' drivers, he was of an impressive size. Eurydice knew just from looking at it that the chest wasn't light, but to him the weight seemed insignificant.

Eurydice helped Annabelle in, and they waited patiently while Ivan secured the chest onto the rack at the back of the coach. The coach shifted slightly as Ivan mounted the driver's seat. Eurydice watched the way Annabelle began to take deep breaths in through her nose and release them from her mouth slowly as she continued to rub the side of her belly once the carriage got under way. Eurydice grew nervous that something wasn't right and thought the sooner they returned home, the better.

"Oof!" gasped Annabelle when they had only gone a short distance.

"What is it? What's wrong?" asked Eurydice with some alarm.

"My water just broke," said Annabelle weakly.

Eurydice frowned uncertainly for only a minute before her eyes rounded in realization.

"*Now?* Can't you hold it? Cross your legs or something until we get home?" she asked with some irritation.

"No, I don't think so," gasped Annabelle, and she put both hands to her stomach as she was gripped by her strongest contraction yet.

Annabelle realized she had probably been in labor since she woke up that morning. She had thought the pains were different, but having never done this before and not having someone to enlighten her, she hadn't thought anything of it. The duchess, Pandora, and Selena had all tried to provide her with information, but there was only so much they could do; some of it simply had to be experienced to be understood. She thought she would have another week or two. Obviously not.

Eurydice pulled back the curtain on one of the windows and looked out. She wasn't overly familiar with Rotherhithe, so she wasn't sure exactly how far they had gone and how far away they were from Westminster and Mayfair. She could tell Ivan to go faster, but the streets were busy. It was unlikely he would be able to do so without having an accident or running someone over. She didn't think they were even out of the dock area yet. She could see several warehouses, but she couldn't see many other buildings. They had just gone through the turnpike, but there was nothing else beyond for quite some distance…just the other traffic on the road. Eurydice could tell, however, that this wasn't a good area. She looked back at Annabelle on the seat beside her.

"Do you think you can make it to the house?"

"No, I don't think so."

"Should we keep going or stop?"

"Ow, oh, I don't know," gasped Annabelle, and she bit her lip to stifle a scream.

"Bloody hell," said Eurydice. She jumped to the other bench and pulled open the small window near the driver's seat. "Ivan, find a place to stop the coach! Quickly!"

Eurydice went back to the seat with Annabelle. Her forehead was beaded with sweat and creased with pain, and she was breathing in panting gasps as she gripped her stomach. Eurydice sighed with relief as she felt the coach come to a stop. Eurydice helped Annabelle lie down on the seat and exited the coach once the girl was situated. She met Ivan as he was climbing down.

"Lady Annabelle is in labor. I need you to take one of the horses and go get help," said Eurydice calmly.

"Lady Eurydice, this area's not safe," said Ivan nervously.

He had stopped the coach in a fairly deserted place. Eurydice couldn't see any buildings nearby. They were off the road under a stand of trees providing shade. She didn't see how there was anything else that could be done. Annabelle could not make it to the house.

"You've the carriage pistol in the box under your seat, yes?" she said calmly.

"Yes, mum," said Ivan evenly, but he was uncomfortable leaving her alone, especially with a woman in labor in the middle of nowhere. He knew she could use the gun if necessary, but he could only imagine what her father would think when he found out Ivan had left her in a position where it *could* be necessary.

"Give it to me, and take one of the horses. Go to the house and get help…the doctor…someone. Dr. Hinton was tending to Persephone when we left; he may still be there. I'll lock the doors, and we'll stay inside until you return. We'll be fine."

Ivan nodded resignedly and climbed up to the seat to retrieve the box and give it to Eurydice. She held the box in her hands as she watched him unhitch one of the coach horses. It was one of their Cleveland Bays, and although it was accustomed to being in harness, it would be manageable. She didn't see how there was a choice in the matter anyhow. Ivan mounted and gave Eurydice one more concerned look before he urged the horse down the road at a fast pace. Eurydice watched until he disappeared from sight, gripping the box to her for a few minutes before she went back into the coach, closed the door, and locked it. She then made sure the other door was locked as well.

Annabelle was still panting, and Eurydice could see she was in a lot of pain. She set the box with the pistol on the other seat and opened the lid. After she made sure it was properly loaded, she turned her attention back to her sister-in-law. They could use some water, but there wasn't any. Eurydice hadn't noticed any streams or springs nearby while she was outside, and she wasn't sure how clean the water would be in any event. There was nothing in the coach...she didn't think. There was a compartment where her father kept whisky and wine, but Eurydice doubted there would be any water. She opened it to look and wasn't surprised to see there was not. She looked at Annabelle over her shoulder.

"Would you like something to drink?" she asked wryly. "We have whisky, brandy, claret, and a Welsh white from our own vineyard."

"Whisky," said Annabelle, and she managed a slight smile.

Eurydice poured some into a glass and held it out to Annabelle, who took it with a grateful smile.

"I've sent Ivan to the house for help. I'm hoping the doctor will still be there, but I don't imagine that will be the case. How are you feeling?"

"That's a bit of a silly question, don't you think?" gasped Annabelle after she swallowed the alcohol.

"Yes, I suppose it is," said Eurydice dryly. "Here, let's get some of this off you. I think you'll be more comfortable."

She removed Annabelle's bonnet and shoes, and then she helped her remove her gown. That was difficult because it required her to sit up, but it did seem to help. The back of the dress was soaking wet, and when Eurydice looked at Annabelle's chemise, she could see it was also wet and slightly bloody. She removed her handkerchief from her reticule and poured some of the white wine onto it to dampen it. It wasn't going to be as helpful as water, but it might provide a little coolness. She dabbed it on Annabelle's face before resting it onto her forehead.

"You're going to smell like you've been carousing," smiled Eurydice.

Annabelle started to smile, but she felt another contraction and could not restrain herself from yelling loudly at the pain. Eurydice winced at the sound, but she took one of Annabelle's hands in hers and patted it soothingly. Eurydice wasn't at all sure she wanted to be here for this, but there was no one else. Like the rest of her family, she would do what needed to be done. She was trying very hard not to panic because it wouldn't be helpful to the situation. She had no notion of what she was to do, but she hoped Ivan would soon return with help.

"Can you tell how long it will be?" asked Eurydice.

"No," panted Annabelle once the contraction had passed. "I think the pains are getting closer together, but I don't know if that means anything. I don't feel like the baby is about to pop out, but obviously, it's coming. Maybe you can look?"

Eurydice raised an eyebrow. The thought was unappealing, but she knew Annabelle couldn't look for herself. Eurydice helped her bend her knees and spread her legs apart, and then she lifted Annabelle's chemise to look. It wasn't as bad as she thought it would be, but she couldn't see anything. She certainly didn't see a baby, and she didn't see anything to indicate how long it would be before she *would* see one.

"I can't tell," she said finally.

She dropped the chemise back into place, but Annabelle seemed more comfortable with her knees bent, so they left them that way. Annabelle screamed as she was racked by another contraction, and Eurydice tried not to put her hands over her ears at the shrill sound in the enclosed carriage. If she had to mark how close the contractions were together by how often Annabelle screamed, they were only three or four minutes apart. She didn't know what that meant. She'd never seen anyone have a baby, and it wasn't something she had ever asked her mother or anyone else about. It wasn't something that aroused Eurydice's interest.

When Annabelle screamed again, Eurydice was almost tempted to put a hand over her sister-in-law's mouth to muffle it, but she suspected it helped somehow. Eurydice didn't see how it could, but she tried to tolerate it. Psyche had told her some of what had happened the night Pandora delivered her twins, so Eurydice wasn't completely surprised by the noise, but it did hurt her ears.

Eurydice was so intent on her sister-in-law that she didn't hear someone rattling the door of the coach until the person had it open. She saw the light coming in from the open door behind her and instinctively reached for the pistol in the box on the other seat and cocked it in one fluid movement. She swung around and pointed it toward the door without hesitation. She was almost surprised when the man in the doorway held a gun leveled at her no less calmly, but she wasn't startled enough to lower her own. A footpad was bound to have a gun.

"Back away from the door, or I'll blow your bloody head off," she said firmly.

Annabelle had quit screaming and lay resting with her eyes closed. Eurydice spared her a brief glance and patted her arm soothingly before she edged toward the door, still pointing the gun at the man. He had lowered his own weapon and put it into his pocket. He held his hands up from his sides as he backed away from the coach as she had instructed, a slight wry smile playing at the corners of his mouth. Eurydice didn't find the situation amusing in the slightest. She gracefully stepped down from the coach onto the ground, keeping the gun aimed steadily at his chest. She closed the door and signaled with the gun that she wanted the man to move even further away.

He seemed familiar to her somehow, but she wasn't sure whether she knew him or not. He was tall and well-built with dark hair and light-colored eyes, but she couldn't tell what color. He was also handsome in a very masculine way, with straight brows, a firm chin and jaw, and chiseled lips. He was wearing a riding coat and boots, a wide-brimmed beaver on his head. Eurydice could see his horse, a chestnut gelding of middling quality, tied to a nearby tree. He had a black leather portmanteau tied to the saddle, but Eurydice couldn't be sure if he was coming from or going to the docks. She also knew looks could be deceptive.

"State your business," she said flatly.

"I should think that would be obvious. I heard a woman screaming from a locked coach on the side of the road and came to provide assistance," he said evenly. She heard Scottish in his accent, and she could tell by the sound of it that he was from closer to Glasgow than Edinburgh. "Lady Eurydice, would you mind lowering the gun before you accidentally shoot someone?"

"If I shoot you, it *won't* be an accident," said Eurydice coldly. Then she frowned confusedly. "How do you know my name?"

"You don't recognize me?" he asked disbelievingly.

"Should I?"

He shrugged. "Perhaps not. It has been almost two years," he said dryly. "I'm Gareth Ellsworth. We met at your parents' dinner party."

Eurydice narrowed her eyes as she looked at him suspiciously. Then she realized why he had seemed familiar. Yes, it was him. She uncocked the pistol and lowered it.

"My apologies, Mr. Ellsworth," she said briefly.

She jumped when Annabelle began to scream again from inside the coach. Yes, she did suppose it sounded as if something untoward were happening inside.

"Bloody hell! Why is she screaming like that?"

"She's having a baby," said Eurydice calmly. "Excuse me."

She turned to open the door and climb back in the coach.

"I think you need to look again," panted Annabelle anxiously when she saw Eurydice.

Eurydice spared Ellsworth a brief glance over her shoulder before she sat down and lifted Annabelle's chemise. She still couldn't see anything, but there was more blood. She still didn't know if that meant anything bad. She put the material back in place and leaned forward to smooth the handkerchief over Annabelle's forehead, giving her an assuring smile.

"Is there anything I can do to help?" asked Ellsworth from the doorway.

"Are you a doctor?" asked Eurydice.

"No."

"Have you delivered a baby before?"

"No."

"Do you have any water?"

"No."

"Then there's nothing you can do to help," said Eurydice evenly.

"Fair enough," said Ellsworth with a tight smile. "Don't you think there are better places to do this besides in a coach on the side of the road?"

"It isn't as if we planned this," said Eurydice tartly.

Annabelle screamed again, and Eurydice winced as she grabbed her hands and squeezed them painfully. She really hoped Ivan arrived with the doctor soon, but it could be hours. At this rate, Annabelle would already have the baby. She chanced another look under Annabelle's chemise. She still couldn't see the baby, but there was a lot more blood, and it was steadily soaking through the thin fabric and onto the seat. She grabbed Annabelle's discarded gown and folded it up. She carefully lifted Annabelle's bottom from the seat and put it beneath her to absorb some of the flow. Eurydice never realized having a baby was so messy. The dress wasn't going to be enough.

Ellsworth still stood in the doorway watching, his arms folded across his chest as he leaned against the frame. Eurydice would rather not have the door to the coach open. They were far enough off the road that passersby wouldn't be able to see in, but they could do with a little more privacy.

"If you're going to stay, you may as well come in and close the door, please," said Eurydice over her shoulder. She felt the coach shift as he climbed in, and the coach became darker when he closed the door. "Thank you." She brushed a hand over Annabelle's cheek and gave her an encouraging smile. "Do you want more whisky?"

Annabelle nodded, and Eurydice got up to retrieve the bottle from the compartment. She poured some into the glass and helped Annabelle lift her head to drink it. Then she looked at Ellsworth.

"Would you care for something to drink?" she asked politely.

He gave her a slightly amused smile. "Whisky will do, please."

He thought the entire situation was odd, but to have her offering him something to drink in that calm tone, as if they were taking tea in the drawing room, was even more bizarre. He was surprised she wasn't hysterical, but she seemed to be almost dispassionate. The way she had looked at him when she had the gun pointed at him, completely calm and in control, had made it easy for him to believe she *would* have shot him if necessary. There were very few women he could think of with that kind of nerve, and they were certainly not daughters of British aristocracy. She poured him a glass of whisky and handed it to him before putting away the bottle in the compartment and turning her attention back to the woman on the other seat.

Annabelle looked at him, uncomfortable at having a complete stranger, much less a strange man, in the coach. Eurydice looked from one to the other.

"Oh, I'm sorry. Lady Annabelle Savage, may I present Mr. Gareth Ellsworth?"

"Savage?" he said in surprise.

"Ellsworth?" Annabelle said in almost the same tone.

Eurydice couldn't believe she had to be responsible for social protocol at a time like this, but it appeared to be necessary.

"Annabelle is Gregory's wife," she explained to Ellsworth. "Mr. Ellsworth is Mrs. Ellsworth's son." She didn't bother to explain that he was now her only son…and *only* living child.

Annabelle was about to say something further when she was hit by another contraction. It seemed to Eurydice that they were getting closer together, and she felt sure it wouldn't be long. She chanced another look under Annabelle's chemise, but she still couldn't see anything. It was possible things *looked* different, but Eurydice couldn't be sure. She needing something else to put under her for the blood, but there were no blankets in the coach. She wasn't sure what was in the trunk from Bermuda, but she couldn't ask Annabelle to let her use it. She looked at Ellsworth.

"I need your coat," she demanded.

He didn't question why she needed it, but he removed the gun and a few other items from the pockets before taking it off and giving it to her. Eurydice folded it up and added it to the gown beneath Annabelle. The seat of the coach was well-cushioned leather, but the blood was going to ruin it.

"Oh, I think I'm going to throw up," said Annabelle, and she started gasping and swallowing as she tried to fight back a wave of nausea. It wasn't going to work.

"Oh, no!" said Eurydice alarmedly. "Give me your hat!" she ordered Ellsworth.

He gave it to her just as Annabelle leaned over the side of the seat to be sick, and Eurydice caught it in the hat rather than letting it go all over the floor. Once Annabelle was done, Eurydice set the hat onto the floor and looked at Ellsworth. He had an astounded expression at what usage Eurydice had made of his hat. He had really liked that hat. Now it was totally ruined. No amount of cleaning would get the smell of regurgitated whisky out of it.

"I'm sorry about that," said Eurydice quietly.

Eurydice looked under Annabelle's chemise, and her eyes widened in surprise. Things looked much different.

"Ooh! I think I see hair," she said excitedly.

"I should hope so," muttered Ellsworth to himself darkly.

"Pardon?" asked Eurydice blankly. He shook his head. Eurydice looked at Annabelle. "Um, I think you're supposed to *push* now?" she said uncertainly.

Annabelle looked confused, but as she felt a contraction, she raised herself up on her elbows and bore down instinctively, yelling and groaning at the exertion. Eurydice smiled as she watched the progress.

"That's it! Whatever that was…do it again," she said excitedly.

Annabelle nodded, gasping for breath. She didn't feel the urge to do it again yet, but she would be ready for the next time, she hoped. Eurydice could see her sister-in-law was tired. She would help her, but she needed to be in front of her for the baby. She turned to look at Ellsworth.

"Can you get behind her and help her sit up?" she asked hopefully.

He nodded silently and stood. As Eurydice pulled on Annabelle's arms to help her lean forward, Ellsworth sat sideways on the seat behind her, his back resting against the wall of the coach, one of his legs bent at the knee on the seat, the other foot resting on the floor. Eurydice settled Annabelle back against him just as another contraction came. She could see she was going to need both her hands.

"Let her hold your hands," said Eurydice hurriedly.

She reached down with her own hands to run her fingers around the baby's head to help guide it out. She just knew if she didn't, something was going to tear; she didn't see how something as large as a baby's head could come out of something that small, regardless of how much it would expand, without help. As it was, there was no guarantee that something *wouldn't* tear. Her face brightened as she saw even more of the baby's head exposed. She looked up at Annabelle with a smile.

"He's got a headful of hair," she said amusedly.

Annabelle laughed and cried, and she was quivering with exhaustion and emotion. She pushed again, groaning and gritting her teeth, and Eurydice could see part of the baby's forehead and then just the bridge of his nose. His hair was dark, but he was also covered with blood and amniotic fluid. She was going to need something to wipe his face. She looked up at Ellsworth once again.

"I need your cravat," she said.

He gave her a dry smile as he unfastened the piece of linen and gave it to her. On Annabelle's next push, the baby rotated to his side and was free down to his shoulders. Eurydice felt an unexpected wave of emotion as she looked at the tiny face and blinked her eyes to control the tears she felt there. She wiped his face with Ellsworth's cravat, and she gave a slight giddy chortle as he released a small whimper. With a final push from Annabelle, Eurydice was able to work him the rest of the way free, and her new nephew was born. She wiped him off as much as she could with the cravat, but there was simply not enough material. She looked up at Ellsworth.

"Not my waistcoat, too?" he said disbelievingly.

The baby began to release a sputtering wail, and Eurydice tilted him downward as she balanced him on her forearm on his stomach to help the fluid in his mouth and lungs drain out. She noticed as he cried and was able to take more air into his lungs, his skin began to lose the slightly bluish tinge it first had and became a rosy pink, almost red. Once the cry became stronger, she took Ellsworth's waistcoat, which he held out to her resignedly, and cleaned the baby off the rest of the way as much as she could. She settled him onto Annabelle's stomach and gave her a grin.

"Congratulations, you have a baby boy," she chortled.

Annabelle began to cry happily as she looked at him, and she lifted him higher on her torso as he wailed, and Eurydice thought he sounded as if he were angry at being removed from his warm, snug cocoon. Annabelle began to examine his fingers and toes to make sure they were all present and accounted for.

Eurydice was left wondering what to do about the umbilical cord. It needed to be cut, but she wasn't entirely sure what to do about it. It was obvious to her that there were veins, and it was tough. She didn't think she could—or should—try to tear it. She reached down to remove the laces from her walking boots and used them to tie off the cord. She wasn't sure what to do about cutting it, though. She looked at Ellsworth.

"Do you have a knife?" she asked hopefully.

He nodded distractedly toward the items he had removed from his pockets onto the opposite seat as he sat looking at the newborn with an expression of utter amazement. Eurydice got up and found a folded pocketknife among the things. She made sure the laces were tied tightly and cut the cord between them. Then the baby was completely free. Annabelle lifted him higher once he was no longer tethered by the cord and rubbed her cheek against the top of his head. He had stopped crying but appeared to be fine.

The placenta still had to come out, and Eurydice was not surprised when after only a few minutes Annabelle delivered that as well. Eurydice thought it had to be the most disgusting thing she had ever seen, but she had positioned Ellsworth's ruined waistcoat to catch it as it came out. The doctor would want to examine it...whenever...*if* he arrived, to make sure it had all come out. Not being a physician herself, Eurydice didn't know what a whole one looked like as opposed to a partial one. She didn't imagine either condition would be an improvement on its appearance. Annabelle was still bleeding, but she didn't seem to be dangerously hemorrhaging, and Eurydice suspected it would continue for quite some time to come.

But she thought the baby needed to be wrapped in something to keep him warm. She hoped when Ivan returned with help, whoever he brought would have thought to bring things like blankets and other items, but she did need something to use in the interim. The items she had already used while delivering him were too dirty to wrap him in. There wasn't anything. Neither she nor Annabelle had worn a pelisse or a shawl. Eurydice looked up in surprise when Ellsworth removed his shirt and held it out to her.

"I had a feeling you were about to ask for it, so I thought I would save you the trouble," he said dryly.

"Well, no, actually, I wasn't going to," said Eurydice simply. "I think decency would demand you at least keep your shirt on, but since you've taken it off...," she said agreeably as she took it from him.

She laid the shirt on Annabelle's stomach and took her nephew from her sister long enough to swaddle him in the shirt before giving him back.

"I imagine he's hungry," said Eurydice practically.

Annabelle looked at Eurydice with a nod, but she was uncomfortable about exposing her breasts in front of a strange man. It was bad enough he had been there for the rest, even though she was grateful.

"We'll just step outside then to let you do that," said Eurydice with a comforting smile, sensing Annabelle's unease.

She stood up to open the door and gave Ellsworth a silent look to let him know she expected him to come out with her. She hoped he had another shirt in the bag on his saddle…or a coat…something. She was used to seeing her brothers without their shirts on…and sometimes even with much less, but for some peculiar reason she found it disturbing to see Ellsworth without his. She tried to keep her eyes averted, but she found herself intrigued.

He was muscular, but not bulky, like someone whose muscles were developed from constant use rather than heavy lifting, much like her brothers. His chest was covered by a matting of hair that narrowed to a thin line down his abdomen only to widen again at his navel and continue below his waistband. He was tanned, but once they were outside the coach, she could see scars that were lighter in a few places. She didn't have any experience with them, but they looked like what she imagined would result from gunshots and being stabbed, especially one scar that was about four inches long and traveled along the lower edge of his ribs on one side. She was curious where they had come from, but she wasn't going to ask him. Even if she knew him better, she wouldn't ask because she wasn't really sure she wanted to know.

The thing she noticed that made her have to bite her lip on a question (which was peculiar for her because she never found much of anything *that* interesting except music) was his back. She saw it as he walked past her to go to his horse to retrieve another shirt. There were a few scars there, too, but what caught her attention was the tattoo. There could be no mistake it was a tattoo because it was a large Oriental dragon that covered much of the upper part of his back between his shoulders. She knew that's what it was because Dorian had one almost exactly like it on his back that had been put there by his valet, Hiroshi, who was from Japan. For someone from Britain to have a tattoo at all was peculiar, but for him to have one like that was highly intriguing.

Eurydice had to wonder where it had come from. She could only assume he had gotten it in the Orient, specifically Japan, and she was puzzled over why he would have been there. Her father had been there several times on diplomatic missions, attempting to establish trade with the reticent country, but the Japanese did not like foreigners and made it clear they were unwelcome. She was curious to know if all the scars and the tattoo were acquired in the same place. She couldn't recall anyone ever even mentioning that Ellsworth had gone to the Orient. It wasn't a place men went on the Grand Tour. And while she could only speculate about why *he* had gotten the tattoo, for her brother it had a particular significance. Considering the similarity between the two, she wondered if Ellsworth had gotten it for the same reason. She didn't see how he possibly could have.

When he turned back to face her from retrieving another shirt and waistcoat from his portmanteau, Eurydice caught the beginning of the movement and turned her attention in a different direction before he completed it. She didn't want him to know she had been staring. While she was objective enough to admit he was attractive, it was only his tattoo and scars that had piqued her curiosity. He strolled toward her as he buttoned his waistcoat, his face impassive. Eurydice smiled politely and folded her arms in front of her in a motion that might have been considered protective.

"You've done that before," he stated with a wry smile as he neared her.

"Well, no, actually, I haven't," she answered simply with a slight shake of her head.

His eyebrows rose. "You seemed to know what you were doing."

Eurydice waved a dismissive hand through the air. "Women have been having babies forever. All I did was catch."

Ellsworth chuckled amusedly. "Is *that* all you did?"

"I think so," she replied evenly.

Eurydice looked to the road as she heard an approaching vehicle. She recognized the crest on the door, not as that of her family, but as belonging to Islington. She sighed with relief. The carriage horse Ivan had ridden away on was tethered to the back, and the driver himself was sitting beside Islington's on the seat. She was assuming from whose coach it was that Ivan had not been able to locate Dr. Hinton. Provided her brother-in-law actually was in the coach, Eurydice wasn't concerned. Islington was a trained physician, even if he wasn't a *practicing* physician, and had even gone to study in Edinburgh for this specific type of medical situation. Eurydice actually thought having Islington was *better* than having Dr. Hinton, given their family physician was a general practitioner. The only person she thought would have been able to provide just as much assistance would have been Pandora's maid, Maiyin.

Eurydice had had enough for one day. All she wanted to do was go home to her room. Unbelievably, she wasn't even sure she wanted to practice her violin. She thought a nap would be just the thing. Then she remembered she still had to go back to Pandora's for Isabey to continue work on her portrait. She felt that under the circumstances she could be excused from going at least for the day. When Islington returned to his house, she would have him pass along her regrets. She would have to go tomorrow, but she wasn't going today if she could help it.

When the coach came to a stop, Eurydice was surprised to see not only her brother-in-law step out but also Psyche, Pandora, and Maiyin. She was pleased Ivan had been able to find assistance, but she didn't think it required *all* of them. She noted Ellsworth's expression of astonishment when he saw Maiyin. Eurydice did suppose it was unusual for her sister to have a Chinese maid. What surprised Eurydice was what he did when Maiyin reached them, and then she had to control her amusement.

"*Konnichi wa,*" he said with a slight bow.

"Humph," said Maiyin disdainfully as she walked past him to go to the coach, carrying a bundle of fabric and other items, rolling her eyes and shaking her head.

Islington shook Ellsworth's hand and quickly said good afternoon before he followed after Maiyin into the coach. Eurydice thought for a moment about going with them, but they wouldn't need her. Annabelle had been conscious for the entire thing, so she would be able to answer any questions they might have. The hard part was over anyhow. Eurydice supposed she should have told them Annabelle already had her baby, but that would be obvious. What was happening *outside* the coach was going to be more entertaining, and she looked interestedly back to Ellsworth from the closed door of the coach.

Psyche and Pandora gave her curious glances as they approached, and both of them were dying to hear the details. They recognized Mr. Ellsworth, but they wondered how he came to be there and why he was missing his coat and cravat. His greeting to Maiyin was also something to make them wonder. Japanese was not a language that could be learned on a European tour, and most people in Britain would be disinterested in learning it anyhow; it wouldn't be particularly useful. It was perfectly understandable to all three of the sisters why Maiyin took offense, even if it wasn't to him.

"She's Chinese," explained Pandora evenly, her lips twitching amusedly when she saw his puzzled expression, "not Japanese." She gave him a slight half-smile as he took her hand to kiss. "Still, one really must ask where you learned to speak Japanese."

Eurydice was glad her sister had mentioned it because she didn't think she would have had the nerve, and it was very curious. It might help her figure out why he had the tattoo on his back as well. She wouldn't mention *that* interesting feature to her sisters because they would ask about it, and then he would know she had been looking at him. Aside from that, Eurydice had the feeling it wasn't something she should tell anyone. She didn't know why she shouldn't, but she had learned long ago not to question her instincts.

"I was speaking Japanese?" answered Ellsworth with a puzzled expression.

All three sisters looked at him in surprise. He did truly seem to be confused, but Pandora, as a skilled actress herself, knew it was an easy enough matter to pretend. Even if the audience knew she was lying, if she could make it seem she believed the falsehood herself, it made it easier to sell the illusion as the complete truth, and sometimes she could get the audience to believe it despite evidence to the contrary. Still, Pandora knew when it was pointless to attempt telling a lie. It didn't seem Ellsworth did.

Eurydice looked at him through narrowed eyes, and Psyche's expression was no less suspicious. Because the two of them weren't prone to being dishonest, for him to so blatantly lie gave them pause. The three sisters looked at each other disbelievingly when he continued to pretend as if he had not said what he did. For one of them to have thought she heard it could have been excused to misunderstanding, but all three of them—and Maiyin—had heard him say it.

Eurydice had to wonder about his character. Their mother and his had been friends for several years, before any of them were even born, and there was no question about the uprightness of Mrs. Ellsworth. Eurydice had to think some of his mother's honor had been bred into him despite what she was seeing. It had been almost two years since the dinner party, but Eurydice didn't recall having the impression that he was prone to fibbing. Of course, Ellsworth hadn't really talked to anyone that night…especially not her, and polite drawing room and dinner conversation really wouldn't have presented a need to lie, not for the average person. His having the tattoo troubled Eurydice. Telling a bald-faced lie about speaking Japanese was something that only added a new knot in the string for her.

Whatever his reasons for being dishonest, she knew he was not what he seemed…whatever it was he was pretending to be, and she wasn't too sure what *that* was, either.

Chapter Three

"It's not fair!" croaked Persephone. "She's *my* best friend! *I* should be his godmother."

Eurydice rolled her eyes exasperatedly and shook her head. "Do you really think this was my idea? I tried to make her change her mind. I *wish* she would change her mind. I don't want the word *mother* associated with my name in any fashion—godly or otherwise."

Eurydice and Persephone had already had this argument several times over the past few days since the unconventional arrival of their new nephew on Friday. Annabelle had decided Eurydice and Ellsworth would be godparents because they were there when he was born. Eurydice tried to convince Annabelle that Persephone would be a better choice, but she wouldn't have it. Now it was Monday, and they were due at the church for the christening. To make matters worse, Persephone couldn't go because she was still sick and unable to get out of bed. She hadn't even seen the baby yet. Somehow, the younger girl had come to blame all of it on Eurydice. For her part, Eurydice did her best to ignore Persephone's foul temper, knowing her sister disliked being ill and was never happy it was unavoidable.

Eurydice didn't know how Ellsworth was taking the request. He was little more than a stranger who had happened upon the two women. She did know he had accepted the honor, but she hadn't seen him since Friday afternoon. She didn't think she would ask him why he had, simply because she didn't know him well enough to do so...and she wasn't so sure he would tell the truth. After lying about speaking Japanese, despite the sisters obviously knowing otherwise, she thought it doubtful.

Persephone blew her nose and coughed several times before Oba poured her something to drink from the pitcher on her night table.

"And who is this Ellsworth person? Why can't the baby have *two* godmothers instead of a complete stranger having the honor of being his godfather? The man won't even care, and the baby's certainly not going to notice," said Persephone with a pout, wiping at her nose with a handkerchief.

"Because that's not the way it works, and you know it," said Eurydice softly. "I really would rather it was you going to the church right now instead of me. You know that."

Persephone slightly relented, her features softening. She did know that. And as unfair as it was, Eurydice did deserve the honor, no matter how much Persephone might wish it were her instead. She also knew it had taken both their parents and Annabelle talking to her repeatedly to convince Eurydice she should be the baby's godmother. While Persephone wouldn't say her sister had an aversion to children, she knew Eurydice considered them a nuisance.

"You better tell me everything that happens as soon as you get home," Persephone ordered, folding her arms across her chest.

"It's a christening, Persy, not a ball."

"I don't care. I want to know if he cries, if he spits up, if he belches, if he farts...*everything*."

"I'll do my best," said Eurydice with a grin.

The whole family was going to the christening, except for Persephone. She was doing much better, but Dr. Hinton had ordered her to stay in bed one more day to make sure she was fully rested. He said putting too much strain on the system for someone of her *delicate* constitution so soon after her temperature returning to normal could cause it to go back up again. For a time, Eurydice wondered if he had her sister confused with another of his patients. Of all the adjectives she would use to describe Persephone, *delicate* was not among them.

Eurydice didn't recall Psyche needing to stay in bed for three days when she caught the influenza the previous season, but then Keung, Maiyin's husband, had tended to her rather than Dr. Hinton. Eurydice preferred Keung when she was ill, too, but now that he no longer worked for her family, it wasn't as convenient. When Pandora married Islington, both Maiyin and Keung went with her, and while they were in town Keung was close, but York was too far from Glamorgan for him to treat them like he used to. Dr. Hinton was an excellent doctor, and far more open-minded than some, especially considering the attitudes of other physicians, but Keung could work miracles.

Eurydice left Persephone's room with the promise she would come see her the minute she returned home. Eurydice didn't anticipate there would be much to report. A christening at a church for a family in mourning seemed likely to be a subdued outing to her.

That did prove to be the case. Gregory Harold Savage was christened without much ado. The service was attended by several of the family's close friends, and the only time he cried was when his mother gave him to Eurydice to be held briefly. Eurydice was no less unhappy with the activity than he, which was probably why he cried. The entire proceeding took less than an hour, but the family was at the church for two hours afterward visiting with friends. Persephone wasn't happy to hear things had been so dull.

The one thing Eurydice didn't bother to mention to her sister was that Ellsworth had asked for his coat back from Friday. He was unconcerned about the rest of the items he had donated, but he was insistent that his coat be returned. Eurydice thought it was peculiar, but he said it was his favorite, and he wanted it back. She wasn't even sure where it was. Someone had probably placed all of it onto the rubbish heap. Either that or it had been burned. But she told him she would see what could be done about finding it, and she would return it to him if at all possible.

He seemed displeased, but Eurydice was unable to guarantee it would be found. She did offer to replace it, considering it probably wouldn't be wearable again even with a good cleaning, but he wanted *that* coat. She again assured him she would do her best to find it. He then told her that he was staying with the Lundeys, along with the rest of his family, and that was where it could be returned. Eurydice thought if the coat had meant so much to him, he should either not have given it to her or remembered to take it with him.

She groaned because it would be yet another thing to keep her from practicing. Over the past few weeks, she had been able to practice little more than one or two hours a day. That was a far cry from the three or four she was accustomed to having. She didn't know where the time was going. Yes, she did. Between portrait paintings, running errands, and delivering babies, she scarcely had time to herself. She was due to go with Psyche to Pandora's that afternoon, and the next, and even more for the next two or three weeks. Then there would be Chrissoula and Stockbridge's reception on Thursday. She could only be grateful they were not attending the Season because at the rate things were going, she would have *no* time for practice at all then.

After Eurydice provided Persephone the details of what had happened at the christening, she began what she was sure would be a futile search for Ellsworth's coat. She went to the mews to ask Ivan, and he didn't recall seeing any discarded clothing in the coach when he cleaned it after their return home. Islington had carried Annabelle to the house, and Maiyin had carried the baby, with Eurydice and her sisters trailing behind. She didn't recall anyone holding Ellsworth's things. She was sure Pandora hadn't touched them, and as squeamish as Psyche could sometimes be, too, Eurydice was sure she hadn't either. She didn't think the clothing could have somehow made its way to Pandora's house. If so, it was certainly gone for good.

She spent two hours looking for the coat to no avail. She had even gone to the rubbish heap to look it over, but she wouldn't go so far as to actually dig through it. If it was buried, *she* was not going to find it for him. She wasn't going to send someone on an errand to Pandora's to ask about it, either. If it was there, Eurydice could ask her sister about it when she went to her house that afternoon. She didn't feel any sense of urgency about it, even if Ellsworth did. She had fairly well decided it was lost.

After looking over the rubbish heap, Eurydice made her way back to her bedroom. She was tired and hoped she would have time for a short nap before going to Pandora's. Because she had spent so much time looking for the coat, she certainly didn't have time to practice. She stopped in briefly to ask Annabelle if she remembered what became of the coat. She didn't, of course, and Eurydice didn't want to stay long because Annabelle was feeding the baby. When she got to her room, she found Agniezka ironing creases out of what appeared to be the missing article of clothing.

"Where did you get that?" blurted Eurydice dumbly.

"From Belinda. She didn't know where it came from, but she knew it certainly didn't belong to Annabelle. I could do nothing for the waistcoat, and there's no getting blood out of white linen well enough for it ever to be worn again in public, but this cleaned. Do you know whose it is?"

Eurydice scratched her forehead confusedly. "I do, actually, and I've been looking for it since I got home. Mr. Ellsworth wants it back."

"Lucky for him it is black. Even if I didn't get all the stains out, they won't show."

"Hmm," said Eurydice noncommittally. She watched as Agniezka continued to press the garment.

"Oh, while I'm thinking about it," said Agniezka as she set the iron aside and went into her small room where she did her mending.

She came back out carrying a small bundle of paper. There appeared to be four or five sheets folded into a square. Eurydice might have thought they were a letter, but there was no seal, and the outside sheet did not have an address. It seemed they were just spare paper he was carrying with him. They were also smeared with blood. Agniezka held the sheets out to Eurydice.

"I found these in the coat just as I was preparing it for the wash."

Eurydice unfolded the sheets and looked. They were all blank.

"That's strange. I thought he removed everything from the pockets before he gave it to me."

"Those weren't in a pocket, actually…not really. I found them in a small pocket in the lining of the coat…at least, I *think* it was a pocket. I might have missed them if I hadn't noticed that it seemed to be particularly stiff where they were."

Eurydice frowned then shrugged. "Oh, well. There appears to be nothing on them, and they're covered in blood. Mr. Ellsworth said he wanted the coat back, but he didn't mention any blank paper. I'll just toss them on the grate."

She put action to words and went to place the sheets onto the small fire Agniezka had lit in the fireplace to heat the iron. The pages fluttered down, not quite landing in the flames but very close. Eurydice was sure they would catch shortly, but she decided to watch, just in case they didn't. She would move them onto the flames if they didn't burn in a few minutes because she didn't want them to stay there until the next fire was lit or until one of the maids came to clean the ashes. Her eyes narrowed then widened in surprise as the heat from the fire began to transform the sheets of paper, making the writing that was hidden on them begin to appear and sharpen into clarity.

"Oh, my goodness!" she gasped as she quickly bent down to remove the pages before they burned completely. She singed the tips of her thumb and index finger on her right hand, and she dropped the pages to the hearth and put her fingers in her mouth with a squeak as she stepped on the edge of the sheets to put them out. They had finally caught fire.

"What? What is it?" asked Agniezka, looking up from her ironing in alarm.

"I burned my fingers," said Eurydice, removing her fingers from her mouth to shake her hand and look at them before putting them back.

She carefully picked up the scorched pages and looked at the words written on them. The ink, and she wasn't sure that's what it was as it had been invisible until it had been exposed to heat, was brown in color. The pages were filled from top to bottom in a neat scrawl interspersed with drawings. Her forehead furrowed as she read, and she felt her heart do an odd fluttery beat. She stood up and looked at Agniezka calmly.

"I'm going to see my father. I'll be back shortly."

"I thought you were going to burn those!" called Agniezka as Eurydice left the room with the pages. She shook her head as she looked after Eurydice for a moment before getting back to her ironing.

Eurydice went down the stairs to the main floor and turned down the hall that would lead to her father's study. He was at home rather than in Parliament because of the christening, but he still had plenty of work to do without going to Westminster. The door was closed, and she knocked briefly before hearing her father calling for her to enter from the other side. Her siblings would have simply walked in without knocking, and Eurydice was sure her father wouldn't have minded, but she thought that was rude. The duke looked up expectantly from what he was writing and smiled fondly when he saw her, setting the fountain pen aside.

"Eurydice, what a surprise," he said happily. "I might have thought you were asleep since I haven't heard you practicing today. Are you feeling well?" His forehead wrinkled with concern when he thought that another of his children might be coming down with an illness.

"I'm fine, Father," said Eurydice quietly, giving him a smile. "I've had things to do that have kept me from practicing, and I'm thoroughly tired of it."

The duke chuckled amusedly at her annoyed tone. Yes, he could only imagine how put-out she was at not being able to practice. Anything that kept her away from her violin was an inconvenience at best, but he had to wonder what it was that was important enough to drag her away from it.

"What can I do for you, dearest?"

"Well, Father, I think you should look at this."

She held out the scorched pages. He frowned slightly as he took them from her, and it deepened even further as he read what was written there. He looked up at Eurydice.

"Where did you get this?"

"On Friday, Mr. Ellsworth gave me his coat to use when Annabelle was in labor. This morning at the christening, he said he wanted it back. Agniezka had cleaned it, so it can be returned to him, but when she was getting ready to clean it, she checked it for belongings and found those." She pointed at the pages in his hand. "They were blank when I first saw them, and I thought to put them on the fire because of the blood, but when the pages got hot...." She shrugged. "I brought them to you straight away."

"Does anyone else know about this?"

"No, Father. I didn't even tell Agniezka."

He nodded approvingly and gave her an assuring smile. "Good, good. You did the right thing. Let's just keep this between us for now, shall we?"

"Of course, Father," said Eurydice with a slight frown. "Why would he have that?"

"I don't know, dearest, but you can be sure I'll find out." He gave her another smile. "You run along now."

"All right, Father," said Eurydice absently, and the frown she wore did not lessen. He seemed concerned, as she had expected him to be, but not nearly as concerned as she might have thought. It was very odd, but her father would know exactly what needed to be done with the situation.

Aberdare watched his daughter leave the room and close the door behind her. He sighed gustily with a shake of his head and moved aside the papers he had been working on and took a clean sheet out of the drawer. He stood up and placed the papers Eurydice had given him into the safe and closed it, and then he went back to his desk, took up his pen and clucked his tongue as he began to write.

"Bloody fool. It's a wonder he hasn't been killed by now."

Eurydice was wearing a dark gray dress, her hair coiled into its usual, unadorned knot. It was the closest she could come to mourning without being too gloomy to attend a wedding reception, and the gray was kinder to her complexion than black. The entire affair would be subdued in any case because Chrissoula was a member of their staff, so she was technically in mourning also. There wouldn't be any dancing or other entertainment, just a simple buffet and champagne punch. Lord Sheerness would be there because Stockbridge was his bosun, and he was also very good friends with Chrissoula's family in Greece. The first mate from the *Medea*, Mr. Higginbotham, and his nephew, Freddie Bunney, would be there, as would Dr. Felton, the ship's surgeon. Otherwise, it would just be the Aberdares, their family, and other members of the staff.

Most people would consider it odd that they would provide and attend a reception for Psyche's maid and a bosun, but the Aberdares considered their servants to be extended members of their family. Not only that, but Chrissoula was considered a member of the aristocracy in her homeland...if it had been common knowledge there that she was still alive. For them not to have the reception would have been unthinkable, and it wasn't as if Society would know, even if the Aberdares cared.

At least for one day, Eurydice wouldn't have to go with Psyche to Pandora's house, but they would be going the following day. She wasn't sure how much more Isabey had to do on her portrait. She was sitting for him three hours at a stretch almost daily. The canvas wasn't large; perhaps that was why it seemed to be taking a long time. In truth, Eurydice hadn't even looked at it. She knew from looking over his shoulder from a distance through the window that he was only about halfway finished with the portrait of Psyche in the garden temple, so Eurydice could only assume he had only made that much progress on hers as well. It seemed her estimate that it was going to be a fortnight before he was finished was accurate.

The reception was no livlier than Eurydice had anticipated it would be. She did enjoy meeting Freddie after hearing so much about him from both Psyche and Pandora, and their younger brothers took to him as well. Freddie was the cabin boy on the *Medea*, but it seemed he was looking forward to one day becoming a first mate like his uncle. Psyche had made sure to warn him beforehand not to mention some of the adventures they had on the ship the previous year, but he was able to tell Cosmo, Christopher, and Damon plenty even after leaving out the most alarming parts.

Chrissoula and Stockbridge seemed very happy with one another, and Eurydice was glad. She knew Chrissoula's history, and she was pleased the young woman would finally have a little joy in her life. As much as she loved Psyche and being with their family, Chrissoula was homesick for her own family. Eurydice hoped one day soon she would be able to see them again.

By the time everyone left, it was late afternoon. Eurydice would not have time to practice. She thought she would at least have time to do more composing before supper. She was making progress on the piece she was working on, but she'd had no more time to play it on the piano than she had for playing the violin. It was frustrating. She believed she was transcribing everything the way she was hearing it in her head, but she couldn't be sure without actually being able to play it. Perhaps once Isabey was done painting her portrait she would finally be able to sit down at the piano and see.

"But, Dad, we *have* to go!" complained Persephone with a pout. "We're going to ruin Psyche's run if we don't, and what about all the people who look forward to using our pavilion?"

"Persephone, you know better than to ask whether we can go to the Derby," said Aberdare calmly. "Your sister's run at picking the winner for ten years won't be ruined if she doesn't even go to make a selection. The people who've come to depend on it will understand why she doesn't this year. It is only a horse race, after all. As for the pavilion, it is going to be set up as usual with Lord Stranraer overseeing the festivities."

"But, Dad—"

"Persephone, I said no, and there will be no further discussion," said the duke firmly.

Persephone tightened her jaw in vexation and stalked out of her father's study, going to the library next door where Eurydice sat in an armchair by the window reading a book. She looked over the top of it at her younger sister as she flounced into the adjacent chair, folding her arms across her chest with a sullen expression.

"I told you that he wouldn't change his mind," said Eurydice quietly.

"Oh, pooh. I just haven't used the right argument yet," said Persephone petulantly.

The Derby would be the following day. Persephone was desperate to go. She had been pleading with her father for weeks, and he had adamantly refused to let her or any of the family attend. Persephone loved to gamble, betting on horses especially. Psyche had been picking the winner for the last ten years, and Persephone always took home a nice sum, as did most of the friends and associates of her brothers and father.

"He's *not* going to change his mind. Believe me. It's only once that you'll have to miss it, Persy. It's not the end of the world."

"Gregory would have wanted us to go…so would Myron."

"It's not a question of whether or not they would have wanted us to go, Persy. We are in mourning. Going to the Derby when one is in mourning is not allowed."

"Rubbish! Sheerness went last year when *he* was in mourning."

"Yes, but Lord Sheerness is a *man.*"

Persephone's expression grew thoughtful. "Yes," she said slowly. She slapped her thighs and stood up. "I'm going to my room."

"Hmm," said Eurydice absently, turning back to the page she was reading. She heard the door open and close and shook her head. "You're going to get into trouble," she said to the empty room.

The following day, Eurydice had enough spare time to go to the piano. She had two hours before she would have to go to Pandora's with Psyche, and she intended to use every minute of it practicing her piece and making any corrections. She had even managed to get in a few hours on her violin, so she was feeling the day was turning out to be very productive, even if she did have to go sit in a chair by a window without moving for two or three hours.

She was able to get through the first movement with only minor adjustments necessary and had started on the second when there was a knock at the door. Eurydice groaned frustratedly and scratched her forehead. Now she would have to start all over again.

"Come in," she called.

Corbie, one of the footmen, entered the room.

"Pardon the intrusion, Lady Eurydice, but there's a Mr. Ellsworth and a Mr. Wilde here to see you."

"Me? They specifically want to see *me*?"

"Yes, mum."

Eurydice frowned. "Oh, all right. Show them in, please, Corbie."

He nodded and left the room, only to return momentarily to show in Mr. Ellsworth and a younger gentleman Eurydice didn't know. At least, she didn't think she knew him. He seemed vaguely familiar, but she couldn't recall ever meeting Mr. Wilde. She knew that happened a lot, though—her forgetting the names of people. Perhaps if she spoke with him for a while, she would determine why she felt like they had met before. She stood up from the piano and went to greet them.

"Mr. Ellsworth, this is an unexpected surprise," she said neutrally as she held out her hand.

"Yes, for both of us," he said cryptically with a wry smile as he brushed her knuckles. He waved his hand in the direction of the other man. "May I introduce my newfound friend, Mr. Percy Wilde? We only just met in Epsom, and I thought I should bring him here to meet you straight away."

Eurydice frowned. That was entirely peculiar. Why would he find it necessary to bring a new acquaintance to meet *her*? They were her nephew's godparents, but she really couldn't say their familiarity with each other was any more than casual. There was no reason she could think of that would prompt him to assume she would want to meet his new friend. She had returned his coat, minus the papers, and she had not heard a word from him that he had noticed anything amiss with the garment. She had not asked her father what he was doing or had done with the papers and finding out why Ellsworth had them. She was sure his grace was more than capable of addressing it without her needing to concern herself with it any further. She hadn't seen Ellsworth since the christening and had honestly not had any expectation of doing so. She was beginning to find that he was something of an enigma, and that piqued her curiosity. She held out her hand to the other man.

"How do you do?" she asked politely. Then she saw the younger man's expression, and her eyes widened in shock. *"Persephone?"* she squeaked. "Oh, my giddy aunt! You went to the Derby, didn't you?"

Persephone took off her hat and shook out her hair before flouncing past her sister to one of the sofas. She carefully removed the fake whiskers she had attached to the sides of her face and rubbed a hand over the skin where the adhesive had irritated it. She gave her sister a mischievous grin and a wink and propped her booted feet onto the edge of the low table in front of her.

"Don't look so smug, Persy! You are in so much trouble!" said Eurydice hotly.

"Oh, calm down, Dicy. I am not in trouble," chortled Persephone.

"Yes, you are," said Eurydice. She looked from her sister to Ellsworth.

"Actually, I don't think anyone else realized what and who she was," he said evenly, and Eurydice's lips tightened when she saw his expression of amusement.

"The two of you think this is funny?" asked Eurydice irritatedly.

"No, of course not," denied Ellsworth, but the way the corners of his eyes crinkled with silent laughter said otherwise.

"I *knew* you were going to do this," said Eurydice, deciding to ignore Ellsworth for the moment and turning back to her sister. "I should have told Father yesterday what I thought you were about."

"I'm glad you didn't. I won five hundred pounds," said Persephone with an unapologetic grin. "Don't look so indignant! It was completely harmless."

"Harmless?" hooted Eurydice. "What if you had been found out? You *were* found out!"

"For what it's worth, I'll not tell a soul," said Ellsworth helpfully.

Eurydice rounded on him. "You stay out of this. You're…you're abetting a delinquent!" Ellsworth laughed outright then. When she heard Persephone's own chortle, Eurydice looked at her. "I think I should tell Father right now!"

Persephone's eyes rounded. "Oh, no! Don't tell him, please!" She could tell by Eurydice's expression that she was perfectly serious, and that Persephone and Ellsworth seemed to be sharing a joke at her expense only made matters worse. Eurydice did not like to be made fun of. "I didn't get caught, and I swear I will never do it again! Just, please, don't tell Dad. Please?"

"It really was harmless," said Ellsworth evenly.

Eurydice turned to look at him. "Thank you, Mr. Ellsworth, for seeing my sister home, but I believe I can take care of this."

His warm expression faded at her cold, dismissing tone, and Ellsworth clasped his hands behind his back. "Of course, Lady Eurydice." He bowed formally, and then he looked past her to Persephone on the sofa. "Try not to swish so much when you walk next time," he said with a slight grin and a wink.

Eurydice bit her tongue on a retort as she watched him leave the drawing room. It was obvious he didn't understand that Persephone needed no encouragement when it came to dressing like a man. Her family was trying to discourage her from doing it quite so often now that she was a young woman of eighteen years, but they all realized they had let it continue for far too long for her to willingly let go of the habit. Now that her older brothers were no longer there to indulge her, she had become even less cooperative on the matter. And it was one thing for her to go around the house in breeches, but to go so far as to put on fake whiskers and risk being seen in public dressed as one was an entirely different matter.

"Dicy, you were positively horrid to him!" said Persephone, rising from the sofa to go stand in front of her sister with her hands on her hips angrily. "It wasn't as if *he* had anything to do with it."

"I was not horrid," defended Eurydice calmly. "I thanked him for bringing you home, and I was polite."

"You were not," argued Persephone hotly. "You dismissed him like the hired help. No, worse; you don't even speak to the servants that way."

"Humph," said Eurydice shortly. "You don't need anyone putting ideas into your head for being naughty, and he was positively applauding you, so you'll have to excuse my not offering to let him stay for tea."

"You don't like him, do you?"

Eurydice shrugged. "I have no opinion one way or the other. There's something not right about him, but I haven't figured out what it is yet. Until I do, I'm reserving judgment. His finding your little charade so amusing is not a point in his favor."

"Mm-hmm," said Persephone, folding her arms across her chest. "Are you going to tell Dad?"

Eurydice looked at her sister consideringly for a moment. She really thought she should tell their father. She had the feeling Persephone's adventure today was only going to be the first of many more, but she couldn't quite decide if telling their father would do anything to prevent them or not. She suspected not. Both Persephone and Ellsworth swore no one but he had discovered she was a female. That was possible. Persephone's disguise had been so effective even Eurydice had almost not recognized her…probably wouldn't have from a further distance. Other than yelling and taking away privileges, she wasn't sure what her father could do about it after the fact in any event.

"You won't do it again?"

"I swear I will never dress up as a man and go to the Derby ever again," said Persephone solemnly.

Eurydice narrowed her eyes as she looked at her sister. She did not miss the implications in the wording of the oath. It left her younger sister with lots of room for further misadventures.

"No, I won't tell Father…this time," said Eurydice resignedly, "but only on one condition."

"Name it," said Persephone with a relieved grin.

"From now until I leave for Vienna, you will not say one word if I want to practice early in the morning. You will not break another violin string or bow, and if you do, I will tell Father everything."

Persephone looked almost as if she would say no, but then she nodded her head. "All right," she muttered.

Eurydice reached up to Persephone's cheek to remove more of the fake whiskers with a slight smile. "You've still got a bit of the man about you. We'd better get it all cleaned off before someone sees you. And you really won five hundred pounds? Wow."

Persephone kept to her word about not complaining when Eurydice practiced early. Eurydice didn't take undue advantage, but she was able to get in an extra hour that she had otherwise been missing. By the middle of the month, Isabey was through, and needing to rise early for practice ended. That relieved her as much as Persephone because Eurydice hadn't liked getting up early, but she had needed the practice…at least, she thought she did.

As for the portrait, Eurydice had to admit it was a good likeness. The twins, Islington, and Sheerness all thought it was an *excellent* likeness. She had no idea what she was going to do with it. She could have it sent to Wilderland to be hung in the portrait gallery, but there really was no rush. Sending it home with her family at the end of the season would be soon enough. Psyche was still unaware that Sheerness knew her own portrait was to be his wedding present, but he didn't know that it was a nude or that it would be painted into miniature on a pocket watch, which Eurydice finally discovered herself. She somewhat hoped she was there when her sister gave it to him. She was sure his reaction was going to be something to behold.

The middle of June was a somber time for the Aberdares. It marked the one year anniversary of Myron's death. The duke and duchess made arrangements to return home to Wilderland for the week to visit Myron's grave, but they didn't require the rest of the family to go as well. They left from London on Friday evening for Glyncorrwg, and they intended to be back the following Friday. Their children would manage on their own; they had been left to their own devices before for much longer periods. It was only the purpose behind this journey that was different.

On Tuesday evening after supper, while the rest of her siblings retreated to their own rooms or gathered in the family's private sitting room, Eurydice went to the drawing room to practice her piece for the piano. She had finally completed it, and she wanted to play through the entire thing to hear if it was cohesive. She was concerned it might not be because of all the interruptions while she was composing it. It was a little late, but only her younger brothers were asleep. If she kept the door closed, she wouldn't disturb anyone. Aside from that, it wasn't a very loud piece. She would be surprised if anyone even heard her playing.

She had just reached the bottom step when there was loud knocking at the front door. She hesitated for a moment with a curious frown, wondering who would be calling at such an hour, especially considering that her family was still in mourning. She continued on her way the short distance down the hall that would take her in sight of the front door on her way to the drawing room and jumped when there was another loud knock. Eurydice could see Tannaz hurrying on his way down the hall from the servants' area, and she gave him a brief smile before turning in the direction of the drawing room. She had to admit she was curious who was at the door, obviously impatient for it to be answered. Tannaz would tell whomever it was that the family wasn't receiving visitors at this hour and send the person on his way.

As Eurydice situated herself at the piano, she felt confident it wasn't anything bad that brought someone to their door at almost eleven at night…at least, not about someone in her family. Their own servants wouldn't knock at the front door, and she couldn't think of any others who would either. As far as she knew everyone was healthy and safe. She put it from her mind as she arranged the sheets of her composition and flexed her fingers to begin playing.

She didn't even make it to the middle of the first page before the doors of the drawing room flew open. She jumped, and her fingers made a discordant sound on the piano as they hit the wrong keys. She was beginning to wonder if the sonata was doomed to remain unplayed forever.

"I need to see your father."

"I'm sorry, Lady Eurydice, I tried to stop him," said Tannaz at the same time.

Eurydice rose from the piano and slowly walked toward the door with a slight frown. The man who had unceremoniously burst in was unkempt, to give his appearance a kind description. He had several days' growth of beard, and his clothing was spattered with mud that had long since dried into place, particularly on his coat, boots, and breeches. As she came closer, she caught the odor of wet leather and horses with a healthy dose of several types of stale tobacco and alcohol, as if he might have recently been spending a large amount of time in a tavern or public house rather than partaking of all of it alone. But then again, she supposed he could have. She had the distinct impression he hadn't bathed for days, and she fought very hard to keep her nose from wrinkling in distaste. If she didn't know who he was or what he normally looked like, she might have mistaken him for a brigand. She gave Tannaz an understanding smile.

"I'm sure you did your best," she said kindly before giving the other man a stony look. "I'll take care of it. You may go, and thank you." Eurydice continued to look at Ellsworth as the footman bowed and left the room. "My father is not here, as I'm sure Tannaz told you when he answered the door. It's also rude to force one's way into someone's home without invitation at any time, but especially at eleven at night, Mr. Ellsworth. Not that I wish anyone ill, but there had better be a death or a serious maiming involved," she finished icily as she folded her arms across her chest.

When he started to laugh and picked her up to swing her in a circle, it was not the reaction Eurydice had anticipated. She began to push at his shoulders with her hands, trying to get him to put her down. That, too, did not produce the result she expected...not really. He did put her down, only to give her a sound kiss on the lips. She was momentarily stunned to inaction, her eyes rounded in surprise. When he lifted his head to look at her, Ellsworth was grinning hugely.

"Mr. Ellsworth!" she gasped. "Have you gone insane?" Now that Eurydice thought about it, it would explain his odd appearance and behavior.

He laughed and kissed her again, and Eurydice thought she might have to take drastic measures of some sort. She didn't know what the cause of his actions was, but he needed to stop them immediately. It was unseemly *and* disconcerting.

"Mr. Ellsworth, I demand that you let me go at once and explain yourself!"

He didn't let her go, and he looked down at her with a wide grin.

"Napoleon's been defeated at Waterloo."

Eurydice's lips parted in surprise, and her forehead wrinkled in confusion at the news. If it was true, it was wonderful. But how would Mr. Ellsworth know? She was so stunned by what he said, she didn't notice he was lowering his head to kiss her again. And when he did kiss her, this time, it was different.

Whereas before the kisses had been close-mouthed and almost impersonal, this time his lips pressed against hers softly, in a way that was entirely intimate. At first, she realized he was kissing her in a somewhat disassociated way; she was still trying to digest the news that Napoleon had been defeated. But then, as he continued to kiss her, the pressure of his lips becoming more insistent, it began to be the sole focus of her attention.

She had never been kissed before, and it affected her on a level she hadn't anticipated. As much as she tried to analyze it, there was a part of her that reacted to it with pure instinct. She noticed several different things. His lips were soft and warm as he slowly darted his tongue into her mouth to play it against her own, in contrast to the roughness of the growth of beard she felt on his chin as it brushed against her face. As dirty as he appeared and smelled, the taste of him was clean and tantalizing, a mixture of whisky and mint that was in no way unpleasant. His hold on her was gentle but definite, and Eurydice found herself having no interest in removing herself from it. As much as she knew this was improper, as much as she knew there was something not quite right about Ellsworth, his kissing her seemed to be as natural as her breathing…or playing music.

When he ended the kiss and raised his head to look down at Eurydice, she slowly opened her eyes, her expression dazed. She felt utterly confused, which was no easy task to accomplish.

"Where is the duke?" he asked softly.

Eurydice's forehead wrinkled. "The what?" she asked blankly.

"The duke? Your father? Where has he gone?" asked Ellsworth slowly, his expression slightly amused at her bemusement.

"Oh, he's gone to Wilderland for the week. He should return Friday," said Eurydice automatically. She couldn't understand why she felt in such a stupor.

Ellsworth grinned and let her go. He ran his fingertip along her jaw before tapping it gently on her chin, and then he turned and left without another word.

Eurydice looked after him at the closed door, and she tried to regain some of her composure. After several minutes, she heaved a huge sigh and turned to go collect her score sheets from the piano. Her desire to try playing the sonata had completely gone away for the moment.

"Well, I certainly didn't see *that* coming," she muttered to herself.

Chapter Four

Over the days that followed, Eurydice tried to put Ellsworth and his actions from her mind, but it wasn't easy. When she went to the family's sitting room to tell them the news, Dorian had been more excited by it than the rest. He had even seemed angry that she didn't tell him Ellsworth had arrived at the house, and it wasn't because she had been alone with the man in the drawing room. That did nothing to help Eurydice reassert her calm perspective.

For some reason, Ellsworth was making her life chaotic. She wasn't sure she liked that. She was accustomed to an orderliness to her days, and he was disturbing that…somehow. She didn't think it was intentional, but he left her feeling mystified. Since he kissed her, Eurydice found herself thinking about him more than was wise, and it wasn't only because he had kissed her. The more she knew about him, it seemed there was less she *understood* about him. She couldn't recall ever experiencing that before, and she wasn't quite sure how a man who had so little contact with her could cause it.

In addition to the confusion he had caused by kissing her, Eurydice was startled to discover that the news Ellsworth had brought of Napoleon being defeated at Waterloo didn't arrive in an official dispatch from Wellington to the Secretary for War until late in the evening the following day, and it wasn't something made available to the general public until the day after that. Again, Eurydice had to wonder how he had known. Unless he was there and had left for London the minute it happened, it was physically impossible for him to have known as soon as he did. She did realize that would explain his appearance perfectly, but if it were true, it would mean her growing suspicions about him were actually realizations. She didn't believe for an instant that it could be due to any type of presentient ability on his part.

And she could only assume he had wanted to see her father to give him that news. Her father did a lot of work with Bathurst and the War Office, as did Dorian, Islington, and Sheerness; although, Sheerness seemed to do more with the Foreign Office. She wasn't sure exactly what it was her father did, and she couldn't imagine asking him, even if she felt confident he would tell her. Considering how momentous Napoleon's defeat was for the country, Eurydice thought it would have been more logical for Ellsworth to want to deliver that news to the Secretary for War and the Regent rather than her father. It was almost as if he didn't want them to know that he knew. She wondered for a time about what her father had done with the papers from Ellsworth's coat, but she still wasn't going to ask his grace about them.

The duke and duchess had returned from Wilderland that Friday as planned, but they had returned much earlier in the day than Eurydice and everyone else had expected. There was no mention of Ellsworth and his news, but Eurydice knew that was why they had rushed back. Her father and Dorian were gone from the house to Whitehall and Downing Street for much of the day until late at night, sometimes not even returning in time to have supper. Eurydice also knew it kept Islington and Sheerness busy. Again, it was disorder and confusion, caused somehow by Ellsworth.

Added to all of this chaos he was bringing to her family, there was the confusion he caused her personally after kissing her. She could not understand for the life of her why he had done it. That the war was over was a joyous thing, but she couldn't say that it warranted his kissing her…possibly not even his kissing someone else for that matter. She had felt something when he did it, and she had not been able to determine exactly what it was. She certainly hadn't mentioned it to anyone in her family, not even to Agniezka. She was still trying to analyze it and decide how she should proceed if she saw him again. That she *would* see him again seemed likely.

Her family's mourning for Gregory was officially over by the middle of July. They could, theoretically, begin attending social functions again, but none of them had any interest in doing so. They were all content to wait until the following Season to begin again. Persephone was relieved her debut would be delayed that much longer. None of the rest of the family had any desire to start into a season that would be over in less than a month in any case. Their mourning was over in time for the family to celebrate the Aberdares' wedding anniversary and the duchess's birthday, and for Psyche to marry Sheerness at the close of the season. Those were the only two social functions any of them really cared about at all in any event.

The duke and duchess did not celebrate their anniversary the previous year because it had only been a month since Myron's death. It had, in fact, been the first time since they had been married that they weren't together on that day. The duchess had remained with most of the family at Wilderland after the funeral, while the duke, Dorian, and Psyche had returned to London. Their anniversary dinner was never a grand production—it only included family and a few very close friends—and this time would be no different. The family and their friends would gather in the drawing room for conversation and aperitifs prior to supper, then supper, followed by some type of musical entertainment in the drawing room. At the last party, the three older girls had sung a song, accompanied by Dorian on the piano, followed by Eurydice playing her violin. This year, Eurydice was going to play her recently composed sonata.

Once the initial excitement over the end of the war had lessened, Eurydice was actually able to play the piece through from beginning to end without interruption. She was pleased to hear it wasn't as jumbled as she was concerned it might be. She had yet to give it a name, other than giving it a number, but something would come to her eventually; it always did. No one else in the family had really heard it yet; she didn't allow anyone else to be in the same room with her when she was playing a piece through for the first time, except for Agniezka, but parts of it would sound familiar to them.

On the night of the anniversary party, Eurydice sat at her dressing table as Agniezka styled her hair. She was already in her gown, which her maid had selected, and she watched in the mirror with only mild interest as Agniezka tamed and twisted her hair. The dress was made of a green and gold woven silk that seemed to change from one color to the other as the fabric shifted in the light. The top edge of the bodice was trimmed with a lighter green mull, almost like a fichu. There was a sash of the same mull at the bottom edge of the bodice, and the bottom of the skirt was intricately embroidered in gold and dark green in a pattern of flowers, leaves and vines. It was one of the new dresses Janet had made for her, and the shade suited her coloring well.

"You'll wear the amber earrings Pandora gave you the year before last and the necklace Psyche brought back for you from Greece, *da*?" said Agniezka as she finished adjusting a gold comb into Eurydice's braided and coiled hair.

"Whatever you think is best," said Eurydice agreeably with a brief smile to Agniezka in the mirror.

"Are you nervous about playing tonight?"

"Only a little," said Eurydice with a shrug.

In truth, she was very nervous. She always was when she played in front of people besides family. The more people present who weren't family, the more anxious she became, and tonight she would be playing her own piece. She wasn't sure how many people her mother had invited, but it was more than just family. She would have to try not to think about it. She was comfortable with the sonata, and there was no reason she should not play it well.

Agniezka put in the earrings, a simple yet elegant pair of silver and amber drops Pandora had given Eurydice for her birthday two years ago. The necklace Psyche had given her a year later for Christmas seemed to be from a matched set separated by thousands of miles. The color and size of the beads matched perfectly, and the amber in both echoed the color of Eurydice's eyes. Regardless of her own opinion of her appearance, Eurydice was the most beautiful of her sisters. Even they would agree without hesitation.

After Agniezka helped her put on her elbow length gloves, Eurydice rose from her seat and went to collect her sheet music from her desk. She didn't anticipate she would need it, but she would look it over a few times more just to be sure. She bade Agniezka farewell and decided to see if Psyche was ready. She suspected not, as was the usual case, but perhaps Eurydice's arrival would prompt her to hurry. They still had fifteen or twenty minutes before they could expect the first guests to arrive, but the duchess wanted them to be downstairs *before* then. She came out of her room just as Persephone was leaving hers, and Eurydice almost didn't recognize her.

Persephone was in an evening dress...unwillingly, judging by her petulant expression. Her gown was made of a reddish-brown silk that almost matched the color of her hair. There was a braided gold cord tied beneath the bodice, and the bottom of the skirt was intricately embroidered with gold foil and a lighter shade of reddish-brown thread in a pattern of scallops, medallions, and leaves that came almost to her knees. The sleeves, which reached the middle of her upper arm, were split, exposing an undersleeve made of gold tissue. Oba had gathered most of her hair to the back of her head and coiled it low on her neck, but the shorter layers at the front were left loose in natural waves that framed her face.

"Persy, you look very beautiful," said Eurydice with a proud smile.

"I don't care," said Persephone darkly.

Eurydice's lips quirked in amusement. "No, I don't suppose you would." She went to her sister to link their arms together at the elbow and started walking down the hall with her toward Psyche's bedroom. "You do realize a few hours in a dress will not prove fatal?"

"I don't know about that," muttered Persephone as she reached up a hand to adjust the bottom edge of her bodice. "This thing's so tight I can't breathe."

"Well, I suppose after all that time wearing waistcoats and men's shirts, having something fastened at that particular location does take a bit of getting used to, but it will eventually get to the point you don't notice."

"Not ruddy likely," said Persephone with a grin. "I don't intend to be wearing things like this often enough for that to happen."

"What about next season? You know Mother and Father will expect you to go somewhere every night, and then there'll be your presentation at court...." Eurydice trailed off. "You may as well start getting used to it now, a little at a time. And it's not as if you've *never* worn a dress before, but evening gowns are constructed a little differently than other dresses."

"Humph," said Persephone doubtfully.

After Eurydice knocked briefly on the door, she walked into Psyche's bedroom and saw to her surprise that only Chrissoula was there, putting things away that had been taken out as Psyche tried to decide what to wear. There were stockings and slippers strewn about, and at least four different gowns were thrown across the bed.

"Has she already gone down, then?" blurted Eurydice as she looked about the room with raised eyebrows.

"Oh, yes, about five minutes ago. She's impatient to see her man," said Chrissoula with a chuckle.

Eurydice and Persephone turned and left the room, closing the door behind them. They went back down the hall to the right to go to the landing and take the stairs to the ground floor.

"Ugh, men," said Persephone disgustedly. "What's so special about *men*? Sheerness seems all right, but why would she want to get *married*?" She shrugged. "They're fine for shooting with, gambling with, racing horses and whatnot with, but *marriage?* Not ever," she finished definitely with a shake of her head.

Eurydice's lips twitched amusedly at Persephone's attitude. Eurydice wasn't so quite against the male population as her sister, and Persephone's opinion would change, whether she liked it or not. Eurydice supposed one day she would fall in love and marry because that was the natural course one's life was expected to take, but there were other things she wanted to accomplish first. She didn't spend her days wondering when it would happen, waiting for it to happen, or what it would feel like when it *did* happen. There was a difference between the love she felt for her family and the way she would feel when she loved a man, but she wasn't sure what the difference was. Judging from the things she had heard from Selena and Annabelle, Pandora and Psyche, it would be obvious.

And that made Eurydice wonder if she really wanted to ever have it happen. It seemed to be quite disruptive…falling in love. She didn't think she would like that. Perhaps it would be just as convenient for her to marry someone she didn't love. It would give her companionship, and the required production of eventual children, except she wouldn't have the uncertainty that seemed to be part and parcel of being in love with her spouse. At least she believed she would eventually marry one way or another. Persephone seemed determined to fight matrimony in any form tooth and nail. Luckily, their parents would never force her to marry if she didn't wish it.

The duke and duchess were standing at the bottom of the stairs when they reached them, and they kissed the girls on the cheek and gave them a hug.

"Happy birthday, Mother," said Eurydice quietly.

"Oh, thank you, dearest," said Julia with a fond smile. "I'm looking forward to hearing you play after supper. After all, it won't be long before I will certainly be missing it." Julia's eyes sparkled slightly as she smoothed a hand down Eurydice's cheek and gave her a loving pat on the shoulder.

"Thank you, Mother," whispered Eurydice.

The duchess cleared her throat and smiled brightly. "Well, in any event, I'll tell you with whom you're to go into supper, and then you can join everyone in the drawing room."

"Who's here?" blurted Persephone.

"Other than family? No one yet. Dorian and Selena are there, and Psyche came down not too long ago. She will, of course, be going in with Sheerness. Persephone, you'll be going in with Baron Lambeth."

"Do I have to?" pouted Persephone.

"And what does that mean? You've never met him," said the duke sternly.

"Yes, I have. Two years ago almost this very night, we were introduced, and he was at Wilderland for Myron's funeral last year. He's obnoxious."

"Persephone, we'll have none of that tonight," said the duchess. "You will go into supper with Baron Lambeth, and you *will* be polite. You will talk, and you will smile. There is absolutely nothing wrong with him."

"But—" began Persephone.

"Enough!" bit out her grace. "We have let you run wild for far too long, and it is telling on you."

"Oh, Mum, I—" began Persephone again with a cajoling smile.

"No!" said Julia firmly. She exchanged a resigned glance with her husband and looked back to her youngest daughter. "Your father and I have been very indulgent with you. But no more," she said ominously. "Beginning tonight, for a year and a day, you will behave like the properly brought up young woman we've raised you to be. There'll be no more boots and breeches. No more gambling or racing. You will wear a dress, and while you may not like it, you will *not* complain. At the end of that time, if you still feel so inclined, you may take back up your pursuits. For now, it ends. Do you understand me?"

Eurydice looked from her parents to her sister, her heart thudding anxiously. She didn't want to witness this. As much as she wanted to believe this was not an eventuality, it had been looming for some time. Her parents had tried reasoning with Persephone, but she wasn't willing to compromise. They had given her freedom to do as she willed, believing she would eventually settle down, but she had only seemed to grow worse, especially since Myron and Gregory had been killed. And now, when her parents required her to do her duty, she was unwilling. For the situation to draw to this conclusion was going to make them all unhappy, but Eurydice knew there would be no other way...there *could* be no other way. It broke her heart to see it.

Persephone looked as if her mother had struck her. Her jaw clenched, and her eyes glistened with tears, and she blinked several times to keep them from escaping. She squared her shoulders and inhaled sharply before giving a slight nod of her head.

"Yes, Mother," she finally answered in a voice barely above a whisper.

"Eurydice, you'll go into supper with Mr. Ellsworth," said the duchess tonelessly, giving Eurydice a brief glance.

"Yes, Mother," said Eurydice mildly.

She might have complained about her mother's choice of dinner companion for her, but there had been enough arguing. For her, Ellsworth was only disturbing...not obnoxious, and she could bear being in his company for the four or five hours the evening would require. She knew well enough how to be polite, even to those she disliked. Persephone truly did as well, but she didn't see a reason for needing to. Now she would have to learn.

After the sisters turned down the hall to go to the drawing room and were out of sight of their parents, Eurydice moved her arm from where she had it linked with Persephone's at her elbow and put it around her shoulders to give her a comforting squeeze. It wasn't that she didn't want her parents to see her offering her sister sympathy; Persephone didn't want them to see.

"Oh, Persy, I'm so sorry," said Eurydice quietly.

Persephone shrugged off her sister's arm and stuck out her chin stubbornly.

"It doesn't matter," she said stonily, and she quickened her pace to walk ahead of Eurydice.

Eurydice looked after her sadly, her own step slowing a bit. It was only going to get worse for Persephone before it got better, she knew, and she wished she didn't. She put a hand to her chest and patted it softly, trying to calm the beating of her heart as she took several deep breaths in and out through her nose. It was at times like this that she wished she could be oblivious. Because even as she knew what was coming, she also knew no matter how much she wanted to prevent the things she saw from happening, they were going to regardless.

It wasn't a fatalistic outlook. It was realistic. When she was younger, when she became aware of what possessed her and *Babushka* Alexa had explained it to her, she had tried to change things, believing that had to be the purpose behind having the Insight. And that was what taught her that she was possessed by the Insight rather than being in possession of it. Because not only was she powerless to control the things she saw, she was also powerless to stop them from happening.

Once she managed to get her emotions under control, she hurried to catch up to Persephone just as she reached the door to the drawing room.

"Persy, wait," said Eurydice, putting her hand over her sister's on the handle. She hugged her younger sister tightly and smoothed a soothing hand over her back. "I love you," she said softly.

Persephone was momentarily overwhelmed by Eurydice's almost desperate embrace, but she returned her sister's hug and gave her a blithe smile when Eurydice released her to look at her face worriedly.

"I'll be fine, Dicy," said Persephone, giving her an affectionate nudge to her shoulder. "It'll only be a year and a day."

"Yes," said Eurydice affirmingly with a slight smile of her own.

The drawing room was full of people as they prepared to go into supper. The air was filled with the sound of many different conversations, and Corbie and Tannaz circulated around the room unobtrusively making sure all the guests had drinks. Eurydice was of the opinion that at least one or two did not require one.

One in particular was Viscount Drake, the son of the Earl and Countess of Lundey. From what Eurydice could see, he would have benefited more from something sobering. She might not have noticed his inebriation if she didn't know him so well, but to her, and everyone else, it was obvious. He had changed dramatically since the previous Season, and not for the better.

Around mid-June of the previous year, only the day before Myron had been killed, in fact, he had married Victoria Manson, a beautiful if somewhat peculiar girl. The Aberdares and their older children had all been surprised by his choice, considering he had once been engaged to her sister, but it wasn't as if they had a hand in the matter. Not long after the marriage, it was announced Victoria was expecting their first child. Not far beyond that it was learned she had a dangerous fall down some stairs and had miscarried. To make the tragedy complete, the loss of her baby had apparently been too much of a mental strain for her, and, while it was not common knowledge to the *ton*, she had gone completely mad. All the Savage girls had been certain Victoria would make him miserable, but none of them had foreseen quite this reason for it.

Before this, Drake had been charming and humorous. He had been friends with the older Savages since they were all children. He had been especially close to Arachne and Myron. Eurydice could scarcely believe he was the same man. Now, more often than not, he was drunk and unpleasant. Tonight was not an exception. The duke and duchess were disappointed, and his parents were embarrassed, when he arrived obviously intoxicated. His dinner companion was Arachne, and it was all she could do to keep him civil. She was hoping that once he had something to eat he might sober a little. If it hadn't been for their years of friendship, she would have had him escorted out.

Another guest who arrived deep in his cups already was Baron Lambeth. However, he didn't become surly when intoxicated; he just became even more charming…at least, he thought he was. From the expression on her face where she sat beside him on one of the couches, Persephone didn't think so. She was doing her best to comply with her parents' wishes, and they had to admit under the circumstances that she was doing admirably.

Eurydice was relieved to find when Ellsworth arrived that he seemed to be completely sober. She had had so little interaction with him that she couldn't recall if she had ever seen him drunk or whether she would be able to recognize it without smelling it on him if he were. She tried to imagine how he would behave. She couldn't tell. Still, two drunks at a dinner party were enough. He bothered her plenty without throwing intoxication into the equation, so she was not going to dwell on it for long. Most men of polite society did not go to social functions drunk. It was bad manners. She could somewhat understand Drake's reason for doing so, but she didn't know enough about Lambeth to determine why he might.

Eurydice tried to delay going to talk to Ellsworth for as long as possible. She really had no reason for needing to avoid him, but part of it was that she wanted to observe how he interacted with the other people first. From what she could tell, he was perfectly normal. He talked. He smiled. He seemed polite and attentive. There appeared to be absolutely nothing out of the ordinary about him. So why did he seem so completely *wrong* to her?

Eurydice stood talking with Pandora and Psyche while she watched everyone. Drake had Arachne somewhat cornered near the piano. They appeared to be arguing, but Eurydice suspected Arachne was doing it willingly in an effort to keep him from arguing with anyone else and causing a scene. Persephone remained seated beside Lambeth on the couch, her hands folded decorously in her lap. She was uncomfortable—both with the situation and what she was wearing, but she was doing her best to smile and talk to him as her parents had ordered.

For the most part, Ellsworth spent his time before supper in conversation with her father and brother, Islington, and Sheerness. She had no notion of what they were talking about, but he did more than just stand and listen. When he eventually moved on to speak with women, he was charming and sociable. She couldn't see that anyone else he spoke to thought there was anything odd about him. It appeared she was alone in her distrust and confusion. Even her father, who knew about the papers found in his coat, did not have any issues.

Psyche and Pandora eventually went to claim their men for supper, and Eurydice went with them in preparation for going in with Ellsworth. Eurydice was almost relieved when her sisters, while polite, both looked at him somewhat suspiciously. They hadn't forgotten his lying about speaking Japanese after all. Ellsworth took her hand and kissed it, and Eurydice raised an eyebrow as he seemed to remain perfectly normal. He also didn't seem to notice that she thought he was peculiar. She did have to admit she tried to keep her expression neutral, no matter what the situation.

"Good evening, Lady Eurydice," he said politely with a slight smile.

"Mr. Ellsworth," she replied calmly.

The six of them stood talking together for only a few minutes before Rajeesh came to announce that supper was served. Eurydice linked her arm through Ellsworth's, and they went into supper. Eurydice found herself seated between Ellsworth and Drake. It did not prove to be a pleasant experience. She willingly talked more to Ellsworth than Drake simply because the viscount was almost unbearably rude when she did talk to him. He had not sobered any since his arrival and continued to drink more wine with dinner. He also made no effort to disguise the fact that he was drunk. She was sympathetic to the problems he had recently been through, and she understood everyone dealt with grief their own way, but she was beginning to find his behavior inexcusable, despite how long she had known him.

Ellsworth, for his part, acted as if none of the strange things he had done had ever happened. While Eurydice couldn't forget them, she was at least able to pretend for the time being, and she did enjoy her meal despite Drake's intransigence. She could hear him arguing occasionally with Arachne, but she couldn't understand what it was about because she would only get bits and pieces of it while she talked with Ellsworth. By the end of the meal when it was time for the women to retire to the drawing room for tea and coffee, she was more than ready to go. She could see that Arachne was as well.

After they left the dining room, she linked arms with Arachne and Persephone as they walked down the hall. Neither of them was enjoying the evening, and they were grateful to be rid of their supper companions for the time being. Eurydice herself thought it was going well, other than how badly it was going for her sisters. She felt ready to play her sonata; well, as ready as she ever would. She was actually looking forward to playing it for her parents and had almost arrived at what she was going to name it. She was nervous about performing in front of all the other people, but she thought if she could forget everyone else, she would be fine.

"Is this going to be a *long* piece?" asked Persephone tiredly.

"I don't know. I've never timed it to see how long it is," said Eurydice dryly. "It's a sonata with four movements in six-eight time. Other than that, I honestly couldn't say. Um, twenty or thirty minutes, maybe?" She shrugged. "It might be longer. I don't know."

"I'm not going to sit by Lambeth a minute longer," said Persephone petulantly. "I don't care if Mum and Dad get angry or not."

Arachne leaned past Eurydice to look at Persephone. "I can't say it would be an improvement, but I will sit by Lambeth if you'll sit by Drake."

"Hmm, trading one drunken eejit for another," said Persephone thoughtfully. She scratched her forehead. "We have a deal."

Eurydice shook her head with a slight smile. This trade was only temporarily delaying things, but they could do with some peace, even if it would put them into a different kind of suffering. Perhaps some pleasant music was what everyone needed. She was sure her sisters were hoping Drake and Lambeth would fall asleep.

Psyche and Pandora were relieved they would not be required to provide the musical entertainment; although, Psyche felt that, by rights, Pandora should. The two of them had placed a wager that she would have twins last year. The outcome would have been that one or the other would have needed to perform the musical entertainment. Psyche had won, so Pandora was supposed to sing at the anniversary dinner the previous year. Then Myron had been killed, and Pandora had gone into labor early and had her twins. The anniversary party had not occurred. Psyche felt it had only delayed Pandora's performance, but Pandora felt the circumstances warranted the entire wager being forfeited. Psyche had finally relented and agreed to call it off. She wasn't happy about doing it, though.

Eurydice spent the time waiting for the men to join them in the drawing room by looking over her sheet music. She was fairly confident she would do fine; she had, after all, composed it. It was only her nervousness about performing in front of people that made her want to study it. She sipped a cup of coffee with cream as she read through it, occasionally making a comment or two or a smile in the conversation her sisters were having nearby with Selena and Amalie. The duchess was talking with the older women near the fireplace, but Eurydice didn't really have anything to contribute to either conversation because they were all talking about children or their husbands. Eurydice had no interest in either.

Eurydice thought it was amazing how less tense the atmosphere seemed without the men, and yet it wasn't caused by *all* the men…only some of them. Lambeth's younger brothers, Jordan and Odoric were there, and Eurydice found them to be very nice. Amalie's new husband, Westerkirk, was present and also very nice. Sheerness's younger brother, Alex, was attending, and he was a lot like his older brother, only much more happy-go-lucky. Several of her father's male friends, who were mostly the fathers of the younger men present, were also easy to socialize with. Islington and Sheerness were fine, as was Dorian. But apparently, when all the men were in the same room with all the women, it was not an agreeable combination, which made her all the more puzzled why any woman would want to be in love with the man she married.

The men soon came to join the women in the drawing room. Eurydice was startled to see that neither her father nor Ellsworth was with them. She saw Dorian walk over to their mother and whisper in her ear. The duchess frowned, but she looked at Dorian and nodded slightly in understanding. Eurydice wasn't too terribly concerned about it at first. The men still needed to get their coffee or tea, and her mother would allow everyone a few minutes to talk with each other. After fifteen minutes, her father had still not come in, and the duchess walked over to speak with her.

"Are you ready, dearest?" she asked quietly.

"Oh, but Father isn't here yet," said Eurydice nervously.

"He may be in before you've finished, but he asked that you start without him," said Julia, giving Eurydice's shoulder a soothing pat.

"But—" began Eurydice again. She might have continued to delay, but after her parents' recent argument with Persephone, she didn't feel that she could. "Yes, Mother," she said obediently.

Eurydice calmly walked over to the piano and sat down. She tried to control her disappointment that her father wasn't going to be there and kept her irritation for Ellsworth in check. That wasn't so easy. She found it difficult not to be angry with him. She knew he was the reason her father was not there and wondered what could have been so important Ellsworth felt he had to take her father away from his anniversary party. She tried to console herself by believing her father wouldn't have gone with him if the business had *not* been important. How could it be that this man had suddenly become so insinuated into the life of her family?

She placed a few sheets in front of her, but only the ones that annotated segments she felt she might have trouble remembering, the ones she had needed to change after originally putting the piece onto paper. She took a calming breath in and out through her nose and flexed her fingers preparatorily. She did her best to put her anger from her mind…and to forget the other people in the room. She could deal with the one afterward if she felt it was necessary, and the other would be gone.

The piano was positioned in such a way that it kept the other people in the room barely within her peripheral vision. Unless she turned her head in their direction, they were little more than a blur out of the corner of her eye. If she kept her eyes focused on the keys in front of her, she couldn't see them at all. It made it easier for her to address her fear of performing in front of an audience. The way the piano was placed had more to do with its arrangement in relation to the other furniture in the room rather than the resulting imaginary screen, but it served the purpose well.

Eurydice began the sonata, and she closed her eyes as she listened to the music. She tried to settle her mind, and she eventually let go of her anger and disappointment. Neither emotion was helpful to the piece. It was flowing and romantic. Too much tension would make her touch too heavy, too passionate. She, for the most part, kept her eyes closed or looked at the keyboard. She had so completely forgotten her audience that she jumped in surprise when they applauded at the end of her performance. When she turned to look at them from the bench, she was unhappy to see that her father wasn't there.

Eurydice consoled herself by believing she would play the sonata for him at some other time, but *this* should have been the time—here, with her mother. The setting and the moment would never be so perfect again. Ellsworth had ruined it. Eurydice tried to keep her jaw from clenching angrily.

After she accepted everyone's congratulations and compliments, she managed to ask her mother if she could go out to the terrace for some air. Their guests would be leaving soon, but Eurydice thought some time to herself would help get her anger under control. She disliked losing her temper, even when it was justified. She wasn't sure that it was at this point. Possibly.

By the time she left for the terrace, her father had still not come into the drawing room. She grabbed a shawl from the closet. It looked like one of Arachne's, but her sister wouldn't mind her borrowing it briefly. She draped it around her shoulders and made her way down the hall toward the terrace. As she reached the door to her father's study, she paused for a moment. She thought about knocking or putting her ear to the door, but instead she sighed frustratedly and continued on her way. She could hear the muffled sound of voices through the door, and she knew interrupting them—whatever it was they were discussing—would be rude...and childish.

She stepped onto the terrace and closed the door behind her. She adjusted the shawl and went to the balustrade. No one else was out, as had been her intention. More people would come out, at least briefly, but she hoped by the time they did she would be back inside. She looked out over the garden and inhaled the scent of her mother's roses with her eyes closed. As she breathed it in, she could also smell the undertones of gardenias and lavender. The hyacinth and jonquils had already bloomed, but Eurydice thought that was when the garden smelled its best. Her grip on the railing slowly loosened, and she thought she would only need a few more minutes before going back inside.

She turned her head to look back over her shoulder curiously when she heard the door open. She wasn't surprised someone else would be coming outside, even though she had hoped she would be gone beforehand. What did surprise her was that it was Ellsworth. He was not who she had expected. She had been alone long enough to sort her feelings so that she was only mildly irritated when she saw him. She would have no trouble being polite.

"Mr. Ellsworth," she said calmly.

"Lady Eurydice," he replied mildly. "Lovely weather tonight," he said as he looked at the sky overhead.

It was true. The sky was cloudless, and the moon was nearly full. The air was cool without chilling, and the only reason Eurydice had worn the shawl was that it was expected for a lady to have one when she went outside. It had been almost unbearably hot over the past few days—Parliament had even dismissed early because of the stench it caused to rise off the Thames. Tonight's weather had been a pleasant change, but it would rain tomorrow.

"Yes, it is," agreed Eurydice in a neutral tone.

"Have people started to leave already, then?"

"I don't believe so, but soon, I imagine."

Ellsworth walked a little closer to her at the railing. Eurydice didn't want to talk to him, but she didn't see how she could avoid it without being rude. Although she felt he deserved it, it went against her nature to be that way.

"So did you learn anything interesting?" he asked her evenly.

Eurydice frowned confusedly. "I beg your pardon?"

"Eavesdropping is a deplorable habit, Lady Eurydice, and at times, a dangerous one."

"I quite agree with you, but I have no idea what you're talking about," she said calmly.

"You were listening at the door to his grace's study. Don't deny it."

"I *will* deny it, Mr. Ellsworth, because it isn't true. I stopped for a moment—mere seconds—at the door on my way out here, thinking to knock, but I wasn't even close enough to reach out with my hand and touch it—let alone *eavesdrop*—before I continued on my way. I have excellent hearing, Mr. Ellsworth, but to have heard what was being said would have required me to have superhuman traits…even had I wanted to know," she said coldly.

Ellsworth narrowed his eyes and looked at her suspiciously. She had a very light step. He hadn't heard when she arrived outside the door, but he did when she left. He didn't know how long she had been there, and until he came out to the terrace, he hadn't been sure who it was. He wasn't happy to see it was Eurydice. She was already privy to far more information than was safe for her, whether she knew it or not. He would have preferred to wait for another time to speak with Aberdare, but the older man had insisted that it needed to be done now. Ellsworth had actually been looking forward to hearing her play the piano and was disappointed to have missed it. He didn't think her father realized she was outside the door, but it wasn't his job to notice things like that.

"You weren't listening?"

"No, Mr. Ellsworth. Why would I want to? I respect my father's privacy, and despite my irritation with you for feeling it was necessary to take him away from his family on his anniversary, whatever business you had with him is none of my affair."

She thought he was responsible for it? He thought about setting her straight but decided to let it lie. He didn't think she would believe him anyhow, and she would be upset to learn it was her father's idea. That wouldn't serve any useful purpose. He wasn't sure just how upset she already was. Even though she said she was irritated, she seemed very self-contained and dispassionate. He might not have even realized it if she hadn't told him. Regardless, she did seem to be oblivious to what they were talking about, and he finally felt able to relax his guard.

"Of course," he finally said. He stood beside her and clasped his hands behind his back. "Your playing went well?"

Eurydice blinked in confusion at his change in subject. "I suppose so," she said evenly. She adjusted her shawl and turned in preparation to leave. "If you'll excuse me, Mr. Ellsworth, I believe I'll go back inside now."

He reached out to put a hand on her upper arm to keep her from leaving. "I'll go in with you."

Eurydice opened her mouth to refuse, but then she decided that would seem very rude. She nodded her head in consent instead.

She thought he was going to place her hand at his elbow, but he surprised her when he instead moved closer to her and bent his head to kiss her. One of his hands still held her upper arm, and she felt him put the other to her waist before moving it to the small of her back. She was stunned to inaction, and she felt the same odd sensations begin that she had experienced the last time he kissed her. She wasn't any more certain why he was doing it this time either. When he lifted his head to look at her, Eurydice had a puzzled frown.

"That was interesting, but I don't know why you keep doing it," she finally said in a musing tone, in all honesty. "I haven't given you permission to do so, and you continuing to do it without my consent is unseemly and rude."

Ellsworth's eyes widened in disbelief for a moment before he started to laugh amusedly. If only she knew that he would like to do more than just kiss her, but her reaction left him wondering why he should want to. She seemed completely unmoved. He released her and put her hand into the crook of his elbow to walk with her across the terrace.

"Lady Eurydice, you are a cold fish," he said finally.

"Well, that was uncalled for," she muttered insultedly. "Just because I'm not happy about you doing something you shouldn't does not make me a cold fish. Perhaps you are accustomed to women fawning over you and letting you take liberties, but I am *not* that kind of woman."

"Oh, no, Lady Eurydice. You are definitely one of a kind," chortled Ellsworth.

Eurydice started to open her mouth and say something impolite, but she clenched her jaw instead as they went through the door to the hallway. She was grateful this might be the last time she would have to see him. She didn't like being laughed at. Even if she did enjoy him kissing her, it wasn't his right, and she felt the less opportunity she presented him to do so the better…since he couldn't seem to stop himself.

≪ ≫

Eurydice woke up and rolled over in bed to look at the wall between her room and Persephone's. She could hear her sister crying, and she thought for a moment to go offer her what comfort she could. In the end, she simply hugged one of her pillows to her and did her best to blink back her own tears. Persephone wouldn't want anyone to know she was crying, not any more than she would want anyone to know the reason for it. Eurydice heaved a shuddering sigh and closed her eyes. She wouldn't be able to go to sleep until her sister stopped crying, and as a single tear slipped out onto her pillow, Eurydice knew there would be one more dream to close in her diary.

Chapter Five

"Chrissoula, where are my slippers?" asked Psyche anxiously as she hurried around her room, looking under the edge of the bed and several other places for the missing items.

"In my hand, where they have been for the last five minutes," said Chrissoula blandly.

Psyche looked up over the edge of the bed and sighed with relief, and then she got up from her hands and knees to take the slippers from her maid and put them on her feet and lace them.

Eurydice and Pandora sat in the matched set of chairs near the window watching Psyche amusedly. She was nervous and excited, and she looked absolutely beautiful.

The slippers were made of a shimmery silver satin, embroidered with small flowers and stars of silver tinsel. The laces were edged with more silver tinsel and ended in tassels of the same material. Her gown was made of a silver tissue overlaid with several layers of silver net, the sleeves reaching to her elbows and made of several ungathered layers. The dress was also embroidered and scalloped along the edges with flowers and lace of silver tinsel. A long train fell at the back that would have to be gathered for dancing. Pandora had thought her wedding dress was beautiful, but her twin's was almost ethereal. Janet had created something that was breathtaking in its workmanship. She had, in fact, only managed to finish making it by the beginning of August and had been working on it since the end of March. Even Eurydice, who didn't care one way or the other about fashion, had to agree the gown was unbelievably beautiful.

Psyche's jewelry was simple. Anything too overdone would have seemed gaudy when combined with the dress. She wore a silver chain and cross around her neck and tiny pearls in her ears. Chrissoula had gathered her hair up and wound through it with a strand of pearls, securing it with filigreed silver combs.

Rather than a bonnet or hat, Chrissoula had attached a lace-edged piece of sheer silk that fell to Psyche's waist.

With her slippers on, Psyche was ready to go to the church to be married, and not a moment too soon. As it was, they would only have fifteen minutes before the ceremony was to begin. The twins, Eurydice, and Chrissoula all left the room and hurried down the front stairs to the entry hall. The duke and duchess were there waiting for them, and their eyes welled with parental pride when they saw them.

The rest of the family had already left for the church, but the house wasn't silent. They could hear sounds of activity as the servants prepared the house for the celebratory ball that would take place afterward. It was only going to be attended by family and friends because the day before had been the last of the season, and most of the *ton* had left for the country, but even still the duke and duchess were expecting nearly one hundred guests. There wouldn't be that many at the service, but the ball was more inclusive.

Jim held open the door on the coach for everyone to enter, and he smiled proudly as he looked at Psyche, almost as if she were his own sister. He'd had a busy day getting all the luggage taken to where it needed to go. Some had to go to the *Medea* in preparation for the honeymoon. Still more had been taken to a river barge that would deliver it to the Isle of Sheppey for after the happy couple's return. He'd only just returned in time to drive the coach to the church, but he wouldn't let any of the other drivers have the honor.

Sheerness had applied for a special license from Canterbury for the wedding. The ceremony was going to be performed at St. Georges, where they attended church every Sunday while in town, by Mr. Hodgson, who gave the sermon every week. The banns had been read, and of course, no one had objected. The duke had wholeheartedly consented to the marriage. The only real reason for it was that both Sheerness and Psyche had wanted to marry after noon. They wanted to have a dinner and ball rather than breakfast to celebrate, and they wouldn't be leaving for their honeymoon until the tide late that night. It seemed entirely logical to them, and the ceremony was arranged to be held at six in the evening.

When they reached the church, Chrissoula hurriedly went in and found her place to sit beside her husband near the back in one of the galleries. The duchess gave Psyche a kiss on the cheek and a tight hug before she went in to find her seat as well. Once they made sure Psyche's train and veil were arranged properly and that she had her flowers, Pandora and Eurydice went in and slowly walked to the front of the chapel where Sheerness calmly stood waiting with Mr. Hodgson. They were to be her bridesmaids. Within minutes, Psyche entered on her father's arm, and everyone stood.

As Eurydice had predicted, Psyche made it to the church just barely on time. The service was lovely, and there was only a brief moment of anxiety when it seemed Sheerness might have misplaced the rings. They were found, and the two exchanged their vows without further mishap. It wasn't difficult to see that both the bride and groom were extremely happy, and Eurydice hugged them when it was done. After they signed their names to the register, Psyche and Sheerness rode back to the house in the coach with the duke and duchess, while Eurydice returned with Pandora and Islington and Lady Bardsey.

When Eurydice returned home, she went upstairs to her room for Agniezka to help her freshen up before the guests arrived in full force. There wasn't much that needed to be done—only a few curls that had decided to go where her maid had not put them.

Eurydice's gown was made of a cream-colored silk, embroidered with small rosettes of gold tinsel all over and edged at the bottom of the skirt with even more. There was a gold silk, tasseled scarf tied beneath the bodice, with slightly gathered sleeves that ended at her elbows. As far as ball gowns went, this one was fairly comfortable, which pleased Eurydice because she would be wearing it until they left for the ship. After Agniezka neatened her up a little, Eurydice went downstairs and made her way to the ball room.

The duke and duchess were in the front hall to greet arriving guests, but the rest of her family was already in the room. Psyche and Sheerness stood talking with Pandora and Islington not far from the open doors to the gallery where the servants had set up the table where all the guests would eventually go in for supper. The Lundeys and Stranraers had already arrived, as had Sheerness's family, and Chrissoula and Stockbridge were also there. The musicians were preparing in their box, and Eurydice recognized them as being the same ones her mother always hired. They did an adequate job, although Eurydice felt they sometimes played the waltzes too quickly.

Eurydice calmly walked over to Pandora and Psyche where they stood with their spouses and joined the conversation. Arachne and Persephone stood talking with the Lundeys and Lord Drake, who seemed to be sober for a change but in a foul mood nonetheless, and Ellsworth and his mother. Once the duke and duchess came in, before the dancing began, everyone would go in for supper. Had there been more guests, Eurydice knew the duchess would have arranged for a buffet instead.

While Eurydice stood talking with her family, Sir James Klein arrived with Lord Georgie and his wife. She had formerly been Lucy Cranston but now proudly bore the title Countess of Plimpton. Georgie fully bore the title Earl of Plimpton, but everyone had known him as Lord Georgie for so long (including himself) that he was referred to that way by his friends and close acquaintances without offense. Lucy would occasionally smooth a hand over her burgeoning belly, as she was excitedly expecting their first child some time in October. All of the sisters, with possibly the exception of Persephone, who hadn't had a chance to know them very well yet, were happy to see the trio, and they were indeed a trio.

It was something that was not common knowledge, and it could be dangerous if it were. To the *ton*, they were simply a very close group of friends. Sir James and Lord Georgie had been best friends before his marriage;

it was only natural that Lucy should become a part of it. However, James and Georgie had been—and were—in fact, lovers. Georgie had married Lucy, formerly one of the most incorrigible gossips of society, simply to produce an heir. Despite her seeming vapidness, though, it had only taken her a few months of marriage to realize the truth. Much to their relief, and contrary to what they had expected to happen, she had actually accepted that part of her husband's life…and encouraged it. They had formed an unusual *ménage à trois* that had so far proven very beneficial and blissful for all of them.

Eurydice, the twins, and Arachne all knew about it. Psyche was very good friends with Sir James, and Lucy was quite fond of Pandora. All four sisters knew about the relationship between James and Georgie before his marriage, and the parties involved had let the information slip in bits and pieces—enough for the sisters to figure out what was happening. None of them could say they would find such an arrangement to their liking, but they were happy it was successful for their friends. They all agreed that the situation had brought about a much-needed improvement in Lucy, and her acceptance of it had caused them all to reconsider their opinion of her and change it for the better.

Once they arrived, Eurydice stood talking with the three of them for several minutes. She wasn't sure, but she felt fairly confident that Georgie and Lucy would have the heir he had married her for. Eurydice didn't tell them that; she wasn't sure they would believe her. Besides, it was only a feeling, not something she had dreamed. Her intuition about things generally turned out to be correct, but sometimes not. She had the impression they would keep trying even if they didn't have their heir this time, so they wouldn't need any direction from her.

The rest of the guests continued to arrive, and the duke and duchess soon entered the ball room. After a few minutes, Rajeesh gave Julia a discreet nod from one of the entryways to the gallery to let her know supper was ready. This was to be their butler's last official function to oversee. After tonight, his son, Tannaz, would be taking over as butler. Rajeesh had held the position for thirty years, before the duke and duchess were even married, in fact, and he was looking forward to spending the remainder of his days puttering around the cottage he shared with his wife and children at Wilderland.

Eurydice happily went into supper with Sir James. He was always an interesting conversationalist. Even though she for the most part had no interest in history, languages, or antiquities, he was usually able to find some type of music-related anecdote to share with her that kept her entertained. She was relieved she would not have to go in with Ellsworth. That dubious honor fell to Persephone. She, of course, was pleased with it, since he seemed to condone her waywardness. To make Eurydice feel even better, Persephone and Ellsworth were seated at the other end of the table from her, making it unnecessary for her to talk to him at all.

Ellsworth was becoming a thorn in her side, one she wanted to remove as soon as possible. Between his lying, seeming inability to keep his hands and other body parts to himself, and disrupting her family, he was becoming progressively more annoying and intriguing to her. What made it even more bothersome was that the effect he was having on her seemed completely unintentional. She didn't need the distraction. She was only grateful that after tonight, she wouldn't need to see him ever again—at least not for a year. Perhaps, if she were lucky, even longer than that could be arranged. She did realize his mother lived in Austria, obviously, since she would be Eurydice's chaperone to Vienna from Venice, but surely the man was old enough he no longer lived in his mother's household and wouldn't be traveling with her. Eurydice also didn't know why her mother had said he was musically inclined. She had noted nothing musical about him, certainly not his conversations. If anything, he was a discordant nuisance.

After supper, the women rose from the table, but instead of the duchess escorting them all to the drawing room for tea and coffee, they went into the ballroom, where several footmen wheeled around carts with the beverages while the doors to the gallery were closed for the men to have their port and tobacco. Eurydice thought that for this once, the entire procedure could have been skipped. Her father and Dorian didn't smoke tobacco. Islington smoked a pipe occasionally. Sheerness didn't smoke, either. She knew more went on behind the closed doors than the smoking of tobacco and drinking of alcohol, but she thought it could have been made elective.

Eurydice was glad her mother had decided to forego dance cards. In truth, the ball was to be an abbreviated affair. A more appropriate description of the celebration would have been *supper with dancing to follow*. She, Psyche, and Sheerness would be leaving shortly after eleven to reach the ship and sail with the tide. The dancing and celebration would continue after they left, but Eurydice's part would end then. That meant she would only have a little less than two hours before she would be on her way to Vienna. She was starting to feel excited, and that put her into a pleasant mood.

The doors to the gallery were opened after thirty minutes, and the men came into the ball room. There was a tobacco-scented cloud of smoke that escaped with them, and Eurydice wondered why they had even bothered to close the doors. She could smell the cherry-scented tobacco from Islington's pipe and another that might be cloves or mace, as well as two or three cigars and something she couldn't quite determine. It contained tobacco, but she didn't think she had ever smelled it before. She didn't know how they had all managed to breathe in the closed room with all that smoke, but the dissipating scent of it was tolerable to her. Small amounts of smoke didn't bother her, but she much preferred the air to be clean and fresh.

Eurydice happened to glance at Persephone shortly after the doors opened, and she caught the almost wistful expression on her face before her younger sister replaced it with the one of petulant indifference she had recently adopted. She looked very pretty in the dark rose-colored ball gown she wore, but Persephone wasn't the least interested in whether or not she was pretty.

Eurydice didn't think it was the smoking and drinking that caused her sister's envy; the men were boisterous as they came out, sharing an easy camaraderie that seemed to indicate whatever they had been doing was *fun.* Wearing ball gowns, minding her manners, and acting girlish weren't things Persephone thought were fun. Eurydice knew at the end of the year and a day their parents had imposed on her, Persephone would loathe dresses.

When the musicians saw the doors were opened, they struck up the music for a minuet. Eurydice wasn't particularly fond of that dance, but she let Alex Nichols take her out for it. She was willing to tolerate it because she would only have to dance four or five dances at most before it would be time for her to go to the ship. Knowing that she would be leaving soon made it easy for her to tolerate things she might otherwise find tedious.

She liked dancing, but like her sisters, she preferred the waltz out of all the ball dances. There were other dances that she liked better than the waltz, but none that were danced by the *ton.* And Eurydice couldn't say she was an excellent dancer. Pandora and Psyche were much better, and so was Arachne. She did dance better than Persephone, but that was because her younger sister did better at dancing the *man's* part rather than the woman's. Eurydice could improve her dancing if she felt inclined to do so, simply by practicing more, but that would require her to take further time away from her music. Her skill was adequate, and that was all that was necessary.

She idly wondered if there was a social season in Vienna like there was in London, and whether or not she would arrive in time to attend it or to miss it. Her mother would know, but it had never occurred to her to ask. It wasn't that important. She felt that as a foreign visitor, she could be excused from it. One season—even only part of one—per year was enough. She hoped she would be too busy studying with a maestro to worry about social functions.

The next dance was an Allemande, and she danced it with Lord Georgie. He was in a very cheerful mood, but then Eurydice couldn't recall ever seeing him when he wasn't. He had still seemed happy even when faced with the prospect of marrying to produce an heir when he had no interest in women or an heir. Eurydice was sure there were times when he was unhappy; he just never seemed to show it. She supposed if one had to choose an emotion to display, whether it was truthful or not, cheerfulness would be a good one. Eurydice herself did not generally show any emotion...unless she felt one.

Once the Allemande ended, Eurydice was thirsty, but she only had about an hour before it would be time for her to leave. She could make do for that long. After the men had left the gallery, the servants had gone in and rearranged things. There were now bowls of champagne punch and lemonade, as well as the wedding cake. Eurydice didn't know when the cake would be served, but presumably before Psyche and Sheerness left for the ship. If she felt thirstier after the next dance, then she would get something to drink. If not, she would get it before they left or once she boarded the *Medea.* It wasn't an emergency.

Lord Georgie escorted her to the edge of the floor after the Allemande, and he was still standing with her when Ellsworth approached them. Eurydice looked at him calmly. She could have hoped she wouldn't have to dance with him, but she was unsurprised. The number of men and women attending was fairly equal, so she wasn't being swamped by requests for each dance, part of the reason the duchess felt she could dispense with using dance cards, and her dancing with him was something etiquette would require…from both of them. There were enough other women he could have asked someone else if he had chosen to do so, though.

"Lord Plimpton, Lady Eurydice," said Ellsworth pleasantly.

Eurydice blinked. It was obvious Ellsworth wasn't in London very often; otherwise, he would know that no one used Georgie's title. Even Georgie seemed confused when he used it.

"Mr. Ellsworth," said Eurydice politely as she held out her hand.

"Might I have the next dance?" he asked after brushing her knuckles.

"Of course," said Eurydice evenly with a slight smile. She would have liked to refuse, but she had no real reason to do so.

He took her hand and escorted her onto the floor just as the musicians began the music for a waltz. Eurydice bit the inside of her lip and tried to keep her features impassive. She would have preferred any other dance with him to the waltz. She liked the waltz; she just didn't want to dance it with *him*. She looked up at Ellsworth and smiled politely as he put his hand at her waist and she placed hers onto his shoulder.

Once they started to glide around the room, she avoided making eye contact with him. Eye contact would require conversation, and she didn't want to talk to him. They didn't seem to have anything in common. She truly didn't know anything about him, so perhaps her opinion was unfair, but it just didn't seem likely. He was a man; she was a woman. He lied; she did not. He seemed to like kissing her, and while she admitted it was pleasant, she wasn't so sure that she liked him doing it.

When he made a sound that might have been one of disgust, she looked up at him. He had a slightly annoyed look on his face.

"Is something the matter?" she asked curiously. She didn't think it was her dancing. Of all the ball dances she knew, the waltz was her best.

He looked down at her. "Oh, it's nothing," he said distractedly. Eurydice raised a doubtful eyebrow. "It's the musicians."

"What about them?" she asked confusedly. They seemed to be doing their usual, adequate job. She was sure no one else noticed.

"They're not very well-trained," he said evenly.

"Oh?" said Eurydice interestedly.

"They're playing this waltz much too quickly, and one of the violinists is playing behind the others by just a hair." Eurydice's mouth was slightly opened in surprise. "Can you not tell?"

Eurydice blinked and closed her mouth. "I can, actually," she said evenly with a slight smile. "I can also tell that the violist is using an incorrect string, even if it is tuned properly."

Ellsworth tilted his head sideways and listened, a slight frown forming between his brows. "No, I don't think that's right."

"Yes, it is," said Eurydice flatly.

"His bowing may lack refinement, but it's not the strings."

"Yes, it is," repeated Eurydice patiently.

"No, it isn't," he replied back.

Eurydice gave him a look of disbelief at the note of petulance in his voice before she finally shrugged. "If you say so," she finally said airily. "After all, how would *I* know?"

Ellsworth tightened his lips exasperatedly, and then he pulled her closer. Then it was Eurydice's turn to become irritated. She pushed at his shoulder in an effort to make him slacken his grip, but it only made him seem to tighten it even further. Without causing a scene, there wasn't much more she could do except ask him to loosen it.

"Mr. Ellsworth, you're holding me too close," said Eurydice calmly.

"No, I'm not; it's a waltz. I'm supposed to hold you close," he said evenly, as if nothing were amiss.

"You're holding me too close," she repeated through clenched teeth.

"Perhaps if you were less prudish, Lady Eurydice, you wouldn't find this dance so objectionable."

"I am not a prude; you are simply a lout who forces his attentions where they're unwanted," said Eurydice coldly.

Ellsworth chuckled. "I am not forcing my attentions," he said amusedly. "We are dancing a *waltz*."

"Humph!" scoffed Eurydice disgustedly, looking away from him. It was pointless to argue with him.

They finished the dance in silence, except for the occasional silent laugh from Ellsworth as he looked at her face set in an infuriated frown and her rejoining sounds of irritation when he did so. For a moment, Eurydice almost thought they might have something in common after all, but his continued enjoyment of annoying her made their interest in music a tenuous and probably useless thing. The more time she spent in his company, the more relieved she was becoming that she wouldn't have to see him again. She couldn't recall anyone ever being capable of making her feel so annoyed before.

When the song ended, Eurydice didn't wait for him to escort her back to the edge of the floor. Without a word, she pried herself loose from his hold and turned her back to walk away quickly. She knew it was rude, but by the end of the dance, she no longer cared if she was rude to him. She was beginning to feel like he didn't deserve her best behavior. She was only at the edge of the floor near one of the doors leading from the ball room to a side hall when Psyche approached her with Sheerness's arm linked through hers.

"I want you to stand watch at the door to the library while I give Sebastian his wedding present," said Psyche excitedly.

"Now?" blurted Eurydice blankly. "Can't you give it to him once you get to the ship?"

"Now," said Psyche with a grin. "I want you to stand at the door so we can have some privacy. It won't take long."

"But—" began Eurydice.

Sheerness looked from one to the other of them with a mild expression. He already knew what his new bride was going to give him, and he was trying to feign ignorance. Psyche's portrait would be a perfect addition to the gallery at Belle Glade. It would require a bit of rearranging, but he thought putting it to the other side of the one of his mother would be just the place for it.

"I promise it won't take long, Dicy. Then we'll have cake and leave for the ship," pleaded Psyche. She was almost bristling with excitement.

"Oh, very well," relented Eurydice. It would take her out of the ball room…away from Ellsworth.

The three of them exited through the door into the hallway and went the short distance to the door of the library.

Psyche left Eurydice at the door and pulled Sheerness by the hand into the room and closed it. He smiled at the way she almost skipped across the room to the table where something tall, narrow, and rectangular was placed on top of it. It was draped in a piece of cotton cloth fastened with a cord at the top. She stood to the side and held out her hand toward it in invitation for him to open it. Sheerness smiled with a shake of his head and moved closer to his gift.

When Sheerness loosened the cord and the cloth dropped, it was unnecessary for him to pretend surprise, and he immediately realized that hanging his wife's portrait in the gallery at Belle Glade was out of the question. For a moment, he was at a loss to decide if there was *any* place at all that he would be able to hang it. It was a wonderful picture, on so many levels, from execution to subject matter, but he couldn't possibly let anyone else see it.

Psyche was reclined on her side on the bench in the garden temple at her sister's home, her torso slightly turned. One of her hands rested on the cushion near her head, while her other arm was draped at her side and rested on her hip. Her hair was loose and flowing, and other than a piece of white silk arranged across her hips, she was completely naked. It was spectacular, and there was no mistake that it was her. The portraitist had not simply painted her head onto the body of another model. Even if Sheerness had not been aware she was having her picture made, he recognized every curve.

Psyche watched nervously. She couldn't tell from his astounded expression if he liked it or not. He had taken to wearing his spectacles more often, and he had them on now (though he didn't wear them for their wedding), so she knew he could see it. When, after a few minutes of his still standing with open-mouthed awe, he had said nothing, Psyche hesitantly reached for the small jeweler's box that was on the table beside the portrait and held it out to him. He only glanced at her briefly to take it from her, transfixed by the painting. As she didn't know what he thought of the portrait, she wasn't sure what his reaction was going to be to what the box contained.

Sheerness opened the lid on the box and finally managed to tear his gaze away from the picture to look inside it. It was a beautiful gold pocket watch, the cover and case etched with fine engraving of acanthus leaves, the edge rimmed with tiny diamonds. He lifted it by the chain from the box and held it in his hand. There were two catches, and he released the first one to reveal the watch face. The workmanship was very detailed, and there was even a second, smaller face inset into the first that provided the seconds. When he released the second catch, he was so surprised he almost dropped the watch. He looked up at Psyche then back to the picture. It was the same as the painting on the canvas, just as detailed, and just as assuredly her.

Psyche began to chew on the side of her thumb nervously. Perhaps she had misjudged. She had thought it would be something he would like. She thought she had come to know her new husband so well. Now she wasn't sure.

"Well?" she said brightly. "What do you think?"

Sheerness put the watch back into the box and closed the lid. Then he turned to look at Psyche and pulled her toward him to kiss her ravenously.

"Oh, *chere,* you should have waited to give this to me when we were on the ship," he said huskily, his arms still around her waist.

"Do you like it?" she asked with a worried frown.

"Absolutely," he purred with a sensual smile, and he moved his hands to cup her bottom and pull her against him. "But nine months without being able to do anything more than kiss you, and then you show me this…?" He lifted her onto the edge of the table and began to raise the hem of her skirt toward her thighs as he began to nuzzle her neck and the tops of her breasts exposed by the bodice. "I just…*can't*…wait," he sighed longingly.

Psyche's expression changed to one of pleasure and anticipation, and she laughed throatily as she began to work at the fastenings on his trousers. She didn't want to wait either. The last nine months had been torture. They'd not had a moment alone together, and they'd been unable to do anything more than hold hands and kiss. After four months of having unlimited access to one another the previous year, Psyche thought it was going to drive her mad. She moaned low in her throat as he moved his hands to cup her breasts and kiss her. Maybe once would be enough until they got to the ship.

≪ ≫

Eurydice folded her arms across her chest and leaned her back against the wall near the door to the library with a resigned sigh after it closed. She somewhat understood why her sister didn't want anyone to walk into the library and see her new husband's wedding present, but she couldn't think of why anyone would decide they needed to go to the library in the first instance. She supposed, considering it was Psyche and Sheerness's wedding celebration, people might wonder where they had gone, especially since it would soon be time to cut the cake, but she didn't expect this would take long. At least, she hoped it wouldn't. After all, Psyche only needed to show him a painting.

She absently began to move the fingers of her left hand where they rested against her right biceps in the fingering pattern for a piece by Mozart that was floating through her head. The musicians were playing a Scotch reel in the ball room, and despite herself, she tried to listen for sounds in the library. So far, there had been none—no talking, no shouting. She couldn't tell if that was a good or bad sign. She wouldn't put her ear to the door, but she was curious. After several minutes, she heard muffled conversation from the other side of the door, followed very shortly by her sister's laugh.

Eurydice shook her head. At least it sounded as if the gift had been well-received. Not seconds after the laugh from her sister, she heard what sounded like the clatter of a chair tipping over and falling to the floor. She frowned and went to put her hand on the door with the intention of opening it, but then she began to hear a few other sounds, and her eyes rounded in alarm. She might be innocent, but she wasn't stupid, and she had no doubt what was occurring behind the door. Her sister should have waited until they got to the ship.

She removed her hand from the knob as if it had turned into a snake, and then she turned her back and rested it against the door. When she could still hear the sounds coming from inside the room, she moved back to the wall, where the sounds were more muffled. She tried to remain calm, but that became difficult when the door from the ball room opened and someone came into the hall. She tried to keep her features composed, but she was sure her cheeks were colored bright red.

"Mr. Ellsworth, can I help you with something?" she asked calmly.

"I'm looking for Sheerness," he said flatly. "I saw him come this way, and I had something I needed to speak with him about."

"He's in the library with his wife," said Eurydice as evenly as possible.

"Very good." He started to go to the door of the library and enter.

Eurydice quickly moved from the wall to put herself in front of the door.

"I'm afraid you can't go in there. She's giving him his wedding present and asked not to be disturbed."

Ellsworth raised an eyebrow. "This will only take a moment," he said dismissively, and he started to move her out of the way.

Eurydice braced one hand against the door frame and put the other over the handle.

"I said you can't go in there," she said firmly.

"And I said this will only take a moment," said Ellsworth testily.

He put his hands at her waist and prepared to physically remove her from in front of the door. Psyche chose that precise moment to say her husband's name loudly enough in a manner that left no doubt what had prompted her to say it. Eurydice's eyes rounded as she looked at Ellsworth, and her cheeks turned a bright shade of pink when she saw his expression. He realized what they were doing, too, and he looked down at her with a knowing smile.

"That must be some present," he said sardonically.

Eurydice tilted her chin and narrowed her eyes at him. "Mr. Ellsworth, if you'll go back to the ball room, I'm sure Lord and Lady Sheerness will be there presently."

"Presently?" he said in the same tone with a sensual smile.

"If you please!" said Eurydice aggravatedly.

Ellsworth tightened his grip on her waist and closed the distance between them. Eurydice wasn't particularly short, but even still, he was nearly a foot taller, and she had to tilt her chin back to look up at him when he stood that close to her. She frowned.

"What do you think you're doing?" she asked coldly.

"I'm about to force my attentions," he said silkily.

Eurydice only had time to blink before he lowered his head to kiss her. Her lips were already parted, and she felt his tongue dart past them to begin an exploration of her mouth. Her hand slipped off the handle as he kept her pressed against the door with his body, and she moved it to place over his at her waist with the intention of pushing it away. Instead her grip tightened, and she didn't move it. His other hand moved lower to her hip before she felt him slowly smooth it up her ribs to rest on her side just beneath her breast. Her other hand eventually left the door frame to move to his shoulder before she curled her fingers into the hair at the back of his head.

What she felt was extraordinary and puzzling. On the one hand, she knew she should stop him. She knew she should be angry. Anyone might happen upon them and see them, and she hadn't given him permission to kiss her. On the other, she felt curiosity and something else. Every time he kissed her was different, and she wanted to know what happened next, wanted to *feel* what happened next, whether she had allowed what he was doing or not.

She sighed softly at the back of her throat when his hand at her ribcage moved to her breast to squeeze it gently, but she knew that was her cue to stop him before he went too far or before someone caught them. Whether or not she allowed it would be irrelevant if someone saw them, even if it were someone from her family, even if it were one of the servants. The curious part of her did not want him to stop, but the practical part knew she should be infuriated.

She almost changed her mind when he began to circle her nipple with the pad of his thumb through the fabric of her gown and chemise to cause a tingling sensation she felt all the way to the pit of her stomach, but her hand over his at her waist eventually began to do what she had intended for it to do, and she tried to get him to loosen his hold.

Her resistance seemed to only make him all the more determined to continue. He shifted his feet and pressed even closer against her, and Eurydice gasped when she felt his arousal against her stomach. She took her hand from over his at her waist and moved it to his shoulder to begin pushing at it, making a muffled sound of protest. She wouldn't say he was being *forceful*, despite what he had said he was going to do, and she had to admit to herself that her efforts to be disengaged from him were only half-hearted. But she *was* trying to stop him, which should have been enough to make him let go.

He did finally end the kiss with a gentle nip to her bottom lip. Eurydice opened her eyes to look up at him with a flustered expression as he stepped away from her slightly. He didn't completely let her go, and he reached up with the hand that had been at her breast to lightly trace a finger along the edge of her jaw to her chin with a thoughtful gaze. Eurydice shied away from the caress and tightened her jaw.

"You should not have done that," she said stiffly.

"No, absolutely not," he agreed absently, his expression still pondering.

"You're not allowed to do that," said Eurydice in a quiet, accusatory voice.

"No, I'm not," he continued in the same tone, still examining her features thoughtfully.

"You're going to get me in trouble," said Eurydice vexedly.

It seemed he was listening to what she was saying, but apparently whatever he was thinking combined with her statements and gave his answers a meaning that was more complicated to him than it was to her. He looked into her eyes then and gave her a somber smile.

"I hope not," he said seriously.

Eurydice's forehead wrinkled slightly with confusion. He gently put a hand to the side of her neck and gave her a soft kiss on the forehead before moving away from her.

"Please, tell Sheerness I would like to speak with him after he is done getting his present," said Ellsworth, his lips twitching humorously, and he turned to go back into the ball room.

Chapter Six

Eurydice stifled a yawn as the coach moved toward the Surrey Docks. She was far more tired than she had thought she would be, and she was looking forward to going to sleep as soon as she was settled into her cabin. There was very limited conversation between herself, Psyche, Sheerness and Agniezka, and as the coach rocked along, Eurydice found herself coming very close to nodding off. They had already crossed the Thames and were well on their way into Southwark. They would be to the *Medea* in plenty of time to sail with the tide just before one.

Eurydice had never been to see the ship. She had seen the outside of it the previous year when Psyche and Sheerness had returned home from Greece, but she had not been aboard to see belowdecks. The burgundy and gold had been striking, and it had still gleamed with newness, despite being more than fifteen years old and having gone to the Mediterranean and back. Psyche had tried to describe the inside to Eurydice, and she promised she would give her sister a full tour the following day once they were under way, from top to bottom. It was larger than the *Julia* had been but not enormous, and Psyche assured her there was more room aboard than there appeared. Eurydice was certain it would be adequate, and anything on the ship was bound to be better than what she would have endured had she made the journey to Vienna over land.

Psyche had told her that Mr. Laing, the ship's carpenter, had seen to making some modifications to the bunk in what would be Eurydice's cabin on instruction from Sheerness. All the bunks had drawers underneath them for storage, and the cabins were not large enough for more than one bed. For Psyche, that had not been a problem because she had no maid with her when she had been on the ship before. However, Agniezka would be traveling with them, and she couldn't stay on the berth deck with the sailors. So, Mr. Laing had raised the bunk a little further and added a trundle beneath it. There was enough room in the cabin that the bed could be pulled out when needed at night and put away during the day when it wasn't without making the cabin impossibly cramped. Eurydice had to agree it was an ingenious idea.

Eurydice didn't mind sharing her cabin with Agniezka. She adored her maid. She attended to everything for Eurydice in order to give her all the time she wanted for her music. She trusted Agniezka's judgment implicitly. Not only that, but Eurydice would often confide things to her maid that she would tell no one else in her family, not even Arachne. Everyone thought Eurydice was always so calm and centered, but it was having Agniezka that made it possible for her. She would have no trouble having her maid with her in her cabin for however long the trip to Venice would take, and even longer than that should traveling conditions to Vienna make it necessary.

When Psyche and Sheerness had come out of the library not long after Ellsworth went back to the ball room, Eurydice had done her best to pretend she hadn't known what they were doing. That had been no easy feat. Neither was disheveled, but they had both appeared flushed and breathless…and satisfied. They had acted as if they had been doing nothing more than looking at a painting, but because Eurydice did know what they had been doing, it was patently obvious. It had taken all her effort to keep from blushing and maintain a calm expression. She had told Sheerness that Ellsworth wished to speak with him, and they had gone into the ball room for cake with no one being any the wiser to their assignation, except for Eurydice…and Ellsworth.

What she had been doing with Ellsworth in the hallway had made it even more difficult for her to keep her composure. Her sister and brother-in-law were too involved with each other to notice that Eurydice was nervous. That and her ability to have the appearance of calm even when she was not gave them no clue. Inside, however, she was a ball of nerves. She had enjoyed it far more than she should have, and he had completely overstepped what was acceptable behavior. She tried to placate herself with the knowledge that she wouldn't have to worry about it happening again after that night, but it didn't really help. There was something troublesome at the back of her mind that told her it was not finished. What was even more disturbing was that she wasn't sure she wanted it to be.

Eurydice jerked slightly when the coach came to a stop at the docks. She had almost fallen asleep. She hoped it wouldn't take long to get ready for bed. She wanted to go straight there. Anything else could wait until tomorrow. She wasn't interested in watching the ship sail down the river because once she was on it, she was on her way. Besides, it was dark, and there wouldn't be much she could see in any case. She just wanted to sleep.

Jim opened the door, and Sheerness stepped out of the coach before reaching back in to help the three women out. Psyche paused in front of Jim and gave him a grin.

"A bit different than the last time you brought me here," she said cheekily.

"Oh, yes, mum," he agreed with a grin of his own. "You have a safe journey, aye?"

Psyche giggled and gave him a quick hug. "Oh, absolutely."

She linked arms with Sheerness, and the four of them walked up the gangway to the ship after saying goodbye to Jim. There were a few lanterns lit on the deck, and Eurydice looked around interestedly as the sailors prepared to get the ship under way. She could see Higginbotham standing on the poop deck near the helm, and Stockbridge was on the waist deck overseeing the crew. After a brief shouted greeting, Sheerness escorted the three women to the aft deck.

Lanterns were lit in the officers' mess, and Eurydice was very impressed so far. The ship wasn't cramped at all and very well constructed, with more height to the ceilings than was found on most. Sheerness had to stoop slightly when walking through the doorways, but he was able to stand upright within the cabins themselves with almost a foot to spare. While Eurydice knew it was a ship and would have no trouble realizing that were she led aboard blindfolded, the furnishings—at least in the after cabins—were almost luxurious. It wouldn't be home, but it would be very home-like. She was pleased and looking forward to seeing her own cabin.

Psyche had told Eurydice that many of the crew from the previous year had readily signed on for another outing. Sheerness had of course kept a few on once they returned to Britain—the officers and Dr. Felton (the ship's physician), Mr. Meals (the cook), and a few of the sailors—to keep the ship in good order, and the men he had managed to assemble the year before had been excellent. When he began to hire on regular seamen for the journey this year, many of them had left new posts—if they were able and in the country—to sign back on with the *Medea*.

Sheerness said good night once they reached the small alcove beyond the officers' mess and went into the captain's cabin to change into something better suited to overseeing the ship rather than evening attire. Eurydice noticed the door opposite her own and suspected she would find out what was behind it when Psyche gave her a tour of the ship tomorrow. She fought back another yawn as Psyche opened the door to her cabin.

Someone had been in to light the lamps on the walls, and Eurydice looked about herself with satisfaction. It would do nicely. The bunk fit into a niche in the wall just around the corner. There was a writing desk on the far wall with a small coffer to the other side of it covered with cushions to use as a window seat. There was a small table, a washstand, and a full-length mirror with a small storage compartment at the bottom of it. Her and Agniezka's trunks were stacked and lashed on top of one another behind the door, out of the way, and there was a small rug on the floor. It almost looked like a room at an inn, and Eurydice would be quite comfortable in it.

"Now, there is a water closet and a shower-bath in my and Sebastian's cabin," Psyche was saying. "I don't recommend simply walking in, but you can use them as often as you like."

"Wow! A shower-bath! That's capital," said Eurydice happily.

She couldn't remember if her sister had mentioned that before, but it relieved her to know it because until then she had thought she would have to be content with washing off with a bucket or a small tub. She did much prefer a tub—a large tub like the ones at home, but a shower-bath was far superior to a bucket.

"Yes, and it uses sea water from the steam bilge pump, so it will be hot."

"Marvelous!" sighed Eurydice.

A hot shower-bath was even better. She was becoming more pleased by the minute that Psyche had suggested she travel by ship at least to Venice. This was going to be much more comfortable than traveling over land and staying at inns. She had thought so before knowing the full extent of the accommodations aboard, but she was positive now.

"Do you want breakfast here, or would you rather dine with the officers?"

"In here, I think," said Eurydice after considering for a moment.

"Fine. I'll be sure to tell Sebastian, and he'll let Freddie know to bring it for you around nine. I would do it right now, but I'm sure the boy is already asleep, and Sebastian is usually up and about before me."

Eurydice blinked. For him to be awake before Psyche was not as simple as it sounded, but Eurydice wasn't going to ask how he managed it. She was relieved and happy her sister had finally found something that made her sleep.

"All right," said Eurydice agreeably.

Psyche hugged and kissed her. "Well, then I'll leave you to get settled in and go to bed. If I'm not on deck in the morning after breakfast, I'll be in my cabin. Come find me, and I'll give you a tour. Good night, Dicy."

"Good night," said Eurydice with a slight smile.

Agniezka had already busied herself with finding Eurydice's things to change for bed. It was apparent Chrissoula had already seen to having her things unpacked and put away in the drawers under the bunk. Agniezka was pleased to see Chrissoula had put them just where she herself would have done. She got out a long-sleeved shift and a dressing gown and laid them out on the bunk, and then she located the hairbrush and box for Eurydice's hairpins.

"Come along, then. Let's get you into bed. You look exhausted," said Agniezka as she turned Eurydice to unfasten the back of her gown.

"I am," affirmed Eurydice, and she put the back of her hand to her mouth as she yawned.

It might not have been noticeable to anyone else, but her maid had learned that Eurydice's displays of anything were subtle. She sometimes even recognized things that the girl's family did not. Agniezka helped her out of her clothes and dropped the shift over her head, and then she had her sit in the desk chair sideways to remove the pins from her hair to brush it and put it into a braid. While Eurydice brushed her teeth, Agniezka pulled back the covers on the bunk. She would get her own bed ready after Eurydice was situated. She was just grateful she wouldn't have to sleep on the floor or a cot. It would not be the first time she had ever needed to do that, but it had been a long time.

Both of them heard the noises that accompanied the raising of the anchors as Eurydice got settled into her bunk. Agniezka extinguished the lantern on the wall above her head, and Eurydice snuggled under the blankets and nestled her head into the pillow. The bunk was very soft, and she closed her eyes tiredly. There was a slight lurch as the sails caught the wind, and Eurydice soon drifted to sleep with the rocking of the ship, completely oblivious to the noise made by Agniezka as she got her own bunk prepared and changed into her shift.

The sun was shining through the window directly onto Eurydice's face when she woke up the next morning, and she wished she had thought to close the curtain that enclosed the nook containing her bunk. The curtain had been hung to afford her some privacy from her maid, which was probably why she hadn't closed it; she didn't think she needed to separate herself from Agniezka.

As for her maid, she was already awake and dressed, the trundle put away, and she sat on the coffer by the window knitting a blanket. She looked up from her work when she saw Eurydice stirring and smiled as she set it aside and stood up. Eurydice thought she seemed a little pale, and she realized it was because Agniezka was seasick.

"I think a turn about the deck in the fresh air will do you some good."

Agniezka waved a hand through the air dismissively. "I'm much better already sitting by the window where I can see where I am going." She smiled. "I am sure I was positively green earlier."

"Oh, Agniezka," said Eurydice concernedly. "Are you going to be all right all the way to Venice?"

"As long as I am by the window."

"But what about sleeping?"

"I'll sleep on the coffer. I actually slept there last night after I realized I couldn't sleep on the trundle. It's not nearly as uncomfortable as you might think, and I have slept worse places."

"Really? Are you sure?" said Eurydice worriedly. "Maybe I can see about Psyche arranging something else for you."

"I will be fine," assured Agniezka with a chuckle.

"It's a shame you can't sleep on the trundle. It's more comfortable than the coffer. What if you slept on the bunk and I slept on the trundle?"

"No, that will not work either. Don't worry. I will be perfectly fine," repeated Agniezka with a small laugh.

Eurydice got up from the bunk and went to the writing desk, where she found her dream notebooks and fountain pen. Before she did anything else, she turned to a blank page and wrote down the dream she remembered with as much detail as possible. She didn't dwell on what she was writing but put it on the page before it slipped away. She would look at it later, if necessary. The most important thing was to write it down. Then she could forget about it.

Agniezka had already removed one of her dresses from a drawer and hung it on the edge of the mirror to begin airing the wrinkles out of it. It was unfortunate they didn't have a clothes-press or a wardrobe, but this arrangement would suffice. She had already discovered that Chrissoula had not unpacked all of Eurydice's things, particularly the ball gowns and the more delicate of her other dresses, and Agniezka would have to make sure to thank her. It did leave Eurydice with a limited number of dresses to wear while aboard the ship, but having fewer things in the drawers prevented the items stored there from becoming more wrinkled than they might otherwise. She could only assume from the things Chrissoula had unpacked that it would not be expected for Eurydice to dress for dinner. It also meant Agniezka would have to make sure the dresses that were out were kept as clean and neat as possible. She didn't expect laundering would be easily done on the ship.

She had just finished helping Eurydice dress and put up her hair when there was a knock at the door. Both women looked at it expectantly, and Agniezka went to open it. Freddie was there with a tray of food for them, and he smiled shyly when he saw them.

"Good morning," he said quietly as Agniezka moved out of the way for him to take the tray to the table and set it down.

He quickly started to leave, made nervous by their silent, serious faces. He knew Lady Psyche's sister was aboard, but he sensed she was different. He didn't think she disliked him, but she wasn't like Psyche. He remembered meeting her at Stockbridge and Chrissoula's reception, and while she was nice then and still seemed so, the way she held herself was not easily approachable. And although it was something that was hard for his young mind to fully grasp, there was something about her eyes, not just the color but the expression, that made her seem sad and somehow apart. It made him uneasy.

"Thank you," called Eurydice as he seemed to flee from the cabin.

She looked at Agniezka in puzzlement, and her maid simply shrugged uncertainly.

She noticed as Agniezka prepared to close the door that the door across the alcove was open, and it seemed to be another cabin. No one was in it, and it didn't appear to be occupied. The bunk in the cabin was placed at the far end of it, near the window. If it wasn't being used, it would be the perfect solution to Agniezka's problem. Eurydice made a mental note to remember to ask Psyche. She didn't like her maid having to sleep on the coffer by the window for the entire trip to Venice, not if there was a bunk by a window available for her to use. She hoped Agniezka's seasickness would dissipate after she became accustomed to being at sea, but Eurydice couldn't be sure that it would.

Eurydice moved the desk chair to the table while Agniezka sat on the coffer, and they enjoyed their breakfast of pancakes, scrambled eggs, and bacon with a pot of coffee. The food was excellent, and again, Eurydice was sure, much better than what she might have been offered traveling by coach. Of course, if she had been traveling over land, by this point, she would still be in England. As it was, they had reached the Channel and were nearing Calais while she enjoyed another cup of coffee and talked with Agniezka.

"Do you think he'll come back for the tray?" asked Agniezka after they had finished eating.

"I'm sure he will," said Eurydice. "He seemed very skittish, though," she said thoughtfully.

"Really? He seemed scared witless to me," said Agniezka amusedly.

Eurydice sighed and shook her head. "Children don't like me."

"Nonsense," said Agniezka dismissively. "Your brothers like you fine. Your brothers *love* you."

"They're my brothers," muttered Eurydice, almost to herself.

"Hunh," said Agniezka.

She knew what it was about Eurydice that made children uncomfortable. It wasn't that they didn't like her. It wasn't even that they thought she didn't like them. Children were impressionable, their senses still fresh and sharp. They could feel that she was special. Her brothers had grown accustomed to it and also shared it, so it didn't affect them the same way. It left most other children, like Freddie, feeling confused. Adults, most of them, no longer believed in magic—for lack of a better description, and they didn't notice.

Agniezka retrieved a shawl for Eurydice from one of the drawers and gave it to her to go for a tour of the ship with Psyche.

"Do you want to come with?" asked Eurydice. "It will give you a chance to walk around a little, get some fresh air. It might help your seasickness."

"No, you go ahead. I think I'll find Chrissoula and visit for a while. I really am feeling much better."

"All right," said Eurydice agreeably.

She looked at the other cabin thoughtfully from the alcove. On closer inspection, she could see two trunks stacked atop one another just beyond the writing desk, so it was apparently occupied after all. She had to wonder by whom and assumed it was one of the officers. Neither Psyche nor Sheerness had mentioned there would be anyone else aboard as a guest besides herself and Agniezka…and Chrissoula, but she—obviously—shared a cabin with Stockbridge. Eurydice was disappointed her maid wouldn't be able to use it.

Once she was in the alcove, she could also see that the door to the captain's cabin was open, and Psyche was not there. Eurydice sighed and turned for the officers' mess to go topside. She startled Freddie in the process of clearing the breakfast dishes from the table, and he dropped the plate he held back onto it. The earthenware made a loud clatter as it landed but, luckily, did not break. He looked at her in round-eyed surprise, and he seemed as if he intended to run away.

"I'm sorry," said Eurydice, giving him a friendly smile. "I didn't mean to frighten you." He shook his head silently. "We are done with the tray in our cabin whenever you would like to go get it, if that's not too much trouble."

He shook his head again. "Yes, ma'am," he said hurriedly.

Eurydice gave him another smile. "Thank you," she said quietly before she continued past him through the room to go topside.

She tried to control the disappointment she felt at seeing the effect she had on the boy. Agniezka was right: he was afraid of her. Eurydice tried to convince herself that it was just as well she frightened him because children were a nuisance, but it hurt just the same. Some of her dislike of children stemmed from knowing that they didn't like her either, not that she had ever gone out of her way to *make* them like her. She could hope that Freddie would eventually come around when she continued to be friendly, but she didn't hold out much hope that he would. Children simply did not like her.

Psyche was lying in one of the launches reading a book when Eurydice went onto the deck. She was wearing a pair of dark-lensed spectacles, and she was situated so that she could look at the stern and poop deck where Sheerness stood overseeing the helm rather than the bow and where they were going. As she approached the side of the launch, Eurydice could see that her sister was dressed in one of her split skirts and a gansey. She did look comfortable, but Eurydice didn't know if she could possibly feel the same wearing them.

Psyche looked up from her book with a smile as Eurydice drew near.

"Good morning! Did you sleep well?"

"I did, yes, thank you, but I think I'll have to draw the curtain on my bunk tonight. The sun was far too bright this morning."

Psyche laughed. "Yes, I noticed that as well, but once we turn east, that shouldn't be a problem. Are you ready to see the ship?"

"Yes, I think so."

"What about Agniezka?"

"She thought she would find Chrissoula and visit. She's a touch seasick," said Eurydice with a slight grimace. No one in her family got seasick.

"Oh, no!"

"It's not too bad. She was looking a little pale when I got up this morning, but she swears she's feeling much better now that she's been able to sit by the window and see where she's going. She slept on the coffer last night, and I think if she could have managed it, she would have slept on the deck under the stars. If the cabin across the way weren't being used already, I'd suggest letting her sleep there, but I'm also hoping it will improve after she's had a little time to adjust."

"I'm sure it will," said Psyche as she marked the page in her book and climbed out of the launch onto the deck. She looked at her watch. "Where would you like to start?"

"Wherever you want to take me," said Eurydice with a smile.

Psyche gave her a tour of the entire ship, including the hold, but she didn't go so far as to show her the bilge. Eurydice was very impressed, especially when she saw that there was a shower-bath for the crew on the berth deck. Psyche didn't tell her sister that she had recommended it to her husband. Eurydice thought the crew's accommodations were better than some that were afforded to the steerage passengers on the packets, possibly even the first class on several, and most definitely better than those provided to the crew on other ships. She had to wonder if her brother-in-law realized that. After some thought, she suspected he had done it on purpose. It meant he would never have want of men willing to hire on, and it would allow him to find the best men available to work for him.

It actually took Psyche quite some time to show Eurydice the ship because she would stop to introduce her sister to the members of the crew. Eurydice wasn't surprised when her sister would ask them about things that had happened in the year since they had seen each other if the men had worked the last trip or to become better acquainted with them if this was their first time aboard. What astounded some people, but didn't surprise Eurydice, was that Psyche actually remembered their names and things about them she had learned the year before. Psyche truly cared about people, all people, and knowing the things that were important to them was a part of that.

Eurydice enjoyed meeting everyone, and she was impressed by the ship, but near the end of the tour, she was impatient to get back to her cabin to practice on her violin. She had decided that being on the ship should not interfere with her playing. Even if she might have to miss a day every now and then, she was not going the entire trip without practicing. She couldn't. She wasn't sure where she would put her sheet music in the cabin, as she had not brought her stand because there had been no way for her to fit it into her trunk, but there would be some way to arrange it. Failing that, she could always practice the pieces she knew without the music.

By the time Psyche finished giving Eurydice the tour, it was time for dinner. Eurydice had seen Freddie busily hurrying up and down the stairs from the berth deck to the waist deck several times as he went to the officers' mess to retrieve things from the dumbwaiter there for their meal. She would catch him looking at her occasionally with an expression that was a cross between curiosity and fear, as if she were a specimen of some rare animal that he couldn't decide was either friendly or intending to gobble him up when his back was turned. She tried to ignore it; she couldn't think of anything she could do to make him less frightened of her because she couldn't think of what she might have done to make him feel that way in the first instance. She had become accustomed to the fact that children inherently did not like her.

Once they reached the waist deck, Psyche and Eurydice went to the poop deck where Sheerness still stood. Psyche went to him to give him a soft kiss on the lips, and he put his arm around her waist as he looked at Eurydice.

"So what did you think?" he asked her with a slight grin.

"You have a very lovely ship," she said with a smile, "and I can't thank you enough for taking me to Venice."

"Thank you, and you are quite welcome."

"Let's go eat," said Psyche. "I'm famished."

Sheerness chuckled and linked their arms. "You are always hungry."

"No, I'm not," said Psyche calmly as they went down to the waist deck with Eurydice following behind them. "It has been hours since breakfast."

"I've been up longer than you, and while I am hungry, I'm not *famished.*"

Eurydice listened to them banter as they went to the after cabins, and she was pleased that Psyche and her husband seemed to be friends as well as lovers. She was sure her sister wouldn't have married him if she didn't like him for more than just sex; although, his ability to make her sleep would have been a very hard-to-resist temptation. Eurydice was not particularly hungry. Mr. Meals had positively blushed when Psyche introduced Eurydice, assuring her sister that he was an excellent cook who made a lamb stew that was to die for. Eurydice was sure she would get to find out before they reached Venice.

The officers' mess was brightly lit by the beautiful, large skylight. The table was set and several people were seated, even though they hadn't started eating yet because they were waiting for the captain and his family. Chrissoula and Stockbridge were there, and Dr. Felton was seated beside Agniezka across from them. She looked much-improved, and Eurydice hoped her seasickness would only be temporary. Mr. Higginbotham was above deck overseeing the helm and would not be joining them. The only officer Eurydice hadn't met was Mr. Broughton, the second mate, but she assumed the man sitting at the foot of the table with his back to her was he. Psyche had explained that he had watched the helm last night and was sleeping. Mr. Blossom, the ship's master, who she had met on her tour, had traded cabins with Stockbridge on the berth deck for the bosun to have a cabin large enough to accommodate himself and his wife. Mr. Rolleston, the gunner, and Mr. Laing, the ship's carpenter, also ate with the crew on the berth deck. Freddie sat unobtrusively on a stool in the corner to clear away dishes or refill glasses, and Eurydice tried to ignore the way his eyes rounded when he saw her. The only seat left available besides those at the top of the table, where Sheerness would sit, and at the left hand of it, where Psyche would sit, was at the left hand of the bottom, beside Mr. Broughton. Eurydice wished she could have been seated by Agniezka, but she should consider herself lucky she had a seat at all. There wasn't room for all the guests and officers to eat at the same time; they needed one more seat.

All the men stood as the three of them came in, and Eurydice calmly waited for her sister and brother-in-law to introduce her to Mr. Broughton. She was surprised when they both went to take their seats instead. Eurydice shrugged mentally and went to take her own seat. She would meet him soon enough, and there was less need to stand on ceremony aboard the ship. Once she had removed her shawl and arranged her napkin into her lap, she looked at him with a pleasant smile that quickly froze.

"Bloody hell!" she gasped in shock, and then her cheeks began to turn red with embarrassment.

The man beside her looked at her with a slow, amused smile, and everyone else looked at her in surprise, particularly her sister and her maid. Psyche didn't think she'd *ever* heard Eurydice say a bad word before, especially not something like that. Agniezka was keenly interested to know what had made her so agitated that she would have said anything at all. An outburst like that for Eurydice was like screaming blue murder for anyone else. She looked at the man at the foot of the table assessingly, knowing he had to be the cause of it. The other men at the table, including Sheerness, were not as shocked at Eurydice's outburst as might have been expected. All of them were familiar with Psyche, and she had never been one to hold her tongue. They didn't know why her sister would be any different. It was simply that they would not expect a woman of her breeding to say something like that at the table.

Eurydice tried to regain her composure as she looked at the man. It was definitely not Mr. Broughton. Oh, how she wished it was. Sitting there looking well-pleased that he had managed to make her forget her manners was none other than Ellsworth. Her forehead creased with a puzzled frown, and she had to bite the inside of her lip to keep herself from asking him what he was doing there and telling him he had no business being there. It only took her a moment to realize he was the occupant of the cabin across from hers, and she tried to control the small ball of panic she felt forming in the pit of her stomach.

"Forgive me, everyone, I'm afraid I don't quite know where that came from," she said quietly as people continued to look at her curiously.

Psyche looked at her with a raised eyebrow, but she picked up her fork to begin eating her macaroni casserole, braised turnips, and ham. She would have to ask Dicy later what had caused it. Whether or not her sister would tell her was open to speculation. After Eurydice picked up her own fork and pretended she hadn't said anything, everyone else did the same, and conversation around the table soon took them away from it.

Eurydice did her best to ignore Ellsworth sitting beside her, trying to eat the food she had lost her appetite for, and speaking with Dr. Felton, Chrissoula, and Stockbridge. While he participated in the same conversations, she didn't speak directly to him or anything he had said. But it soon came to the point that she could not continue to ignore him without seeming rude after everyone else moved on to their own conversations. That was unfortunate because she didn't want to talk to him. She gave him a polite smile before taking a sip of wine from her glass.

"You seem surprised to see me," said Ellsworth casually, taking her smile to be an invitation to talk to her, which she had intended. She would have been happier if he hadn't been able to realize that because she wasn't going to speak unless he did first.

"Yes, actually, I am," said Eurydice honestly. He was the one that mentioned it, so she didn't feel rude by saying so.

Ellsworth frowned slightly. "You didn't know I was sailing on the *Medea* to Venice?"

"No, I didn't," said Eurydice flatly.

"But I talked to Sheerness about it more than a month ago."

"Perhaps you did, but I'm not Sheerness," she said in the same flat tone before eating more of her food. She really wasn't hungry. "It is his ship, so why would he feel it was necessary to inform me about the other passengers he would be taking on?"

Ellsworth looked at her amusedly. "Maybe he thought you wouldn't come if you knew."

Eurydice managed to contain her snort of disbelief and looked at him doubtfully. "You are giving yourself far too much credit to think your presence would dissuade me from going some place I have wanted to go since I was twelve years old. As I said, it was—and is—not my concern who Sheerness decides to take aboard his ship."

"Point taken," said Ellsworth dryly with a slight smile. She really was a prickly chit, and he couldn't understand why she fascinated him so much.

"Why could you not travel with your mother?" she asked evenly, putting butter onto a roll.

"Because she's not leaving on the packet from London until the thirtieth, and I needed to make the arrangements for our trip from Venice to Vienna."

"You'll be traveling with us then?" blurted Eurydice, barely managing to avoid dropping the butter knife.

"Of course. Why would you expect that I wouldn't?" asked Ellsworth, his lips twitching amusedly at her dislike for the idea.

"I don't know. I just thought…. Oh, never mind," said Eurydice dully.

The entire situation was completely unexpected. She had thought she would be rid of him after the ball, once she left London. Now, to find out she would have to endure his company longer made her uncomfortable. What made it worse was that he would be much closer—aboard the ship, just across the alcove; on the journey from Venice to Vienna, possibly in the same coach. She hadn't even considered that something like this might happen. She had thought the worst thing she would have to endure would be the children. She was beginning to believe she would rather bear the company of an entire dozen of children than his.

And yet she couldn't understand what it was about him that she found so disturbing. It was a combination of many things, but from a distance, they were things that could be easily managed. Beneath the surface, however, when she let her feelings come into play, he made her nervous. She couldn't recall anyone ever having the effect on her that he did. There was nothing that had prepared her for it. She couldn't even recall having a single dream about this, but depending on how long ago it had been, that would be understandable. Of course, that's what her notebooks were for. She had them all with her, and she thought she might look through them, just to see if there might be something there to give her some direction.

As she thought about that, she also realized the easiest way to reduce the nervousness she felt when she was around him would be to remove some of his mystery. She might not be able to avoid him on the ship or on the journey to Vienna, but he also would not be able to avoid her. There were things about him that were very suspicious, and she was going to find out if what she thought was right. She would have to be stealthy about it. She had the distinct impression she would learn nothing if he found out she wanted to know something. But if she could understand more about him, Eurydice thought she would be able to deal with him more objectively.

"I'm sorry you find my company so distasteful, Lady Eurydice, but it's not as if I can find an alternate means of transport from the middle of the ocean."

"On the contrary, Mr. Ellsworth," said Eurydice calmly, "I have no interest one way or the other in your company."

Ellsworth looked at her doubtfully. She didn't seem overly expressive of any emotion, but he was good at interpreting subtlety. It seemed dislike was the one she most often used for him. He did realize that was just as well. There were several reasons he needed to stay away from her, and if she didn't like him, it would reduce the temptation…in theory. Of course, it wasn't going to be so easy to do for the next month, perhaps even longer.

Chapter Seven

After four days aboard the ship, Eurydice was feeling sleep-deprived. While her maid's seasickness kept her from getting a good night's rest, Eurydice had discovered in a disconcerting way that the walls of her cabin were not as well-insulated as they should be. She hoped she would eventually become accustomed to it and ignore it, but she hadn't yet.

The wall beside her bunk was shared with Chrissoula and Stockbridge's cabin, and their bunk was along the same wall. At night, if she didn't fall asleep before they went to bed, she could hear them making love. She couldn't hear them when they were talking or at most any other time, but at night, for that particular activity…. It was apparent they both got a lot of enjoyment out of it. She understood they were married—and it was a natural part of that relationship, but she certainly didn't want to listen to it.

It was too embarrassing for her to mention to Chrissoula that she could hear them, and she would definitely not say anything to Stockbridge. Chrissoula would be no less bothered to discover they had an audience than Eurydice would be in telling her. So, Eurydice suffered in silence, praying they would stop being so frequent and enthusiastic. She was only grateful that she couldn't hear the same activities from the direction of the captain's cabin because listening to one happy couple was enough. She thought if things did not improve shortly, she might mention it to Psyche. Chrissoula would take the news better from Psyche than from her.

They had stopped in La Coruna that morning to re-supply and arrange for correspondence to be mailed home, but they had only stayed long enough to tend to that and had sailed with the tide that afternoon. Eurydice had spent the time they were moored taking a nap to make up for her lack of sleep the previous night. Psyche had told her that Sheerness tried to stop every five days in the nearest, largest port to re-supply and send home mail, but Eurydice didn't think she could go five days in succession without a proper amount of sleep, not for an extended period of time. She was almost tempted to join Agniezka on the coffer. It seemed her maid wasn't able to hear it. Either that or it was something that simply didn't bother her as much as it did Eurydice. After thinking about it, Eurydice thought that was likely.

The weather was not cooperating for a speedy journey. It hadn't been stormy; other than a brief thunderstorm during the night before mooring in La Coruna, it had been mild and clear. But up until that day, there hadn't been enough wind to keep the sails taut. Psyche had told her that the previous year by that point in their trip, they had already reached Vigo, and that was even after having to endure a ferocious storm in the Bay of Biscay. Eurydice still thought they seemed to be making excellent time, and the wind had picked up a bit after the rain.

She was somewhat discouraged about her practice on her violin. She hadn't been able to play nearly as much as she had anticipated she would. She would have thought, considering she was aboard a ship with nowhere to go and nothing else to do, that she would be able to practice more than she had so far. She was barely managing an hour or two a day. She didn't know where her time was going, but it seemed to slip through her fingers. An hour or two a day was better than none at all; it did at least keep her fingers flexible and kept her from forgetting how to play.

Supper that night was most excellent, a wonderful pork roast with creamed potatoes, Brussels sprouts, and a delicious pumpkin custard with whipped cream afterward. Eurydice could tell they had re-supplied because they had been eating things like lamb stew and fish caught from the ocean as they sailed. Still, she knew even that, especially for the crew, was much better than what the typical fare was aboard a ship, and she was not going to complain. She wouldn't be getting anything better if she were traveling over land.

She tried to calculate where she would be at that moment if she were traveling by coach. Probably still somewhere in France, and there was no telling who she would have managed to have as a chaperone. Agniezka would have been traveling with her regardless, but she couldn't be considered an appropriate chaperone because she was a maid, even though she was married. It might take her a little longer to get to Vienna going by sea, but it was infinitely better than going the entire way by coach, even having to tolerate Chrissoula and Stockbridge...and Ellsworth.

Eurydice hadn't been going out of her way to avoid him, but she also had not been making a point of seeking him out, either. She saw him at meals, and occasionally when she was taking a turn around the deck. He was always polite and kept his hands to himself, but there was little risk of him doing otherwise with other people present.

She still fully intended to learn more about him and combine it with what she already knew, but she didn't feel it was necessary to rush. She wanted him to become complacent, to think he was familiar enough with her behavior and presence that he would believe she was innocuous. That would make it much easier for her to get him to say or do something that would tell her what she wanted to know.

Eurydice still wasn't sure what that was, however. How he knew Japanese and why he lied about it would be one thing; how he got the tattoo of the dragon on his back would be even better. Why he had those papers in his coat would be helpful, but why her father hadn't seemed as concerned about it as she thought he should be would be even more so. How he knew Napoleon had been defeated before the official dispatch had arrived from Wellington and why he had felt it necessary to tell her father before anyone else was puzzling. The more she thought about it, the more she realized that getting him to provide any of this information, even were he unsuspecting, was not going to be easy. They weren't the kinds of things she could bring up in typical conversation. It would take all the finesse she could muster to get him to tell her all those things. Either that or she would simply have to confront him with what she suspected and perhaps shock him into admitting the truth. Neither way would be easy.

She tried to think about all the things she knew about him already, and there really wasn't much. She knew more about his family than him personally. She didn't know if he had an occupation. She would assume he did not. She wasn't even sure how old he was. Her mother and his mother had gone to finishing school in Austria together, but Mrs. Ellsworth had married much younger than the duchess. Myron would be twenty-five this November, were he still alive, so Eurydice knew Ellsworth had to be at least in his late twenties but definitely not older than thirty-five. He seemed to be more knowledgeable about music than she had originally thought after his comments at the wedding reception, but he could simply have a good ear. That summed up everything she knew, and even that was nothing concrete.

Mrs. Ellsworth had four children, three boys and one girl. When her husband had died unexpectedly after twenty years of marriage, she had packed up the three younger children, Gareth among them, and moved to Austria. Staying at their estate in Renfrewshire apparently held too many painful memories. Her eldest son, Samuel, had remained behind in Scotland to oversee the property and continue his father's business dealings in tobacco and other commodities in Glasgow. Seven years later, he died in a horrible accident while cleaning a gun. To Eurydice's knowledge, after his funeral, the family never went back to Scotland, and the estate had fallen into disrepair, with a goodly portion of the house even being gutted by a fire shortly after Samuel's death. Mrs. Ellsworth's sanctuary on the continent was almost taken away when two years after their arrival there, her youngest son, William, had drowned after falling through the ice on a lake. His body couldn't be recovered until the spring when the ice thawed. He had only been nine years old. Then her daughter, Natalie, had died only the previous year in the carriage accident, and Mrs. Ellsworth was left with one child…and four grandchildren to raise.

After Eurydice thought about things with all of that tragedy in mind, she could begin to understand why Ellsworth stayed with his mother. Even now she couldn't be sure that he lived with her, but Eurydice had the impression he was at least staying very close. She didn't know if he had before his sister's death, but it seemed for the immediate future that would be the case. She didn't think he did it for his benefit, but Eurydice imagined Mrs. Ellsworth was very anxious about the safety of her last child. She would want to have him close so she could see for herself that he was well. Considering some of the things Eurydice thought he was up to, his mother probably spent many nights up pacing the floor…if she were aware of his activities.

As she got ready for bed that night, Eurydice wondered what she would like to learn first, more general things about his background and interests, or go directly to the heart of the matter and satisfy her curiosity about all the other things that puzzled her about him. That would be more interesting, but it would also be more difficult. She yawned and stretched before closing the curtain on her bunk to block out the sun that, while it didn't shine directly into her eyes since the ship had changed direction, did make the cabin too bright for her liking early in the morning. She would have to come up with a plan, but she still had plenty of time, and a good night's rest would help.

Then she could hear Chrissoula and Stockbridge on the other side of the wall. She sighed fitfully and put one of her pillows over her head to block out the sound. With those two in the adjoining cabin, she was *never* going to get a good night's rest.

By Saturday, Eurydice was desperate for sleep. She had taken to napping for an hour or two during the day just after dinner to make up for what she was missing at night. No one in her family had been prone to napping regularly during the day, especially once they left the nursery, but she was at her wit's end. It was something of a vicious circle for her. If she took the nap during the day, she was too awake to fall asleep quickly and avoid the "night music," but if she didn't take the nap, she was too exhausted by bed time to fall asleep. It made her short-tempered when she didn't get enough sleep. Agniezka had noticed her napping, but she hadn't commented about it, even though she was curious. Eurydice was too embarrassed to tell her maid the reason.

Her lack of sleep was making her unpleasant company. It wasn't really that she was in a foul mood or unable to speak civilly. She simply *wouldn't* speak, and things that normally wouldn't bother her in the slightest tried her patience. One thing was the happiness and affection that abounded from both Psyche and Sheerness and Chrissoula and Stockbridge. Eurydice was glad they were so happy together, but after having to listen to Chrissoula and her husband every night for over a week, watching them all hug and kiss and hold hands annoyed her. Not only that, but it seemed Dr. Felton had taken a shine to Agniezka. While he had been nothing but polite and courtly—as far as she knew, Eurydice could tell her maid wasn't displeased by his attention, but Eurydice was. Had she been well-rested, Eurydice would have been overjoyed for Agniezka. The woman deserved some happiness.

Dr. Felton was a nice man. He was intelligent and kind, and he was handsome. Eurydice thought he was in his late twenties, not much older or about the same age as Agniezka. He was a little taller than average and slim. She wouldn't say he was muscular though definitely athletically built, but she thought her brothers and brothers-in-law, even Ellsworth, were more so. *Proportionally fine* would be a good description. It was obvious he spent more time reading or indoors than outside involved in manly pursuits, as would be expected for a physician, but he didn't look sickly or bookish. He had curly, light brown hair and gray eyes with a high forehead and a straight nose, but the thing about his features that Eurydice thought made him most attractive was the compassionate, serious expression he often wore. Had she had more sleep and Eurydice would have been very hopeful for Agniezka.

Another thing which tried her patience was that Freddie had still not become accustomed to her. He still acted like a startled rabbit in her presence. She was at a loss. She didn't know what she could do to remedy the situation. She'd not said a cross word, not said one unfriendly thing. She was always amicable and kind, but he was still nervous around her, his expression one of awe and fright. She had asked Psyche to speak with him and explain that he didn't need to be afraid of her, but it apparently had done no good. He seemed to have become on good terms with Agniezka but not Eurydice. It baffled her, and without enough sleep to make it more bearable, it began to exasperate her.

Then there was Ellsworth. He had taken to walking with her when she took a turn around the deck, if he was topside when she did it. It wasn't that he was unpleasant, but they didn't talk during their stroll. He would simply put her hand into the crook of his arm, and they would walk a time or two around the deck, stopping occasionally to look out at the ocean or the land when they were close enough to the coast to see it. His walking with her presented the perfect opportunity to question him, but she was too frazzled from lack of sleep to think properly.

Eurydice thought for a time about asking her sister why she had failed to mention Ellsworth would be sailing with them, but she decided not to. It was more than likely Psyche wouldn't have considered it something to be of concern, and there had been other things to occupy her concentration. Eurydice's feelings about Ellsworth traveling with them would have been very low on the list, and Psyche thought Eurydice wouldn't have had feelings about the matter at all.

They were coming very close to the Strait of Gibraltar and the northern coast of Africa, and Eurydice began to see more ships on the horizon as they neared it because it was the only way to get to the Mediterranean by water. The look-out in the crosstrees became more attentive as they neared the coast of Africa because of the pirates. Great Britain was finally at peace with both France and the United States, but the Barbary corsairs were willing to attack anyone. They knew ships had only one way to go to reach the Mediterranean, and they prowled the mouth of the Strait like sharks.

But there were also ships from the navies of several countries patrolling the waters; Britain, France, Spain, Portugal, and the United States all had frigates and ships of the line in the vicinity to protect their citizens and trade routes. Once into the Mediterranean, after they were further away from Morocco with more open water, the risk of pirates would lessen, at least until they neared Algiers. The *Medea* was equipped with cannon, and the gunner, Mr. Rolleston, had plenty of weaponry for the crew should it become needed, but Eurydice was confident it would be unnecessary. She didn't feel threatened in the slightest, and she felt positive there would be no altercations on their journey. It wasn't that she had dreamt about it, but she still felt completely safe.

As Eurydice climbed into her bunk that night, she tried to go to sleep as quickly as possible, but it was as if her body had become attuned to anticipating the sounds from the cabin next door. She could not get herself to relax enough to go to sleep, and of course, once she heard Chrissoula and Stockbridge, it was impossible. She put her pillow over her head to block it out, but she had become hypersensitive to it, and she could still hear them through the down and cotton. She was on the verge of bursting into tears.

After thirty minutes without the end in sight, she sat up and opened the curtain frustratedly. Had anyone seen her at that moment, they would have been surprised by the put-out expression on her face. Agniezka was sound asleep on the coffer, resting comfortably in spite of her sleeping conditions, and anything was better than the alternative. Eurydice got out of her bunk and went to sit on the small storage box at the bottom of the mirror, resting her forehead in her hands. She could still hear them, although not as loudly. Had she not been listening to it already, she probably wouldn't have noticed. Eurydice wanted to sleep. She was desperate for sleep, and she was willing to do just about anything to get it. If she couldn't find a solution soon, then she would have to talk to Psyche, no matter how embarrassing it might be.

As it was, she sat on the box for some time trying to decide what to do. She had thought Agniezka would sleep on deck because of her seasickness if she could have gotten away with it. That would have been a perfect solution for Eurydice as well, were it not for the fact that she would be alone on deck with the crew. She didn't think they would misbehave, but it might be unladylike. The ship wasn't like a house; it wasn't as if there was another room farther away to which she could go.

Then she lifted her head quickly in realization. There *was* another room…two of them, in fact. One was the room where extra rope for the deck, cannonballs, and other ammunition were stored. The other was the pantry, where Meals kept most of the food stores for the crew, particularly the grain and flour and more perishable items that could be damaged by the less controlled conditions of the hold and berth deck. She thought that, of the two rooms, the pantry would be the more comfortable.

It would be odd and would come to an end should anyone find out. There *was* something unseemly about it. She was an early riser, though. She felt fairly sure she could go there to sleep for a few hours while her neighbors went to sleep, and then she could come back to her cabin without anyone being any the wiser. It wasn't perfect, but it would be tolerable, and it would spare her the embarrassment of talking to her sister about Chrissoula.

She went to her bunk to retrieve her pillow and a blanket and closed the curtain just in case Agniezka woke up while she was gone. After checking that her maid was asleep, Eurydice quietly padded to the door and opened it. It glided on silent, well-oiled hinges. It was very dark in the alcove, but she was able to feel her way to the door to the officers' mess. Once she had it open, the skylight brightened the room considerably, and she was to the doorway on the other side in no time. She couldn't hear Chrissoula and Stockbridge there, but she couldn't sleep on the dining table. She entered the short hall that would lead abovedecks or to the two rooms and turned right. She trailed her fingers along the wall to guide her way. She had it out slightly ahead of her rather than beside her so she wouldn't walk into the door in the pitch black of the hall.

When she reached the pantry, she realized she should have brought a candle or a lantern. She had no idea where anything was located. She knew there were lots of shelves and large sacks stacked in the room, as well as barrels, smaller casks, and a rack that held several kinds of wine, but she wasn't sure where it all was because she had only seen it once. She didn't want to accidentally trip over something and damage it. She only wanted to sleep.

She slowly felt her way around with her hands and feet in the darkness after she closed the door, trying to find a likely spot. She stubbed her big toe on a barrel at one point and bit her lip to muffle her yelp of pain. She finally located the large sacks that held oats, rice, barley and flour. They would be harder than a mattress but better than the floor. Besides, it would only be for a few hours. She settled herself onto the sacks as comfortably as she could with her pillow and blanket. After a sigh of relief, she was sound asleep.

Eurydice woke up when she landed on the floor with a thump. She looked around herself confusedly in the dark before she remembered where she was. It took her another minute or two to realize the reason she had fallen to the floor was that the ship was rocking. At some point after she fell asleep, the weather obviously had changed. She could hear thunder, muffled by the closed confines of the room, and the ship was definitely not rolling *gently* along.

Eurydice stood up and grabbed her pillow and blanket. Her back was a little stiff, but she at least felt like she had gotten some sleep. She wasn't sure how much she had gotten, but enough time had passed that Chrissoula and Stockbridge would be quiet. It was likely the bosun had gone topside because of the storm. If the storm would let her, Eurydice fully intended to go to her cabin and go back to sleep. She only knew she couldn't stay in the pantry because someone—Agniezka—would wonder where she was.

She nearly fell and slid when the ship yawed to portside as she made her way down the short hall, but she managed to regain her footing by grabbing onto the door jamb for the officers' mess. Once the ship righted somewhat, she started across the cabin, which even with the skylight had become darker because of the storm. She was almost to the door of the alcove when it opened. Eurydice jumped in surprise when she saw Sheerness. He wasn't expecting anyone to be there either and was therefore not looking where he was going. He nearly ran into her and knocked her over.

"Bloody hell!" he yelped. "What are you doing out of your cabin?"

"Uh—" said Eurydice uncertainly.

"You don't need to see the storm," he said irritatedly. "Get back to your cabin and stay there."

Eurydice nodded dumbly, and she watched after him as he strode across the cabin, muttering under his breath about silly women who *liked* the feel of rain on their face and the risk of getting struck by lightning. Eurydice suspected his annoyance stemmed from something Psyche had done and his surprise at finding her in the officers' mess more than anything she might have done personally. He obviously didn't notice she held a pillow and blanket or that she had on a shift and dressing gown; otherwise, he wouldn't have thought she had been trying to go topside. He wasn't wearing his spectacles, and that probably accounted for it.

Eurydice got to her cabin without further incident, and she was not surprised to find that Agniezka was awake on the coffer, but she was not in any condition to be observant. The roiling sea had caused the same effect in her stomach, apparently, and she had her head in a bucket and was vomiting. Eurydice quickly went to her bunk and tossed the blanket and pillow onto it before Agniezka noticed, and then she went to her maid to provide her with what assistance she could. So much for going back to sleep.

The storm lasted well into the day and did not break up until almost five in the evening. Eurydice was more exhausted than she had been before. She had stayed up helping Agniezka, and at one point after the sun rose, Psyche came into the cabin for a little while as well. She was dressed in a linen shirt and trousers, her stockinged feet bare. Eurydice thought Psyche might have come in to talk to her to take her mind off of her husband on the deck in the storm. Eurydice didn't mind the reason behind it, but she was almost too tired to have an intelligible conversation. As it was, her sister didn't stay long because Agniezka was frequently vomiting into the bucket she kept nearby. It wasn't pleasant to hear or see.

Freddie had figured out that he could travel from the berth deck to the after cabins without being exposed to the storm by using the dumbwaiter, and he was able to bring them food for breakfast and dinner. Agniezka, obviously, did not eat, and Eurydice was too tired to eat much, but she appreciated that Freddie had brought them food. Considering he was so afraid of her, she felt like she had to eat at least something when he brought it or run the risk of making the situation even worse.

She couldn't play her violin, although there were times she wanted to try. By the time it was over, she was too exhausted. Agniezka got a little better once the storm ended, and Eurydice was going to take a nap to compensate for the lack of sleep she'd had the night before, but she was concerned if she did, she might not be able to sleep that night, even if she went back to the pantry to do it. If she wasn't tired, she wouldn't sleep, no matter if it was quiet.

Supper was served on time, and Eurydice was impressed with Meals' culinary talents. It was only lamb stew, but that he had been able to prepare it regardless of the storm could not have been easy. When they were given cherry pandowdy for dessert, she had to agree with Psyche that the man was an excellent cook. She didn't know if she could place him into the same category as Mrs. O'Flaherty, but she could definitely say that Meals was far above what she would expect on a ship. Agniezka didn't eat because she was still a bit under the weather, and Eurydice could tell Dr. Felton was disappointed she didn't join them. If Eurydice could remember, she would mention it to her maid as casually as possible. That would make Agniezka feel even better.

When Eurydice went to bed that night, she was—for once—able to go to sleep before any noise started from the cabin next door. If they made any once she was asleep, she was blissfully unaware. She also didn't know when they finally sailed through the Strait of Gibraltar and entered the Alboran Sea. In fact, when she woke up the next morning, Eurydice thought she'd had the best night's sleep since her first night on the ship. She knew her reprieve was temporary and was sure the next night would be back to normal, but getting enough sleep put her into a pleasant mood the following day.

Eurydice was practicing Beethoven's *Spring* sonata before dinner. It was a piece she had played many times before, and although she had her music arranged on the closed top of her desk as a substitute for her stand, she wasn't looking at it; she had it there from habit more than anything else. She had actually been able to get a couple hours of practice in, which caused her to have a soft smile that never quite went away.

Agniezka had recovered enough from the previous day that she was almost back to normal...well, as normal as she had been for being aboard the ship with seasickness. She sat on the coffer by the window knitting methodically as Eurydice played. She had become so accustomed to Eurydice's playing that it didn't bother her to be in the same room, not even if she went through the same piece over and over again; Agniezka simply ignored it if it got too tedious. She did, however, need to go to the water closet. She set aside her work and went to the door as Eurydice continued to play unconcernedly, facing the desk.

When Agniezka opened the door, Freddie tumbled to the floor in the cabin from where he had been crouched outside of it, bumping into Agniezka's legs and nearly knocking her over. He jumped up quickly, his eyes wide with fear. Eurydice stopped playing at the commotion and turned to look.

"Oh," she said softly in surprise. The boy started to flee the room. "Stop right there, Freddie," she said calmly.

She gave Agniezka a brief nod, and her maid left to do what she had intended, her lips twitching amusedly. She almost regretted she wasn't going to be there to listen. Eurydice had decided enough was enough, and having a full night's rest had put her into a frame of mind that made her more capable of addressing it. She pulled out the chair from her desk and turned it. Then, she gestured toward it as she looked at Freddie neutrally.

"Come sit." He clutched his hands in front of himself nervously, and she could see his little chest heaving anxiously, just like an animal caught in a trap. "It's all right," she said softly with an encouraging smile.

Freddie hesitantly did as he was told, and once he was seated, he clasped his hands together between his thighs and hunched his shoulders as he looked up at her. Once he was seated, Eurydice set her violin and bow in their case on the table and sat on the coffer and faced him. She gave her forehead a thoughtful scratch as she tried to decide how best to begin this conversation and accomplish her goal.

"Freddie, were you listening outside my door?" she asked gently.

Freddie shook his head, his eyes rounding. "Oh, no, ma'am!" he said anxiously.

Eurydice arched an eyebrow and chewed the inside of her lip to bite back a smile as she watched his ears begin to turn a bright shade of red. She wasn't familiar with him at all, but knowing how Psyche reacted to telling a lie, Eurydice suspected Freddie had a similar, less traumatic condition.

"Freddie, I'm not angry," soothed Eurydice, "but I will be if you lie to me." She folded her arms across her chest and gave him as stern a look as she could muster without trying to be terrifying. "So, were you listening outside my door?"

Freddie was almost on the verge of tears, and Eurydice watched as his lower lip began to tremble.

"Yes, ma'am," he finally whispered.

"Do you do that often?"

"Yes, ma'am," he squeaked. Eurydice made a sound of impatience as she watched a tear slip down his cheek.

"Oh, Freddie, why are you so afraid? I'm not angry. I'm not going to punish you."

"No, ma'am," said Freddie in the same tone, looking down at his feet.

"Do you like listening to me play?"

"Yes, ma'am."

Eurydice nodded once briefly and stood up. She went to the table and picked up her instrument. Once she had it settled beneath her chin, she began to play the Beethoven again. Freddie's head jerked up in surprise when he heard the music, and his expression began to change to one of fascination and delight as he watched her effortlessly draw the music from the violin. Her technique was so flawless, her familiarity with the piece so intimate, to Freddie it seemed magical. Hearing it through the door had been wonderful, but to *watch* her make it was even more so. Eurydice glanced at him and gave him a slight smile, heartened to see that perhaps she was finally beginning to get through to him.

Agniezka finished in the water closet, but when she returned to the doorway to the cabin and saw the blissful expression on the boy's face, she smiled to herself and decided she would take a turn about the deck, perhaps visit with Chrissoula for a while before dinner. Seeing Dr. Felton would not be such a bad thing either, especially since her mistress had mentioned he was disappointed she hadn't been at supper. She had the distinct feeling that Freddie was not going to be afraid of Eurydice anymore.

Ellsworth was coming from topside to his cabin to tend to a few things before dinner while Eurydice was playing, and he paused with his hand on the knob to watch and listen. He could tell she was playing her Stradivarius, even if he wasn't close enough to see it clearly; the tones from it were so much warmer than those from the Stainer she usually practiced with, and the instrument seemed to be so perfect for Beethoven. She was turned in profile to the door, playing for her enraptured audience of one, and Ellsworth had to admit he was almost as enthralled as Freddie, though definitely not for the same reasons, he was sure. There was so much more about her than her music that captivated him, and he was beginning to find her harder to resist.

There was something magical about her music. When she played, it could be heard all over the ship, though not as loudly as in the after cabins, and the entire crew would listen. Even if the men didn't care for that type of music, it almost seemed as if she enchanted them when she played. In her hands, pieces he had heard many times before became new and infused with an emotion he had never noticed. It was extraordinary.

Yet he knew she was going to Vienna to find a maestro. He didn't know what could be done to improve perfection. There were violinists twice her age who didn't possess half her skill, men who would sell their souls to play as well as she did. He heard her play a piece the other day that he had never heard before, and when he asked her sister about it, Psyche said it was a piece Eurydice had composed herself. She was a musical prodigy. There was nothing more she could learn; she needed to be *heard,* and he couldn't understand why she felt she needed to learn more. He honestly didn't think there was anyone in Vienna—or anywhere else—who *could* teach her.

After he listened for several more minutes, he finally shook his head to clear it and opened the door to his cabin. He could never grow tired of listening to her play, but he did have things to do. Sheerness had informed him that they would be mooring in Melilla to re-supply either some time during the night or early in the morning. He had several letters to write, and he wanted to have them done before they reached port.

When Eurydice finished playing, she lowered her violin and smiled warmly at Freddie.

"That was lovely," he sighed.

Eurydice chuckled. "Thank you."

Freddie's expression grew thoughtful, and his forehead creased slightly. "I guess you're a good one after all."

It was Eurydice's turn to frown. "I beg your pardon?"

"Well, I could tell you have a touch of the Other about you, but I couldn't tell if it was good or bad."

"The *Other?*" said Eurydice softly, and she could feel a knot forming in the middle of her chest.

"Uh-huh. Me mum used to tell me there are some people who are special because they are touched by the other world. When they were babies in their cradles, they were kissed by a spirit, either a demon or an angel." He shrugged. "Both of 'em are touched by the Other, but the ones who are kissed by demons are always bad, and the ones kissed by angels are good." He grinned. "Me mum said I was kissed by an angel because I'm so good with animals. You must have been, too, because only an angel can make music like that."

Far from making Eurydice feel better, as she was sure Freddie intended to do, she could feel the skin tingling on her cheeks as the blood drained out of them, and the knot in her chest only grew tighter. It wasn't his fault; he was only a child. He had been afraid of her before he heard her play, and she knew it was the Insight he had sensed as "a touch of the *Other*," as he called it, not her music. She couldn't tell him that. It seemed they were on their way to, if not becoming friends, then at least getting on without him being scared. If she told him what he had really felt, that would end. She didn't know what his mother could have been thinking to tell him something like that. She gave him a smile she hoped was appreciative because she didn't feel like smiling at all.

"Thank you, Freddie, that's very sweet."

"You're welcome!" He stood up. "I've got to go now. Meals is probably wondering where I am. I'm supposed to be helping with dinner."

"I won't keep you then," said Eurydice softly. "Don't feel like you have to sit outside the door anymore, Freddie. If you want to come in to listen, you are welcome any time."

"Thanks!" he said happily. "Goodbye!" he called over his shoulder as he skipped from the room.

"Goodbye," said Eurydice dully.

She put her violin into its case and went to sit on the edge of her bunk. It was superstitious nonsense. There was nothing angelic about her playing, not any more than there was something demonic about the Insight. At least, that's what she tried to tell herself. There was no *Other*. There were no kisses to babies from angels or demons that made people good or bad. A person's destiny was determined by himself—or herself, by the choices made...not by some capricious smooching performed by spirits. There was nothing evil about her dreams. Her *babushka* had them. Her siblings had them. None of her family could ever be considered bad by any stretch of the imagination. And neither could she. At least, that's what she tried to tell herself.

Chapter Eight

Over the days that followed, Eurydice did her best to put Freddie's words from her thoughts. As he remained friendly, his fear of her forgotten, it became easier to do. She didn't mention what he had said to anyone because if she did, it would be as if she were giving credibility to the misguided nonsense of a child. She didn't want to belittle him, and she didn't want to believe him, so the best thing she could do was forget he said it.

Eurydice sent letters home to her family when they stopped at Melilla, and Psyche was even able to coax her off the ship to walk with her through the town. Eurydice didn't get as much enjoyment from it as her sister, but it was nice to get some exercise that offered a broader variety of scenery than the deck of the ship. They made a feminine outing of it, taking Chrissoula and Agniezka with them. Freddie came along as well, and he happily guided Psyche's dog Cupid along on his leash as he skipped along with them, going in and out of shops that Psyche had been unable to visit the previous year. After they were finished with their shopping, they delivered their packages to the ship where it was moored at the dock, and then they went for a stroll along the beach and collected seashells. Eurydice didn't really find much to interest her in the stores or the market, but Agniezka was able to convince her to make a few purchases here and there by giving her casual suggestions.

Once Eurydice discovered her new place to sleep, her attitude improved greatly. She would wait until she was sure Agniezka had gone to sleep, and then she would slip from the cabin with her pillow and blanket and go to the pantry. It was as if she had a mental clock that would wake her after she had slept for a few hours, around two or three in the morning, and she would quietly slip back into her cabin and her bunk without anyone being the wiser.

By Saturday, they were sailing between Tunisia and Sicily. When Eurydice asked Sheerness about it, he thought they would be to Venice in less than a week, provided the weather and the wind remained good. They had made excellent time on their journey. There had only been the one bad storm before they entered the Strait of Gibraltar, and they'd not encountered any of the corsairs. Eurydice could not compare it to previous trips, but she thought they had been very lucky.

Shortly after dinner, Eurydice was in her cabin practicing her violin when she heard the sound of the anchors dropping. She lifted her bow from the strings and frowned curiously. To her knowledge, they weren't anywhere near dry land. She looked over to Agniezka, who was in her usual seat on the coffer, still knitting her blanket. Her maid was frowning as well. The weather was pleasant, very balmy and sunny, and even Agniezka knew a ship would weather a storm better drifting than at anchor in an open port. Eurydice could see nothing out the window.

She was about to go topside when the door to her cabin opened, and Psyche came in, her face excited.

"What's the matter? Where are we? Why have we stopped?" asked Eurydice concernedly.

"Nothing's the matter," said Psyche with a grin. "We're at Pantelleria, and I've convinced Sheerness we need to stop for a few hours and swim."

"Swim?" said Eurydice confusedly.

"Well, yes. We stopped here last year to teach Freddie how to swim, and I found some very interesting things while I was diving. I just thought it would be fun to stop again for a while and swim. We've been pent up on this ship for weeks, and I'm sure the crew will enjoy it. They certainly did last year."

"Oh, but—" said Eurydice.

"I know, you'll need something to wear," said Psyche with a grin.

Eurydice snapped her teeth together and lifted her eyebrows. "Actually, that hadn't occurred to me, but now you mention it…."

"Then what were you going to say?"

"I was just…it's just…the crew…."

"Pssh," said Psyche with a grin, waving a hand through the air. "They'll stay on the starboard side of the ship while we're on this side. We'll be using your window to get to the channel to go in and out of the water though, if you don't mind. They should be rigging the ladder any minute now."

Eurydice sighed with relief. She had thought *everyone* would be swimming together and that she would have to go onto the deck to get into the water. It wasn't that she thought the crew should remain separate, just that the women and men should remain separate, especially considering what she typically wore to swim—which was nothing. She didn't care at home, but she didn't know these people. It seemed Psyche had thought of everything, and any reservations Eurydice might have had disappeared. She did love to swim, and it had been almost a year since she'd had the chance.

"I'll go get you something to wear," said Psyche. She looked over Eurydice's shoulder to Agniezka. "What about you? Want to swim?"

"That would be nice, actually, but I don't know what I'll wear."

"No need to worry. I have a costume for you, too, I think. If I don't, I think Chrissoula has a couple."

"What, exactly, does this costume look like?" asked Eurydice thoughtfully.

"Oh, it's wonderful, you'll see," grinned Psyche as she left the room.

Eurydice looked at herself in the mirror in her cabin. Psyche had brought her a "swimming costume," and it was not what she had expected. At home, she didn't wear anything when she swam in the lake. Neither did anyone else in her family. She knew that was unseemly, and most people "bathed" clothed. Her family didn't *bathe* in the lake, though; they swam, and since it was only her family, there was nothing to cause them to be self-conscious. She knew that, too, was unseemly. When most people went to the seaside or to swim in public, they used bathing machines and wore articles that weren't any more revealing than regular clothing. That was fine if all they intended to do was stand in the water or dunk their head under it, but Eurydice thought it would be impossibly uncomfortable to swim in something like that. It would be dangerous, too. She didn't think, however, that polite society would condone what she was presently wearing.

It was composed of two pieces made from black cotton. The top had a bodice that was twisted and shirred to provide the coverage for her breasts, and it was covered in beautiful, heavy embroidery to increase the opacity of the fabric and lined with silk. But the bodice didn't go around all the way to the back, and there were no sleeves. It was actually little more than two "cups" to contain her bosom. There were strings at the top edge to tie around her neck and strings at the sides to tie around the back to keep it on and in place. There was a piece of fabric at the bottom edge of the bodice that was gathered and hung loosely all the way around to where the strings attached at the sides to tie at the back. It was made of a sheer black mull rather than the opaque linen of the bodice, and was edged at the bottom with more of the fine embroidery Eurydice was sure Chrissoula had done. While it was fairly long, it only came down to her navel. She didn't think the hanging fabric served any useful purpose, other than for modesty, but it really wasn't very helpful for that if one were to consider it for a moment.

The bottom half of the costume was no less bizarre, and no less immodest. It was almost a pair of trews, but not quite. There was a fitted yoke at the top, and then there was gathered fabric that loosely hung down from it to form the legs. From a distance it could almost be mistaken for a very short skirt—even kilts were longer. The legs only came to about the top of her thighs, enough to cover her buttocks but not much else. The pants were held on by lacing in the yoke, which allowed them to be adjusted to the proper tightness to keep them in place. The bottom edges of the legs were embroidered to match the bodice.

As Eurydice looked at herself, she had to agree that wearing it would be as comfortable for swimming as she could get without being naked, but once she had it on, she was almost tempted not to swim at all. She was glad the men would be swimming on the other side of the ship because the costume was almost as bad as being naked. Actually, she thought it might have been *less* provocative were she to go swimming naked. Although she was sure it hadn't been Psyche's intention when she designed it, the costume accentuated and flattered body parts that men admired without assistance. She couldn't think of anyone on the ship that she wanted to have admiring her.

Eurydice had never seen anything like it, and she was sure no one else had either. One of the main problems she had with it was that it had been made for Psyche. While it didn't leave Eurydice overly exposed (relatively speaking), the bodice didn't cover her breasts as well as she was sure it would her sister's. The lacing and ties actually proved quite practical for allowing it to be adjusted to fit several different women or one woman whose figure might change for some reason, and it did allow the costume to fit snugly enough that Eurydice didn't feel like it might come loose at some point. But there was all the exposed skin to consider.

Agniezka stood nearby watching Eurydice turn this way and that as she looked in the mirror. She had on a costume very similar to the one her mistress was wearing in a sapphire blue color, and she wasn't any more comfortable having that much skin visible than Eurydice. She did have one advantage in that the costume she wore was made for Chrissoula, who was better-endowed through the torso, which gave Agniezka more coverage from the bodice rather than less. If she forgot the indecency of it, though, Agniezka did think the costume was very flattering to Eurydice. Even though it was made entirely of black, there was enough of her golden skin exposed that it made her look very feminine and alluring. Eurydice turned from the mirror to look at Agniezka. She relied on her maid's judgment for clothing matters, but she didn't think this required any deliberation.

"Well?" she asked.

"I suppose it's better than wearing nothing," said Agniezka with a shrug, "and it won't be quite so obvious once we're in the water."

After a brief knock, Psyche came into the cabin with Chrissoula. Both were dressed in their own costumes, a burgundy one for Psyche and red for Chrissoula. Eurydice was somewhat relieved to see that her own costume covered more than Psyche's; the fabric on the top was several inches above her sister's navel. Chrissoula had several towels in her arms, and she took them to the coffer and set them down where they could be easily reached from the channel just outside the window.

"Psyche, what possessed you to come up with something like this?" asked Eurydice bluntly without preamble.

Psyche grinned. "I saw it on a Greek vase. Actually, the one on the vase didn't have the material at the bottom of the bodice; it was more of a bandeau, really. I think it was just a piece of fabric tied at the back over the breasts, but I couldn't see the back of it to say for sure. And the trews? Well, much less coverage, and I think these will prove to be more comfortable in the long run."

"Yes, but why not a costume more like everyone else wears?"

"You can't swim in that. You know that. I used a modified chemise last year, which worked fine, except that it wasn't very easy to pull up over my hips and all the excess fabric would float about if it wasn't belted and gartered. I saw this on a vase, and Chrissoula helped me to make it a little more modest."

"Modest?" hooted Eurydice.

"Oh, pooh," said Psyche, waving a hand through the air. "It will be perfectly fine, and you can be sure no one is going to say a word, especially not Sheerness or Freddie. Consider this: if all four of us are wearing it, you are less likely to be conspicuous."

"Sheerness and Freddie?" said Eurydice with a frown.

"They're both swimming on the other side of the ship right now, but I'm sure they'll come over to our side before long, and so will Stockbridge…and Ellsworth," she trailed off thoughtfully and scratched her forehead. She saw her sister's troubled look. "Honestly, there is nothing to worry about. It will be fine. Now, let's swim. We've only a few hours before we have to set sail again. Sheerness wants to be to Valletta very early tomorrow to re-supply. We are behind schedule this year."

Eurydice shrugged resignedly. Both Agniezka and Psyche were right, of course. She had to agree that the oddness of the costume wouldn't be noticed once she was in the water, and it was unlikely anyone would complain about the decency of it if all four women were wearing it. Freddie was too young to care, and Sheerness and Stockbridge were too interested in their wives to notice other women. As for Ellsworth, Eurydice could only hope he stayed to starboard. Of all the men on this ship she didn't want to see her so scantily clad, he was at the top of the list. She again thought about not swimming at all.

The four women climbed through the window onto the channel and looked down at the water through the shrouds. A sailor had climbed down from the deck to attach a jacob's ladder to the deadeyes before Psyche brought Eurydice and Agniezka their costumes. When Eurydice looked back over her shoulder toward the deck, she could just see over the gunwale and promptly turned back to face the water. There were quite a few naked men running around up there, and she would just as soon not have that image planted in her mind if she had to speak with them when they were clothed later.

The water was very blue and clear, and it looked like it was going to be very warm. She could see all the way to the bottom, where there was white sand peppered with dark rocks. She could see crabs scuttling about, and she wondered if Meals would catch some while they were stopped; she loved crabmeat. The island did seem to be the perfect place to stop for a swim.

Psyche gave her a grin and dove from the platform into the water. Eurydice soon followed, and Agniezka and Chrissoula joined them. Of the four, Agniezka was the least capable swimmer, but the buoyancy of the salt water made it very easy for her to stay afloat. The four women swam around and splashed and played for a while. Eurydice had to admit that the costume

Psyche had designed was highly suited to swimming. She almost didn't notice she had it on.

She had dove to the bottom to look at some of the creatures she saw there, and when she came to the surface, she heard a man's laughter. She had been hearing it on and off distantly while they swam because the men were on the other side of the ship, but this was from a man on their side. Once she had her eyes adjusted and she looked around herself, Eurydice saw Sheerness treading the surface near Psyche. Freddie and Stockbridge were there as well, but she fortunately did not see Ellsworth.

When Sheerness saw she had surfaced, he grinned at her.

"Did you find any treasure?" he asked.

"I saw a very pretty pink and orange anemone, and I really wish Meals would catch about two dozen of the crabs I saw down there to cook for my supper. I didn't find any gold or jewels, though."

Sheerness laughed. "Meals *is* catching some of the crabs, actually, but I don't think you'll have two dozen all for yourself, though. He intends to use them to make crab cakes. Even as abundant as they are here, it would take entirely too many to have enough for the crew to have their fill without more time to catch them."

Eurydice tried to hide her disappointment. Crab cakes would suit, but she much preferred it picked from the shell, dabbed in melted butter with just a little garlic. She almost thought about catching her own, but she did realize it wouldn't be fair.

≪ ≫

Ellsworth walked into Eurydice's cabin without knocking or checking to see if anyone were there. The door was open, so he didn't feel like he was intruding. He hadn't gone into the water yet. He had been contemplating whether he should. It wasn't that he didn't like swimming because he did. He simply didn't want to wear what he was wearing. Trews or nothing was best, but he *had* to wear this. It would cause too many questions if he didn't. It would be best to dress like everyone else and save himself the trouble.

He frowned slightly as he looked around himself at the room. Eurydice confused him. He knew she was leaving her cabin at night for several hours. She was very quiet, but he often had trouble sleeping and was very observant, so he had noticed. He wasn't sure where she was going, though. Seeing as how they were on a ship, there were only so many places it could be. Considering she seemed to wait until everyone was asleep and returned only a few hours later, the one thing that seemed logical was going to be with a lover.

Who? It would have to be someone in the after cabins. She would have been discovered by now otherwise, he was sure. Aside from that, the crew quarters were too open and public for her to have the privacy to be with a lover. It had to be one of the officers. Of those men, the only one who seemed likely as a tryst mate was the doctor. Higginbotham and Broughton were too old. Ellsworth did know stranger things had happened, but he simply couldn't see her becoming involved with men who were old enough to be her father, if she were to become involved with anyone at all. He couldn't be sure it was Felton, though. The wall of Ellsworth's cabin adjoined the doctor's, and he had heard no noises from there after Eurydice had left her cabin. He couldn't see either of them being that quiet. He couldn't be…not for that.

What confused him was that while her leaving her cabin for an assignation seemed to be the only logical conclusion, he couldn't believe Eurydice would do something like that. She seemed entirely too prim and fussy to take a lover. He did know from personal experience, however, that looks could be deceiving. If she had a lover, it had just started. She had seemed far too inexperienced in London for him to think this had been going on for much more than the time on the ship, which made Felton seem all the more likely. Then again, her innocence could have been an act, too. It simply puzzled him that she would feel it was necessary to take the charade to such an extremity, and why she would conduct one in the first instance, particularly one like that. If it *was* all simply an act to cover her unsavory habits, Ellsworth had to admit he was impressed with her skills. He knew she was the daughter of a duke and was expected to be modest and chaste, but her indifference sometimes bordered on frigidity, which was why he honestly couldn't believe she had been pretending to be how she was. Perhaps another part of him was simply unhappy that if she *had* taken a lover, she had not chosen him.

Ellsworth had begun taking walks with her around the deck hoping he would unnerve her enough for her to say something that would tell him who it was or perhaps by some sign—some change in demeanor—show him who of the crew it was. It didn't work, though, and he didn't think it ever would. She was always perfectly calm and self-contained. They rarely spoke to each other, and when they did, it was only about things on the ship or that they saw as they sailed. She couldn't be as placid as she appeared, but he had discovered there were only certain things he could do to make her express her emotions. None of them could be done on the ship in full view of the crew.

He started to go to the window to climb onto the channel when the several notebooks sitting on her open desk caught his attention. He only hesitated for a moment before he picked one up and opened it. Some might call it unscrupulous; Ellsworth considered it an occupational hazard. He quickly realized it was a journal or diary of some type. Each entry was marked at the top with a date. Some went for a few pages, some barely a page. Without reading the contents, he put down the first one to look for another, more recent one. The first one had been filled five years ago. He found one that looked like it had not been completely filled yet and opened it, finding that it was current, the last entry being made that day.

He flipped through the pages until he found the first entry made after they set sail. It seemed she wrote every day, and he had to admire her consistency.

Some people he knew who kept diaries sometimes managed to write only an entry or two a week. She had five notebooks, and he could only assume they were all journals. He began to read the entry, intending to confirm whether or not she was involved with Felton or some other member of the crew.

As he skimmed through the entry, he began to frown. Whatever it was about, it certainly wasn't regarding her sexual activities. He read the next one, and the frown didn't go away. They seemed to be short stories of some type, but unlike anything he had ever read before. After the third one, he flipped back to the days before they sailed. There was only more of the same.

He put down the current notebook and picked up the first one again. In this one, he could see where comments in the margins had been made on some of the entries in a different ink but still her handwriting. Some even had addendums, as if the story were continued at a later time. He read one she wrote when she was about fifteen with only a very brief paragraph added to the end of it. He could feel the blood draining from his face as he got to the last of it, and he read the entire entry again to be sure he was not misunderstanding what she meant.

"Myron was killed today, 18 June 1814. If only it had been just a dream."

He read another of the entries that had been modified, and he could feel the hairs on the back of his neck rising as if a cold wind were blowing across it. After reading four or five and finding only more of the same, he closed the notebook and put it back on the stack exactly as he found it. He brushed his fingers across the leather cover contemplatively and looked at the window where the sound of women's laughter was carried in on the wind. He didn't think any of the laughter belonged to Eurydice, and after finding the notebooks and realizing what they were—what they meant, he began to see her in a different light that illuminated certain things about her so much clearer.

It still did not, however, answer his original question of who she had taken for a lover. Despite discovering what he just had, Ellsworth could still only believe she had one and that it had to be Felton. He could think of no other reason why she would leave her cabin in the middle of the night, and he certainly didn't think she was sleepwalking. She had to be meeting someone, either in the man's cabin or somewhere else.

Ellsworth climbed out the window onto the channel. Freddie was sitting there taking a rest, and the boy looked up with a smile when he saw him. He was dressed in only a pair of breeches, and as he looked at Ellsworth, his forehead wrinkled slightly with a frown at his clothing. Freddie didn't say anything about how odd it seemed, though.

"Are you only just swimming?" asked Freddie.

"Yes, only just. I had some things I needed to do in my cabin first."

Freddie shrugged. "Oh."

Ellsworth looked down at the water. He could see Sheerness, Psyche, Stockbridge, and Chrissoula not far from the ship near the ladder. Agniezka was a little further away from the ship, treading water and looking beneath the surface. He didn't see Eurydice anywhere, and he had to wonder where she was. She certainly wasn't in her cabin. After a minute or two still without seeing her, Ellsworth dove off the platform into the water.

As soon as he was in the water, he knew what he was wearing wasn't suitable for swimming, and he had to wonder how people did so. The flannel was heavy, and if it weren't for his being a capable swimmer, it was possible to believe it would drown him. He surfaced near Psyche and Sheerness, and the two of them looked at him pleasantly. Ellsworth could see that Sheerness was only wearing trews, and he was envious of the man being able to do so. He looked at what Psyche was wearing, what little of it he could see in the water, and he realized there wasn't much of it *to* see. It was definitely not a normal bathing costume, but he could see where it would be practical for swimming, and while it wasn't something society would consider modest, he thought it was at least decent for what it was.

"Hallo, Ellsworth," Psyche grinned. "Did you not have any trews? Breeches would have been suitable, too. There was no need for you to wear that."

Sheerness gave her a dryly amused look. "Have you ever thought, *chere*, that perhaps there are still some people in the world who are modest? Perhaps even *shy?*"

"Hah!" hooted Psyche amusedly. Her face grew serious as she looked at Ellsworth. "Are you really?" she asked in surprise.

Ellsworth managed to look bashful. He didn't think he had ever been called shy or modest by anyone who really knew him, but it was a perfect reason for him to be wearing the bathing costume, even if it wasn't the *real* reason. But as Psyche continued to look at him, he could tell she didn't believe him, even if her husband did. She was very good at reading people, a skill she shared with her father apparently. He thought she might even be better at it. He was beginning to realize something about the females in Aberdare's family: they were all extraordinary in some fashion, it seemed, but Eurydice was perhaps the most extraordinary of them all. Even if Psyche didn't believe him, though, she was too polite to outright accuse him of lying.

"I'm sorry, you wear whatever you feel most comfortable in," she said after a minute.

Ellsworth had been talking with the Sheernesses for two or three minutes, and there was still no sign of Eurydice. He tried not to be concerned because her sister didn't seem to be in the slightest, but he wondered if that was because she was preoccupied and didn't realize Eurydice was missing. About that time, Psyche looked beyond him to where Agniezka was treading water.

"Is she *still* down there?" Psyche called amusedly.

"Yes. It must be a very interesting anemone. Either that or she's managed to find something else to entertain her," returned Agniezka, no less amused.

Sheerness laughed. "And I thought *you* had gills," he chortled. "How long can she hold her breath again?"

Psyche grew thoughtful. "I don't know, really. Seven minutes, maybe."

No sooner had she said that when her head suddenly bobbed under the water, her expression one of surprise. She soon surfaced again, laughing amusedly, with Eurydice beside her.

"I was expecting you to do that," burbled Psyche.

"Of course you were," said Eurydice dryly with a slight smile.

Then she realized that Ellsworth was there, and she gave him an assessing look. She saw that he was wearing an actual bathing costume, which surprised her. She didn't believe for an instant that he would have been concerned about modesty, not from the way he had behaved toward her thus far. She thought it would be more likely that he would swim in the buff. She realized without thinking about it too hard that he wore it to hide certain things, like all the scars, and especially the tattoo. They would cause questions, and it was apparent from what he was wearing that he didn't want to answer them. Psyche didn't know anything about that, but Eurydice did. She could also see that while he appeared to be an excellent swimmer, the costume was making it difficult for him to even tread water.

Ellsworth could see that Eurydice was wearing a costume like her sister's, except hers was black. It was very seductive on her, and he could feel his heart beginning to thud against his ribs as he looked at her. He tried to control it, though. *She is not for you,* he could hear a voice in his head telling him, but she was proving to be very irresistible without even putting forth any effort to make herself that way. If anything, she seemed to be trying very hard to make herself as untempting as possible.

"How far are we from shore?" Psyche asked her husband.

"Not very...about two hundred yards or so...probably less."

"Would you like to race?" she asked with a grin.

Sheerness laughed and shrugged. "I don't know about that."

"Come on. We'll all go. Would that make it fair? At least then there's bound to be *someone* you can beat," she teased.

Sheerness laughed again and splashed water in her face. "You better behave, or I will have the crew lift anchor and sail off without you."

Psyche giggled. "They wouldn't do it, and you know it. They'd be more likely to tie you up and drag you off the stern," she bantered back. She looked past Eurydice and Ellsworth to Chrissoula and Stockbridge. "Would you two like to race to the shore?"

"No, I think we're done for now," said Chrissoula with a smile. "I'm feeling a bit waterlogged."

"I'll go," said Freddie excitedly, looking down from the channel, and he jumped into the water with a loud splash.

"See? There. You can definitely beat Freddie," teased Psyche. Sheerness shook his head and gave her a look of pretended disgust. Psyche ignored it and looked at Eurydice and Ellsworth. "What about you two?"

"I suppose," said Eurydice agreeably. Two hundred yards wasn't that far.

"I'm game," said Ellsworth mildly. It might be fun, and he could use the exercise.

Eurydice turned to look at Agniezka. "What about you? Do you want to swim to the shore?"

"Eh, no," said Agniezka as she swam toward them to go for the ladder. "I think I'll take a nap on your bunk while we are stopped."

Eurydice grinned. "It is calm here, isn't it?"

"Yes, I noticed that earlier," chortled Agniezka.

"So, there are five of us," said Psyche to Sheerness. "That should give you respectable odds."

"You are so pushing your luck," he chortled amusedly. "Very well."

"Huzzah!" said Psyche enthusiastically. "We start when we get to the rudder. No rules on stroke. The best way you can get there."

"Agreed," said Sheerness, "but what am I going to get if I win?"

Psyche swam closer to him to whisper in his ear, and Eurydice watched curiously as his face turned a bright shade of pink. Whatever his prize would be, she had the impression it was something he would consider to be worth any effort. Psyche turned to look at everyone else.

"For the rest of you, I have a very nice watercolor of the Acropolis in Athens."

Eurydice raised an eyebrow. She had no idea what she would do with a watercolor of the Acropolis, but she couldn't be sure that she would win in any event. She hadn't done any swimming for a year, and while she had other exercise to keep herself fit, she was too out of practice to do her best. Still, it would be fun, she was sure. She loved to swim, as did everyone in her family.

The five of them began toward the stern, and Eurydice took her time, kicking with her legs mostly to propel herself with an occasional stroke or two with her arms to keep on course. Freddie wasn't far away from her, and he looked over at her with a happy grin as he paddled along. He was rather small, and two hundred yards was quite a distance for someone his size, but he seemed to be doing well so far.

As they rounded the stern, Eurydice lined up on the shore, intending to aim for the rocky cove just to the right of the rock formation that resembled an elephant dipping its trunk into the water. There was actually a spit of rock that jutted out on the other side of it that she thought might be closer, and as they reached the rudder, she aimed for it after taking a deep breath.

Eurydice began the race with a simple frontward crawl she used when she wanted to cover distance quickly, but she soon grew tired of it and decided to change. Without losing much of her pace, she glided onto her back and switched to a backstroke that she found much more relaxing and allowed her to look at her surroundings. With the crawl, it kept her insulated from what was going on around her and kept her focused on swimming only. She was far enough away from the ship that she could tell some of the men there were naked, but they weren't close enough for it to bother her. She also noticed with some surprise that she had quite a lead on both Psyche and Sheerness, who seemed to be keeping pace with each other fairly well. The distance between her and Ellsworth and Freddie was even larger. What shocked her even more was to see that Ellsworth was trailing behind Freddie. She would have thought he would be a much better swimmer than that, but there it was. She glanced back over her shoulder as she swam to get a bead on where she was, and she found it hard to believe that she was within fifty yards of the shore. She really hadn't been putting all her effort into the race. Perhaps she wasn't as out of practice as she had thought she was.

As she continued to watch the swimmers behind her, however, she began to realize Ellsworth's lag was not due to lack of skill. The bathing costume he wore was simply too heavy and was about to drown him. She slowed her pace with a slight frown, and Psyche and Sheerness soon caught up to her.

"Tired already?" chortled Psyche as she came abreast of her. "You're almost there!"

"Hunh," said Eurydice flatly. Her sister obviously was not aware of Ellsworth's difficulty.

She reluctantly changed her direction and began to swim back toward the ship, toward Ellsworth. Freddie soon neared her, swinging his arms and legs in the water enthusiastically. He was enjoying himself, even if he wasn't going to win. He frowned slightly when he realized she was not going toward the shore.

"Where are you going?" he asked confusedly.

"Don't worry. Keep swimming to shore," said Eurydice calmly.

By that point, Ellsworth was very far behind, too far away from the ship to go back, and too far away from the shore to reach it without help. She quickened her pace to get to him, just as he began to sink under the water, only to bob to the surface again. He was tired but still determined not to admit he was in trouble, even as he went under the water a second time.

"You're going to drown," said Eurydice bluntly when she got within earshot.

"No, I'm not," panted Ellsworth.

"That costume is only good for bathing in water that doesn't go over your head. At least take off the shirt, or you're going to drown," said Eurydice firmly, changing to a side stroke as she reached him, easily keeping pace with him as he continued to struggle stubbornly.

"I'll take off mine if you take off yours," he panted.

"Mr. Ellsworth, this is no time for levity," said Eurydice flatly, and she watched as he sank under the water again. This time, he didn't come immediately back to the surface. "Bloody hell," she muttered, and she took a breath to go under and retrieve him.

He was several feet below the surface, trying to get back, but the weight of his clothes competed against the strength he had left and was winning. Even with the buoyancy of the salt water, he was sinking further. Rather than pull him back to the surface, though, Eurydice grabbed the bottom of his shirt and pulled it off before she attempted any type of rescue. That wasn't so easy to accomplish because he actually fought with her to keep it on. She had always thought her sister, Persephone, was the most obstinate person she knew, but she was beginning to believe Ellsworth might possibly be even worse. When it came down to a choice between keeping on his shirt or drowning, however, he finally let her remove it. When Eurydice held the weight of it in her hands, it felt like lead ballast, beginning to make her sink, and she let it go, watching it continue to the bottom. Fabric shouldn't sink like that, she thought, especially not something intended for use in water.

For a few seconds, Eurydice thought about removing the pants as well, but she couldn't be sure what he had on underneath, if anything. She decided against it. She would get him to the surface, and if the weight of the pants proved to still be too much, not having him in the shirt would at least make it easier for her to haul him to shore. Losing the shirt had helped a lot; he gained some positive buoyancy and rose slightly toward the surface. She grabbed him by the arm and kicked her way to the top.

Ellsworth spluttered and coughed when he reached the air, and Eurydice kept a hold on his arm with one hand, while she used her other arm to sidestroke toward shore. She kept her lips tightened in a grim line, trying her best to refrain from scolding him for being such an idiot. She couldn't believe he would actually risk drowning for the sake of avoiding questions about a silly tattoo, which made her all the more determined to find out how he got it. She was fairly sure she already knew because she didn't think there could be any other reason for it than the one she had in mind, but she would like to hear it from him. In the minutes it took her to heave him toward the shore, she tried to formulate a plan for getting him to tell her. Nothing came to mind.

She could see Psyche standing on the shore with one of her hands on her hip, the other shielding her eyes from the sun. She was wearing a concerned frown, and Sheerness and Freddie beside her were doing the same. After a few more yards, the water was shallow enough that Eurydice could stand, and she put her feet down and continued to haul on Ellsworth.

"What happened?" asked Psyche worriedly.

"This is what happens when an idiot wears a lead bathing costume," grunted Eurydice in Japanese, relievedly releasing Ellsworth's arm as he was finally able to move on his own toward the shore without the risk of going under again. "No, this is what happens when an idiot decides to wear a lead bathing costume to swim," she corrected herself, and she heaved a tired sigh, putting a hand to the stitch that had developed in her side from the effort of rescuing him. He would be heavy even without the lead pants.

"I am not an idiot," panted Ellsworth tiredly, heaving himself onto his back on the rocks. The heat of the sun had warmed the basalt nicely, and he would be happy to just lie there and sleep for a couple hours if given the chance.

Psyche raised an eyebrow as she looked between the two of them, and several thoughts came to her mind. She had the feeling her sister had used

Japanese because she wanted to find out whether or not Ellsworth actually did understand it, and the strange day her nephew had been born came back to her. If he hadn't understood Japanese, he wouldn't have said what he just did. Whether he wanted to deny it or not, he knew the language. With that confirmed, her curiosity about *how* he knew it began to build.

Another thing she wondered about was Eurydice's attitude toward the man. For some reason, she didn't like him overly much. Psyche remembered her reaction to finding out he was aboard the *Medea*. And just now, her calling him an idiot really hadn't been necessary, even if Psyche did agree that wearing the bathing costume had been foolish. She didn't believe him when he implied he was modest, much less shy, and what really might have prompted him to wear it made her curious. Even if Eurydice had been trying to get him to give away that he understood Japanese, Psyche couldn't recall her sister ever resorting to name-calling, not even the few times she had ever seen Eurydice lose her temper. She had to wonder what had happened between the two of them for Eurydice to feel that way toward him, and for her to express that dislike when she usually kept things like that to herself.

"Ellsworth, are you all right?" asked Sheerness, seeming to be the only one who was concerned about that.

Ellsworth lifted a hand into the air and waved it tiredly, his eyes closed as he soaked up the sun. "I'm fine."

Psyche gave Sheerness a puzzled glance when she noticed all of Ellsworth's scars. Sheerness shook his head quietly to let her know she shouldn't mention it. Psyche didn't see where there would be any harm in doing so, but she would let it go for now. She wondered if that was the reason he had worn the bathing costume. That would have been downright silly, but some people were that vain. There were so many of them, but they weren't disfiguring—just peculiar. Psyche looked at Eurydice and tilted her head at Ellsworth, wondering if her sister had noticed them as well. She was somehow unsurprised to see that Eurydice had seen them and wasn't dumbfounded by them, like she had already known they were there. Then Ellsworth sat up, and Psyche saw his back. She couldn't restrain herself.

"What is that tattoo doing on your back?" she blurted.

"I have a tattoo on my back?" said Ellsworth dryly. "What does it look like? Obviously, someone must have put it there while my back was turned."

Eurydice snorted derisively, unsurprised he would resort to flippancy. She also knew her sister wasn't going to let it lie. She hadn't expected Psyche to take up the quest for answers, but Eurydice was willing to let her try.

"Bollocks!" hooted Psyche persistently. "Why have you got that?"

"I went to India for a couple months many years ago. I went out for a night with my friends once, doing things I probably shouldn't have, and woke up the next morning with that."

Psyche and Sheerness both looked at each other. That made Sheerness as aware as his wife and sister-in-law that the man was lying because Sheerness truly *had* been to India. All three of them knew that while Indians did tattoo, they didn't do tattoos like that. To anyone who knew, the dragon was blatantly Oriental—specifically Japanese or Chinese, not Indian. Like Eurydice, Psyche knew about Dorian's tattoo and why he had it. Ellsworth's looked almost identical. The only real difference was that their brother's was mostly red and blue; Ellsworth's was mostly red and green. Something that large and detailed was not done in an hour or two, not even a day or two. It took months to create a tattoo like that, and it wasn't something that could be accomplished without the person being tattooed being aware of it. One would have to be quite literally comatose not to realize it was being done.

Psyche was beginning to suspect that what made her sister dislike the man so much was that she was already aware of things like the tattoo and other dishonesty on his part. Certain things began to make much more sense.

Sheerness gave her a warning glance and shook his head when it seemed she intended to continue her questioning. He was just as curious as she was, admittedly, but he was also aware of a few things that made him think it would be best to let Ellsworth keep his secrets to himself. Aside from that, he suspected Ellsworth would not give them an honest answer even if she did ask more questions. Sheerness wasn't sure if that would be because he *couldn't* give them one or *wouldn't*. He liked Ellsworth; he didn't want to see the man continue to dig a deeper hole for himself. Sheerness could see that his wife and Eurydice did *not* believe him. That wasn't a good thing because Sheerness knew, especially with Psyche, once they wanted to find out the truth about something, they would be relentless…and sneaky, and they *would* find out.

Chapter Nine

Without his shirt, Ellsworth was able to make it back to the ship without assistance once he had rested for about an hour. Eurydice and Psyche had gone with Freddie to climb around the edge of the cove and walk out onto the elephant while he did that. It was fairly easy to manage, and they had a very nice view of the ocean once they reached the part of the rock formation that resembled the elephant's rump. Psyche and Eurydice thought about diving from the rock into the water, but Psyche's fear of heights made her change her mind, and Eurydice honestly thought there might be too many shallow rocks beneath the surface to make it safe. By the time they climbed back down to the beach, Ellsworth was rested enough for them to return to the ship.

He was actually relieved they were aware of his tattoo. From that point on, if he should go swimming again, he would be able to wear trews, which would be much more comfortable. The questioning about the tattoo was not as bad as he had thought it would be. He had the distinct impression none of the adults believed a word of what he said about how he came by it, but they were willing to let him keep up his pretense. That was the only part that mattered for him. As long as they didn't press him, they could think what they wanted.

He could tell Eurydice, particularly, didn't believe a word of it. She had a disdainful expression when she looked at him, as if a foul odor had passed beneath her nose, and while she was polite, she didn't make any effort to be friendly or to speak to him directly at all for that matter. He really did hate that she had such a low opinion of him, and he knew it was his own fault. She had caught him in several lies. There were so many things she had discovered by accident that he wished she didn't know because, regardless of whether she knew it or not, it wasn't safe for her. He had become careless because of her— but only with her, and it only made things more complicated.

Yet there was a part of him that was irritated with her for looking at him in that superior way. She was keeping her own secrets. She was pretending to be innocent when she wasn't, and that made her no better than him. Actually, she was worse because he at least had a legitimate reason for the things he did while her only reason was duplicity. He had to wonder what her family would say and do if they knew the things about her that he did, but he knew he would never tell them.

It wasn't long after they made it back to the ship before the anchors were raised, and they were under way to Valletta. The sun had started to set, and the sky was colored in brilliant shades of pink and orange. It was spectacular over the crystalline blue of the water, and Eurydice went to the deck after she changed clothes to watch it. She couldn't recall ever seeing a sunset with quite those colors before, and she didn't know if it was because of where they were or something about the weather. Once the colors had faded, she went to her cabin to begin writing letters home to her family before supper.

Sheerness didn't think they would reach Valletta before sunrise, but as long as they reached the city on Malta early enough to re-supply and sail with the evening tide, that would be soon enough. Once they left Malta, instead of continuing east as they had done the previous year, they would sail north between Italy and western Greece into the Ionian and Adriatic Seas. Provided the weather remained good, they would be to Venice by Wednesday.

After supper, Eurydice went to take a shower. It was a bit ridiculous to be bathing in sea water after swimming in it for most of the afternoon, but she needed to wash her hair. It didn't feel quite as clean as it did when she washed it using fresh water, and rain water was even better, but her shampoo would remove quite a bit of the salt and make it not feel quite so stiff and heavy.

She was coming out of the captain's cabin into the alcove, wearing her shift and dressing gown, just as Ellsworth was going to his own cabin. She looked at him and gave a slight nod of her head in greeting.

"Mr. Ellsworth," she said evenly.

"Lady Eurydice," he said in the same tone.

"I trust you are all recovered from this afternoon?"

"Of course," he said with a self-deprecating half-smile.

"Good," said Eurydice calmly. "Well, good night, then."

"Good night."

Eurydice went into her cabin and closed the door. Agniezka put away her knitting and grabbed the brush and comb to plait Eurydice's hair before she went to bed. Once that was done, Eurydice climbed onto her bunk, turned off the lamp on the wall over her head, and snuggled under the blankets after closing the curtains. She would love to stay there to sleep, but she wouldn't be able to because of her neighbors. Before long, Agniezka turned off the other lamp, and Eurydice began her wait until she could go to the pantry.

She spent the time while she waited thinking about Ellsworth. He had risked drowning to hide a tattoo, a tattoo he had lied about when eventually questioned on it. If he was going to lie regardless, why bother hiding it in the first instance? She was still no closer to finding out her answers about him, but she did at least now know for certain that he understood Japanese. That wasn't very helpful. He could have used the same lie about how he got the tattoo and still admitted he got it in Japan, but it almost seemed as if he didn't want anyone to know he had even been to the country. That made absolutely no sense. It wasn't as if it were illegal for him to have gone there.

She curled a hand under her cheek on the pillow as she continued to think. Relations between Japan and Great Britain were nearly non-existent. Perhaps he didn't want anyone to know he had been there because the length of time it would have taken to have the tattoo put onto his back would have been a bit longer than what might be considered typical. Then, added to that, would be the length of time he would have needed to be there to find someone willing to do it, especially if he got it for the same reason Dorian did. When Eurydice thought about it, if he got the tattoo in Japan, for the same reason her brother did, he would have needed to be there for at least a year. The more she thought about it, the more she realized it would be even longer than that, at least five years. That was way beyond the length of time any Westerner would be there for any practical reason. But most people wouldn't know that, and the only reason Eurydice knew was that her father had been there several times. None of his stays had ever lasted more than a month at a time at most, though. The Japanese simply did not like foreigners, and they tended not to let them stay very long. Some hated foreigners so much they would just as soon kill them as tolerate their presence.

So how and why had Ellsworth been there that long? Considering the tattoo and why Eurydice thought he had gotten it, that part was simple enough, but she couldn't think he had gone there *only* for that without some guidance. That would be the *how* part of the question. Japan was very insular; its culture and customs were still largely unknown. In order for him to go to the country for only that reason would have required him to have knowledge of it from someone who had already been there or came from there. There weren't many of either…at least, not in Britain.

Then another piece clicked into place, and Eurydice frowned troubledly when it did. She didn't like how it fit into the puzzle at all. Her father. He was a piece as well, despite her not wanting to think so. What made her frown was seeing that he fit into it very well and was a far larger part of it than she would like him to be. She sighed frustratedly and scratched her forehead. Without asking either man outright, there was no way to confirm it, but in her heart she knew it would only be confirmation of the truth. With it being the truth, she knew she couldn't ask them.

Once she stopped thinking for a moment, she could hear that Agniezka's breathing had changed and she had gone to sleep. Eurydice sat up on her bunk, took the blanket she kept folded at the end of it, grabbed a pillow, and silently put her feet on the floor. She was leaving not a minute too soon; the sounds next door were just beginning. She had hoped their swim that afternoon might have exhausted them enough for them not to carry on for too long; *she* was certainly exhausted. She really wanted to sleep more than just three hours in her bunk. She was starting to develop a stiffness in her back from sleeping on the sacks in the pantry.

The next morning, they docked in Valletta around nine. After breakfast, Psyche convinced Eurydice to go shopping with her. Chrissoula and Agniezka went as well, as they had done in Melilla, and Freddie came along, leading Cupid on his leash. Eurydice was not sure why her sister thought she would want to come shopping. Valletta was a beautiful city, much prettier than Melilla. Agniezka would tell her the things she needed to buy, and Eurydice would dutifully purchase them, but by the time they were finished, the number of packages she had was not nearly as many as those of her sister.

They found a respectable coffeehouse to stop at for dinner not far from the Grand Master's Palace and resumed shopping afterward. Sheerness had told them they would be sailing with the evening tide, and while the women weren't sure when that would be, Freddie was able to tell them it would be around seven that evening. They got back to the *Medea* just shortly after six, and Psyche was relieved she had been able to conduct her business without all the excitement of the previous year. Sheerness was no less relieved.

Once Eurydice helped Agniezka put away her new things, she intended to practice for an hour or so on her violin before supper, but she also wanted to watch the sunset. She couldn't do both…or so she thought. Just as she had picked up her violin to begin practicing, Psyche came into her cabin.

"Come watch the sunset with me. I've never seen them look like this," she said excitedly.

Eurydice lifted an eyebrow. So, it apparently wasn't due to their location, not if Psyche, who had been there before, thought they were different.

"But I haven't practiced all day," said Eurydice in a discouraged voice.

"So bring it with you. It won't bother the crew, I'm sure. You've been doing remarkably well on not playing the same bit over and over again to an annoying degree."

"I don't do that," said Eurydice affrontedly as she followed her sister through the after cabins.

"Yes, you do. As much as I like *Eine Kleine Nachtmusik*, there have been times after hearing you practice it that I thought I would never want to hear it again," said Psyche amusedly.

Eurydice narrowed her eyes at her sister's back but kept silent. After she thought about it for a minute, she supposed her sister was right. She knew she was wont to play a section several times if it bothered her, until she felt comfortable with it, but she never realized how *many* times she was playing it. And while she knew the sound of her violin carried, she was only beginning to realize it was heard more loudly by everyone than she thought, even with her door closed. Now she could understand why Persephone was prone to coming into her room to break her strings; her room at Wilderland and in town was directly beside Eurydice's. Eurydice still didn't think she did anything differently than someone else might do, though.

The thing about playing on the deck that concerned Eurydice was that she would be aware she was playing for an audience. In her cabin, she knew the crew could hear her, but she didn't have to *see* them. Her palms were slightly sweaty as they took the stairs onto the waist deck. Freddie had started coming to her room occasionally when he could, but playing for Freddie was no more nerve-racking than playing for her brothers or anyone else in her family. She was almost tempted to go back to her cabin.

The two of them climbed to the poop deck, and Sheerness was standing near the helm with Higginbotham and Ellsworth. That made Eurydice reconsider even more that she should go back to her cabin, but when she looked over the taffrail at the sky she decided to stay. It was just as spectacular as the day before, if not more so, with streaks of orange and crimson and a band of steadily darkening blue above it. She quickly decided that if she watched the sunset and not the deck, she could forget about the crew...and Ellsworth.

"In an effort to make amends for my annoying repetition," she said dryly as she looked at Psyche with a slight smile, "what would you like to hear?"

Psyche clapped her hands and bounced on her feet excitedly. "Ooh, something of yours!" She chewed on the side of her thumb for a minute as she thought, and then she snapped her fingers. "I know, *The Faerie Air.* I like that one."

"Really?" blurted Eurydice, mildly surprised.

"Oh, absolutely," grinned Psyche. "Play that one, please."

Eurydice shrugged, but agreed to her sister's request. It was one of her older pieces that she'd composed when her *babushka* was still alive. Whereas *Le Papillon* was soothing and peaceful, *The Faerie Air* was fun and exuberant, much closer to folk music than a classical composition. It used a lot of interesting bowing, while the fingering was very lackadaisical. Eurydice liked it and enjoyed playing it, but she wouldn't consider it one of her better pieces.

Eurydice smiled wryly at her sister as she nestled the violin beneath her chin and drew the bow across the strings. She began to tap her foot as she played, and she tried not to laugh and lose her concentration as Psyche began to dance. She tried to get Sheerness to join her, but he obviously didn't know the steps and shook his head with a chuckle. Psyche then moved toward Eurydice and tried to get her to join in, which she did...somewhat. Her steps were not as energetic as her sister's; otherwise, she wouldn't have been able to play her violin. But the dance didn't require arm gestures or curtsies, and Eurydice actually knew the folk dance better than ball dancing.

Before long, those of the crew who didn't have duties to tend to gathered on the waist deck near the railing to the poop deck to clap and watch the sisters. Eurydice could hear them clapping to the music, but she kept her attention focused on her sister and her instrument. It had been a long time since she had this much fun, and she didn't want her anxiety over an audience to spoil it.

Freddie grinned as he scurried across the deck to the after cabins to retrieve things from the dumbwaiter for supper, and once he had them out and in place, he hurried up to the poop deck, where Psyche tried to teach him the steps of the dance. After watching for a little while, Sheerness caught on and joined in as well. Eurydice was only marginally surprised when Ellsworth began to dance, too. It was, after all, Scottish in origin. For him not to know it would have been more surprising. Psyche laughed amusedly when Sheerness lifted her into the air, and Eurydice shook her head with wry humor.

When the song ended, the crew applauded loudly, and Eurydice tried not to blush in pleasure and embarrassment. She curtsied shyly with a slight smile and nod of her head. She looked at Ellsworth with a raised eyebrow when he whistled through his teeth and grinned widely, clapping his hands with the rest of the crew. Sheerness was also applauding appreciatively but not nearly as exuberantly.

Once everyone got back to what they were supposed to be doing, Eurydice went down the steps to her cabin to get ready for supper. She nodded politely as the members of the crew smiled at her, but she did not stop to talk to anyone. She made it to the alcove just as Ellsworth caught up to her.

"Lady Eurydice, that was spectacular," he said enthusiastically.

Eurydice blinked. "I will take that to mean you liked it rather than not, so thank you."

"Of course, I liked it. It was a bit more to gaff standards than I would expect from you, but it was wonderful."

Eurydice narrowed her eyes at him. "Mr. Ellsworth, forgive me if I sound rude, but how could you possibly know what to expect from me? And I take exception to you referring to my composition as gaff-like."

Ellsworth rolled his eyes and sighed exasperatedly. "Honestly, I meant no offense by any of it, Lady Eurydice. I told you I liked it. There you go being prudish and offish again. Perhaps if *you* weren't so critical of your music, you wouldn't think anyone else was either." He nodded curtly and went to his own cabin and closed the door.

Eurydice looked at the closed door with a startled expression after he left. She really thought it was unfair of him to insult her like that without giving her the opportunity of a response. Perhaps she was offish, but she wasn't prudish, and neither had anything to do with his telling her the song had sounded like something that would be played in a cheap music hall. She finally shook her head and went to her own cabin to put away her violin and wash her hands before supper.

Eurydice woke up the next morning feeling stiff and tired. She was glad they were almost to Venice. Although sleeping in the pantry was giving her more sleep than she would get if she stayed in her bunk, the sacks were uncomfortable, and because she had to move back and forth between the pantry and her cabin, the sleep she was getting was not uninterrupted. She had to remind herself that in less than a week, she wouldn't have to worry about it anymore.

Agniezka's seasickness was somewhat better. After so long without any improvement, Psyche was able to acquire some ginger for her while they were in Valletta to make her a tea. Agniezka still wasn't quite ready to try sleeping on the trundle, but she thought she would by Tuesday. Eurydice thought it was unfortunate they had been unable to arrive at this solution earlier. Although Agniezka had never complained, Eurydice knew sleeping on the coffer all that time could not have been comfortable. Of course, if Agniezka *had* been sleeping on the trundle, it would have made it more difficult for her to go the pantry undetected. Once her maid started using the trundle, she didn't know how she was going to manage it. She supposed she would have to tolerate not getting much sleep for the remainder of the trip.

Eurydice hadn't talked to Ellsworth much at supper. After what they had said to each other in the alcove, neither felt like talking. Eurydice did concede she was critical of her music, but it was practicality to be that way. She felt it would be conceited and foolish to not examine it with a critical ear. How could anyone else think it was good if she didn't? Why did he think that was a bad thing? Fortunately, they didn't talk to each other very much even when they were feeling cordial toward one another, so no one noticed a difference.

The weather was clear and mild as they started to sail through the Ionian Sea, but by noon, Sheerness could see a storm on the horizon. It was moving slowly, but it would be large, and as the day wore on, the clouds continued to darken to the point that he could see it wasn't going to be a gentle one, either. He had the crew reef most of the sails to delay going into it for as long as possible. They would be nearing the Strait of Otranto soon, and while it wasn't as narrow as the Gibraltar, he didn't want to risk their sailing through it in the dark during the storm. As slowly as the storm was moving, and as slowly as they were traveling toward it, he was hopeful they could delay meeting up with it until tomorrow morning.

Eurydice was mostly oblivious to the weather. She had noticed their speed had dropped, and when she looked out her window, she could see the clouds, but they had already been through two storms, one of them rather severe, and she didn't think anything about it. She might have been more concerned if she had known Sheerness thought this storm might be worse than the one they had encountered the previous year that had done serious damage to the ship.

As they sat down for supper, conversation was subdued, but Eurydice didn't place any importance on it. The rocking of the ship was no more than usual. Actually, it wasn't rocking as much as it usually did because they weren't moving as fast. No one mentioned any concerns about the impending storm, so she thought everyone was just feeling untalkative.

She went to bed that night after taking a shower and waited for Agniezka to fall asleep on the coffer. Eurydice thought she fell asleep much quicker than she had been and suspected it was because of the ginger tea and because the ship was moving more smoothly. Eurydice was pleased about that; this had not been an easy journey for Agniezka because of her seasickness and sleeping conditions, and she would still have the trip over land in a coach to tolerate. Traveling sickness was traveling sickness, on land or sea, and neither was easy for her maid to tolerate. Eurydice was hopeful that once they reached Venice Agniezka would have a week or two to recuperate from the sea voyage and perhaps begin taking the ginger tea a few days in advance of their starting for Vienna to avoid further illness. Once Agniezka was asleep, Eurydice took her blanket and pillow and went to the pantry. Just a few more days, she sighed to herself. Just a few more days, and she would be able to sleep on a nice fluffy mattress that wasn't moving.

Eurydice awoke when she rolled off the sacks onto the floor. It was apparent the ship had pitched violently because rather than landing directly beside the sacks, she rolled and slid across the floor and slammed the small of her back into the edge of the wine rack. She was disoriented from being awakened so unexpectedly, and her back ached from hitting the rack, and she only had a few seconds to remember where she was before the ship pitched again and rolled her back across the floor into the sacks. Obviously, they had finally reached the storm they had been waiting for all day, and it was a bad one. She had no idea how long she had been sleeping.

She carefully stood and retrieved her pillow and blanket. She put a hand out in front of herself in the darkness and balanced her feet apart as the ship pitched again. She hurried across the floor to the door, and as the ship yawed to portside, she had to cling to the knob as her feet slipped from under her. The floor in the hallway was wet and slick from rain that had seeped around the sill of the door to the waist deck, and Eurydice could feel her heart beginning to thud against her ribs nervously. Making her way to her cabin in this wasn't going to be easy, and she wished she had known the storm was going to be this bad. If she had, she would have stayed in her cabin because she would have known Stockbridge wouldn't be able to stay with Chrissoula.

Once the ship righted somewhat, she hurried to the doorway to the officers' mess and went in. The chairs at the dining table had been secured to keep them from tumbling about, and Eurydice was thankful for that because there was no light coming into the room from the skylight. She kept a hand out in front of her to keep herself from walking into something, and she sucked in air through her teeth when the ship pitched to starboard and her hip slammed into the edge of the table. She really needed to get to her cabin. This storm was worse than the last one, if the way she had trouble keeping her footing was anything to go by. She considered herself to be fairly agile, but maintaining her balance in the dark as the deck rolled violently beneath her feet was not easy.

When she got to the alcove, she had just put her hand on the knob to the door of her cabin when the ship yawed again. Her feet slid out from under her, and her hand slipped off the knob, sending her tumbling across the alcove into the door to Ellsworth's cabin. The door flew open at the impact, and she went rolling across the floor, her blanket and pillow flying. She lodged against the bottom of his bunk on the floor, and the back of her head slammed into it after one of her knees banged against the corner of his writing desk. Eurydice gasped at the pain and felt slightly dizzy. She braced one hand and her feet against the floor as the ship began to rock the other way and lifted the other hand to her head. The skin didn't seem to be broken, but she was going to have a headache. Her knee was throbbing, and she sucked in air through her teeth at the pain when she tried to bend it. The door slammed shut with the movement of the ship, and Eurydice jumped at the noise.

"Bloody hell!" said Ellsworth as he looked down at the floor in the darkness. "Who is that?"

Eurydice squeaked in surprise when she felt him reach down to grab her by the collar of her dressing gown and shift and lifted her off the floor. He picked her up as if she weighed nothing.

"So sorry to burst in, Mr. Ellsworth," she said meekly.

"Lady Eurydice? What are you doing out of your cabin? Don't you realize this is a bad storm?"

"Um, yes, I had noticed that," she said dryly.

He was still holding onto her collar, and when the ship pitched to starboard again, she barked her shins on the edge of the bunk and tumbled onto it…and Ellsworth. She was flung across his chest, and his back was pressed into the wall. She put a bracing hand against his chest as she slid even further onto the bunk and pressed even closer against him. She tried to straighten and sit up, but it was useless until the ship righted itself.

Eurydice hadn't realized when she went to sleep in the pantry that it would be such a dangerous thing. She had aches everywhere, and she didn't doubt for one minute that there would be bruises to mark every one of them.

"You still haven't answered my question," said Ellsworth once the ship straightened somewhat.

"I told you I had noticed it was a bad storm," said Eurydice simply.

"No, the other question. Why are you out of your cabin?"

Eurydice's teeth snapped together, and she was glad he couldn't see the way her cheeks colored. She couldn't tell him why she wasn't sleeping in her cabin. If she couldn't tell her sister, she certainly couldn't tell him.

"You couldn't take a miss on that for one night? What would your sister think?" he grated out angrily when it became obvious she wasn't going to answer, and he realized exactly why she had gone.

Eurydice frowned. How had he known what she was doing? Her cheeks colored even further in embarrassment. He must have heard her either coming or going from her cabin at some point, at least once. Judging by what he said, apparently several times. But she didn't think he knew *why* she had been sleeping in the pantry. Still, it was bad enough that he knew she had been. She wondered why he hadn't told Psyche or Sheerness.

"Well, it is a bit improper, and we're almost to Venice, so…," Eurydice trailed off uncomfortably.

"Hunh," said Ellsworth disgustedly. He thought *improper* was a mild description for what she had been doing.

The ship began to tilt again, and he braced a foot against the railing at the front of the bunk to keep his back against the wall and put an arm around her waist to keep her from tumbling to the floor again. His other hand was still at the back of her neck where he had been holding her collar. Her face was only inches from his, and he could feel her breath as she exhaled. Her hand was still resting against his chest, and she smelled heavenly. He was trying to ignore how it felt to have her pressed against him, but it wasn't easy. That he was angry with her only marginally helped.

She had just as good as admitted she had gone to be with a lover. He still, for the life of him, could not be sure who it was. He still thought the only logical one would be Felton, but he didn't know. He had never heard any telling noises from the doctor's cabin. Of course, since he slept with his head near the opposite wall, which adjoined the captain's cabin, it wasn't easy to tell. He could hear quite well when the shower-bath was being used because it was directly beside his bunk, and he could distantly hear when Sheerness and Psyche were making love. Relievedly, their bed was far enough away that the sound was muffled enough he could ignore it. If it were closer, he would have started sleeping in one of the launches on the deck a long time ago. There had been nothing like that from Felton's side of his cabin.

Eurydice could tell he was angry with her, something that was confirmed when the lightning flashed and illuminated his face, showing her the way his jaw was tightly set and the furrows between his eyebrows. She wasn't sure why her sleeping in the pantry would make him angry. If he knew the reason why she had been doing it, being a man, he would think she was a silly female. He would also think it only confirmed his opinion that she was a prude. Eurydice shrugged to herself. Once Agniezka started sleeping in the trundle tomorrow night, Eurydice would have to tolerate it for the remainder of the trip.

The skin on his chest felt warm against her palm, and the skin on her cheeks tightened as they colored even further when it occurred to her that he had nothing on beneath his blankets. She should not be in his cabin, and she needed to get back to her own. As badly as the ship was rolling, Eurydice knew Agniezka was no longer sleeping. She only hoped her maid wasn't in the cabin alone with her head in a bucket.

The ship rolled back to starboard, and she pushed her hand against his chest to keep herself from sliding closer to him. Her breasts were already pressed against his chest, and his foot braced against the front of the bunk crossed over the top of her legs kept her effectively pinned there. Lightning flashed through the window, and she looked at it with a start as the thunder that accompanied it followed almost without pause. Then she turned her head to look at Ellsworth in the dark, and that was when he kissed her.

She really wasn't surprised when he did it. She suspected the only reason he hadn't kissed her before then while they were on the ship was that he hadn't been alone with her long enough. It was as if he couldn't help himself, and despite her thinking he shouldn't be doing it, she enjoyed it. And whether she wanted to admit it or not, she had missed having him do it.

At first, he was almost leisurely as he kissed her, gently nipping at her lips with his teeth, as if he were tasting them. Then he began to sample the inside of her mouth with his tongue, and Eurydice sighed at the back of her throat. Her hand on his chest slowly moved across the skin to the side of his neck in a caress, and her other hand moved up his arm to his shoulder. She felt tingly all over, and her stomach felt fluttery as he moved his hand at the small of her back in a slow circle before moving it to cup her bottom.

Ellsworth kept his foot against the railing at the front of the bunk, and he turned slightly to press Eurydice closer against him. The ship continued to rock violently, but they were wedged closely together, caught up in what they were doing, and neither seemed to notice. Eurydice couldn't understand how they could be doing this. There was something about her that he apparently didn't like, and she certainly didn't trust him for a minute, but he wanted her just as much as she wanted him despite that. It was completely illogical to her, but as he continued to kiss her, she decided she wasn't going to try understanding the logic of it. She just didn't want him to stop.

Ellsworth smoothed his hand over her hip between them, and he untied her dressing gown and moved the fabric out of the way. He moved his hand up her ribs and placed it over her breast, and Eurydice instinctively arched her back toward his touch. The blankets had shifted until Ellsworth was for the most part uncovered, and as the ship rocked to starboard and pressed Eurydice closer against him, she could feel his erection, and she gasped because the only thing that separated them was the thin cotton of her shift. The fluttery feeling in her stomach grew even more intense, and she trembled excitedly.

He soon left her lips to begin placing kisses along her neck, and Eurydice tilted her head back to make it easier for him. His lips were soft and warm as they traveled across her skin, and she wanted to allow him all the access he needed to keep using them in whatever way he saw fit. He moved his lips along the skin at the edge of her shift, and then he untied the strings that fastened at the front for it to gape open and expose one of her breasts. He took the tip into his mouth and rasped his tongue against the nipple, and the hand that Eurydice had on the side of his neck moved to the back of his head to clutch in his hair convulsively. She bit her lip to stifle a moan, and she felt like she was drowning from the sensations he was causing.

He reached down to begin smoothing a hand up her leg to her hip beneath her shift, and he could feel that her leg had no hair on it and felt softer than silk to his touch. She jumped when he clutched at her bare bottom to press her against his erection excitedly. She was almost panting as her heart thudded in her chest. She enjoyed the feel of him close to her, and there was something about it that felt so completely, perfectly natural. She knew where this was going. She knew what he wanted to do, and she wasn't unwilling. In fact, to her astonishment, she was more than willing.

Ellsworth moved his hand from her bottom to between her thighs to begin teasing her, and he felt her tremble against him with a soft whimper. He had been hesitant to touch her there, knowing she had just come from being with someone else, but as he stroked her, he could feel that she was wet from excitement but not from another man. Either they had been interrupted, or they had used a condom.

He knew he couldn't be doing this, for many reasons, and that he shouldn't want her as much as he did, knowing she already had a lover and yet was willing to be here doing this with him, but the way he felt about her went beyond simple wanting. He *needed* her, and he was willing to take her any way she would let him.

Eurydice began to quiver as she orgasmed, her hands clutching at him feverishly, and he covered her mouth with his to muffle her sounds of pleasure. He didn't think anyone would hear her in the storm, but he didn't want to take any chances. She put a gentle hand to his cheek and brushed her fingers along his jaw, down his neck, to smooth across his chest. She seemed almost awed by her orgasm, as if she'd never had one before, and he wondered if her lover was that inconsiderate. A woman like her deserved to be pleased—any woman did, but her especially.

Eurydice thought her heart had stopped beating when the tension she felt at his touch finally released. It was ecstatic. She hadn't known what to expect, but she could never have imagined that. Did every woman feel that? Is that what had made Psyche so lonesome for Sheerness, why they couldn't wait until they were on the ship? Eurydice was slowly beginning to understand.

As Ellsworth nuzzled her cheek and smoothed his hand across her thigh to place her leg over the top of his, she could feel they weren't done yet, if she'd had any doubt about the matter. He still had an erection, and his moving her leg brought it to rest between her thighs. He brushed against her, and Eurydice's lower lip quivered and she inhaled sharply at the sensations it caused. She rubbed herself against him mindlessly, finding it exquisitely pleasurable. She shouldn't be here doing this with him, but there was nothing to stop them. It wasn't as if someone would come in and catch them because the storm would keep everyone otherwise occupied.

At that thought, Eurydice's eyes flew open. *Agniezka.* She was alone in their cabin. Even if she wasn't sick because of the storm, she would realize Eurydice wasn't there, if not already, then very soon. She would be terribly worried. As much as Eurydice would like to stay, she needed to go, and she felt ashamed that she had stayed as long as she had. She was being completely irresponsible. She put her hands to Ellsworth's shoulders and tried to disentangle herself from him.

"I've got to go," she said hurriedly.

"*Go?*" he blurted out in shock and disbelief.

"Agniezka is looking for me," said Eurydice breathlessly as she got herself free. She retied the strings on her shift and tumbled off the bunk onto the floor with a thump as the ship continued to rock with the storm.

"You can't leave *now*," said Ellsworth irritatedly.

"I've got to go," repeated Eurydice distractedly as she tried to feel around on the floor for her blanket and pillow. They had to be somewhere.

"You manky quean," he bit out angrily.

Eurydice looked up at him over the edge of the bunk, her eyes round in shock. "I beg your pardon?"

"You can't just leave a man like this."

"But I've got to go," said Eurydice quietly, hurt by the insult, and it wasn't as if she *wanted* to go.

"You're worse than a whore. At least that kind of woman would stay to see the job through to the end."

Eurydice felt tears sting her eyes at his harsh tone. Even as his words hurt her feelings, he wasn't being unfair when he said them. She was innocent but not completely ignorant. She hadn't meant to disappoint him or to cause him any pain. If she thought she could stay longer, she would do so without hesitation because she *wanted* to see this through to the end. But her time had run out long ago.

Agniezka wouldn't leave the cabin to go looking for her, but Eurydice fully expected that her maid had long since realized she wasn't on her bunk behind the curtains, and she was probably frantic. At least Eurydice would have her blanket and pillow with her and the real excuse that she had been sleeping in the pantry. Otherwise, the consequences of what they had been doing would not be good. She finally found her blanket and pillow, and she clutched them to her chest as she rose unsteadily from her knees on the floor.

After there was a brief flash of lightning to give her bearings, she reached out a hand toward him to brush against his cheek, but she wasn't surprised when he flinched away from her touch with a sound of irritation and disgust.

"I'm sorry," she whispered brokenly, "so very sorry."

Chapter Ten

"Where have you been?" asked Psyche angrily as soon as Eurydice entered her cabin.

Eurydice felt disoriented for a moment. Both of the lamps had been lit, and it took several seconds for her eyes to adjust to the brightness. She had been in the darkness so long, she had forgotten the ship had lamps. Added to that was finding her sister there and knowledge of what she had just been doing with Ellsworth. Agniezka was curled up on the coffer, looking at Eurydice with a worried frown, but it didn't appear that the motion of the ship was making her unbearably sick any longer, which relieved Eurydice. Psyche stood in the middle of the cabin with her hands on her hips, her feet balanced apart. She was dressed in linsey breeches and a man's shirt and waistcoat, her stockinged feet shoeless. The curtain on Eurydice's bunk was pulled open, and Chrissoula was sitting there in the corner, her expression no less worried than Agniezka's. Only Psyche seemed to be more angry than concerned.

Eurydice wondered how long the women had been there waiting for her. She had thought the only one she would have to tell of her activities was her maid; now, it was apparent she was going to have a larger audience, and she had truly hoped she wouldn't have to talk about it in front of Chrissoula. She colored slightly as she walked further into the cabin.

"I was sleeping in the pantry," mumbled Eurydice quietly.

Psyche's eyebrow shot up in surprise. "Why were you sleeping in the pantry?" she demanded.

Eurydice went to put her blanket and pillow on the bunk, and her face colored even more when she briefly looked at Chrissoula.

"Because it's the only place I can go to get a decent night's sleep."

"What's wrong with your bunk? If your bunk was uncomfortable, you only had to tell me or Sebastian. We would have had Mr. Laing fix it for you immediately," said Psyche, her anger dissipating somewhat.

"No, no. It's not the bunk. It's very comfortable, exactly the way I like it," said Eurydice hurriedly.

"Then *what* is the problem?" asked Psyche exasperatedly. "We've been worried sick about you."

"There are noises at night that make it impossible for me to go to sleep. After a few days, I thought I was going to lose my mind if I didn't get some rest, so I thought sleeping in the pantry was the best solution."

"What *kind* of noises?" asked Psyche confusedly. She'd never noticed any bothersome noises on the ship, just the usual creaking and snapping.

"Um, at night, through the wall...I can hear...uh...," stuttered Eurydice, and Psyche blinked because she'd never seen her sister so perturbed. Eurydice took a deep breath and blurted it out. "I can hear Chrissoula and her husband."

"Oh," said Chrissoula softly, her eyes rounding, and her face began to turn a shade of red that was even brighter than Eurydice's.

"Oh, my giddy aunt!" peeped Psyche in surprise. "Well." She blinked.

"They're married, so it's not as if they aren't allowed. I just *couldn't* say anything," said Eurydice, and she clutched her hands in front of her and gave Chrissoula an apologetic glance.

"Oh, Dicy, you should have told me," said Psyche, going to her sister to put her arm around her and pat her shoulder comfortingly. "I could have given you my sleeping draught."

"But—" began Eurydice.

"Believe me, it will put you to sleep whether you want to or not, *no matter what*." Considering how uncomfortable her sister was with the conversation they were having, Psyche decided she wouldn't give her proof. "You could have been sleeping in your bunk all this time. I'll go get it for you."

She left the cabin and returned shortly with a small vial. It was over half empty, but Psyche knew there was enough there to last at least the rest of the trip to Venice and possibly for a month or two beyond.

"You can take some now, and I guarantee it will even let you sleep through this storm."

"No, thank you," said Eurydice. "I'm not very tired any more."

"Fine then," grinned Psyche. "I'll just put it here in your desk. Three drops in a cup of water is all you need when you're ready. Keung made it, so you know it will work." She closed the top back on the desk and turned to look at her sister. "Now, I've got to tell Sebastian that I've found you."

"Sheerness knows?" blurted Eurydice with a frown.

"Yes, he knows. After Freddie went overboard last year in a storm not unlike this one, I thought it would be best to tell him you had gone missing."

"Oh," said Eurydice dully.

"Don't worry. I won't tell him *why* you've been sleeping in the pantry...unless he asks me."

Psyche giggled as she left the cabin, and Eurydice was glad someone at least was able to find some humor in this. She turned to look at Chrissoula.

"I'm sorry you had to find out like that. I didn't want to embarrass you."

Chrissoula waved a hand through the air and sat up. "Eh, it's not too bad. I'll just make sure not to mention it to Wills. He would positively faint," she said with a chuckle. She stood up from the bunk and began to make her way across the cabin to the door. "Now that we've found you, I'm going back to bed. The best way to wait out a storm is to forget there is one."

Eurydice watched her leave, and then she turned to look at Agniezka. She really was happy to see that her maid was no longer seasick. It was only unfortunate it had taken most of their trip to find cures for both their maladies. Agniezka gave her a wan look.

"You weren't leaving to sleep elsewhere because I've been sick?"

"Oh, no, Agniezka. Absolutely not. It's just that those two *really* enjoy having sex with each other…endlessly."

Agniezka chuckled and shook her head. "Well, I suppose if you are to be married, enjoying the pleasure you can give to each other is part of what makes it worthwhile." She distractedly rubbed a hand across the pale, jagged scar on her forehead. "What is even better is if there is more than that."

"I'm sorry, I didn't mean to stir up memories for you," said Eurydice quietly, going to sit on her desk chair.

She thought the storm was calming somewhat. The ship was still rocking, but it no longer seemed as if it intended to go keel up. Perhaps after a little while, if it continued to slacken, she would try to go back to sleep. She didn't know if she would be able to, though. Her mind was buzzing with thoughts, and she wasn't sure she would be able to get them to quieten down enough. She had no notion of what time it was. It was still dark outside, but that could be due to the storm.

Agniezka waved a hand through the air dismissively at Eurydice's apology. "Memories are only that. They can't hurt you."

Eurydice took Agniezka's hand in hers and gave her a smile. Agniezka had been through a lot in her life. She was only sixteen when she became Eurydice's maid, and she had been through far more by then than anyone should have to. She and her brother, Nickolai, had come with Aberdare from Russia when he returned from one of his endless trips. There had been a bandage across her forehead then, and for months after she arrived, even after her injuries had healed, she would jump at the slightest unexpected noise. Eventually, her nervousness had faded like her scar.

It had taken several years before Eurydice finally asked what had happened. Agniezka had married a man who was handsome and wealthy. She had thought he loved her, and she had thought she loved him. Almost from the beginning, however, she discovered that wasn't so. He would beat her and mistreat her, often locking her in the cellar for days at a time. Then Nickolai and their father discovered the way Agniezka's husband, Sergei, had been abusing her when she managed to escape from him and arrived at their door bruised and bloody. Nickolai nearly beat Sergei to death with his bare hands, and the authorities would have arrested him if Eurydice's father hadn't arranged for Agniezka and her brother to return to Britain with him.

Agniezka was very beautiful, and Eurydice didn't notice the scar. Judging from the attention she received from the men on their staff, no one else did either. She was shorter than Eurydice by an inch or two, slender, and fine-boned. Her hair was a silvery blond, and her almond-shaped eyes were a startling shade of pale blue, a testament to her Scandinavian ancestors. Her features were very delicate, and they reminded Eurydice of a porcelain doll. She wore her hair short at the front to cover the scar on her forehead, but it wasn't very obvious even without the hair to hide it. She seemed very fragile, and it brought out the protective urge in every man who met her. Eurydice couldn't recall Agniezka expressing an interest in any of the men who worked for her family or anyone else, though…until Dr. Felton. Because even though no one else noticed her scar, Agniezka did.

If the doctor decided to make an offer for her hand, Eurydice tried to think of who he would go to for permission. Then again, in order for him to make an offer, Agniezka would have to be free of Sergei. Even though she had left him, they were still married. Not to anyone's knowledge had he petitioned for divorce, and he hadn't died, either. Eurydice wasn't sure how divorce was addressed in Russia. In the end, she decided it was pointless to be overly concerned about it until the time arose when it was necessary to find out.

Eurydice did her best to avoid Ellsworth over the days that followed. It didn't prove to be that difficult because he was making the same effort to stay away from her. What also made it easy for her to avoid him was that once Sheerness had discovered what she had been doing (sleeping in the pantry, that is), he made sure someone kept an eye on her at all times to prevent any further mischief. Until she departed for Vienna, Eurydice was under his protection, and he intended to make sure she *was* protected. Eurydice thought it was a bit ridiculous, but perhaps it was for the best.

Psyche's sleeping draught did prove to do the trick. If Chrissoula and Stockbridge continued their nightly activity (and Eurydice hoped that her mentioning she could hear them had not caused them to curtail it), she was completely oblivious. Agniezka was sleeping on the trundle, and both women were overjoyed to be getting a comfortable, full night's rest. Eurydice wished she hadn't been so hesitant to mention the situation to her sister. This could have all been addressed ages ago, and it might have prevented what had happened between her and Ellsworth.

She didn't know how she was going to tolerate traveling all the way to Vienna with him. She supposed she would worry about it when the moment arrived. Psyche did tell her that he would be their guest at the palazzo in Venice while awaiting his mother's arrival, but Eurydice was hopeful it would be large enough she wouldn't have to see him, except at meals perhaps. The best thing for both of them would be to stay as far away from each other as possible.

Her mother had described the palazzo to them, and Selena had tried to describe it as well, since she and Dorian had gone for their honeymoon, but Eurydice had never been. Neither had Psyche. Although they had a general idea of its appearance, they didn't have a very clear picture of it in their minds. The caretaker was aware they were coming, so it would be prepared and staffed for their arrival, but neither sister knew much of anything about it.

The duchess told them it had been a very lovely place to live. It wasn't on the Grand Canal, but in a quiet, respectable neighborhood. She also said it was very old, and when Julia's father had inherited it after his mother's death, it had been in a sad state of disrepair. He had spared no expense in restoring it, and it was very comfortable. After her father died and left the palazzo to her, the duchess had gone even further in remodeling it, adding several of the amenities her family had come to appreciate, like a boiler for supplying hot water for bathing and rooms specifically for that purpose. Eurydice was very much looking forward to seeing it.

They arrived in Venice very early Friday morning. Eurydice woke up to find that the *Medea* was no longer moving, and when she looked out the window, she could see the city. Agniezka was already awake and had begun to pack their things back into their trunks. There wasn't much that needed to be done as most of it had remained packed. When she saw that Eurydice was awake, Agniezka helped her dress, and then Eurydice helped her finish packing while they waited for Freddie to bring their breakfast. She couldn't believe how impatient she was to be off the ship. Perhaps it was because she knew once she was actually *in* Venice, Vienna would be next.

Freddie was very quiet when he brought in the tray with their food. He seemed to be very sad as he set the tray on the table, and Eurydice looked at him thoughtfully.

"Are you feeling well, Freddie?" she asked concernedly, reaching out a hesitant hand to pat him comfortingly on the shoulder.

"Yes, ma'am," he said glumly.

"You seem rather down in the dumps."

"I'm just sad everyone is leaving is all."

"The captain and Psyche will be back before long, and I should think everyone being off the ship for a while would give you a chance to rest," said Eurydice soothingly.

"Yes, ma'am," said Freddie agreeably, but he wasn't any more cheerful.

"Can you not come with us then?" asked Eurydice, trying to think of a reason why he couldn't.

"Oh, that would be lovely, ma'am, but I do have responsibilities and all…helping Meals and cleaning and whatnot."

"If I can convince Sheerness to allow you to come, would you like to, at least for a few days?"

"Yes, ma'am," said Freddie with a grin.

"I'll go speak with him as soon as I've finished with my breakfast."

"Thank you, ma'am."

Eurydice watched him leave the cabin with a spring in his step. She couldn't believe she was actually going to talk to Sheerness about having the boy come with them. Before she had been on the ship, she would have done whatever she could to avoid being around children. She was still leery around them, she supposed, but she had grown accustomed to Freddie. He was almost like a little brother. She really could see no reason why he couldn't come with them. If there were no guests aboard the ship, there were no cabins that required straightening, and the crew was able to tend to their own cleaning. Eurydice actually thought Sheerness should get another cabin boy besides Freddie. He worked entirely too hard for his size. Having at least one other small pair of hands to help would be useful, and it would also provide him with some companionship his own age.

Once she finished breakfast, she prepared to find Sheerness. Psyche was coming out of her cabin into the alcove at the same time, and Eurydice blinked because her sister was wearing a normal gown. Eurydice had become so accustomed to seeing her sister in split skirts and breeches that she almost didn't recognize her in the dress. She briefly explained her idea to Psyche, and Psyche agreed it was wonderful, both having Freddie come along and getting another cabin boy. They both went to speak to Sheerness.

Sheerness was at first reluctant to agree to either idea, but with both sisters arguing with him about it and both of them capable of providing him with entirely logical reasons for why he should agree, he was left with little choice but to do so...if only to get them to leave off. He actually had already been thinking about getting another cabin boy, but he wasn't sure how he was going to acquire one. Once he said yes, Psyche told him he should leave it to her to hire the boy. That made Sheerness nervous, knowing her penchant for acquiring strays of any kind, but he did trust her judgment.

It took Sheerness a little time to arrange for transportation to the palazzo, but he was able to find it. All of Eurydice, Agniezka, and Ellsworth's belongings had to be taken, while Sheerness, Psyche, Chrissoula, Stockbridge, and Freddie only needed to take the things that would be necessary for their stay. Other than the Grand Canal, a lot of the *rios* were very narrow, some barely wide enough to allow one boat. It took three just to transport their luggage, and a further two to carry the people. Before it was over, Sheerness found himself wishing the canals were wider; then he could have simply sailed the *Medea* to the door and been done with it. Psyche had giggled when he said that, and she knew he had only said it out of frustration. She knew he didn't actually believe he could sail the ship through the canals of Venice, but what a tale it would have been to tell.

Eurydice found herself in the gondola with Ellsworth, Agniezka, and Freddie. She didn't mind her maid and the boy, but she would have rathered

Ellsworth not be there. If it weren't for Freddie chattering away and Cupid's occasional barks, the ride would have been very quiet. As it was, Eurydice discovered Ellsworth was very familiar with Venice. She didn't know how it had happened, but she wasn't going to ask, either. Despite herself, she listened to what he was saying to Freddie, but she tried not to make it obvious.

Eurydice was disappointed when they didn't stay on the Grand Canal but turned onto one of the narrow *rios*. In fact, they didn't even make it to the Grand Canal. Her mother had said the palazzo wasn't there, but she was hopeful they were taking a shortcut. She would like to at least see some of it. She didn't think she would leave the palazzo once she arrived, so their journey there would be her only chance.

The side canal was interesting, and there were some very pretty palazzi, but it felt very confined. The sun barely managed to reach them as they were prodded along, and there was nothing but endless building façades—no grass, no trees. There were window boxes with bright flowers and herbs to at least break the monotony, but there weren't enough of them. Eurydice wasn't so sure that Arachne would like Venice…unless she stayed on the Grand Canal where things weren't so crammed together.

It took them some time to arrive at the palazzo, but Eurydice knew when they did before they even stopped. They were nearing an adjoining canal, and a large palazzo loomed at the far corner of the intersection. She knew that had to be it because her Grandfather Sanders would have liked something that would have been set apart. Being on the corner would have kept him separated from his neighbors, at least on that side. It would have made him feel like he had more privacy. If nothing else, her Grandfather Sanders liked his privacy.

It was beautiful. The walls of the water floor were made of a rusticated pink stone, but the floors above it were covered in a creamy yellow stucco. All of the tracery, columns, and framing around the windows were made of a bright white marble. As Eurydice looked at it, she agreed with her mother that it was very old. Judging from the arches and other architectural details, she thought it was Gothic. Psyche and Sheerness would know for certain, Eurydice was sure.

It was also larger than her mother had led her to believe. Counting the water floor, there were five, and the façade facing the canal on which they traveled was almost one hundred feet long. The façade facing the side canal was no less ornate than the front, but there weren't any entrances from the water floor. Something else that set it apart from the neighboring palazzi was that the water floor appeared to be slightly higher above the canal than those surrounding it, making it seem even taller and grander. That was another thing that let her know it was the palazzo; in addition to liking his privacy, Grandfather Sanders appreciated *grandness.* Eurydice had to wonder why this palazzo had not been built on the Grand Canal; it was out of place on the narrow canal where it was located.

There were five-arched loggias on the first and second floors, but Eurydice didn't see any glass windows, just shutters. The doors that opened onto the loggias were made of very finely-carved mahogany, glazed with diamond and circular leaded panes. At least whatever rooms those were would be bright, but she didn't expect hers would be one of them. She hoped the wooden shutters over the windows actually hid glass. If not, staying in the palazzo was going to be worse than belowdecks on a ship. The only consolation would be that she wouldn't have Chrissoula and Stockbridge sleeping next door or Ellsworth across the hall…she hoped.

There was a recessed, colonnaded loggia at the main doors, but Eurydice could see a set of wrought iron gates with gilded ornamentation nearby that opened onto an area where the family could keep their personal boat (or boats) securely moored. She was sure there was a much larger—and just as elaborate—landing there. She was very much looking forward to seeing the inside of it, and she was disappointed her parents had never taken any of the girls to see it after all these years.

The entrance doors were made of solid mahogany, but they were carved in a pattern of diamonds and circles that matched exactly where the glass was located on the upper loggias. They were flanked by leaded windows that matched the others, and that gave Eurydice some hope that there were real windows hiding behind the wooden shutters.

The doors were opened almost immediately by a man who introduced himself as Signor Montenegro, the caretaker. He appeared to be in his fifties, but Eurydice had never been good at guessing ages. Psyche and Pandora were much better at that. His black hair was graying at the temples, and an interesting streak of the same color ran down the center of his short, pointed beard, but his mustache was still solid black. His eyes were dark brown, and his skin was swarthy, but his rounded cheeks had a slightly rosy color and the corners of his eyes were wrinkled in a way that suggested a jovial disposition. He was about Psyche's height and rotund, his body reminding Eurydice of a water barrel. From the minute she saw him, Eurydice had the impression he was a man who enjoyed life very much.

"*Benvenuto al Ca'Bon dei Pesci Felici,*" he said with a smile, throwing open his arms.

His voice was warm and melodious, and it made Eurydice think of a viola. There was just something about him that made her feel very warm and cozy…safe. She could recall ever feeling that way on first meeting someone only once or twice in her entire life. It usually took a little while longer for that feeling to develop for her with people. There was absolutely nothing romantic about it, as none of the others had been, but Eurydice immediately decided she liked him and that he could be trusted completely.

When they heard the name of the house, Psyche and Eurydice looked at each other with raised eyebrows, and Sheerness's lips twitched amusedly. Their mother had never told them the palazzo had a name. She had always simply called it "the palazzo."

"The happy fish?" they both said in puzzlement at the same time.

Signor Montenegro laughed and stepped out of the way for everyone to enter and to let the boatmen begin unloading their belongings. He had brought a few male servants and the housekeeper with him to have the things taken to the appropriate rooms. He thought it would be best if everyone moved out of their way. He quickly issued instructions and then smiled to the new arrivals.

"You'll see," he chortled.

The *portego* was breathtaking. The floor was for the most part covered in tiles of black and green travertine, but at the center near the bottom of the stairs was a beautiful, rectangular mosaic created of different geometric patterns centered around a bright red and orange sunburst. There were Corinthian columns made of the same white marble used on the façade, and it was used for the railing on the stairs and the treads themselves. Beyond the mosaic, going beneath the first landing on the stairs, was a tunnel-like hallway that ended in a delicate, gilded iron gate. Eurydice could see trees and flowers, and the sound of birds echoed down the hall toward her. She knew the back of the palazzo should be spatially further away than what she was seeing, and she realized the house was centered around a courtyard, what appeared to be a large courtyard that allowed for lots of sunlight.

Signor Montenegro saw her eyes brighten when she looked down the hall, and rather than showing them to their rooms, with a warm smile, he took them down the hall and opened the gate.

"Oh," gasped Eurydice when she walked in, her eyes rounding.

"Wow!" blurted Freddie, his expression no less awed than hers.

It was nothing short of magical. It was easy for Eurydice to see her mother's hand in the design. She could also now understand why the palazzo seemed so large from the outside—to hide this jewel at its center. There were cherry, orange and lemon trees, lilacs and gardenias, hibiscus and oleander. She could smell roses and see beds full of multiple colors of geraniums. There were gladiolus and several different kinds of lilies, and other flowers were blooming everywhere.

At the very center was a fountain, the basin made to look like a small pond with a gently arching footbridge to cross it. The edge was flush with the grass—bright green, soft grass that Eurydice imagined would feel heavenly between her toes, and there were sunken baskets with potting material because cattails and marsh reed were growing at the margins. The fountain itself appeared to be nothing more than a pile of rocks, the water gently gurgling up from among them to pour into the pond as if it were a natural spring. The surface was dotted with rich purple water hyacinth and different shades of water lilies. When Eurydice walked closer to the edge of the fountain and looked into it, she saw where the house got its name.

"Koi!" she said excitedly.

"What?" blurted Psyche, rushing up to her.

Eurydice pointed down at the pond, and they could see at least a dozen large fish, most of them over a foot long, swimming beneath the surface, gliding about, twirling around each other almost playfully as they searched the bottom and surface for food. Some were one color, while others were covered in three or four. There were dazzling shades of orange, black, white, and gold. The sun shining down made them sparkle, almost as if they were gilded.

"What are those? Carp aren't they?" said Sheerness as he came beside Psyche to casually drape an arm over her shoulder.

"Well, yes, but these are Japanese *nishikigoi*…we think. They breed them to make all of these interesting colors," said Psyche. "In Japanese, the word for carp is *koi*, but there is another word in Japanese that sounds exactly the same but spelled differently, and it means love and affection. These fish are *nishikigoi*, brocaded carp, rather than your common carp, and are symbols of love and friendship in Japan. Some of them are also very expensive, worth far more than you would want to spend for a meal," she said with a giggle.

"Hunh," said Sheerness doubtfully. "Which ones?"

Psyche looked at him exasperatedly. "I don't know. I'm not a breeder of koi," she chortled.

"Really? Because sometimes you are awfully good at *being* coy," said Sheerness with a grin before giving her a kiss on the cheek.

"Boo," groaned Psyche with a giggle.

Ellsworth walked onto the bridge and looked down at the pond and the fish for a moment thoughtfully. He finally pointed a finger at one of the larger ones.

"That one, with the mostly black and white except for the red spot on his head. He's the most expensive one."

"How do you know?" asked Eurydice evenly.

He looked up at her with a grin. "Just a guess."

They looked at the fish and the garden for a few more minutes, but then Signor Montenegro wanted to show them a few more of the common areas in the palazzo before taking them to their private rooms. They went back to the *portego*, and he showed them the area where the family's boats were kept, just where Eurydice thought they would be. He didn't take them there directly, but he explained where the kitchen was, where the servants quarters were on the water floor, and the store rooms. Then he took them up the stairs to the great hall, which served as the drawing room as well as dining room.

Eurydice walked into the room and looked around. Every surface, except for the furniture and the plaster on the ceiling, was made of marble. But rather than one color, there were several. The floor was covered in a beautiful red. The walls were covered in shades of white, green, cream, pink, and black. And there was carving and tracery everywhere. Eurydice didn't think she had ever seen such ornate stonework, other than in some churches. Not even Wilderland had stonework this elaborate. The room stretched across the entire front of the palazzo. She supposed it could be used as a ball room as well…unless there was an actual ball room somewhere.

Signor Montenegro next showed them the music room, which Eurydice enjoyed seeing because it contained a piano; the library, which Psyche enjoyed seeing and was eager to explore for anything she hadn't already read; the study, which her father used as his office when he was in town; the chapel, which was very lovely, and almost as ornately carved as the great hall; and a small sitting room, which seemed to be much like the one at Aberdare House. That had taken them around the courtyard and brought them back to the great hall.

Through an archway was another stairwell as ornate as the one from the water floor, and it led to the second floor. This, it seemed, would be the floor where everyone had rooms. Eurydice's concern that she wouldn't have enough light in her room had lessened while they toured the first floor. She was amazed at how much light actually entered the rooms. The windows facing the courtyard received plenty of light, and there were loggias and more windows on the back and the side facing the other canal. It seemed the only rooms that might want for light would be those on the left side of the house, which abutted the wall of the neighboring palazzo. Unless it was a corner room or had a wall on the courtyard, it would have no windows. She was hopeful that hers would not be one of them.

He first took Sheerness and Psyche to their room. Eurydice was curious, but she wasn't sure she actually wanted to see it. After Freddie and Ellsworth, and Chrissoula and Stockbridge followed them, she shrugged and did the same with Agniezka. It was situated above the great hall, and while Eurydice wouldn't say it was as large as the room below, it came very close. The walls were covered in a brocaded russet with white, painted wainscoting beneath. The floor was covered in beautiful wood parquet, and the biggest bed Eurydice had ever seen was situated on a raised platform along one wall. The ceiling was covered in beautiful painted plasterwork, and as she looked around, she somehow suspected this was the room her mother and father used when they stayed at the palazzo together. Sheerness and Psyche's trunks must have been taken up by the servants while they were exploring the garden and touring the rooms on the floor below because they were stacked neatly not far from the door.

Psyche went to a door on the wall facing the side canal, seeing that it was a dressing room, or a room where a maid could stay or work. Another door on that wall revealed a similar room, only decorated in a fashion more suited to a man—a valet. Unfortunately for Sheerness, his valet, Clements, was on holiday. Psyche went to the wall on the left side of the palazzo and opened the door to peek in. It was a very large closet. When she opened the next door, however, she began to bounce up and down on her feet excitedly.

"Sebastian! Come see this!" she said, beckoning with her hand.

He did as requested with a slow smile and a shake of his head, and she grabbed him by the hand to pull him into the room when he was near enough. His jaw dropped in surprise, and then he smiled appreciatively.

"Very nice," he drawled.

Everyone else had followed him after Psyche's excitement, and Eurydice peeked around the door frame without actually going in to see it was their bathing room. It was lovely, decorated in a style similar to the bedroom, and Eurydice hoped it wasn't the only one in the palazzo. Scheduling when she could bathe around Psyche and Sheerness had been problematic enough on the ship. She was hoping things would not be so complicated at the palazzo.

"Is that a pool?" asked Freddie uncertainly.

Psyche giggled. "No, that's a bathing tub."

Freddie scratched his forehead in befuddlement. "Really?"

Psyche tousled his hair and then turned him and everyone else toward the door to leave the room and their bedroom. She took Cupid's leash from Freddie's hand with a grin. Signor Montenegro still stood near the door to the main room, waiting patiently as they explored. Psyche spoke to him briefly about when dinner would be served, and then she politely asked everyone to leave her room so she could be alone with her husband. Eurydice didn't have to wonder very much about what it was she wanted to be alone to do. Eurydice almost groaned and shook her head exasperatedly, but she didn't. Psyche told Chrissoula she could come to help her unpack her things and get settled in after she and Stockbridge were settled into their own room, but there was no hurry.

The next room Signor Montenegro showed them was for Chrissoula and Stockbridge. It was on the right side of the house, with the side canal. This room was, obviously, not as ornate as the room given to Psyche and Sheerness. Eurydice would be surprised if there was another bedroom in the palazzo as ornate as theirs, but it was beautiful nonetheless. The walls were covered in red and gold brocade, while their bed was covered with a luxuriant, matching red velvet. The floor was covered in cream-colored tile, and as Eurydice looked at it, she realized it was marble. They, too, had adjoining rooms for a valet, a lady's maid, and bathing. Eurydice was sure Chrissoula found a lady's maid having a room for a lady's maid humorous. Eurydice began to grow hopeful she would have her own bathing room as well.

As they began to walk toward the next suite of rooms he would show them, Eurydice idly wondered where he intended to put Freddie. She didn't think the boy needed to stay in the servants' quarters on the water floor. She didn't imagine the palazzo had a nursery, but she could be wrong. Even if it did, it would likely be on the next floor, and Eurydice wasn't so sure Freddie would feel comfortable sleeping there alone. She didn't think Signor Montenegro intended to put him in a room as sumptuous and large as the ones they had seen so far. She fully expected staying alone in a room like that would make him more uncomfortable than staying in the nursery.

Signor Montenegro led them to a door on the back side of the palazzo and opened it.

"These are your rooms, Lady Eurydice," he said melodiously as he moved out of the way.

Eurydice hesitantly walked into the room. She had a few misgivings about Ellsworth coming in, but this would be the only time he would see it, and she wouldn't see his, so she supposed she would be able to tolerate it. She looked around herself and sighed. It was beautiful. The walls were covered in gold satin brocade. The floors were covered in a brown, gold, and green mosaic that seemed to radiate outward in a widening circle…at least, what of it she could see. There were several Turkish rugs colored predominantly red on the floor. The ceiling was coffered and decorated with ornate plasterwork that had been tastefully gilded. The bed was large and looked like it was going to be soft and comfortable. It was a tester, but rather than being draped in heavy brocade curtains, it was lined with golden, gossamer silk. The coverlet was made of gold satin brocade similar to that on the walls. The other furniture in the room was upholstered in a velvet that matched the shade of red in the rugs.

She walked to one of the doors of an adjoining room, on the wall facing the side canal, finding that it was a brightly lit sitting room, decorated in shades of yellow and lavender, with windows on the canal and the back of the palazzo. Walking to another, she saw, to her relief, that she would have her own bathing room. It was decorated similarly to the main room, using a little more white and cream and red. The tub looked very comfortable, and she was looking forward to bathing in something other than salt water, and soon.

Eurydice went to the matching doors on the other side of the room, opening the one that would allow for windows on the back of the palazzo, and saw that it was a room for a lady's maid. She waved Agniezka over to look at it. Her maid smiled when she saw it, thinking it was going to be very comfortable. She would be happy in that room, decorated in white, green, and gold. The next room was for a valet. The only difference Eurydice saw in her rooms and the other two she had seen was that she had a separate sitting room and no closet. She didn't mind. The only thing she had been hoping for was a bathing room, and she had one.

"Thank you, Signor Montenegro. This is lovely," said Eurydice with a smile.

"*Bene*, I'm glad you like it," he said with a pleased smile of his own, clasping his hands in front of him.

He started to leave with Ellsworth and Freddie, and Eurydice could see the boy was growing anxious. It wouldn't hurt to ask.

"Signor Montenegro, before you go, I thought I would ask where you intend to lodge Master Bunney?"

"I had thought to put him in the nursery on the next floor," he said calmly.

Freddie's eyes rounded, and Eurydice could see the thought of staying alone in a nursery didn't appeal to him in the slightest. She knew without question there was no nanny—not that Freddie had ever had one of those before and probably wouldn't feel comfortable with one either. She hadn't realized when she invited him to come with them how far out of his own world it would take him. She felt responsible for him, and she didn't want him to feel too misplaced.

"If you don't mind, I'd like for him to stay here with me, in the valet's quarters, at least temporarily, until more children arrive to keep him company.

He's not used to all of this, and I think it would make him feel more comfortable to stay here."

Signor Montenegro smiled kindly and nodded. "Of course, Lady Eurydice. I'll have someone retrieve his bag from there and bring it here."

"Thank you," said Eurydice with a smile, and Freddie's face brightened immediately.

Ellsworth had stood in the doorway with his shoulder leaned against the frame as Eurydice explored her rooms. He didn't feel any more at ease walking around in what would be her rooms than she did having him do it. He was still stinging from her sudden departure from his cabin, and he supposed it had been Fate's not-so-subtle way of telling him he needed to stay away from her. Until things were different, and he didn't know if they ever would be, she was forbidden fruit.

He thought it was very kind of Eurydice to allow the boy to stay with her. Judging from the awed expression he had been wearing almost from the moment they had left the ship, Ellsworth was sure Freddie had to find all of this overwhelming. He knew it had been her and her sister's idea for the boy to come with them, and he wondered if they had fully thought their plan through. Freddie was a cabin boy, not a son of the manor; this world was as strange to him as becoming scullery maids would be to them, he was sure. He straightened up and smiled agreeably when Signor Montenegro turned to show him to his own rooms. His only disappointment was that he knew his rooms would probably have no windows. That was going to make things difficult.

Chapter Eleven

Over the next two or three days, Eurydice became accustomed to her new surroundings. She absolutely loved her bathing room. The piano in the music room had a rich tone, and she hadn't realized how much she had missed being able to play while she was aboard the ship. She had taken to playing her violin in different places around the palazzo, trying to find the location that gave her the best sound. So far, it seemed the inner courtyard did. That suited her perfectly. She had found that the grass *was* very soft between her toes.

Later in the day of their arrival, she had discovered that there was a second, smaller courtyard at the back of the palazzo. When she had opened a set of the doors on the loggia and stepped out onto the balcony, it was obvious there was a fair distance between their palazzo and the next one. When she looked down, she saw another garden, not as large as the one in the inner courtyard, but every bit as lovely. There was a stairway at one end of the loggia that wound in a spiral to the ground to gain access, and Eurydice had taken it.

The stairway was very beautiful, composed mostly of the pink stone of the water floor, but with open arches and railing made of white marble. When she reached the garden and looked up at it, she had been amazed. It looked very delicate, but she knew from using it that it was very solid. It wound down to the ground, but it also went to the very top floor of the palazzo, where it culminated in an observatory. There was access to the loggias on every floor from the stairway, but there was no access to the back garden from the water floor…at least, none that she could see. The stairway was open at the bottom, and the room there had been furnished with a small table and chairs for dining. She had climbed to the very top of the stairway to the observatory, and it had given her a wonderful view of the neighboring rooftops. She had even tried playing her violin there, but she decided she didn't like the acoustics.

Ellsworth was frequently gone from the palazzo making the arrangements for their journey to Vienna, Eurydice could only assume, and the only time she usually saw him was at supper, sometimes not even then. She wasn't complaining. There had been no opportunity for them to speak about what had happened on the ship, and she thought that was for the best. It would be even better if she completely forgot it had ever happened. Although it was her intention to do so, she hadn't yet. When he was at the palazzo for supper, he would speak when spoken to, but he was usually very quiet and seemed preoccupied. She wasn't going to ask him by what because even if it were any of her concern, he wouldn't tell the truth anyhow.

The day after they arrived, Chrissoula got a pleasant surprise when her brother, Nikos, and his family arrived from Greece. Although they exchanged frequent letters, they had not seen each other for more than ten years, not since Chrissoula had fled the country for her safety. It was a tearful reunion. Eurydice was happy the siblings were together again, even temporarily. Psyche and Sheerness had arranged for them to come because Chrissoula seeing her brother while they were in Greece would have been problematic. They just thought it would be such a shame for them to have come all this way, to be so close, and not be able to see each other.

Nikos and Ioanna, his wife, had five children, and all of them were girls. When they were introduced to Eurydice, their reactions were mixed, and it wasn't necessarily in order of age. The youngest, Yelena, who was almost two, walked over to Eurydice and wrapped her arms around Eurydice's legs before looking up with a happy grin. Eurydice gave her a lopsided, uncertain smile of her own. The little girl continued to keep her arms wrapped around Eurydice's legs until Psyche had to remove her in order for her sister to be able to walk, much to Yelena's displeasure. Eurydice was at a loss. She'd never had a child react to her with such instant affection. If anything, especially with babies, they often began to cry and would run away...if they could.

Odette, the next youngest, who was almost four, didn't run away, but she looked at Eurydice with round-eyed awe, and Eurydice thought her final reaction could go either way. The identical twins, Evangelina and Euphamia, who were five, did not like her...at least, Eurydice didn't think so. They kept a tight grip on each others' hands and whispered things to each other as they looked at her. Eurydice was fairly sure they were comparing notes, and the results were not favorable. Stefania, the eldest, who was eight, looked at her with the same round-eyed expression as Odette, but she walked toward Eurydice and looked up at her thoughtfully before beckoning with her hand for Eurydice to lean down and closer for Stefania to speak to her.

"Are you a lampad?" Stefania whispered.

Eurydice blinked and looked at her in surprise. The girl reached out to shyly touch Eurydice's hair and then ran a finger across her cheek near one of her eyes. At first Eurydice was upset, thinking the girl had asked her if she was one of the nymphs of the underworld because of their association with witchcraft. As Stefania continued to look at her features wonderingly, Eurydice realized she had asked because of their association with something else: fire and light. They were also thought of as fire nymphs, residing in volcanoes and lava. Eurydice gave her a slight smile then put a finger to her lips.

"Shh," said Eurydice secretively.

Stefania's eyes grew even wider, but she smiled and nodded her head. Psyche hadn't missed the exchange, and when the children went with their parents and aunt to the inner courtyard, she looked at Eurydice amusedly.

"That would explain so much," Psyche chortled.

Eurydice gave her a dry smile. "I didn't want to disappoint her."

"Mm-hmm," said Psyche amusedly as she linked her arm with her sister's at the elbow, and they both started toward the courtyard themselves. "They all seem quite taken with you."

"I don't know about all of them. I think Euphamia and Evangelina have decided I'm a tricky one."

Psyche chuckled. "Oh, no. They like you a lot, but they're not quite sure whether you're a fairy or a nymph, so they don't know what kind of presents to get to appease you." Eurydice looked at her in alarm. "None of them think you're human, Dicy," she giggled.

"Psyche, that's not funny," said Eurydice quietly.

"Oh, pooh," said Psyche with a wave of her hand. "They've just never seen someone colored like you, and you are very pretty. Then there's that look you have."

"What look?" asked Eurydice confusedly.

Psyche shrugged. "Oh, I don't know. Sometimes you get this expression. It's hard to explain. It's sad and distant…like you have seen more and know more than anyone should have to. It makes you look ancient, Dicy," said Psyche, her humor dulling somewhat. "Not old, but as if you've seen the woes of the world, and they've broken your heart."

"Oh," said Eurydice breathlessly.

Psyche had upset her sister, and she bumped her shoulder against Eurydice's companionably and gave her a teasing smile.

"I also told them that when you lose your temper your hair turns into flames and your eyes glow, so they had better be nice to you."

Eurydice gasped in disbelief, and her shoulders began to shake with silent laughter. "You're terrible, Psyche."

"No, really, they do," averred Psyche with as serious an expression as she could muster, scratching at a red patch on her arm.

Even with the arrival of the Andreanopouli, Freddie remained in the valet's room in Eurydice's suite. There were more children, but they were all girls, and they didn't speak English. He enjoyed playing with them, but he didn't feel comfortable sleeping in the same room with them. He was still at the age when he thought of girls as a nuisance, much like Eurydice's younger brothers, but it wouldn't be long before that changed. As Eurydice had no need for the room, she was content to let him stay there.

Dr. Felton came to call on Agniezka on Sunday, and Eurydice did her best to make herself invisible to give them some time alone. She had found an interesting medieval treatise on music theory in the library, and she took it back to her sitting room to read, curling up on a settee by one of the windows to listen to the sounds of activity from the canal below through one of the open windows. She was enjoying a very relaxing afternoon, and doing nothing all day was making her feel sinfully lazy.

Psyche and Sheerness and all their other guests, with the exception of Ellsworth, had gone on an outing to the Piazza San Marco and Basilica. Eurydice had thought to go, but then she found out they would be walking for all of it, and she decided not to. If they had decided to go on a tour of the Grand Canal by boat to see the palazzi there, she would have gone with them, but Eurydice didn't feel like walking all afternoon. She preferred to get her physical exercise from swimming and *t'ai chi chuan*. Ellsworth had left the palazzo early that morning, shortly after breakfast, on more errands for their trip to Vienna, she assumed.

Eurydice was actually on the point of dozing when there was a knock at the door to her suite. She looked up from her book with a frown, knowing it wouldn't be Agniezka. Freddie might knock, but he had gone with her sister and everyone else, as far as she knew, and they had not returned. She marked the page in her book and went to the door to her bedroom. She was taken aback when she saw Dr. Felton standing there...without Agniezka.

"Dr. Felton, where's Agniezka?" she asked confusedly.

"She's in the inner courtyard at the moment. I left her there so that I might come have a word with you, if you don't mind."

Eurydice frowned. "This is highly improper, Dr. Felton."

"I know, Lady Eurydice. I wouldn't have done it, but she insisted I should come see you immediately." Eurydice's frown only grew deeper. "It really is important, and I promise I won't take much of your time."

"A-all right," said Eurydice hesitantly, and she moved out of the way for him to enter. "We'll go to my sitting room."

"Thank you," he said relievedly.

She left the doors to her bedroom open. She was uncomfortable having him in her room, but it must be something very important for her maid to send the doctor to see her. She took him to her sitting room, and she left that door open as well. There was no one else in the house, except for the servants, but she knew the Catholic view on things was far sterner than in London, and most servants enjoyed a bit of lurid gossip. It was, in fact, the way a lot of news travelled through a city. Dr. Felton had promised he wouldn't take much of her time, so hopefully the issue could be dealt with quickly, and she could shoo him out before anyone was aware he had been there. She invited him to take a seat, and when he chose the settee, she took a nearby armchair.

He cleared his throat nervously and tapped the ends of his fingers together as he thought of what to say, and then he stood up quickly in preparation to leave with a shake of his head, changing his mind. Eurydice was startled and stood as well.

"Perhaps I should wait and discuss this with the captain," he said hurriedly.

"Dr. Felton," said Eurydice concernedly, "if Agniezka asked you to speak with me about it, then whatever it is, you can be sure I will listen."

"It's not that I don't think you'll listen," he said dully. "It's simply...it's just...," he stammered. Eurydice thought he was turning green.

"Dr. Felton, please, tell me," she said levelly, and she raised a hand and directed him to retake his seat. "You're obviously anxious about something. Once you've told me what's troubling you, then we can decide what to do or if there's even anything I *can* do." He reluctantly went to take his place on the settee again, but he didn't seem any closer to speaking. Eurydice grew slightly impatient. "I can only assume, since my maid sent you to me, that whatever it is you have to say has something to do with the two of you and the attachment you have formed for each other?" she supplied coaxingly.

He nodded wordlessly.

"You want to marry her," stated Eurydice calmly.

"Yes, I do...very much," he said earnestly, lifting his head to look at her.

While she had no doubts, she thought she would ask. "And she is agreeable?" He nodded again, but the glumness to his features didn't change. Eurydice tried to choose her next words carefully. "You are aware of how things stand in Russia?"

"Yes, I know she is already married."

"Then all that needs to be done is to dissolve that marriage," said Eurydice simply, not seeing the difficulty about the matter.

Felton looked at her directly then, and he ran a finger between his neck and cravat, as if it had suddenly grown very tight. She quickly realized from that one, brief action that it wasn't going to be that simple.

"Yes, we understand that, but there is a...uh...slight development which...uh...necessitates—"

"Oh, for pity's sake, Dr. Felton!" said Eurydice impatiently. "Will you just tell me what it is already?"

"Agniezka is with child," he blurted.

"Oh," squeaked Eurydice, her eyes rounding in surprise. "That was fast," she said dryly after a minute. "Between her being seasick and whatnot, how ever did you arrange to have the time for *that*?" He started to reply, and Eurydice quickly held up a hand, thinking of her own interlude with Ellsworth. Where there was a will, a way could be found. "You're sure? I mean, has it been long enough for you to know?"

"She has said that she is, and while it is not my area of specialty, she has started to show some of the symptoms."

Eurydice scratched her forehead thoughtfully. "If Agniezka has said that she is, it's fairly safe to say she is not mistaken. Obviously, since it had to have happened aboard the ship, she cannot be very far along...weeks at most."

Dr. Felton was startled by the calm way she discussed the matter. He had thought it a highly inappropriate topic to discuss with someone like Eurydice—innocent...and nobility, but Agniezka had insisted *she* was the one to talk to. He watched as she stood and began to pace back and forth as she thought, listening as she talked about the matter to herself.

"Hmm," she muttered. "Were it not for this *slight development*, as you called it, dissolution of her marriage to Sergei could be dealt with in due course. Now, it needs to be cleared quickly. But who to talk to...? Hmm.... Need to have someone who knows how these things work legally in the country, someone with a bit of finesse...and charm."

"You aren't going to dismiss her, are you?" asked Felton, interrupting her train of thought.

"What?" she asked absently. Then she shook her head and waved a hand in the air. "Don't be absurd. I would no more dismiss Agniezka than I would wear a hat made of banana leaves."

Felton blinked and watched as she began to pace again.

"This is going to take discretion, tact, and probably a bit of *real* diplomacy. Hmm. If she's only weeks along, it will give us possibly three months before anyone even begins to notice. With the right clothing and other things being equal, possibly longer." She stopped pacing with a final nod of her head and folded her arms in front of her as she turned to face him. "Which came first, the baby or the marriage?"

"I beg your pardon?"

"Did you want to marry her before you discovered she was with child?" she asked patiently.

"Yes, of course. I had asked her while we were aboard the *Medea*, and she had accepted. We were going to do what we could to dissolve her marriage while she was with you in Vienna so that by the time you returned home, she would hopefully be free for us to marry. She wanted to tell you from the very beginning, but I convinced her to wait until she was divorced, or annulled, or whatever needed to be done. Now...." He raised his hands. "She only told me when I came to call on her today that she was pregnant. I think *she* wanted to be sure first."

"Hmm. Agniezka should have been rid of Sergei a long time ago, but there didn't seem to be a need." She tapped her chin. "This *is* something I'll need to discuss with the captain, but only because I think he can help with a few things. I hate to bother him on his honeymoon with this, but we cannot afford to waste time. Right now, I think we need to go see Agniezka."

Eurydice tried to keep the thought to herself that they could be worrying for nothing. Although she would not wish for it, there could be a miscarriage before it ever became obvious Agniezka was pregnant. It happened all the time. Some women miscarried without even realizing they had been pregnant to begin with, not even realizing they had miscarried sometimes. She knew without question that her maid would never do anything to intentionally make it happen, and that was also not something Eurydice would wish for. But nothing was certain, and the sooner they started the process, the better, just in case. It was something that should have been done a long time ago, but Agniezka had been afraid Sergei would find out where she was and come after her or Nickolai. She had thought it would be best to let sleeping dogs lie.

Eurydice and Felton were just entering the hallway from the doors to her suite when Ellsworth turned the corner on the way to his own rooms. When he saw the two of them together, his expression turned stony, and he clenched his jaw angrily. He also couldn't keep the jealousy he felt from stabbing him in the midsection. Both of them colored guiltily, and any doubts he may have had about their being involved with one another were quickly dashed.

"Mr. Ellsworth!" said Eurydice in surprise.

"Lady Eurydice. Felton," he said tonelessly.

She could tell from the look on his face what he thought. Of all the people who might see the doctor coming out of her rooms, she wouldn't have wanted Ellsworth to be one of them. She opened and closed her mouth wordlessly because she couldn't tell him the true reason why Felton had come to see her, and trying to explain that it wasn't what it seemed would be trite. From the expression on his face, he wouldn't believe anything she had to say anyhow. She didn't know why she should be concerned about his opinion of her, but she was, and she wasn't happy to know he thought even less of her when what he thought he was seeing now was added to her fleeing from his cabin.

When neither tried to offer him any explanations, and the silence stretched interminably, Ellsworth simply nodded curtly and continued on to his rooms.

Eurydice and Felton went to the inner courtyard to see her maid. She tried not to think about Ellsworth and what he thought he saw. She would have to address that later. She could only handle one crisis at a time, and this one was more important. Agniezka had been pacing anxiously before their entrance, and Eurydice could see she was afraid of what her mistress's reaction might be. Eurydice went to her and put her arms around Agniezka in a soothing embrace.

"We'll find a way," said Eurydice comfortingly. "We will get this sorted out."

Two days later, it seemed the matter *was* on its way to getting sorted out. When Psyche and Sheerness had returned from their outing, Eurydice had asked to speak with them alone. She had made sure she had Agniezka's permission before she mentioned it in front of Psyche, and she didn't really think it would be something Sheerness would be able to keep from his wife in any event. She also suspected it was something that Chrissoula would find out, if Agniezka hadn't told her already.

Sheerness had wanted to dismiss his doctor when she first told him, but Psyche managed to calm him enough to see that the ship needed a doctor. She also mentioned a few choice words about he who is without sin casting the first stone, and Sheerness quickly lost his bluster. He knew as well as she did that this could have just as easily been them last year, except there was no husband to contend with. Eurydice assured him that while the affair might have proceeded at an alarmingly fast pace, Agniezka and Felton cared for each other a great deal. Psyche didn't need convincing on that; she was aware of Agniezka's past, and she thought she might tell her husband about it later. Sheerness promised he would begin making enquiries immediately.

In the meantime, they decided they would mention nothing of Agniezka's condition to anyone. When Mrs. Ellsworth arrived to escort Eurydice to Vienna, Agniezka would still go with her. If things weren't sorted by the time she began to show, they would worry about what to do when the time arrived. Being married did protect her reputation somewhat, but everyone knowing she wasn't with her husband did not. It really was something that would have resulted in her being dismissed had she been employed anywhere else.

Eurydice didn't think it was something she should mention to her parents in a letter, and Psyche agreed wholeheartedly. Their parents wouldn't want to dismiss Agniezka, but it would only worry them. It was selfish of her, but Eurydice thought if they knew, they would demand she return home. That would mean she couldn't go to Vienna, and she was almost there. There really was no point in going home.

Tuesday was Eurydice's birthday. There had been correspondence waiting for everyone when they arrived at the palazzo, and most of what Eurydice received was wishes for many happy returns. She didn't like a big to-do made over her birthday, and she never expected presents, even though she usually received several. She had asked Psyche to let her quietly celebrate the day, but from the moment she awoke, she got the impression her sister had completely ignored her request. Her first clue that would be the case was when a maid brought her breakfast in bed. Eurydice resigned herself to the day being out of her control from then on, which meant she would not get any practice done on her violin or anything else she might have thought to do.

The second thing that let her know Psyche had ignored her was when the younger Andreanopouli all came to find her in the inner courtyard to present her with gifts. She was standing on the footbridge over the pond, watching the fish and becoming mesmerized by their slow twirling and undulation, when the girls came through the archway in a line, holding the packages in their hands. She glanced up from the fish as the children approached her, and she thought it seemed like a processional, as they were arranged by age and height, with Yelena leading the way and Stefania the last. She smiled and walked onto the grass. When Yelena reached her, she grinned and held out her package.

"Happy birthday," said Yelena joyfully.

Eurydice took the package from her, and she went to sit on a nearby bench. It was a small wooden box, which was very pretty by itself, and she suspected Psyche had helped Yelena select it. When she opened the lid, Eurydice gasped in amazement. It contained a rock, a little larger than a quail's egg but imperfect in shape, and it was the most beautiful, unusual rock she had ever seen. She couldn't tell what it was. It was mostly a shiny black, like obsidian, but it had streaks of bright colors, in every shade of the rainbow, that sparkled across its surface like flames. She almost thought it was an opal, but she knew it couldn't be. As she looked at it, she realized it was probably very rare, which meant it was probably very expensive, but she could tell it was simply a rock Yelena had found, a rock she had selected from a collection of other rocks she had in her possession. Eurydice wasn't so sure she could keep it, but when she saw the hopeful, happy look on the little girl's face, she knew she couldn't give it back. She leaned forward to give her a kiss on the forehead.

"*Eycharisto, mikros,*" she said softly.

Yelena beamed proudly and moved out of the way for Odette. Her present for Eurydice was slightly larger, wrapped in a piece of beautiful red and gold silk. When she had it unwrapped, Eurydice found that it was a shell. It was a very pretty shell, mostly white with golden brown bands and lots of spiny protrusions. It was just small enough to fit in the palm of her hand with a little hanging over the end of her fingertips. It almost looked like a flower. When she turned it over to look at the bottom, the inside of it had a pearly sheen, and it made it seem as if the shell were lined with gold. Eurydice thought it was, again, something from a personal collection. She only hoped it wasn't the little girl's favorite.

"Thank you, Odette. It's lovely," said Eurydice softly.

Next were Euphamia and Evangelina. They had only one gift between them, and it was large, easily as tall as they were. Eurydice eyed it nervously when they held it out to her. It was covered in a beautiful piece of dark blue brocade satin. She smiled amiably as she took it from them and placed it on the bench because she could tell carrying it had taken a lot of effort for them. For its size, it wasn't at all heavy to her. There was a handle at the top where the fabric had been tied in place with a ribbon. Eurydice took an anticipatory breath and untied it. The satin fell away, and she gasped in surprise.

"Oh, my," she breathed.

She didn't think it was something from their personal collection…at least, she hoped not. As she looked at her gift, she was at a loss to determine how the two little girls *did* come by it. Opening the wrapping had revealed a cage, and inside it was a bright scarlet macaw. It was the most beautiful bird Eurydice had ever seen, and she had absolutely no idea what to do with it. Removing the fabric cover had woke it (she didn't know if it was male or female), and as she curiously peered into the cage, the parrot looked back with just as much curiosity. After the two of them eyed each other for a minute, she looked at the twins, who were holding each others' hands, eagerly awaiting Eurydice's reaction.

"Um, wow, thank you," said Eurydice uncertainly. "It's very pretty. You wouldn't happen to know if it's a boy or a girl, would you?" she asked hopefully. The girls giggled and shook their heads negatively. "No? I suspected not," she said dully.

"Do you like it?" they asked her in unison.

Seeing the look on their faces, she couldn't disappoint them.

"I love it. Thank you," she said, giving them what she hoped was a sincere smile.

Stefania practically skipped toward Eurydice to give her the last present, and Eurydice was relieved to see that it wasn't as large as the previous one had been. It was larger than those of Yelena and Odette, but Eurydice had some comfort in knowing it couldn't possibly be another animal. She unfastened the ribbon holding the emerald green silk around it to reveal a very pretty set of panpipes. She wasn't sure what kind of wood they were made from, but they had been very finely carved across the surface. Eurydice set aside the piece of cloth and tried to play them. She ran through a scale and managed to make it sound passable. They had a much warmer, organic sound than her Quantz, and she was looking forward to learning how to play them.

"Thank you, Stefania, this is just perfect," said Eurydice with a pleased smile. "Thank you to all of you. These are all very lovely gifts."

The girls all blushed and beamed happily, and then just as quickly as they came, they departed.

After they'd gone, Eurydice turned to look at her new pet and scratched her forehead thoughtfully. The bird sat preening its feathers, but when it became aware she was looking, it stopped to look at her. Then it spoke and nearly made Eurydice jump out of her skin.

"Ciao, bella signorina."

"Oh, my!" gasped Eurydice, putting a hand to her chest. *"Ciao?"* she said hesitantly.

"Amo i vostri occhi," squawked the parrot.

"Grazie," said Eurydice with a wry smile.

"Amo le vostra labbra," continued the parrot.

"Hmm," said Eurydice, pursing the mentioned feature.

The parrot sidled a little closer to the side of the cage where Eurydice stood.

"Scopiamo."

"What?" shrieked Eurydice, her eyes growing round in shock.

"Ariamo, mia bella," said the bird.

"Oh, my giddy aunt!" gasped Eurydice in alarm. "Hush!"

It wasn't done, however. Eurydice listened in dismay as the parrot proceeded to ask for the same thing several more different ways. She was just preparing to go have a word with Psyche about the bird's origins when her sister came into the courtyard. Eurydice folded her arms across her chest and gave Psyche an irritated glare.

"Where did this parrot come from?" she asked without preamble.

"We bought him in the market yesterday. The twins thought it was the perfect gift for a lampad," said Psyche with a teasing grin. "Do you like him?"

"He's very pretty, but he is a dirty bird."

"He looks fairly clean to me," said Psyche, walking to the side of the cage to give the parrot a once-over with a slight frown. There were a few nut shells in the bottom of the cage, but other than that, he appeared to be healthy and very well-kept.

"No, no. It has a vulgar tongue."

"Ooh! He talks? The man we bought him from didn't say that he talked," said Psyche excitedly, and she began to make noises, trying to coax the macaw to say something. When he did, Psyche blinked in consternation. "Well!"

"See? Just like Casanova…only with feathers."

Psyche began to giggle amusedly. "I guess you know what to call him then," she chortled.

"I can't keep a bird that talks like that! It's unseemly."

"Well, we can't take him back to the man who sold him, and Euphamia and Evangelina would be crushed if you tried to give him back to them."

"But—"

"Just try not to provoke him."

Eurydice groaned frustratedly. "I didn't do anything the first time," she mumbled.

Psyche helped her carry the rest of her gifts to her room while Eurydice carried the parrot. Thankfully, he remained silent as she carried him through the palazzo. She would be perfectly happy if he never spoke again. She cleared off a spot on top of a table near the doors to the loggia to set the cage down. She made sure he had water in his dish and found some fruit to put in the cage for him to eat. He didn't try to attack her or escape when she opened the door to his cage, and she was relieved he was well-behaved, his language notwithstanding.

Agniezka eyed the bird and the cage doubtfully when she came out of her own room and saw it.

"Agniezka, this is…erm…Casanova. My best advice is just to pretend he isn't even here."

"Hunh," said Agniezka.

"How are you feeling?" asked Eurydice concernedly.

Agniezka had awakened feeling sick to her stomach, and when the maid had brought in Eurydice's breakfast, Agniezka had run from the room with a hand over her mouth. It would eventually go away, but it would be two or three months more she would have to endure it. Eurydice and Psyche both knew it was only just beginning.

"Better now. The ginger tea helps a lot," said Agniezka, "and I think once I am actually able to eat something, it settles my stomach even more."

The three of them sat talking with each other for a while about babies and pregnancy. Eurydice felt a bit out of her element on the subject. She was anxious for Agniezka, but also excited and hopeful. To know she had found a good man who seemed to care for her a great deal made Eurydice very happy. To know that Agniezka had found someone she could care for in return made her doubly so. Psyche mentioned that she and Sheerness were trying to have a baby, and Eurydice gave her a sober look.

"Wait until you're at least on your way home," she advised sagely.

"Why? What have you seen?" asked Psyche nervously.

"Nothing bad," assured Eurydice. "I just think you'll want to be stationary when you go into labor. Actually, being in one place at least a month or two beforehand wouldn't be a bad idea."

"Why?"

"Honestly, it's nothing bad," repeated Eurydice. "I swear." She tried to keep her lips from twitching with amusement. "Just remember that you *like* children," she said cryptically.

She wouldn't say anything more on the subject, and Psyche would occasionally look at her sister with a thoughtful frown as she chewed on the side of her thumb. Eurydice knew she probably shouldn't have said anything, but she also knew it was probably too late for Psyche to worry about it in any event, which Eurydice was sure her sister would find out soon enough on her own. Eurydice felt confident Psyche and Sheerness would be back to Britain in plenty of time, but it would be close. She didn't want to tell her sister the reason she needed to stay in one place for a month or two was that she would be spending the time in bed. That would make her panic, and things were going to be fine.

They were still talking when there was a brief knock at the doors. The politely expectant expression on Eurydice's face froze when she opened it to see Ellsworth standing there. He hadn't spoken to her since he saw her and Felton coming out of her room, not even at supper. She knew it was too late to explain things, and she really couldn't do it without telling him about Felton and Agniezka, and that was none of his business. She still couldn't understand why his opinion of her mattered so much to her.

"Oh, good, Mr. Ellsworth," said Psyche happily as she came behind Eurydice at the doors.

"Lady Sheerness," he said evenly.

Psyche blinked, momentarily confused because she was unaccustomed to her title. She almost turned around to look for her mother-in-law.

"Yes, well, my sister wants to see the palazzi on the Grand Canal, and I thought you would be just the one to take her."

Eurydice's eyes rounded in alarm as she turned to look at Psyche. Her sister had a completely unassuming expression, but Eurydice had the distinct impression she was plotting something. She was also obviously oblivious to the tension between Eurydice and Ellsworth. Either that or she simply chose to ignore it.

"Oh, but—" began Eurydice hurriedly.

"Of course, Lady Sheerness," said Ellsworth calmly with a slight smile. He looked at Eurydice. "I'll meet you in the *portego* in fifteen minutes," he said politely, his face impassive.

"A-all right," said Eurydice dully.

She had been tempted to refuse, but she had the feeling that one way or another, Psyche would make her go. She did want to see the palazzi, and it would be a nice treat for her birthday. She just would have rathered to go with anyone but Ellsworth. She could tell the feeling was mutual, and she wasn't sure how much she would enjoy the outing if he continued to look at her in that disdainful way.

After he left, Agniezka guided her to the dressing table to put a few stray hairs back where they belonged. The ruffled, beige mull morning dress she wore would be fine, and Agniezka found a pair of crocheted gloves, and a bonnet, shawl and parasol to make her ready. Psyche grinned as Eurydice prepared to leave the room with a glum expression to accompany her outfit.

"Have fun, and I don't want to see you back before sunset," said Psyche as she looked at the watch on the chain around her neck.

Eurydice didn't see how it could possibly take that many hours, but her sister's words did nothing but confirm she was up to something, despite Eurydice's pleas not to make a big to-do for her birthday. She eyed Casanova in his cage before she left the room, wondering how much worse things could possibly get.

Eurydice took her time walking down the stairs to the entry hall. She didn't think she was late, and she didn't expect Ellsworth to be awaiting her arrival with baited breath either. She would almost be willing to bet he was hoping she wouldn't show up, and she wouldn't be surprised if he wanted to *dunk* her in the Grand Canal.

When she reached the *portego*, Ellsworth was standing with one hand clasped casually behind his back, the other holding his pocket watch as he looked at it critically. He looked up in surprise just as she reached the bottom of the stairs. She had been so quiet he didn't hear her coming until she was almost beside him. He didn't realize he had been that distracted. He could think of very few people who could move that quietly. None of them were women. Without a word, he offered her his arm and went with her through the archway that led to the palazzo's private dock.

An oarsman was already there waiting to take them out in one of the family's gondolas. The wrought iron gates stood open in preparation for their departure. Ellsworth stepped into the boat and reached back to help Eurydice step in. They had taken their seats and were starting away from the steps when Freddie came running in with a small, cloth-wrapped package.

"Lady Eurydice, wait!" he called as he ran down the steps to the water's edge and held it out toward her.

Eurydice started to stand up and reach for it, but Ellsworth put a hand on her shoulder to stop her.

"I'll get it, or you're liable to tip the boat," he said flatly with a sigh.

Eurydice snapped her teeth together and clenched her jaw on a retort. Then she watched as he stood up and gracefully leapt from the moving boat to take the package from Freddie and hopped back into it. The part of this entire feat that caused her amazement was that he managed to do it with barely a wobble to the boat. There were very few people she knew who could have done that: Dorian, Hiroshi, and Keung…and most likely Hiroshi's siblings and mother. Most everyone in her family, including her, could have done it without *tipping* the boat, but to do it without rocking the gondola—or barely even making a *sound*—took special talent. She spared him a brief, suspicious glance through narrowed eyes as he sat back down before looking over her shoulder at the boy on the steps.

"Thank you, Freddie!" she called with a smile and a wave.

Freddie grinned happily and waved until the gondola turned left into the *rio* and disappeared from sight.

Ellsworth held the package out to Eurydice, and she took it from him, still eyeing him distrustfully. She started to say something, but he wouldn't tell her the truth. He never did. In her heart, she already knew the answer anyhow.

She looked at the package. It had been wrapped in another piece of the red and gold satin that Odette had used, tied with a red velvet ribbon. She carefully unfastened the bow and opened the cloth to reveal a small, carved wooden box, very similar to the one Yelena had given her. As Eurydice looked at it, she wondered if the two might be part of a matched set. The box didn't hold another rock, however. When she opened the lid, she sighed in wonder, and she knew, while Freddie may have chosen it, only Psyche or someone else could have bought it.

It was a figurine of a phoenix, slightly less than three inches long. It was made of beautiful, translucent pink jade that was almost deep rose in color. The detail in the carving was exquisite, and it was very old, which was why Eurydice knew Freddie could never have bought it himself. She ran her fingers over it before putting the cloth and ribbon inside the box and closing the lid.

"That looks like an expensive bauble," said Ellsworth neutrally after he saw it.

Eurydice looked at him. She had almost forgotten he was there.

"Yes, I suppose it is," she said thoughtfully.

"Makes one wonder how he came by it."

"Oh, I know Freddie didn't buy it."

"No?"

"Of course not. He could never afford to buy something like that, and I know he certainly didn't steal it or just find it somewhere. He may have given it to me, but it came from someone else," said Eurydice with a secretive smile.

Ellsworth tightened his jaw and looked away from her. It appeared she and Felton were now involving Freddie in their affair. He thought he should have a word with Sheerness about the business. After he had seen the doctor coming out of her room the other day, he could see they were becoming more brazen and more careless. It was obvious she had no concern about her reputation, but he thought she would at least have a care for the scandal it would cause for her family. Perhaps this evening, after they returned to the palazzo, he would be able to talk to Sheerness in private…discreetly.

At the very least, he thought Sheerness should dismiss the doctor…and lock Eurydice in her room. If she was that determined to carry on with the physician, perhaps she should even marry the man, despite their difference in station. Ellsworth didn't want to mention that thought to Sheerness, simply because he found the idea of her being married to anyone disturbing. He knew he couldn't have her, but he didn't want anyone else to have her either. As it stood now, there was still a chance. If she were married, there would be none.

When they reached the end of the *rio,* the gondolier steered the boat right, and he began to prod it along the Grand Canal. Ellsworth did his best to give Eurydice an entertaining tour, as her sister had requested. He found that she listened attentively and asked questions. They eventually relaxed enough in each others' company to smile and even laugh occasionally as he provided her with anecdotes regarding some of the buildings they saw. She tried to keep her features impassive when he pointed out the palazzo where the real Casanova had stayed. If he had still been living there, she would have been tempted to go knock on the door and demand whether or not he knew of a certain foul-mouthed red bird. They didn't go up the entire canal but covered a major portion of it, and by the time they turned onto the *rio* to return to the palazzo, the sun was indeed setting.

Ellsworth stepped out of the gondola after the oarsman pulled it to a stop and got out also to begin tying it to a nearby metal ring. Ellsworth reached out a hand to help Eurydice alight after she had gathered her things.

"Thank you, Mr. Ellsworth. I had a wonderful day," said Eurydice softly, giving him a warm smile. She was hopeful they were on their way to a reconciliation of some type after he had been so kind and polite all afternoon.

Ellsworth placed her hand into the crook of his elbow as they entered the *portego* and began to climb the stairs to the great hall.

"You're welcome, Lady Eurydice. If you would like to see more of the city while we are here, it would be my pleasure to show you."

Eurydice gave his arm a slight squeeze, and she smiled happily. "Thank you. I think I would like that."

When they entered the great hall, Eurydice wasn't at all surprised when Psyche and everyone else jumped out from their hiding places to yell just that, but she could tell Ellsworth was as she felt him jump slightly and tense beside her. She smiled dryly as the children gathered around her laughing and jumping excitedly. She let go of Ellsworth's arm to tousle Freddie's hair and give him a smile.

"Thank you very much, Freddie, for your gift. You have excellent taste." He grinned bashfully and blushed.

She looked at Ellsworth and saw his bemused expression. He seemed to have quickly relaxed when he realized he knew the people in the room.

"What's all this, then?" he asked perplexedly.

"This, Mr. Ellsworth," said Psyche with a grin as she grabbed Eurydice's hand to pull her further into the room, "is my sister reluctantly celebrating her birthday." Eurydice finally relented and quit dragging her feet as Psyche gave her hand a coaxing squeeze.

"Birthday?" he blurted.

"Yes," said Psyche, and she lifted her watch to look at it. "In exactly fourteen more minutes, Dicy will officially be twenty years old." She laughed as she took the things Eurydice carried in her hands and placed them on a nearby couch. "Two decades! A score! One-fifth of a century!"

"Thank you, Psyche. You make me feel so young," said Eurydice dryly with a sardonic smile. Psyche laughed amusedly with a shake of her head and handed Eurydice a glass of champagne.

The dining table had been covered in a beautiful gold cloth and decorated with several bouquets of flowers from the inner courtyard. A nearby table had been covered with more of the cloth and was overflowing with gifts. As Eurydice looked at them, she knew they couldn't have all come from the people staying at the palazzo, not even if the children gave her a second set of gifts.

"You know, Psyche, I said I didn't want a fuss," said Eurydice softly.

"Yes, I know. You say that every year, and every year you get one anyhow," chortled Psyche. "Were you surprised?"

Eurydice gave her a lopsided smile. "Not for a minute."

When fourteen minutes had passed, Psyche tapped the edge of her glass with her wedding band to get everyone's attention. She also did it to get the children, who had champagne glasses filled with lemonade, to settle down. She had told them what she was going to do, and they had practiced what they were supposed to do when they heard that sound. She smiled amusedly when she saw them all line up in a row, barely containing their giggles as they waited excitedly.

"To my beautiful, sweet sister on her twentieth birthday, whose smile is a rare treasure, whose heart is endlessly open, and whose spirit is generous and pure, I wish many, many happy returns."

"To Eurydice," chimed everyone and drank from their glasses.

Eurydice swallowed an emotional lump in her throat and kissed her sister on the cheek and hugged her. This had already been the best birthday ever.

Chapter Twelve

Eurydice sat at the dressing table, patiently waiting as Agniezka brushed and braided her hair. She'd taken a nice long bath after the party, and now she was ready to sleep. She had been so sleepy before bathing, in fact, that she had started to doze in the tub. Agniezka had needed to prod her in the shoulder to wake her after she had lounged in the tub until the water grew tepid.

When it had been time for her to open her gifts, she discovered the reason there were so many was that friends and family had sent them with Psyche to give to her. They had all been just as lovely as the ones given to her by the children, and Eurydice was a bit overwhelmed by everyone's thoughtfulness and generosity. At times, she wasn't so sure she deserved it.

Her parents had sent a new bow and composition pages. She was always in need of both. Pandora and Islington had sent a metronome inlaid with mother-of-pearl and gold. Dorian and Selena gave her a beautiful matched set of earrings and a necklace made with amber and marcasite. Persephone gave her lots of new strings (not just G) for her violins. Arachne gave her a new notebook, bound in leather overlaid with brocaded and beaded red velvet on the front. Annabelle had given her a lovely dark red, cashmere shawl.

Cosmo, Christopher, and Damon had all gone in together to buy her a watch, but it was musical, with a glass window for her to see the movement for both the watch and the music. As far as she could tell, the music would play on the hour, and she wondered what the piece would be. Whatever it was, simply because of the size, it would be brief. Once she had set it and wound it, to her delight, she discovered that it played the opening notes of *Adelaïde*. The children had all clapped gleefully and had wanted her to make it play again, but Eurydice was afraid she might break it.

Lord Georgie, Lucy, and Sir James had sent a folio containing several compositions from the Renaissance. Eurydice was looking forward to learning them. Lady Bardsey had sent a cuff bracelet with an oval of cloisonné at the center. When Eurydice examined it, she discovered it was a locket that opened to reveal miniatures of her nephews, Alex and Myron. Maiyin and Keung sent a box that contained her much-anticipated perfume with other grooming items scented to match. As she removed the stopper to smell it, she couldn't quite decide what the scent was. Between her, Psyche, Chrissoula, and Agniezka, they were finally able to agree that it was orange blossoms and chamomile. She absolutely loved it.

Then she opened the presents from the people at the palazzo. Psyche and Sheerness gave her a beautiful, ornately-carved wooden chest. When she opened it, she saw that it was lined with velvet and padded, with places to store six violins, a niche for her bows, and another for storing her rosin and spare strings. She only had five violins, but it would be perfect to store them in at home and would take up much less room than having individual cases for all of them, and she would immediately know where they all were. Psyche proudly announced that Sheerness had designed it, and Eurydice thanked them both happily. Chrissoula and Stockbridge gave her a set of filigreed silver earrings...and some zils. She immediately put them on her fingers to make them chime and loved the clear tones. Nikos and Ioanna, who she hadn't thought would give her anything because she barely knew them, gave her a gold silk scarf trimmed in beautiful embroidery and beadwork. She suspected Ioanna had done the work herself. Agniezka presented her with the blanket she had been knitting while they were sailing to Venice. It had lots of complicated stitches and patterning and was made of a very soft mohair yarn. When Eurydice opened it and held it in her hands, she immediately rubbed it against her cheek and hugged it.

The only person who didn't give her anything was Ellsworth. She was not upset that he didn't. She had far more presents than she had any right to expect, especially when she hadn't been expecting any. She knew he didn't know it was her birthday, and as he wasn't family—barely a friend despite everything—there had been no reason for him to give her anything. Besides, his taking her on a tour of the Grand Canal had been present enough.

Supper had been delicious, with lots of pasta, cream sauces, and vegetables. Eurydice's favorite part of it, however, was probably the dish that had been composed of lobster with bits of tomato and zucchini in a rich cream sauce served over *farfalle*. She absolutely adored lobster. When dessert had been brought, she wasn't sure she would be able to eat another bite, but she did manage to find room for the sponge cake with layers of custard and amaretto cream. There had been lots of wine and champagne, and by the time Eurydice left the great hall for her room, she was feeling very drowsy. She thought she might even be the least bit tipsy.

Once Agniezka was done with her hair, Eurydice brushed her teeth after she said good night to her maid. She could tell Agniezka was tired. Eurydice thought she might be missing Felton just a little as well. He had not been to see her since Sunday, and Eurydice thought he was trying to avoid Sheerness, to give his employer a little time for his anger to lessen over the doctor's impropriety. Things would work out for the best, and Eurydice hoped the two lovers would be able to spend more time together before she and Agniezka left for Vienna because they would be apart for several months then.

Eurydice wasn't sure when they could expect Mrs. Ellsworth. She had only just left London two days before the *Medea* arrived in Venice. Although she was traveling by packet, and they were built to travel faster than the *Medea*, it would be at least two weeks, provided the weather and wind were favorable. That meant they wouldn't leave for Vienna until the first of October. That would give Agniezka and Felton almost a month together before they were separated, and Eurydice hoped Sheerness would be able to find some information and have things well in hand for Agniezka's divorce.

What if Agniezka had to go to Russia to make the petition herself? Eurydice wasn't so sure she would go. She had committed no crime (apart from her adultery with Felton), so there was nothing legally to keep her from safely entering and leaving the country. But she was terrified of her husband. If getting a divorce meant she would have to see him face to face to get it accomplished, Eurydice didn't think Agniezka would be able to do it. She might, considering the circumstances, but Eurydice couldn't say one way or the other. Hopefully, Sheerness would be able to tell them more before it was time to leave. Austria *was* closer to Russia.

Eurydice snuggled under her blankets and fluffed her pillows. The night was slightly cool, but not uncomfortably so. She had a small fire lit, and she was very cozy under her blankets. She heard a soft tinkling as her new watch struck the hour, and Eurydice idly wondered what hour it was exactly. The birthday celebration had lasted several hours, and she had spent quite some time in the tub. She thought it might at least be one, perhaps even two, but she didn't think it was much beyond that. She was almost asleep when she heard Casanova.

"*Buona notte, mia bella,*" he squawked.

Eurydice popped one eye open and looked at the cage on the table. Several minutes passed without further chatter, and Eurydice began to relax and drift off again.

"*Bacilo, per favore,*" said Casanova. "*Bacilo con la lingua.*"

Eurydice groaned aggravatedly and rolled onto her back with a shake of her head as he started into his repertoire of the colorful language he had used earlier in the day. She got out of bed and put on her dressing gown. She stalked over to the cage and looked at the bird.

"Shh!" she hissed. "*Dormite!*"

But he wouldn't be quiet or go to sleep. It seemed that once he started, he was compelled to finish. She found the piece of fabric it had been wrapped in and draped it over the cage. The bird finally stopped, and Eurydice leaned her forehead against the side of the cage with a sigh of relief. She didn't know why the bird had decided to start speaking. She would have thought the room was dark enough to make him sleep but apparently not. She hoped the cloth over the cage would keep him silent for the rest of the night. Something would have to be done about his vocabulary.

Eurydice's head snapped up in surprise when she heard noises from outside. It was distant, but she could hear shouting and the sound of a whistle blowing shrilly. Eurydice frowned. Venice was a lively city, but that was a bit extreme for two in the morning. As she listened, it seemed the sound was coming closer, from the direction of the Grand Canal, and it almost sounded like an alarm. She listened for a few minutes more to the commotion, with the noise coming steadily nearer to the palazzo. It sounded as if the people were on foot, traveling the narrow streets and alleys rather than by water. She finally shrugged and began to make her way to the bed. Whatever it was, it was none of her concern. She'd gotten Casanova to be quiet, this new disturbance would pass soon enough, and she was extremely tired.

She was crossing in front of the doors to the loggia when they opened, and a dark figure stepped into the room. As Eurydice looked, she felt a disorienting dizziness and put out a hand to steady herself and found the edge of the nearby table. She should be frightened, but she couldn't be. For the life of her, she couldn't bring herself to scream. She was reliving a dream, and she felt completely disconnected from the present, as if it were entirely separate. She wove unsteadily on her feet, and her hip bumped the edge of the table. That brought her presence to the attention of the man who had entered her room. He quickly moved toward her and put a hand over her mouth with a curse.

"Don't scream," whispered Ellsworth. "It's me."

Eurydice shook her head and moved his hand. Without a word, she feverishly began to push him toward her bed, something in her subconscious guiding her actions. She didn't remember this dream as one she wrote in her notebooks, but she let it guide her, knowing there was no other way, somehow sensing that his life depended on it. He was dressed in black from head to foot, and Eurydice could not at first determine how the clothes were cut or fastened, knowing only that they were made of some soft, stretchy, woven material. She began clawing at his clothing as she continued to steer him toward the bed in the dark, tugging at gloves, a hat, finding buttons here and there, which she popped from their threads as she tried to take things off.

"Eurydice? What–?" he began in surprise.

"They're coming for you. We don't have much time," she muttered almost mindlessly. "Must...have you...in my bed."

"What?" he gasped. "Eurydice, are you even awake? Let me go to my room. Forgive me for bursting in uninvited, but now is not the time for this."

"No, in bed...now," grunted Eurydice as she succeeded in pulling off his shirt and tumbling him onto the bed on his back. "Search your room...not good. Alibi," she muttered.

She kicked the things she had already removed under the edge of the bed, and she pulled at his shoes to remove them and put them there as well.

Ellsworth gasped when she grabbed his calf to remove one of them, and she could feel a wetness beneath her hand. He was injured. That was how they were following him, and there was probably a trail of blood that would lead them to the palazzo. It was just a matter of time. She loosened the drawstring on the pants he wore and pulled them off to kick them under the bed with everything else. Once she was sure they were well hidden, she reached for the bottom of her shift and tore off the ruffle that was attached to the edge of it, the thin lawn making a soft hissing noise as it ripped loose from the seam.

"Now, see here!" said Ellsworth in consternation.

He was frowning, looking at Eurydice worriedly, even as he struggled to get away from her and leave. He had not anticipated that she would be awake when he decided to cut through her room to his own. Like her, he could hear the sound of the police following him, but they wouldn't be able to find him, especially now that he had reached the palazzo. The events of the night had already been strange enough, and now to have her behavior added to it....

She was not herself. If he didn't know better, he could almost think she was asleep...or drunk. Her movements were somewhat jerky, but she seemed to know exactly what she was doing—whatever that was. There wasn't anything seductive at all about it, either. He couldn't see her face clearly in the mostly dark room, but it was almost as if she were demented. And yet, the things she was saying to herself made disturbing sense.

"Shh!" hissed Eurydice. "Not much time now. Have to hurry," she muttered. "Must hurry."

She grabbed the handkerchief she always kept on the night table by her bed and put it over the wound in his leg, and then she used the ruffle from her shift to bind it on and stop the bleeding. There was nothing she could do for the trail outside. She could only hope it hadn't bled bad enough to lead them directly to the doors to her room. The patterning on the rugs would hide any stains that might have occurred once he came inside. She pulled off her dressing gown and draped it on the bench at the foot of the bed, and then she removed her shift and used what was left of it to wipe off any blood that might be on his leg not covered by the bandage to keep it from getting on the sheets and to wipe it off the floor before shoving the garment under the bed with his clothes.

She could hear them in the rear courtyard now, and when she looked to the windows of the loggia, she could see the flicker of torches and lanterns reflecting off surfaces outside as their search neared its conclusion. She could also hear activity inside the palazzo itself. She could hear lots of shouting in English, German, and Italian, including the voice of her sister, as well as Cupid barking excitedly. There wasn't much time now. If they could wait just a few more minutes—even a minute—that would be enough. She had to have time to create an illusion, to make things seem to be something they weren't, even if she only completed it a few seconds before the door was opened.

She put Ellsworth's legs onto the bed and placed them beneath the covers to hide the bandage, and then she climbed on top of him and straddled him at the waist and pulled the cover over herself. She leaned on her elbows to either side of his head on the pillows.

"You've been here since half past midnight, and we're having sex," she whispered quickly before covering his mouth with hers.

Ellsworth was bewildered and dizzy, and her kiss muffled the protest he tried to make at her actions. He didn't think he'd been in her room more than five minutes, and he was utterly confused. He could hear the shouting voices then, too, and he realized with shock what she seemed to know from the moment he came into her room. They had managed to find him. The sounds he had thought were simply fruitless searching were, in fact, them tracking him. If he had gone to his room, they would have discovered him. If they had searched his room, it would have made things even worse. Somehow, she knew he needed an alibi. She didn't ask him any questions about how he was injured or why the authorities were after him, but she was protecting him. And it was all wrong. It would save him, but he didn't think she fully understood what it was going to cost. Either that or she simply didn't care because her morals had slipped so far it seemed perfectly fine.

The feel of her against him, the feel of her bare breasts brushing against his chest as she kissed him, was irresistible. He was only a man, and she was a beautiful, willing woman. She smelled intoxicating, and despite his worry over what was about to happen, he began to kiss her back with a groan of delight. He moved his hands along the soft skin on her thighs to her hips before lightly trailing his fingers across her back to her shoulders. He rolled them over to place her beneath him, and he began to kiss and nuzzle her neck before taking the tip of a breast into his mouth. Eurydice moaned and arched against him excitedly, her fingers clutching in his hair. He knew people would be coming soon, but he intended to enjoy as much of her as he could while he had the chance, and she had said they were having *sex*, so....

That was the scene the police and everyone else came upon when they burst into Eurydice's room from the hall and the loggia. The shouting died, and there was an immediate, collective gasp of shock before there was almost a full minute of complete silence.

"What is this? Son of a bitch!" shouted Sheerness angrily.

"Oh, my giddy aunt!" gasped Psyche in dismay.

It wasn't difficult for Eurydice to color brightly, and Ellsworth gave her a somber, apologetic smile before he rolled off of her onto his back to look at their audience with a sardonic half-smile. Eurydice pulled the covers up to her chin as everyone continued to stare in open-mouthed disbelief. Psyche, Sheerness, Stockbridge, Chrissoula, and Signor Montenegro were the only faces she recognized, but there were six or seven more people with them, and some of the men had guns in their hands. Eurydice sank even further beneath the covers as Ellsworth relaxed against the pillows and casually folded an arm behind his head.

"Is there a problem?" he asked calmly.

Eurydice watched as Psyche silently put a restraining hand on her husband's arm to keep him from attacking Ellsworth.

"*Scusi, signor, signorina,*" said a man dressed in a uniform holding one of the lamps…and a gun, "I am Captain Bustamente."

Eurydice nodded slightly in understanding. Ellsworth continued to lounge in his seemingly relaxed pose.

"We are looking for a criminal responsible for the murder of Signor Ermete Merletto on the Riva del Carbon. Do either of you know this man?"

Eurydice shook her head negatively, and she paled slightly. She hadn't realized what the offense was, but she wouldn't betray Ellsworth. Things had progressed too far for her to change her mind now in any event.

"I've never heard of him," said Ellsworth calmly.

"The murderer was found standing over the body just seconds after the crime. We were able to wound him as he fled, and we were able to track him to this very palazzo," continued Bustamente, his eyes narrowing as he looked at Ellsworth. "All the other male inhabitants of this household are able to account for their whereabouts over the past two hours, leaving only you, signor."

"He's been here with me," said Eurydice softly, "since half past midnight."

"*Stavamo scopando,*" whispered Ellsworth loudly.

Eurydice blushed a bright shade of red and turned her face away.

"You quiffing shite," breathed Sheerness unbelievingly.

Psyche tightened the pressure grip she had on his arm as she felt him tense in preparation to pounce. She was ready to do the same thing, but what she really wanted was a moment alone with her sister.

"I see," said Bustamente neutrally.

He lifted his lantern to look around the room. Nothing appeared to be out of place. He went to the open doors of the sitting room and bathing room to look in. He thought the bathing room was peculiar, but nothing seemed to be out of the ordinary otherwise. He went to the closed doors at the other end of the room, those of Agniezka and Freddie's rooms, and Eurydice sat up slightly in the bed and held out one hand toward him in a staying gesture while she used the other to keep the blankets pulled up.

"If you could, please, do that quietly," she said hurriedly. Bustamente turned to look at her, lifting an eyebrow. "There's a nine-year-old boy sleeping in one, and my lady's maid is in the other. If they're not already awake, I would appreciate it if you could just let them continue to sleep."

Bustamente tilted his head slightly in acquiescence and softly opened each of the doors to look in. When he saw things were just as she said, no one hiding in the shadows, he turned his attention back to the main room. He went to the wardrobe and opened the doors. He moved some of the clothes hanging there out of the way to make sure no one was hiding behind them and closed it back. Then he noticed the large square object on the table near the loggia doors covered in the blue cloth. It was conceivably big enough to hide a person.

"Don't!" gasped Eurydice in alarm when he pulled it off, and she held her breath in anticipation for what the bird would choose to say.

"*Vaffanculo!*" squawked Casanova.

Eurydice shook her head and put a hand over her face in embarrassment. Ellsworth turned to look at her with a sardonic grin. That must have been one of the presents she received for her birthday, and he could only imagine who had given it to her.

Bustamente turned to look at her after he put the cloth back over the cage. "Colorful bird that," he said dryly.

He looked at the two of them in the bed suspiciously for a few minutes more before he signaled with his head to his men that it was time for them to go. He had found nothing to be anything more than what it seemed. The criminal he was looking for did not appear to be there, but he had the feeling another crime had been committed at the palazzo that night and needed to be taken care of without his presence or that of his men. He stopped in front of Sheerness with an apologetic smile.

"We are sorry to have bothered you, Lord Sheerness. It seems the man has escaped for the time being."

Sheerness nodded curtly, never taking his eyes off Ellsworth in Eurydice's bed, a nerve ticking in his jaw. He was glad the captain was leaving because he felt ready to do murder, and he certainly didn't want a policeman to witness it.

Signor Montenegro left with the officers to escort them from the palazzo, and Chrissoula and Stockbridge left for their own room and to go back to sleep. Nikos and Ioanna had remained upstairs with their children after the police had gone through the rooms and scared them all without finding their suspect.

"You will put on some clothes, and then you will drag your worthless hide to the study, where I will have a word with you," bit out Sheerness coldly before turning on his heel and leaving the room.

Psyche stood with her arms folded across her chest, waiting for Ellsworth to do what her husband said. She would gladly help him along if she had to. After a minute, she realized he was waiting for her to look away because he had on no clothes. Psyche snorted derisively, but she moved away from the door to the hallway and went to look out the doors of the loggia, watching as the light of the torches and lanterns of the police faded into the night.

Ellsworth looked at Eurydice somberly and ran a hand across her cheek before giving her a soft kiss on the forehead once her sister's back was turned. He climbed out of the bed, quickly grabbed the things from where she had shoved them beneath the bed—including her shift, and limped to the door. Eurydice could see a red stain on the makeshift bandage she had provided for his leg and frowned slightly with concern. She really thought a doctor should look at it; there was an awful lot of blood. He quietly closed the doors and was gone, and when he was, Psyche rounded on Eurydice with a dismayed expression, wringing her hands.

"Oh, Dicy, what have you done?"

Eurydice scratched her forehead confusedly. "I don't know. It's all a bit of a blur, really. I remember him coming into my room, and removing clothes, and climbing on top of him on the bed at one point, but it's all a bit jumbled exactly how it got from one thing to another."

"Please, tell me you love him," said Psyche hopefully as she walked closer to the bed.

"Of course not," said Eurydice simply. "Why should I?"

"Oh, Dicy," said Psyche brokenly as she climbed onto the bed with her sister. "You'll have to marry him."

Eurydice frowned disconcertedly. "But I don't want to marry him. I don't want to marry anyone."

Psyche shook her head. "I'm afraid you have no choice. This can't be washed out. Too many people saw. Granted, it was only us and the police, and we're not in Britain, but it can't be ignored."

"But I *can't* marry him!" said Eurydice in alarm. She could feel her heart thudding against her ribs as she began to panic. What *had* she done? "I just.... He isn't...," she stammered.

Psyche wrapped her arms around her sister and smoothed a hand over her hair. "I'm so sorry, Eurydice. I would never have wished for something like this for you. I would have wished for you to find your own Sebastian."

"He doesn't even like me," moaned Eurydice.

Psyche's lips pursed slightly with a smile. "Um, obviously, considering what you were just caught doing, it is a fair assumption that he *does* like you…at least something about you. The only time at least liking someone won't enter into an activity like that is when it's being paid for on Drury."

"I don't trust him at all."

"But you seem to get on well…most of the time," soothed Psyche. She really didn't know what to say to comfort Eurydice because she didn't trust him either. "Is this the first time you two…?"

Eurydice looked at her sister and colored slightly. She shook her head negatively. There was no point in trying to hide it now. She actually felt relieved that she was able to confess to it.

"Once, on the ship, we almost…, but I was worried about Agniezka, and I left his cabin before he…," she trailed off with a glum expression. "He wasn't very happy with me."

Psyche chuckled briefly. "Well, I suppose you've made up for it now," she said mildly.

"But we haven't…I mean, we didn't…," stammered Eurydice uncomfortably.

Psyche's eyes rounded in dismay. "You mean you're still intact?" she gasped. Eurydice colored even more before she nodded. Psyche hugged her again and rubbed her back soothingly. "Oh, Dicy, this is all so unfair. Why did someone have to choose tonight of all nights to trail blood to our palazzo after killing someone? It makes me so angry that your life is going to be changed the way it is because of some idiot. I'd like to see the man responsible so I could bust his nose…and worse," she muttered.

≪ ≫

Ellsworth had rewrapped his leg with a better bandage once he went to his room. The gunshot had gone through the muscle in his calf without damaging the bone. It hurt, and it bled quite a bit, but he'd had worse. It was completely survivable, and one more scar wasn't going to make a difference. With concentration, he was able to walk with barely a limp, and no one would be any the wiser. He calmly walked to the door of the study and went in after only a brief knock. Sheerness had demanded his presence, after all.

When he entered the room, Sheerness sat behind the desk writing a letter, a glass of brandy sitting at his elbow and the half-full bottle within reach. Ellsworth could only imagine what he was writing and to whom, but none of it boded well for him. There was one letter he had already written, sealed and addressed, sitting nearby. It was to Aberdare, and Ellsworth didn't even want to think about what Sheerness told him, especially if he was still furious. His life had suddenly, completely spiraled out of his control, and he wasn't sure how to get it back. He shouldn't have gone to see Signor Merletto. That was his first mistake. He should have taken his chances and gone to his room. That was his second mistake. That he would have been arrested for Merletto's murder while the real criminal went free would have been a certainty, but at least then his suffering would be over.

Sheerness finished the sentence he was writing before he set aside the pen and removed his spectacles to look at Ellsworth disdainfully. After three glasses of brandy, he had managed to somewhat calm his temper. He felt speculative that he would be able to address this matter in a rational manner. He was supposed to be on his honeymoon! Yet here he sat with another unpleasant chore, and he found this one to be more distasteful than the matter of Felton and Agniezka.

"What do you have to say for yourself?" asked Sheerness flatly without preamble.

Ellsworth took a seat in one of the chairs across the desk. He'd managed to stop the bleeding, but standing for too long would start it again. He folded his arms across his chest and gave Sheerness a level glance.

"I have nothing to say," said Ellsworth evenly.

"You need to come up with something better than that," said Sheerness coldly. "You've ruined the innocent daughter of a duke, a peer of the realm, with apparent disregard for her reputation."

Ellsworth scoffed. "Someone's already ploughed that field before I got to it," he said sarcastically.

Sheerness angrily slammed a hand against the top of the desk and stood up to come around it. He thought he would be able to maintain his composure, but this man pushed him to the edge of tolerance. Upstairs in her room, Ellsworth's attitude and things he had said made it seem he thought Eurydice was little better than a trollop. And now, saying that made it obvious. Sheerness could think of no one more proper and modest than Eurydice…no one, and to have this man imply she wasn't was an insult.

"You will *not* speak about her like that!" he bit out. "That girl was as innocent as the day is long until *you* changed it."

"I think Felton would disagree with you on that."

"Felton has nothing to do with this. He hasn't laid a finger on her. That one thing I know without question." Sheerness pinched the bridge of his nose and took a deep breath in an effort to calm himself. "In any case, *he* is not the one who was caught in bed with her. *You* were. I'm sending a letter to her father to apprise him of events, and I am also sending a letter to Canterbury to obtain a special license because *you* are going to marry her…here…as soon as it can be arranged."

"No, I'm not."

"Bloody hell you're not!" shouted Sheerness furiously

He reached out to grab Ellsworth by the front of his shirt and lifted him out of the chair. Sheerness was going to throttle him, plain and simple. He was going to kill him, and then Eurydice wouldn't have to be saddled with the worthless bounder.

Ellsworth calmly reached up with a hand to grab Sheerness by the wrist and extend his arm out behind him to force Sheerness to bend forward with his face on the top of the desk or have his arm broken.

"Don't do that again," warned Ellsworth softly before he let him go.

Sheerness straightened up and looked at Ellsworth angrily. Psyche had told him about Ellsworth, or what she suspected about him, so Sheerness really wasn't surprised by what the man did. He would simply have to tell his wife that she had not been wrong. Sheerness really wished she had been though, because he would have dearly loved to batter the man.

"You are going to marry her," Sheerness repeated, "and if you don't, *I* am not the one you will contend with." He gave Ellsworth a dark smile and a brief shake of his head. "Really, right now, *I* am the least of your worries."

Ellsworth folded his arms across his chest, apparently unmoved. Actually, he was thinking of the contention his marrying Eurydice would cause. He was in a quandary about whether or not refusing to marry her would cause less. Everything had happened so quickly he hadn't been able to think. *She* had made it impossible for him to think, and now she had put them both into a position that made it impossible for things to be any other way. He didn't think she had done it purposely, but he had no way of knowing what had been going through her head. There had been times while he was in her room that he had wondered if *she* even knew.

"Don't think it wouldn't give me great pleasure to shoot you where you stand and put the entire matter permanently to rest. At this moment, to me, that would actually be a joy and a privilege, except I don't have access to a gun. So, as her guardian, this matter rests solely at my discretion to resolve however I see fit, and I am attempting to do that as reasonably as possible."

"I wouldn't agree that forcing two people to marry against their will is reasonable," said Ellsworth darkly.

"Perhaps you should have thought about that before you decided to swive her."

"I didn't *choose* this!" bit out Ellsworth.

"No? You are not honestly going to expect me to believe that *she* seduced *you*, are you?"

Ellsworth gave him a sardonic half-smile. *If you only knew,* he thought humorlessly.

"She's no innocent," he said flatly.

Sheerness sighed exasperatedly and ran a hand through his hair. "I don't know what it is you *think* you know about her, but you are mistaken," said Sheerness coldly. "Lady Eurydice was immaculate before you sullied her, and there is *nothing* you can say that will make me think there was someone else responsible for that. You took advantage of her, even if you didn't force her."

Ellsworth clenched his jaw and looked away sullenly as he folded his arms across his chest. She was *not* innocent. He didn't know how she had managed to pull the wool over the eyes of so many people. It annoyed him that he was being made to seem like some lecherous profligate. Perhaps he would accept that role if she truly was untouched, but he knew she wasn't. Getting him into her bed had been entirely her idea, not his.

"You have dishonored her. If you don't marry her, you will continue to do that and bring dishonor to her family as well."

That touched a nerve for Ellsworth, but he remained silent. He kept hoping Sheerness would admit defeat and leave him be.

"It is obvious you have no regard or respect for her, much to my confusion. If this weren't the right thing to do, I would not wish you upon her for all the tea in China. She deserves so much more than to be made miserable by a sorry drip like you."

Ellsworth clenched his jaw angrily. He knew all of this discussion was just prolonging the inevitable. Sheerness wasn't going to let him *not* marry her. He had always thought he would marry one day, but not right now; he had thought it would be a few years, once he was done with his job. He wanted a wife and children like most men did, but his life was too uncertain, too unstable, and too complicated for now. Having a wife would only make things worse, and marrying Eurydice rather than someone else was going to compound that exponentially. He finally sighed resignedly and ran a hand over his face.

"Fine. I'll marry her."

"Too right you will," said Sheerness firmly.

Chapter Thirteen

Eurydice woke up the next morning feeling confused and anxious, not to mention tired. The results of what she had done the night before had still not fully settled in yet. She didn't want to marry anyone, least of all Ellsworth, but she realized she had no choice. She had always thought she would marry someone she didn't love, but she thought it would be in the future, after she had gone to Vienna. She certainly had never thought it would come about the way it had. She had never imagined she would have to marry someone she didn't love to save her reputation and avoid scandal. She had simply assumed she would settle for a suitor who was agreeable in temperament and breeding when the time came. While she knew Ellsworth's breeding was agreeable, despite his untitled status, his temperament was often found wanting. And now she was going to be stuck with him for the rest of her life.

She was pouring through her notebooks when Agniezka came in, trying to find any reference to the dream that had prompted her actions. There was nothing. It was one of those she didn't remember until they happened. Her maid sat with open-mouthed shock and dismay when she heard what was to be Eurydice's fate. She couldn't believe she had slept through all of that. She did her best to determine a way to keep it from happening, but she could think of nothing. She knew, like Sheerness and Psyche, there was no other way. However, she also knew Eurydice wasn't completely averse to her future husband. She knew there was something about the man that provoked some emotion in Eurydice that definitely wasn't dislike. While she wasn't quite sure it was love, there was something, and that gave Agniezka hope it wouldn't be a completely unhappy union.

Psyche had stayed with Eurydice for an hour or two discussing her impending marriage. There was no planning for a trousseau or honeymoon, no guest list. Eurydice didn't feel she was being deprived by not doing those things, but she was still in a bit of a daze.

When the maid brought Agniezka, Freddie, and Eurydice's breakfast to the sitting room, the friendly greeting and smile she usually had for Eurydice were absent. They were replaced by a stone-faced disapproval and silence. Whether any of the servants had been present in her room last night or not, they knew what had happened. She was a fallen woman, a *puttana*. Eurydice tried not to let the change in demeanor bother her. It was to be expected.

She had written a letter to her parents, and when Sheerness asked to see her after breakfast, she gave it to him to be delivered with his own letter and Psyche's. She didn't want to think of what her parents' reaction was going to be to this news. She made sure to tell them that the responsibility for it was hers alone, that Sheerness and Psyche had not fallen lax in their duty as her guardians. Her parents would be disappointed. They had trusted her enough to let her go across the continent, and she had betrayed them.

Eurydice also apologized to Sheerness. Although he didn't seem to be angry or disappointed, she knew that he was. So far, his honeymoon with Psyche had been one disaster after another for him to sort out, and it could have been avoided if he had simply not taken Eurydice with them. She knew he had been up all night composing letters and making arrangements for their delivery to Britain with as much haste as possible.

Sheerness only grew angrier with Ellsworth when she apologized. Psyche had told him what Eurydice had said the night before. He had no reason to doubt she was telling the truth. The marriage would take place regardless of whether or not she was still a virgin because of the position in which they had been caught, in *flagrante delicto*, as it were. Saying she was intact wouldn't make a difference, only to make Sheerness angrier with Ellsworth for insisting she was glaringly and brazenly not. It only confirmed the man had taken advantage of an innocent, and she had no reason to apologize.

Sheerness wasn't sure how long it would take for the license from Canterbury. Signor Montenegro was able to provide him with a trustworthy man to travel to Britain. Once he arrived in the country, he would engage another courier to have the letters delivered to Aberdare at Wilderland, and then he would contact Sheerness's solicitor to handle obtaining the license. He had provided the man with enough funds to pay for changing horses as often as necessary to get it done quickly and for passage across the Channel.

He disliked that it was necessary to send someone to Britain, but there was no other way. There was no diocese or bishop nearer to hand. Even with the special license, it would be at least two—possibly even three—weeks, and Sheerness wanted to make sure this was legally binding. He wanted to have some kind of license, even if they didn't need one to be married in a foreign country. There was no parish to have the banns read, and he wanted to see this done before they left for Vienna. That wasn't to punish Ellsworth; it was to protect Eurydice.

He had already made enquiries at the new consulate in Venice to find out if there was a member of the clergy available to perform the ceremony once the license had been received. There was, much to his relief, and Sheerness would be going to meet with him that afternoon. It would take some finesse to explain the situation to the man, but Sheerness actually thought it was going to be one of the easier parts of this mess to sort out.

Eurydice was standing on the bridge in the inner courtyard after she'd met with Sheerness. She had thought about bringing her violin or one of her other instruments, but she wasn't in the right frame of mind to practice. Perhaps later, once her thoughts were more settled. She didn't know why, but watching the koi calmed her, and she never grew tired of it. She was so lost in thought she didn't hear Felton until he stepped onto the bridge.

"Dr. Felton," she said brightly. "Do you need me to fetch Agniezka for you? I know she wanted to see you."

"No, Lady Eurydice. In fact, I've just come from talking with her."

"Oh! All right," said Eurydice uncertainly.

"I just wanted to say I'm sorry about everything."

"Oh, Dr. Felton, these things happen. You can't choose who you love. Just ask my sisters," she said with dry amusement. "You and Agniezka will be very happy together. Even with all that's happened, she is already so much happier having found you. That, to me, makes everything else insignificant."

"Really?"

"Absolutely, doctor. I just want to say I'm sorry this whole other marriage business is going to delay things, but trust Sheerness. He will get it sorted out."

The doctor impulsively took her hand and kissed it. "Thank you."

"You run along back to where you were," said Eurydice mildly with a soft smile. "I think you need to spend every minute you can."

He smiled appreciatively and turned to leave, nearly colliding with Ellsworth. "Oh, pardon me, Ellsworth," he said amiably as he stepped around the other man to go back to Agniezka in the rear courtyard.

Eurydice looked at Ellsworth guardedly as he walked onto the bridge. His jaw was set in the position it often was when he was angry with her, and she honestly couldn't say she was surprised. She rested a hand on the railing and calmly waited for him to say something. She had no doubt that he would.

"We are to be wed," he said flatly.

"Yes, so it would seem," agreed Eurydice evenly.

"I don't want you seeing Felton anymore."

"I'm afraid that's not possible," said Eurydice politely.

"You're to be my wife, and I'll not have you see another man," he bit out.

Eurydice clenched her fingers around the railing to keep herself from slapping him. She longed to discuss what had happened the night before and so many other things, but his words directed her attention elsewhere.

"I'm not any more pleased about this than you are, but there are a few things that I feel I must say now so there will be no misunderstanding later," she said stonily. "Firstly, I am not your property, especially since we aren't married yet. I won't be after, either. Secondly, I will see whom I choose, when

I choose. My friends and family mean a great deal to me, and I am not going to let marrying you force me to sever my ties with them...ever. Finally, do not pretend that this is anything more than an arrangement of convenience. Do not try to tell me that any control you try to exercise over me or my actions is due to some form of care or affection on your part because we both know better. In return, I will be honest, loyal, and as undemanding as possible."

Ellsworth clenched his hands into fists at his sides, and he looked at Eurydice with an arctic glare.

"Since we are laying things out for each other, I have a few for you," he said coldly. "Firstly, you will conduct yourself as a married woman. I will not tolerate infidelity, brazenness, or anything that would cause a scandal. Secondly, you will not question me about anything I do, anywhere I go, or anyone I see. Finally, you *will* do your duty as my wife and provide me with an heir. If I am to be married to you from now till doomsday, I want a son. In return, you may continue with your music; I'll see your needs are provided for; and I will not mistreat you."

Eurydice blanched slightly. The first item, she didn't foresee as causing any difficulty at all. The second and third ones, though.... Questioning him would be pointless no matter because he would lie. He always lied. She wondered if she could add that as a condition—that he would have to be honest with her, just as she had promised she would be with him. Perhaps she could broach that later. As for providing him with an heir, while she had recently become more comfortable around children, she still wasn't sure she wanted any of her own. She knew it was expected, though, so at some point she supposed she would have to have at least one.

She was relieved he didn't intend to make her give up her music. If he had made that a condition, she would never marry him, reputation be damned. She would move to Siberia first. As for providing for her needs, she didn't have many, and her allowance more than covered what she required. And what, exactly, did he mean by not mistreating her? If he meant he wouldn't treat her the way Sergei had treated Agniezka, he would have a very hard time accomplishing that even if he tried. She didn't think he would treat women that way, but he would be in for a surprise if he did. In the end, she thought it all sounded reasonable, and it really wasn't any more than she had expected to have eventually...except with someone else.

"All right," she said calmly after she thought about it.

Ellsworth raised an eyebrow in surprise. "All right? That's it?" he said disbelievingly.

"What more is there to say?" she asked simply with a slight shrug. "I accept your terms."

"Hunh," said Ellsworth doubtfully. He turned to rest his elbows against the railing, looking down at the pond. "So, we are to be wed," he stated mildly.

"Yes, it would seem so," repeated Eurydice in a dry tone, resting her elbows on the railing to look down at the fish as well.

This time, however, it seemed both of them were slightly less abhorred by it. Eurydice tried not to dwell on the fact that he hadn't said whether or not he would honor her own terms.

Two weeks later, Eurydice sat at her dressing table as Agniezka styled her hair. She was wearing a simple white gown made of mull. There was a white silk ribbon gathered beneath the bodice, and beautiful, intricate embroidery in silver and white cascaded down the front of the skirt in the shape of feathers and flowers before circling the bottom hem. Agniezka was weaving a strand of pearls through her hair in a style that was looser than she usually wore, and soft tendrils curled at her nape and near her ears. Eurydice was indifferent.

The man Sheerness had sent to Britain had returned that afternoon with the license. As soon as he arrived, arrangements were made for Mr. MacNaughten to come perform the wedding ceremony in the chapel at the palazzo. The only people who would be attending were those staying at the palazzo and the vicar's wife. As the service was being performed in the evening, they would have supper afterward. Eurydice didn't see the point of all the fuss.

After their discussion on the footbridge, Eurydice and Ellsworth had agreed to spend at least an hour with each other every day. The results were mixed. At times, they were able to behave amicably; at others, one or the other didn't see how they could possibly spend their lives married. That day, unfortunately, was one of the latter kind, and it still had to do with Eurydice's refusal not to speak to Felton. Ellsworth still thought she was having an affair, and she couldn't tell him the man had impregnated and become affianced to her maid. Perhaps, if she discussed it with Agniezka and Felton and they were agreeable, since Ellsworth was to be her husband, she could tell him the truth, but it rankled her that he had such a low opinion of her morals. That it was a violation of her second condition also irritated her. She was feeling rebellious.

As Agniezka and Eurydice left her room for the chapel, she was completely calm. There was none of the jittery nerves a bride was supposed to feel on her wedding day. There was no excitement or anticipation for the future that lay ahead. She was simply ready for the entire business to be over, and she knew Ellsworth was expecting a wedding night. She supposed they had to have one, and while she somewhat knew what she could expect, she wasn't impatient for it. It was only one more formality to have over and done.

His things had been moved from the rooms where they had been to Eurydice's. She had the better rooms was one reason. That she would have more to relocate was another. She should have expected that they would share a room once they were married. Most married couples she knew did...unless they loathed each other. While she couldn't say she loathed Ellsworth, at times she found his company disagreeable. Still, about the only time they would have to be in the room together was at night, and she thought that would be tolerable.

Psyche and Sheerness were waiting outside the doors to the chapel when she and Agniezka arrived. After giving Eurydice a brief hug and a kiss,

Agniezka went in to find a seat beside Chrissoula. Psyche turned to look at her sister expectantly.

"Are you ready?" she asked quietly.

"Do I have a choice?" asked Eurydice with rhetorical sarcasm.

"You look very pretty," said Psyche encouragingly.

"Eh, Agniezka chose it," said Eurydice dully. "Does it look bridal enough?"

"Very much so," said Psyche with a grin.

She held out a small bouquet of white lilies and freesia. Eurydice reluctantly took it. Sheerness put her hand into the crook of his arm to escort her to the altar with an encouraging wink. He patted her hand soothingly as they walked, and Eurydice looked up at him to give him a wan smile.

When she looked at Ellsworth standing with Mr. MacNaughten, she was startled to see him wearing a kilt. He was wearing a full, traditional kit, complete with sporran, sgian dubh, and ghillies. She never thought of him as being that tied to Scotland. He still had his brogue, but she'd never heard him talk about the country of his birth. She didn't object to him wearing it; it was actually a very attractive look for him, but it was a surprise.

Sheerness relinquished his hold on Eurydice's hand and gave her a kiss on the cheek before he went to stand beside Psyche. He took Psyche's hand in his and gave it a kiss and a squeeze, thinking how different this wedding was from their own. Ellsworth had no love or respect for Eurydice, and if there could have been any other way to do things, Sheerness would have found it. Psyche kept hoping there would be something to stop the marriage from taking place. It would be miraculous, but she didn't want to see her sister unhappy.

The reverend proceeded with his opening commentary and the solemnization of matrimony, and both said "I will" to their declarations of intent. Psyche and Sheerness thought it sounded so hollow. When it came time to exchange vows, there was a brief moment when Eurydice hesitated on the words "to love and to cherish," but she did say it. Mr. MacNaughten had just taken the rings to bless them when there was a loud noise as the doors to the chapel flew open.

"*Wait*! I'll have a word with those two before this business goes one amen further!"

"Father!" gasped Eurydice.

"I say, steady on," bleated Mr. MacNaughten.

"Oh, my giddy aunt," sighed Psyche, and she tightened her hold on her husband's hand.

Aberdare was road worn, with mud spattering his clothes and caked to his boots. It was obvious he had ridden across country without stopping any more than absolutely necessary. Despite the tiredness in his features, it was evident he was furious. As Psyche looked at him, she didn't think she could recall her father ever looking that angry, not even when she had helped Pandora run off to Edinburgh. That he had traveled all the way from Britain over land to interrupt the proceedings wasn't a good sign. And yet Psyche was hopeful his arriving would mean Eurydice wouldn't have to marry Ellsworth. The duke walked further into the room, down the aisle, to confront his daughter and pending son-in-law. Mr. MacNaughten had never met the duke, but he could tell the man was in no mood for nonsense. Aberdare pointed at Eurydice.

"I'll talk to you first," he said shortly.

Eurydice simply nodded obediently and followed him from the room. He took her to the doors of the recessed loggia at the rear of the palazzo and opened them to go outside. As soon as the doors were closed behind them, he pulled her to him in a tight hug.

"Oh, dear heart," he sighed emotionally.

"Papa!" she choked out, and she blinked her eyes to hold back her tears as she hugged him back. She was never so happy to see anyone.

"My dear, sweet girl," he said as he gently held her away from him at arm's length, looking her up and down sadly. "Your mother is worried to distraction, and I am not far behind her. I want you to tell me everything that happened."

Eurydice bit her bottom lip hesitantly. She couldn't lie to her father. He was the only one she could explain it to honestly. She knew she had to tell him…she had to tell *someone*.

"They would have killed him, Papa. Signor Merletto, whoever that is, was murdered, and they thought Ellsworth did it. He was wounded and bleeding, and they would have found him out because of it. I had to make them think he wasn't the one responsible, and there wasn't any other way."

"Oh, Eurydice," sighed Aberdare, putting a hand to her cheek. "You have no idea—"

"I know what he is, Papa," she said quietly. She put her hand over his. "At least, I know that—somehow—he works for you, and I don't think you would have wanted anything to happen to him."

"Did he tell you?"

Eurydice shook her head. "I've seen the scars…and his back, and enough other things. He didn't have to tell me." She shrugged and smiled tremulously. "I know he wouldn't tell me, even if I asked."

"I can't stop this," he said sadly.

"I know," whispered Eurydice brokenly, and she drew her bottom lip between her teeth and took a steadying breath. "Don't be angry with Psyche and Sheerness, Papa. It wasn't their fault."

He hugged her again with a deep sigh. She rarely called him that. It was always *father*. She only ever called him *papa* when she was frightened or sad…or extremely happy. Of all his children, even though Aberdare would never admit it if asked, she was his favorite. He didn't want this for her, but he couldn't stop it. It broke his heart. He finally let her go and kissed her cheek.

"Don't be sad, Papa," she whispered. "I'll be all right."

He gave her a loving smile and swallowed emotionally before giving her a slight nod.

"You run along now, and send him out here," he said softly.

Eurydice nodded and squeezed his hand before going inside. Aberdare heaved a gusty sigh and rubbed a hand over his face to compose himself. He turned to look at the rear garden, resting his hands on the railing as he took a deep breath and closed his eyes. He was tired, and he had never felt so old. He heard the door open and close behind him, and the first thing he did when he turned to face Ellsworth was deal him a backhanded blow to his cheek.

"How...dare...you!" hissed Aberdare.

Ellsworth reached up to wipe away the trickle of blood from the corner of his mouth before clasping his hands behind his back, his face impassive.

"You violated my trust. You violated my *daughter!"* roared Aberdare furiously. "She thinks this is happening because it was the only way to save you, but we both know that isn't true, don't we?" he said acidly.

"I'm sorry, your grace," said Ellsworth woodenly, unable to look him in the eye. "I never intended—"

"Bah!" interrupted Aberdare with an irritated wave of his hand. "You let it happen!" he bit out, poking Ellsworth in the chest. "You were careless, and if I didn't know better, I would think you did it on purpose!"

"She knows things!" said Ellsworth, finally showing some anger of his own. "I *am* careful, especially around her. The other night, she *knew* they were coming for me, and she...it was almost as if she were possessed."

Aberdare looked at him sharply, tempted to hit him again.

"You want to die, don't you?" he flatly said instead.

"No, your grace. I hope to die a man so old I won't even notice when I piddle myself."

"Boy, you are on dangerously thin ice already. This is no time for levity."

"I'm being perfectly serious, your grace."

"You should not have allowed this to happen," said Aberdare, his tone becoming more modulated.

"I know, your grace."

"You are marrying *my* daughter."

"Yes, your grace," said Ellsworth evenly.

"If any harm befalls her, I will kill you," promised Aberdare stilly.

"Yes, your grace."

"If *you* hurt her, I will kill you."

Ellsworth narrowed his eyes as he looked at Aberdare.

"Yes, your grace."

Aberdare looked at him angrily. He was still of a mind to end Ellsworth. If he weren't aware of the younger man's occupation, he might not have minded the marriage...provided it hadn't come about the way it had. Ellsworth was an honorable, decent man, his occupation notwithstanding. But Aberdare did know, and compromising his daughter to save himself was contemptible. No matter what either of them said about the plan being her idea, Ellsworth could have found another way. Aberdare suspected he hadn't wanted to.

"You haven't asked if I care for her," said Ellsworth after a few minutes.

"You better," warned Aberdare stonily.

Aberdare held out his hand in the direction of the doors to go back inside, and Ellsworth opened them for the two of them to enter. They silently walked back to the chapel. Eurydice stood at the front talking with Psyche and Sheerness as they came in, and when she saw them, she frowned as they approached her, noting the bruising beginning to develop on the left side of Ellsworth's face. She had to wonder what had taken place. Mr. MacNaughten looked skittishly at the duke, but Aberdare calmly went to take a seat in the front pew behind where Psyche and Sheerness stood.

"Continue," he ordered benignly, circling a finger in the air.

Mr. MacNaughten cleared his throat nervously and blessed the rings. Eurydice and Ellsworth gave the rings to each other, reciting their pledges, and then Mr. MacNaughten proclaimed them man and wife and blessed the marriage. Once they stood, Ellsworth leaned toward Eurydice to give her a soft kiss on the lips, and she blinked with momentary confusion.

For some reason, after her father arrived, Eurydice felt a panicky fluttering begin in her chest that made it difficult for her to breathe. Outwardly, she appeared as calm and dispassionate as she had before, but inside, there was a nervousness, almost as if it were just beginning to dawn on her that she *was* getting married—forever—to a man she barely knew. She would be bound to him now, and she would never be with her family in quite the same way ever again. Even though she knew she would see them again, as often as she liked, there was something about her connection to them that had been severed. While she would never be his property, she *belonged* to Ellsworth now. She felt lost and frightened, and she felt terribly alone.

There was no register for them to sign, and after the Lord's Prayer, Mr. MacNaughten dismissed them with a final amen. It was done. She was now Mrs. Ellsworth. For better or for worse. There was none of the usual happy congratulations and well wishes, except from the children, who knew nothing of the reason for the wedding. They didn't know it was all a sham; they were still innocent enough to believe that love was the only reason two people married. Eurydice had lost that delusion a long time ago, but she had always thought two people who married should at least *like* each other.

Once the ceremony was over, her father excused himself to go clean up before supper. Psyche and Sheerness offered to vacate their rooms, but Aberdare said he would be fine staying in the rooms recently occupied by Ellsworth. He would stay at the palazzo until Mrs. Ellsworth arrived and Eurydice left for Vienna. Although circumstances had changed, and whether or not she would be able to continue to pursue her original purpose for going was uncertain, it was where Ellsworth lived. He had promised she could continue with her music, but Eurydice was not confident he meant it.

Supper was a sedate affair. It wasn't somber, but there was no toasting of the bride and groom, no revelry and celebration. Eurydice didn't have much of an appetite. She quietly sat beside Ellsworth, mostly picking at the food on her plate and only managing to eat an occasional bite. She still, outwardly, appeared perfectly serene, but she had always been good at keeping her emotions contained. She would speak when spoken to, but she didn't offer conversation of her own.

The children were excused from the table for bedtime, and Chrissoula went with them to see they were all tucked in properly, including Freddie. There was no separate drawing room for the women to retire to to allow the men their drinks and tobacco, so when the time came for that, the women left for the inner courtyard…most of them. Eurydice was going to prepare for bed.

Psyche gave her a hug and a soothing pat to her back when she told her good night.

"You're married now," said Psyche quietly with a tremulous smile.

"Yes," agreed Eurydice neutrally.

"Be happy, Dicy," said Psyche earnestly, brushing a hand down her arm. "Even if it's not what you would have chosen, try to be happy."

Eurydice nodded with a wan smile. She bade the other women good night, and she and Agniezka left for her room. When they reached it, Agniezka went to the bathing room and drew a tub full of water for Eurydice. It was hot enough to make her skin red and tingly, and the scent of her new perfume curled up on tendrils of steam from the oils Agniezka had added to the water. She didn't stay in the tub as long as she normally did. Normally, she dozed while she was in the tub until the water grew cold, but Eurydice wasn't sleepy. She couldn't relax enough to feel sleepy, but she did feel a little less tense.

After she got out, Agniezka provided her with a shift and dressing gown. They were made of soft, white silk, with lots of ruffles and delicate embroidery and openwork. She didn't recognize them as her own—she usually wore cotton, and Agniezka told her that Psyche had purchased them. Eurydice supposed, since it was her wedding night, a special outfit was required, just like for the ceremony. They were very pretty and feminine, and Eurydice did like the feel of the silk against her skin.

Once Agniezka had brushed and braided her hair, Eurydice brushed her teeth and turned to look at her maid, who stood nearby watching her with a pensive expression.

"Well, I guess I'm ready for bed," said Eurydice dully.

Agniezka walked toward her and hugged her comfortingly. Even if no one else could see it, Eurydice was afraid, and Agniezka knew there was nothing she could do to make it go away. Agniezka let her go to look at her solemnly.

"I'll be just in the next room," said Agniezka softly. "If you need me for *anything….*"

Eurydice nodded quietly. She watched Agniezka go to her room and close the door, and then she looked around herself at her own room with a resigned sigh. Casanova's cage was covered to keep him silent. A small fire burned on the grate to remove the slight chill from the air. A lamp burned lowly on one of the night tables by the bed, and the blankets had been turned down. It all seemed exactly the same as it had many nights before, but there was something different: she was still waiting for something that wasn't there yet.

She walked to the bed and removed her dressing gown to drape it over the bench at the foot. She climbed onto the mattress, and then she settled herself beneath the covers, turning her back away from the lamp, lying slightly to one side of the bed rather than in the middle of it as she usually did. She curled a hand beneath her cheek, and then she began to wait.

Her mind began to drift, and her eyes began to lose their focus on her surroundings even though they were still open. She tried to make her thoughts go to something less constraining than her circumstances, and she began to hear the notes of a melody in her head. It was soft at first, like a whisper or a sigh, and too faint for her to even tell the instrument. Then it began to grow louder, and she smiled softly to herself when she recognized that it was a violin. She had been hoping the next song she heard would be for the violin.

Eurydice jerked in surprise and lost her concentration when the doors to her room opened and closed quietly. She couldn't see who it was, but she knew it was Ellsworth. She listened as he moved about the room, making barely a sound, as he got ready for bed. The only noise was caused by the things in his surroundings as he used them rather than from him directly: drawers being opened and closed, the distant sound of the water closet from where it was located in a corner of the bathing room. It was only those noises that let her know it wouldn't be long.

She lay stilly and barely breathed when he turned off the lamp and got into bed. She felt the mattress shift as he moved across it toward her, and she nearly jumped out of her skin when she felt him smooth a hand up her thigh to her hip. He placed his lips close to her ear to whisper, and Eurydice felt a tingle work its way up her spine at the warmth of his breath.

"Turn around. I want to kiss you."

Eurydice rolled over to face him, and he pulled her close to begin kissing her ravenously. Eurydice moaned at the back of her throat, partially in protest, partially in surprise, as he began to plunder her mouth with his tongue. There was no gradual progression from softness to this heated exploration as she had become accustomed to, but she withstood it and moved a hand up his chest to the side of his neck as she tried to follow him. He smoothed a hand across her hip to press her against him excitedly, and she could tell he was naked. She felt him begin to tug at the material of her shift, and he stopped kissing her and began to use both his hands to remove it.

"Take that off," he panted impatiently.

Eurydice slowly sat up and pulled the shift over her head, reaching out her arm to let it fall over the side of the bed onto the floor. She blushed when she saw the hungry expression on his face as he looked at her, and she had to try very hard not to reach up and cover herself. She gasped when he put a hand to the back of her head to bring her mouth to his and resume kissing her.

Eurydice felt as if she couldn't breathe as he continued his onslaught. He rolled over to place her beneath him, and she was panting for air when he left her lips to run his tongue down her neck to her breastbone before moving to the peak of one breast to worry the nipple with his teeth and tongue as he began to tease the other with his fingers. Eurydice moaned and raised her back from the bed, clutching at his shoulder with one hand while the other clenched in the hair at the back of his head.

He was almost feverish and frantic as he touched her, and Eurydice was overwhelmed by the unrestrained need. She was confused and uncertain, wondering where it had come from and what she was supposed to do with it. She was slowly beginning to feel a fluttering in her stomach, especially as he continued to play with her breasts, but she was dizzy from the manic pace of his lovemaking. She just felt he was going entirely too fast for her to catch up, and she didn't know how to tell him to wait.

He shifted his position as he continued to worry her breasts to settle more solidly between her thighs. She could feel his erection pressed against her, and Eurydice moaned as it rubbed against her button. Her hands fluttered over his shoulders in a caress, and she trembled as he smoothed a hand down her thigh to put her leg around his waist. He ran his lips up her neck, back to her mouth to kiss her hungrily, and then he thrust into her with a groan of satisfaction.

Eurydice tensed, and her eyes flew open. His mouth over hers muffled the sound of surprise and protest she made as she felt a searing pain between her legs. Her hands desperately clutched at his shoulders as she tried to make him stop, but Ellsworth continued to drive into her relentlessly. Eurydice was in agony, and she pushed at his shoulders and tried to maneuver her legs to make him get off her, but he didn't seem to realize she was trying to make him stop. Either that or he simply didn't care. When he moved a hand between them to begin teasing her button as he continued to do what felt like stabbing her with a knife, it only added insult to injury, and Eurydice whimpered and squeezed her eyes shut to keep herself from crying.

Ellsworth lifted his head to look at her, but Eurydice couldn't bring herself to look back. She bit her lip and tried to block out the sounds of pleasure he made, and she began to pray it would be over soon. She was in pain, and she felt used and ashamed.

"Oh, you feel so good," he sighed delightedly. "So hot...so wet."

He lowered his mouth to her neck to suck at the soft, sensitive skin excitedly, and Eurydice flinched as she felt him tense and begin to quiver with a soft moan of relief as he orgasmed. His movements slowly stopped as the last of it ebbed away, and Eurydice's chest was heaving as she breathed in and out quickly through her nose to keep herself from sobbing uncontrollably. Ellsworth nuzzled her neck adoringly before running his lips along her jaw to kiss her softly on the lips, completely oblivious to her distress.

Ellsworth finally got off of her, and Eurydice rolled over on her side facing away from him with a shuddering sigh, almost curling up in a ball. She ached physically and emotionally, and she didn't think she had ever felt so mishandled. She tensed nervously when she felt Ellsworth moving. He turned on his side to spoon behind her, placing an arm around her waist to pull her against him possessively and nestling his head onto the pillow near hers. Eurydice kept her eyes closed, and she began to cry silent tears that she couldn't stop from coming anymore.

Chapter Fourteen

Eurydice woke early the next morning. The sun was up, but she didn't think it had been for long. Ellsworth still remained sleeping close behind her, his arm draped loosely over her waist. She carefully eased herself off the bed and grabbed her dressing gown from the bench to put on, wrapping her arms around her waist as as she quickly headed for the water closet.

The pain between her legs had subsided to a dull ache, and as she sat on the bowl, she could see dried blood on the insides of her thighs. After she finished with the water closet, she went to run water into the tub. Using a flannel and water would be sufficient, but she just felt like she needed a bath.

She was in the water up to her chin with a distant, dazed expression when Agniezka hurried in. She first went to the water closet to vomit and relieve herself, and then she came to sit on the low stool at the edge of the tub.

"Why didn't you wake me to draw your bath?" scolded Agniezka.

"Because I am perfectly capable of doing it myself, and you need your rest," said Eurydice calmly. She watched as Agniezka quickly rose from the stool to go back to the water closet and vomit again. She gave her maid a sympathetic smile when she came back out. "I am fine in here alone. Go make yourself some tea to settle your stomach. By the time you get done with that and bring me some clothes, I'll be ready to get out."

"You're sure?" asked Agniezka uncertainly.

"Quite sure," said Eurydice dryly.

Agniezka started to leave the room, but she stopped in the doorway to look back. "How was—?"

"I don't want to talk about it right now," cut in Eurydice flatly, lowering her eyes. "Go get your tea," she said quietly.

Agniezka nodded unhappily and went to do as she was told. She had hoped things would go well, but to find Eurydice in the tub and hear her response, they obviously had not.

Eurydice continued to lounge in the tub, in no hurry to begin another day because at some point she would have to face Ellsworth.

There had to be something wrong with her. None of the women she knew who had been with men had ever mentioned the act being so painful. She didn't think it was some secret they kept to themselves, and it was obvious they wouldn't enjoy it so much if it were. She wasn't as well-read on such topics as Psyche and Pandora, but she had read a few things, none of which had ever mentioned it either. Everyone she knew seemed to take great pleasure from it, even her parents (which she tried not to dwell on too long). Ellsworth had unequivocally enjoyed last night, and she didn't think he had intentionally hurt her. Therefore, it had to be her.

When they were together on the ship, when he had touched her, she had experienced ecstasy. She suspected what she had felt then was the thing that made it so wonderful to everyone else, and she couldn't understand why she had been unable to feel that last night. She did realize it had been her first time, but none of her sisters had ever mentioned the intense pain and bleeding. At least Psyche would have warned her. Perhaps she was the prude Ellsworth had accused her of being. She only knew she couldn't bear to do it again.

And that put her into a quandary. She had promised Ellsworth she would provide him with an heir. There was only one way she could do that, and if she couldn't stomach doing it, she would break her word. She had never done that before. She realized rather dismally that she would have to tolerate it, at least occasionally, to fulfill her promise. She would have to be more observant about her cycle, but a bit of judicious planning would be all that was needed to reduce how often she'd have to suffer through it. Once she had provided him an heir and kept her side of the agreement, she would never have to do it again.

She heard small feet trundle across the floor of the bedroom and realized Freddie was awake. She hoped the noise didn't wake Ellsworth. She wasn't ready to face him yet. She knew Freddie was going to the inner courtyard to play, and she didn't doubt the younger Andreanopouli were already there. She was glad Freddie had playmates, and she was sure he was enjoying his stay at the palazzo much more than he would the ship in the lagoon.

Eurydice idly wondered how Psyche's search for another cabin boy was faring. She hadn't made any mention of it, but things at the palazzo had been far from settled since their arrival. Her sister would probably wait until they returned to Britain to hire one. Freddie would have no assistance this time out. Eurydice regretted that would be the case because he was so in need of it.

She waved her hands back and forth beneath the water and tilted her head against the edge of the tub with her eyes closed. The water was still deliciously hot, and it would be awhile before Agniezka returned to help her out. The tune she had heard in her head the night before returned as she sat in stillness. After she was dressed and had breakfast, she would begin to write it down.

≪ ≫

Ellsworth woke up when he heard the door close. He opened his eyes and realized Eurydice was no longer in the bed. There was still an indentation in the pillow where her head had rested, but the place where she had been was cold. She had apparently been gone for a while. He rolled over onto his back to yawn and stretch languidly and looked around the room. She was nowhere to be seen. He didn't think there was anyone else in the suite besides him.

He heard a soft tinkling noise as Eurydice's watch struck the hour, and he wondered what hour that was. The sun was shining outside the windows, but it wasn't shining directly in, so it had to at least still be morning. He wasn't upset Eurydice was not there, but he had hoped she would be. He had enjoyed last night, and he wouldn't mind an encore. He contentedly sighed with a half-smile. There would always be tonight, and the next, and the next, and the rest of their lives. There was no need to be greedy.

He threw the covers back to get out of bed, and his eyes widened in shock. There was dried blood on the sheet. There wasn't a copious amount of it, but there was enough that it couldn't be missed. It still had a bright red tinge to it rather than a dull brown, letting him know that it was fresh, definitely less than a day old. It couldn't have been caused from the night two weeks ago. He looked at the bandage on his leg and saw that it was still pristinely white. The wound there was healing well, so he hadn't really expected that to be the cause of the stains. Then he looked at his yard, and his heart skipped a beat. He felt a queasiness in the pit of his stomach and rubbed a hand over his face.

She was immaculate before you sullied her. Sheerness's words came back to him like a slap in the face. She had been untouched, and all the things he had thought about her were proven egregiously wrong by the bloodstain on the sheets. *You violated my daughter.* At the time, he had needed to clench his jaw to keep himself from disputing that, knowing Aberdare would have killed him with his bare hands, but now he knew that he had. She had never tried to correct him on the matter, either. The modesty and primness he had thought affected were genuine. He really had dishonored her, even before last night, simply by thinking and saying the things he had about her.

Ellsworth poured through his memories of last night then, and the sickness he felt only grew worse. He had never taken a virgin before, but he knew it required a certain amount of finesse and patience to be done correctly. He had exercised neither. He had made love to her on the assumption that she was well-acquainted with the act. He had not been gentle. He had not even been considerate. He had ploughed into her like a stag in rutting season.

He thought about Eurydice's actions the night before, and he broke into a cold sweat. She must have been in so much pain, and there was no question she had received no pleasure from it. He recognized now that she had tried to get him to stop, and he hadn't given her the chance to tell him. Sullied and violated her? Oh, yes, he was guilty of that. He had done little better than rape her, and that was probably what she thought about it, too.

Ellsworth rose from the bed to go to the bathing room. He would get dressed, and then he would go find her. He had to make amends somehow, beg her pardon at the very least. He could only hope she hadn't told her father what had happened. He had hurt her in so many ways Aberdare would gladly kill him if he found out. After a moment's thought, though, Ellsworth suspected she wouldn't. He was sure she would feel too embarrassed and ashamed.

He stopped short on his way out because the object of his quest was reclining in the bath. Her hair was loose and hanging outside the tub to nearly touch the floor, and she was relaxed in the water up to her neck. She appeared to be sound asleep. He had to wonder how long she had been there.

He slowly walked closer to the side of the tub, and despite himself, he began to peruse her body. She was magnificent. Her breasts were perfect—full and round and pert, slightly more than a handful and—he knew—with just the right amount of heft. Her ribs ended high to create a long, narrow waist only to flare out gently at her hips—baby-making hips. Although he couldn't see it because of her position, he knew her bottom was exquisitely rounded and firm and as soft to the touch as a baby's. She had beautiful long legs, much longer than would be expected for her height, and the shape of them was graceful from the exercise they received when she swam. They were also hairless, and Ellsworth had to wonder how she accomplished that. He didn't think she used a razor. Despite her innocence and modesty, her body was sinful, and she was all his.

Ellsworth looked down and cursed with a shake of his head when he saw that he was semi-hard. He went to a cabinet to retrieve a flannel and carefully dipped it into the water at the foot of the tub. He used it to wash himself off, and by the time he was finished he had managed to get his member back under control. He had just put the flannel into the laundry hamper when there was a startled squeaking noise in the doorway, and Agniezka averted her eyes and put a hand to the side of her face, her cheeks turning red in mortification.

"I am *so* sorry," she said abashedly before turning to leave.

The sound woke Eurydice, and when she realized he was in the room, she put up her arms to cover her breasts and shifted her legs to hide her ware. She turned her face away when she saw he was naked, and her cheeks began to turn a bright pink.

"Get out, please," she said quietly.

Her turning her head exposed the lovebite he had put on her neck, and he was filled with renewed remorse for what he had done.

"I'd like to talk to you once you are dressed," he said evenly.

"Only if *you* are," she muttered.

Ellsworth's lips twitched slightly with amusement, and he really could not fault her for her distaste. He was feeling a bit disgusted himself. He started to leave the room, but he paused to bend down and place a gentle kiss on her cheek.

"Please," he said softly, and then he left.

Eurydice put a hand to her cheek where his lips had been, and she blinked confusedly. That...she hadn't minded so much. Of course, she had always enjoyed his kisses...until last night, but it wasn't kissing him that had hurt.

She idly wondered what he wanted to talk about. She could only speculate, but she didn't want to argue. She couldn't think of anything she had done since the previous day that would have made him want to do that. She had been more than compliant and obedient...like a wife was expected to be. Their marriage had taken place, and their wedding night, and there would be no honeymoon. Eurydice hadn't expected one, but it obviously wouldn't be something they needed to discuss. Nothing came to mind after she thought about it for a few more minutes, and she eventually shrugged dismissively.

Agniezka soon returned to help her dry off and dress. As she slowly closed the fastenings at the back of Eurydice's dress, she cleared her throat.

"He's very well put-together, your husband," she said casually.

Eurydice frowned slightly. "I suppose so," she said dully.

She had never disputed that Ellsworth was attractive. Even now, after last night, she wouldn't argue the point. She suspected, though, the feature that had prompted Agniezka's comment was not his wavy, dark brown hair, pale blue-green eyes, strong jaw, or sensual lips. It wasn't even the sinewy muscle and commanding height or the way it was all composed like a living symphonic masterpiece. He was what Pandora had unabashedly used to describe her own husband: *well-hung.* Unfortunately, knowing that Pandora had no complaints about her own similarly-endowed spouse, Eurydice couldn't use that as the reason she had found last night so unpleasant. She was still left with the knowledge that there had to be something wrong with her.

"Let us go brush your hair," said Agniezka quietly once she had Eurydice's dress fastened.

Eurydice went to the dressing table in her room and sat down. She didn't see Ellsworth anywhere, but she wasn't concerned about it. She was actually relieved he wasn't in the room. Two of the house maids had come in to change the linen on the bed and other chores around the room. Agniezka had removed the cover from Casanova's cage and fed him, and the women would look at the cage with expressions of outrage and disgust as he would occasionally squawk something offensive. Eurydice was slowly learning to ignore him. They quickly finished their task and left the room, twittering to each other about the bird needing to have its neck wrung.

Eurydice watched in the mirror as Agniezka styled her hair, methodically braiding and twisting it up on her head. There was something meditative about this ritual for both of them, and Agniezka always did such wonderful work. When she saw the mark on her neck as Agniezka steadily pinned up her hair, Eurydice paled and looked instead back to Agniezka's face in the mirror, trying to ignore it. Her maid had noticed it, too, and once she was done with Eurydice's hair, she retrieved a small container of tinted maquillante to begin skillfully applying it to her neck. Eurydice's skin was so flawless the harmless, unleaded paint was rarely used other than to cover an occasional blemish when she was attending a social function. Agniezka had not missed Eurydice's reaction when she saw the mark, and she knew the younger girl thought it was much more embarrassing than a pimple.

"Do you…do you want to talk about things?" asked Agniezka hesitantly.

Eurydice looked at her maid in the mirror pensively. She was uncomfortable discussing the subject, but she needed *someone* to explain things to her. She knew Psyche and Pandora, even Arachne, discussed things like sex and men, pregnancy and childbirth with Maiyin and their mother's maid, Lucia. Eurydice had never been interested in knowing. She knew what the different body parts were and how they went together and what happened when they did, but most of it mystified her.

"The first time…," began Eurydice nervously. "The first time you were with Sergei, did you enjoy it?"

Agniezka smiled slightly. "I would have to say that I did."

"Was it the first time you ever did…that?"

"Of course. I married him when I was fifteen, almost sixteen…not so very young for Russia. It was a little uncomfortable at first because I had to get used to him being there, but after that…." Agniezka shrugged. "Things did not become unpleasant until later."

"And what about with Felton?"

Agniezka gave her a half-smile. "I've always enjoyed it with Simon."

"The first time, did you bleed at all?"

"Not at all," said Agniezka. She frowned slightly as she looked at Eurydice. "You did?"

Eurydice nodded discomfittedly.

Agniezka put her hands on Eurydice's shoulders and squeezed them soothingly. "Well, you are getting ready to start your courses. Maybe that's what caused it."

Eurydice nodded again, but Agniezka's words didn't provide her any comfort. There had to be something wrong with her. Agniezka had said discomfort for a few seconds; hers had been from the first second to the last, and it had really been at a fairly consistent level the entire time. She had to be frigid. It was the only thing she could think of to explain it. Maybe the bleeding could be accounted for by her courses, but the pain could not…at least, she didn't think it could. She didn't see how it possibly could.

A maid came in to bring their breakfast to the sitting room, and Eurydice noticed she was back to her usual friendliness and smiles. Eurydice supposed now that she had been made an "honest" woman, all was forgiven. It was a good thing the maids were unaware Agniezka was with child by a man who wasn't her husband. They would be merciless.

Ellsworth and Freddie were both apparently taking breakfast in the great hall since neither came in to join them. It didn't surprise Eurydice. Freddie was always playing with the girls, so it made perfect sense he would eat breakfast with them, too—less interruption to playtime that way. As for Ellsworth, she didn't care if he ate breakfast or not…or where he ate it.

Once Eurydice finished her meal, she had delayed long enough on speaking to her husband. She left Agniezka knitting baby clothes in the sitting room and went to the great hall. No one was there. She went to the inner courtyard, but only the children were there playing with Cupid and a ball. They all greeted her, but she didn't stay. She went back to the first floor and stood in the middle of the great hall with her hands on her hips as she tried to decide where Ellsworth would be. She would not do a room-to-room search. She shrugged and went back to her rooms to begin composing the song she was hearing. If it was something important, he would come find her.

She was still there composing when the maid brought her dinner, with still no sign of Ellsworth. Psyche came in with a huge smile not much later.

"Hallo," she cooed brightly.

Eurydice looked at her with a raised eyebrow. "You are very cheerful."

"I think I may have found a cabin boy."

"When have you had time?" asked Eurydice dryly.

Psyche chuckled. "Well, I don't know that I've actually found one yet. Papà happened to mention there was an orphan asylum not far from here."

"An orphan? Really?" said Eurydice doubtfully.

"I just thought: if I'm going to acquire one here rather than waiting until I returned to Britain, an orphan would be the only solution. I couldn't imagine taking him away from his family, and it would be highly inconvenient to return him here and collect him next time we happen through, don't you think?"

"I suppose," said Eurydice evenly.

"This way, he will learn a trade, and he will be cared for, and Sebastian pays his cabin boy."

"He does?" asked Eurydice with some surprise. She couldn't think of anyone else who did.

"Not very much, but yes, Freddie is paid."

"Hmm," said Eurydice speculatively. "I wish you luck."

"I want you to come with me."

"Now?" blurted Eurydice, looking at her composition. She had transcribed most of what she had heard so far, so she would have to wait until more came to her, but she had thought to play it through.

"Yes, I don't want to go by myself, and you are as good at judging character as I am—better, so I would like your opinion."

"But Ellsworth said he wanted to speak with me."

Psyche waved a hand through the air dismissively. "Eh, he's been in the study with Papà, Nikos, and Sebastian for an hour or two now. Men and politics. I wouldn't be surprised if they remain there till supper."

Eurydice thought about it for a moment. Agniezka was visiting with Felton in the rear courtyard. She really had gone as far as she could with her piece, and if Ellsworth was otherwise engaged….

"All right, I'll come with you. Let me get my things."

Psyche clapped gleefully, and she followed Eurydice out of the sitting room into the bedroom as she grabbed a bonnet, shawl, and gloves. She also took a reticule with some money. She didn't think she would need it, but it was always good to have it just in case. Once she had her things, she went with Psyche to her own rooms to get her things as well, minus a shawl. They went to the loggia on the first floor and took the stairs down to the rear courtyard. Agniezka was there, sitting on a bench with Felton.

"I'll be back shortly," Eurydice told her. "Psyche is going to inquire about a cabin boy."

"Good luck," said Agniezka with a smile.

Psyche and Eurydice went through the gate at the back wall and went a short distance to the left before turning right onto another street. They were only on it for a short distance before Psyche turned them to the right again. Eurydice frowned slightly.

"Do you know where you are going?"

"Of course, I do," said Psyche with a grin. "The way this city was built, it is a bit like a maze. Sometimes you have to go backwards to go forwards. Trust me. I know where I'm going."

"Hunh," said Eurydice noncommittally.

Psyche linked their elbows together as they strolled, and Eurydice was already finding the excursion interesting. She did like the buildings in the city. They walked across a bridge, and Eurydice thought it was taking them over the canal that went beside their palazzo. She certainly hoped her sister knew where she was going, because Eurydice was becoming completely lost.

"So, you haven't said how it was last night," said Psyche conversationally.

"It's done," said Eurydice dully.

"You were all the talk among the maids."

"I was? Why? Because Ellsworth made an *honest* woman out of me?" she asked darkly.

Psyche chuckled. "No, because of the sheets."

Eurydice frowned. "What about them?"

"They had blood on them."

Eurydice colored. "Oh, I didn't realize…." She supposed it would only stand to reason. "Why would that make the maids talk, other than complaining about how hard they will be to clean?"

"It proved you were a virgin, so to them, your honor has been exonerated."

Eurydice looked at her sister with a frown. There were several things she noticed. The first was that the maids seemed to be happy she had stained the sheets they would have to clean. Actually, they were probably ruined, but it was work for the maids nonetheless. The second was that her bleeding on them somehow indicated to the women she had been intact. The third was that this didn't worry or surprise Psyche at all. She scratched her forehead thoughtfully.

"How does my bleeding prove anything?"

Psyche stopped to look at her in surprise. "Do you not realize?"

"No," said Eurydice dully. "Did you bleed the first time you were with Sheerness?"

"No, but it's to be expected," said Psyche as they began to walk again.

"Why is it expected you wouldn't, but I would? And you still haven't explained to me *why* the maids are so pleased."

Psyche groaned. "I can't believe you don't know. Where have you been?"

Eurydice narrowed her eyes at her sister. She remained quiet because she was hopeful at least *something* was going to be explained to her.

"The hymen is a membrane, but it isn't entirely whole. It lines the edges so that there is an opening for your courses and other things to drain. Sometimes that opening is large; sometimes it can be small. The point is, it's a membrane, which means it's thin and fragile, and therefore can be easily damaged...by things like riding astride and other physical activity."

"Oh," said Eurydice dully. Yes, Psyche was far more physical than she was. She rarely rode Amati, and she always rode aside, like a proper lady.

"It can also be damaged by the insertion of things," said Psyche evenly. "You use a belt and cloth, which for the life of me I cannot understand, when a cotton wool tampion is so much cleaner and simpler."

Eurydice looked at her sheepishly. "I just...it never...."

"I have brought some with me, and you must try them." She sighed deeply. "I don't think I'm going to need them for a while." She stopped to look at Eurydice anxiously. "You *swear* nothing bad will happen if I am pregnant?"

"You are, aren't you?" asked Eurydice knowingly with a slight smile.

"I don't know," said Psyche glumly. "It's too early to say. I am several days late, but not so very. Although, I never have been before...always right on schedule, Pandora and I both." Eurydice decided not to mention it was the same for her as well. Even Persephone and Arachne could mark the calendar by their courses. "I haven't even told Sebastian yet because I'm not sure," continued Psyche, "but it seems very likely. If the first arrives without my flowers arriving as well, or I begin cascading everywhere like Agniezka, I think it will be safe to say that I am."

Eurydice kissed her cheek. "I'm very happy for you," she said softly, "and yes, I do swear nothing bad will happen." Psyche brightened, and Eurydice patted her arm as they began to walk again. "So, continue with my biology lesson, please," she said with a wry smile.

"Well, there's not much more to tell. As I said, it's a membrane, easily damaged and all that. When you are *intact*, that's exactly what it means. So, when you are with a man for the first time, provided you've not done anything else to cause it, that tears it—pfft!—no longer intact, and because it tears it, depending on the thickness of the membrane, how large it is, et cetera, it can bleed, and that's it."

Eurydice felt her heart fluttering with relief to have at least some of what troubled her so much explained so easily.

"There used to be a time, not so very long ago, when it was customary and traditional to hang the bed sheets out the window after the wedding night," said Psyche amusedly, "to display that the bride had been pure. Of course, for those who weren't so very, there was always a bit of animal blood to be readily found." She gave Eurydice a teasing grin. "Just be glad that doesn't go on anymore."

"Too right," chortled Eurydice. Her face grew serious after a moment. "Would that tearing bit...would that hurt, do you think?" she asked as nonchalantly as possible.

Psyche shrugged. "Oh, I wouldn't imagine so. It's very thin, so while it might hurt for a brief moment, that would be the extent of it."

"Oh," said Eurydice dully.

"Here we are," said Psyche brightly, stopping to look up at a building.

"Are you sure?" asked Eurydice doubtfully. Psyche rolled her eyes and shook her head before tugging on Eurydice's arm. Her father had given her excellent directions.

They walked into the *portego* and were met by a Dominican friar. Psyche explained why she had come, and his face brightened. Before he took them to see the children, he asked if Psyche would let the boy continue to practice his faith. She smiled amusedly. Considering her family employed Hindus, Muslims, Buddhists, Shintos, and a host of other faiths, Catholics were rather pedestrian. Even though she was no longer at home, she had no bias toward someone practicing the religion of his choosing. It wouldn't be a problem.

He took them to a large room on the first floor, where there were several children, all boys, milling about. He excused himself for a moment, but soon returned with a boy, gently guiding him by the shoulder toward Psyche and Eurydice. The boy looked about twelve years old, with dark hair and eyes and a slight frame. He looked at the sisters shyly and fidgeted with his hands in front of him. Psyche looked down at him with a kind smile.

"What is your name?" she asked gently.

"Jacopo, *signora,*" he said quietly.

"I understand you speak English."

"Yes, *signora,* I speak the English," he said, using the language.

"Has the father told you why I am here?"

"Yes, *signora.* Father Anselmo say that you are looking for a boy to work on a ship and to go to live in the *Inghilterra.*"

"Would you like that? You would be paid; you would learn a trade; and when you are not at sea, you would be allowed to go to school."

"That sounds very nice, *signora,* but I cannot go," said Jacopo sadly.

"Can you tell me why?" asked Psyche gently after exchanging a glance with Eurydice.

Jacopo turned slightly and pointed to two other boys standing not far away. One appeared to be about ten, the other eight. Eurydice could immediately see the family resemblance.

"Those two, they are my brothers, Milo and Ambrosi. They are hard workers, but they no speak the English so well. We have no one else but us, and as much as I would like to do what you say, I cannot leave them behind."

Psyche and Eurydice looked at each other questioningly and turned away slightly to talk in private.

"Well?" asked Psyche quietly.

"The choice is entirely yours," said Eurydice evenly, "but we can't separate that boy from his only family. He does seem to be very sweet and good-natured, though."

"I agree," said Psyche thoughtfully.

They turned back to face Jacopo, and Psyche smiled.

"I believe it is said many hands make light work. Your brothers may come as well. Would that suit?" she queried.

Jacopo's face brightened, and he turned to wave at his brothers for them to come over. Father Anselmo was happy he had found a home for the three boys. They had been at the asylum for more than three years, and he had begun to despair that they would not leave. There would have always been a place for them in service to the Church, but now they had a choice. Psyche and Eurydice both made very generous donations to the asylum, and after completing a little paperwork, they left with the three boys hurrying along behind them carrying the few possessions they had among them: a Bible, a small picture of their mother, and outer coats. The only clothes they had were those on their backs.

Not far from the asylum, they found a store selling secondhand clothing. It took some searching, but they were able to find more clothes for the boys to wear that weren't too worn and of the right size. By the time they left, the boys were each carrying packages that contained two changes of clothing for them. After examining their shoes, Psyche decided they would need new ones before the *Medea* sailed, but there would be time to locate those soon enough.

When they got back to the palazzo, Eurydice took the stairs to the second floor and entered her rooms from the loggia. Psyche was going to take the boys to Sheerness to introduce him to his new employees, and then she would introduce them to Freddie. The sun was on its way to setting, and it wouldn't be long before it was time for supper. Eurydice hoped she might have enough time before that to play what she had written down of her composition. She was sure that she would, provided she didn't encounter any massive errors in her transcription. That had never happened before.

Agniezka was taking a nap in her room, and Eurydice decided not to wake her. If she didn't wake on her own by time for supper, then Eurydice would do it. She was on her way to the sitting room to retrieve her composition when the doors from the hall opened, and Ellsworth came in. He did not look pleased.

"I told you I wanted to talk to you," he said shortly.

"Yes, you did, and I went looking for you and couldn't find you. Then I spent several hours here waiting for you to come find me, which you did not. I got tired of waiting," she said simply.

He walked closer to her, his expression softening slightly. "Can we talk now?" he asked evenly.

"Of course," said Eurydice with a slight nod. She folded her arms in front of her, holding her elbows. Ellsworth thought it looked like a protective gesture.

"Why didn't you tell me you had not been with a man?"

Eurydice blinked at his bluntness. Of all the things she had thought he might wish to discuss, that was not among them. She blushed slightly and lifted her chin.

"You didn't ask."

"You should have told me," he said flatly.

Eurydice narrowed her eyes at him. "Mr. Ellsworth, why would I need to *tell* you that? I am—or was—an unmarried woman, raised to comport myself modestly and according to propriety. That I had not been with a man should have been something that needed no clarification. The only time I have ever behaved improperly was with you," she said stiffly.

Ellsworth blanched slightly. She was right. He had assumed too much. He had taken things as they appeared to be, when he should have known that things weren't always what they seemed. If he'd had any question, he should have asked her. Otherwise, he should never have assumed she was not a virgin.

"Where were you going when you left your cabin on the *Medea*?" he finally asked.

Eurydice found this turn in what seemed to be another direction confusing.

"To sleep in the pantry. I was unable to sleep well in my cabin, so I went there for a few hours."

"Why couldn't you sleep in your cabin?"

Eurydice colored and cut her eyes away for a moment before she looked back.

"There were certain noises aboard the ship at night that kept me awake. I found I didn't hear them when I slept in the pantry."

Ellsworth looked at her questioningly for a moment, but he then realized what the *noises* had been. Yes, he could see where that might have bothered her enough that she would want to sleep elsewhere. He could recall his own feelings about the noises he had heard from the captain's cabin. Chrissoula and Stockbridge had been directly beside her. Had he been in the same predicament, he would have been sleeping on the deck.

"Why was Felton in your room here?"

Eurydice sighed tiredly, now understanding why he was asking the questions he did. "He came to see me on a personal matter. I talked with him in my sitting room. The doors to my suite and the door to the sitting room were open the entire time. He sat on the settee, and I sat in a chair."

"What sort of personal matter?"

"I'm sorry, I am not at liberty to tell you that. It is a *personal* matter."

Ellsworth frowned. "You said you would be honest with me."

"I am being entirely honest. If you would like to know what we discussed, then I suggest you ask Felton. I leave it for him to tell you. I am *not* at liberty to say," she said coldly.

Ellsworth tilted his head, relenting. He rubbed a hand across his jaw thoughtfully as he tried to choose his next words.

"About last night…it wasn't quite what it was supposed to be," he said slowly.

Eurydice paled. "No, it wasn't," she said hollowly. "I know I promised I would provide you with an heir, but I cannot do…*that*, even though I know it's the only way the other will happen. I have never broken my word, so I will let you know when the time is best for me to successfully conceive."

"I see," said Ellsworth quietly, and he felt a knot forming in his stomach.

She rubbed a hand across her forehead. "I know that a man has needs, but I don't think I can attend to yours," she said neutrally. "So," she sighed, "if you want to take a mistress to see they are addressed, you will find that I won't complain," she finished quietly.

Ellsworth looked at her with an unreadable expression. She hoped he wouldn't say she had failed to uphold their agreement. She hadn't technically done that. She still intended to give him a son. She thought she was trying to comply as best she could and be as undemanding as possible in the process.

But Ellsworth wasn't angry. Not with her. This was his fault. He had damaged her. She thought there was something wrong with *her*. He could tell. She hadn't felt that way before last night. He knew. He felt so unbelievably ashamed of what he had done. He would have to fix it…somehow, but he wasn't sure how he would be able to do that.

"We will still share a room and a bed," said Ellsworth evenly.

"If you like," said Eurydice calmly. She wanted to say no, but if he wasn't going to argue about the rest, she would tolerate it.

Ellsworth only nodded stoically and turned to leave the room. As long as he could keep her in the same bed, then maybe he could find a way to repair this. Now all he would have to do is figure out how he was going to do that without making things even worse.

He went to the rear courtyard to have a moment of peace to himself before supper—to think. He preferred the inner courtyard, but the children were often there. Even though he liked children, he wanted to be alone. He'd scarcely had any time alone since he woke up that morning, and he was craving it.

Shortly after breakfast he met with Sheerness to offer him an apology. He didn't provide specific reasons for the change in his opinion of his new wife, but Sheerness didn't need him to; he'd heard about the sheets. Sheerness accepted the apology, but he couldn't quite forget everything. He wanted to. He had liked Ellsworth before this debacle, but he wasn't happy that Eurydice had needed to prove she was untouched before Ellsworth would believe it.

After Ellsworth met with Sheerness, Aberdare met with him privately and demanded an accounting of what had happened to Signor Merletto. Ellsworth wasn't entirely sure. He had made arrangements to meet with the man, but he was dead when Ellsworth arrived. What's more, the authorities were there within seconds of Ellsworth's arrival, and he had been unable to do any searching for clues that might tell them who the real culprit was. It didn't take much deduction on their part for Ellsworth and Aberdare to realize the meeting had been a trap, which meant someone knew what Ellsworth was and was determined to stop him, either by death or imprisonment. As for who that was, considering the anonymity of everyone who shared his occupation, it would take some effort to discover.

When he had finished his meeting with Aberdare, they had met Nikos and Sheerness in the great hall, and that had led to a discussion of the situation with the Ottomans and Greece that, to Ellsworth, had seemed to last an eternity. All he had really wanted to do was find Eurydice and talk to her, only to discover once he had the chance that she had gone out with her sister.

Their conversation really wasn't any more than he should have expected. All day, he had hoped things weren't so bad, but they were, and he had been fooling himself to think anything else. He had never intended to hurt her, not by anything he had ever done, but he had been doing his job too long. He had forgotten there were still pure, still breakable people—particularly women—in the world. Perhaps he may have peripherally known they were there, but he had forgotten he might come into contact with them. He had never thought someone like that would care for him.

He had no delusions that Eurydice loved him, but he did believe she cared for him in some fashion. He didn't think she would have done what she did to save him otherwise, but he also realized he had probably ruined his chances of it growing into something more by what had happened last night, not if he couldn't fix it. He knew she already didn't trust him, and he had made it all the more difficult for that to change.

Perhaps he should just accept he was not meant to return to a normal life, that he wasn't meant to have the things everyone else took for granted: honesty, happiness, love. In his world, those were not guaranteed, and perhaps he had lost his right to expect them. There had been so many things he had done because of his job, bad things that, despite his doing them for the right reasons, had left their mark on him. Perhaps after all this time he no longer *deserved* to have the things everyone else took for granted.

And he could not seem to quit. Just when he thought he would be able to leave it all behind, there was always one more thing, one more mission. Perhaps it was because he was so good at what he did, but no one wanted him to quit, not even himself, if he were to be honest. He had begun to thrive on it, and for him, it wasn't that he was making a difference for the greater good. For him, it was the danger and uncertainty. He had become addicted to it, no matter what he would say to the contrary if asked, and Aberdare *had* asked him.

Aberdare, his mentor and now his father-in-law, was the only one in the game who was not enthusiastically encouraging him to stay at it. He didn't refuse to let Ellsworth work. He didn't ask him whether he should think about quitting, but Ellsworth had noticed a certain hesitation before he assigned a new task. Sometimes Ellsworth thought the only reason Aberdare didn't tell him to quit outright was that he knew there was no one better. He had trained his protégé too well. But now that Ellsworth was married to Eurydice, both men knew it was time for it to end. Even if it were still unspoken, it was understood. Aberdare couldn't bear the thought of possibly making his daughter a widow, and Ellsworth was ready to quit.

Ellsworth shook his head and looked around. Twilight had come while he sat thinking, and he realized it was time for supper. He felt calmer after his time to himself, and even if nothing had been resolved, he had a clearer idea of what needed to happen. He had only been married one day, and Eurydice had made his already complicated existence become almost unbearably so. She had no idea.

He looked up at the back of the palazzo as he walked toward the stairs. The curtains were drawn on the windows and doors of the suite he shared with Eurydice, but someone was opening a few of them, and the lamps had been lit. He could hear the muted sound of a violin, and when he looked to the windows of the sitting room, he could see Eurydice playing. He couldn't clearly hear the tune, but he didn't think it was anything he recognized. She had a studious frown as she played, and he suspected it was a new composition. He paused for a moment at the bottom of the stairs to listen and decided he liked it.

She was a musical genius, and she deserved to be heard as more than just a bit of drawing room entertainment. She was much more than that. While he knew she wanted to find a maestro in Vienna (which he didn't think she needed), he had no notion of what she intended to do once she felt she had learned enough. He couldn't imagine she would be studying and practicing so much with no intention of doing anything with it. As he continued up the stairs, he wondered if she would be willing to perform for the public. Society did frown on things like that, but in her case they would make an exception. To hide a talent like that from the world bordered on the criminal. He could think of at least one or two people who would agree with him.

He went to the doors of their suite and went in. Agniezka was doing things around the bedroom, putting the cover over the bird cage and organizing a few odds and ends. She smiled slightly when she saw him, but she continued with what she was doing without speaking. He knew the relationship she had with Eurydice was more than just that of mistress and maid. He knew this because Agniezka had far more privilege than a typical lady's maid would have. A lady's maid didn't share meals with her employer, not even when they were on holiday. They were also very familiar with each other. His own mother's maid didn't speak to her the way Agniezka talked to Eurydice. She would have been dismissed a long time ago if she had even tried.

He went to the sitting room to listen to Eurydice play for a little while before supper, but when she became aware he was there, she stopped.

"Don't stop on my account, please," he said with a half-smile when she looked at him with mild annoyance. "Is that new?"

"Yes, it is," she said flatly as she started to put the sheets away. "It's not finished. I don't allow anyone to hear a piece until it's finished."

"Oh," said Ellsworth, his lips twitching with amusement. He started to tell her it was impossible to keep anyone from hearing it but thought it best to remain silent. "Would you play something else then? We have a little time before supper."

Eurydice blinked. She wasn't sure she wanted to play for Ellsworth, but she did want to keep playing her violin.

"If you'd like," she said finally. "Any preference?"

"Surprise me," he said mildly as he took a seat on the couch.

Eurydice shrugged. She raised the violin to begin playing a piece by Bach. She wouldn't have time to play all of it, but she thought she could get through the first movement. She didn't look at Ellsworth while she played, and she tried to forget he was even in the room. As she played, to her surprise, she found she didn't mind so much that he was there. She waited for the nervousness she usually felt when she played in front of strangers, but it never came. It was the oddest thing.

She stopped once she reached the end of the movement, and then she looked at Ellsworth with a puzzled frown. He sat relaxed against the back of the couch with his eyes closed, a slight smile on his lips. When he realized she wasn't going to play any more, he opened his eyes and the smile widened.

"Outstanding," he said with quiet admiration.

Eurydice blushed with pleasure and embarrassment at the compliment, and she turned to put away her violin. They would be late if she didn't hurry.

"Thank you," she said evenly. She wasn't sure if he was trying to flatter her, but she decided to take it for what it seemed.

Agniezka had already gone when they entered the bedroom. Ellsworth offered Eurydice his arm to go to the great hall, and she took it gingerly.

"Have you ever played with accompaniment?" he asked casually as they walked down the hall toward the stairs.

"Dorian has played piano with me on occasion, but if you mean anything else, such as an orchestra or even a chamber ensemble, the answer would have to be no. Most of my sisters are not musically inclined, except for Arachne. She has a wonderful contralto, which she doesn't like to use very often." Ellsworth smiled slightly. "Why do you ask?"

"Just curious."

"I've composed pieces with accompaniment, and I've even written a few symphonies, but I can't say they're any good," she supplied conversationally.

"Why not?"

"Because I've never heard them played. I've played the individual parts, and they seem passable separately, but I can't say how they are all put together."

"Hmm," said Ellsworth thoughtfully.

Eurydice looked up at him with slight bemusement. She had the impression he was trying to gauge how dedicated she was to her art, and she had to wonder why. He had said he wouldn't interfere, and he seemed to like her playing, but his curiosity made her uncomfortable.

The children were in the great hall when they arrived, but they were about to leave for the nursery, where they would be fed their own supper before bathing and bedtime. She was pleased Freddie appeared to be getting on well with Jacopo, Milo, and Ambrosi. Actually, they were getting on splendidly. When Freddie saw Eurydice, he ran over to her with a happy smile.

"Thank you for finding the Geniseos!"

Eurydice smiled amusedly. "It was entirely my sister's doing," she said dryly.

"Now that they're here, I'll be moving to the nursery. I don't think I'll mind it so much now."

"If you're sure you want to," said Eurydice cautiously. She didn't want him to feel like she couldn't wait for him to go before he was ready.

"Oh, yes, ma'am," averred Freddie. "Milo said he would teach me how to speak Italian," he said proudly.

"All right," said Eurydice kindly. "What about your things?"

"Agniezka has already taken them up for me."

"Well, if you change your mind, the room will still be there."

Freddie grinned. "Yes, ma'am."

Eurydice watched after him for a moment when he went back to the three brothers and the Andreanopouli. She didn't think there was going to be any problem with them getting along in the same room. Eurydice only hoped there was room enough. There would still have to be places for Ellsworth's nieces and nephew when they arrived, too. She doubted the palazzo had seen so many residents in quite a long time, but there would still be room for several more if necessary; the rooms on the top floor were still unused.

Psyche walked over to them then, watching after the children as they followed Chrissoula and Ioanna out of the room.

"So, does Sheerness like the new cabin boys?" asked Eurydice mildly.

Psyche's expression changed to mild annoyance. "He will," she said determinedly.

Eurydice frowned. "How could he not? Those are very nice boys."

"It's not the boys themselves he's taken exception to; it's that I acquired *three* of them."

"He'll come around," said Eurydice sagely. "Once he sees how hard they work and the improvement in keeping the ship in order, he'll think it was his idea all along."

"Yes, I know, but he wasn't very happy. He was most disagreeable." Eurydice watched in alarm as Psyche's face crumpled as she tried to keep herself from crying.

"Oh, there," said Eurydice uncomfortably, patting her sister's shoulder. "It can't be so bad as all that. Would you like me to speak with him?"

"No," squeaked Psyche. "I don't know why I'm so upset. I really shouldn't be." She took a deep breath in an effort to calm herself. "I just can't seem to help myself these days. Today has been particularly trying for me."

Eurydice looked at her with dawning recognition. To her, the cause of her sister's distress was obvious. She tried not to laugh because it would only upset Psyche all the more. It was one of the few things she had read about, and seeing her sister being taken by it was somewhat comical. She was even worse than she had been when she was separated from Sheerness before they were married. She took Psyche aside to whisper in her ear, and Psyche's eyes grew round before her features brightened happily. She looked at Eurydice.

"Are you sure?" she asked hopefully.

"I can't guarantee it. You could always send a letter to Pandora if you wanted to wait that long, but you should ask Ioanna, or even Agniezka would probably know."

"Oh, I feel so much better now," sighed Psyche with relief.

Eurydice smiled amusedly. "For now," she said dryly.

Psyche chuckled and kissed Eurydice's cheek before walking over to Sheerness to link her arm through his and give it a gentle squeeze. He looked at her suspiciously as he continued his conversation with her father, but he didn't say anything. He thought they were supposed to still be angry at each other because of her indulgence in cabin boys. Eurydice clasped her hands behind her back as she watched them.

"What was that about?" asked Ellsworth curiously.

"Oh, nothing," said Eurydice, shuttering her features.

"She seemed a bit…I don't know…hysterical," he persisted.

"It's nothing," repeated Eurydice flatly.

Ellsworth compressed his lips in irritation. Despite saying she would be honest, she was keeping far too many secrets: the private matter with Felton and now this with her sister. The only reason he didn't pursue it was that he was keeping far too many secrets of his own, and she had not pressed him for any answers on those. He finally inclined his head in acceptance.

Supper proved to be an agreeable event, despite everything that had happened recently. While it may not have been lively, everyone was at least polite, and there was no lull in conversation. When the meal was done, the women excused themselves and went to the inner courtyard while the men stayed behind to have tobacco and port.

Eurydice wasn't sure if any of the men actually smoked. Her father and Sheerness didn't, and she was fairly sure Nikos didn't either. She couldn't say whether Stockbridge or Ellsworth did. Stockbridge didn't strike her as the type. She had no notion of whether Ellsworth was the type or not.

She thought it was strange that she wouldn't know something like that about her own husband. Yet even as it was peculiar she didn't know that about

Ellsworth, there were so many other things she also didn't know about him. There were things she knew about him that she probably shouldn't, but little things, like whether or not he smoked, his favorite color, what he liked to eat—things that might actually be worth knowing—she was clueless.

Psyche spoke to Ioanna while they were in the courtyard, and Eurydice could see from her excited reaction that Ioanna had confirmed what Eurydice had told her. Eurydice had never been in any doubt. Psyche was pregnant, and Eurydice expected she would deliver around the end of April. Not quite her due date, but close enough. Her delivering early wouldn't be caused by anything bad, just as she had swore to Psyche, but she was in for a bit of a shock when the time came. She could have hinted and told Psyche not to make any wagers on numbers with Pandora, but Eurydice didn't want to spoil the surprise.

Eurydice didn't wait for the men to rejoin them. She had wanted to say good night to her father, but she would talk to him tomorrow. She was actually very tired, and Agniezka was as well. She said good night to everyone, and the two of them went upstairs. She didn't feel like she needed a bath after having one that morning, but she washed her face and brushed her teeth after Agniezka helped her dress and braided her hair.

She wasn't able to fall asleep once she got into bed. She was wondering what was going to happen once Ellsworth came. He had agreed to what she said, but she couldn't be sure he meant it. She only knew she couldn't go through what she had gone through last night again so soon. She also knew she couldn't stop him if he wanted to, but she could make it very difficult. If he went that route, as embarrassing as it would be, she would tell her father, and Ellsworth would have to answer to him. Eurydice somehow didn't think Ellsworth would want to do that. She would have to wait and see.

She heard him when he came in, and she saw him when he did because she was lying on her side facing the door. The lamps on both sides of the bed were lit because she hadn't thought to turn hers down for the night. She closed her eyes and pretended to be asleep when he glanced in her direction, but she wasn't sure she was convincing. She was again struck by how quiet he was, and despite herself, she opened her eyes to see what he was doing.

He was undressed except for his pants, and she watched as he walked across the floor to the bathing room. If she hadn't seen him moving, she wouldn't have even realized he was there or that he was walking. It was uncanny, and until last night, she had never noticed. And it wasn't as if he were moving about with the intention of being so quiet. It seemed to be something he did unconsciously, as if it were second nature, and he was very graceful about it. It was again something—like his feat with the gondola—that took special talent. People did not naturally move that quietly.

She heard the sound of the water closet, and then she heard a few other noises as he washed his face and brushed his teeth before he came back into the room. She thought he was going to take a bath, but she realized it would be more practical for him to wait to do that in the morning. She narrowed her eyes to just slits, until it seemed they were closed, but she could still see what he was doing. She watched as he removed his pants and took them to the nearby chiffonier to put away. She started to close her eyes, but curiosity made her keep them open.

She supposed Agniezka was right. He was well put-together, and it wasn't the part of his anatomy that had drawn her maid's attention that made Eurydice realize it. She actually tried to avoid looking at that particular item because of what had happened the night before. As odd as it was, she found she liked the tattoo on his back; it somehow seemed to complete the "composition." She found it fascinating, and she absently wondered if she could feel the places where the colors changed from one to another or if it would be smooth. It would be interesting to find out, but she wasn't going to make a special effort. She didn't think that would be wise.

After Ellsworth put away his pants, he walked around to the side of the bed behind her and turned off her lamp. She was actually glad he had done that. Then he went to the other side, turned off the lamp and got into bed. Eurydice tensed and held her breath when he moved closer to her on the mattress. Then she felt him gently pull her toward him, as if he didn't want to wake her, resting her head onto his chest and cradling her against his side. She frowned slightly, but it seemed harmless enough. He kissed the top of her head and smoothed his hand down her back to her thigh to drape it across his. Then she heard him yawn and sigh tiredly.

It was not an uncomfortable position. She could hear the slow beat of his heart beneath her ear, and it soon began to lull her to sleep when she realized that was the extent of what he intended to do and let herself relax. As she drifted off, she unconsciously snuggled closer and smoothed her hand down his side to rest it at his hip. It felt like a natural place for it to be. Actually, being held close against him like that seemed like the most natural place to be, despite everything that had happened, and she was soon sound asleep.

Ellsworth knew she wasn't asleep when he came in the room, but he hadn't wanted to let her know that. He wanted to let her become accustomed to him, to become comfortable with his being there at her own pace, helped along by nudges from him to guide her in the right direction. It was going to be a slow process, but if he rushed it, it might put him right back to where he began. He had the patience to take his time, but he didn't have the patience to start over again. It was going to take all he had to see it done right the first time, and he wanted to do it right. She deserved that.

She had said she would let him know when the time was best for her to conceive. He didn't know when that would be, but he wasn't sure she would be ready by then. It wasn't important to him for them to have a child right away. It would be best for them to wait until he had completed this one last assignment before that happened. There was too much that could go wrong, and he didn't think he could handle one more difficulty. He didn't know how long it would take—any of it, but he needed to have things less complicated before he added something new.

He thought this entire enterprise might be fun in the long run, and he knew what it was about it that made him feel that way. There was going to be a certain degree of difficulty, finesse, and danger involved, and those were all things that made him like his job so much. And the reward? He had the feeling the reward was going to be worth the wait.

Chapter Fifteen

Eurydice jerked awake confusedly. For a moment, she wasn't sure where she was, but she quickly remembered she was in bed with Ellsworth when she heard him muttering unintelligibly. She lifted her head to look at him, seeing he was still asleep. He was dreaming about something, and whatever it was didn't seem to be pleasant. He wasn't thrashing about, but Eurydice would never get back to sleep with him muttering like that.

It was their third night of being married, but this was the first time he had talked in his sleep, as far as she knew. Like the night before, he had pulled her close to his side when he got into bed, but she hadn't pretended to be asleep this time. He had kissed her gently on the lips and told her good night, and that was the extent of it. She had snuggled against him and gone to sleep contentedly, deciding she could easily become accustomed to the arrangement.

When he continued to mutter, Eurydice hesitantly patted a soothing hand on his chest, hoping it might lighten his sleep enough that he would stop. He wasn't making enough noise that it might wake Agniezka in the next room, but it was loud enough it would keep Eurydice awake. She couldn't understand a word of what he was saying, but he seemed to be having a very interesting conversation with himself.

"Shh," whispered Eurydice, adding it to the patting. It wasn't working.

She sighed tiredly, continuing to pat and soothe, wondering when it would work. If nothing else, she would completely wake him, and that would keep him quiet long enough she would be able to fall back asleep. She was just about to try that when his eyes flew open, and he put a hand around her throat and began to strangle her. It was easy enough for him to get a good grip with just one hand because Eurydice's neck was fairly small in comparison to the size of his hand, and he was very strong.

Eurydice was gasping for air, and she pounded on his chest in an effort to get him to wake up. She didn't think he was awake, and her trying to make him settle had only made it worse. He kept the hold on her neck, and she could feel herself going dizzy from the lack of air. When pounding on his chest didn't have any effect, and she feared he was going to kill her, she reached up to put a pressure grip on his wrist to make him loosen his hold, and once she got him to do that, she sat up a little higher and slapped him across the face with the other hand. It was difficult to get the leverage to do it properly, but when she saw the lucidity come into his features, she decided it was good enough.

"Bloody hell!" he gasped.

When Ellsworth woke up and saw he had his hand around her neck, he quickly let go, and Eurydice put a hand to her throat, coughing and gagging as she tried to get air back into her lungs as she weakly collapsed onto the mattress. Ellsworth got up and went to get her something to drink, but at the moment, Eurydice didn't want anything except to breathe, which she was finally able to do somewhat normally after a few minutes. Ellsworth set the glass on the night table, and he pulled her close to cradle her against him and began to rock her soothingly.

"Jesus! I am so sorry, Dicy," he sighed contritely.

She weakly patted his cheek as she continued to get her breathing back to normal.

"'Sall right," she wheezed. "Bad dream."

Knowing that he had been dreaming when he did it didn't make Ellsworth feel any better because if he had done it once, he could do it again. He had already hurt her so much, and to know he could have killed her while he slept and have no memory of it terrified him. She felt so fragile as he held her against him, and he couldn't believe she wasn't upset by what he had done. He let her go long enough to reach for the glass he had gotten and gave it to her to drink. Eurydice drained it, and she gasped and wheezed as her eyes watered.

"What was that?" she choked out, and she began to feel dizzy all over again as it began to take effect.

"Whisky," said Ellsworth as he continued to look at her worriedly.

He got up again and went to put some wood on the fire. It had burned down to just embers, and he was feeling very cold. He went back to the bed and got under the blankets. Eurydice was very limp as he pulled her against him, both of them lying on their sides facing each other, and he realized it was a combination of the alcohol, tiredness, and nearly being strangled to death. He gently ran his fingers over her neck, and while there was no swelling and it didn't feel as if he had done any damage to the fragile bones and cartilage, her neck would be bruised. He would be very surprised if it wasn't. He shuddered uncontrollably as the waking image of his hand around her throat came to him again.

Eurydice knew he was anguished by what he had done, but she didn't blame him. He had been asleep and hadn't known what he was doing. She was all right. Her neck was a little sore, but she could breathe, and other than the intoxication from the whisky, she felt almost back to normal. She wanted him to know that. She didn't want him to punish himself. She reached up a hand to gently smooth it down his cheek.

"I'm fine," she whispered soothingly. "It wasn't your fault."

"I could have killed you," he said unevenly.

"But you didn't," said Eurydice, continuing to caress his cheek.

"It could happen again," he said dully.

"Then we'll cross that bridge when we come to it," said Eurydice simply.

Ellsworth took her hand from his cheek to place a kiss on her palm. She really shouldn't forgive him. Regardless of whether or not he had done it in his sleep, the violence was there inside him, and he had meant it when he said he could do it again. Only next time, she might not be able to stop him. He couldn't bear the thought of something like that happening; he would never forgive himself.

Eurydice hesitantly leaned toward him to give him a soft kiss on the lips. It seemed like the right thing to do, and she wanted him to feel better. For some reason, she didn't like seeing him so unhappy. She wanted him to—if not forget it—at least not feel so tormented by it.

Ellsworth tried to keep himself under control as she continued to kiss him, doing his best to let her set the pace. It wasn't easy as she gently nipped at his lips with her teeth and smoothed her hand down his cheek to his chest in a caress. He didn't want her to feel threatened. As hard as it would be, he wanted her to decide how far things went. He didn't imagine they would go as far as he would like, but her initiating a kiss was excellent progress. That could have so easily been lost by what had just happened. He couldn't afford to lose any more. He returned her kisses with restraint, and he lightly moved his hand to her waist before letting it slide to the small of her back.

Eurydice was enjoying herself. She thought she might be a little tipsy from the whisky, but she had always liked kissing him. Now that they were married, she didn't see any reason why she couldn't. She appreciated that he wasn't trying to force her to do anything, and it made her willing to explore a little more than she might have otherwise. She left his lips to begin placing small kisses along his jaw to his ear, where she gently nipped at the lobe. His hand tightened at the small of her back, and she heard the breath catch in his throat.

"I like that," he sighed.

When she heard that, Eurydice wondered if she should stop, but when he still didn't try to press her into anything, she let her curiosity convince her to do a little more. She slowly let her fingers play over his chest, and she lightly ran them across one of his nipples. He didn't need to tell her he liked it; the soft moan at the back of his throat let her know that he did. She left his ear to trail her lips down his neck to his collarbone, and then she began to kiss his chest and grazed a nipple with her teeth before lightly licking at it. She was amazed at the way it hardened, and she sucked it into her mouth. Ellsworth startled her when he grabbed her by the shoulders to gently push her away. She made a sound of protest at the interruption.

"You have to stop," he gasped, his breathing ragged.

"But—" began Eurydice confusedly.

Ellsworth took one of her hands in his and slowly guided it down his chest to his stomach, and then he lightly placed it onto his erection. He had started to become aroused when she first began kissing him, and as she had continued to explore, it had only progressed until he was now throbbing. He had thought he could let her set the pace, but he had overestimated his self-control.

"Oh," said Eurydice softly, her face coloring.

"I'm only human, Eurydice. I can't...I can't not want you," he said quietly.

Now, Eurydice felt bad because she had only been trying to make him feel better. Instead, it seemed she had done the opposite. She couldn't have sex with him. Not only was the thought of it not appealing to her, but she was also having her courses. She knew enough to realize he was feeling very uncomfortable at the moment, and it would be awhile before he didn't, not if something wasn't done. She had felt terrible leaving him that way on the ship, and she knew what he had thought of her when she had done it. Eurydice finally came to a decision, and she gently tightened her fingers around his arousal.

Ellsworth inhaled sharply and tried to remove her hand.

"Oh, Eurydice, I'm already in pain; don't make it worse," he groaned.

Eurydice put her hand to his cheek and kissed him softly. "I want to...help you," she whispered uncertainly, "but I don't know what to do."

She almost panicked and changed her mind when he kissed her hungrily, but he soon ended it and rested his forehead against hers, almost panting.

"Just touch me," he sighed. "I'll let you know if it's working," he said with a half-smile before giving her another kiss.

Eurydice frowned slightly, thinking that wasn't very helpful at all. She had told him she didn't know what to do. It wasn't as if she had ever done something like this before. After a moment of consideration, she gently pushed him onto his back, deciding that would be more convenient. She sat up on her knees and looked down at him with a thoughtfully raised eyebrow. She had no idea where to begin.

Ellsworth waited with anticipation. He knew when she said she wanted to help him that she didn't mean to tup. It was too soon to expect that, but he was overjoyed she seemed willing to pursue other avenues of pleasure. It surprised him that she would; he would have thought her too prudish, but he was beginning to realize all the assumptions he had ever made about her were off the mark. That intrigued him, because he had always thought he was excellent at reading people. Eurydice continued to provide him with one surprise after another. Sometimes that was really bad, but sometimes—such as tonight—it was very, very good.

Eurydice lightly ran her fingers over his chest, and she lowered her head to begin teasing his nipple again. Ellsworth gasped and clenched his fingers into the sheets. She slowly let her fingers play over his stomach to lightly brush them over his erection. It was interesting that the surface was so soft, like silk, and she would never have imagined a man could have skin so soft anywhere. And it was warm, almost hot, as she continued to skim her fingers up and down the shaft. He was long and thick, the tip resting on his stomach just below his navel, and she hadn't realized it would change the way it did between when he was aroused and when he was not. She had never seen a man when he was aroused—never mind touched one, and she hadn't realized there would be a difference. She wrapped her fingers around the circumference and glided her hand up and down, fascinated by how hard it felt while the texture was so smooth and silky. She couldn't understand how something that felt so lovely could hurt so bad.

"Oh, that feels nice," sighed Ellsworth.

Eurydice moved her lips up his chest to his neck to his ear as she continued to touch him, and she felt him quiver. She thrilled with the knowledge that she was able to provoke him. Knowing he was probably a man who was very experienced and that she could make him tremble with pleasure made her feel powerful. She continued to move her hand up and down, her grasp gentle but firm, and a slight smile formed on her lips as she heard him begin to pant excitedly.

"Will you take off your shift?" he asked softly. "I want to see you."

Eurydice thought about it for a moment before she straightened up and let him go. She slowly pulled the garment over her head, laying it to the side. She colored slightly when he looked at her lustfully, but the temptation to cover herself that she had felt on their wedding night wasn't there. She thought it was only fair that she was naked as well, considering what she was doing to him, and she was his wife.

"Just lovely," he whispered appreciatively.

He slowly reached out a hand to lightly run it up her thigh to her side to cup her breast and knead it gently. Eurydice felt the fluttering in her stomach grow at his touch, and she closed her eyes as she savored the feel of it. She leaned forward to kiss him heatedly as she began to stroke him again. She eventually left his lips to go back to his chest, and Ellsworth shuddered as she teased one of his nipples with her teeth before placing kisses along the edge of his ribs and tracing the scar at the bottom edge with her tongue. Ellsworth moaned softly, and Eurydice's smile returned.

She expected something was supposed to happen eventually, but she didn't know when or what. She wasn't too concerned; she was content to keep doing what she was. She kissed his stomach, tracing the ridges of muscle with her tongue. She could feel it rising and falling quickly as he breathed, and from the erratic pace of it, she had the feeling it wouldn't be long. She licked at the indentation of his navel before placing her lips around it and sucking, and she felt Ellsworth's hand go to the back of her head to clutch weakly in her hair.

"Oh, God, Eurydice," he moaned, "I don't know how you figured that out, but…it…feels…divine."

Eurydice briefly chuckled with amusement, but she didn't want to lose her concentration. He was almost writhing as she continued to touch and kiss him, and Eurydice tingled with pleasure. She was amazed that she could feel so excited when he had done no more than briefly touch her breast, but she almost ached from it. She cautiously licked the tip of his erection, and she was startled when his hips bucked involuntarily.

"Oh, yes!" he hissed slowly, and Eurydice looked up at his face to see his eyes were closed, his lips curved in a smile of delight.

As she continued to stroke him with her hand, she ran her tongue around the ridge where the tip met the shaft, never taking her eyes from Ellsworth's face. She flicked her tongue against the underside where she had felt an interesting indentation near the tip, and she watched as his features became blissful as he sighed and moaned. She sucked the tip into her mouth and rasped her tongue against that same spot, and Ellsworth's hips rose off the bed. That was, apparently, a particularly sensitive location. She repeated the teasing a few times, and Ellsworth only grew more agitated.

"Oh, God," he gasped, "I'm going to come!"

Eurydice had him in her mouth at that moment, and she was surprised when she felt something warm hit the back of her throat. She almost choked, but she realized what it was. There wasn't a large amount, and rather than spitting it out and getting it onto the sheets, she swallowed it. She didn't *think* there was anything about it that would make her sick. It had the most peculiar flavor, faintly like cherries and brandy, and she recalled the compote they'd had for dessert. It was extraordinary. She slowly stopped stroking him after a few seconds and removed him from her mouth with a final lick to the tip, and Ellsworth lay with his eyes closed, his chest heaving. He twitched occasionally from the intensity of his orgasm, and he was covered with a light film of perspiration.

He gently grabbed her by the shoulders after a minute or two and pulled her up his body to lay her on top of him, and he kissed her appreciatively before rubbing his nose against hers adoringly.

"Thank you for helping me," he purred with a roguish smile. "Any time you want to help me in the future, do not hesitate."

Eurydice was propped up on her elbows to either side of his head on the pillows, and she looked at him with an uncertain frown.

"Was that good?" she asked hesitantly.

Ellsworth chuckled amusedly and kissed her again. "Oh, sweetheart, that was outstanding." He smoothed his hands down her back to rest them on her bottom, and Eurydice tried not to squirm as he began to circle his fingers lightly over the skin. "I'd like to return the favor," he said softly.

"I can't," said Eurydice with some disappointment, which surprised Ellsworth.

He put a hand to the back of her head and kissed her gently. They had already made progress far beyond his expectations, and he didn't want to force the issue. That she seemed disappointed at having to refuse gave him hope that it wouldn't be long before he was able to repair the damage he had caused.

"Whenever you're ready," he said earnestly, brushing a hand down her cheek.

He helped her slide off of him onto her side, and he spooned behind her with an arm over her waist and twined their fingers together.

Eurydice woke up the next morning to the pleasant sensation of Ellsworth placing light kisses along her neck and shoulder while he gently toyed with one of her nipples. She inhaled sharply, and her eyes flew open. She turned over to look at him.

"I can't do that," she said quickly.

Ellsworth gave her a half-smile, and then he lowered his head to kiss her. It was passionate without being overwhelming, and Eurydice felt herself going dizzy. She put her hand to his shoulder and weakly pushed at it to get him to stop. He nuzzled her cheek and smiled amusedly.

"Good morning," he drawled.

"Good morning," said Eurydice breathlessly.

Ellsworth looked down at her with a soft smile, and he ran his fingers down her throat. Her neck was ringed by an obviously hand-shaped bruise, but it didn't seem to be bothering her. She was looking up at him thoughtfully, but he didn't imagine she would tell him what was on her mind.

"What time is it?" she asked quietly.

Ellsworth shrugged. "Morning…some time. The sun hasn't been up very long."

Eurydice frowned. "Did you not go to sleep?"

"No."

He had been afraid to go back to sleep, and he had enjoyed holding her. It wasn't that long ago, so he'd only missed two or three hours of rest. He had been impatient to wake her, and it had seemed to take forever for the sun to rise. She continued to look up at him with a frown.

"I wasn't sleepy." He could tell she didn't believe him. "I'm going to take a bath," he said finally. "Do you want to join me?"

"No, thank you," said Eurydice quietly, her cheeks coloring.

Ellsworth grinned and bent down to kiss her before he got out of bed. "Suit yourself."

Eurydice watched as he sauntered across the floor to the bathing room. It really was wonderful to see him in motion; he was very graceful. Before long, she heard the sound of the water closet, and then she heard the sound of water being run into the tub. For a fleeting moment, she had considered joining him in the tub, but she just hadn't felt comfortable doing that…not yet. He was proving to be far more considerate than she had thought he would be, and it was making it very easy for her to feel at ease with him. She stretched lazily and yawned before she sat up and brought her knees to her chest and rested her cheek on top of them.

Last night had been very strange. First, there had been the strangulation. He said he hadn't gone back to sleep because he wasn't tired, but Eurydice knew he was afraid it would happen again. It was possible that it could, but next time she would know better than to try to wake him or calm him in some way. She didn't think it would have happened if she had left him alone. Then there had been the love making. She had enjoyed it very much, and she hadn't been afraid. The only part of it that had disappointed her was that she had been unable to feel the same thing he had felt—that ecstasy. She didn't know if she could feel it again or if the time on the ship had been a one-off. She had become excited, much to her amazement. In any event, she was happy she had been able to please him without having actual intercourse, and she didn't think she would mind so much doing it again.

She finally got out of bed and went to write in her notebook. She felt fairly confident it really had been just a dream, but she wrote down all of them regardless, just in case. She had noticed since coming to Venice that she hadn't been dreaming as much. She usually had at least one dream a night that she could remember, but not so much lately. She wasn't concerned about it, and she really wouldn't mind if she had even less of them.

Then she went to change her tampion. Eurydice thought it was odd Psyche and Pandora would decide upon the name for it that they had, but it did seem appropriate somehow. Even though it wasn't something they had invented (courtesans used them quite often, and it was Lucia, formerly of that occupation in this very city, who had introduced them to the item), the name was apparently all their own. Eurydice supposed it was better than calling it a plug...or a stopper. Actually, stopper wasn't so bad when she thought about it, and it was somewhat appropriate. Eurydice supposed a more correct term for it would be pessary, but it wasn't medicated.

When she had started her courses yesterday, she had been tempted to just use the belt and cloth she had always used, but she was curious about what made Psyche's tampions so much better. She had gone to see her sister, and Psyche had given her the supplies she needed with instructions for how to insert them, how often to change them, and how to make more. It did all sound simple enough, and now that she had tried them, Eurydice had to wonder, like Psyche, why she hadn't been using them all along. They were cleaner and simpler, and Ellsworth hadn't even known she was having her courses. They weren't uncomfortable, and they worked better. Psyche had made her a convert, and Eurydice had already thanked her for suggesting them.

Once she had that done, she put back on her shift and dressing gown, and then she went to the doors of the loggia and onto the colonnade. The air was slightly cool, but not uncomfortably so, and she looked down at the garden with its few remaining flowers. It seemed it was going to be a lovely day.

Agniezka was coming out of her room when Eurydice came back in and closed the doors, and she had to stop her before she went to the water closet because Ellsworth was in the tub. Agniezka promptly turned around and went to use the chamber pot in her room, but she soon returned. She didn't give Eurydice more than a cursory glance until after she had gotten Eurydice's clothes from the wardrobe and began to help her into them. When she did, the bruising on Eurydice's neck was obvious.

"What has he done to you?" gasped Agniezka with a horrified expression.

Eurydice's hand flew to her throat. "It was an accident," she said calmly.

Agniezka pulled her over to the mirror to let Eurydice see it. "That was no accident!" she said angrily, pointing at her reflection.

Eurydice turned to Agniezka and put a soothing hand on her shoulder.

"It was an accident," repeated Eurydice earnestly. "He was having a bad dream, and I tried to wake him. He didn't know what he was doing."

"Hunh," said Agniezka doubtfully, and she glared at the doorway to the bathing room, tempted to go have a word with him, naked or not.

"I swear," averred Eurydice. "It was an accident. He felt horrible about it. He would never do anything to intentionally hurt me."

Agniezka looked at Eurydice's sincere expression. Considering the circumstances behind her marrying Ellsworth and how unhappy she had been to do so, Agniezka had to believe she wouldn't lie to protect him, not that Eurydice had ever been prone to lying about anything at all. Ellsworth being abusive would be the quickest and easiest way for Aberdare to joyfully put an end to it. Agniezka finally relented with a huge sigh and a shake of her head.

"He just better hope he doesn't cause any more *accidents,*" said Agniezka shortly as she resumed helping Eurydice get dressed, "because *I* am not the one he will answer to."

Eurydice realized who she meant, and her eyes rounded. "Oh, no! Can you cover it up? Is there anything that can be done?" she asked worriedly.

Agniezka guided her over to the dressing table and put her in the seat. She looked at Eurydice in the mirror. "I can't cover that," she said softly. "It's a simple enough matter to cover a lovebite or a pimple, but that...." She shook her head negatively.

"Then I'll have to make sure I tell Father that he didn't do it on purpose," said Eurydice determinedly.

"Yes, I'm sure you'll let me know how that goes," said Agniezka dryly.

"Isn't there at least some way we can make it less obvious?"

"You don't have any jewelry big enough to cover it. We might be able to find a pelisse with a high collar that will cover it, but it's not likely."

Agniezka brushed and styled her hair, and once it was up, it only made the bruising even more blatant. His grace was going to be furious when he saw it. Eurydice would just have to explain. It was unsightly, and she knew her father was going to have a hard time believing it wasn't done purposely. If she didn't know the truth of it, Eurydice would as well.

Ellsworth came out of the bathing room while Agniezka was putting up Eurydice's hair, a towel wrapped around his waist. When he saw the maid, he collected his things to get dressed and took them to the valet's quarters to put them on. He had shaved, and as he walked past Eurydice, she caught the scent of his shaving lotion. She couldn't quite decide what it was, but she liked it. She was able to detect lime, but there was something else, some spice, that she couldn't recognize. He winked at her when they made eye contact, and Eurydice blushed.

When Agniezka saw that, she relaxed. Despite anything that may have happened on their wedding night, or last night, Eurydice was starting to like her husband. Actually, *like* was probably a mild word for it, considered Agniezka upon reflection. Eurydice would never feel that way about the man if he were mistreating her, and the more Agniezka thought about it, the more she realized Eurydice wouldn't *tolerate* a man mistreating her. Seeing her reaction made Agniezka happy and hopeful this arranged marriage would have a pleasant outcome after all.

Once she was done with Eurydice's hair, Agniezka went back to the wardrobe to look for a pelisse. Just as she thought, there wasn't one with a high enough collar to hide her neck that wouldn't also make Eurydice so unbearably hot she would faint, but she was able to find one with a collar that might make it seem less obvious.

By the time Agniezka was done dressing her, a maid came with breakfast and took it to the sitting room. Ellsworth came to join them, and the three of them had an enjoyable meal, despite Agniezka's disapproval over what he had done to Eurydice's neck. Ellsworth convinced Eurydice that she should go see the Doge's Palace with him, and while she wanted to work on her new composition, she found she wouldn't mind spending some time with him.

Eurydice asked Agniezka if she would like to go, but her maid decided she would stay at the palazzo and do some knitting and embroidery. Eurydice didn't need to guess what kind. She thought Agniezka would have plenty of time to get things like that done, but Agniezka still wasn't feeling well and would spend at least some of the time while Eurydice was away to take a nap. For Agniezka's sake, Eurydice hoped that wouldn't last much longer for her. Then Agniezka would have the traveling sickness to contend with in the coach on the way to Vienna in addition to the pregnancy sickness. It didn't seem fair at all. Eurydice also suspected Agniezka was hoping Dr. Felton would come for a visit.

Eurydice and Ellsworth went to the great hall, where she would wait while he went to make arrangements for a gondola to take them to the Piazza San Marco. It would be just as easy to walk, but Eurydice didn't want to walk. She could do with some exercise—she hadn't had much since leaving Britain, but she just didn't feel like it today, and it really was quite a distance. Then there would be the walk back. She just thought going by boat would be more pleasant.

She had been sitting for a while when her father came into the great hall from the direction of the study. She smiled happily when she saw him and got up from the couch to kiss him on the cheek. She opened her mouth to wish him good morning when he saw the bruising on her neck, and he tilted her chin up with his fingers to look at it before she could say a word.

At almost the same moment, Ellsworth came upstairs from the water floor. The duke's face went through several color changes from white to red when he saw her neck and then his son-in-law. Without a word, he strode toward Ellsworth, wrapped his hand around the man's throat, and shoved him against the wall.

"I warned you!" ground out the duke.

"Father, no!" shouted Eurydice with alarm, rushing toward them.

She wrapped her arms around the duke's in an effort to make him let go, but he wasn't going to. He had told Ellsworth what would happen if he hurt Eurydice, and it was glaringly obvious his warning had been ignored.

"Papa, stop it!" she gasped, still trying to make him let go.

Ellsworth's face was starting to turn a bright shade of red as Aberdare continued to choke him, and Eurydice anxiously tried to pry her father's fingers loose before he killed her husband. When she couldn't get him to let go, she used a pressure grip on his wrist, and his fingers loosened enough that she was able to get his hand off and shove it away, and then she got between Aberdare and Ellsworth to keep her father from attacking him again.

"Move out of the way, Eurydice," said Aberdare angrily.

"No, Papa. Leave him alone!" said Eurydice bravely, trembling nervously. She looked over her shoulder at Ellsworth concernedly, and he was leaning with his back against the wall with a hand to his throat, gasping for air. "You didn't give me a chance to explain."

"Did he do that to your neck?" asked Aberdare shortly.

"Yes, but—"

"Then there's nothing to explain. Move out of the way."

Psyche and Sheerness had come in when they heard all the yelling, and Psyche's eyes grew round when she saw Eurydice standing between the two men. She was close enough that she could see the bruising on her sister's throat, despite the collar of her pelisse, and she felt a knot forming in her stomach when it brought to her mind Lady Morecambe.

Georgiana Jeffries Marsh, the Marchioness of Morecambe, had been their brother Myron's lover. They had been in love, but she was a married woman. That she was married was bad enough. What made it worse was that her husband was Ector Marsh, the Earl of Hendon, an insane criminal who took great pleasure in abusing his wife. He was also their brother's murderer, and Georgiana had been the cause of it. Seeing her sister's neck reminded Psyche of the night Lady Morecambe had come to a dinner party given by Pandora with her neck in a not dissimilar condition. It had marked the beginning of the end for Myron.

She blindly reached over to take her husband's hand and squeezed it nervously. She didn't want to jump to conclusions. It appeared Eurydice was trying to protect Ellsworth from their father. She didn't think her sister would do that if he had intentionally abused her.

"I will not let you hurt him, Papa," said Eurydice unevenly. "It was an accident, a misunderstanding—if you will—that has been addressed between me and my husband."

Psyche frowned thoughtfully. She knew all about accidents and misunderstandings involving one's husband. Albeit, most of hers with Sheerness had happened *before* they were married, but it was difficult to misunderstand someone tightening his hand around one's throat hard enough to leave bruises.

"That was *not* accidental," said Aberdare stilly, pointing at her throat.

"Yes, it was," said Eurydice determinedly. "He was asleep when he did it, so I don't know what else it could have been."

Psyche shared a glance with her husband. Sheerness did not take well to being abruptly woken from a sound sleep. He had a tendency to thrash like a fish out of water if waking him was not done gradually and gently. Psyche had learned that the hard way, and she'd had a bruise or two to prove it before she figured it out. There had been a time when Nikos and Ioanna thought he was abusing her, too, and it had been nothing like that.

"Papà," she began hesitantly, "if Dicy says it was a misunderstanding, at least this time, perhaps we should give it the benefit of doubt."

Aberdare looked at her, and then he looked back to Eurydice and Ellsworth. It pained him to see his daughter like that, but he had to believe she wouldn't defend the man who had done it without good reason. She said he had been asleep. Aberdare supposed that was possible. He didn't think she would lie about it. He knew his daughter well enough to realize that. In any event, she wasn't going to let him hold Ellsworth accountable for it. Aberdare straightened the front of his waistcoat and sleeves and took a deep breath in an effort to get his temper under control.

"Fine," he said finally, "just this once, I am willing to overlook it." He looked at Ellsworth stonily. "However, next time I see *anything* that looks like you've mishandled my daughter—so much as a *hair* out of place—accident or not, I will end you."

"And just what makes you think you can issue threats like that to my son?" asked an imperious woman's voice from the top of the stairs to the water floor. "I'm the one who brought him into the world, and only God or I will be the one to take him out of it."

Everyone turned to look as Mrs. Ellsworth walked toward them, carrying a little girl in her arms. Signor Montenegro was with her, and they were followed by a woman who appeared to be a nanny, carrying another small girl and followed by another girl and a boy, and another woman Eurydice assumed was Mrs. Ellsworth's lady's maid. They had expected Mrs. Ellsworth's arrival any day, but it was still a surprise. She looked from the duke to her son as she continued to stroll across the floor, her face expectant.

Ellsworth went to her to place a dutiful kiss on her cheek. "Hallo, Mum," he said quietly.

"Don't you 'hallo, mum' me," she said sternly. "Aberdare's sounding as if he could do murder. Have you been up to your tricks again?"

"Cora, I think it would be best if you and the children were settled in before we discuss this. It's a bit complicated," said Aberdare neutrally.

Mrs. Ellsworth looked from the duke to her son again, and then she looked at Eurydice. All of them had uncomfortable expressions.

"Hmm," she said thoughtfully. "Thirty minutes, and it had better be good," she said firmly.

Chapter Sixteen

Mrs. Ellsworth did not take the news well that her son had married Eurydice. She was infuriated when she found out the reason for it. Her anger wasn't directed at her new daughter-in-law, however. It was all for her son. To Eurydice's confusion, Mrs. Ellsworth had a very low opinion of her son. She thought him a wastrel and a spendthrift, irresponsible and reckless. Eurydice thought the woman had Ellsworth confused with another man. Eurydice had never felt he was any of those things. In fact, she thought he was the exact opposite, and she shared as much responsibility for their marrying as he did. It was her actions that had caused the compromising situation they had found themselves in, not his. She could have let him go to his rooms.

The four of them had met privately in the study to discuss things, and Eurydice had needed to bite her tongue when Mrs. Ellsworth proceeded to berate her son in front of Eurydice and Aberdare. She didn't like seeing his mother talk to him that way, not when she believed it was completely unwarranted. She talked to him as if he were little better than a simple-minded idiot, and that made Eurydice angry. She decided she would wait until Mrs. Ellsworth had time to adjust to things before she said something. Perhaps the woman was just talking out of anger. If that proved not to be the case, however, Eurydice would have a word with her.

Ellsworth introduced Eurydice to his nephew and nieces later that afternoon, and she wasn't surprised by their reactions. The oldest, Simon, who was six, greeted her politely, but she could tell he was frightened. Mary Kate, the next eldest, who was four, took one look at Eurydice and ran to hide on the other side of one of the beds in the nursery. Cassie, the two-year-old, started crying and wouldn't let go of her uncle. The only one who didn't seem bothered by her new aunt was the youngest, Corinna, who was one. She went directly into Eurydice's arms and hugged her around the neck as if she didn't intend to let go.

Freddie, the Andreanopouli, and the Geniseos were all puzzled by the Windhams' fear of Eurydice; although, Yelena was jealous when she saw Eurydice holding Corinna. Eurydice supposed that, like Freddie, it would take them some time to get used to her. She wasn't bothered the older ones were afraid of her. She was accustomed to it, but they would eventually have to adjust because she was now their aunt. There wasn't any need to rush, though.

With the arrival of his mother, Eurydice could see a change in Ellsworth that was almost immediate. He became quiet and withdrawn, and to Eurydice, he just seemed very unhappy. Part of it could be due to his mother's treatment of him, but Eurydice didn't think all of it was caused by her behavior. Just her presence seemed to affect him. Eurydice didn't understand the relationship between the two of them yet, so she couldn't decide what was causing the change and what she could do to stop it. She had always thought Mrs. Ellsworth was a nice woman, but she was not very nice to her son.

That night when they went to bed, Ellsworth snuggled close behind her after kissing her good night. Eurydice put her arm over his around her waist and twined their fingers together. She drifted off very quickly, a contented smile at the corners of her mouth. If nothing else, being married had the benefit of having someone to keep the bed warm in the cold months.

Eurydice woke up at some point during the middle of the night only to realize she was alone. She felt the mattress where Ellsworth had been, and it was cold. She slowly propped herself up on her elbows to look around the room by the dim light of the dying fire in the fireplace, but she didn't see him. He wasn't there, and she didn't know why or where he had gone.

She pulled the blankets over herself with a frown. She didn't know the hour, but it was no time to be up and about. She waited to see if he had gotten up to go to the water closet, but she knew he hadn't. The bed was too cold for him to have made a brief trip there, and he would have been back already in the length of time she had been awake. It was the cold that had awakened her. She believed he would be back, but his being gone troubled her.

She had agreed she wouldn't ask him about anywhere he went or anything he did, but that didn't mean she couldn't worry. She remembered what had happened the last time he made a secretive foray to somewhere in the night: a man had been murdered and Ellsworth had nearly been killed. She wanted to believe he had a good reason, but since she couldn't ask, there was no way to tell. Although she wasn't clear on what he did for her father, she couldn't ask that either. She could ask her father, but she expected he wouldn't tell her.

Eurydice shivered and curled up in a ball under the blankets, covering her nose to warm it with her breath. She hadn't realized the air was so cold when Ellsworth was there. She thought about getting out of bed to put more wood on the fire, but she was too cold. She waited several more minutes to see if Ellsworth would return, but when he didn't, she went back to sleep, too tired to stay awake despite her worry.

The next time she woke, the sun was up and Ellsworth was there behind her, lightly running his fingers up and down her thigh through her shift. He started just above her knee and trailed them along to the edge of her bottom, and Eurydice could feel her heart starting to beat a little faster. He nuzzled her ear before nipping at the lobe with his teeth, and the breath caught in her throat as she felt the fluttery sensation begin in her stomach.

She turned over to look at him, and Ellsworth lowered his head to kiss her languidly, teasing her lips with his teeth before gently sucking at the bottom one. He slowly moved a hand up her stomach to cover one of her breasts, and Eurydice moaned softly at the back of her throat as the nipple puckered almost painfully. He was very good at finding pleasant ways to wake her. She put her hand to his cheek and slowly drew her lips away from his.

"I can't do that," she panted.

Ellsworth smiled slowly and moved his hand back down her stomach. Eurydice quivered as he moved it lower to lightly brush his fingers against her button through her shift. She bit her lip and put her hand over his to stop him.

"That feels wonderful," she sighed, "but I can't."

"Sure you can," he purred against her ear. "You know you want to."

He was right. She was tempted, but she couldn't...not yet, and she wasn't sure she would be able to try having intercourse. She couldn't bear the thought of it hurting again, and if it did, they would be doing it at a time when she wasn't fertile, so it would be enduring pain for nothing.

"I'm having my courses," she said quietly.

Ellsworth lifted his head to look at her with a half-smile.

"No, you're not."

"Yes, I am. Since Thursday," she said evenly.

Ellsworth slowly ran his hand from her waist to her thigh until he found the bottom edge of her shift. Never taking his eyes from hers, he moved his hand beneath it across her bare skin along the inside of her thigh. She colored hotly as he went higher, and she saw his eyes widen in surprise when he felt the drawstring.

"Told you so," she said dryly.

He removed his hand, and then he lowered his head to nuzzle her neck.

"I beg your pardon," he sighed.

By Tuesday, Mrs. Ellsworth was still treating her son the same as the day she had arrived. Eurydice couldn't understand where it came from, and what puzzled her more was that Ellsworth withstood it without saying anything. She could see it bothered him, and she knew it was unfair and unwarranted. She understood it was his mother and he wanted to treat her with respect, but Eurydice felt the respect should be reciprocated. Clearly, it wasn't. Mrs. Ellsworth was nice to everyone else at the palazzo, including Eurydice, but when it came to her son, she had not one kind word. Every comment or compliment was backhanded.

Until that evening, Eurydice had simply done her best to avoid the woman, whether Ellsworth was present or not, because any mention of him was more of the same. Regardless of whether or not she knew her husband well, Eurydice knew the man Mrs. Ellsworth described and the one she had married were not the same, and she was beginning to find it intolerable. She disliked spite directed at anyone when it was undeserved, but she especially disliked it being directed at Ellsworth. The only reason she had managed to go as long as she had without saying anything was that Ellsworth was tolerating it.

They were eating supper, and other than the comments Mrs. Ellsworth made about her son, the conversation was pleasant and lively. Dr. Felton had joined them, which made Agniezka happy. Aberdare had calmed considerably and was able to speak with Ellsworth in a manner that was almost friendly. Ellsworth's attitude toward Felton had greatly improved once he learned the doctor and Eurydice were not involved with one another. There was laughter and teasing. The food and wine were delicious. Everything was lovely.

But when Mrs. Ellsworth made a comment that implied she thought her son was a coward, Eurydice was full-up.

"Enough!" she said exasperatedly, and she hit her hand against the tabletop hard enough to make the silver rattle and stood up, throwing down her napkin. "You may talk about my husband any way you like when I am not present, but I will not have you say one more unkind thing about him around me! I regard him as one of the most kind, decent, honorable men I know, and I will *not* tolerate you belittling him any more! Do you hear me?" she said angrily.

All the conversation at the table ceased when she began her tirade, and everyone looked at her with astonishment. No one had ever seen her lose her temper like that. Her family and Agniezka had seen her angry, but she had always expressed her displeasure in a modulated, calm manner. For her to have an outburst like that, she had to be furious. For anyone else, this would be the point where she caused physical harm to the object of her wrath.

Eurydice spared Mrs. Ellsworth one more meaningful glare before she turned and left the room. She was going to take a bath, and then she was going to bed. She hoped by the time she was through in the tub her temper would have calmed enough she would actually be able to go to sleep. She probably should have remained silent, but Mrs. Ellsworth had pushed her beyond the point she could bear. She couldn't recall anyone or anything making her quite so infuriated before.

She went to the bathing room to start the water for her bath when she reached her suite. Then she went to undress, take down her hair, and get a shift and dressing gown. By the time she was done, the tub was ready, and she sank into the water up to her chin. She took a deep breath and rested her head back against the edge of the tub with her eyes closed. The warmth of the water began to relax her, and the frown she had etched into her forehead steadily began to fade. She would start to wash in a few minutes, but for now she didn't want to do anything.

She didn't know how long she sat like that, but her eyes flew open in surprise when Ellsworth bent down to kiss her lingeringly. She didn't think she had fallen asleep, but she didn't hear him come in. She didn't even know he was in the room until his lips touched hers. After her initial start, she sighed at the back of her throat and reached up to clutch at the lapel of his coat. When he lifted his head to look at her, Eurydice opened her eyes and saw that he had a soft, thoughtful smile playing about his lips.

"I'm sorry I talked to your mother like that," she said quietly. "I'll apologize tomorrow."

His smile changed to one of amusement. "She didn't say another word the whole meal. She's not used to being put in her place."

Eurydice colored with embarrassment. She didn't know what had come over her. She never talked to anyone like that, and she had to do it for the first time to her mother-in-law.

"Don't take this wrongly, but please, tell me she will not be riding in the same coach with us to Vienna," she said hopefully.

"She won't," he chuckled.

Ellsworth took off his coat and rolled up his sleeves, and then he sat on the low stool beside the tub. Eurydice looked at him curiously. Since he had come to their suite, she expected Agniezka would be there soon to help her wash and get dressed for bed. She knew she should feel uncomfortable with him seeing her naked, but she couldn't. It wasn't as if he had never seen her before, and they were married. He reached for a flannel and the soap, and then he took one of her hands in his and began to wash her arm.

"Agniezka will be in soon to do that," said Eurydice a little nervously.

"No, she won't," said Ellsworth with a slow smile. "I told her she could go to bed."

Eurydice's eyes widened in surprise, and he released her hand to take the other one to begin washing her other arm.

"I'm surprised she listened. She takes her job very seriously."

"I don't think she likes me."

"Agniezka is very protective," said Eurydice evenly. "She's been my maid since I was nine."

He moved further down and lifted one of her legs to begin washing it, resting her foot on his shoulder. She enjoyed his hands as they glided over her skin, and she could feel a knot of excitement beginning to grow in her stomach. After he had soap on her leg, he ran his fingers lightly along the surface and looked up at her face.

"How do you do that?" he asked thoughtfully.

"Do what?" asked Eurydice perplexedly.

"How do you remove the hair from your legs like that? You don't use a razor."

"I used to," said Eurydice calmly. "I'm very good with a razor, actually, but I don't use one any more. Too much work. Pandora concocted a depilatory in the solarium about five years ago. It smells very bad, but fortunately it works quickly and I only have to use it about every fortnight."

"Courtesans do that, you do realize?" he asked with a sensual smile.

"Oh, sure, they do," said Eurydice agreeably, "but so do Muslims and a few other cultures. It's very hygienic."

"It also feels very nice," he said warmly, placing a kiss on her leg near her ankle.

Eurydice colored, and the knot in her stomach began to grow. He put her leg back into the water and picked up the other one to wash. She was enjoying this a lot. He was being very gentle but thorough, and the touch of his hands was seductive. She was starting to have a difficult time conducting a logical conversation.

He had her lean forward and lift her hair out of the way for him to wash her back, but he couldn't quite reach all of it because of the level of the water in the tub. Eurydice got up on her knees to make it easier, and Ellsworth smiled appreciatively as he looked at her. He ran the cloth over her in slow circles, and he especially enjoyed smoothing it over her bottom, loving the way her skin glistened from the soap and water.

When he was done with her back, he reached around her to wash the front of her torso. He ran the cloth over her skin, gliding it down across her stomach to wash between her thighs, and he smiled slightly when he felt her shiver excitedly. He set the flannel aside and smoothed his hands up her stomach to cup her breasts, toying at the nipples with his thumbs until they hardened to almost feel like pebbles. Eurydice's head lolled back to rest onto his shoulder, and Ellsworth's smile grew wider. She moaned softly at the back of her throat and arched her back to press her breasts into his hands. He smoothed his hands back down her waist to her hips and turned his head to whisper in her ear.

"Time to rinse."

Eurydice's eyes sprang open with a start. Her cheeks were flushed, and the quivering in her stomach was almost unbearable. She sank back into the water to rinse off the soap, and then she let the water out of the tub and stood to let Ellsworth dry her with the towel he had waiting for her. Once he had her dry, he tossed the towel aside and lowered his head to kiss her temptingly, gently resting one hand against the side of her neck while the other moved to the small of her back. Eurydice leaned toward him with a soft sigh, and she thought her legs were going to give way.

She gasped in surprise when she felt him lift her in his arms to carry her from the bathing room to the bed. She put an arm around his neck to steady herself, and her eyes were round as she looked at his face. He climbed onto the mattress on his knees to gently lower her onto it near the middle, and Eurydice weakly put a hand to the back of his head when he kissed her again.

"Will you help me undress?" he whispered.

Eurydice nodded, and she began to unfasten the buttons on his waistcoat while he untied his cravat. He removed the linen from around his neck and tossed it over his shoulder to have it land on the floor, and Eurydice slid the waistcoat from his shoulders and did the same. She pulled his shirt loose from the waistband of his pants as Ellsworth kissed her, and she smoothed her hands up his chest beneath it as she raised it to pull it over his head. Once she had off his shirt, Eurydice lowered her head to tease one of his nipples, and she heard Ellsworth gasp when she nipped at it lightly with her teeth. He sat down on the bed to remove one of his boots while Eurydice pulled off the other, and they soon landed on the floor with a thud, followed not long after by his socks. He undid the fastenings at the waistband of his pants, and Eurydice tugged at the bottom of the legs to get them off once she had the buttons there undone.

Once he was naked, he pulled Eurydice toward him as they were both on their knees and kissed her slowly, letting his hands trail down her back to cup her bottom. He lightly ran his fingers over the soft roundness, and Eurydice quivered as she felt chill bumps rise on her skin. He pulled her closer, and she could feel his erection pressed against her stomach, but she wasn't worried. She wrapped her arms around his neck and moaned softly at the back of her throat and leaned against him.

Ellsworth slowly guided her onto her back against the pillows, lying on his side, and he let his lips trail down her throat to the hollow at its base. He gently moved one of his hands up her side to one of her breasts, and Eurydice arched her back as he began to tweak the nipple between his fingers. He soon kissed his way down her chest to take the nipple into his mouth as he kneaded the fullness of her breast. Eurydice whimpered with pleasure, and Ellsworth lifted his head to look at her.

"Do you like that?"

"Yes!" gasped Eurydice.

Ellsworth moved his other hand down her stomach to begin teasing her button, and he felt her jump before she gasped and sighed at the back of her throat.

"Oh, God, that's…I can't…breathe…," she panted mindlessly.

Ellsworth smiled as he flicked at her nipple with his tongue, and he looked up at her face. Her eyes were closed, her features blissful. As he continued to tease one of her nipples with his fingers, he moved his mouth to the other, all the while toying with her button. She was trembling and sighing, and he could feel a light sheen of perspiration forming on her skin. He slowly kissed his way down her stomach then carefully eased one of her legs over his shoulder. Eurydice's eyes flew open in surprise, and she looked down at him when he began to play her with his mouth before her head fell limply back to the pillows.

"Oh, Ellsworth," she sighed weakly.

"Call me Gareth," he said softly with a sensual smile before he resumed what he was doing.

Eurydice clutched one of her hands into his hair while she smoothed the other across her forehead in disorientation. She really did feel as if she couldn't breathe. She was dizzy from the sensations he was causing, and she wasn't sure she could remember how to take air into her lungs. She felt a momentary shock when he gently glided one of his fingers inside her, but it didn't hurt, and when he slowly began to move it in and out as he continued to tease her, she found that it only enhanced the experience.

"Gareth," she whispered hoarsely as she began to orgasm, and she felt as if her heart were going to explode from the intensity of it.

Ellsworth felt it when she began to come, her thighs quivering as her back arched off the bed, and her fingers tightened in his hair as she seemed to vibrate with pleasure. He slowly kissed his way back up her body to her lips, and Eurydice wrapped her arms around his neck as she returned it passionately. He nuzzled her cheek before he lifted his head to look at her.

"I want to be inside you," he whispered softly.

Eurydice opened her eyes to look at him solemnly and put a hand to his cheek.

"I don't think I can—" she began, and Ellsworth began to gently tease one of her earlobes with his teeth. Eurydice gasped as she felt the excitement flutter in her stomach again.

"Let me try," he whispered soothingly. "If it hurts, if you don't like it, all you have to do is tell me." He began to place nibbling kisses along her neck. "I'll stop. I promise."

Eurydice lightly ran her fingers over his shoulder blade as she thought about it. Other than on their wedding night, he had always stopped doing something when she asked him to. He had never tried to take advantage of her or force her to do anything she didn't want to do. What he had just done was heavenly, and since their wedding night, he had been very gentle with her. He had never done anything to intentionally hurt her, and for whatever reason, she trusted that he never would. It was one of the few things that she *did* trust about him. Ellsworth kissed her gently on the lips and rested his forehead against hers as he looked into her eyes.

"Let me show you the wedding night that should have been," he whispered earnestly.

Eurydice looked at him pensively and softly ran her fingers down his cheek.

"All right," she whispered finally.

Ellsworth gave her an ardent kiss, and Eurydice could feel her heart starting to thud in her chest with excitement and nervousness. She desperately wanted him to be right, but she was afraid he wouldn't be. He continued to kiss her and caress her until the fluttering she felt in her stomach began to suffocate the worry, and she was soon trembling with need for him.

She panicked for a moment when he settled himself between her thighs, but she soon relaxed as he touched and teased her. She could feel his erection pressed against her, but she didn't let it frighten her. He was being so considerate, so generous, and she knew he had to be aching. She slowly ran her fingers down his back to trail them over his buttocks, and she heard him groan excitedly as he rubbed against her. He lifted his head from her breast where he had been lapping at the nipple to look at her, and Eurydice reached up a hand to trace his features with her fingertips.

Ellsworth gently moved a hand down her flank to her calf to place her leg across the back of his thighs. He kept his eyes on hers as he positioned himself, and he slowly began to push into her. Eurydice pulled her bottom lip between her teeth when she felt the insistent pressure as he began to enter her, waiting for the pain to start. Ellsworth kept his eyes on her face for the slightest sign of discomfort, but she continued to look up at him with that nervous anticipation. After what seemed like an eternity, Eurydice began to wonder if he was going extremely slow. She steadily began to have a sense of fullness, but there was no agony like she had felt on their wedding night. Ellsworth lowered his head to kiss her thoroughly. When he lifted his head, Eurydice had a puzzled frown.

"What's wrong?" he asked concernedly.

"Are you...? Aren't you...?" she said confusedly.

Ellsworth grinned and nuzzled her neck. "I'm in," he whispered.

"You are? All the way?" blurted Eurydice with surprise.

"Oh, yes," he drawled slowly with a slight chuckle.

Eurydice smiled relievedly and released a small, giddy laugh, but Ellsworth knew there was still plenty of room for things to go wrong. He raised himself and slowly thrust into her. Her eyes grew round with surprise.

"Oh!"

"Did that hurt?" asked Ellsworth worriedly.

"Uh, no," said Eurydice thoughtfully. "I don't think so." Ellsworth did it again a little faster. "No, that doesn't hurt," said Eurydice decidedly.

Ellsworth smiled wryly and shook his head. He began to thrust in and out of her with a slow, steady pace, and he watched as a look of wonder came over Eurydice's features. He gradually began to go faster, and he watched pleasure begin to replace it. She soon had her eyes closed, a smile of enjoyment playing about her lips, and Ellsworth smiled happily. She clutched at his shoulders and wrapped her other leg around his waist as he continued to move in and out of her, and Ellsworth lowered his head to place a line of kisses up her neck to her mouth. He was still kissing her when she began to orgasm, and Eurydice returned his kiss heatedly as it seized her.

"Oh, Gareth!" she gasped, and Ellsworth loved seeing the euphoria that filled her features.

He reached his own climax as hers ebbed away, and Eurydice reached up to put a hand against his cheek as he shook with a soft sigh of gratification. She smoothed her hand down his neck, and she lifted her head to kiss him affectionately. He slowly lowered his head to nestle his forehead in the crook of her neck and shoulder, kissing the side of her throat. Eurydice wrapped her arms around him with a slight smile.

"That...was...marvelous," she sighed contentedly.

Ellsworth lifted his head to look at her and traced a finger along her jaw before tweaking the end of her nose with an amused smile.

"Do you think you'll still have trouble doing that?" he asked.

"Oh, no, I don't think so," said Eurydice agreeably.

"Does that mean I can forego finding a mistress?" he asked with a roguish smile.

"I will have to say that now I shall complain if you do," said Eurydice seriously before giving him a smile of her own.

Ellsworth laughed, and he rolled off of her after giving her another kiss. He pulled her close to his side, and Eurydice laid her head on his chest, giving the skin beneath her cheek a kiss before snuggling closer. She was really starting to like her husband.

Eurydice woke up the next morning, as she usually did, to the sensation of Ellsworth running his hands over her in a titillating fashion. This time, instead of worrying about what it might lead to, she hoped it would. She didn't know why it had hurt so much the first time, but last night had been incredible. She now had no difficulty understanding why everyone she knew liked it so much. She smiled as she opened her eyes, and she lifted her head to kiss him warmly.

"Good morning," drawled Ellsworth lazily.

"Good morning," purred Eurydice, and she shifted her position to lie on top of him and kiss him some more.

"Mm, Mrs. Ellsworth, you hussy," said Ellsworth amusedly as he smoothed his hands down her back to squeeze her bottom.

Eurydice lifted her head from where she had been teasing his ear to look at him worriedly.

"Do you not like this?"

Ellsworth chuckled and kissed her soundly. "Why don't you slide back a little further and find out?"

Eurydice raised an eyebrow questioningly, but did as he suggested. She didn't have to move very far before she felt his erection pressing against her. She began to kiss down his neck to his chest and gently worried one of his nipples with her teeth.

"Why, yes. Yes, you do," she said with a slow, impudent smile before she resumed what she was doing.

Ellsworth had been hoping she would be of the notion to make love when he woke her, and to find that she had needed no convincing made him very happy. He hoped it meant they would be able to put their wedding night behind them. That it appeared she was willing to behave everywhere except in bed also made him happy. He was really starting to like his wife.

She surprised him when she took his erection in her hand and slowly settled herself onto it. She released a soft sigh of pleasure as she closed her eyes and sat up, and Ellsworth grinned lustily. He smoothed his hands up her ribs to cup her breasts and tease the nipples with his thumbs. Eurydice quivered excitedly and threw her head back, thrusting her breasts into his hands and causing her hair to brush against his thighs erotically. Ellsworth sucked in air through his teeth and moved his hands down to her hips. He lifted up on them to get her moving, and Eurydice slowly began to raise and lower herself.

It was a little uncomfortable, but she realized it was due to his size and her position rather than anything else. It hadn't hurt last night. When he began to tease her button with his thumb, it made it easy for her to ignore the discomfort. She leaned forward to kiss him, and she found that eased the pressure she felt, and she began to move a little faster.

"Oh, Eurydice, you are sublime," he sighed.

Eurydice smiled mischievously and began to nibble on his ear as she tweaked his nipples. She loved the way he shuddered and gasped, his hands clutching at her hips. He brought a hand to the back of her head to bring her mouth to his for a ravenous kiss, and Eurydice moaned and nipped at his bottom lip as she began to orgasm. She was amazed that it was still as wonderful, still as intense, as it had been the night before. She just didn't think it could be possible.

She continued to move as the last of the spasms she felt began to wane, and she gently ran her fingers through his hair. He wore an expression of pleasure and concentration, his jaw clenched, his breathing ragged. He was *so* close. She kissed him softly as she smoothed a hand down his chest, lightly raking it with her nails. She felt him tense as he reached his climax with a soft moan of pleasure that almost sounded as if he were in pain. Eurydice nuzzled his jaw tenderly before she placed a kiss on his neck and slowly stopped moving. She eased herself off of him and propped her head on her hand to look at him. He lay with his eyes closed, breathing heavily, trying to get his heart to slow down.

While she waited for him to do that, she began to lightly trace his scars with a fingertip. There weren't a lot of them; it didn't look as if he had been riddled by bullets and stabbed a dozen times, but there were enough, more than any one man should have. They were also in places—some of them—that let Eurydice know he had come close to dying at least once or twice. That made her anxious for some reason. There was one on his shoulder that had a corresponding exit scar on his back. There was the long scar at the bottom edge of his ribs, and there was also a scar on the same side that looked as if someone had slipped a knife *between* two of his ribs. That was one of the scars that made her anxious. He had another scar from a bullet on the same side, a little higher, which would have hit his heart if it had been only a few more inches to the left.

When she looked up from what she was doing with a thoughtful frown, she saw him watching her with a guarded expression. She knew he was waiting for her to ask about the scars, how he had gotten them. She could only imagine, and she knew he wouldn't tell her the truth if she asked, despite certain things that had changed. She wanted to tell him she knew what he was, but she couldn't because she didn't *really* know. She only had her suspicions really, even if they were right. Instead, she leaned toward him and gave him a gentle kiss before resting her head onto his chest with a resigned sigh.

Ellsworth looked down at the top of her head contemplatively. The way she had looked at him, so sad, so knowing. It was such a world-weary expression for someone so innocent. She wouldn't ask him about the scars…or the tattoo. Not yet. But it wasn't because she hadn't noticed or that she didn't care. It was because—somehow—she already knew. She might not know the stories behind them, but she knew why. There were so many levels at which that bothered him.

There had only been one time he had been truly careless, the day Annabelle delivered her son, and he had left some very important documents in his coat. Somehow, chance had let her see them. He might have been a little careless by letting her know about Napoleon at Waterloo, but Ellsworth had been so happy, thinking everything was over. He had thought everything would finally return to normal. He had been wrong, of course, at least for him. When he thought about it, he realized he had been extremely careless around her, and he found himself re-examining his actions with everyone, wondering if he really had become as careless as Aberdare had accused him of being. He relaxed only a little when he felt confident he hadn't. Only with her. But of all the people it could have happened with, she would not have been the one he would have chosen.

He knew, though, that it wasn't all his doing. Because of her gift, or even her intuition and intelligence, she knew things whether he had been careless or not. And she probably knew just enough to make it dangerous for both of them. She seemed very capable of being discreet, but it would only take one thing said to the wrong person. She had apparently said something to her father about the night Signor Merletto was murdered, as close to the truth as she could come without graphic detail and appearing insane. She had told no one else, and he didn't think she had done it simply because Aberdare was her father. It seemed she had discovered that much as well, and Ellsworth was curious exactly how much she *did* know. The only problem was trying to find a way to learn that without telling her more and making it worse.

Chapter Seventeen

Eurydice finally had the opportunity to apologize to Mrs. Ellsworth later that day. She accepted the apology and seemed as if she truly hadn't been upset by Eurydice's outburst. She would not, however, tell Eurydice why she didn't like her son, and her opinion hadn't changed because of Eurydice's anger. Eurydice didn't want to pry. She would have several years to find out what had caused it. If not, as long as Mrs. Ellsworth didn't insult him while Eurydice was around, she would be satisfied to leave well-enough alone.

With his mother's arrival, Ellsworth began to spend more time away from the palazzo making final arrangements for their journey to Vienna. They would be leaving the last day of September, which would be arriving shortly. He was often gone from just after breakfast until just before supper, and Eurydice found herself missing him. She would practice on her violin, play the piano in the music room or her flute or panpipes, work on composing the latest piece she was hearing, socialize with her family and everyone else, and still, all day long, she would find herself growing impatient for him to come back. It was peculiar. It wasn't as if she wanted to spend every waking moment with him or that she couldn't bear to have him out of her sight. It was just the knowledge that he was there—nearby—that she found herself missing.

But his being gone during the day wasn't really what troubled her. It was his leaving at night when he thought she was sleeping that made a nervous ball form in the pit of her stomach. Wednesday and Thursday night, he left their bed to go somewhere. On Wednesday, Eurydice awoke to find him gone as she had in the early hours of Saturday morning. She knew it had something to do with Signor Merletto's murder and whatever he had gone to see the man about. On Thursday, she found herself unable to go to sleep, and she was awake when he left through the doors to the loggia and back courtyard after running a hand down her thigh and giving her a soft kiss to her shoulder. It had taken her at least an hour after he had gone before she was finally too tired to stay awake any longer. She didn't know when he came back, but both times, he was there to wake her when the sun was up, acting as if he had been there the entire night while she slept.

She didn't know how he was managing his midnight forays and staying up all day as well, but he never seemed tired. Unless he was near his mother, he was always good-tempered and pleasant, and he always had the energy to make love to her at night and sometimes in the morning. Eurydice grew suspicious that part of the time he was supposedly out making arrangements for their trip he had found some place to get a few hours sleep to make up for the ones he lost at night. She didn't know why he didn't just take a nap at the palazzo, but then she realized people would wonder why he was sleeping during the day. He thought *she* would wonder why he was sleeping during the day. She could have saved him the effort, but they were both still pretending she didn't know about his secret life.

She had to wonder what was going to happen when they got to Vienna. She had the feeling it would only be more of the same. She could be wrong, but she didn't think it likely that she was. That was where he lived, so it only stood to reason that was where he did most of his "work." How much longer would it have to go on? She didn't know how she felt about him doing it in the first instance, other than the occasional nervousness it caused her, so she couldn't say what she thought of it continuing indefinitely. Surely, now that Napoleon had been taken in hand, it had to end soon. What more could there be for him to do? Europe was now at peace, as far as she was aware. She only knew she didn't want to be a widow any time soon, and that was what she was afraid would happen if he didn't stop. She hadn't had any dreams that she remembered, but she hadn't remembered the dream that had saved him the night Signor Merletto died.

When Saturday morning arrived, Ellsworth woke Eurydice by slowly placing kisses up the inside of one of her legs. He was to her knee before her eyes opened, and she looked down to see him watching her with a salacious grin. She pursed her lips to hide her smile and shook her head with mild exasperation. If he had left at some point during the night, she didn't remember; she had been exhausted when she fell asleep, thanks to him.

"Good morning, Mr. Ellsworth," she said softly after he let go of her leg and moved up her body to kiss her soundly on the lips.

"Good morning, Mrs. Ellsworth," he answered with an amused smile. He tilted his head sideways as he looked at her. "I still find that strange."

"What?"

"That you are Mrs. Ellsworth. Sometimes when I wake up with you in bed beside me, it takes me a moment to remember I have a wife."

Eurydice put a hand to his cheek. "Well, then, you'll be relieved to know I find it no less surprising I have a husband," she said dryly with a slight smile.

He lowered his head to rub his nose against hers affectionately. "But I suppose if I am to have one, you'll do."

Eurydice laughed amusedly and rubbed her leg against his thigh enticingly. "Likewise," she chortled.

Ellsworth looked at her wonderingly. "That's the first time I've ever heard you laugh."

Eurydice frowned disbelievingly. "Surely not."

"No, really, I've never heard you laugh. Not in London, not on the ship, not here. I've seen you smile...sometimes with genuine happiness. You've chuckled briefly...snickered, but not one laugh," he said seriously.

"Oh," she sighed, her eyes widening in surprise.

Ellsworth lowered his head to kiss her neck. "I like your laugh," he mumbled as he began to make his way to her breasts. "I should like to hear it more often."

Eurydice put a gentle hand to the back of his head, and she closed her eyes with a deep sigh as he began to tease one of her nipples. She had never thought she didn't laugh very much. She didn't consider herself unhappy or somber, but perhaps she seemed so. She didn't think it would make her conscientious about trying to do it more often—an affected laugh was worse than none at all to her mind. Perhaps it was that she hadn't had much to laugh about lately.

They left for Vienna not long after breakfast. It involved many tears from Psyche and the younger Andreanopouli. Yelena did not want to let go of her neck when Eurydice picked her up to give her a hug, and it took Psyche and Chrissoula to get her to let go. It left Eurydice feeling flustered. Freddie was trying to be brave, but he was ready to start crying, too. The Geniseos politely said goodbye and shook her hand. She hoped being with Psyche, Sheerness, and Freddie would be good for them. They were too young to have already led such unhappy lives. Aberdare shook hands with Ellsworth, giving him a silent, meaningful glance, and then he hugged his daughter tightly and kissed her cheek. Eurydice had a very hard time not crying herself at that point. She was going to miss him so much.

Sheerness shook Ellsworth's hand as well and wished him luck. When he hugged Eurydice and kissed her cheek, he whispered in her ear to be careful. She gave him a puzzled nod at the advice, but she didn't need him to explain. When he stood away from her, he promised he would send her a letter in Vienna as soon as he heard anything about the matter he was addressing for her, but he didn't know how much he would be able to accomplish until he returned to Britain. When Aberdare arrived, Eurydice and Sheerness had informed him of what had taken place, and Aberdare said he would help as well. Eurydice didn't doubt that her father had just as much capability as Sheerness in taking care of the matter, possibly even more. Ellsworth looked at the two of them suspiciously but remained silent. He could ask her later.

She received hugs and kisses from everyone else staying behind, and she hoped this wouldn't be the last time she saw them. If she didn't see them again, she determined it wouldn't be through any fault of her own. Despite everything that had happened there, her stay at the palazzo had been one of the most memorable and enjoyable times of her life, and she hoped she would be able to come back soon. One of the nice things about living in Vienna, she supposed, was that it was much closer to Venice than Britain was.

Rather than using two or more smaller gondolas to take them across the lagoon to Mestre, Ellsworth had hired just one larger boat that was capable of carrying everyone. Two other boats of a similar size had been used for their belongings and left the palazzo before they did to meet with the coaches and wagons that would be used for transporting them and have everything loaded on, hopefully before the arrival of their boat at the same point. The boat that carried them was very comfortable, with an awning to block the sun and well-padded seats. It required two oarsmen to operate, and it took them some effort, as weighted down as it was. They would be very tired by the time they reached Mestre, but hopefully their return trip to Venice would be easier.

Eurydice enjoyed her last ride on the Grand Canal. She got to see the rest of the palazzi she had missed on the tour that Ellsworth had given her on her birthday. The journey was slow enough that he was able to point things out to her as they traveled and to answer questions if she had any. The Ponte Rialto was absolutely beautiful, and the ride on the canal was the perfect way to end her visit to the city.

Ellsworth sat on the same cushioned seat with her, an arm draped casually over her shoulders, and Eurydice relaxed against him without a thought. She had become so accustomed to and comfortable with him in the short time they had been married that she could sometimes scarcely believe how recently the exact opposite had been true. There were still things about him that she questioned, but she was beginning to trust him despite that uncertainty. She had begun to realize that for the things that mattered, he was completely honorable and attentive. Despite how they had come to be married, she could have done a lot worse for a husband.

When they reached Mestre, their baggage was loaded. Eurydice couldn't believe how many vehicles there were. Two high-sided wagons were packed with their trunks, other than items they would need on their journey. The wagons wouldn't be traveling with them; they would travel directly through, rather than stopping at night like the Ellsworths, and they would hopefully be to Vienna and unloaded before the family's arrival. There were only two coaches for the people because they weren't all adults. It would have taken more if all ten of them were full-sized. Ellsworth, Eurydice, and Agniezka would travel in a smaller one, while Mrs. Ellsworth, her lady's maid, the nanny and the children would travel in the other. Casanova in his cage would be in the coach with Eurydice. She couldn't trust that he would arrive safely if he were carried with the baggage, and she couldn't put him in a coach full of women and children, even if most of them wouldn't understand what he was saying.

After Ellsworth paid the boatmen the rest of their fee, the family set off for Vienna. Eurydice didn't know how long it would take to reach the city. They would stop periodically throughout the day to change horses and to eat dinner, but they would also stop at night to sleep at inns. She wasn't sure how far Vienna was from Venice, and she didn't imagine they would travel quickly. She knew how fast the mail coaches were at home and how long it took her own family to travel to and from Glyncorrwg to London, but this was different. She didn't know the condition of the roads, bridges, or anything else. She only knew that the amount of time she would have needed to spend in a coach was greatly shortened by having taken the *Medea* to Venice. Granted, the overall length of her journey would be longer time-wise, but she was enjoying it more.

Eurydice sat on the seat behind the driver with Ellsworth while Agniezka sat on the seat facing forward with Casanova in his cage beside her. Eurydice had the cover off for the time being because he was behaving himself, but if he started to talk rudely, she would put the cover back on. Eurydice preferred the forward-facing seat, but Agniezka needed it because of her traveling sickness, and Eurydice wanted to sit by Ellsworth. She couldn't have both.

The seats of the coach weren't as cushioned as the ones in those belonging to her family, and this coach was also smaller. It was just large enough for two people to sit per side with barely a foot of space between them on the seat. Agniezka was somewhat crowded with Casanova's cage sitting beside her. She barely had enough room to pull out her knitting and move her elbows, but she did at least have a window. The leg room between the seats was comfortable, and they didn't have to tolerate bumping their knees against those of the person across from them. Their coach was only pulled by two horses, whereas the one carrying everyone else was pulled by four. It was also much larger, and Eurydice imagined the seats were more comfortable, too.

They stopped for dinner in Treviso and changed horses. Eurydice was astonished to see that it also had canals because of its location at the merging of the Botteniga with the Sile. There were definitely not as many as in Venice, but it made the city very picturesque. The people who lived there didn't depend on the canals for transportation as they did in Venice either.

They had a very interesting meal, and Eurydice had never tasted anything quite like it. They were first served bowls of ravioli filled with a mixture of basil, pine nuts, and other spices covered in a sauce made from cream and lemon juice. That was delicious, but the main dish was the one she thought she could eat every day. It was a very large flat bread made with yeast, coated with a tomato sauce seasoned with oregano, garlic, basil and olive oil. That, by itself, would have been wonderful, but it had been covered with cheese, ham, ripe olives, and peppers. When it was brought to their table, cut up and served, Eurydice had no choice really except to eat it with her fingers. Mrs. Ellsworth thought it was rustic for them to serve that particular dish, but Eurydice thought she had died and gone to heaven. When she asked Ellsworth if he knew what it was, and he saw her blissful expression as she began to devour a second piece, he chuckled and told her it was pizza. After the heaviness of the meal, dessert was a simple biscuit called *zaleti* made from cornmeal, currants, and nuts.

Eurydice liked them so much she took a few extra with her to eat in the coach should she become hungry again before they stopped for the night and supper. She didn't think she would, though.

Once they left Treviso, they began to take a direction to the northeast, skirting along the foothills of the Venetian Alps. The land they traveled over was fairly flat, but Eurydice could see the mountains in the distance. It was also heavily veined with rivers and streams making their way to the gulf. Even in early fall, the land was still green and patchworked with fields that had been ploughed and sown with cover crops to prepare for the next growing season. The air smelled so pure with a hint of spice and citrus. It was marvelous.

They stopped for the night at Sacile, another town that had been built at the confluence of two rivers. They were able to find an inn with room enough to accommodate them located not far from the duomo on the Livenza. It was almost dark when they arrived, and yet it was barely six in the evening. Eurydice couldn't possibly go to sleep that early, but she might change her mind after supper. If they were served a meal as heavy as the one they had at dinner, she would be more than ready to sleep.

The nanny was put into a room with the children, while it was arranged for Agniezka to share a room with Mrs. Ellsworth's maid, Edith. Eurydice and Ellsworth, of course, were in the same room together, and Mrs. Ellsworth had her own. Eurydice was disappointed the drivers of the coaches wouldn't have a room, but would instead stay in a large, dormitory-like room where several single men stayed together. It was better than having to sleep in the barn, and it was cheaper than letting another room. The men didn't seem unhappy that was to be their accommodation, so Eurydice was willing to not say anything.

By the time everyone was settled into their rooms, it was nearing eight. They went to the common room for supper, and apparently Saturday night was a time when a lot of people came to that particular inn to socialize. They were able to find tables to sit at for their meal, but if they had arrived just a little later, that might have been problematic. There was a trio of amateur musicians playing in a corner not far from the fireplace, and the room was filled with a steady level of noise from conversations. Mrs. Ellsworth would have preferred to eat in her room, but Eurydice wasn't bothered; neither was Ellsworth. The children were round-eyed at all the activity, but they were well-behaved.

Eurydice wouldn't have minded pizza again, but instead they were first given *risotto* with asparagus, followed by braised pork with tomatoes, cream and porcini mushrooms with side dishes of artichoke *parmigiana* and potatoes roasted with black olives and garlic. That was followed by a salad made from fennel with a bowl of fruit for dessert. Eurydice would have still preferred pizza, but the meal was entirely satisfying. Her eyelids were heavy by the time she and Ellsworth left for their room.

Agniezka was going to come with Eurydice to help her get ready for bed, but she told her maid she could manage without her and that she could go to her own room. Edith heard the conversation, and Eurydice could tell she was scandalized and just the least bit envious. Mrs. Ellsworth fully expected her maid to help her dress and undress morning and night…or at any point in-between when it was necessary. Eurydice thought it was a waste of time to get into her shift; Ellsworth would be pulling it off of her at some point soon. The only thing she really needed Agniezka's help with was braiding her hair, and Eurydice didn't mind going without occasionally. Her hair did tend to become tangled while she slept if it wasn't braided, but it wasn't a necessity. Agniezka was tired, and it would be more likely for her to be sick if she didn't have rest.

When they got to their room, Ellsworth pulled Eurydice toward him to kiss her warmly as he began to work at the fastenings on the back of her gown.

"I have been wanting to do that all day," he purred as he slid her dress from her shoulders to let it drop to the floor.

Eurydice gave him a smile. "Which? Kissing me or getting me out of my dress?"

"Yes," said Ellsworth distractedly as he nuzzled her neck and grabbed her bottom to press her against him.

Eurydice chuckled and reached up her hands to remove the pins holding up her hair as he moved lower to begin placing kisses along the edge of her chemise. She playfully maneuvered out of his grasp to put the pins on the dressing table with the rest of her toiletries where they could be found in the morning, and Ellsworth came behind her to wrap his arms around her waist and begin to pull her backward toward the bed. Eurydice laughed at his impatience and managed to turn herself to face him and reached up to unfasten his cravat, pulling the linen loose from his neck and letting it fall to the floor. She had started on the buttons to his waistcoat when they reached the edge of the bed, and she tumbled on top of him onto the mattress. Eurydice laughed so hard she snorted when she inhaled. Ellsworth looked at her amusedly.

"Did you just *snort*?" he chortled.

"Did I?" she asked with a barely controlled innocent expression.

He laughed. "You did!"

Eurydice lowered her head to kiss him temptingly, and then she sat up on her knees to either side of him to remove her chemise and let it fall to the floor after she disentangled her hair from it. She reached down to unfasten the last two buttons on his waistcoat, and then she pulled his shirt loose from his pants. She lifted it and lowered her head to one of his nipples, and Ellsworth gasped as she sucked it into her mouth and rasped her tongue against it. She sat up and tried to remove his clothes.

"I want you naked," she panted excitedly.

Ellsworth grinned lecherously and put his hands to her hips to flip her off of him onto her back on the mattress then stood up.

"In a jiffy," he assured, pulling off his waistcoat.

Eurydice lay with her cheek propped on one of her hands as she appreciatively watched him undress by the light of the fire. She was tempted to help when he had difficulty removing his boots, but he soon had them off along with his pants. He rejoined her on the bed, and Eurydice sighed contentedly when he leaned over her on his knees, one hand balanced near her head, and kissed her. She had been waiting for bedtime no less impatiently than he had, she was sure. She weakly put a hand to the back of his head and ran her fingers through his hair.

Ellsworth laved one of her nipples with his tongue, and Eurydice arched her back with a soft moan. She trailed one of her hands down his chest to his stomach, but she couldn't quite reach what she was searching for. She shifted herself on the mattress to move further beneath him, and then she could put her hand around his member. Ellsworth groaned and nipped at her breast. He was not fully erect yet, and she slowly began to stroke him. After only a moment, though, Eurydice decided she wasn't happy with her position and let go. She startled Ellsworth when she managed to flip him over onto his back and reversed their positions.

"How did you do that?" he asked in amazement.

"My brother, Dorian, taught me," she said distractedly as she began to kiss her way down his neck to his chest.

She teased one of his nipples as she slowly let her fingers trail down his stomach to take his erection in her hand. She began to stroke him again as she slowly ran her tongue down the ridge of muscle in his stomach to his navel. She circled the indentation with the tip of her tongue before sucking at it, and she smiled satisfactorily as she felt him begin to grow harder and heard him sigh with pleasure. She loved that she could make that happen.

Ellsworth had a slight frown as she continued to tease him. He was greatly enjoying what she was doing, but she shouldn't have been able to do what she did. Not only because she was a woman, but because of *how* she had done it. She was completely nonchalant, as if what she had done were nothing unusual, but it was, especially that it had seemed so effortless and instinctive. She said her brother had taught her. As Aberdare's son, Ellsworth could see where Dorian might have learned it himself, but he had to wonder if their father was aware of what the man had been teaching his sister. He also had to wonder what else her brother had taught her.

He soon lost the ability to think about that or anything else when Eurydice took his erection into her mouth while she stroked him with her hand. She may have been innocent when she married him, but she was quickly becoming skillful. She might be modest, but she was obviously not prudish or frigid. She let her intuition and senses direct her actions when they were in bed together, and she didn't have any concern that some of the things she did might be viewed as improper for someone of her position to enjoy. He couldn't believe his luck in discovering how wrong his assumptions had been.

He took her by the shoulders and drew her up his body to kiss her hungrily before rolling over to place her beneath him. She wrapped her arms around his shoulders and nuzzled his neck, and then she put one of her legs around his waist and rubbed against him ardently. Ellsworth smiled teasingly and positioned himself to thrust into her, but he didn't. Eurydice made a sound of frustration and put her hands on his buttocks to push against them, but still he waited. Ellsworth lowered his head and kissed her neck with a soft laugh.

"Now," she moaned. "I want you *now.*"

Ellsworth pushed into her a little further, but he continued to withhold himself. He was relishing the expression of longing on her face, but he wouldn't make her wait much longer. He was having a hard time maintaining his control, and he sucked in air through his teeth when she scratched at his buttocks with her fingernails.

"When you say now, do you mean you want me *right* now?" he asked with a wicked smile.

Eurydice groaned frustratedly, and she wrapped her other leg around his waist and lifted herself from the mattress to bury him within her as she kissed him, nipping at his bottom lip.

"Yes!" she drew out on a desperate sigh, and she moved against him hungrily.

Ellsworth chuckled lowly and began to drive in and out of her, matching the pace she had started. Eurydice sighed relievedly and smiled with pleasure, running her hands across his shoulders to grip his upper arms tightly. He felt her nails dig into the skin as she began to orgasm with a choked whimper, and he watched as her back arched off the bed in an uncontrollable spasm of ecstasy. He quickened his pace slightly, and he soon joined her, lowering his head to suck at the soft skin of one of her breasts. He wrapped his arms around her waist as he rested his head on her breasts, and Eurydice softly ran her fingers across the skin on his shoulders. Both of them were sweat-soaked and breathing exhaustedly, and they were feeling entirely satisfied.

Ellsworth eventually managed to find the energy to move off of her onto his stomach on the mattress, but neither could find the strength to get under the blankets just yet. He had one of his arms draped across her waist, his head resting close to hers on the pillow, and Eurydice lightly ran her fingers up and down his forearm in a caress, her eyes closed as she tried to get her breathing under control. She was starting to doze off, but when she managed to open her eyes and turn her head, she found Ellsworth looking at her.

"What?" she asked softly.

"I was just wondering something," said Ellsworth casually.

Eurydice rolled onto her side to face him and rested her arm over his around her waist with a slightly amused smile. "And what were you wondering?"

"Did your brother teach you anything else?"

Eurydice arched an eyebrow, finding the question unexpected. "One or two things, but I didn't have time to learn more. I had other things to study."

"Does your father know he taught you that?"

Eurydice gave him a dry smile. "No, probably not."

"And where did your brother learn what he taught you?"

"He learned it from his valet."

"His valet?" asked Ellsworth in surprise.

"Yes, his valet, Ashikaga Hiroshi, is from Japan—Utsunomiya," said Eurydice as she propped herself up on her elbow to look down at him.

She began to lightly trace her fingers over the dragon on his back, and she was unsurprised that she couldn't feel where one color ended and another began. She lowered her head to trace one of the areas with her tongue, and she couldn't feel a difference that way either. It was a beautiful piece of work.

"Does your father know your brother's valet taught him that?" he asked stilly.

"Of course," said Eurydice as she continued to examine his tattoo. "Dorian has a tattoo exactly like this one," she said absently as she touched and tasted, "but his is blue and red. I've never seen it, but Hiroshi has one, too. His entire family has them."

When the muscles beneath it rippled, it almost seemed the dragon was alive. It was extraordinary. Ellsworth surprised her when he turned over to look at her.

"Your brother and his valet have that tattoo?" he asked breathlessly, his features pallid.

"In blue and red, yes," she said casually with a shrug, "as do Hiroshi's brother, Yoshio, and his sister, Keiko. Their mother, Michiko, also has one, but hers is a little different because she is from a different clan—Asano. I'm not sure what design it has, but it is also blue and red." She shrugged again. "It may not mean anything to you—perhaps it does, but the Ashikaga and Asano are of the same ilk as the Hattori in Iga, the clan of Hiroshi's paternal grandmother...who have the tattoos in red and green. Hiroshi gave the tattoo to Dorian...once he completed his training. It took a very long time...for both...years," she said softly. Ellsworth looked at her guardedly, but he didn't say anything. "It took a lot of effort...for both...and pain, but it was the *only* way either could be done."

"You knew I was lying," he stated dully.

Eurydice gently ran her fingers along the edge of his face, down his neck, to his chest. "Of course," she said quietly. "We all did, except for Freddie."

"And you let me do it."

Eurydice gave him a wan smile. "You thought you needed to." Ellsworth leaned toward her and gave her a soft kiss. When he lifted his head, Eurydice looked at him solemnly. "I know what you are," she said quietly.

Ellsworth gave her an indulgent smile, trying to seem unconcerned, but his heart was thudding against his ribs uneasily. "And what am I?"

"You're a spy." She looked at him pensively. "Perhaps even an assassin."

He started to laugh when she said it, but when she looked at him with that same...*ancient* expression, the laugh slowly faded, along with the smile, and he closed his eyes defeatedly.

"I really wish you hadn't said that," he said softly.

"I know you work for my father," continued Eurydice, deciding to tell him all her suspicions. "He probably even recruited you."

"Stop," said Ellsworth in an airless tone, and he really did feel as if he couldn't breathe.

"You had papers with French troop movements written in invisible ink hidden in your coat. You were at Waterloo."

"Stop," he repeated a little more forcefully.

"And whatever you're doing now, Signor Merletto was a source...or an agent, and he was—"

"Stop!" repeated Ellsworth, and he put a hand over her mouth and rested his forehead against hers. "Shh. Don't say another word," he whispered gently.

He had hoped she didn't know. He had hoped she wouldn't discover the truth, but he had been fooling himself. It had probably all begun to unravel from that day in the coach in Rotherhithe, and every time he had been even just a little careless had only given her more clues. She hadn't needed second sight to figure it out. He had made it easy for her.

Now he knew that she knew the truth. What was said could not be unsaid. He could try to play off what she had said as foolishness, but it would be useless. It was too late for that. And what was he going to do about it? He wasn't so sure she wouldn't tell anyone what she knew. He wanted to believe she wouldn't, but there were ways to make people talk, even if they didn't want to. And if someone ever became suspicious and tried to get to him through her.... He couldn't bear the thought of it.

She would have to be protected...watched, but it would have to be done subtly. She wouldn't tolerate it, thinking he was trying to control her. If it were too obvious, it might also make it easier for others to discover what he was and make them all the more determined to harm her to get to him. At least now he had no doubts about what she knew. In some ways, that would make things easier. In others, it was going to make them all the more complicated. Ellsworth didn't think he could handle things more complicated.

"We can't talk about this," he said quietly after he removed his hand from over her mouth.

"But I—" began Eurydice worriedly, and Ellsworth put two fingers back to her lips.

"Shh. I really wish you didn't know, but I can't change that. You must never say a word to anyone."

"But I—" she started again with a frown.

"To *anyone*," he said firmly.

Eurydice's heart was fluttering anxiously as she looked at him. She hadn't asked, but he hadn't really admitted it either, so they were technically in the same place. The only difference was that before there had been deniability. He couldn't—or wouldn't—deny it now. A small part of her had wished she had been wrong. She didn't know all the details of what his occupation involved, but it was dangerous. Knowing about his scars and the death of Signor Merletto, Eurydice was almost panicked to find out he was involved. She didn't like that feeling. She knew she shouldn't be...for so many reasons.

Ellsworth continued to look at her with that grave expression, so serious and pleading and sad. Maybe she shouldn't have said anything—about his tattoo or his spying. It was going to change something in their relationship, and it had only just started to get to the point where she felt they were compatible with one another. Now, since they couldn't speak about it even though she knew the truth, it was going to leave a void that would have to be skirted around or risk falling in.

Eurydice finally nodded resignedly and gave him a brief kiss. They got under the blankets then, and she snuggled close against him, putting his arm around her and laying her head onto his chest. Listening to the slow, steady beat of his heart calmed her only a little, and it took a long time before she finally went to sleep. When she did, the dream she had did nothing to make her feel better.

Chapter Eighteen

The family started out early the next morning after breakfast. The air was cool, but the sky was clear, and the weather would be perfect for traveling. The road was in good repair and traffic was light, making it possible for them to keep a fairly decent pace over the plain they crossed at the base of the Alps. Tomorrow, however, would not be so easy because they would be starting into the mountains Eurydice could see to the north and east, directly ahead of them. They looked beautiful from a distance, but traveling through them and over them would be slow.

They stopped shortly after one to have dinner at Palmanova. The land was too flat for them to see it, but Ellsworth explained that the city walls had been built in the shape of a nine-pointed star, a design that made it easier to defend from attacks. The irony was that it had never been attacked from the time it was built in the sixteenth century. When Napoleon arrived, it had surrendered without a shot being fired. Even without seeing the entire design of the city, Eurydice thought what of it she could see was pretty. As a matter of fact, she had yet to see anywhere in the country that she didn't think was just lovely.

After dinner, they continued eastward, the mountains coming ever closer. They stopped for the night at the base of the mountains in Gorizia after they crossed the Isonzo. It was nearing six in the evening, and Eurydice didn't realize the sun set so early until they left Venice. Seeing that and combining it with the chill that was beginning to constantly hang in the air confirmed for her that autumn had arrived.

The inn they stayed at was just as nice as the one had been in Sacile, and when Eurydice looked out the window of their room, its location gave her a beautiful view of the sunset over the plain they had just crossed. They had a very nice supper completely different from the one they had the night before. They were first served a wonderful soup with seasonal greens and pasta, followed by a main dish called *cevapcici*, which were somewhat like grilled sausages and served with *polenta.* Dessert was a delicious *gnocchi* stuffed with cherries and plums that Eurydice ate so much of she could scarcely move.

Mrs. Ellsworth, again, thought the food was beneath what she felt should be served. Eurydice was not so discerning. If it was edible and satisfying, that was all she required. She had yet to be served anything as fabulous as the pizza they had eaten in Treviso, but everything was entirely adequate. She was actually enjoying the opportunity to sample the different regional dishes. She had been able to do that somewhat at home because of the servants they had from different countries, but Eurydice was never averse to trying more.

That night when they went to bed, Eurydice was glad to have Ellsworth to snuggle against. It was her understanding the weather in Gorizia was comparatively mild because of its location, but she was cold. The blankets were warm and they had a fire, but neither warmed her quite as pleasantly as her husband. After they made love, he spooned behind her and held her close, and she felt very cozy. But she couldn't go to sleep.

Ellsworth woke up that morning pretending they had never talked about what he did for an occupation (or pastime—Eurydice wasn't sure what it was). She tried to do the same, but she couldn't...not quite. She wanted to know when he had started, *why* he had started, and when it would end. She especially wanted to know when it would end. But he had told her they couldn't talk about it. She understood why not, but she couldn't forget what she knew, and knowing only made her want to learn more.

Then she had the dream last night. She hadn't been able to remember all of it that morning when she wrote it down, but she wrote down what she could. As much as she had disliked what she saw, she found herself hoping she would dream it again. At the same time, she hoped she didn't. She rarely saw a vision more than once, but the few times she had, it always meant it would happen...soon. She didn't want this one to *ever* happen. She wanted to believe it was only a dream caused by what she and Ellsworth had been talking about before she went to sleep, but she could tell the difference. It was a vision. The only reason she wanted to have it again was that she had missed the end. The rest of it had worried her enough that she *needed* to know how it ended.

She finally snuggled against Ellsworth with a tired sigh and twined their fingers together. Ellsworth had long since fallen asleep, and she envied that. Until recently, she'd never had a problem falling asleep. Maybe once they were settled in Vienna instead of sleeping a different place every night, then she would fall asleep easier. If not, she still had Psyche's sleeping draught.

It was overcast when they left from Gorizia the following morning. Eurydice was hopeful the skies would clear as they traveled further east, but the sky was so gray she wasn't sure which direction the clouds were moving. It didn't improve as the day wore on. It was still gray when they stopped in Ober Laibach for dinner, but it didn't start raining until after they stopped at Podpetsch for the night. Even then it didn't start until they were in bed.

It involved a lot of thunder and lightning and howling wind, and Eurydice usually found that kind of weather soothing, but she didn't that night. She didn't have the dream again last night, but she had a different one. It wasn't good either, but it wasn't what she wanted. She *needed* to have the dream again, but she couldn't make herself do it. She had no control over what she saw. She tried to console herself by thinking if she didn't have the dream again perhaps it meant she had a long time before it happened. She had nearly five years with Myron before the vision she had about his death came true. Eurydice was sure of what would happen with Psyche's pregnancy because she'd dreamt about it five times already. That was the most she had ever dreamt about anything. When her *babushka* died, she'd only dreamt it twice.

Sometimes she could tell when a vision would happen because of certain things within it. If it involved people she knew, she considered how they looked: were they older? If there was more than one person, had she or the other people in the dream met yet? What were the surroundings like? It could be tricky, but sometimes it could be done.

The only things she knew from the vision she wanted to have again was that it involved her and Ellsworth; it was dark and very cold; and it was going to be dangerous. She didn't know what kind of danger and what would happen to either one of them because of it. She needed to know. Even if it was bad, she needed to know.

They were lying in bed together, and Eurydice was trying not to fidget. She was watching the flames in the fireplace and listening to the storm, hoping they would lull her to sleep, but she wasn't having any success. She started slightly when Ellsworth smoothed a hand up her thigh and across her hip to her stomach as he placed a kiss on her ear. She thought he had gone to sleep.

"It's just a storm," he whispered soothingly.

She had apparently not been as still as she thought she was. She put her hand over his and snuggled against him.

"I'm not bothered by the storm," she said quietly.

"Then what is it? You've seemed preoccupied since we left Sacile. Are you missing your family?"

Eurydice turned over onto her back to look at him. "I will always miss my family when I am away from them. I've accepted that."

Ellsworth ran a gentle finger along her jaw with a thoughtful expression. She had that look on her face again. He was beginning to learn it never meant anything good.

"What is it?" he asked softly.

Eurydice looked at him consideringly for a moment, and she knew she couldn't tell him. The Insight wasn't something she liked to discuss…with anyone. Her family knew about it, and most of them shared it to some degree. Agniezka knew about it and accepted it, but she knew Eurydice wasn't comfortable talking about it. She knew it was both a blessing and a curse to Eurydice, and it was a part of herself Eurydice had learned to live with, even if she didn't like it. But it was something not everyone could understand or tolerate. It wasn't so very long ago that people burned women like her at the stake. Now, they would simply classify her as insane and lock her away in an asylum. She didn't want Ellsworth to think that about her. It was hard enough trying to pretend she didn't know he was a spy; she didn't want the Insight to come between them as well. She still didn't know him well enough to decide whether it would or not.

"It's nothing," she said dully, not looking him in the eye. "I'm having trouble sleeping. That's all."

Ellsworth knew she wasn't telling the truth. It was obvious something was bothering her. She had been somewhat distant when they left Sacile, but it had improved by the time they reached Gorizia. This morning, though, it was back worse than the day before, and it had only grown more so. He was sure part of it had to do with his being a spy and their not being able to talk about it, but it involved something more than that.

"You're lying," he said bluntly…if not unkindly.

Eurydice looked at him calmly, but she felt a mild annoyance for him accusing her of lying when he was wont to do it himself without a thought.

"I can't tell you what's bothering me because I don't know."

That was the truth. Until she had the dream again, she couldn't know why it made her so uneasy. She didn't know why this particular dream bothered her so much. She'd had bad visions before about people she knew, about people she *loved,* about herself, and none of them had ever affected her the way this one did. She didn't know if it was because she didn't know the whole story or something else.

Ellsworth looked at her suspiciously. He didn't think that was the whole truth, but it was as close to it as he would get her to come for now. The only reason he didn't press her was that she was respecting his request not to talk about his occupation. He did realize it wouldn't be fair, but *she* had promised she would be honest. He hadn't because sometimes he couldn't right now.

Eurydice put a hand to his cheek and lifted her head from the pillow to kiss him. "I don't know yet," she whispered.

Ellsworth nuzzled her neck and smoothed a hand up her side to rest it on her ribs just below her breast. Maybe she wasn't being completely honest, but her tone had been frightened. That was what she was trying to hide, for whatever reason. He didn't think it was him, and he didn't like that she felt that way. He trailed his fingers down her side to her thigh to find the bottom of her shift, and Eurydice sat up to let him pull it over her head. She didn't feel like making love, but he could change her mind. Actually, it might help…maybe.

He leaned his back against the headboard and pulled her toward him, and Eurydice straddled his lap on her knees. She wrapped her arms around his neck as he began to kiss her and pressed herself against him, her skin tingling as her breasts brushed against the hair on his chest. She loved the feel of him pressed against her. She smoothed a hand down his chest to his stomach before wrapping her hand around his erection, and she moaned softly when he gently bit one of her nipples as he rasped his tongue against the tip. She slowly began to stroke him with her hand, and Ellsworth grabbed her by her shoulders to ease her backward onto the bed as he kissed his way down her stomach. She soon had to let him go, and she sighed when he began to tease her with his mouth.

"Gareth," she whispered, and she clutched her fingers in his hair as she felt the ache growing in the pit of her stomach.

He smoothed a hand up her ribs to knead one of her breasts, and Eurydice moved one of her hands to place it over his before she lifted it to her mouth to place a kiss on the palm and move it to her cheek. He glided one of his fingers inside her as he played her, and Eurydice arched her back and trembled as she began to orgasm with a soft moan.

Ellsworth pulled her back onto his lap and into a sitting position, and Eurydice clung to him weakly as she kissed him. She rubbed herself against his erection as she tweaked one of his nipples before she let her fingers trail downward to take him in her hand. She moved onto her knees and raised herself up before slowly settling onto him. He groaned softly with pleasure and put his hands to her hips to hold her still.

"Wait," he whispered. "Don't move yet."

Eurydice put a hand to the side of his neck and teased his lips with her teeth, and then she clenched her internal muscles around him with an impudent smile. Ellsworth sucked in air through his teeth and tightly clamped his hands on her hips.

"You are evil," he sighed.

Eurydice's playful expression faded somewhat, and she lightly ran her fingers down his cheek before kissing him gently on the lips.

"No, I'm not," she said dimly.

Ellsworth frowned when he saw her expression, and he ran his fingers from the small of her back to her nape in a caress before bringing her mouth to his to kiss her warmly. He then wrapped an arm beneath her bottom to keep her pressed against him and rose up on his knees to turn and settle her onto the pillows. He slowly began to move in and out of her, and he loved the expression of need that filled her features. She ran one of her hands from his shoulder down his arm and twined their fingers together while she clutched the other in the hair at the back of his head. She wrapped her legs around his waist, and her breath came out in short, panting gasps as he plunged into her.

She cried out his name when she began to come, and as Ellsworth felt it, he lost what control he had and joined her. He kissed her with a soft moan as he slowly stopped moving, and they were both trembling. He weakly rested his head onto her breast, and Eurydice wrapped her arms around him, giving him a soft kiss to his forehead. They drifted off to a satiated sleep, oblivious to the storm and the cold.

Ellsworth woke with a bit of a start when it was still dark outside. The rain had stopped, and the air was very cool. The fire had burned down to only embers, and although he and Eurydice were still tangled together, he felt cold. He carefully felt for the edge of the blankets to pull them up without moving too much and waking Eurydice, and he frowned when he couldn't find them. He gently eased himself off of her, and he decided since he was moving, he might as well put more wood on the fire. Once he did that, he got back into bed and pulled up the blankets. He carefully pulled Eurydice closer and settled her head onto his chest and sighed relievedly as he began to grow warmer.

He was starting to drift off again when he heard Eurydice make a strange sniffling noise. He looked down at the top of her head, but he couldn't see her face. He didn't think she was awake; she hadn't been when he got back into bed, and he had been careful when he moved her. She was actually a rather heavy sleeper. After listening for a moment, he could hear that her breathing didn't have the same slow, even tempo he was used to hearing. It was fast and shallow, and if she were awake, he might have thought she was panicked. He softly smoothed a hand over her cheek, and he felt that it was wet.

Ellsworth frowned concernedly. She was having a bad dream, bad enough that she was crying in her sleep. He ran his hand up and down her back in an effort to soothe her, but he didn't notice any change in her breathing, and he could feel her tears beginning to dampen his chest. He finally decided the only thing he could do was wake her. He didn't think what she dreamt about could be anywhere near as violent as what he dreamt about, but he didn't like to see it. Her reaction to being awakened was not likely to be dangerous, either. He gently shook her by the shoulder and called her name.

Eurydice jolted awake and sat up, her chest heaving. She had a wild, disoriented expression, and then she looked at him in dismay.

"You woke me up!" she whispered brokenly.

Ellsworth looked at her worriedly and tried to pull her toward him to calm her, but she pushed his hands away.

"Oh, no, no, no," she moaned anxiously, shaking her head, and she began to crawl off the bed. "Have to hurry," she muttered to herself.

Ellsworth watched with bewilderment and concern as she lit a rush from the fire then used it to light the lamp on the desk. She got out her notebook and pen and began to write, unmindful that she was naked and it was cold. Ellsworth wasn't sure she was even awake as he listened to her continuing to mutter unintelligibly. He definitely didn't think so when he realized she was muttering in Russian. He hadn't even known she spoke Russian. He got up and went to her to get her to come back to bed. She pushed his hand away distractedly when he placed it onto her shoulder.

"Leave me be," she said shortly. "I've got to write this down."

"Dicy, come back to bed," he soothed.

"I've got to write this down," she repeated tersely. "You shouldn't have woke me."

"What are you writing? Can't it wait until morning?" he asked bemusedly.

She stopped writing for a moment and wiped at her cheeks and cleared her throat before she turned to look at him. He could see she was angry but also afraid, and he had never seen such a sad, knowing expression on a face so young.

"No, it can't wait. I'll forget, and I'm missing enough already. As for what it is, it's none of your concern," she said quietly.

"The hell it isn't," said Ellsworth flatly. "Whatever it is gave you a nightmare and has you acting like a madwoman. I would say it *is* my concern."

Eurydice tightened her jaw and narrowed her eyes at him. "Until you can give me a full accounting of everything you do, then you've no right to demand it of me," she said coldly, and she picked up her pen to begin writing again. The longer she waited, the more likely it was that she would forget what she had seen, and she needed to remember every detail she could. She still hadn't seen the end.

"That's not fair. You know why I can't," he said softly, his expression troubled as he looked at her back.

"Humph," said Eurydice derisively. "And in the future, I would appreciate it if you not refer to me as *mad.* Go away, please."

Ellsworth continued to look at her as she scribbled. He could *make* her come to bed, but she wouldn't stay, and she would only be all the more angry with him if he did. She was obviously disinclined to see reason. He didn't know what she was writing, but he recognized the notebook and knew what she used it for. He didn't understand how her gift worked, but it seemed the things she saw came to her in dreams. Whatever she had seen had apparently disturbed her a great deal, and he wanted to know what it was. She usually wrote in her notebook in the morning after she first got out of bed, but this particular vision must have bothered her so much she felt it couldn't wait. He hadn't looked at the diary since they had been aboard the *Medea.* Several pages had been filled since then; she was almost to the end of it. He didn't think he would be able to look at it again before they reached Vienna, but he would have to at some point. He finally sighed resignedly. He gently put his hands on her shoulders and kissed the top of her head.

"Fine," he said neutrally, and he went back to the bed and got under the blankets.

He turned his back to the light, but he didn't go to sleep. He wouldn't be able to until she came back to bed. As he lay there thinking, he realized rather humorlessly that they were a fine pair. He was bothered by dreams of things that had happened, while she was bothered by things that might. He knew part of the reason she didn't want to tell him was that she thought he didn't know about her gift...or curse. He wasn't sure how she viewed it. He knew it was what had provoked her to do the things she did the night Signor Merletto was murdered. Considering the way Eurydice was currently behaving, he didn't know how she could possibly think of it as a blessing. He wouldn't.

Eurydice sat at the desk for another thirty minutes or so, trying to make sure she had written down everything she could remember. There had been more at the beginning, and she was able to recall more from the middle—the part she had already seen, but the end was still missing. She still needed to see more. She knew now from seeing it more than once it was going to happen soon, but she didn't know how soon. Since she already knew it was coming, it was pointless to be worried she might see the vision again. Now she found herself hoping she would and knowing she needed to, especially now that she had seen more of it without seeing the most important part.

There was the same darkness and cold. She remembered snow and water. Seeing the snow let her know it would be winter, but would it be this winter or some other winter? Where was the water coming from? It seemed more like a river or a stream rather than a lake, but she didn't think it was in the countryside. It seemed bound...contained. And still there was her and Ellsworth, but there was someone else. She had almost seen his face. It was a man, and he was the source of the danger. She had seen a little more of what that danger would be, and it frightened her, especially since there was nothing she could do to stop it. That's why she needed to see the end, and Ellsworth had awakened her before she could.

She finally turned off the lamp and went back to bed. She looked at Ellsworth's turned back as she climbed onto the mattress. She tried to control her anger and annoyance. The annoyance was for him waking her before she could finish the dream. She couldn't be too upset with him for that because he hadn't known; he thought he had been helping. The anger was for the rest. He could talk about the fairness of things, but it was unfair he thought he could have all the secrets he wanted and yet she should be entitled to none. Then, to say she behaved as if she were mad was uncalled for. She had simply been agitated...not crazy. If nothing else, it only made her all the more convinced she couldn't tell him about the Insight.

Eurydice settled under the blankets facing the fire, her back turned to Ellsworth. She didn't know what time it was, but she hoped she could go back to sleep and that she would be less angry by morning. As for the dream, she hoped she would have it again, as many times as she had dreamt about Psyche's pregnancy would be good, or as many times as it would take for her to finally see the end of it. She only prayed she would see the end before it really happened. She was fairly sure it would happen in winter; it was still early autumn. Maybe she had a little time.

They left from Podpetsch early the next morning. Their breakfast had been served earlier, and they were able to leave about an hour sooner than they had been. They were going to need the extra time. The road wasn't in very good condition after the rain the night before, and while they were still able to keep to a fairly decent pace, they weren't going as fast as they had been. Even that hadn't been as fast as a mail coach might go in Britain, but it saved them from having to change horses quite so often, and it was less strenuous for the children.

Eurydice was starting to like her new nephew and nieces. The older children were slowly coming around, and Corinna always wanted to go to Eurydice when she was within sight. The only time she saw them was at dinner and supper, but there would be plenty of time to become better acquainted when they reached Vienna. She still missed her own family, but she knew she couldn't be with them and the Ellsworths were now her family, too.

Agniezka was finding the coach she shared with Ellsworth and Eurydice uncomfortable. The birdcage took up much of the seat, and the seat itself was not well-padded. Eurydice had hoped Agniezka would be all right for the short time it would take them to reach Vienna, but when they stopped for dinner in Maria-Pletrowitsch, she watched as Agniezka got down from the coach with a limp from the stiffness in her back. The ginger tea was helping immensely for her traveling sickness and her pregnancy sickness, but Eurydice had noticed yesterday morning that her eyes were beginning to develop dark circles from the strain the journey was putting on her.

Eurydice asked Agniezka if she would like her to speak with Mrs. Ellsworth about letting Agniezka ride in the other coach. The seats were better cushioned. Although it was carrying seven people, at least Corinna and Cassie were sitting on someone's lap. She was sure there was room, and if there wasn't, she was not averse to letting someone in the other coach come sit in the one she shared with Ellsworth...as long as it wasn't his mother. She didn't mind having someone else ride with them, but she wasn't sure how well the person would handle Casanova. He was being very well-behaved without the cover on his cage, but he would sometimes feel like talking and say something rude, requiring that the cover be put back. Eurydice could usually ignore it, but it was harder to do now that she and Ellsworth weren't talking.

Agniezka decided she would stay in the carriage with Eurydice and Ellsworth for the time being. She liked Edith, who she was getting to know fairly well from their sharing a room, but she didn't want to impose on anyone. She preferred to be with Eurydice, especially since she had noticed that morning that the girl and her husband weren't speaking to each other very much. Eurydice hadn't mentioned they'd had words, but it was obvious something had happened. By the time they stopped at Windisch-Feistritz for the night, however, Agniezka had changed her mind. Eurydice talked to Mrs. Ellsworth at supper, and she had no objection to Agniezka riding with them in the other coach. There was plenty of room.

That night, Eurydice and Ellsworth did not make love. They weren't even holding each other when they went to sleep. Eurydice dozed off with her back turned toward him, watching the fire. They hadn't talked much in the coach after they left Podpetsch. They had been polite at all their meals and in the coach, but there was a distance. They were both still angry, and neither wanted to apologize. Not only was Eurydice angry, she was also unhappy because the things she had feared would come between them had done exactly that, and there wasn't any immediate remedy to the situation.

She didn't think she was asleep for long when Ellsworth woke her. It was raining heavily again, but after being awake for only a minute or two, she knew it was her husband that had disturbed her. He was having a bad dream. She rolled over to look at him, listening to him mumble in his sleep, and she had to wonder about the things he had seen—the things he had done—to cause those dreams. She couldn't immediately understand what he was saying, and she frowned when she realized he was speaking Gaelic.

His family was Lowland Scots, from Renfrewshire, and only on his father's side, if she was remembering what his mother had told her correctly. His mother's family was from Durham. Even his father's ancestors weren't native Scots, but they had been there since the fifteenth century. That wasn't all that recent, but a lot of the families who had been there longer still thought of them as foreigners. She hadn't even realized he spoke Gaelic, and it was as odd to her as his wearing a kilt to their wedding had been. She wasn't so sure this dream was caused by his employment, though.

Even though she understood Gaelic, she couldn't understand what he was dreaming. Although the language was something she could decipher, most of it was incomprehensible muttering. She waited a few minutes to see if he would quieten, but he didn't. She was hesitant to do anything, remembering what had happened the last time she had tried to calm him, but she needed sleep. She wouldn't do any shushing or patting. She would just hold him. If that didn't work, then she would sleep in the coach tomorrow. It wasn't as if they were speaking to each other.

She sighed tiredly and charily edged toward him. He had his back turned toward her, just as she had done to him, and she carefully spooned behind him. She managed to work her arm beneath him and put the other over his waist and rested her cheek against his back. This wasn't as comfortable a position for her as it might be for him when he did it, simply because of their difference in size, but she didn't know what else she could do. Too much jostling would risk waking him, and the bruises she had on her neck had only just faded. Even if it was uncomfortable, she did feel warmer snuggled against him, and when he finally settled down, she easily went back to sleep.

Ellsworth didn't wake her when he got up the next morning. Eurydice opened her eyes to find herself lying in the middle of the cold bed alone. He hadn't even bothered to put more wood on the fire so she would have at least *that* to warm her. Fortunately, she only stayed that way for a few minutes, with the blankets up to her nose, before Agniezka came in with a tray carrying their breakfast and added the last of the wood to the fire. Once Eurydice could breathe with her mouth from under the covers without seeing a puff of vapor when she exhaled, she got out of bed and went to stand in front of the fire.

"I don't suppose you've seen my husband, have you?" she asked casually.

"He's having breakfast in the common room with the children and Nanny Rigsby," said Agniezka as she poured Eurydice a cup of coffee and added lots of cream and sugar.

"Oh," said Eurydice dully as she took the cup from her.

Agniezka busied herself getting out Eurydice's clothes. She was moving around quickly in an effort to keep herself warm in the cold room, but the fire was beginning to remove the chill. As it slipped further into October and they traveled north, the air had only become cooler, especially as they went through the mountains, and Agniezka was glad she had remembered to set aside some of the warmer pelisses for Eurydice to wear, the ones that would have been too hot to wear in Venice and cover the bruising on her neck. After they finished breakfast, Agniezka helped Eurydice dress and began to style her hair.

The ginger tea was doing wonders for Agniezka's nausea, and—the motion sickness notwithstanding—she thought it might be getting better even without the tea. Felton had told her the sickness would last for a few months, so she was hoping it would be gone by the end of October. Her waist was still narrow, and she might have until Christmas before it became obvious she was with child. Her breasts were getting fuller, but not so full yet that her dresses wouldn't fit. She hoped Sheerness would be able to obtain her divorce from Sergei very soon. She might be able to hide her condition until the beginning of the year, but after that, without taking drastic, dangerous measures, it would be impossible. Marrying Felton would be a perfect present for Christmas.

Agniezka looked at Eurydice's preoccupied expression in the mirror as she styled her hair. She wasn't too concerned because her mistress was often preoccupied—by her music or one of her dreams, but she knew Eurydice and Ellsworth weren't speaking. They had seemed to be doing so well that Agniezka could only wonder what had happened. She was fairly sure the problems they'd had on their wedding night had been resolved satisfactorily. This was something new.

"Is there anything wrong?" she asked softly.

Eurydice looked at her in the mirror for a moment. What could she say? There were so many things that were wrong, and most of them were things she couldn't discuss. She trusted Agniezka completely, but she could no more tell her maid Ellsworth's secrets than she could tell Agniezka's to him.

"I think I'm going to begin a diary," said Eurydice absently.

Agniezka smiled amusedly. "You already have one."

"No, that's for my dreams. Recently, I've found there are things in my head, cluttering it so I can't think clearly."

"You can always talk to me," said Agniezka soothingly. "I am not so wise and smart as some, but I listen very well."

"The problem is that I cannot talk about these things, no matter how much I might wish to do so, but I *can't* keep them in."

"Ah," said Agniezka comprehendingly with a slight smile. She added the final pin to Eurydice's hair, and then she set aside the brush and put her hands onto Eurydice's shoulders as she looked at her in the mirror. "Then perhaps you do need a mute confidant. Just remember what happened with the barber who knew the king's secret, though." Eurydice frowned uncertainly, and Agniezka's expression grew sober. "He dug a hole to leave the secret in and buried it, but then the reeds grew and whispered the secret for all to hear every time the wind blew: *the king has donkey's ears.*"

"I heard it another way," said Eurydice quietly.

"Oh?" said Agniezka with a raised eyebrow.

"It was his queen."

They left from Windisch shortly after nine, which was a later start than they usually had. The roads were not improved after the rain from the previous night, and the sky was cloudy with the threat of more. Still, traveling wasn't too difficult as they skirted along the edge of the Bach Mountains, known as the *Pohorje* to the local Slovenes. They crossed the Drava at Marburg and started into the hills of the *Slovenske gorice*. There was no valley to pass through, but the grades were gentle enough it went well. They stopped to eat dinner at Ehrenhausen just before they reached the Mur once they were across the hills, and although there were still hills and mountains all around them, the road would continue northward through the river valley.

Once they left Ehrenhausen, Eurydice spent the time looking out the window at the countryside. Without Agniezka in the coach, Casanova sat in his cage on the rear-facing seat, and Eurydice and Ellsworth were on the forward-facing one. The coach was also very quiet, other than the occasional expletive from the parrot. While they were stopped for dinner, Eurydice thought about looking for a book, but she enjoyed looking out the window. A nap would not be out of the question either.

"Did you and Agniezka have a disagreement?" asked Ellsworth shortly after they passed through Leibnitz.

Eurydice turned from the window to look at him. "No," she said calmly.

"Then why is she riding in the other coach?"

"Because the seats in this one are too uncomfortable for her."

Ellsworth frowned thoughtfully and pushed his hand against the squabs. They were leather, and while they weren't overly padded, they weren't bare wood. The coach wasn't well-sprung, but it wasn't unbearably jarring. He'd ridden in worse. The roads were in good condition, even after the recent rains.

"I think you coddle your maid," he said flatly.

Eurydice narrowed her eyes. "I do not *coddle* my maid. I treat her like a human being rather than an appendage." Ellsworth looked at her doubtfully, and she groaned. "Her back was broken when she was sixteen, and now it bothers her to sit for long periods of time, as in a coach, particularly when whatever she sits on is not well-cushioned. Perhaps you haven't noticed her hobbling every time we've stopped and gotten out of the coach, but your mother has, and she was most agreeable and kind in letting Agniezka ride in the other coach, where the seats are more comfortable and the springs are better. Added to that is her traveling sickness, which you've also apparently failed to notice, and the pain in her back only makes it that much harder for her to cope with the nausea. Easing her *suffering* is not *coddling.*" She turned to look back out the window, her jaw set angrily, and folded her arms across her chest.

"I'm sorry. I shouldn't have assumed," said Ellsworth quietly after a time, and Eurydice looked at him over her shoulder.

"Too right you shouldn't have," she said scathingly. "You know, for a spy, you really aren't that observant sometimes."

"How did she break her back?" he asked calmly, trying to keep his own temper in check.

"I'm not at liberty to say," said Eurydice evenly.

Ellsworth raised his hands frustratedly and shook his head. "Why do you *always* do that?" he asked in exasperation.

"Do what?" she asked quizzically.

"Why do you never tell me anything? You said you would be honest, and yet you consistently keep secrets from me!"

Eurydice turned around fully then to look at him. "I am being perfectly honest with you. I have never lied to you, even when I should have…many times. When a person tells me something in confidence, then I owe it to them to maintain that confidence, be they a member of my family, a friend, a ship's doctor, or a lady's maid. Perhaps gossips and tale-tellers make your line of work easier, but I am not either one. If it's not necessary for you to know something, then I don't need to tell you."

"I am your husband!" he said aggravatedly.

"To you, dear sir, I say kiss my arse," said Eurydice shortly. She held up her left hand and wiggled her ring finger. "You have one of these, too, hubby of mine, so you remember that the next time you demand I tell you something that is none of *your* business!"

"You know why I can't talk to you about what I do," he said stiffly.

"Then let me ask you something that should be easy for you," said Eurydice tartly. "Why do you speak Gaelic?"

Ellsworth frowned. "How do you know I speak Gaelic?"

"Because you were jabbering away in your sleep last night."

"My grandmother was a Sinclair, and she made all her grandchildren learn it. Why do you speak Russian?"

"Because my *babushka*, my father's mother, was from Tver."

"Do you understand Gaelic?"

"Yes. Do you understand Russian?"

Ellsworth smiled slightly. "Yes."

"See? Ask me a question I can answer, and you will see that I am very forthcoming," said Eurydice, smiling slightly herself.

"Likewise," said Ellsworth dryly.

Chapter Nineteen

Despite her misgivings yet feeling compelled, Eurydice started a new diary that night when they stopped in Graz. With the others, she did nothing but write down her dreams. In this one, which she used the notebook Arachne had given her for her birthday to begin, she would write down only her thoughts and things she could tell no one else. She simply couldn't keep them in her head any longer, and the number of things continued to grow to the point there was barely room for anything else. But she wasn't going to make it easy for the reeds to whisper should anyone happen by—she wrote it in Arabic.

Graz was a larger city than some of the others where they had stayed, and the hotel was able to provide Eurydice with a bath, much to her relief. She was blissful as she soaked, letting the water grow tepid until Agniezka had to come wake her. She almost felt like she was at home. She did feel guilty that she was able to have a bath but Agniezka couldn't. Her maid was accustomed to frequent bathing as well, as most of her family's servants were. If she had an opportunity for another bath before they reached Vienna, she would remember to not spend as long to let the water stay hot enough for Agniezka. She had no idea what the bathing conditions would be once they reached their destination, but they wouldn't be anything like those at home.

Eurydice and Ellsworth's truce only went so far. She told him her grandmother had taught her to play the violin and had given her the Stradivarius. He told her liked Scotland, and, were circumstances different, he would be living there rather than Austria. That was the extent of their peace. She made the mistake of asking him what circumstances those were, and he made the mistake of asking if there were anything else she had inherited from her grandmother. Neither question had been asked to poke a tender spot, but that was the end result.

They spent most of the night sleeping with their backs turned to one another, until Ellsworth—again—woke Eurydice with a bad dream. She didn't even fully wake up when she snuggled closer to him. He had at least turned over to his back at some point, so she was able to get into her comfortable position she had been missing with her head on his chest. He was mumbling in Gaelic again, but Eurydice was too tired to make an effort to listen. She still didn't think this nightmare was due to his occupation, and it was peculiar this one seemed to bother him more often than the one that had prompted him to strangle her. She could only imagine what was causing it, and she wasn't sure she wanted to know. She wasn't complaining, though; she would take Gaelic rambling over being choked to death whenever given a choice.

Ellsworth was at least still in the bed when she woke up the next morning, but he made no effort to wake her. When Eurydice woke up, she said good morning and moved away from him to get out of bed and write in her dream diary. She had not had the dark dream again since they left Podpetsch, and she was concerned she might not have it anymore. She wouldn't have been so worried if she at least knew the outcome. She did have other dreams, though, and she dutifully wrote them down so she wouldn't have to think about them anymore. Of the two she remembered, one might be a vision, but the other was just a dream. Ellsworth got out of bed and dressed and left the room without saying a word while she was writing. Her pen paused on the page for a moment when she heard the door open and close. She had heard him getting dressed, but she didn't know he was leaving until he was already gone.

She couldn't understand why they were so at odds over this. He couldn't accept that she couldn't betray a trust. Felton and Agniezka had confided in her, and it wasn't something Ellsworth needed to know. Depending on how things went for Sheerness and her father in arranging Agniezka's divorce, it *might* become necessary to tell him, especially if Agniezka had to go to St. Petersburg. If it wasn't done before it became obvious Agniezka was pregnant, she would have to tell him then, too. But until then, Eurydice could keep their secret. It also wasn't her place to tell Ellsworth that Sergei had nearly beaten Agniezka to death and that she had needed to crawl on her hands and knees most of the way from her husband's home to her father's through snow and ice to escape him. She couldn't see where it would ever be necessary for Ellsworth to know that. As for Psyche being pregnant, she hadn't even told her husband she was expecting their first child, one Eurydice knew they had been impatient to create since the previous year. If Sheerness didn't know, why should another man know first?

She would no more break those confidences than any Ellsworth gave her. She would never tell anyone what he did. The only reason she had talked to her father about the night Signor Merletto was murdered was that she knew he was involved. She wouldn't have told him simply because he was her father. She had never mentioned any of the things she knew about Ellsworth to anyone. She didn't expect him to tell her what he was doing, what the objective was of whatever assignment he had. She wouldn't care anyhow. All she wanted to know were the peripheral things, like why and how long. She felt those were things he could tell her without endangering his mission and, other than Agniezka, who might she tell?

Living in Vienna was going to make her very isolated. She might as well be living in the middle of a desert. She would have no one except Agniezka. She would be able to write to her family and receive letters. She would be able to visit them occasionally, but then there would be no one. She liked Mrs. Ellsworth, and they were getting on well together now that the woman didn't harangue her son in front of Eurydice. (She didn't know what happened when she wasn't around.) But it wasn't as if Eurydice could turn to her for help should she need it. And Ellsworth? She didn't know how long their current estrangement would last, but considering things, it would be more likely for him to cause her need for help rather than provide it. She would have no one but herself, and she wasn't sure she was capable.

They left from Graz after breakfast, and the coaches traveled slowly. There was a road—barely—following along the edge of the river through the valley, but because of its condition, the horses were frequently unable to do more than move at a walk. Eurydice would have thought the road would be in better condition. Graz was a large city, and the route they were taking was the most direct one between it and Vienna. It would be like the road between London and Edinburgh being impassable. By the time they stopped for dinner in Rothleiten, their slow pace was tiring to Eurydice. When they stopped for the night in Kapfenberg, she was exhausted.

She had nothing new to add to her life diary before bed. Ellsworth had, for the most part, slept while they traveled, and she had spent her time looking out the window at the passing countryside. They did, as usual, occasionally speak to each other, but it was always about something inconsequential. They could have been strangers traveling together by post for all the warmth they showed one another. That had been as tiring to Eurydice as the slowness of their journey. After Agniezka went to her own room once she helped Eurydice get ready for bed, Eurydice washed her face and brushed her teeth and relievedly climbed into bed. Ellsworth hadn't come in yet.

The inn where they were staying was nice, as all of them had been so far. They had yet to stay at one where Eurydice might be concerned about what could be sleeping in the bed with her besides her husband. This one, however, was a little drafty, and Eurydice soon pulled the blankets up to her nose and curled up in a ball to keep herself warm. There was a fire burning, but because of the draft, she would occasionally feel a warmth against her face followed soon after by a blast of ice. There was no warming pan to at least thaw her toes, and she clenched her jaw occasionally to keep her teeth from chattering. As tired as she was, she couldn't go to sleep because she was so cold. She was almost tempted to get out of bed to put her dressing gown on over her shift and sleep in that as well when Ellsworth came to their room.

She watched as he got ready for bed, washing his face and brushing his teeth before getting undressed. He didn't look at the bed, and he probably thought she was asleep. He seemed tired. She didn't know how he could be, considering he had slept most of the day in the coach. Then again, the bad dreams he had been having were keeping him from getting a restful night's sleep. When he got into bed, Eurydice thought about it for only a few minutes before she moved toward him and snuggled against his side, putting his arm around her and resting her head onto his chest. She felt him start in surprise when she did it.

"I'm cold," she said meekly by way of explanation.

"Is that what you've been doing the last few nights? Using me as a bed warmer?" he asked with mild annoyance.

"No," she said flatly. She yawned hugely and put a hand to her mouth to stifle it. She felt much warmer pressed against him, and now she was sleepy. "You've been having bad dreams. The same one...over and over again...I think," she mumbled.

Ellsworth looked down at the top of her head where it lay on his chest with a frown. He had wondered why she had been cozied up to him the last few mornings. He hadn't thought she had done it as some sign of affection, but now, he supposed she had...in a way. She had said he was talking in Gaelic in his sleep, and while he didn't remember the dreams, he could guess what had caused them. He was surprised she would have tried anything to soothe him after what had happened the first time, and he was relieved that hadn't happened again. She had already fallen asleep, and he smoothed a hand down her back to her hip and hugged her closer against him.

How were they going to get past their disagreement? He didn't like that she kept things from him, even if he had to admire her scruples. He suspected that part of the reason she wouldn't tell him things, though, was that he wouldn't tell her anything. She couldn't understand he was trying to protect her. Despite how they had come to be married, he did care about her...a great deal, and if circumstances had been different, he would have asked her to marry him...if Aberdare would have let him. If he could have waited and asked her when he was ready to, there would have been no need for all this secrecy. She need never have known what he did. She didn't seem to understand or care that the reason he didn't want to talk to her about his occupation was that the more she knew the more dangerous it could become for her.

Even though he could look at her diary to know what the dream was that had troubled her so much (and he still hadn't been able to do that yet), there was still the rest of it: Felton, Psyche, Sheerness, and Agniezka. He felt frustrated he had to—in essence—*spy* on her to discover things. Obviously, considering his occupation, she should know she could trust him with a secret, and he was her husband. Somehow, he had to make her trust him.

He missed making love to her, despite it only being a few days. When he woke up yesterday morning with her breasts pressed against his back, it had been all he could do not to turn over and ravish her. He didn't think it would have been welcomed, so he had left their room before he lost his senses and did it regardless. This morning when he woke up to find her pressed against him yet again, he had hoped it was a sign she missed him, too, but then she had tersely said good morning and got out of bed. While he enjoyed being close to her, he wanted to get *much* closer, and he wasn't sure how much longer he could wait. He wanted his wife.

Ellsworth finally managed to go to sleep, bothered by her being next to him yet enjoying it at the same time. He was warmer with her snuggled against him than without, and maybe this was the way they were going to eventually move beyond their secrets.

Eurydice woke up the next morning still cozy beside Ellsworth. Her head was nearly buried under the blankets because he had them tucked over his shoulder on the opposite side from her. When she tilted her head back to stick her nose above them, she could feel the cold. She spared a glance at Ellsworth's face and saw with some surprise that he was still sleeping. The fire had burned to nothing, and she didn't want to leave her warm place. He had at least not been bothered by a bad dream, or if he was, it wasn't bad enough to talk in his sleep and wake her.

She frowned slightly when she realized she'd not had a single dream she could remember. It didn't overly concern her because not having them had actually become more frequent of late, but she wished she had dreamed the dark dream again. If she couldn't see the end of it, she would at least like to know who the man was that would cause it. She didn't remember seeing his face in the dream, but it was possible she would know him if she met him—in the same way that she sometimes acted on dreams she didn't remember until they happened. She would like to have a little bit of forewarning.

"Unless you're going to screw me, would you please stop that?" said Ellsworth drowsily.

Eurydice started in surprise at the sound of his voice, and she realized when she stopped her woolgathering that she had absently begun to tweak one of his nipples. She removed her hand, and she frowned and looked up at him confusedly.

"Screw?"

Ellsworth leered at her. "Swive, shag, wap, join giblets, grind, knock, tup…fuck. Shall I continue?"

Eurydice's cheeks had turned a bright shade of pink. "No," she said abashedly. "Why do you call it that?"

"I don't always. There are so many words and phrases, why use just one?" he asked rhetorically with a grin. "Why do you call it sex?"

"Because that's what my family and I have always called it. It's much shorter than sexual intercourse and more polite than anything you just said."

Ellsworth chuckled amusedly and smoothed his hand down her back to cup her bottom. "Don't ever feel like you need to be polite with me on that subject, sweetheart. You can be as nasty as you want to be," he said with rakish charm.

Eurydice gave him a half-smile and lifted an eyebrow as she looked at him. She leaned forward and kissed him temptingly before she removed his hand from her bottom and got out from under the covers.

"I'm not going to screw you right now," she said dryly as she went to put on her dressing gown and add more wood to the fire.

"Maybe later?" asked Ellsworth hopefully, propping his head up on his hand.

Eurydice looked at him over her shoulder with wry amusement, but she didn't answer him. Instead, she went to sit at the writing desk and make an entry in her life diary. She heard Ellsworth sigh resignedly after a time and get out of bed. Even though her back was turned, she knew he was getting dressed, and she soon heard the door open and close as he left. Maybe she would give him what he wanted when they stopped for the night—depending on whether or not they got into any further arguments in the coach on the way there. She was missing it, and that surprised her. The entry she was writing was very short, and she was just finishing it as Agniezka came in carrying a tray with their breakfast.

They left from Kapfenberg within the hour, and Eurydice noticed that while they were still traveling through a valley, it had widened greatly from what it had been, giving room for fields to line the edges of the river that meandered through it. If they continued in the same direction, however, there would be mountains and forest ahead of them. She didn't know how long that would continue, but it would make their progress slower.

They had to be getting closer to Vienna. This was their seventh day of traveling, and even though they had been going slowly, Eurydice had enough understanding of the geography of the region that she knew it couldn't be long before they reached it. She didn't know the exact distances between cities or even what the distance was they had gone already, but it had to be nearing. It couldn't possibly be more than two or three days away. She was impatient to get there for so many reasons, not the least of which being that she had been unable to practice on her violin since leaving Venice.

By the time they stopped for dinner, they had traveled the length of the river valley to Muerzzuschlag, where the wider valley split into two narrower ones, one taking a northerly direction still following the river, the other going eastward. Their meal was very filling, consisting of roasted pork with dumplings, sauerkraut—which Eurydice found she could tolerate when it was eaten with a bite of the sausage that accompanied it at the same time, a pumpkin soup, and apple strudel. She was unsurprised the children didn't like the sauerkraut, and Mrs. Ellsworth thought the meal was particularly good. Her mother-in-law thought the food they were given in Graz was good as well, which let Eurydice know they were getting closer to Vienna. Eurydice missed pizza, but she wasn't choosy.

They left Muerzzuschlag shortly after two, and Eurydice was feeling drowsy from their large meal. She shouldn't have eaten so much, but Ellsworth told her their supper wouldn't be as grand because the midday meal was always the biggest of the day. She had managed to acquire some pumpkin seeds and an apple she sliced using Ellsworth's knife for Casanova, and he sat in his cage eating his food quietly. He was tolerating their journey well, and the cold didn't seem to be bothering him.

They had only been traveling for a little over an hour when there was a sudden lurch, and the coach came to an awkward stop. Ellsworth quickly put his arm around Eurydice and braced a foot against the opposite seat to keep them from being thrown about inside the coach. Casanova flapped his wings and squawked excitedly, but he was steady in his cage, which had been strapped into place. When the coach completely stopped moving, it was easy to notice it no longer sat evenly. Ellsworth looked at her concernedly.

"All right?"

Eurydice nodded. "I think so."

Ellsworth opened the door and stepped out, and then he turned back to help Eurydice do the same. When they looked back at the coach, the problem was obvious. One of the rear wheels had—somehow—lost a spoke, and when it did, it caused several others to cant. The iron strake and rim of the actual wheel still appeared to be sound, but the missing spoke and one or two of the others would have to be replaced.

Eurydice looked up the road in the direction they had been traveling. The coach carrying the rest of the family was no longer in sight. She didn't know how far ahead it was, but there would be no calling it back. They had just passed through a village, but she couldn't remember if there had been a wheelwright. That hadn't been something she thought she needed to know, and it had been a small village. If there wasn't a wheelwright, there might be someone else who lived there who could provide assistance in repairing the wheel. Eurydice didn't know how far it would be to the next village or if that one would be able to provide help either.

She looked around herself as Ellsworth and the two drivers spoke to each other about their situation. Then she looked at her watch. It was almost four in the afternoon. They would only have an hour and a half—possibly two— before it was dark. Beneath the trees, it was already gloomy. She wasn't sure how the footpads were in Austria, but the isolation of where they were would be perfect for them in Britain. With the sun starting to dip toward the horizon, the air was becoming cooler, and she rubbed at her arms through her pelisse. When Ellsworth was done talking to the drivers, one of the men turned to go back the way they had come on foot at a fast walk. Ellsworth walked over to her and looked her up and down.

"Are you warm?" he asked.

"I'm a little cold but tolerable," said Eurydice calmly.

Ellsworth nodded and went to close the door on the coach. The driver had managed to stop near the edge of the road so the coach wouldn't be blocking other vehicles should they come past. Their belongings were as secure as could be accomplished, given the circumstances, and the other driver would remain with the coach to stand guard. He had a carriage pistol should he need it, but their journey had been blessedly without criminals so far.

"Let's go," said Ellsworth, walking in the direction they had been traveling.

"Go? Go where?" asked Eurydice confusedly, not moving.

"Gloggnitz is not far ahead of us. We're going to walk there and see if we can get transportation the rest of the way to Neunkirchen."

"How far?" asked Eurydice charily.

"No more than three or four miles I should think," said Ellsworth calmly.

"But I'm not wearing the proper shoes to walk that far," hedged Eurydice.

Ellsworth looked at the slippers on her feet. "Those will do fine. The road is soft. If not, just walk on the verge."

"I don't want to walk that far," said Eurydice stubbornly. "Why can't we just stay with the coach?"

"Because my mother and everyone else will be worried if we don't arrive within a decent amount of time. I don't know how long it's going to take the wheel to be repaired, and the temperature is falling. We can't stay here."

"But that's a long way," complained Eurydice with a frown.

"That is not a long way," said Ellsworth with mild annoyance. "We can be there within the hour."

"But—" began Eurydice again, but Ellsworth didn't give her a chance to finish.

He walked back toward her and hefted her over his shoulder. The air whooshed out of her, and she was so surprised that for a moment she couldn't do anything except look at the dirt and gravel of the road. He started walking up the road again with her over his shoulder, not saying another word.

"Hey! Put me down!" she said indignantly. Ellsworth continued to walk without a word. "I said put me down, please!" she said tightly.

"Are you going to walk?"

"No," said Eurydice stubbornly.

"Then this is the way you'll get there."

His tone was a mixture of amusement and exasperation, and Eurydice could only imagine the expression on his face.

"Put me down!" repeated Eurydice, and her hands hung at just the right distance that she could smack him on the buttocks.

"Ow! Stop that!" he said, and he smacked her back on her own bottom where it rested at just the right height near his shoulder.

"You manky Scots eejit!" said Eurydice angrily, and she smacked him again.

"You rammish Welch shrew!" he yelled back, and he lifted the back of her clothes to expose her bottom and smacked the bare skin.

"Ow! Let me go! Put me down!" she bit out, her eyes watering from the stinging tingle in her backside, and she began to struggle, trying to lift herself off his shoulder and kick him.

"Lord, preserve me from lazy, silly females," muttered Ellsworth, and he tightened his hold around her thighs to keep her legs immobile.

"I am not lazy or silly, you bully!" argued Eurydice. "You can't carry me all the way there!"

"We'll see about that," said Ellsworth determinedly.

"Why are you being so mean?"

"All you have to do is tell me you'll walk, and I'll put you down," said Ellsworth reasonably.

"Fine. I'll walk," said Eurydice shortly.

Ellsworth stopped in the middle of the road and put her down. Eurydice felt a little dizzy when she was rightside up again, and she wove a little unsteadily. Her face was red from all the blood that had rushed to her head, struggling to get free, and embarrassment. She wouldn't look Ellsworth in the eye, and she set her jaw and folded her arms across her chest and started walking up the road. For the moment, she wasn't cold anymore.

Eurydice kept to a fairly fast stride as she walked, her eyes directly ahead of her on the road, and Ellsworth was easily able to keep pace with her. She could tell he was looking at her occasionally as they walked, but she had nothing to say. That was entirely uncalled for, and she was furious. He owed her an apology, and she *might* forgive him.

"How's your bum?" he asked after they had walked about a mile.

"It's fine," said Eurydice stiffly. "How's yours?"

"A little sore. You've got strong hands," said Ellsworth amusedly.

Eurydice cut her eyes toward him briefly with a disdainful expression. She was not appeased.

"Perhaps I shouldn't have done that," he said quietly after a few minutes. "I apologize."

Eurydice rubbed a hand across her forehead and sighed tiredly. "Apology accepted," she said dully.

She'd never been accused of being a shrew before. If anything, she always tried to be very agreeable, often to the point of doing things she didn't want to even when she could have said no and not been thought any worse for it. Eurydice had begun to realize, though, that with him she often lost her temper. She'd never been prone to name calling, much less hitting before. She had always tried to be reasonable and not become angry because it never solved anything and usually tended to make things worse. The disaffection they had for each other at the moment only made that obvious.

The wind was starting to blow, and Eurydice looked up at the sky. She couldn't see much because of the trees, but she didn't think it was going to rain. She clenched her jaw to keep her teeth from chattering and adjusted the collar on her pelisse when a particularly strong gust blew against the back of her neck.

"I thought you were warm," said Ellsworth with a frown.

"I was when we just stepped out of the coach," said Eurydice dryly. "You didn't give me time to get a cloak...or change my shoes."

Ellsworth sighed and removed his coat. "Here," he said as he held it out to her.

"But you'll be cold," said Eurydice simply.

"I'll live," said Ellsworth with a slight smile.

"So will I," replied Eurydice evenly. "Keep your coat."

Ellsworth shook his head and draped the coat over her shoulders. When he did, a strange series of things happened. The strings to Eurydice's hat hung loosely from their tussle, and she hadn't bothered to retie them, instead holding onto them when the wind blew to keep the hat in place. The collar of his coat displaced the back of her hat at about the same time a gust of wind blew. The end result was that the hat blew off her head and into the woods.

"Oh, dang!" said Eurydice in dismay, and she took off after it.

It was made of dark green velvet, and she had trouble seeing it in the gloom and the foliage. She had a general idea of where it had gone, and she hurried after it when the wind blew again and picked it up to move it further into the woods, showing where it had gone.

"Eurydice, come back!" called Ellsworth from where he still stood on the road.

"Not until I have my hat!" she yelled back, keeping her eye on the item. "I'll only be a moment!"

She didn't have to go much farther when she caught it just before it went into a stream. Eurydice grinned victoriously as she picked it up and put it on her head. As she looked at the stream, she realized it was being supplied from a spring pouring from a cleft in the rocks to form a very pretty waterfall. After looking at it briefly, she shrugged and turned to go back to the road.

Ellsworth startled her when she found him behind her. He moved so quietly and she had been so intent on what she was doing, she hadn't realized he had followed her. She lost her footing and began to topple backward into the stream when Ellsworth grabbed her. She looked up at him in round-eyed surprise. He was very fast.

"It's too cold to swim," he said with a teasing smile.

"Oh," said Eurydice breathlessly.

Ellsworth thought his wife looked very beautiful. Her cheeks were rosy from the cold and her chase after the hat, and she was looking so utterly kissable that he had to. He felt her jump slightly when he touched his lips against hers, but she didn't try to stop him. He held onto the ribbons on her hat as much to keep it from blowing away again as to keep her close. He lightly nipped at her bottom lip, and he began to deepen the kiss. Eurydice moaned softly at the back of her throat and wound her arms around his neck.

She had missed kissing him. She had been unable to resist that morning, and right now, she could feel her heart starting to beat a little faster as he continued to explore her mouth with his tongue. She felt him move a hand beneath his coat over her shoulders to smooth it down her back and place it onto her bottom to pull her closer. She was growing dizzy with need for him, and she had no hesitation in kissing him back.

She felt him lift her feet from the ground to carry her further away from the stream as he continued to kiss her, and then when he put her back onto her feet, he slowly began to guide her to the ground with him onto their knees. He removed her hat and set it on the ground, and then he moved his lips to her ear to nip at the lobe. Eurydice knew she should be worried someone might see them, but they were well into the woods, far off the road. The chances of anyone seeing them, especially with darkness coming, were unlikely. She slowly smoothed a hand down his chest and lower until she could feel his semi-aroused member through his pants. She heard Ellsworth moan excitedly at her touch, and he lifted his head to look at her.

"Do you really want to do this right now?" he asked softly.

"Oh, yes," sighed Eurydice as she continued to touch him, feeling him grow harder. "I want you to shag me right now, please."

Ellsworth grinned rakishly and lowered his head to kiss her hungrily. She felt him unfastening the buttons on her pelisse, enough of them for him to reach his hands beneath it and undo the fastenings at the back of her gown. Then he managed to slide all of it down far enough to expose her breasts, and he took one of her nipples into his mouth and worried it with his teeth. During his fumbling with her clothes, she removed her gloves and undid the buttons at the front of his pants and wrapped her hand around him to stroke him.

Ellsworth released her long enough to lay his coat on the ground, and then he laid her onto it on her back, settling between her thighs. He pulled up the front of her skirt by brushing his hand along her flank, and Eurydice sighed when she felt his erection brush against her button. She was already aching for him, and she rubbed against him excitedly, hooking her leg behind his thigh. She hadn't realized how much she had been missing this, despite it only having been three days. Ellsworth thrust into her with a pleasurable groan, and he lowered his head to kiss her ravenously as he began to plunge in and out of her.

Eurydice slid her hands down his back to push against his buttocks, and she loved the feel of the muscles flexing as he drove into her. She felt dizzy and breathless, and even though this was technically a public place, she wanted him so much she didn't care. It was cold and night was coming, but she couldn't wait. She slid her hands beneath the waistband of his trousers and put her hands against the bare skin, digging her nails into it as she sighed and breathed in excited gasps.

"Oh, Gareth, faster," she panted, and she moaned ecstatically as he did his best to comply.

He lifted one of her legs to hook it in front of his arm, and Eurydice gasped at the pleasurable sensations it caused. He had never done that before. She grabbed the front of his waistcoat to pull his mouth to hers, and she began to quiver uncontrollably as she orgasmed, her back arching as she whimpered in ecstasy. She felt as if her heart had stopped beating, and she traced her fingers over his cheek wonderingly as it continued to thrum through her. She was looking into his eyes as Ellsworth started to come, and the expression on his face was so blissful and awed, Eurydice felt an emotional lump form at the back of her throat.

He lowered his head to gently kiss her lips, and then he rubbed his nose against hers lovingly before resting his forehead onto her shoulder. He was still breathing heavily, and Eurydice was still waiting for her heart to quit palpitating. She felt him shiver slightly when the wind blew, and she could tell from the gathering gloom that it wouldn't be much longer before dark. She ran her fingers through his hair and put her lips close to his ear.

"We should go," she said quietly.

Ellsworth wrapped his arms tightly around her waist and rested his head onto her chest, listening to the beat of her heart.

"Just one more minute," he mumbled.

Eurydice smiled with exasperated amusement and pushed at his shoulders. "We can continue this later."

Ellsworth raised himself up on his elbows to look down at her with a boyish grin. "Do you promise?"

Eurydice chuckled as she put a hand to his cheek and lifted her head to give him a playful kiss. "I promise."

Ellsworth got off of her then, and Eurydice sat up with a shake of her head. She was able to put her chemise and dress back into place, but she had to have him refasten the back. She buttoned her pelisse, and once she made sure her hair wasn't too disheveled, she put her gloves and hat back on. Ellsworth tied the ribbons for her and gave her a soft kiss once he was done. There was a minor disagreement about which one of them was going to wear his coat, with the end result being that Ellsworth wore it and draped his arm over her shoulders. That proved to be much warmer for both of them.

After they returned to the road, Gloggnitz proved to be not much farther. They were able to get a ride on the back of a wagon hauling pumpkins, and within an hour they arrived in Neunkirchen. They were only a little later than they would have arrived had their coach not lost a wheel, so everyone was becoming concerned but not overly worried.

The inn they were staying at was large enough to provide Eurydice with another bath. She knew she had one in Graz, but she thought she could use another after all the walking she had done. After supper, she went up to her room with Agniezka. She let her maid get in first. Agniezka protested, but Eurydice insisted, knowing she hadn't had one since they left Venice. Eurydice was sure the heat would feel good on Agniezka's back.

There was a privacy screen blocking it from view of the door where it had been set up near the large fireplace. Eurydice stood watch as Agniezka washed, just in case Ellsworth came in while she was in the tub. She wasn't in very long, but she appreciated that Eurydice had let her wash first. She knew if she worked for anyone else, she wouldn't have gotten a bath at all. Agniezka protested even more when Eurydice told her she could go to bed before she had her own bath.

"You are too good to me," said Agniezka brokenly.

Eurydice rubbed her shoulder soothingly and smiled. "Only because you would do the same for me." She turned Agniezka in the direction of the door. "Now, go to bed."

"Good night, and thank you," said Agniezka before she went to the door.

"Good night," said Eurydice with a fond smile.

Agniezka had already set out her shift and dressing gown, and once Eurydice was undressed, she settled into the water with a sigh of relief and closed her eyes. Its closeness to the fire and the screen worked well to block any drafts, and she felt very relaxed and comfortable. But the water wasn't going to stay hot for long. After soaking for only a few minutes, she reached for the soap and flannel to begin washing.

She looked up in surprise when Ellsworth came around the screen completely naked and settled into the other end of the tub. It wasn't very big, and with both of them in it, the water came very close to splashing over the top.

"No, of course I don't mind if you join me," said Eurydice dryly with a half-smile.

"I didn't think you would," said Ellsworth with a grin and a wink.

He was right, of course. They took turns washing each other, and despite the threat of water splashing onto the floor, they made love as well. By the time they got out of the tub, the water was cold, and their fingers and toes were pruny. Ellsworth added more wood to the fire, and then he joined Eurydice in the bed. They snuggled together under the blankets, and she put her head onto his chest. Neither one of them was ready to sleep yet.

"Are we done fighting now?" asked Ellsworth quietly.

Eurydice lifted her head to look at him pensively. "I don't think we were ever fighting," she said softly.

"Weren't we? You want me to talk about what I do, and I can't. I want you to trust me, and you won't," he said disappointedly.

"That's not it at all," said Eurydice evenly. "I do trust you. It's just that the secrets you want to know are not mine to tell." She smoothed a hand down his cheek and shrugged. "I suppose I can now tell you at least one thing you wanted to know. I imagine she's already told her husband, and if she hasn't, she will have by the time we see them again. I imagine it will be fairly obvious."

"What are you talking about?" he asked with a puzzled frown.

"You wanted to know what I was talking about with my sister. She and Sheerness are expecting their first child. How fair would it have been for another man to find out before her husband did?"

"It wouldn't have been," said Ellsworth dully. She had told him it was nothing, and—really—it was. "What about Sheerness?"

"What about Sheerness?" she said with a puzzled frown of her own.

"What is he working on for you?"

"He's not working on it for me. It's for Agniezka, and—again—I can't tell you what it is. All I can say is that I needed someone with his diplomatic connections." Ellsworth tightened his jaw in frustration, and Eurydice put a hand to his cheek. "If it were for me, I would tell you. I swear. But that is the difference between the secrets we keep. Yours belong only to you."

"I can't—" began Ellsworth, and Eurydice put her hand over his mouth.

"I don't want to know what you're doing. I don't want to know about Signor Merletto or what your assignment is. I don't care about that."

"Then what is it that you want to know?" he asked confusedly when she removed her hand.

"I want to know about *you*. I'll tell you what I think, and you can answer yes or no. If I'm wrong, you don't even have to tell me in what way. Just tell me I'm wrong. All I ask is that you answer me truthfully." She gave him a soft kiss on the lips. "Just yes or no," she whispered.

"And what will I get in return?" asked Ellsworth softly.

"I will do the same, but you have to remember it has to be questions about me—not Agniezka, not Felton, not anyone else."

She sat up and removed her shift, and then she lay on top of him, propping herself up on her elbows to either side of his head. She wiggled against him and gave him an impudent smile.

"Are you trying to distract me?" he asked with a raised eyebrow.

"No, sweetheart, I'm doing this because I want to fuck you," purred Eurydice as she lowered her head to nibble on his ear.

"Ooh, you naughty wench," gasped Ellsworth admiringly, and he moved his hands to tighten them at her hips.

"Let's start at the beginning, with your…travels. You speak Japanese because you went to Japan, and that's also where you got your tattoo," said Eurydice as she placed light kisses all over his face.

"Yes," said Ellsworth softly.

"You were there at least three years…more likely five."

"Yes."

"I don't think you went to a *ryu*. I'm thinking you learned from one of the secret clans, like Hiroshi and his family are from, but you were at least taught *jujutsu*. Actually, I think it is more likely you are *shinobi no mono*. As an outsider, you wouldn't have been accepted by a *ryu*. You would have been thought of as *hinin…gaijin*. It wasn't easy for you to find someone willing to be your *sensei*. Am I right?"

Eurydice was caressing him and kissing him as she talked, and while she was exciting him, her words were also causing Ellsworth's heart to race. So far, she hadn't been asking him questions, only stating things she already knew, and what she already knew astonished him.

"Yes," he sighed after a moment, his fingers curling in her hair as she kissed his chest. "How do you know all this?"

She looked up at him as she licked one of his nipples. "Because Dorian is, and I asked him and the Ashikaga about some of it…out of curiosity. You wear the mark of the Hattori. You learned from the relatives of the Ashikaga. Your tattoo and theirs and Dorian's are far too similar for it to be otherwise." She continued to move lower on his body, and Ellsworth looked at her with a slight frown. "You wouldn't have been able to find someone to teach you if my father hadn't given you direction. He took you to Japan at some point…and left you there with the intention of you learning this. He is—or was—friends with Hattori Yasuzumi and his father, the late Hattori Yasuhiro. Yasuzumi, I think, was your *sensei*."

"Yes!" gasped Ellsworth as she began to kiss and suck his navel.

"My father wanted you to learn these skills specifically for what you do now." She took his erection in her hand and began to kiss down his thigh. "For whatever reason, my father created you…the perfect instrument…the perfect weapon."

"Yes," moaned Ellsworth.

He was extremely hard in her hand as she lightly stroked him, and she could hear him panting excitedly as he clenched his fingers into the sheets. She lifted one of his hands to put it to her breast, and she sighed in gratification as he began to knead it and toy with the nipple. When she looked up at his face, his eyes were closed, his features anguished. She wasn't sure how much was caused by her teasing and how much by her talking, but she was almost done with both. She kissed her way up the inside of his other thigh, and he trembled occasionally as he struggled to maintain control.

"I don't think you wanted to go. I don't think you volunteered. I think, for whatever reason, my father thought you *needed* this, and he left you there alone. I'm sure he knew the Japanese *could* have killed you, but I suspect whatever it was that led him to do this to you would have definitely done the same thing. He thought it was the only way he could save you."

She moved her mouth to his erection and lightly flicked her tongue at the sensitive point on the underside where the shaft met the tip, and she put a gentle, steadying hand to his hip as he arched off the bed. She could hear him breathing in and out quickly through his nose, and he wouldn't be able to wait much longer.

"Oh, God! Yes!" he choked out almost desperately.

That mostly answered everything Eurydice wanted to know. She didn't want to know the specifics of what he was doing. She might not know what the thing was that her father had saved him from, but judging from the extremity of what the duke had done to accomplish it, whatever it was must have been very bad. Her father wasn't a cruel man. He must have thought that at least in Japan, Ellsworth would stand a chance. She knew enough about why he had become what he was, how he had become what he was, and about how long he had been doing it. Her father had not been back to Japan (to her knowledge) for at least five years. Ellsworth had been spying longer than that. He was too young to have been doing it since the beginning of the war, but that didn't mean he couldn't have been sent to Japan then. Maybe one day he would fill in the missing pieces, or perhaps she would arrive at her own conclusions once she had time to think about it, now that her initial suspicions were confirmed.

She kissed her way up his body and lay on top of him, and then she slowly guided him inside her. Ellsworth sighed with relief as Eurydice remained still, and he clamped his hands onto her hips to make sure she stayed that way for the moment. She gently ran her fingers through his hair with a tender smile. His eyes were closed, and his jaw was clenched as he took several calming breaths, a slight frown of concentration furrowing the space between his eyebrows.

"I have no more questions for now," whispered Eurydice as she nuzzled his neck. "That was all I wanted to know."

Ellsworth opened his eyes to look at her in surprise. "That was it?"

"Yes," said Eurydice distractedly as she moved along his collar bone, kissing down his chest to gently graze her teeth against one of his nipples.

Ellsworth sucked in air through his teeth, and she felt his hands tighten even further on her hips. "Stop that," he sighed. "Wait just a few more minutes."

Eurydice lifted her head, and she folded her arms across his chest and propped her chin on her forearm to look at him patiently. She could have put them to either side of his head, but that would have required her to move off of him, and she didn't want to move for his sake as much as her own, enjoying the feel of him inside her. She could wait until he was ready, provided it wouldn't take too long.

"Can I ask questions now?" he asked calmly, his eyes closed again.

Eurydice gave him a wry smile. "Now you're trying to distract *me*."

"Absolutely," he agreed wholeheartedly. Eurydice chuckled, and Ellsworth frowned at the sensations it caused. "Ooh, don't do that," he gasped.

"Poor sweetie," said Eurydice sympathetically. "You have my undivided attention."

"Do they have to be yes or no questions?"

"That would only be fair, but I'm willing to give you some latitude," said Eurydice calmly.

"I just don't know how to ask you what I want to ask you," said Ellsworth, opening his eyes to look at her thoughtfully.

Eurydice looked at him with that knowing gaze. He couldn't ask about her other secrets, so that left only one. She knew what it was he wanted to ask and couldn't, and she hoped he wouldn't. She would tell him, if he asked, and she wouldn't lie to him.

"Are you happy?" he asked instead.

Eurydice smiled wryly. "At this moment, I am *very* happy, but show me someone who is always happy, and I will show you someone who is not mentally all together."

"Are you ever surprised?"

Eurydice released a brief snort of humor and shifted her chin on her hands with a raised eyebrow. "Sometimes I am *very* surprised."

"Do you sleepwalk?"

"What?" she hooted in amused disbelief. "What an absurd question. Of course not."

"But sometimes you have nightmares?"

She shrugged her shoulders. "I only have dreams. Sometimes they're good, sometimes bad."

"And sometimes they come true," said Ellsworth gently.

Eurydice looked at him, and the humor slowly drained out of her features. She knew he wouldn't leave it alone. She should have known he would figure it out.

"You do realize that sounds completely insane?" she asked softly.

"Yes, but it's true. Isn't it?"

"Yes," she finally whispered, not able to look him in the eye.

"Do all of them come true?" he asked curiously.

"No. About half...so far." She shrugged. "Sometimes, a dream is just a dream."

"How long have you been having them?"

"Probably since the day I was born, but I can't remember that far back," said Eurydice dully. "The first one I can remember was when I was five."

Ellsworth frowned. "That long?"

"Yes."

"Are they all bad?"

"No. Like all dreams, sometimes they are good, sometimes bad."

"And they always happen exactly as you see them?"

"Yes."

"Haven't you ever tried to change things you've seen, to stop them?"

Eurydice rubbed her cheek against the back of her hand. "Yes," she whispered.

"And?"

She looked at him then. "I can't."

He looked at her doubtfully. "There's nothing you can do?"

She tried to move then, but he kept his hands on her hips and held her still. She didn't want to answer any more of these questions, but he wasn't going to stop. She took a deep breath in an effort to dislodge the lump that had formed in her throat.

"I saw my *babushka* die. I saw my brother, Myron, die. Now, do you think for one second if there had been anything I could have done that I wouldn't have?" she said brokenly, her eyes glistening.

"Of course not," said Ellsworth sadly. "I'm sorry. That was a stupid question." He moved a hand from her hip to brush a finger down her cheek. "How do you...how do you live with that?"

She gave him a somber smile. "I either live with it, or I go crazy."

He smiled slightly. "And you write them down in that notebook every morning?"

"Yes."

"That night I came to your room at the palazzo, you dreamt that?"

"I must have."

"You mean you don't know?"

Eurydice sighed deeply. "If I remember a dream, I write it down. Sometimes I don't remember a dream until it happens. Either I don't remember having it at all or I forget it before I can write it down. That's why I try to write them down as soon as I wake up. It helps. That way if it's bad, I can get it out of my head. If it's good, and I forget it, I can read my notebook and see what I have to look forward to. What happened that night was apparently something I dreamt and didn't remember at all. I don't like those."

"Why not?"

"Because they make me very confused," said Eurydice in a vague tone. "Sometimes, like that night, I have no control over what I do when what I've dreamt and reality merge. It's like I'm watching it and yet I'm a part of it. I know what I'm doing, and then I don't." She gave him a self-deprecating smile. "It's not very fun."

"Does that happen very often?"

"Not so very because it only happens with dreams that affect me directly in some way. There have been very few dreams that I don't remember until they happen, but they always involve me. That's why I don't like them and why they always make me so disoriented."

"That night in Podpetsch, what was that dream about?" he asked thoughtfully.

"I'm not sure yet," said Eurydice evasively. "I've not seen the beginning or the end, and seeing only part of a dream is a bit like a rumor—if you know the truth, the rumor is usually distorted and nothing like it."

"But it wasn't just a dream, though, was it?"

"No, it was a vision," she said quietly.

"You seemed very frightened."

"I've had it more than once, so I know it will happen soon, but I don't know what causes it or how it ends. Those are the most important parts."

"So it was bad?"

"I don't know. The part I remember wasn't good, but I'm missing pieces. The end could be very happy, which would make what I saw not quite so bad, but I don't know," she repeated.

"You don't want to tell me what you saw, do you?"

"No. I'd rather not," said Eurydice evenly. She looked him in the eye. "I'm not trying to be secretive, I swear. It's just it's not all there. I keep hoping I'll have it again. I know it's going to happen soon, so dreaming it more isn't going to make a difference, but I can't control what I see."

"So if you have a vision more than once, that means it will happen sooner than something you've only dreamt once?"

"Usually. Sometimes, once is all it takes. I had the dream about Psyche five times, so I know it will happen with this pregnancy rather than another."

"You had a dream about your sister being pregnant?" he asked amusedly.

"Yes."

"And what was it about?"

"I can't tell you that. I didn't tell her, and since it was about her, it just wouldn't be fair if I told you. It wasn't bad. That's all I can say."

Ellsworth conceded she had a point, but he was curious. He just added it to the list of things he would look for when he went through her notebook.

"The dream you had in Podpetsch, you've dreamt it more than once?"

"The night in Podpetsch was the second time…in less than a week. That can't be a good sign."

"Is it about you? Is that why you're so worried?"

"I wouldn't say I'm worried. I'm just…concerned."

Ellsworth gave her a sardonic grin. "I know what it's about."

"How could you?" she asked confusedly.

"You're worried that Beethoven will die before you ever have the chance to meet him," he teased.

Eurydice smiled. "Oh, I don't imagine I'll ever meet him."

Ellsworth smoothed his hands down her hips to her thighs, and then he lightly ran them over her bottom. She tried not to squirm. She lifted one of her hands to his face to run her fingers down his cheek with a pensive expression.

"You don't think I'm crazy," she said with a hint of wonder in her tone.

Ellsworth moved her hand to his mouth and placed a kiss in her palm. "Sweetheart, you saved my life. I would *never* accuse you of being crazy," he said with a soft smile.

He rolled over to place her beneath him and kissed her thoroughly, and then he moved his mouth down her neck to her breasts to take one of them into his mouth. Eurydice moved one of her legs to put it around his waist and sighed pleasurably as she shifted against him.

"Does this mean we can shag now?" she asked breathlessly.

Ellsworth raised himself and thrust into her with a lusty grin. "I think I've corrupted you."

"But you said I could—" she started with a frown.

Ellsworth leaned down and kissed her as he continued to plunge in and out of her.

"I didn't say I didn't like it," he purred. "I appreciate a woman who can be a lady in public and a wench in bed."

Eurydice smiled impudently and moved her other leg behind his thigh. She gasped when he sat up on his knees and raised her hips off the bed until only her head and shoulders were on the mattress as he moved in and out of her. It caused an entirely new set of sensations, and she gurgled with pleasure and dug her hands into the sheets.

"Oh…God…yes!" she gasped in blissful abandon. "Oh, right there!"

Ellsworth chuckled softly, enjoying the sounds she made, loving the joy on her face. He raised one of her legs to drape it over his shoulder to free his hand and used it to tease her button, and he soon watched as her back arched even further off the bed as she orgasmed, her expression one of euphoria. He could feel her trembling as the spasms coursed through her, and he was gratified to know he could cause that. He slowly eased her back onto the mattress and placed her legs around his waist. His head was near hers as he drove into her, and Eurydice put her lips near his ear.

"Come for me, sweetheart," she whispered seductively, and she nibbled his earlobe while one of her hands slid down his chest to tweak one of his nipples.

Ellsworth completely lost control and began to orgasm with a low groan of release, shuddering pleasurably. Eurydice put a hand to his cheek and gently brushed it down his neck. He slowly stopped moving and collapsed on top of her, resting his head next to hers on the pillow as he wrapped his arms around her waist.

"You are the *perfect* woman," he gasped appreciatively.

Eurydice chuckled amusedly, her eyes closed. "Just wait until I know what I'm doing," she chortled tiredly.

He moved his head closer to kiss her neck. "Anytime you need to practice, I am always at your service."

Eurydice laughed. "And I'm sure that pun was not intended."

"Oh, no, I meant it," he mumbled as he continued to kiss her neck, one of his hands trailing to her breast.

"Again? Already?" she asked in surprise.

"I can't help it," he sighed as he kissed down her shoulder on his way to her chest. "You're an enchantress, and you have cast a spell on me. I am…your slave."

Eurydice laughed amusedly. Now that he knew about the Insight and had not been put off by it, she didn't take offense at what he said. There were still a few secrets they kept from each other, but she felt they would now be able to move beyond them, having reached a better understanding of one another. As he began to do things that made it impossible for her to think clearly, she realized her entry in her life diary tomorrow was going to be very long. She smoothed her hands across his shoulders and smiled.

"Practice makes perfect," she sighed happily.

Chapter Twenty

They arrived in Vienna late the following afternoon. There was a fairly flat plain that opened out in front of them once they left the river valley at Gloggnitz, and they were able to move quickly. The coach they had abandoned was repaired and waiting for them when it was time to leave Neunkirchen that morning. Casanova had spent the night in his cage inside it, but it had been covered, and he seemed none the worse for wear from the cold. Eurydice was glad the drivers had been able to find someone to help them repair the wheel and that nothing had happened to them while that was being done. She would have felt terrible if something had. She also hoped they hadn't needed to spend the night in the coach. It had been particularly cold. She hadn't thought to ask them that morning before they set out, and now she realized it was too late for it to matter.

Eurydice hadn't minded the journey so much. If it had been longer, she might have grown weary of it, but only a week had been bearable, even if the seats of the coach hadn't been very comfortable. She was glad she would be staying in one place for a while, though. As much as she had enjoyed seeing the countryside and sampling the different foods, she didn't want to go anywhere again any time soon. She would wait until next summer before she went back to Britain to visit her family.

When they arrived in Vienna, Eurydice was surprised by the size of the town house. She counted three floors above the ground floor, which was only partially above street level, and it seemed there were rooms in the attic as well. It was narrow, but wider than those it abutted to either side. There was no yard at the front. Instead, it had a short flight of stairs down to the sidewalk from the covered, recessed entrance. As Eurydice couldn't see the back, she didn't know if there was a yard there. She didn't imagine it would have an inner courtyard like the palazzo. It was much too narrow to accommodate something of that size and probably anything similar of even a smaller size. She hoped it had a small garden...something at the back. It didn't even have window boxes. Even though Eurydice wasn't fond of outdoor pursuits, not even gardening, she did enjoy being able to view nature, which was why she had been so happy the palazzo in Venice had the inner courtyard and the rear courtyard. Nothing but stone and wood was entirely too sterile for her liking.

Since they arrived in the dark, she could only assume the house was in a respectable neighborhood. It was unlikely it would be otherwise. It was inside the city walls, but as she wasn't familiar with Vienna, it would take her some time to grow acquainted with where everything was located, such as the shops, parks, and theaters...bad neighborhoods. There were much larger houses outside the city walls, located in one of the outlying areas within the Linienwall that were steadily enlarging and beginning to merge into the Old Town, houses with a bit more distance between them, because she had seen them as they drove in. In London, Aberdare House didn't adjoin the houses beside it, and it had a small front yard between it and the street, and it had a very lovely, large garden at the back. It was also at least twice as wide as this house, but Eurydice supposed the Ellsworths didn't need something quite that large.

The coach stopped in front to let them out and unload their belongings. Eurydice didn't know what the arrangement was between Ellsworth and the drivers. She could only assume they would return to Venice after they'd had a night's rest. She wasn't sad to see the last of the coach she'd ridden in with Ellsworth. She'd discovered that afternoon that the seats weren't comfortable for making love at all, but that hadn't stopped them from doing it anyhow. They'd had nothing better to do, and no one was there to see them; they saw no reason why they couldn't. If they ever made love in a coach again, they would either need seats with better padding or become more creative on positioning.

Ellsworth showed her to their suite when they arrived. It was on the second floor on the left. It was of a decent size, with an adjoining sitting room and a room that would serve as both her dressing room and the room where Agniezka would sleep. Eurydice was disappointed. It would make things very cramped and inconvenient for Agniezka.

There was also a room for Ellsworth's valet, Schellen, who Ellsworth introduced her to when they walked into the room. There was a brief flicker of surprise in the Austrian's eyes when his employer introduced his new wife, but his features remained impassive and polite as he greeted her. He seemed very stuffy, and she couldn't tell if he liked this new development or not.

The room was suitable, but there weren't enough windows. Eurydice didn't know how she would tolerate not having the light and would have to become accustomed to it. One would think they would know it would be cheaper to run their household without the expense for candles and lamp oil the lack of windows caused. Ellsworth saw her disappointed expression.

"We can change things, if you'd like, if it would make you feel more at home," he said softly as he came over to her and put his arms around her waist.

"No, no, the furniture is fine," said Eurydice quickly.

"Then what is it? You don't seem happy with it."

"The room is fine, but it would be better with more natural light," said Eurydice hesitantly. She really did hate to complain.

"I'm afraid every room in my mother's house is the same, other than the public rooms on the first floor," said Ellsworth evenly.

"Oh," said Eurydice dully.

Ellsworth looked at her consideringly and gave her a soft kiss on her forehead. "Once I am done with what I have to do, perhaps we can see about finding a place of our own."

"Why not now?" asked Eurydice with a frown.

"Because for now it suits my purposes to live here," said Ellsworth flatly.

"Oh," said Eurydice softly. "When will you be done then…do you think?" she asked uncertainly.

"I don't know. I'll be done when I'm done," he said shortly with a frown.

"There's no need to gnaw off my head. I was only asking so I would know how long I might expect to be living in a cave," said Eurydice tartly.

Ellsworth sighed tiredly and pulled her to him in a hug, resting his chin on top of her head.

"I'm sorry. I don't know," he repeated softly. "Six months. A year. I hope not any longer than that." He gave her a squeeze. "Perhaps we could even move back to Britain…to Scotland. I don't know if there's any repairing my family's home there, but I'd like to try…that is, if you want to go back."

Eurydice tilted her head back to look up at him with a slight smile. "I never intended my stay in Vienna to be permanent, and neither did my parents. I *would* like to go back, but I will go where you are, I suppose."

Ellsworth grinned boyishly and gave her a sound kiss. He was glad she wasn't attached to Vienna. He knew she had only been there less than an hour, so she could change her mind, but he had the feeling she wouldn't. He had never liked that his mother had moved to Vienna, and if it hadn't been more convenient for him to be there than in Britain, he would have gone back a long time ago. He could understand why his mother had done it, even if he didn't agree with it, but at the time, he hadn't been in a position to disagree…unlike his brother, Sam.

Once they were settled in, Ellsworth gave her a tour of the first floor, showing her the drawing room, music room, library, and the family's private sitting room. Of the rooms he showed her, only the drawing room had a respectable number of windows. The library had none at all, which Eurydice found particularly useless. He had no office or study, and she couldn't see that he ever had. Since his father was dead before their moving here and his mother would have no need for one, no accommodation had been made for him once he became old enough he might need one himself. The music room seemed adequate, with a piano and harpsichord, as well as several windows. Ellsworth assured her both instruments were tuned properly. Eurydice was almost tempted to play the piano, missing the opportunity over the past several days.

She restrained herself, deciding tomorrow would be soon enough. The wall between the drawing room and music room was actually made of doors and curtains, which could be opened to join the two rooms together. That made it convenient if there was to be music for an evening's entertainment. It also made the room large enough that Mrs. Ellsworth could have a small ball, possibly…perhaps not.

Eurydice missed having Agniezka at the table with her for supper. It was a very quiet affair, with only Eurydice, Ellsworth, and his mother. The children were fed in the nursery. They talked with each other, and Mrs. Ellsworth even managed to be polite to her son, but Eurydice could tell it took her some effort.

They mostly talked about things they had seen on their journey that day, but Eurydice also learned from Mrs. Ellsworth that Vienna did have a social season. To her dismay, it began in November. What made Eurydice all the more anxious was that Mrs. Ellsworth anticipated her new daughter-in-law would be taking part. Eurydice wasn't enthusiastic despite how calm she appeared. Ellsworth didn't expect that she would attend many functions if she could avoid them, but it might be good for her to go to at least a few, perhaps make a few friends so she wouldn't become lonely.

Now that he was back in Vienna, he would have to continue his work in earnest, both to finish it in the amount of time he had told Eurydice it would take and to keep it from becoming irrelevant. If Signor Merletto hadn't been killed, it would have saved him a lot of time and effort. His murder had only compounded the chore, and it meant he would have to be gone from the house a lot. He might be able to conceal some of his absences from Eurydice but not all of them. If she had friends to occupy her, then perhaps she wouldn't notice or mind so much. She would have her music, but it would only go so far.

Agniezka had gotten settled into her room by the time they went upstairs to get ready for bed. She had lots to say about some of the other servants she had met at supper, mostly that they all seemed very nice, but also that most of them hadn't been working for Mrs. Ellsworth very long. Their pay was adequate, but their employer followed the same policy as most did who had servants by not calling them by their real names, deciding it was too much effort. She called all the upstairs maids Anna and all the downstairs maids Ingrid. There were four upstairs and three downstairs. The footmen were all known as Wilhelm. There were three. The cook was simply known as Cook. There was no butler, but the housekeeper was actually called by her real name, Frau Geiger. The only other servants called by their own names were Edith, Mrs. Ellsworth's lady's maid, and the nanny, Nanny Rigsby.

The reasons they didn't work for the family long was that Mrs. Ellsworth didn't allow her employees to be married, and they couldn't have children. They also had to speak English. Most were young, and they soon left to marry or work for someone who didn't demand their undivided attention. While they did speak English, it was a second language, and most felt that as Vienna was a city where German was the one spoken everywhere, that should be the one used. So, although their pay was adequate, they felt they received it on very hard terms.

Eurydice might have been shocked if she didn't know her family was exceptional. They had servants who had worked for them for decades. They could marry and have children, and some had cottages on the grounds rather than rooms in the servants' quarters to accommodate that. They had entire families that worked for them. Their butler, Rajeesh, had been replaced by his son, Tannaz, who had been a footman, and Rajeesh's daughter, Shailesh, was one of the downstairs maids. He had a wife and a younger daughter who didn't work. Their stable master, Tajik, had a son, Tewfik, who worked in the stables with him, and Tajik's sister, Intisar, was an upstairs maid. There had never been a servant who had left the service of her family, unless it was to follow a branch of the household, like Maiyin, Keung, and Kwan leaving with Pandora, and Jim, Mary, and Chrissoula going with Psyche. The servants had never left due to some dislike of working for the Aberdares.

Part of the reason her family had servants who gave them such unquestioning loyalty was that they called them by their real names. All their servants could speak English, but the family could converse with them in their native language if they preferred. They could practice the religion of their choosing, and their time when they weren't working was their own to do with as they pleased. Respect was something that had to be given to be returned, and the Aberdares knew this. But not everyone cared to try. Any slaves the family had owned were given their freedom and an income by Eurydice's grandfather when Eurydice's father was still quite young. Some of them or their children still worked for the Aberdares. Oba, Persephone's lady's maid, was one of them. At times it all seemed Utopian, but it was very successful.

Eurydice thought she would make a point of learning all the servants' real names. She didn't imagine Mrs. Ellsworth would follow her example, but Eurydice couldn't call them all Anna, Ingrid, or Wilhelm, especially after Agniezka told her none of them actually had those names. She didn't know how long she would be staying in the town house. Until Ellsworth finished his assignment, she would have to make her stay as pleasant as she could.

She asked Ellsworth about it when they got into bed. He was surprised to learn they didn't have the names they were called. He had noticed the faces changed, but the names never did, but he hadn't thought anything of it. She was consoled to see he didn't like finding out their real names were different either. She would tolerate the situation as best she could, but she intended to follow her family's example when she established her own household.

Both of them were too tired to make love for once. They didn't get much sleep the night before, and neither one of them had slept in the coach either. Eurydice was content to snuggle beside her husband, resting her head onto his chest, and both of them were soon sound asleep. She would have at least one errand to run tomorrow, in addition to practicing, so a night of just sleeping would be perfect.

Ellsworth stayed to have breakfast with her the following morning, but he left shortly after, saying he had business to attend to and would not be back until late evening. Eurydice was disappointed, but she wasn't surprised. She did want him to finish what he had to do, but she wasn't keen on encouraging him—not after having her Dark Dream. What happened in the dream had to do with his occupation, regardless of whether or not she had seen the entire thing. There was nothing she could do to stop it, but she kept hoping it would change.

She'd only had the dream twice. After the night in Podpetsch, she'd not had it again. She didn't know if that should relieve her or concern her. She hoped to have it again for several reasons. One was that she wanted to see the beginning and the end. Another was that she hoped she would be able to determine *when* it was going to happen. Winter was not sufficient. What winter, and where? The last was that she wanted to know who the man was who would cause it. If she could see his face, perhaps she could warn Ellsworth. She didn't know what good that would do, as she hadn't seen the beginning or the end of the dream, but she had the feeling he needed to know.

Most of her dreams recently were about mundane things or at least were currently unimportant. She had a bizarre one about her mother, but she suspected it was just a dream. It had felt like a vision—mostly, but it had been very peculiar. That's why she thought it was only a dream. She had a terrible one about Viscount Drake that she hoped she never had again. The poor man had suffered so much already, she felt sorry for him. They had been friends since they were children, and he deserved some happiness. There were others about people she didn't know. She sensed they were related to her in some way, but she didn't know how, and judging by one or two things she had seen, they would not be happening for a long time. When she had dreams set that far in the future, she was always at a loss to describe what she saw, simply because it was so foreign, but she did her best.

After breakfast, she spent time working on her composition for the violin. She was only half through, but the delay had been caused by her not being able to work on it rather than the music not being in her head. She could play it through without the sheet music, but she needed to get it transcribed. If she could devote the same amount of time to it every day for another week, she thought she would be finished. As she didn't really have anything else to occupy her, she felt it would be something that could be accomplished. She also played a few pieces on the piano, simply because she had missed playing and needed the practice.

Shortly after dinner, she made arrangements for a carriage to take her to Waehring. She was going to pay a call on Leilah Mahone. It was Sunday, not a day considered appropriate for calling, but it needed to be done as soon as possible. Eurydice and Aberdare had both sent her letters from Venice to let her know she would no longer need to be a chaperone, but Eurydice felt she owed it to the woman to talk to her in person. Miss Mahone had needed to rearrange things in her own schedule to do it, only to find out at the equivalent of the last minute that she hadn't needed to. Eurydice wanted to wait until after dinner to be polite. She didn't know how things were done in Vienna as far as social etiquette was concerned, but in London, coming to call before dinner would be rude. She was pushing the boundaries of acceptability just by calling on Sunday.

She enjoyed the ride through the city, part of it taking her on the same route they had used last night. The carriage turned west before reaching the city walls, and it took her past several churches and the Hofburg, as well as one or two theaters. The houses and buildings didn't become more widely spread out until they left the city and crossed the Glacis onto Waehringer Gasse. She could see, however, it wouldn't be long before this area, too, would be filled with more housing and businesses.

Once they crossed the Alser Bach and completely left the environs of the city by passing through the Linienwall, it was obvious they had left it behind. There were woods and fields, but not many houses. Because Mrs. Ellsworth and Miss Mahone were friends, the driver was familiar with the location of her house in Waehring. Eurydice was glad because she had no idea. When they got to the village, the driver went all the way through down the main street and exited the other side. They were heading for the hills of the Wienerwald when he turned down a narrow, tree-shaded lane to the left that began a gradual climb upward. When the trees cleared and their path leveled, it wasn't long before they came to a stop. Eurydice looked out the window and sighed wistfully. She almost wished she was staying with Miss Mahone, regardless of whether Ellsworth went with her or not. It seemed very peaceful.

Miss Mahone's house was bigger than a cottage, but not what could be called a manor, more like a small villa. It had three floors, but because the house was built on a slope, the ground floor was mostly basement. It was made of stone covered by warm ochre-colored stucco. There were lots of windows and niches and nooks to its outline, and the roof changed to accommodate it, some portions having Dutch gables, others having Mansards. Eurydice wasn't sure how old it was, but she didn't think it was recently built. The trees had been cleared at the front just enough to afford sunlight for the many plants and shrubs growing nearby in a garden that was obviously well-kept by its simply not appearing to be so. Even though it was well beyond the time of year when flowers would be blooming, just the greenery was very pretty, and ivy was growing up the sides of the house. It was just lovely, and Eurydice wished Mrs. Ellsworth had chosen to live in a place like this rather than in the city.

The driver opened the door to let her step down, and she smiled at him briefly before she walked up the short flight of steps to the porch. She lifted the handle of the knocker and hit it against the plate loudly just twice, and she patiently folded her hands in front of her and waited for it to be answered. It only took a few minutes before the door was opened by an older woman wearing a work apron. She looked at Eurydice with a slight frown.

"*Ja?*" she said slowly.

"Good afternoon. I'm Lady Eurydice Sa—Ellsworth, and I'm here to see Miss Mahone. Is she receiving visitors?" she asked politely in German.

The woman's frown disappeared, and she raised an eyebrow in surprise as she looked Eurydice up and down assessingly. She moved out of the way and motioned for Eurydice to enter.

"If you will follow me, I will show you to the sitting room, and then I will go get her. I am Frau Kouts, the housekeeper…among other things," said the woman kindly as she guided Eurydice down a short hall past the stairs.

Eurydice smiled thankfully and followed her, looking interestedly at her surroundings. The inside of the house was just as lovely as the outside. The furnishings were tasteful and unpretentious, and Eurydice could see the house was intended to be a home rather than a place for display of conspicuous spending. She would have been very happy staying there, and while she was optimistic about how things would bode at the Palais Crantzdorf, where the Ellsworths lived, this house enveloped her in calmness. If she and Ellsworth stayed in Vienna, she would like to live in a place like this.

Frau Kouts opened a door at the end of the hall, leading Eurydice into a room bathed in afternoon sunlight. It was irregularly shaped, with only two walls. The interior wall was straight, while the outside wall was a semi-circle almost completely lined with windows. The curtains were open to allow light to enter, and a glass door opened onto a balustraded terrace that matched the shape of the room. The walls were painted a rich salmon color, with the trim painted white. There was a fireplace on the interior wall with a cozy fire crackling to remove the chill and draft from the windows. The floor was wood, covered by an intricately figured Persian rug of predominantly blue and gold. The part of the interior wall not taken by the fireplace was covered in paintings of various sizes, some people, some landscapes. The wood of the furnishings was chestnut and maple, and the upholstery was in varying shades and patterns of mostly blue. Eurydice liked this room.

"I will let Miss Mahone know you are here," said Frau Kouts pleasantly.

Eurydice smiled and nodded her head, looking out the windows at the breathtaking view as the housekeeper quietly left the room. The house was situated with the back facing the downward slope of the hill, and it gave her a wonderful view of the surrounding countryside. She removed her gloves and placed them into her reticule then walked toward the windows. After gazing out for a few minutes, she turned her attention back to the room and looked at the paintings on the wall. Eurydice didn't recognize most of the people in the paintings, but she did see her mother and father, Mrs. Ellsworth, and—to her surprise—there was a painting of her *Babushka* Alexa. They all looked quite a bit younger than she could recall ever seeing any of them. She sighed and went back to gaze out the window.

She turned to look expectantly when the door opened. Frau Kouts moved out of the way to let Miss Mahone enter. Eurydice had seen her many times before when she had come to Britain, both in London and at Wilderland. She was a beautiful woman and did not look the age of fifty. Eurydice knew she was that old because her mother had once said Miss Mahone was five years and five days older than herself. She had ash blond hair and dark blue eyes with few wrinkles. She was slightly taller than Eurydice with a figure that was still slender and shapely. Eurydice wondered why the woman had never married. She was sure Miss Mahone had numerous suitors in her time, but Eurydice would never think of asking such a personal question. Miss Mahone gave her a warm smile as she walked toward her which Eurydice returned. The older woman gave her a hug and kissed both her cheeks then held her hands and stood back from her to look her up and down appraisingly.

"Lady Eurydice, you look more like your grandmother every time I see you," she said kindly.

Eurydice blushed. "Thank you, and thank you as well for seeing me on a Sunday, Miss Mahone."

The older woman waved a hand through the air dismissively and shrugged. "Eh, one tends to blend into the next for me these days, so I don't stand on ceremony so much," she said with chuckle in her lilting Irish accent. She turned to look at the housekeeper. "Could you bring some coffee, please?"

Frau Kouts nodded and closed the door as she left the room. Miss Mahone took Eurydice by the hand and guided her to take a seat beside her on the couch near the fireplace.

"Now, first things first, you must call me Leilah. You're of an age and married now, and I have just decided we are going to become good friends. Your mother and I have known each other since before she married your father, so she and I are as close to being sisters as can be arranged without having common blood."

"All right," said Eurydice with a hesitant smile and a brief nod. "Then you should call me Eurydice, or Dicy, as my family calls me."

"Ooh, I like Dicy," said Miss Mahone with a grin. "Second, you must tell me how you came to be married. I received letters from your father and yourself, and his held more information than yours. Yet the only thing I was able to glean from both together was that it wasn't planned."

Eurydice blushed as Leilah looked at her with friendly curiosity. "Well, yes, I would say it was definitely unplanned. I…um…well, how shall I put this delicately…?" she stammered. That was a question she hadn't thought someone would ask, but she should have known someone eventually would.

Leilah chuckled amusedly. "Oh-ho!" she chortled with a wave of her hand. "Say no more! I can see it perfectly. It's got to be Venice. There must be something in the water or the air there that makes people love foolish because I know so many people who found themselves married after going there." She put her hand over Eurydice's where it rested on the couch and squeezed it warmly, giving her a soft smile. "I know it wasn't your father who caught you because you wouldn't be married right now if he had."

Eurydice scratched her forehead thoughtfully with her other hand. "No, I suppose not," she said with a slightly amused smile.

"And how are you finding it? Being married, I mean," asked Leilah softly.

"It's taking a bit of adjustment. I suppose it wouldn't require quite so much if it hadn't been so unexpected," said Eurydice dryly.

Leilah smiled understandingly. "And what of Gareth? Is he proving to be at least halfway decent as a husband?"

Eurydice blinked in surprise. "Well, yes," said Eurydice matter-of-factly. "I didn't think we could get on at all before we married, but now I don't think I could have chosen better if I had tried. Actually, I might have done worse."

Leilah raised a doubtful eyebrow. "Really?" she said in surprise. "And his drinking and all that—you don't take exception to that?"

"Drinking?" said Eurydice, frowning confusedly. "I've not noticed that he drinks...at least, not any more than anyone else."

Leilah looked at her doubtfully for a moment before she gave a resigned shrug. "Perhaps marriage was just what was needed to undo things then."

"I'm sorry? Undo what?" asked Eurydice blankly.

"I'm surprised you don't know this, but I suppose you were too young at the time it began for it to be of any interest to you." Eurydice still had a lost expression. "I don't know if I should be the one to tell you, bearing tales and all, but maybe if you know, then you won't be surprised if things go off."

"I don't see how they could possibly *go off*, as you say, but anything you could tell me about my husband would be helpful. He won't tell me anything," she said dully.

Leilah smiled comfortingly and gave her hand a soothing pat. "Well, I'll tell you what I know, and then you can decide if it's helpful." Eurydice nodded her understanding. "He's never been the same since his younger brother, William, died nearly thirteen years ago. He was always very cheerful when he was a boy—always laughing, very mischievous, but never mean-spirited at all."

Frau Kouts returned with a tray then, and Leilah paused for a moment while the housekeeper poured their coffee and handed them their cups before leaving again. Eurydice looked at the coffee. She usually took cream and sugar, and it appeared the beverage already contained them. When she took a small sip, her eyes widened in surprise. It had more than just cream and sugar.

"This is delicious! This is coffee?" asked Eurydice in amazement.

Leilah laughed. "It is. They've turned coffee into a masterpiece in Vienna, lass. There's cream, chocolate, a little sugar, and a few spices, which Kouts refuses to tell me what they are. I know it has at least cinnamon."

"Well, I think it's absolutely wonderful," averred Eurydice, "and so is your home. I meant to tell you that first thing, and also that I'm truly sorry I'll not be staying here, especially now I've had this coffee."

Leilah laughed. "Well, thank you. I'm glad you like them both, and you can come to call any time you wish. I'll be sure to have Kouts make coffee." She sighed deeply. "Now, where were we? Oh, yes, I remember. Gareth was a sweet scamp when he was a boy, even after his father died and Cora decided to take him and his younger brother and sister away from everything they'd ever known, including their older brother, Sam, who Gareth idolized.

"In the same way he looked up to Sam, so did William look up to Gareth. He was eight years older, and William always followed him everywhere he went. Being the baby, though, William was spoiled rotten. He wouldn't listen to anything unless he wanted to, and Cora could see no wrong in him. He was a good child at heart, but he was still too young to learn that things could not and would not always go his way and that one has to accept responsibility for one's choices. Gareth was so not that way he often let his younger brother do things he shouldn't. Sometimes he did it because he was just as indulgent as everyone else, sometimes because he hoped his brother would learn a little compassion and accountability if the consequences of the things he chose to do were unpleasant.

"When Gareth was seventeen and William was nine, they came here with their mother and sister for a visit. It was December, and we'd had our first really cold spell for the year. You can't see it from here because of the trees, but down the hill is a bach that runs into a small lake. Cora's children liked to come here to go to the lake to ice skate. So that's what they did."

She paused for a moment to pour them both more coffee. She also placed a small lemon tart onto a plate and set it on the table in front of Eurydice.

"You must try at least one. Frau Kouts is also my cook, and she will be unhappy if you don't," she said with a smile. She took a sip from her cup and gave a slight shake of her head before setting it on the table. She could still remember everything about that day so clearly; she could still hear the voices.

"Natalie had a slight cold at the time, so Cora wouldn't let her go. The ice was thick enough on the lake at the far end from where the bach fed it, but where there was current from the flow into it, it wasn't. Gareth told William that, but he wouldn't listen. He wanted to skate from one end of the lake to the other, despite his brother warning him repeatedly not to go on the ice at that end. It cracked, and William fell in. Gareth was at the other end when it happened, and it took him a minute to get to his brother. By the time he got there, William had gone under. He couldn't swim very well, you see, and the water was so cold. Gareth went in after him, but it was too late. He nearly drowned himself trying to find William beneath the ice, but he couldn't. They weren't able to retrieve his body until the spring when the ice melted.

"Gareth managed to make it back here, nearly frozen solid from the cold and wet, poor thing. When he arrived in that state...sobbing...without his brother, we knew something terrible had happened. When he told his mother, the first thing she did was backhand Gareth. She blamed him for it, and even though he had warned his brother not to go, even though he nearly died trying to save William, he blamed himself, too." She shook her head sadly. "To see him crying like that, almost a man...just *weeping* uncontrollably...well, it almost broke my heart," she said softly.

She swallowed and cleared her throat. "Cora was furious with him. Both Natalie and myself were here when she *told* him that it was his fault, that if he hadn't been able to save his brother, then he should have died, too. At the time, I think she meant it, she was so grief-stricken. Eventually, the anger softened, but the blame was still there, *is* still there...I think."

"Oh," sighed Eurydice, and she felt a tightness in her throat and chest. She could never have imagined what had happened.

"His brother's death, his mother's blaming him for it, his own guilt—it all changed him...almost overnight. He couldn't bring himself to end his own life outright, so he started doing it slowly, by bits and pieces. As young as he was, he started to drink heavily, associating with an unsavory crowd, gambling. I suppose he should consider himself fortunate he has an intolerance for opium because he would have tried that, too. Less than a year after William died, Gareth was well on his way to joining him.

"Cora didn't know what to do with him. She was beside herself because she resented him for what had happened to William, but Gareth was still her son and she still loved him. After he got in trouble with the law a few times because of things he had done, she finally told him he had to leave her house and not to return until he could act more like his father's son. He came here."

She shrugged and shook her head. "I wasn't any more capable of managing him than his mother. At least here he was away from the criminal element he had begun to call friend. His other friend, though, alcohol, was easy enough to find when it suited him. I wrote to your mother and father for direction. Cora wouldn't. Needless to say, I was surprised when your father arrived on my doorstep."

"You mean he just showed up?" blurted Eurydice in surprise.

Leilah smiled and nodded. "In the middle of a war with most of Europe being overran by Napoleon's army, and there he was at my door looking fresh as a daisy and smelling like a rose." She chuckled. "That's you're father, though. Mere mortals cannot compete, which is why I'm not surprised your mother married him. Anyhow, he was here to take Gareth off my hands. I didn't know what Aberdare planned to do with him, but I was hopeful a masculine hand at the reins would be all that was needed to put him right.

"We let Cora know Gareth would be with Aberdare. She seemed relieved the man was taking her son to parts unknown. He was gone five years. He didn't come back until we got word Sam had died in another terrible accident."

"He was cleaning a gun, wasn't he?" asked Eurydice thoughtfully.

"That's what Cora was told. He was at Ellsworth Park in Scotland when it happened, supposedly alone. We can only believe what we heard, but I've personally never thought that was the truth of it."

"What do you think happened?" asked Eurydice with a frown.

"I think he was murdered. I don't think he shot himself, accidentally or otherwise. He didn't have the temperament for suicide, and he was much too careful to do it while cleaning a gun."

"Hmm," said Eurydice thoughtfully with a slight frown still creasing the area between her eyebrows.

"When Gareth came back, he was somewhat improved, depending on how one wants to view it. He's not slowly trying to kill himself anymore, but he's become a bit of a ne'er do well. Being responsible and dutiful? Well, those things apparently died with William because he seems content to have nothing worthwhile left to show at the end of his life.

"He's drinking…a lot…I would expect; although, I don't think I or Cora have seen him inebriated once in the past eight years, and I ask her occasionally just to find out if she has. He doesn't appear as wrung out as someone would expect him to look if he spent all his nights in a bottle, but perhaps it's not been long enough," she said, tapping the end of her index finger.

"Whoring. There's a particular brothel on Juden Gasse that he frequents, managed—if you will—by a certain Anneliese Rathmueller. She calls it a gentlemen's club, but last I knew, Boodle's doesn't allow women, and her establishment has *lots* of women. She manages to keep her reputation as one slightly above that of a courtesan, but not by much. He's gone till all hours of the night, sleeping all day." She tapped her middle finger on the same hand.

"Gambling, I can only assume, which is one of the other entertainments Fraulein Rathmueller provides. He inherited from his father and also received everything from Sam when he died, including the remains of Ellsworth Park and its estate. It would be hard to reach the end of all that, but it would be a shame for him to bet it all away. Cora has her own income, so she'll not have to worry about moving into the street if he loses every penny.

"Sometimes he disappears for weeks at a time without a word, but Lord only knows what he's doing while he's gone. He comes in looking like he's spent the better part of it sleeping under a bridge, but if what he's doing is criminal, he's improved his technique while he was gone because he's not had the authorities call on Cora since he's been back.

"His mother let him move back into Palais Crantzdorf when he returned from wherever your father had taken him, but I don't think she feels there's been much of an improvement in his behavior for all the five years he spent under Aberdare's guidance." She waved her hand, showing all five fingers.

"But, when he is at home, he is respectful and attentive to his mother. He's not been after any of the house maids. He is on his best behavior. Before, he would come in belligerent, arguing with Cora, chasing after the help. I can't say they are affectionate, but Cora has never been wont to display her softer emotions, even before all of this. Cora's willing to let him stay, even if he is a profligate, simply because he hasn't brought it back under her roof."

Leilah lifted her cup and gave Eurydice a wink over the rim as she took a sip.

"And now there's you…and how you came to be the younger Mrs. Ellsworth," she said with an amused chuckle.

Eurydice blinked. "Oh," she sighed.

"There you have it. All I know about your husband; well, everything he wouldn't *want* you to know," she chortled. "Was it helpful?"

"Oh, yes, thank you so much," said Eurydice gratefully. "So many things make so much more sense now." Leilah raised an enquiring eyebrow and gave her a slight smile. "Well, I noticed his mother's behavior toward him was far less than affectionate, and I'm afraid at one point I yelled at her about it."

Leilah laughed with hilarity. "You *yelled* at her?" she chortled.

"Yes, I did, at the dinner table in front of everyone." Leilah continued to giggle. "I thought she was being unfair. I still do. I couldn't tolerate it any longer," defended Eurydice. "She had not one kind thing to say about him from the moment she arrived, and while my relationship with my husband might not be one graced with undying affection and devotion, I know he's not the man she thinks he is."

"That is true, I suppose," said Leilah thoughtfully. "Perhaps you are just what is needed to mend things between them." She patted Eurydice's hand. "Now, enough about that. There will be more to say eventually. What about your music? Do you still intend to study?"

"Oh, yes," averred Eurydice. "Ellsworth has said he would let me, but I've no notion of where to begin."

"You'll find no end of maestros in Vienna," said Leilah with a smile. "I don't think you could throw a rock without hitting one," she chortled.

Eurydice smiled. "Yes, but hitting one willing to teach me is the important part."

"Well, I've heard you play, and it's safe to say you can forego any for beginners. You need a true master to make it worth the bother. Did you know Salieri lives one or two houses down from you?"

"No!" gasped Eurydice in astonishment.

"He does," affirmed Leilah with a slight nod. "One of his current pupils is a gifted young man, about your age, named Schubert, I believe. Of course, Salieri is also one of the few that Beethoven will admit was his teacher, and don't you believe for a minute any of that tripe about the rivalry between him and Mozart. It's complete rubbish," she said firmly. She gave Eurydice a determined look. "You should go to him."

Eurydice looked at her doubtfully. "Oh, no, I couldn't," she said weakly. "He would never take me as a pupil."

"You won't know unless you ask," encouraged Leilah. "You do yourself a discredit to think you're unworthy to have him as a teacher. You forget I've lived here for more than twenty-five years. The life's blood of that city is music. If it were a living, breathing thing, the streets would be its veins, and they flow with it constantly. I've heard both the mediocre and the majestic, and you, my dear girl, are far beyond anything. Any master in this city would be blessed to find you thought him capable of teaching you anything."

Eurydice blushed. "I appreciate the flattery," she said slowly, "but as a woman—"

"That you are female is beside the point," interrupted Leilah flatly. "It only makes your talent all the more extraordinary, and even though I'm Irish, I am not prone to flattery. I don't tolerate nonsense well, and flattery *is* nonsense." She could see that Eurydice was still not convinced. "However," she said calmly, "if you feel you are not up to Salieri's sphere, then I might have a few other names to suggest."

"Thank you," said Eurydice appreciatively.

Chapter Twenty One

It was dark by the time Eurydice left Leilah's. She hadn't intended to stay so long, but she had found the older woman so easy to talk to. She had been able to tell Eurydice so many things, about Ellsworth, music, and her parents. As the coach crossed the Linienwall, she couldn't believe how fortunate she was to have Leilah there. She truly did regret she wouldn't be staying with the woman. Although Mrs. Ellsworth was kind, she lacked Leilah's warmth, and Eurydice didn't feel nearly so at ease in her company. Eurydice didn't know if Mrs. Ellsworth had been different before all the troubles she had endured, but Eurydice also suspected she would never find out.

She didn't tell Leilah in what other ways her story of what had happened to William had helped. She had wondered what her father had saved her husband from. Now she knew, and it had been just as terrible as she had thought it would be.

She couldn't believe his mother would have said what she did to him, in front of Leilah and Natalie, and Eurydice could understand the relationship between them so much better now. Leilah had thought Eurydice might be able to help them mend the estrangement between them, but she didn't see how she could. She didn't know if his mother's behavior toward him was caused by lingering blame for William's death or because of what she thought he had made of his life since then. If it was because of the latter, the situation could be made better if he simply told his mother what he was really doing. Eurydice knew he wouldn't do that…*couldn't* do that.

She didn't know how much of what his mother and Leilah thought he was doing since coming back to Vienna was accurate. The disappearances for weeks at a time were due to his job. She couldn't believe he was a drunk. Not only had she never seen anything to indicate that he was, he couldn't possibly do his job well if he were inebriated. Then again…. As for the gambling and whoring…those were things she wasn't sure about. She couldn't ask, either.

She would have to wait and see. They'd only been in Vienna for a day. His mother and Leilah thought he was no longer trying to kill himself, but Eurydice wondered if his occupation might have become his chosen form of destruction.

Leilah had been able to recommend more than just a *few* names for a teacher. The slip of paper in Eurydice's reticule had closer to twenty. There were a few she immediately knew she could mark off, or at least leave until all the others had turned her away. Eurydice couldn't believe Leilah had even thought they would be interested: Salieri, Czerny, Hummel…and Beethoven. She didn't want to go to Czerny in any case, simply because he specialized more in piano than anything else. She wasn't familiar with the other names on the list, but starting tomorrow, she would begin at the top and make her way to the bottom until she found someone willing to teach her. She was hopeful she could find someone before the end of the month. Maybe then she could avoid the social season.

When she arrived home, Ellsworth had still not returned from attending to his business. She tried not to let it concern her. He had said he would be late; Eurydice thought she was particularly late returning from Waehring, though. She hoped he would be back before supper. She found herself missing him. In the meantime, she went to their rooms and visited with Agniezka for a while before she went to the writing desk in the sitting room and worked on her composition. She wanted to play it through, but she would wait until tomorrow morning after breakfast.

When it was time for supper, Ellsworth still had not come home. She had a slight frown as she walked to the drawing room, and she was surprised when she entered to see that Mrs. Ellsworth had guests. There were two couples close in age to her mother-in-law, and she introduced them as Mr. and Mrs. Smith and the Count and Countess von Heide. Of all of them, only the count was not English, and she wasn't sure what nationality he was. His title originated from Holstein, which was part of Denmark, but he seemed German. She also wasn't sure what their mostly being British signified. They were all nice, but she had to try hard not to feel uncomfortable under their scrutiny. Apparently, Leilah and Mrs. Ellsworth weren't the only ones who were aware of her husband's reputation and incorrigible pursuits. All through supper, she felt one or the other of them looking at her as if she were some new species or perhaps even a bit insane to have married him. For her part, Mrs. Ellsworth seemed completely unconcerned about her son's absence. No one asked where he was, and only Eurydice even seemed to care.

After the meal, Mrs. Ellsworth asked her to play something on the piano. Eurydice started to refuse. She didn't know their guests; she had no prior notice that she would be playing; and she didn't really *feel* like playing. But she agreed. She chose a cadenza by Diabelli. It was over quickly enough, and she was never so relieved to go to her room. The Smiths and von Heides were amazed by her skill on the piano, and it made them stare at her all the more. Eurydice was almost tempted to run when she left the room.

She had told Agniezka before she went to supper that she would like a bath. Eurydice missed her family home. The tub had to be put in Agniezka's room, and the water had to be carried up in buckets from the kitchen. Eurydice wouldn't be able to bathe frequently because she simply couldn't bring herself to make the servants do that much work. Not only was she unhappy with the bathing conditions, but she also missed the water closets. There was a garderobe down the hall from her rooms, or she could use a chamber pot. She had been thoroughly spoiled by her family.

Despite the size of the tub, Eurydice enjoyed her bath, and she didn't spend too long in order to keep the water warm enough for Agniezka to have a bath, too. She was sure Mrs. Ellsworth did not encourage her servants to bathe frequently, and they would frown on Agniezka doing so, thinking she was putting on airs. As Eurydice bathed, she wondered how she was going to tolerate living like this. She would have to adjust to it, for however long it would be. She could only hope it wasn't forever. She realized rather sadly that unless she moved back in with her family, it probably *would* be forever. By the time she got out of the tub, Eurydice was longing for home.

She climbed into bed after writing an entry in her life diary. She was thankful that at least the bed was comfortable, but it would be even better with her husband in it. Even when they were having their disagreement, she had become accustomed to his being there beside her. Even when they were in Venice and he would leave in the middle of the night after he thought she was asleep, he was there when she went to bed and when she woke. She was amazed she could miss his presence so much; they hadn't even been married a full three weeks yet. She didn't know how it was possible.

She didn't know how long she lay there unable to fall asleep. She let her mind play over the remainder of the violin composition, and she eventually started to drift off. She had apparently fallen asleep or come very close because she jumped in surprise when she felt the mattress shift as Ellsworth got into bed. She hadn't heard him come in. He carefully pulled her toward him, and she snuggled against him as he put his arms around her. Her nose wrinkled, and she frowned with her eyes closed.

"You smell like stale cigars," she mumbled groggily.

Ellsworth smoothed a hand over her hip and kissed the top of her head. "I'm sorry. I didn't mean to wake you," he said softly.

"I wasn't that asleep," said Eurydice dryly. She wasn't going to ask *why* he smelled like cigars. "I had a nice visit with Leilah Mahone this afternoon."

"Did you? How is the old girl?" he asked thoughtfully. It had been ages since he had been to see her himself.

"She had some delicious coffee and a lovely house, and she was able to give me the names of some music teachers," said Eurydice absently as she smoothed a hand over his chest.

"That's good," said Ellsworth slowly. He put his hand over hers to stop what she was doing and brought it to his mouth to kiss the palm. He knew what she wanted to do, but he was exhausted. "Sweetheart, I just want to sleep," he said tiredly.

"All right," she said quietly, trying to contain her disappointment.

She snuggled her head onto his chest and put her arm around his waist and sighed fitfully. She had missed him all day, and while she would like to make love, she would be satisfied with just being close to him. She would definitely not tell him what Leilah had told her that afternoon. He wouldn't appreciate Leilah had done it, and he would find mention of it upsetting. Maybe they could make love in the morning.

Ellsworth was already gone when she got up. She was unhappy to see that, and it wasn't only because she had wanted to make love. She had only been able to spend breakfast with him the previous day, and she wouldn't even have that today. He had left no note to tell her where he had gone (not that she thought he would) or when she might expect him back.

She didn't know why she felt so upset he wasn't there, and as she ate the breakfast Agniezka brought to the sitting room, Eurydice determined she would not let it bother her anymore. They had a marriage of convenience, and it was silly for her to act as if they had some form of affection for each other. While making love with him was wonderful, and she did have to be honest and admit she did care about him, there was nothing more. It wasn't possible there was anything more, and it was obvious there wasn't for him either.

Agniezka was beginning to feel better. She still had nausea when she woke in the morning, but she was able to keep the contents of her stomach where they belonged, especially now that she was staying in one place. With the ginger tea, the nausea was quickly remedied as well. She wasn't showing yet, which Eurydice had noticed last night while she sat talking with Agniezka as she bathed, but her breasts were larger. Before, they had been about the same size as Eurydice's.

Eurydice hoped they could have Agniezka's marriage dissolved before she started to show, but Eurydice began to think of what they were going to do if it wasn't. Knowing Mrs. Ellsworth's attitude toward her own servants, Eurydice could only imagine how she would react to discovering Eurydice's maid was pregnant. She only knew that Mrs. Ellsworth had no say in whether or not Agniezka was dismissed. When they were in Venice, Eurydice had discussed Agniezka's employment and wages with her father. She was now paid from Eurydice's own allowance, and her employment was at Eurydice's sole discretion. But that didn't mean her mother-in-law couldn't be angry or that she couldn't refuse to let Agniezka remain under her roof. Eurydice had no qualms about finding a new place to live if that happened, whether Ellsworth thought it convenient or not. There was also the matter of how the other servants would react should they find out Agniezka was with child. Eurydice didn't want to think they would be mean, but it was possible. She wouldn't want to let Agniezka have to suffer that.

Something she had discussed with her father—and Ellsworth—while in Venice was her dowry. She had peripherally known she would have one, but she had never thought about how much it was or anything else. It was something that would be discussed between her father and husband, and she was surprised when Ellsworth asked her to be present when he talked to her father about it. It was a large sum, almost as much as she had inherited from Grandfather Sanders, and she had been flabbergasted when Ellsworth told her that he didn't want it. He told Aberdare to instead arrange for it to be placed into Eurydice's own accounts.

She thought that was very generous of him, but she didn't need the money either. She received an allowance of one hundred pounds every month from her inheritance from Grandfather Sanders, an amount that was less than the interest that accrued on the original sum and more than adequate to meet her needs, even with now being responsible for Agniezka's income. Should things not go well with Agniezka's divorce and Mrs. Ellsworth didn't react kindly to finding out Agniezka was with child, Eurydice supposed the funds would be helpful for establishing her own household. They would be useful for doing that when she and Ellsworth finally were able in any event.

After breakfast, Eurydice worked on transcribing more of her composition. She was almost finished, and she was pleased it was going so well. She wasn't sure what to name it yet, but something would come to her. Once she had the last little bit written down, it would come to her. As it was, she was able to play it through to the very end, only needing to play the last of it from memory. She was curious what the next thing would be to come to her after she finished the violin piece. She was already vaguely beginning to hear a symphony, but Stefania's panpipes were a part of it…and zils, and she wasn't sure that was practical.

She had Agniezka make sure her hair and clothes were satisfactory, and then she put the slip of paper Leilah had given her into a reticule, placed several of her compositions into a portfolio, and took *La Ragazza Dolce* in its case. She arranged for the carriage to be readied for her use, and the same driver from the previous day, who she discovered was named Etzel, was there to help her into it when she went out the front door. It would have been possible for her to walk from one place to another, but she wasn't familiar with the streets yet, and she had no notion of where to begin.

Agniezka had dressed her in a simple white gown with a beautiful olive velvet pelisse. It was feminine without being frivolous—just the thing to be worn for an interview. Eurydice was nervous about going to see these strange men, but she would have to do her best to remain calm. The worst that would happen was that they would say no, and she would be no worse off than before. But, someone could just as easily say yes, and that would be marvelous. Still, she had to make sure the teacher who accepted her would be someone she could learn from. She wasn't unwilling to work hard, but it would be pointless if what he wanted to teach her wasn't what she needed to learn.

The first teacher she went to see, Herr Seckinger, flatly told her no without even giving her an opportunity to play anything or looking at any of her compositions. It was obvious he did so only because she was female. He was polite when she first arrived, offering her coffee and inviting her to take a seat. By the end of the interview, however, he was impatient for her to be gone. He did tell her the reason he wouldn't teach a female, and Eurydice had to bite her tongue on an angry retort. He said women lacked the determination to be serious musicians. They would be diligent for a month or two, but they always left for marriage. He didn't have time for that nonsense.

The next name on the list, a man called Schellig, did at least look at some of her compositions, but he wouldn't let her play and refused to believe the compositions were hers. He was convinced they belonged to a male composer, and that she either borrowed them or stole them in some quest to dupe him. He did offer to teach her piano, and Eurydice was even angrier when she left his house than she had been when she left Herr Seckinger's. At least Seckinger hadn't accused her of thievery.

The next teacher she went to see was Herr Fehrin. She was hopeful when she met him. He politely looked at her compositions, and not only did he consent to listen to her play the violin, requesting she play a piece of her own as well as one by Beethoven, but he also asked her to play a piano composition of her own and one by Beethoven again. When she was finished, he was quiet for several minutes, but he kindly told her that he couldn't be her teacher. When she asked for the reason, he only said again that he *couldn't* teach her. Eurydice was disappointed when she left. It made her wonder if her technique was so unmanageable that it would take too much effort to shape it into something that wasn't.

The next teacher she met, Johannes Bracher, had the same opinion—there was nothing he could teach her. By the time she left his house, the sun was setting, and Eurydice was feeling entirely deflated. The only consolation she had was that the anxiety she felt at the beginning of the day had dissipated by the time she played for him. As the day wore on, she realized being told no several times was a somewhat liberating experience. It might have been strange if it weren't so pathetic.

When she arrived home, the sun had dipped below the roofs of the houses, and the air was looking as gloomy as Eurydice felt. Etzel wasn't able to drop her directly in front of the door because there was a carriage already there. It was fancy, with lots of polished brass and glass. The curtains were open, and she could see the seat was well-cushioned and covered in rich red velvet. She frowned slightly as she looked at it, but she supposed it was a caller for Mrs. Ellsworth. She had discovered at supper last night that her mother-in-law had a very active social life.

She was preparing to go up the stairs when a woman exited the house. Eurydice looked at her calmly and smiled politely, but the woman sneered disdainfully when she saw Eurydice. After the day she'd had, Eurydice didn't let it bother her. She judged the woman to be possibly in her twenties but definitely not beyond her thirties. Where Eurydice's hair was a dark, rich auburn, hers was a shade much brighter, closer to copper, and her skin was very pale. She had bright green eyes, almond-shaped and slightly tilted at the corners, making her appear feline. She was the same height as Eurydice, but her figure was more curvaceous, with larger breasts and wider hips. Eurydice thought she would be pretty if it weren't for the snide expression she wore.

She didn't say a word as she walked past Eurydice down the stairs in a cloud of heavily-scented perfume, and Eurydice turned to look perplexedly when she heard the woman laugh amusedly as the carriage pulled away. Eurydice stood with her hand resting on the rail, looking after the vehicle with a thoughtful expression. She had no idea who the woman was, but she apparently had known Eurydice, even if they hadn't been introduced. She finally shrugged and went inside.

She could hear raised voices coming from the drawing room as she closed the door, and she realized without much effort that it was Ellsworth and his mother. The door to the room was open, and while she was tempted to go in to see her husband, she didn't want to intrude on what was obviously an argument. As it was, she couldn't help but hear it as she went to the bottom of the stairs to go to her room.

"Keep your voice down, please, Mum. Do you want the servants to hear?"

"I don't care! Let them hear! I will *not* have that rank slut in my house again!" said Mrs. Ellsworth angrily.

"I didn't invite her here," said Ellsworth calmly.

"Then just you make sure you keep it that way, and tell her not to *ever* come back! What you do with your drab elsewhere is one thing, but think about your wife! That girl deserves better than to have you throw your trash in her face!"

Eurydice didn't stay to listen to the rest of the argument. She wore a frown as she made her way up the stairs and went down the hall to their rooms. She took her violin and portfolio to the sitting room, and when she came out, she took off her hat and gloves to set them on the dressing table. She rubbed a shaking hand across her forehead, and then she first walked one way then the other confusedly before she went to the couch in the sitting room. She drew her knees up to her chest and rested one of her cheeks on top of them as she absently looked out the window.

She didn't think the day could get any worse. Despite her best efforts not to, she had missed seeing Ellsworth all day. She had been refused by all four teachers she had visited, one refusing because she was a woman, another accusing her of being a fraud, and two telling her she was unteachable. Then she returned home to be looked upon with contempt by a woman she discovered was none other than her husband's mistress. Eurydice didn't know if she was Anneliese Rathmueller or called by some other name, but it didn't matter. The disappointing part of it was that Ellsworth had a mistress.

Eurydice was sure the relationship had started before they were married, but it didn't seem he intended to end it now that they were.

She was still sitting like that, curled up small at the end of the couch and staring at nothing by the light of the small fire burning on the grate when Ellsworth came into the room. He started in surprise when he realized she was sitting there.

"What are you doing sitting here in the dark?" he asked with a concerned frown, going to sit beside her.

Eurydice shrugged dejectedly. She didn't really want to see him at the moment. She didn't want to see anyone.

"How long have you been home?" he asked softly, smoothing a hand down her arm. Eurydice resisted the urge to pull away from him.

"I don't know. Not long," she said smally.

"I take it things didn't go well finding a teacher," he stated gently, giving her a sympathetic smile.

"No, they didn't, but I've only just started looking," she said evenly.

Ellsworth got up to use a rush to light the lamp on the nearby table, and then he came to sit beside her on the couch again, his expression pensive.

"Maybe you shouldn't get one," he said quietly.

"What?" said Eurydice disbelievingly.

"I don't think you should get a teacher."

Eurydice felt as if the wind had been knocked out of her, and a lump began to form in her throat. She thought the day couldn't get any worse. Apparently, she was wrong.

"But you said I could continue with my music before we were married," she said as calmly as she could.

"I think finding a maestro is a waste of your time," said Ellsworth flatly. "Of course, you should play and compose, but what could anyone teach you?" he asked reasonably.

Eurydice felt as if he had just slapped her. She thought he liked her music and her playing, and it hurt to find out he apparently thought of her as nothing more than drawing room entertainment like everyone else. It seemed she was the only one who thought she could be so much more, that she was the only one who wanted her to be more, except for her family. She had hoped for so much when she came to Vienna, and it seemed it just wasn't going to be everything she had wanted. She looked away from him and rested her cheek onto the top of her knees again.

"I think I'd like to be alone now, please," she said quietly.

"But—" began Ellsworth impatiently.

"Please, go away," she whispered.

Ellsworth looked at her perplexedly. Why couldn't she understand that she needed to perform? There was nothing she needed to learn. Her technique was flawless, both as a musician and a composer. Why could she not see what was so apparent to everyone else who heard her? What would it take to make her see that? It was obviously something beyond his capability. He smoothed a hand down her arm, and then he stood up and leaned forward to kiss the top of her head.

"All right," he said quietly, and then he left.

Eurydice sat for several minutes after he'd gone, crying silent tears. It had only been two days, and she was already wishing she had never left Britain. She missed her family. She even found herself becoming maudlin at the thought of Persephone breaking her violin strings. Her family might have become irritated with her constant practicing, but there was never any question that they thought she was an excellent musician or that they believed she could be more than a parlor trick. She didn't imagine she would ever be comparable to Beethoven, Mozart, Haydn, or Salieri, but she would be happy if she could— just once—play for an audience of complete strangers and have them applaud. If she could have that *just once*, it would be enough for her to feel accomplished. She would gladly go back to playing her violin in her bedroom after that.

Agniezka came into the room after she had been sitting there crying for several minutes, and Eurydice quickly wiped her hands across her cheeks and blinked her eyes in an attempt to disguise what she had been doing. Her maid was far too observant not to realize she was upset, though. She went to Eurydice and put her arms around her, running a soothing hand over her hair.

"What is it, *malutka*?" asked Agniezka softly.

"No one wants to teach me," said Eurydice sadly. "My husband doesn't want me to learn," she said brokenly. She took a deep breath and rested her head onto Agniezka's shoulder. "And he has a mistress."

Agniezka felt tears sting her own eyes as she whispered soothing noises and patted Eurydice's back and rocked her. Agniezka knew she wouldn't cry out loud. She rarely did, and it always broke Agniezka's heart when she heard it because there was never a sound so forlorn. For Eurydice to weep out loud meant she had lost all hope, and for that to happen it meant there truly *was* no hope. In the nearly eleven years she had been Eurydice's maid, Agniezka had only ever *heard* her cry twice. As it was, the silent tears were bad enough because those were almost as rare, and she couldn't help but feel angry Ellsworth had driven her to them. Eurydice had never said she loved him, but Agniezka knew she had to care for him more than just a little for him to make her cry. As she continued to comfort her mistress, she had to wonder if he even realized how special that made him.

≪ ≫

Ellsworth sighed tiredly as he walked up the stairs to the building on Juden Gasse. He didn't go the night before, simply because it had been Sunday, and he never went on Sunday. He hadn't intended to go tonight; he had planned to stay home with his wife for the evening, at least until she fell asleep, but she hadn't wanted him there. So he thought he would go to Rathmueller's for a few hours instead. He didn't feel it was a fair trade. He briefly knocked on the door, and it was answered by a hulk of a man who seemed squeezed into clothing a few sizes too small. Ellsworth always thought he was sausage-like.

"Hallo, Bruno," said Ellsworth casually, giving him a lazy grin.

"*Guten abend,* Herr Ellsworth. It is good to see you back," said the giant pleasantly, moving out of the way for him to enter.

"Is the lady of the house about?" asked Ellsworth calmly as he removed his hat, gloves, and outer coat to give them to Bruno.

Ellsworth always received no end of amusement about Bruno. His official position was footman, but he was also a bodyguard, expelling guests who misbehaved. Bruno could be nice, but he really enjoyed his work. Ellsworth had never had to find out exactly how well Bruno was able to do his job.

"The fraulein is in the red drawing room," said Bruno with a smile.

Ellsworth clapped him on the shoulder appreciatively and headed for a set of heavy, oak-paneled doors to the right of the stairs. Rathmueller's, while a "public" establishment, had once been a private residence. There were five floors, not including the ground floor. The top two floors were still a private residence, being Anneliese's own home where guests weren't allowed. (Ellsworth had been there.) The rest of the floors, however, had been remodeled somewhat.

The ground floor still housed the kitchens and storage rooms and had windows that could be peered into and opened. The first floor had four drawing rooms, all of about the same size, two to either side of the staircase, designated by the main color of the décor: red, blue, gold, and green. None of the windows opened. In fact, the windows had all been blocked up, and the only way to know where they had been inside was that curtains were hung at their former locations, and the wall had been painted with trompe l'oeil depicting various scenes.

Not only were the drawing rooms distinguished by their color, but also by the entertainments that could be found in each of them. The gold drawing room was where a man went if all he wanted to do was drink. There was at least a pianist, sometimes a quartet, to entertain. The red was where he could go for cards or other games of chance. The blue and green offered entertainments of a more carnal nature—dining tables with food on platters that were naked women or where they were on display to be sampled and chosen outright to be taken to a room on one of the other two public floors for a more personal form of entertainment. Ellsworth had been to all the drawing rooms on one occasion or another, but he preferred the red. He was glad that was where he could find Anneliese.

He walked into the room, and it was easy enough to find her—she was the only woman seated at a table playing cards. There were other women in the room, to be sure, but they were there as decoration or to convince guests to spend more money, be it on alcohol…or themselves. Anneliese was just finishing a round when he entered, and she stood up and gave him a sensual smile as she sauntered toward him. She took him by the hands and kissed him warmly on both cheeks.

"Inga, please get whisky for Mr. Ellsworth and myself," she called as she led him to a seat beside her on a couch near the fake window. "It's good to see you again," she purred, leaning close to him and running a finger along his jaw.

"My mother was put out you came to her house today," said Ellsworth with a dry smile.

Anneliese laughed amusedly. "That old fly-by-night is easily put out," she said cattily.

"Hey, steady on, that's my mum," said Ellsworth softly, but his tone wasn't critical.

Inga brought their drinks, and she gave Ellsworth a wink and an impudent smile before she returned to her place at the elbow of a man at a table playing *pochen.* Ellsworth was acquainted with her but completely uninterested.

"A little bird told me you had returned, and I had to come see for myself," said Anneliese with a slight pout. Her hand moved to the back of his head, and she clenched her fingers with only marginal playfulness in his hair. "Especially when I heard you had returned with a *wife.*"

Ellsworth shrugged and took a sip from his glass. "Yes, well, that wasn't intentional," he said dryly.

Anneliese laughed again, and while it was amused, Ellsworth could also detect anger. "I saw your little *frau* when I was leaving this afternoon. I suppose she's pretty in a pettish kind of way, but a very poor imitation of *me.*"

"You saw her?" asked Ellsworth calmly, keeping his lackadaisical pose, but he wasn't feeling very calm or lackadaisical.

"Oh, yes. The simple cow *smiled* at me, and what—exactly—is wrong with her eyes?" She took a sip from her glass and leaned even closer against him. "Honestly, darling, her coloring is—quite simply—*off.*"

Ellsworth looked at her through slightly narrowed eyes, the only indication he gave of how angry he was to hear her talk about Eurydice that way. He was trying to resist the urge to push her onto the floor. It wasn't easy.

"She does look a bit unusual, doesn't she?" he said evenly.

Anneliese laughed throatily. "*Unusual?*" she sighed. "You're just saying that because she's your wife, and you can't bring yourself to say she looks downright bizarre," she chortled. She leaned close and nuzzled his neck and moved a hand up the inside of his thigh toward his crotch. "Darling, if you wanted a redhead, I've been here all along," she whispered seductively.

Ellsworth withstood her touching, but he was growing tired of her insulting Eurydice, especially because he knew it was jealousy that caused it. She could never hope to compete with his wife in *any* way.

"Liese, love, you know those days are over for us," he said softly, and he put his hand over hers to calmly move it away from his completely disinterested member.

She lifted her head to look at him with a pout. "Oh, you weren't serious," she said dismissively.

"Yes, I was," said Ellsworth calmly.

"I can make you change your mind," she purred.

"You can try," said Ellsworth lazily, "and while you're at it, you can tell me if you know anyone who's been to Venice lately."

Eurydice fell asleep shortly after she went to bed. She was emotionally wrung out after the day she'd had, and supper only made it worse. When she had told Ellsworth she wanted to be alone, she hadn't meant she wanted him to leave the house, but when she went down to the drawing room before supper, she discovered that was what he had done. Mrs. Ellsworth again had guests, even more than the night before, and she again expected Eurydice to play the piano. She chose Beethoven's "Moonlight" sonata, deciding it suited her mood. She still felt all through the meal and afterward as if she were a specimen on display, and she left as soon as it could politely be accomplished.

She didn't know what time it was or how long she had been asleep when Ellsworth finally returned home, but she woke up slightly when he got into the bed. She apparently hadn't been asleep that long. She thought about moving away from him after what he had said about her music that afternoon, but she wanted to be held and hoped she had misunderstood what he meant. He pulled her toward him into her usual position, with her head nestled onto his chest, but she wasn't that way for long before her eyes flew open and she was wide awake. Her hand resting over his side near his hip balled into a fist, and she had to blink several times as a lump formed in her throat. Last night, he had smelled of stale cigars, which Eurydice had found unappealing but tolerable. Tonight, the smell of stale cigars was still there, and whisky, but there was something more. He smelled like *her.*

Eurydice lay there for a moment unable to decide what she should do. She knew how she *wanted* to react, which was why she had her hand balled so tightly her nails bit into the palm. After several minutes of trying to control her tears and her anger, the only firm thing she could decide was that she wouldn't be able to sleep like that, if it were possible for her to sleep at all.

"Are you awake?" asked Ellsworth softly.

Eurydice jumped at the unexpected sound of his voice, and she could only nod her head, not trusting her voice to speak. It was pointless to pretend she was asleep. She tensed when she felt him move his hand down her back to her bottom and slowly began to play his fingers across it. He moved his other hand down her arm to where her hand rested at his hip in its little ball and lifted it toward his lips. She didn't uncurl her fingers, and he gave her a kiss on her wrist instead. It was obvious he didn't realize how distressed she was. He gave her arm a coaxing tug.

"Give us a smooch, Dicy," he whispered.

Eurydice couldn't bear it, and she sat up and away from him, pulling her arm out of his touch. She couldn't look at him, and she couldn't speak, and she was trying to keep the tears from spilling out of her eyes onto her cheeks. She moved as far away from him as she could on the mattress and turned her back, but she only lay that way a few seconds before she decided it wasn't far enough. She got out of the bed and went to the sitting room, where she curled up in a ball on the end of the couch near the dying embers of the fire. It was cold, but she couldn't bear to be near him. She wiped a hand at her cheek as she rested her head on the arm of the couch, but she soon lifted it as Ellsworth came into the room.

"What's wrong?" he asked flatly.

Eurydice couldn't speak. The emotional lump in her throat had grown so large she couldn't seem to make her mouth move, and she looked around herself in wild-eyed panic as she fought to regain control of herself. She was breathing in and out quickly through her nose, her chest heaving, and her hands gripped tightly at the arm of the couch.

"If this is about your music, why is it so hard for you to realize you need to—" began Ellsworth plaintively.

Eurydice finally found her voice. "My *music?*" she hissed furiously. She got up from the couch and stalked toward him. "You manky, shagging—!" she ground out, and Ellsworth had to grab her wrists to keep her from clawing at his face.

She struggled to make him let her go, but he was stronger and more than capable of keeping her restrained. She finally leaned her forehead against his chest defeatedly, and her shoulders shook with quiet sobs. He let go of her wrists once she stopped fighting him, and her arms dropped limply to her sides. She eventually lifted her head to look at him, and she inhaled a shaky breath.

"This is about you coming to *my* bed smelling like another woman! I don't need to break any promise I've ever made to know where you went, who you saw, and *what* you've been doing," she said huskily. "I'm going to sleep with Agniezka, and don't you *dare* try to stop me."

She proudly lifted her chin and stepped around him with her back stiff, and she didn't let herself slump until she made it to Agniezka's room and closed the door. Agniezka started in surprise when Eurydice climbed under the blankets with her, but she didn't ask any questions. They wrapped their arms around each other, and Agniezka cried silently as Eurydice buried her face in Agniezka's shoulder and began to weep.

Chapter Twenty Two

Eurydice was exhausted when she woke up the next day. She couldn't bring herself to go looking for a maestro. All of the rejection she had suffered the previous day from the moment she woke until the moment she finally managed to sleep could not bear repeating. She would go tomorrow, after hopefully getting through at least one day without any further upset.

Ellsworth was gone when she left Agniezka's room, and Eurydice was only marginally relieved. He hadn't tried to pursue her into Agniezka's room. He didn't try to deny what he had done. Of course, Eurydice didn't see how he possibly could. It wouldn't have hurt so much if he hadn't flaunted what he had been doing, if he hadn't led her to believe he wouldn't have a mistress, if she hadn't thought they were happy. It had all been lies…again.

Agniezka brought her a tray with breakfast to the sitting room. She sat making her entries in her diaries and writing letters to her family while she ate. The entry in her dream diary was brief and only a dream. The one in her life diary, however, was more extensive, filling several pages, even though Arabic took less room than English. She wrote letters to her mother and father and each of her siblings. She didn't imagine Psyche would receive hers quickly, but after a moment's consideration, Eurydice addressed it to her at the home of the Andreanopouli in Greece. She felt it was likely her sister had already left Venice for Thessaloniki. She didn't expect Psyche's stay there would be very long, and she would not be going to Egypt…yet again. Now more than ever, Eurydice missed her family, and she wished she could see them. Despite how she sometimes felt they didn't quite understand her, they loved her and accepted her regardless. She needed that right now.

Once she finished with her diaries and letters, Eurydice took the time to practice her *t'ai chi*. She hadn't been able to since she had been in Venice, and since she couldn't swim, it gave her the exercise she had been missing and also helped to clear her head of some of the things that were bothering her. Her thoughts were jumbled and useless, and it had been hard to concentrate on writing. She couldn't work on her music in that condition.

With her thoughts more focused, she then turned to her composition. She was almost finished, and she was determined to get done that day. She had no intention of leaving the house or seeing anyone, and she saw no reason why she couldn't get it written out. Agniezka sat in a chair by the fire in the sitting room knitting while Eurydice worked at the desk, and it proved to be a very peaceful day with just the two of them. The solitude was helpful and did much to improve her spirits. She still didn't want to see Ellsworth, but at least now she would find it bearable if she had to.

Eurydice had told Agniezka what happened, why she was so upset and had gone to her maid's room to sleep. Agniezka had been sad and sympathetic, and she felt Ellsworth should consider himself lucky he hadn't been in the room when she left her own that morning. He had caused far too many tears for Eurydice. Worse, he had made her weep. The two times Agniezka had seen her like that before had been when her *babushka* and Myron had died. What had caused her sobbing hadn't been their passing but that she had known it was going to happen and had been unable to save them. *Hopelessness.* He had made her feel hopeless, and that wasn't right.

Eurydice wrote the final note on the page slightly after five. The sun had started to dip below the roofs of the nearby buildings, and Agniezka had lit some of the lamps to keep the gloom at bay for a little longer. Eurydice read through what she had written, and then she took her Guadagnini from the case and made sure the strings were tuned properly. She had been practicing with her Stainer while she wrote, but she thought the composition was better-suited to the tones of the Guadagnini than to either the Stainer or the Stradivarius.

She managed to play through the sonata without having to stop for any corrections, and she was satisfied what was on the page matched what had been in her head. She was glad to finally have it out because a symphony was impatiently waiting to be composed and had started to compete with it. She wasn't sure how well its transcription would fare, however, because she was hearing things in her head, like her panpipes and zils, that weren't typical. She would do her best to write down what she heard, though, because she had to. Once she looked at her watch, she decided she would have time to begin work on that before supper and got started.

Not once throughout the day, to Eurydice's knowledge, did Ellsworth come home. Other than to use the garderobe, she didn't leave the sitting room, so the only way she would have seen him would have been if he came to their suite. He didn't. Agniezka brought both her breakfast and her dinner to the room, and if her maid had seen him at any point, she didn't mention it. Eurydice had no notion what she would say to him when she did finally see him again, but she wasn't looking forward to it. She didn't know where he had been going all the time since they had arrived in the city, but she could guess where he was going at least part of the time. She tried not to think about it.

She was so immersed in working on the symphony that she was late leaving her room for supper. She hoped the clock was set wrong, but by the time she got to the drawing room, she was dismayed to see no one there. She walked as quickly as she could without running to the doors of the dining room, and her cheeks colored a bright pink when she saw that Mrs. Ellsworth and her guests were already seated and eating the first course. There was a place for her at the table, and she gracefully walked toward it, feeling mortified that all the men at the table had to stand as she went to take her seat. Ellsworth wasn't among them, but she was overjoyed to see Leilah Mahone was there, and while Mrs. Ellsworth again had a table full of guests, Eurydice was relieved to see she had met them all except for two. Including herself, sixteen were at the table.

"I'm sorry to be late," she said quietly as she took her seat.

"I was beginning to wonder if you intended to eat supper there as well," said Mrs. Ellsworth with an amused twinkle and a smile.

Eurydice blushed. "Again, I apologize. It is simply that I was almost done with one piece, and another is impatient to be born, so…." She colored even further when everyone turned to look at her, and she realized what she said sounded a little crazy. She picked up her spoon to begin eating her soup. "It won't happen again," she said quietly.

"I dislike when they do that myself," said the man beside her after a time, slightly inclining his head toward her to speak confidentially. "One's fingers can only move so fast," he said as he lifted his hand to wiggle his graceful—if short—digits in the air, "and while *I* can understand how it reads, it makes it difficult for someone else to do so. Don't you agree?"

"Oh, yes, absolutely," said Eurydice wholeheartedly with a nod and a smile.

He shrugged and smiled, too. "But as long as *we* know…."

Eurydice relaxed slightly and began to calmly eat her meal. She looked across the table to Leilah, and she gave Eurydice a smile and a wink. After his comment on composing, the man to her right didn't say anything further throughout the meal, even though there was conversation all around him. He was one of the guests she hadn't met before, and she supposed they would be introduced after the meal. As he seemed to be more interested in his food than conversation, she didn't want to impose.

Count von Heide sat to her left, and he requested that instead of her playing the piano after supper, he should like to hear her play the violin. Mrs. Ellsworth had told him that her skill on that instrument was even better. Eurydice was sorely tempted to say she had no intention of playing any instrument at all that evening as she wasn't a performing monkey, but that would be rude, and it wasn't as if she had anything to do after supper other than go to her room and to bed. She had some consolation in that he had at least requested it before the end of the meal rather than waiting until after it, as Mrs. Ellsworth often did, leaving Eurydice to decide what to play on the spur of the moment. By the time dessert was served, a wonderful torte with layers of cream and chocolate, Eurydice decided she would play a piece of her own. Not the one she had just finished but *Le Papillon*.

When the meal was over and the women retired to the drawing room for tea (Mrs. Ellsworth did not serve coffee…at any time, much to Eurydice's disappointment), Eurydice briefly excused herself to go upstairs for a violin. Agniezka was in the sitting room knitting by the fire when Eurydice came in, and she looked up in surprise. Eurydice retrieved her Stradivarius and made monkey noises as she left. Agniezka giggled amusedly and shook her head. She was pleased to see some of Eurydice's good humor was returning, but it was only due in part to her husband's absence for the entire day.

Eurydice had just enough time once she returned to the drawing room to make sure the violin was properly tuned. She was nervous to be playing, as usual, but something she had learned that seemed to help was to ignore the people in the room…to just pretend she was the only one there. Standing sideways instead of facing her audience directly, which put them just at the edge of her vision, made that easier to do. She wasn't sure if that could be done were she ever to play for more people than just enough to fit in a drawing room, though.

Leilah came to speak with her just as the men were rejoining them.

"Are you excited to be playing?" asked Leilah.

"Not especially," said Eurydice flatly. "Mrs. Ellsworth has had me play after supper the last two nights. The only difference tonight is that it's violin instead of piano." She grimaced.

Leilah laughed and rubbed her shoulder. "If it bothers you, just say no. She really won't take offense if you do. Sometimes Cora has a tendency to take advantage of a good thing. You are a *very* good thing. And why are you not calling her Cora yet?"

"Because she hasn't said that I could," said Eurydice simply.

Leilah laughed girlishly and shook her head. "Oh, lass, you must learn to speak up for yourself!" She gave Eurydice's arm an encouraging squeeze. "You can't tell me you have no gumption. I know the stock you come from, and it's there! And I know you can use it when it suits you!" she chortled.

Mrs. Ellsworth had the servants bring in enough chairs for everyone to be comfortable, and the men were served their tea as the servants tended to that and opened the doors and curtains to the music room.

"No, I don't like tea," said the man who had been sitting beside Eurydice to the right at supper. "I want coffee," he said shortly. Eurydice didn't hear the maid's reply, and the man apparently didn't, either. "What kind of establishment is this that doesn't serve coffee? Are we not in Vienna?"

Eurydice looked at him in puzzlement, and she heard Leilah's slight sound of sympathy. Eurydice looked at her.

"Poor thing's almost completely deaf now," she said softly, putting a hand to her chest. "It just breaks my heart."

"Who is he?" asked Eurydice curiously.

Leilah looked at her in surprise. "You mean you don't know?" she gasped.

"No, I—" began Eurydice, but she was interrupted as Mrs. Ellsworth joined them.

"Are you nervous?" she asked excitedly.

Eurydice frowned confusedly. "Not any more than usual," she said dryly.

She continued to look as another maid quickly rushed in with a cup containing coffee to give to Mr. Right. Since they had still not been introduced, and he had sat on her right at dinner, she had no other name for him. Eurydice knew, because Mrs. Ellsworth didn't serve it, that the maid had brought the coffee from the servants' personal stores. It was a bit rude of him to demand special treatment, not to mention peculiar that the servants would be willing to part with their own things to accommodate him. Eurydice didn't think they did it because they believed Mrs. Ellsworth would be angry with them if they hadn't. It was strange.

Leilah seemed surprised she didn't know who he was, but Eurydice couldn't understand how she was expected to; he was at least Austrian— possibly German. She had never been here before. She judged him to be somewhere in his forties, with dark brown eyes and hair that had possibly been black or dark brown but was starting to fade to gray, swept back from a broad forehead to stand out in just about every direction. He had broad features with strong eyebrows and a prominent chin, and although the corners of his mouth were turned down in a permanently serious expression, his whole face brightened when he smiled, and it revealed even, white teeth. She hadn't seen him standing, but she knew from sitting beside him at the table that he stood not much taller than she. Either that or he had long legs and a short torso. His frame was stocky without being heavyset. *Sturdy.* Sturdy would be a word to describe his build. He could be a nobleman or something, but she was clueless.

"Are you ready to play?" asked Mrs. Ellsworth, giving her shoulder an encouraging squeeze.

"I am," said Eurydice evenly with a slight nod.

Leilah and Mrs. Ellsworth went to their seats as Eurydice went to the nearby table where she had placed her violin. She flexed her fingers momentarily before she lifted it from the case and took a deep preparatory breath. She calmly nestled the instrument beneath her chin and began to play. She stood not far from the piano at what had been made the front of the room by the placement of the chairs Mrs. Ellsworth had brought in. The curtains had been drawn, so she couldn't look out the window, but she kept her attention on the dark green brocaded satin in that direction for the most part. She would occasionally look at Leilah and Mrs. Ellsworth and give them a slight smile as they watched her play with delighted expressions. At one point she made the mistake of looking in Mr. Right's direction and saw him sitting with his eyes closed. To her irritation, he appeared for all the world to be sound asleep, but his eyes sprang open suddenly when she was finished, and he applauded with everyone else.

She had turned and was putting away her violin when she heard a collective gasp of surprise behind her. She certainly hoped it wasn't because they expected her to play another piece. She turned back to face the room and was startled when she was nearly toe-to-toe with Mr. Right. He gave her a slight smile.

"Do you know the sonata in C minor?" he asked with quiet politeness. Eurydice frowned in puzzlement. "For violin and piano?" he tried to clarify.

She wasn't sure by which composer. "By Beethoven?" she asked, it being the only one that came readily to mind. He nodded, and Eurydice's frown lessened. "Yes, I do," she said evenly with a slight nod and smile.

He put his palms together in front of himself happily, and then he turned to take a seat at the piano, fanning out his coat behind him with a flourish. Eurydice followed after him slowly, and she spared a puzzled glance to Leilah and Mrs. Ellsworth. Both of them looked ready to start bouncing in their seats, which seemed very incongruent for two women their age, and they offered her no hints on what it meant. She was very familiar with the piece—there weren't many by Beethoven that she wasn't, but she wasn't sure about Mr. Right. She didn't know him. They'd never rehearsed together. But he seemed determined they should play. She remembered Leilah had said he was almost completely deaf, so the entire enterprise was making her nervous. She would survive if it was terrible, but she didn't want to see him embarrassed. Despite his demand for coffee, he did seem nice.

She stood near the piano, turned sideways, facing him as he sat on the cushioned bench. They made eye contact and nodded slightly to each other when they were both ready. Eurydice thought she detected a slight twinkle of mischief in his eyes.

He began the first few simple bars at the beginning, and Eurydice waited for her moment to enter the piece, when things would quickly become complicated for him. That the sonata tended to rely on the violin part taking its cues from the piano rather than the other way around was not lost on her. If he was as hard of hearing as Leilah implied, it would be less likely for him to miss if he were in the lead.

When she began to play as well at just the right moment, her eyes widened in surprise as she looked at him. It didn't take her long to realize he was a very accomplished pianist, better than anyone she had ever played with, and despite his impairment, she needn't have worried. She felt almost giddy as they played through the first movement, and she couldn't resist smiling happily, especially when she saw he was receiving as much enjoyment from their playing together as she was. She didn't have to put any effort into forgetting there were other people in the room, and as they began the scherzo that was the third movement, she found it difficult not to giggle, especially when he was laughing. When they completed the finale, Eurydice found herself out of breath, feeling as if she had just run a race. It was one of the few times she had ever played when she could find nothing wrong with her performance.

Everyone rose from their seats, applauding loudly, and Eurydice jumped in surprise as she turned to look at them, her eyes round and her cheeks flushed with excitement. Mr. Right rose from his seat at the piano and went to take her hand and place a kiss on it. He startled her when he took her by the shoulders and soundly kissed both her cheeks as well before laughing uproariously.

"Very good!" he shouted as he turned to look at the rest of the dinner guests and raised a hand in the air. "Very good!"

Eurydice was a bit amazed and overwhelmed by the tumult. As everyone came toward them to shake his hand and kiss hers and express their appreciation to both of them, she felt somewhat dazed. Leilah kissed both her cheeks and took her bow and violin to put them in the case for her before she dropped them, and Eurydice looked around herself uncertainly. The other man she hadn't been introduced to that evening was the last to come offer his compliments, and then he took Mr. Right by the elbow as he discreetly held up his watch. Mr. Right turned to Eurydice with a kind smile and kissed her hand again before giving it a squeeze.

"I must be going now, young miss," he said quietly.

"It's Eurydice," she said evenly, trying to contain her disappointment that he had to leave. "My name is Eurydice."

"Ah, Eurydice" he said softly with a charmed smile. "Goodbye."

She watched as the two men left the room. She hoped to see him again. She hoped to play with him again. Tonight had been very special for her, and she would never forget it. She didn't know if he was capable of teaching with his infirmity, but if she ever saw him again, she would like to ask. She thought she could learn something from him. Leilah stood at her elbow and leaned toward her to whisper in her ear.

"So, do you know who he is now?"

Eurydice looked at her with a slight frown and shook her head. After their playing together, she had still not learned his name, even though she had finally been able to tell him hers. Leilah linked her arm through Eurydice's and gave it a slight squeeze and smiled amusedly.

"Dicy, that was Beethoven," she said softly.

Eurydice's eyes rounded. "No!" she gasped in disbelief. Leilah nodded her head affirmingly. "Oh, my giddy aunt," sighed Eurydice breathlessly, and she could feel herself going dizzy.

Leilah chuckled and tightened her grip on Eurydice's arm. "Easy does it, now," she chortled. "I'm not big enough to keep you from falling if you faint."

"But...how...he...I," stammered Eurydice incoherently.

Leilah continued to laugh as she directed Eurydice to a chair. "Breathe, lass!" she chuckled.

"Why did no one tell me he was coming?" asked Eurydice disappointedly.

Leilah raised an eyebrow. "Judging from the way you nearly fainted dead away just now when you found out who he was, are you sure you really wanted to know?"

Eurydice frowned thoughtfully. "Well, I would have at least chosen something different to play."

"Dicy, I didn't know you had become Cora's entertainer-in-residence," chortled Leilah. "He was only invited so you could meet him. Everything else was entirely unplanned. Aside from that, what you played was perfect. Obviously, *he* thought so, or he wouldn't have wanted to play with you."

"But——" she started, and then she pressed her lips together, and some of the color drained from her face when she saw that Ellsworth was there.

He stood talking with Count and Countess von Heide not far from the door. She didn't know how long he had been there. From the moment she had picked up her violin, everything and everyone else in the room had faded, especially once she had begun to play with Beethoven. While Ellsworth was conversing with the von Heides, he was watching her as she talked with Leilah.

"Perhaps you're right," she finally said dully with a noncommittal smile when Leilah sat waiting expectantly for her to say something.

Leilah didn't miss the way Eurydice had paled and the excitement had faded from her expression. She knew it was because of Ellsworth, and she was concerned about what had happened between Sunday afternoon and that night. From the way Eurydice had been when she came to call, Leilah thought the two of them were getting on well with each other. Now she wasn't so sure. He seemed sober, if tired, and she actually thought it was early for him to be home. She hoped the disagreement between the two of them was a minor one, but judging from Eurydice's reaction, Leilah had the feeling it wasn't. She would have found it hard to believe there would be anything capable of sapping Eurydice's high spirits if she hadn't seen it herself.

"It's time for me to take my leave," said Leilah on a sigh as she put her arm around Eurydice's shoulders to give her a hug before standing. "Waehring isn't very far, but it has grown late. I want you to call on me this week...*any* time this week," she said with a fond smile.

"Oh, yes," said Eurydice assuredly as she stood as well. "I need coffee...badly."

Leilah chuckled. "There are lots of coffee shops in this city, you do realize? Particularly on the Graben. But I'll tell Kouts to make herself well-stocked on chocolate and cream." She patted Eurydice's shoulder and gave her an encouraging smile. "Remember what I said about gumption, lass," she said softly.

Eurydice nodded as she watched her leave before heaving a tired sigh and smoothing a hand across her forehead once she had gone. Eurydice was feeling exhausted. All of the guests were leaving—there were only the von Heides left, so she suspected the hour was drawing close to eleven, more likely later than that. Her own sonata had been close to twenty minutes in length, and the one she had played with Beethoven slightly longer. Before she left London, especially during the Season, it was nothing for her to stay up well beyond one in the morning, but these days, anything beyond midnight was a chore. Added to the lateness of the hour was that she had not slept well, and it had been an eventful evening. She went to Mrs. Ellsworth to tell her good night.

"I'm going to bed now, Mrs. Ellsworth," she said quietly.

Mrs. Ellsworth surprised her when she gave her a brief hug and kissed her cheek. "Good night, dear," she said affectionately. "I'll be sure to have the servants get you several copies of the newspaper tomorrow."

Eurydice frowned confusedly. "Why would I need even one copy?"

"Because Herr Bakkeman said he would be writing something for tomorrow's edition. That's why he didn't stay to speak with you; he wouldn't have been able to get it to the press in time if he hadn't left when he did."

Eurydice's frown deepened even further. "I still don't understand."

"Eurydice, dear, Herr Bakkeman is a music critic," said Mrs. Ellsworth with a proud smile.

"What?" said Eurydice dully.

"We've been friends for years, and I had only invited him and his wife to supper last night because I was recently back in town and wanted to see them. Needless to say, he was surprised to find I had such a gifted new daughter-in-law. After you played with Beethoven this evening, he asked if I thought you would mind his writing a review, and I said no, even though I doubt it would have stopped him anyhow. It is off season, and this is not a salon or a theater, but I'm sure it will still be worthwhile to read. Naturally, I am assuming you will want copies to have for yourself and to send home to your family."

Eurydice's hand flew to her throat in dismay. A *music* critic? "Oh, no," she moaned, shaking her head. She felt nauseous.

"Eurydice, are you feeling well?" asked Mrs. Ellsworth concernedly, rubbing her shoulder.

"No, Mrs. Ellsworth, I am not feeling well," said Eurydice in a flat voice as she put a fluttery hand to her stomach, hoping to soothe the roiling she felt there. "Since I arrived at the table, I have felt ambushed. First, to discover you invited Beethoven without telling me, and now to find you allowed a *critic* to write an article about a performance that was intended to be private."

"Herr van Beethoven didn't mind Bakkeman was going to write about it," defended Mrs. Ellsworth mildly.

"Beethoven is a respected, *professional* composer and musician, while I am—" Eurydice was saying as calmly as she could.

"Is something wrong?" asked Ellsworth as he approached them with a concerned frown after he noticed the way Eurydice was fidgeting. The von Heides had gone, and the three of them were alone.

"It's nothing," said Eurydice stiffly.

"Bakkeman is going to write an article about this evening, but Eurydice isn't happy."

Eurydice clasped her hands together in front of her and took a deep breath in an attempt to calm herself. She would rather not have Ellsworth involved in this conversation. She would rather not have him anywhere near her.

"I didn't know he was Beethoven, and I certainly didn't know there was a music critic among the dinner guests," said Eurydice evenly.

"What difference should that make?" asked Mrs. Ellsworth confusedly.

"I am a musician, not a pet monkey!" said Eurydice heatedly, and she took another deep breath. "It is hard enough for me to be taken seriously because I am a woman," she said in a more modulated tone. "If I am ever going to get past that, I cannot afford to make mistakes, especially not *publicized* mistakes, and I can't avoid those if I'm not informed I could make them. I am not ready to per—"

"Yes, you are," cut in Ellsworth impatiently. Eurydice looked at him stonily.

"You are," agreed Mrs. Ellsworth with a warm smile and a nod. "Just look at what happened. You played with Beethoven! And Bakkeman wouldn't have wanted to write about you if all he thought you were was drawing room entertainment. He wouldn't waste his time...not even to write something about Beethoven."

"But what makes you so sure that what he is going to write will be complimentary, Mrs. Ellsworth?" asked Eurydice dully. She couldn't make them understand.

"How could it not be?" chided Mrs. Ellsworth.

Eurydice desperately hoped she was right. Something unkind could ruin any chance she had of ever finding a maestro. Despite what they seemed to think, she wasn't ready to perform for the public. There was still so much to learn. She gave Mrs. Ellsworth a brief, uncertain smile.

"Well, I suppose we'll see tomorrow," she said evenly. "I'm going to bed." She turned to leave the room.

"Good night, Mum," said Ellsworth, quickly giving his mother a peck on the cheek and following Eurydice.

Eurydice folded her arms beneath her breasts as Ellsworth caught up with her in the hall. She didn't look at him as he matched his stride to hers. She would have rathered he stayed with his mother in the drawing room, at least until she was ready for bed and gone to Agniezka's room. She would eventually feel like talking to him but not at the moment.

They would have to come to an understanding at some point because she had promised she would provide him with an heir, but she was thinking it could wait awhile—even years—before it became necessary. He hadn't said he would be faithful, except in his marriage vows, and Eurydice could think of very few couples of upper society who even took them seriously, especially the men. When they came to their personal understanding beforehand, she had agreed she would be faithful, but she had basically given him carte blanche. She had no room to complain, but it still hurt...a lot.

When they started up the stairs, Ellsworth moved to put a steadying hand at the small of her back, and Eurydice sidled away from him.

"Don't touch me," she said flatly.

"Eurydice, if—" he began softly, putting his hand back at her waist.

She slapped his hand away and glared at him. "I said don't *touch* me!" she hissed.

"It's not what you think," he said evenly.

Eurydice scoffed. "No? What could I possibly misunderstand about you smelling like jasmine and ambergris?"

"I'm not—" he began patiently.

"Shut up," said Eurydice flatly. "Don't try to tell me all you did was kiss her hand, Gareth! You smelled like her even without your clothes on! You didn't get that way from waltzing," she said coldly.

"No, I didn't," he said evenly.

Eurydice made a noise of disgust and shook her head as they reached the top of the stairs.

"You're not going to believe anything I tell you, are you?" he said neutrally.

She had her fingers on the handle to open the door to their room, and she turned to look at him.

"Why should I?" she asked sadly. "All you ever do is lie. You never admit to anything until you're caught, and even then you're stingy." She opened the door and went in then turned to look at him. "So, you go ahead and do whatever it is you want to do. Obviously, that's what you've intended all along. You made me promise I wouldn't care when I married you. I don't."

"That's not what I wanted," he said softly.

"I'm tired. I'm going to bed," said Eurydice flatly, and she turned to go across their room to the door of Agniezka's room.

"Eurydice, don't—" he started, but she had already gone into the other room and closed the door.

Ellsworth knew she wouldn't be coming back out. He sighed wearily and rubbed a hand over the back of his neck. As tempted as he was to go drag her back out, he could see she wasn't going to listen, and he couldn't blame her. Maybe he could try talking to her about it again in a few days, but he hoped she wouldn't remain sleeping with Agniezka that long. He undressed and got into bed, but he couldn't sleep, just like he hadn't been able to the night before. He had known being married to her would make his life more complicated, but he didn't want to lose her.

After lying in bed for more than an hour without being able to fall asleep, he threw back the blankets and went to the sitting room and closed the door. He lit a rush from the fire and used it to light the lamp on the writing desk. It was littered with score sheets, and he could see she was writing a symphony. He opened a drawer and found her diaries. He lifted out the one he recognized as being current and flipped through the pages. He started with the most recent entry and began to work his way backwards after he sat down in the chair.

As he read, he again appreciated how descriptive she was, and her diligence, but most of the entries were incomprehensible to him. There were one or two of them, as he read them, he had the impression she hadn't understood them either. He had to wonder what she thought about some of the strange things she saw in her dreams. He also had to wonder if her family knew about them. He would be surprised if they didn't. What had she thought when she realized she had this talent? She said the first dream she could remember having that came true happened when she was five. He could only imagine, depending on what it was, that she had been frightened.

He finally came to the entry she had written the night they stayed in Podpetsch. Compared to some of the others he had just seen, this one was fairly long, and he wondered if she hadn't been truthful when she said she hadn't seen the whole dream. He frowned as he started to read, and the furrows between his eyebrows only grew deeper the more he read. He gasped at one point, and he could feel a knot starting to grow in the pit of his stomach. Then he got to the end of the entry, and he read it all again. He quickly flipped back through the pages until he found the entry for the night they had stayed in Sacile, when she apparently first had the dream, to see if there was anything more. When he was done, he leaned back in the chair and rubbed a hand over his face and let out his breath in a loud gust.

"Bloody hell," he sighed.

He had intended to find one of the entries she'd made about Psyche, but he was done. He didn't know what more she needed to see. He had certainly read enough. He had known he needed to protect her, even as just a precautionary measure, when he found out she knew he was a spy. Now, he knew she couldn't be left alone, and he hoped, just this once, she was wrong. He *prayed* she was wrong. He could feel a cold sweat on his skin, and he shivered as he put the notebook back where he'd found it.

He started to close the drawer again when he recognized the notebook she had been given by one of her sisters as a birthday present. It was being used. He frowned as he picked it up, wondering if he really wanted to see what was in it. The diary he had just looked at still had a few blank pages left, and the last entry was from that morning, so he didn't think she had started a new one yet. He opened it, and his eyebrows shot up in surprise.

"What the—?" he muttered perplexedly.

It was in Arabic. He didn't understand it, either reading it or speaking it, but he had no trouble recognizing it. He hadn't even known she knew it, and he had to wonder *how* she knew it. He didn't think she had discovered he was reading her diaries, which led him to believe that whatever she was writing in the notebook were things she didn't want *anyone* to read. The chances of someone just happening upon the notebook and being able to decipher it were slim, and he knew this was the kind of diary he had hoped to find when he discovered her notebooks on the ship. The other diaries were just dreams, which may or may not be truthful. This was the diary that contained her thoughts…her secrets, and some of the secrets she kept were not as mundane as those some other woman might. Apparently, she knew that, too.

He closed the notebook and stood up to go to the fireplace. He started to throw it onto the dying embers, admiring her discretion for using such an uncommon language but thinking she should have known better than to write it down in the first instance, but he hesitated because he knew it probably had answers to some of his own questions. He shook his head and started to put it on again because he had no way of reading it, which made it useless to him, but again he hesitated as he tried to calculate exactly how slim the odds were that anyone else could read it either. Other than the Savages, he couldn't think of anyone he knew who might speak or understand Arabic. A few scholars and learned men at some university or another, but not many; someone from the region where it was spoken, and finding someone like that in Vienna was as rare as hen's teeth; someone who might have been a soldier there, but he couldn't think of any he knew who had been there who had learned to read or write the language or even acquired more than a minute understanding of a few spoken words and phrases. He smoothed a hand over the cover for a moment contemplatively, and then he sighed and went to put it back in the desk and closed the drawer.

Ellsworth made sure everything was exactly as he had found it, and then he turned off the lamp. He went back to the bed and lay down again after he added a little more wood to the fire and got a large glass of whisky. He folded one of his arms behind his head and looked up at the ceiling, thinking. He had thought that reading her diary would be something relaxing to help him go to sleep, but he was even worse off than before; hence, the whisky. He really wanted to know what was in the diary he had almost burned, but he knew he couldn't take it to someone who could decipher it for him, even without his reading it. Perhaps it was for the best no one but Eurydice knew what was in it.

Chapter Twenty Three

True to her word, the next morning Mrs. Ellsworth had one of the upstairs maids, whose real name was Ottilie, deliver Eurydice five copies of the *Wiener Zeitung*. Eurydice could not, however, bring herself to read it so soon after waking. She wanted to wait at least until after she had breakfast. That way, if she lost her appetite, her stomach would already be full, and she would hopefully have regained it in time for the next meal.

Agniezka, however, couldn't wait to see it. Eurydice had told her what happened the night before, and Agniezka had been overjoyed. She knew, of all the composers, Beethoven was the one Eurydice most admired, living or dead. She knew how to play the piano and violin parts for everything of his ever published that she could get her hands on.

The only other composer Agniezka could think of that she appreciated as much was Joseph Haydn, and Eurydice had been unhappy when he died because she would never hear any more music from him. The duke and duchess had met him, had even had him to dinner on a few occasions, the two times he had come to perform in London. The duchess was pregnant with Eurydice on his last visit, but he had gone and never returned by the time she was born. By the time she was old enough to go to Vienna, he was dead.

Agniezka had some difficulty reading the article once she found it, as her German was not quite so fluent as Eurydice's and the font was very decorative, but she was able to understand most of it. Eurydice tried not to pay any attention while her maid was reading, but she grew curious as Agniezka continued to read, keeping her features as inexpressive as possible. Eurydice continued to write her entries in her diaries and eat her breakfast, but her head kept turning to look at Agniezka occasionally as she sat curled up on the couch reading nearby. When she was done, she folded up the paper and set it aside without saying a word. Eurydice couldn't stand it.

"Well?" she said nervously. "What did it say?"

"Oh, I don't think you want to read that," said Agniezka mildly.

"Why? What did he say?" asked Eurydice worriedly.

"It's not good," said Agniezka softly with a neutral expression. Eurydice quickly grabbed up the paper to find the article and begin reading. "It's outstanding," said Agniezka with a proud smile.

Eurydice's lower jaw went slack, and she began to find it difficult to breathe as she read the article. A fluttery hand went to her throat, and her cheeks began to turn a bright shade of pink as her skin began to tingle. She couldn't believe what she was reading. She had been hoping it wouldn't be too disparaging, but she could have never imagined it would be so glowing.

And yet it wasn't insincere flattery. As she read, she could tell Herr Bakkeman was well-informed and discerning. She knew from meeting him that he was serious and straightforward, and she could well understand what Mrs. Ellsworth had meant when she said he wouldn't have written something if he had felt it would be a waste of his time. She didn't know how highly regarded his critical opinion was by those in Vienna, but she appreciated it. His praise was warm without being effulgent. The one negative criticism he mentioned (that of her failure to attempt to engage the audience or even acknowledge they were there) was constructive without being harsh. The few facts he provided— and there were very few—were accurate. He didn't mention her name, only her initials, but that wasn't an uncommon thing. Eurydice couldn't have asked for a better review.

"Oh, my," she sighed when she was finished.

"I don't think you'll be Mrs. Ellsworth's parlor monkey for very much longer," chortled Agniezka amusedly.

Eurydice was momentarily befuddled. She didn't know what else she should be doing. She would certainly have to offer Herr Bakkeman her sincerest thanks, either in person or by a short note. She didn't know if that was done, but she felt she had to say something. She and Agniezka both looked up in surprise when Mrs. Ellsworth burst into the room.

"Have you gotten the paper?" she asked excitedly.

"Yes, Ottilie brought me several copies," said Eurydice dazedly.

"Who?" quipped Mrs. Ellsworth in confusion.

"One of the Annas," clarified Eurydice.

"Oh. Did you read it?"

"Only just," said Eurydice evenly. "It was wonderful."

Mrs. Ellsworth smiled chidingly. "And you thought it would be terrible. Ignatz is a shrewd critic. I told you that you had nothing to worry about."

"You were right," said Eurydice mildly.

"Do you feel up to playing tonight?"

"Is Beethoven coming again?" asked Eurydice hopefully.

Mrs. Ellsworth chuckled. "No, dear. It wasn't easy to get him to come last night. If another appointment hadn't been canceled, he wouldn't have been here."

"I don't see why I can't play again," said Eurydice agreeably, "but would you like violin or piano?"

"Whichever suits you." She gave Eurydice an amused smile. "And I think it is time for you to begin calling me Cora. Leilah said last night the only reason you hadn't was that I hadn't said you could, so there you have it."

Eurydice blushed. "Of course, Cora."

"Ah," she said softly. "I was beginning to think you didn't like me," she chortled. "Well, I shall leave you to other things now. I just wanted to be sure you had seen the paper."

"Thank you," said Eurydice with a slight nod and a smile as she left.

Eurydice and Agniezka exchanged speculative glances with each other after she'd gone. She really was a nice woman. Eurydice couldn't think less of her because of how she ran her household. Most everyone did the same...except Eurydice's family. The only thing she could feel disappointment over was Cora's relationship with her son. Eurydice couldn't accept that she would still blame him for William's death and hold it against him after all this time. If she was angry with him for his current behavior, that...Eurydice could better understand and appreciate after what had recently happened.

Eurydice began to work on her symphony. For all the length and complexity of it, it was flowing out surprisingly fast, and she thought she might be done with the overlay very soon. It wouldn't be something that anyone but she—or her family—could appreciate because of how exotic it was, but it was pointless not to write it down. It would stay in her head until she put it on the page, and it wouldn't let her write anything else until she did. Even if another composition were to come to her, the symphony would drown it, she was sure.

That's why she needed a teacher. She couldn't believe other composers would have this problem. There had to be a way to control that. She couldn't believe other composers let their work be controlled by fancy, especially not if they were given a commission to create a specific type of work. A patron would not find the trade of a sonata for an opera acceptable. Her livelihood wasn't dependent on her ability to sell her work—it wouldn't matter if she never wrote for anyone but herself, but other composers—most composers—*did*. She didn't feel she could consider herself as anything more than an amateur until she learned how to control it.

Despite how insistent the symphony was to be put onto paper, Eurydice only worked on it for a few hours before she went down to the music room to play the piano after dinner. She would play the sonata she had written for her parents' anniversary, and she wanted to practice before supper. She had finally been able to play it for her father when they were in Venice. He had liked it as much as she had thought he would, but she still regretted he hadn't been able to hear it on his actual anniversary. She would have to play it for her parents when they were together one day, but she didn't know when that would be.

She thought about going to look for a maestro again. She still had all the names left that Leilah had given her, Beethoven among them. She hadn't realized his hearing was failing him. She had heard about it, of course, but she never suspected he was almost deaf. Before she knew who he was last night, she had thought she would be able to learn something from him. Discovering who he was, she believed it more than ever. But, despite how much she had enjoyed playing with him, she hesitated to think he would be willing to take her as a student. She would try more of the other names on the list first. Now that Herr Bakkeman had given her a favorable review, provided some of these other teachers had read it, perhaps she would find one agreeable to teaching her.

≪ ≫

Ellsworth was on his way down the stairs to the first floor from visiting his nieces and nephew in the nursery with the intention of going out for a few hours when there was a knock at the front door. He frowned as he pulled out his watch. It was mid-afternoon. That wasn't too late for callers, but his mother didn't usually have people come to visit her during the day. She went out to visit them, or they came to supper. He didn't think it would be anyone coming to see Eurydice. She didn't know anyone…yet.

As long as it wasn't Anneliese coming to see him again. He was fairly sure he made it clear she was never to come to his mother's house again, no matter what she heard. He suspected when she had done it on Monday, it wasn't because she had heard he was back in Vienna with a new wife; it was because she knew it would make his mother angry…and him, too. After a moment of thought, maybe it *was* because she had heard he had a wife. He had always known she was a woman prone to letting her emotions cloud her judgment, something that wasn't helpful in her business.

He was growing weary of Anneliese. She had been entertaining at first, but not anymore. Added to that was the fact she was no longer useful as a source of information. She was a snitch of opportunity. Her loyalty rested with whoever paid her the most…or was the best lay. Until recently, Ellsworth liked to think he had been both. Lately, though, even before he had gone to London, information she had given him had not been as reliable as it had once been. He suspected she had found a better provider of either one or the other form of currency. In any case, he was no longer interested in her physical favors, and her informational ones had about run dry. She might still prove to have a little more use, so he wasn't quite ready to completely sever his connection with her.

He was almost to the bottom of the stairs when Frau Geiger went to answer the door. He could hear Eurydice playing the piano, and he thought he would go see her, at least peek around the door, before he left. Passing that way would also let him hear who was at the door without whomever it was seeing him…just in case it *was* Anneliese again. He had already told Frau Geiger if the fraulein called again—at any time—he was not at home. He could hear Frau Geiger speaking, and when she was answered by a man, Ellsworth frowned.

"You have a musician who lives here," stated the man with moderate impatience.

"Yes," said Frau Geiger calmly.

"I want to speak with him," said the man brusquely.

Frau Geiger looked slightly to the side at Ellsworth. He quietly inclined his head toward the drawing room and began to walk in that direction. The music room was in the same direction, and he still intended to look in on his wife before he spoke to the man. After Ellsworth spoke with him, then he would decide if he needed to bother Eurydice.

"May I inform him who is calling?" Frau Geiger asked the man, not bothering to correct him on the gender.

"Antonio Salieri, Kapellmeister to His Imperial Majesty," he said formally.

She invited him into the entry hall and took his things. "If you will wait here for a moment, I will inform him you are here," she said evenly.

≪ ≫

Ellsworth walked down the hall to the music room and stood in the doorway watching Eurydice. She was playing a piece he didn't recognize. He didn't know if it was new, but he liked it, just like anything else she had composed. She had finished the violin sonata yesterday. He had heard it…distantly…from the nursery. He didn't leave the house as much as she thought. He was often either in the library or the nursery visiting the children. They were just places she didn't go often enough to realize he was there. She looked tired, and he knew she'd not had a nap in the library like he had.

He hadn't missed her performance last night, of either her sonata or the one she had played with Beethoven. He would never forget how vibrant and happy she had looked. It had truly been magical to hear them play, as if two halves of the same being had been joined together. He had also not missed reading the review Bakkeman had given her. She didn't know it, Ellsworth was sure, but Bakkeman was one of the most well-respected critics in Vienna. He hadn't mentioned her name or much of anything else identifying about her in the article to quickly get it past the censors, but he did say the performance had been given at a residence on Singer Strasse, which was probably the reason for their caller. Ellsworth was hopeful that after last night she would finally begin to have as much faith in her ability as everyone else did.

He stood with his shoulder leaned against the door frame, his arms folded across his chest as he watched her play, completely forgetting that he should be going to the drawing room to meet their caller. Frau Geiger touched his arm to get his attention, and he leaned his head down for her to speak in his ear quietly so as not to disturb Eurydice. His eyes widened when she provided him the name of their visitor.

"Bloody hell!" he blurted loudly, and Eurydice made a discordant sound on the piano when it made her jump in surprise and look to the door.

She gave him an irritated glare. "Are you *spying* on me?" she asked archly.

"Yes…no…sorry," said Ellsworth uncertainly. "I'll be back."

He turned to leave with Frau Geiger, and Eurydice watched him go with a frown. She was left wondering why people had to watch her furtively. First there was Freddie on the ship, and now Ellsworth here. It wasn't as if she minded people listening to her play, unless she was composing or playing a new piece, and then the only person she didn't mind being there was Agniezka. Of course, she was sure the reason Ellsworth slinked was partially from habit, partially from him knowing she didn't want him near her. And, what— exactly—did he mean when he said he would be back?

≪ ≫

Ellsworth straightened his waistcoat and adjusted the sleeves on his coat before he went into the drawing room. He combed his fingers through his hair and hoped it didn't look like he'd just recently been rolling around on the nursery floor with his nieces and nephew. He looked in the mirror over the fireplace and sighed with relief when he saw that it was fine. Frau Geiger opened the door for the Kapellmeister to come in not long after. He walked toward Ellsworth, and Ellsworth held out his hand to shake Salieri's.

"Herr Kapellmeister," said Ellsworth respectfully.

Salieri took his hand and turned it this way and that without preamble, examining his fingers.

"Yes, long, graceful fingers," said Salieri, almost to himself, "and strong."

"I am Gareth Ellsworth," he said with a slight frown as Salieri continued to examine his hand.

"English, hmm?" he asked rhetorically. Ellsworth didn't bother to correct him that he was Scottish. He was too confounded by Salieri's interest in his hands. "Those are unusual calluses, but not from fingering," said the Kapellmeister. "You are left-handed?" he asked as he dropped that hand and picked up the other, only to see the other hand had the same kind of calluses but none that would have been acquired from fingering the strings on a violin.

"No, Herr Kapellmeister," said Ellsworth evenly. "I am not the musician."

"Well, where is the musician?" asked Salieri irritatedly as he dropped Ellsworth's hand. "It has taken me four days to find this house!"

Ellsworth's eyebrows shot up in surprise. "Four days?"

"Yes, since Sunday I've been hearing music, and every time, just when I thought I was going to find its source, it would stop. Now I find the house, and you tell me you aren't the musician when that is who I came to see. Where is he?" asked Salieri impatiently.

"My apologies," said Ellsworth, trying to control the amused twitching of his lips at the Kapellmeister's almost fretful expression. "I'll be right back."

"Humph!" said Salieri with no small amount of annoyance.

Ellsworth grinned and almost started laughing after he left to go down the hall to the music room. Eurydice was sitting at the piano playing once again when he went in, but she had her eyes on the door and wasn't surprised when she saw him. She removed her fingers from the keys and raised an enquiring eyebrow.

"There's someone here to see you," he said evenly.

"Who is it?" she asked flatly. She couldn't imagine why anyone would come to see her; she didn't know anyone.

"I think you should come see for yourself," said Ellsworth secretively.

"Is it Beethoven? Did he come back?" she asked excitedly, rising from the bench to walk toward him.

Ellsworth smiled amusedly. "No, it's not Beethoven, but I don't think you'll be disappointed. There's no need to look at me like that."

"Like what?" asked Eurydice evenly as she walked down the hall with him.

"Like I just told you there will be no Christmas this year," said Ellsworth drolly.

"I'm not looking at you like that," said Eurydice mildly, trying to school her features into something more neutral.

Ellsworth chuckled. "Yes, you are," he said softly in her ear as they walked through the door to the drawing room.

As it had always been since she arrived in Vienna, she didn't recognize the older gentleman who was standing impatiently waiting for them. He turned to look when they entered the room, and the scowl he wore only deepened further.

"Herr Kapellmeister, may I present my wife, Lady Eurydice Ellsworth?" said Ellsworth politely, and then he turned slightly to look at her, trying to keep his features as impassive as possible. "Eurydice, this is Herr Antonio Salieri, Kapellmeister to His Imperial Majesty."

"Oh!" she squeaked breathlessly, and Ellsworth almost burst out laughing when he saw the expression on her face, even as he began to grow concerned he might have to catch her if she fainted.

Salieri politely took her hand to place a kiss on it, but he seemed most unhappy.

"Herr Ellsworth, while I am pleased to meet such a beautiful woman as your wife, I believe you were going to bring me the musician. If you aren't going to do that, then I shall take my leave and try another day when I might be confronted with less nonsense," he said coldly.

Eurydice's mouth worked silently as she tried to speak and couldn't. Ellsworth put a steadying hand to the small of her back and took her arm.

"Herr Kapellmeister," said Ellsworth mildly, "my wife *is* the musician."

"No!" gasped Salieri in disbelief.

Ellsworth lifted her limp left hand and held it out to Salieri to examine, which he did. He noted the slender gracefulness of her digits, the way her nails were feminine but short, and when he looked at the pads of her fingers, there were the unmistakable calluses of a practiced violinist. When he saw them, his whole countenance changed to one of utter happiness. He raised her hand to his lips, and then he placed it in both of his to give it a squeeze.

"My dear, I am honored to finally make your acquaintance," he said warmly.

"B-bu-but…," stammered Eurydice in astonishment and confusion. How could he even know who she was?

"Herr Kapellmeister has been looking for you since Sunday," supplied Ellsworth helpfully. He rubbed his hand at the small of her back in an effort to get her to calm down. He still didn't think she was breathing yet. Her eyes were round, and her cheeks were flushed, and he could feel her shaking.

"You compose as well?" asked Salieri interestedly. Eurydice could only nod dumbly. "Might I see some of your work?" He chuckled slightly with amusement. "I believe I've heard some of it, of course, but I should like to see."

"O-of course," stammered Eurydice. "If you'll just give me a moment…," she said dazedly.

Ellsworth excused himself for a moment and went with Eurydice into the hall, guiding her by the hand on her arm and at her back. He didn't think she would have been able to walk otherwise. He turned her to face him and smoothed a soothing hand down her cheek.

"Calm down," he said encouragingly. "Deep breath."

Eurydice nodded weakly and tried to do as he asked. He started to kiss her, and Eurydice jerked her head away. Ellsworth sighed resignedly and turned her in the direction of the stairs and gave her a gentle swat to her bottom.

"Don't be long," he called softly as he watched her start up the stairs slowly. "We'll be in the music room."

Eurydice tried to quicken her step, but she was still dazed by Salieri's arrival. She felt as if she were walking in a fog as she went to her sitting room. Agniezka wasn't there, but Eurydice could tell she had only stepped out for a moment; her knitting rested in the chair by the fire. Eurydice thought about waiting for her to return to tell her who was in the drawing room, but she remembered Ellsworth's request not to take too long. She started to go through her compositions to choose her best ones, but she felt that was taking too long as well; she simply took her entire portfolio. As an afterthought, she picked up *La Ragazza Dolce* in its case and took that with her as well. She didn't know if Salieri would want to hear her play, but it would be best to be prepared. She nearly collided with Agniezka as she was leaving the sitting room.

"Are you going to interview with a teacher?" asked Agniezka when she saw the things Eurydice was carrying. "You're not dressed to leave the house."

"He's here!" said Eurydice quickly. "Salieri is here! I've got to go."

Agniezka chuckled to see her infused with so much excitement and moved out of her way. "Good luck," she said with a grin.

Eurydice went down the stairs, taking several deep breaths as she went in an attempt to compose herself. She couldn't believe she was meeting a second great master in as many days, and she wasn't sure what Salieri's coming to see her meant. She could only assume he had read Herr Bakkeman's review, and since he only lived a few houses away, he thought he might come see if she would be a worthy student. But, Ellsworth had said Salieri had been looking for her since Sunday; Bakkeman's review only came out that morning. *Why* had he been looking for her?

She carried her things into the music room and found Ellsworth and Salieri talking together.

"Ah, that's why your name sounds familiar," Salieri was saying to him, and Eurydice looked from one to the other of them bemusedly.

Ellsworth was glad to see she seemed to have calmed down quite a bit. Her cheeks were still rosy, and her eyes were bright, but she didn't have the paleness of threatened fainting beneath it. She was still nervous and excited, but she wasn't prone to letting herself be carried away for long. Underneath her placid expression, he could only imagine she was bubbling with emotions.

Salieri looked at her kindly, and Eurydice took her portfolio to the table near the windows to give him light to see them. Ellsworth put a calming hand on her shoulder as the Kapellmeister looked at her work, and despite her feeling an urge to push it off, it had the effect he was trying to provoke. Salieri would occasionally make thoughtful sounds as he examined one piece after another, sometimes even humming a few bars, but he didn't say anything at first.

"You play both violin and piano?" he finally asked as he continued to look through the sheets.

"Yes, Herr Kapellmeister," said Eurydice evenly. "I also play the flute, but I can't say I'm anything more than passable with it. I'm familiar with the harp and most other orchestral instruments, but I don't play them on a regular basis."

"When did you begin playing the violin?"

"My *babushka* first put a violin in my hands when I was one, but I didn't actually begin playing it until I was two," said Eurydice with a slight smile. "At least, that's what I was told." She shrugged. "I can't remember a time when I didn't play the violin. I began to learn the piano when I was three. I wrote my first composition when I was five."

"You say your *babushka*? Your grandmother? She was Russian?"

"Yes, Herr Kapellmeister, my grandmother was from Tver, a lady-in-waiting to Tsarina Catherine prior to her marriage to my grandfather."

He nodded. "And what was the piece?"

"A sonata for violin and piano," she said calmly as she moved beside him to the portfolio. She leafed through the sheets to pull out one of the very bottom compositions. "This one," she said as she gave it to him.

As Salieri looked at it, he hummed and nodded his head, and he looked at her appraisingly. "You actually *wrote* it, transcribing it?"

"Yes, Herr Kapellmeister," said Eurydice evenly.

"When did you first compose anything? Something that someone else had to write down for you?"

"A bagatelle for piano when I was four." She found it in the portfolio and gave it to him.

He looked at it, then her, and then he looked at the portfolio. "These are arranged by when you composed them, with the earliest at the bottom?"

"Yes, Herr Kapellmeister, they should be."

"And with whom have you studied?" he asked thoughtfully.

"My *babushka* was my only teacher. She died five years ago, when I was fifteen," said Eurydice quietly. "I've not had any other teachers. That's why I came to Vienna."

"You've had *no* formal training?" asked Salieri with astonishment, his eyebrows rising.

"No, Herr Kapellmeister."

"Then both you and your *babushka* are remarkable women, but you especially," said Salieri wonderingly.

Eurydice colored at the compliment. "Thank you, Herr Kapellmeister," she said quietly. "So, would you be willing to become my teacher?" she asked hesitantly after a moment.

Salieri's eyebrows shot up, and he gave a brief shake of his head. "No, my dear girl, I cannot be your teacher," he said definitely.

Eurydice was crestfallen. "Oh," she said softly. "I see." It had been too much to expect that a man of his reputation would want her as a student.

"My dear," said Salieri gently when he saw her disappointment, "I cannot be your teacher because there is nothing I *could* teach you."

Eurydice's eyes widened in surprise. "Oh, but there are things I need to learn," she said huskily as she felt her throat tightening. "I cannot make the music stop. It is always in my head, and I can't write a concerto or a sonata unless that is what I'm hearing," she said brokenly. "I can't control it. I need you to teach me how to make it *stop!*"

Salieri smiled in wonder and took one of her hands to give it a gentle, soothing pat. "If it is as you say, then you have been blessed by God. Do not worry if you can only write what you hear because what you can hear—"he put a hand on top of the score sheets—"is divine. There are men who spend their lifetimes praying to make it *start.*"

Ellsworth put his hands on her shoulders and gave them a reassuring squeeze. He could feel her trembling. He had never known how long she had been playing or how she composed, and he realized that her music—like her dreams—was one more thing that possessed her. It was as if she were a cipher, with no meaning of her own until they gave it to her, and one or the other was always there, controlling her. It was one more thing to explain why she was always so self-contained; her emotions were the one thing *she* could control. It also explained why she couldn't believe she was as gifted as she was: it had always been there. She didn't feel as if she had worked hard enough to earn being good.

Salieri leafed through the compositions and began to pull out a few.

"There will be a concerto for violin, a symphony, and a—hmm…yes, this one—another concerto…for piano," he mused as he put them in a pile.

Eurydice frowned. "I don't understand," she said confusedly, scratching her forehead.

Salieri looked at her and smiled happily. "My dear, I came to find you because I want you to perform for the Court."

Eurydice's eyes widened in panic. "Oh, I couldn't," she said breathlessly. "I've never performed anywhere but a drawing room. I'm not ready."

"Enough of that," said Salieri sternly. "We've just discussed that, and at my age, I do not have the time to constantly repeat myself. You will perform an *akademie* for the Court the first Monday after the start of the Season, which, I believe, will be the thirteenth." He gathered up the sheets in his hands. "I will return these to you as soon as I've had them to the copyists. I cannot say for certain where you will perform, whether it will be at the Burgtheater, Redoutensaal, Kartnertortheater, or possibly even Schoenbrunn, but I will let you know as soon as it's arranged. It will be tricky, but I *will* get it arranged," he said determinedly.

"But I become very nervous in front of strangers," said Eurydice anxiously.

Salieri laughed. "Who doesn't?" he chortled. He gave her a considering look. "Perhaps what you need, then, is an opportunity or two more to play for the public before that time…in more intimate venues." He nodded decidedly. "Yes, perhaps that will be just the thing. Let me talk to a few people, and I will call on you tomorrow, if that is agreeable?"

"That will be fine," said Eurydice with a slight nod.

Salieri took her hand and kissed it. "Trust in God, my dear."

Ellsworth gave her shoulders a comforting squeeze before he removed his hands to walk with Salieri to the door. Eurydice watched them go with a slight frown. She was slowly beginning to realize she was the only one who thought she needed to learn anything further. Considering who had just refused to be her teacher because he didn't think he *could* teach her, perhaps she needed to reassess her opinion. After so long believing otherwise, it wasn't easy. She went to the bench at the piano and sat down numbly.

Ellsworth came back to the music room and sat down beside her on the bench. She didn't look at him as she moved a little further away. She was tempted to get up and leave, but she was at least able to bear his presence now. Anything else was unlikely, like his trying to kiss her before she went upstairs, but at least the sight of him didn't turn her stomach anymore.

"Do you understand now what I've been trying to tell you?" he asked quietly after several minutes.

She turned her head to look at him. She had misunderstood what he meant…every time he had tried to tell her, and it hadn't been because he had been unclear, either. She had simply not been listening properly. She had let what she thought of her music color what he had been telling her—what everyone had been telling her—with a meaning that wasn't there.

"Yes," she said softly. "I'm sorry."

She turned to look back at the keys in front of her and put her fingers onto them. She sat at the bass end of the keyboard, and she vaguely thought how peculiar it was to be sitting there. When she sat at the piano with Dorian, he always sat there. She looked out the window as the sun began to make its way behind the nearby buildings. The sky was streaked with an unusual assortment of colors, mostly green and orange, and she couldn't decide if it was because of the bad air in the city or not. She hadn't noticed the air was particularly bad. She absently began to tap the keys with her fingers as she thought about how strange her life had become since coming to Vienna. She had gone from being excited to be there to wishing she could go home. Now she wasn't sure.

Ellsworth surprised her when he began to play the treble part of a sonata for four hands written by Beethoven, and she realized when he did it that the notes she had unconsciously been playing in front of her were those of the bass. It was a piece she played often with her brother. She started to lift her fingers away but instead began to pay attention to what she was doing and played with him. She was astonished as she watched him play, and despite herself she began to smile slightly as they raced through it. It was a very fun piece. When they were done, she looked at him thoughtfully.

"You play the piano," she stated.

Ellsworth looked at her somberly. "You started it," he said quietly.

"You've had lessons," she said in realization.

Ellsworth looked back at the keyboard and softly brushed his fingers on the keys with a deep sigh. "My mother wanted a concert pianist, so...when my father died, she brought me to Vienna to study," he said pensively.

"What happened?" she asked softly. She thought she knew, but she wanted to hear what he said.

"I studied for a time, and then my brother died. I didn't feel like playing anymore," he said dully.

They sat silently for a while, looking at the keyboard. Eurydice could understand why he hadn't wanted to play. What had happened when William died was tragic, not just losing his brother but everything that had gone with it. When her *babushka* had died, it made Eurydice all the more determined to play; it was the only thing she could think to do, but she could have just as easily gone the other way. She could only imagine what his life would be like—what he would be like—now, if it hadn't happened. She now understood why her mother had said he was musical. He could have been a great pianist.

"I want you to come back to our bed," he said softly after several minutes.

Eurydice looked at him. "No," she said flatly.

"Eurydice, Agniezka's bed is too small for both of you. Even one side of our bed is bigger than hers." Eurydice narrowed her eyes at him. "I won't touch you, I promise," he said stoically. "You can stay on your side, and I'll stay on mine." He gave her a self-deprecating smile. "It's not as if we haven't done that before."

Eurydice started to refuse again, but she knew he was right. Agniezka's bed was fine for one person or for two people who were very close—which they were, but it was bothering Agniezka's back for Eurydice to be sleeping with her in that narrow bed. Eurydice didn't want to make things more difficult for her. Her own bed was large, and comfortable, and there was no reason she and Ellsworth couldn't share it without actually *sharing* it. They might be speaking to each other again, but she wouldn't let him touch her as long as he had a mistress. She wouldn't know how long that would be…unless he told her, and he never told her anything unless she asked. That would be one thing she would not ask him. Aside from not really wanting to know the answer, she had promised him she wouldn't ask him about anyone he saw. Even were he to discard his mistress and not pick up another, she still didn't know if she would want to, not for a while. After thinking about it for a few more minutes, she sighed resignedly.

"All right," she said evenly, "but you are to keep your hands to yourself."

"Of course," said Ellsworth with a slight incline of his head.

Chapter Twenty Four

Salieri did return the following afternoon to see her. He brought a young man with him who he introduced as Franz Schubert. Eurydice was surprised by his appearance. He was younger than she, or, if not, he *looked* younger. He stood not much taller, with dark, curly hair and brown eyes. He had delicate, almost feminine features, with a snubbed nose, full lips, and a small, dimpled chin. He wore spectacles, and his expression was sensitive and friendly. After his introduction, Salieri did not, at first, tell her why the young man was there.

Salieri informed her that he had spoken with the manager of the Theater an der Wien, who had agreed to let her at least give an afternoon performance a week from the following Monday. If it was well-received, they would be willing to let her give a similar performance every Monday after that until she performed at the Burgtheater (which Salieri clarified for her). If the first performance was a failure (which he didn't think it would be) then she wouldn't do any further performances at the Theater an der Wien…and Salieri had told the manager that he would make up the difference in lost profits for that one failed outing. Regardless, she would still perform at the Burgtheater.

Eurydice's eyes widened in dismay, and she told him she couldn't let him bear the cost, that she would pay the expense of lost profits if necessary. She also told him she didn't want any part of the proceeds from the performance— should there be any. Instead, she asked that the money be given to a worthy orphan asylum or one for the deaf, mute, and blind. She had no need for the money, and considering her class, it made her uncomfortable to even think about being paid for it.

Once Salieri told her where she would be performing, he then explained why he had brought Herr Schubert. The orchestra would play with her at the Burgtheater, but he thought sonatas and other shorter pieces would be better for the Theater an der Wien, and rehearsing an orchestra enough to sound suitable took time…more time than she would have before her first performance there.

Schubert was an excellent sight reader and was to be the player of the second part for those pieces that required it. Salieri had every confidence Schubert would be up to the task. He had Eurydice bring him her portfolio again, and the two men looked through it to select likely compositions: one for violin, one for piano, and two for both instruments together.

Eurydice tried to get Salieri to tell her how many people the Theater an der Wien would hold, but he wouldn't. That concerned her. He said it was smaller than the Burgtheater and that it was just outside the city in Mariahilf. Because she was giving an afternoon performance, it was doubtful the theater would be full because it typically wasn't for a daytime engagement. It had lovely acoustics, even if it tended to be a bit drafty. It was very popular with both the nobility and the commoners. But he wouldn't tell her how many people she might expect to see in front of her when she walked onto the stage. She was anxious to know because he had put so much effort into arranging this for her, and she didn't want to disappoint him. He had so much confidence in her ability she only hoped it wasn't misplaced.

Ellsworth was there for much of the conversation, but he left shortly after she began to rehearse with Herr Schubert. They had slept in the same bed the night before. True to his word, he had not touched her. The bed had been comfortable, but she had been cold, and he had woken her with a bad dream. She had started to move over and comfort him, but she didn't. Instead, she lay there listening to him mutter to himself for quite some time before she was finally able to go back to sleep. It was in English rather than Gaelic, and while most of it was unintelligible, she understood enough to know it was caused by his job. While she listened, she had been left wondering why anyone would willingly want to do a job that gave them nightmares.

When she woke up that morning, he was gone, but he came into the music room shortly after Salieri had arrived, and he only left after everything had been arranged for her performances. She supposed, as her husband, he had a right to know what she was doing, but she thought it was unfair he should know her business, and yet she wasn't entitled to the same courtesy from him. Of the two of them, she was the least likely to do something she shouldn't. That was patently obvious from the current state of their marriage.

Her practice with Schubert went well, better than she had thought it would, considering he had never played the piece before and that they had never played together before. She could see why Salieri had thought he would be able to learn the pieces quickly enough for them to perform in less than two weeks. Herr Schubert was a marvelous pianist, and as they practiced together, she discovered he was also a composer. She expressed an interest in seeing some of his compositions, and he said he would bring a few the following day when he came to practice.

It was strange to Eurydice to hear someone else play something she had written, and to hear both parts of the sonatas played together was even more bizarre. She had never played her own music with Dorian. It had been a bit disorienting to hear the two parts together at first, but she soon found it thrilling. She still wasn't sure she was ready to perform in public, but at least the thought of it wasn't leaving her terrified.

At least, that was what she had convinced herself into believing until the appointed Monday arrived. When the day came for the first performance, she was so nervous she couldn't eat breakfast...or dinner. She had tried to eat her breakfast, but it only stuck in her throat before coming back up. She wasn't pacing or shaking. As Agniezka styled her hair before she left for the theater, Eurydice sat at the dressing table looking for all appearances perfectly composed. But Agniezka knew she was anxious, almost to the point she didn't want to play at all. Agniezka would have given her something to drink to calm her nerves, except Eurydice didn't have a high tolerance for alcohol. She wouldn't be able to play if she was drunk.

Agniezka put Eurydice into a simple ball gown in soft gold silk trimmed with black grosgrain ribbon and white lace threaded through with gold foil. The color complimented her complexion, and the style of it would not be too uncomfortable to play in. Agniezka had thought for a time about putting her into a morning dress and pelisse, but the amount of fabric might be too constricting. She would see how Eurydice felt about playing in the gown this time, and if it proved to not be to her liking, they could change things for the next time. She kept her jewelry simple, with only pearls in her ears and a cross on a chain around her neck. Anything larger would be in the way.

When it was time to leave, Eurydice went with Ellsworth, Cora, and Agniezka to the coach. She wouldn't go without her maid. Agniezka was a calming influence, simply by being there, and Eurydice's stomach was twisted into such a tight knot as it was, to not have Agniezka would be unthinkable. The only one who had been able to keep Eurydice from calling a halt to the entire thing had been her maid, just by gently prodding her along.

Salieri and Schubert would meet them at the theater. Schubert had had the chance to play the piano there, and he assured her it was of an excellent quality, well-tuned with a similar sound to the Ellsworths'. She would have liked to practice on it herself prior to the performance, but she trusted Schubert's judgment. Both instruments were Broadwoods, just like the piano she had composed on at home. She was lucky for that. Instruments that used different actions could change the music and make it completely unlike what she had intended, and not necessarily for the better.

Leilah had assured Eurydice she would be there. Eurydice had gone to see her on Friday, the day after Salieri had come to tell her where she would be performing. She had gone to see her two more times after that, and Eurydice was glad the older woman would be coming. Eurydice had grown very fond of Leilah. She had gone from simply being a friend of her mother's to being one of Eurydice's own friends. If Eurydice still had an aunt, she imagined the woman would be a lot like Leilah. She told Eurydice she had a box at the theater, and that was where Ellsworth, Cora, and Agniezka would sit. Leilah was very excited, and it only made Eurydice more nervous about performing well.

Cora had told all her friends Eurydice would be performing, and they all said they would be there, too. They had all read Herr Bakkeman's review, and they were looking forward to hearing her somewhere other than the drawing room. As she calculated how many people were going to be there just from being friends and acquaintances of Cora and Leilah, it was making Eurydice nervous. The only consolation she had was that she did at least know them.

What would have pleased her more would have been if her family could be there to see her. She had written letters to everyone letting them know she would be giving her first public performance. She didn't think they would get the letters until well after she had already done so, but she still wanted them to know. She also sent them copies of the review Herr Bakkeman had given her. Her copy was in a small wooden chest where she kept her mementoes and souvenirs. She was sure her family would be proud.

Ellsworth sat beside her as they left the city for Mariahilf. He held her hand in his, resting on top of his thigh, but Eurydice was too distracted to notice. He had recognized, just as Agniezka did, that she was extremely nervous. He didn't think holding her hand would really help to calm her, but anything was worth a chance. She didn't even notice she was squeezing it so tightly it was cutting off the circulation to his fingers. If she had noticed he was holding her hand, she probably would have removed it. She wasn't comfortable with him touching her these days...at all.

They continued to share the same bed. There had even been a few times when he had awakened to find her snuggled against him. He didn't know which one of them had moved on the bed to cause it or why, but since he was always gone before she was awake he didn't think she even realized it. He wasn't going to make her aware of it, either, because she would make an extra effort to keep it from happening. That morning had been one of the times she was pressed close against him, and he had lain there for several minutes just enjoying her beside him, not wanting to move.

She still showed no interest in forgiving him or listening to anything he had to say about Anneliese. He had tried to broach the subject a few times, and she had simply walked away or looked at him stonily. They were polite to each other, sometimes even friendly, but she wasn't willing to resume their intimacy. Their marriage had been reduced to exactly what it started as: an arrangement. It wasn't what he wanted, and he was growing impatient to have her listen to what he had to say.

He didn't know if she'd had the dream from Podpetsch again. He had not looked at her diary recently to find out, but he was taking a risk every time he opened it. He didn't know how she would react if she discovered he had been reading it, but it wouldn't be good. Considering how things already were between them, he could only imagine that she might leave him. Perhaps not, because he knew she was aware of what society expected of her. Her husband having a mistress wouldn't be a good enough reason. But it would ruin any chance he had of her forgiving him, whether he had actually done anything that required forgiveness or not.

They arrived at the theater and took one of the side entrances that would lead them to the back of the stage. Eurydice looked up at the building as they stepped out of the coach. She couldn't tell how big it was. There was one square block of construction that she thought might be the theater, with several floors, but there were also smaller buildings attached to it. She couldn't tell if they were part of the theater or separate businesses. Even if they weren't, the portion she was sure was part of the theater was large enough. It was on a corner, with a small river across the street. She couldn't see the front of the theater; otherwise, that might have given her a better estimation of how large it was. The streets along the side and in front of the building were busy with vehicles and foot traffic, and Eurydice wondered if the wings attached to the theater were other businesses to account for all of it.

The four of them walked down a hall that led them back stage. Salieri and Schubert were there waiting for Eurydice. She gave them both a weak smile, but she could feel her stomach beginning to churn as the sound of the audience reached her. It seemed disconcertingly loud. She couldn't see the curtain at the front of the stage, and the stage itself seemed large and cavernous, even though it was filled with set pieces and backgrounds for what she assumed was an opera to be performed that night. Eurydice was beginning to believe Salieri had intentionally misled her about the size of the theater, and she was also beginning to believe she was going to be sick and fail miserably.

She tightly held the handle of the case containing her Stradivarius in one hand, and the other was wound tightly through Ellsworth's elbow as they followed Salieri down a partially open hall that went along the side of the stage, the openings being places where set pieces could be added or removed, or for performers to enter or exit. They soon reached a narrow opening at the front edge of the stage that would allow her to walk onto it in front of the curtain. The audience was even louder, and Eurydice could only imagine how many people were there—far more than she had ever played for in her entire life combined, she was beginning to think. As she heard the noise, she began to wonder what she possibly could have been thinking to believe she would be capable of performing in front of that many people.

"The piano is directly in the center of the stage with the bench facing this way," Salieri was saying, either oblivious to her anxiety or choosing to ignore it. They were standing right stage. "The main curtain is up, but a background is dropped slightly behind the front of the stage to give room for the piano and yourself without showing the pieces for tonight's performance. You'll not have much room, so try not to move about too much. We wouldn't want you tumbling into the orchestra pit."

"That will not be a problem," said Eurydice weakly, and she wondered if she looked as green as she felt.

She wasn't even sure she would be able to walk onto the stage in the first instance, let alone need to worry about falling off of it. Agniezka took the violin case from her hand and opened it for Eurydice to make sure the violin was tuned and to tighten and rosin her bow. Eurydice started to lift it out, and then she put the empty hand to her stomach and swallowed nervously as she felt her skin become clammy.

"Oh, I don't think I can do this," she said breathlessly.

"Nonsense," said Salieri dismissively, giving her an amused smile. "It's all been arranged, you have rehearsed, and all those people are here to listen to you play."

"I know. That's the problem," said Eurydice, and she fanned a hand in front of her face as she fought a wave of nausea.

Salieri chuckled. "My dear, you will be perfect. I will stand right here to watch the entire time." Eurydice nodded, and she took a deep breath in through her nose and let it out through her mouth in an effort to calm herself. It wasn't helping. "Franz will be there with you for more than half of it, so it's not as if you'll be all alone."

Schubert gave her an encouraging smile and a wink. "For me, it always helps if I imagine the audience naked."

Eurydice's eyes widened in shock. "Oh, that won't help me at all." She shook her head and rubbed a hand across her brow. "Oh, why did you have to say that? Now I'll not be able to get that image out of my head," she moaned.

Everyone laughed, but they could see she was beginning to panic. Ellsworth gently turned her to face him and smoothed a hand down her cheek.

"Calm down, Dicy," he soothed. "All those people are here for *you* because they can't do it themselves." She nodded hesitantly, and he gave her a soft kiss on her forehead before moving his lips to her ear to whisper. "Play for me…please?"

Eurydice frowned slightly and released a deep sigh. She moved away from him to give him a troubled look. He had been very supportive and encouraging during the days leading up to this. He was always there for at least an hour or two every day while she practiced with Franz, and he hadn't offered his opinion unless she asked, which she greatly appreciated. When he did give his opinion, he was never critical, and what he had to say was usually very helpful. He was still keeping his distance from her in their bed, and she hadn't noticed any further incidents of him smelling of another woman's perfume despite his frequently going out at night—sometimes before she was in bed, sometimes after when he thought she was asleep. Even though he wasn't doing it purposely, he was beginning to make her feel guilty for keeping her distance from him. She could almost forget he had a mistress…almost.

"I-I'll try," she said quietly.

He grinned happily and ran a finger along her jaw. "Leilah's box is the sixth one down to your left on the second tier. If you just look for us that should make it at least *seem* like you're paying attention to the audience."

"All right," she said evenly, and she finally removed her violin from the case to make sure it was still properly tuned.

"Speaking of, we should go there now," said Cora. She gave Eurydice a kiss on the cheek and smiled as she squeezed her shoulder encouragingly. "*Hals und Beinbruch.*"

Agniezka did the same, and then Ellsworth gave her a gentle hug and lingering kiss on the cheek.

"You can do this," he said quietly in encouragement.

Eurydice watched as they made their way across the darkness of the stage behind the background to a doorway on the other side to reach the box. She could look out in front of the background and see the stage and the orchestra pit. She could only see a small portion of the audience from her location, but that was enough. She counted five levels of boxes, not counting the floor seats, and the seats she could see were all full. She could feel her palms beginning to sweat, and she had to resist the urge to wipe them on her dress.

Salieri looked at his watch, and then he looked at the two young people in front of him. "It's time," he said quietly, giving them a smile.

Franz walked onto the stage, and Eurydice listened as the crowd first grew silent, followed by polite, quiet applause as he went to take his seat on the bench at the piano. Then she took a deep preparatory breath and walked onto the stage herself. The theater wasn't as bright as she had expected it to be, which helped...somewhat. She had an uncertain smile which froze in place as she looked at the audience. The theater wasn't quite full, but even still there were *hundreds* of people. Hundreds of *strange* people, all there looking at her, to listen to her, and she began to break out in a cold sweat.

She immediately began to look for Leilah's box, grasping for something familiar in the sea of strange faces. She could barely hear the applause of the audience above the ringing in her ears, and she tried to take deep breaths in and out through her nose before she fainted. She sighed with some relief when she found the box and saw Ellsworth, Agniezka, and Leilah sitting at the front of it, all smiling encouragingly. Franz sat at the piano, slightly turned as he looked at her and smiled also, and she stopped when she reached the side of it.

She tried to forget the rest of the people and to think of only the people she knew. She settled her violin beneath her chin, and she and Franz nodded to each other when they were ready. She began the piece with high, drawn-out notes that quickly dipped lower to an arpeggio where Franz joined at exactly the right moment. It was one of her more dramatic, intense compositions, and it required a lot of her concentration. Eurydice had wondered if it were the right piece to begin, but Salieri had insisted that it was. It was one of her older compositions, which she had written shortly after her *babushka*'s death. It was composed of four movements, alternatingly fast and slow. There was no scherzo, but there was a rondo, with a finale andante. She had written it at a time when she had not been able to find anything playful or humorous. She had titled it "*Le Loup et la Lune.*"

When the sonata ended, the audience erupted in loud applause, and Eurydice turned to look at them in surprise. It wasn't that she had entirely forgotten they were there, but she hadn't expected them to be so enthusiastic. She was unknown, the music was unknown, and she hadn't felt it was one of her better pieces. Obviously, she had been wrong. She smiled slightly and gave the audience a partial curtsy.

Franz rose from the piano and exited the stage. Eurydice waited for the audience to quiet, and she once again settled her violin into place. She turned herself so that she was more directly facing them, but she kept her attention on the box where her family and friends sat. This piece was no less passionate than the first, but there was a playfulness about it, with a tempo that was for the most part allegro with a scherzo and finale presto. It was shorter in length than the first sonata had been by about half, but Eurydice knew from having written it that it had taken nearly as many score sheets to transcribe it. She called it the "Chase" Sonata, and she was indeed a bit out of breath when she reached the end. Again, the audience applauded loudly, if not more loudly than after the first, and Eurydice smiled and curtsied again, her cheeks flushed.

She was surprised when the crowd emitted sounds of disappointment as she momentarily walked to the side of the stage, but she returned after giving her violin to Schubert to hold for her while she performed the solo piano sonata. He had just a brief moment to give her shoulder a squeeze and to tell her she was doing wonderfully, as did Salieri. When the audience saw her return, they cheered appreciatively, and Eurydice gave them a sheepish smile and a brief wave as she went to take her seat on the bench.

This piece was one she had written for her *babushka* as a present for her birthday. The first movement was composed with the instruction *adagio con amore*, and Eurydice remembered the first time she had played it. It had, in fact, been her *Babushka* Alexa's last birthday; she died almost three months later. But Eurydice hadn't known that when she wrote the song. She had known how her grandmother would die, but she hadn't known when. The song was written full of love and joy—no sadness, and Eurydice preferred to remember her *babushka* that way.

When she finished, she was overhwelmed by the reaction of the audience. There were whistles and shouts of *brava*, and it seemed the more they heard, the more they liked. She looked at them in round-eyed astonishment and put her hands to her cheeks as she rose from the bench. She looked to Leilah's box, and they were all cheering as loudly and appreciatively as everyone else. Eurydice curtsied with a grateful smile, and then she looked to the side of the stage as Franz returned for the final sonata carrying her violin. Eurydice took it from him as he gave her a grin, and then he took his seat at the piano.

The final sonata was, for the most part, as lively as the solo violin composition, but with a different theme. This one was almost celebratory, and indeed, she had written it last year after Napoleon had been exiled to Elba. As she thought about it while she played, she realized the celebration had been a bit premature. Now, hopefully, it wasn't. Napoleon was being sent to Saint Helena in the middle of the Atlantic and may have already arrived. She was certain her government had finally learned he needed to be watched more carefully, and she expected he wouldn't be able to escape so easily next time.

The crowd rose to its feet, cheering loudly at the end of the sonata. Eurydice put a hand to her chest emotionally and smiled gratefully as she gave them a deep curtsy. She turned to take Franz's hand in hers, and she gestured to him to make the crowd cheer even louder. Both of them bowed and curtsied, and Eurydice began to tell them thank you in every language she could think of, starting with German and working her way to the more obscure…like Yoruba. She couldn't believe their response, and she tried not to start crying. She looked to right of stage and saw a man she didn't know standing with Salieri. She looked to Leilah's box and saw everyone leaving it to go back stage. Eurydice and Franz curtsied and bowed one more time, and then they exited.

Salieri introduced the man as Count Palffy, the manager of the theater. She was even more amazed when Salieri informed her that he also managed the Court theaters. Eurydice was confused. If they were Court theaters, yet they were controlled by the count, did that mean they were actually Court theaters or public theaters like the Theater an der Wien? If they *were* controlled as public entities, how had Salieri arranged for her performances at any of them so quickly, and was the count responsible for the performances at all, some, or none? That was something she felt she shouldn't be asking at the moment. She thanked Palffy for allowing her to perform at his theater, and the count took her hand to kiss it lingeringly. Eurydice looked at him suspiciously.

He was a very dapper fellow, dressed in the latest fashion. She judged him to be somewhere in his forties, with curly, light brown hair; large, blue eyes; and a ruddy complexion. He had a high forehead, and his lips were pursed almost primly as he looked at her, even as he smiled. It was a very peculiar expression, almost as if he had just sucked a lemon, and she wasn't quite sure what to make of it. He seemed to be nice enough, but she found the way he continued to warmly hold her hand in both of his slightly unnerving. She couldn't be quite sure, but she had the feeling he was trying to be forward with her. It was so subtle, and she could be completely wrong.

"Lady Eurydice, it is an honor to meet you," he said expansively, giving her hand a slight squeeze.

"Likewise, Count Palffy," said Eurydice evenly. She still wasn't sure. Perhaps he was just being kind and sincere.

"I must admit I was a bit skeptical when Herr Kapellmeister put forward his proposition to have you perform here today, but I am happy to say I was well-pleased by the outcome."

"As was I," agreed Eurydice relievedly. It was miraculous the way her nausea had vanished the moment she walked off the stage.

"Would you be the female Herr Bakkeman reviewed recently?" he asked curiously.

"I would expect so," said Eurydice calmly.

"Ah," he said understandingly. "From England are you?"

Eurydice started to clarify that she was from Wales, but it would probably be lost on him. "Yes." He was still holding her hand, and she couldn't quite decide the best way to go about removing it from his grasp without seeming rude. "If you'll excuse me a moment, I'm just going to put away my violin," she said with a slight smile, politely trying to remove her hand.

"I'll take care of that for you, my dear," said Salieri with a warm smile, gently removing the Stradivarius from her other hand.

Eurydice started to protest, but that, too, could not be accomplished without her seeming rude. Salieri was just being kind, but he had foiled her plan of escaping Palffy.

"I was wondering if you would care to join me for supper?" asked Count Palffy politely.

Eurydice didn't quite trust him. Actually, she didn't trust him at all. There had been nothing about his behavior to indicate he was being anything more than kind, but there was something at the back of her mind telling her that he was a tricky one. Her first impressions of people had never been wrong before. Maybe she was wrong this time, but she'd rather not find out. Other than his intention to permanently keep possession of her hand, there really was nothing.

"I'm sorry, I truly appreciate the invitation, but I'm afraid I have other plans," said Eurydice kindly.

"Speaking of, I'm afraid I have some of my own," said Franz, looking at his watch. He took her other hand to give it a playfully gallant kiss, since Palffy wouldn't let go of the one he had claimed, and gave her a grin. "I think we can take time off from rehearsal tomorrow, don't you?"

Eurydice smiled back. "Absolutely. You were marvelous tonight, by the by. I shall see you at our usual time on Wednesday then?"

"Of course," he assured with a smile.

He stopped to speak briefly with Salieri before he left for the rear of the stage after he turned to look back at her and give her a wave. She liked Franz; he was very humorous and kind. Eurydice could hear the audience exiting the building, and when she looked through the entrance onto the stage, she could see workers preparing everything for the performance of the opera.

"Are you sure I cannot change your mind about supper?" asked Palffy disappointedly.

"I'm sorry, I'm afraid not," said Eurydice neutrally. She *really* wanted him to let go of her hand. It was starting to become hot and sweaty from being held so long. "I have plans with my husband and family, which we made well before this evening." It was a fib, but he wouldn't know that.

"Oh, that's too bad," said Palffy with a crestfallen expression.

Eurydice could hear women giggling excitedly in the darkness on the stage, and she was relieved everyone was finally coming to join her. She couldn't help wondering what had taken them so long. Salieri had finished putting away her violin, but Palffy still did not want to let go of her hand. She would occasionally tug at it discreetly to try to dislodge it, but he held fast.

"Have you been in Vienna long?" asked Palffy politely.

Eurydice scratched her forehead with her free hand and sighed. "No, actually, I only just arrived a little over a fortnight past," she said calmly.

"Truly?" blurted Palffy in surprise, and for once Eurydice did not find his reaction suspect. "Who was your teacher in England, then?"

"Only my *babushka*," said Eurydice, "Alexa, Duchess of Aberdare."

Palffy frowned thoughtfully. "No formal training?"

"Well, my *babushka* was a very good teacher," said Eurydice evasively.

Salieri chuckled. "Indubitably," he said with amusement.

Everyone soon arrived, and Agniezka, Leilah, and Cora all hugged her and kissed her cheeks with lots of proud smiles and watery eyes. Eurydice was happy not only to receive their congratulations, but also because their arrival freed her hand. Ellsworth surprised her when he picked her up and spun her in a circle, and then once he set her on her feet, he gave her a sound kiss on the lips. She looked up at him bemusedly, too stunned to say anything or even decide if she should be angry. She finally managed to turn in his arms, which he still had around her waist, to look at Count Palffy and introduce him to her family and friends. Seeing Eurydice's husband and the way he continued to keep an arm around her waist, Palffy decided to take his leave. He still just seemed to be ingratiating, but Eurydice was glad he was leaving. For once, she didn't mind that Ellsworth wasn't keeping his hands to himself.

"Well, I believe I'll be going now," said Palffy. He took her hand, just after she'd finally gotten it back, and gave it a kiss that wasn't as long as the first. He released it rather quickly, too, much to Eurydice's relief. "I shall expect to see you back here next two Monday afternoons," he said with a smile, "and at the Burgtheater on the thirteenth."

"Thank you, Count Palffy, of course," said Eurydice with a slight incline of her head and a smile.

He started to leave, but then he turned back to look at her. "There is one more thing," he said thoughtfully. "Herr Kapellmeister has said you don't wish to be paid?"

"Yes, that's true," said Eurydice evenly. "If there are any funds due to me, I should like them to be given to a charitable society of some type, particularly for orphans, foundlings, or those with sensory impairment."

"That's very...generous of you," said Palffy slowly. Eurydice had the impression he didn't mean it.

"It's simply that I don't need the money, so I thought it should go somewhere it could do some good. Is there any money due to me?" she asked curiously. She hadn't really thought about it until then. In all her plans for pursuing her music, being paid was something that escaped her.

"Yes, actually, there is...quite a bit...and more to come, if your other two performances here go as splendidly as today's," said Palffy dully.

"Oh!" said Eurydice in surprise. She looked up at Ellsworth questioningly. "I should like to see it go to an institution for the deaf, if there is one."

"There is…in Wieden," he confirmed.

"That's capital," said Eurydice happily.

"Well, that's settled, then. I'll just send the payment to the Taubstummen Institut in your name," said Palffy kindly.

"Thank you so much," said Eurydice gratefully.

He gave her a slight nod of his head and a smile and left. Salieri was ready to leave also. He told her she would need to begin rehearsal with the orchestra at the Burgtheater as soon as possible. He had already given them the scores for the two concertos and the symphony, but he wanted her to begin practice with them and to also make sure the copyists had made the transcriptions properly. Eurydice said she would like to rest tomorrow, but she would meet with him and the orchestra on Wednesday morning. Then she would return home to practice with Franz that afternoon. Salieri thought all of that sounded fine, and he told her goodbye after kissing both her cheeks and giving her a proud smile.

When they left by the entrance they'd come through, Eurydice was surprised to find several people waiting at the door to meet her. Some were members of the audience who wanted to tell her personally how much they had enjoyed the performance, but most were journalists. Eurydice scratched her forehead disconcertedly as they began to ask her questions. They were polite, but their waylaying her was unexpected. She had to wonder what they were doing there. She supposed some of them were intending to stay for the opera and had arrived early; it was the only thing she could think of to account for it. She kindly answered their questions but found it to be a nuisance. She wanted to go to a coffeehouse, and then she wanted to go home for supper. She was famished, but she would really like a cup of coffee first.

Cora was at first reluctant to go, but Leilah tutted her old friend into coming along. They went to a coffeehouse on the Graben, and Eurydice closed her eyes and inhaled deeply as they walked into the establishment. The scent of coffee permeated the air, and it was absolutely wonderful. They enjoyed coffee (except for Cora, who had tea) and a plate of chocolate-dipped orange slices, and Eurydice had no trouble getting it to stay down. She hadn't anticipated that she would—her performance was over and done.

When they arrived home, Eurydice and Agniezka went to their rooms. Eurydice put away her violin and made a quick entry into her life diary before Agniezka neatened her hair and clothes before supper. She would put in a longer entry in the morning. She had several copies of the handbill given out for her performance, and she would send them home to her family and keep a copy with her mementoes. She was still giddy from how well everything went as she walked down the stairs. There were one or two things she thought she might like to improve for her performance next week, but overall, she felt it had gone splendidly.

She was surprised when she reached the drawing room and saw Ellsworth was still home. As she thought about it, she realized this was the first time, other than the night they had arrived, that she would be eating supper with her husband. None of their guests—and there were a lot—seemed surprised to see him, but Eurydice knew they had to be. The more she thought about it, it occurred to her that she'd not shared any meals with him since breakfast the day after they had arrived. She supposed it was a special occasion, but she was still amazed.

Her surprise over her husband's presence was only surpassed by how taken aback she was when the guests all applauded when she walked into the room. She colored a bright pink, and for a moment thought about leaving again. She hadn't realized when she performed in public for the first time that she would become the focus of such adulation. It made her uncomfortable, and she didn't know if she would ever become accustomed to it.

Something she was made aware of before going into supper was that Cora's friends—a large portion of them—were involved in the theater or music in some fashion. Herr Bakkeman was there with his wife, and Eurydice thanked him for the glowing review he had given her for her drawing room performance. He assured her there would be another for the one at the Theater an der Wien, not in the next morning's edition, but in Wednesday's. Eurydice was looking forward to seeing it, and not with the dread she had felt over the first one. Another of Cora's friends was a music publisher, Herr Hohler, and he wanted to talk to her about putting the pieces she had performed into print. Eurydice was astounded, and flattered, and she made an appointment to go see him tomorrow afternoon. She would have put it off until Wednesday, but that day was already becoming entirely too full with things she had to do, and she still had to find time to compose her symphony. Cora counted two playwrights, a painter, and a librettist among her friends as well. All this time Eurydice had been dining with these people, and she never knew.

Supper was lively and enjoyable, with lots of conversation and laughter. There was also lots of wine and champagne, and Eurydice could hear a slight ringing in her ears and felt a little dizzy by the time the meal was through. She hadn't realized she had drunk so much until she stood up. She walked to the drawing room with her arm linked through Leilah's, and she was glad for the support because she felt unsteady on her feet.

When the men joined them, tea was served, and many of the conversations that had begun at the table were continued. Eurydice kept waiting for the servants to open the doors and curtains to the music room in preparation for her to play something, but they didn't. It wasn't that she wanted to play, but it had become such a frequent occurrence that things just seemed off when it wasn't done. Truthfully, she was a little too tipsy to play anything, and the tea wasn't as helpful at reducing the buzzing in her head as coffee would be.

She stood talking with Countess von Heide and Frau Bakkeman, and other guests would occasionally come over to again offer their compliments and take their leave. Then the two women collected their spouses and did the same. Eurydice suppressed a yawn as Leilah came over to her, and the older woman chuckled amusedly. She was their only remaining guest, and Ellsworth stood talking with his mother. What surprised Eurydice about it was that they were *talking*—not arguing but having what seemed to be a genuine conversation.

"What are you going to do when the Season begins in three weeks?" chortled Leilah. "You will never last."

"I am somewhat hoping to evade the Season," said Eurydice dully.

Leilah laughed. "You must at least go to one redoute," she cajoled. "There is nothing like a masked ball. If they'd had them in London more often, I might have stayed in Great Britain," she chortled.

"That doesn't sound too bad," conceded Eurydice with a slight smile.

"Speaking of masks and the home country, I believe Cora is intending to have a party of some type on Halloween. She doesn't usually, but I think because of the children, she thought it would be nice. The Viennese don't do anything to mark it themselves, but I do admit I miss *Oíche Shamhna.*"

"Ooh, that sounds fun. Because of all the different servants, my family has the best traditions from everywhere for Halloween. We always have a large bonfire, and when I was younger, we children would go guising to the cottages on the estate. Cosmo, Topher, and Damon still do. I don't imagine we can do any of that here."

"No, I think a large fire in the middle of the street would be frowned upon," chortled Leilah, "but I'm sure we can bob for apples and whatnot."

Eurydice chuckled and gave a slight shake of her head. "I'm not very good at bobbing for apples. I generally end it without the apple and very soggy, but it's still fun."

Leilah smiled and gave her a hug. "Will you come to call this week?"

"I shall try. Salieri has said I need to begin rehearsal with the orchestra at the Burg. Depending how that goes, I may not have time to do much of anything."

"I'm sure it will go swimmingly."

Leilah said goodbye to Ellsworth and Cora, and then Eurydice said good night to Cora and walked up the stairs to their rooms with her husband. She went to Agniezka's room to dress for bed, and by the time she came out to brush her teeth, Ellsworth was already in bed. He sat with his pillows propped against the headboard, reading a paper or journal by lamplight, one of his arms folded behind his head. Eurydice went around the foot of the bed to her own side and settled under the blankets after fluffing her pillows and turning off her lamp. Her head was clearer, but the alcohol she had drunk was making her very sleepy.

"Good night," she said quietly.

Ellsworth didn't say anything at first, and Eurydice thought he was simply engrossed in what he was reading, but she could see him putting it away, and he soon turned off his lamp.

"I was so proud of you this afternoon," he said softly.

"Thank you," said Eurydice, and he couldn't see in the dark the way her cheeks colored.

He surprised her when he reached over to pull her toward him. Eurydice resisted, trying to pry his fingers loose from her arm, but even as he was being gentle, his grip was firm. She couldn't get free, and she pushed at his chest to put some distance between them when he had her pressed against him.

"No," said Eurydice firmly, still trying to get loose.

He kissed her gently on the lips, and Eurydice began to struggle even more, simply because she wanted to give in, and she couldn't let herself do that. She managed to turn her head away and arched her back against his arm around her waist in an effort to make him turn her loose.

"Come on, Dicy, kiss me. Please?" he sighed longingly. "Just one kiss, please? I miss you."

Eurydice momentarily stilled, realizing there was little she could do to get away from him without resorting to violence, and while he was forcing himself on her, he wasn't being forceful. That he wasn't, that he was being gentle and pleading, was making him very hard to resist. He began to kiss her again, smoothing his hand down her cheek before moving it to the back of her head to keep her from turning away. She hesitantly responded, not struggling, but trying her best not to encourage him either. He finally gave up and rested his forehead against hers.

"Why won't you kiss me?" he said unhappily.

"You're still seeing that woman," said Eurydice quietly.

"Yes, but—" he began.

"Then how could you even think to ask me why I won't?" she said sadly. "As long as you're seeing that woman, you don't need me."

"But I *do* need you," said Ellsworth intensely as he lifted his head to look at her in the dark.

"No, you don't," said Eurydice flatly. "You might want me, but you don't need me. There's a difference."

Ellsworth sighed with disappointed frustration. "You won't let me explain."

"What is there to explain? As long as you're seeing her, there's nothing more to say. We may have an arranged marriage, but I didn't agree to share my bed with a third person."

Ellsworth groaned quietly with exasperation. There was no middle ground with her. She wouldn't let him explain in what way he was still seeing Anneliese.

"Why are you so upset I'm seeing another woman?" he finally asked vexedly. "You said you don't care, and we have an arranged marriage, so why should it make a difference?"

"Because you led me to believe you wouldn't have a mistress when you had one all along. You lied to me. While you've lied to me before, it was due to some misplaced belief that I would betray a confidence. When you misled me on this one thing, it was because you thought you could have your cake and eat it, too."

"I didn't lie to you," said Ellsworth with barely controlled patience, breathing out heavily.

"Not outright, no. You just failed to mention it. Instead, I had to find out by seeing her leave our house and smelling her on you!" said Eurydice in a heated whisper. She took a deep breath in an effort to calm down. "Even a man in an arranged marriage doesn't like to find out he's been made a cuckold. So, tell me, as a man with just such an arrangement, if you found out I had a fancy man, how happy would you be?" Ellsworth clenched his jaw and didn't say anything. "That's exactly what I thought you would say," she said flatly.

Ellsworth put a hand to her cheek and rested his forehead against hers. He closed his eyes and sighed defeatedly. He wanted to tell her everything, but he couldn't. The only way he could tell her would be as an affirmation of something she determined on her own, and he didn't see how she would possibly ever be able to figure it out. He could simply stop seeing Anneliese, but he hadn't reached the point that he felt he could do so.

As much as he hated it, he had to keep Anneliese's other occupation concealed. It was one thing for Eurydice to know he was a spy, or even that he worked for Aberdare. That she knew he had been trained for it in Japan was acceptable. But, he couldn't expose another spy. He wasn't confident Anneliese had extended him the same courtesy, but he couldn't do something that might jeopardize her safety because she was one of those valuable commodities that worked both sides. Her line of work enabled her to gather remarkable amounts of information, and some of it had proved very helpful. For now, she seemed to be working for the same side he was on, and until he found otherwise, her involvement had to remain hidden. He hated that he couldn't tell his wife because it was causing a rift between them, and Anneliese was so contemptible. He had never loathed his job as much as he did in that moment.

He turned over onto his back and pulled her against him, settling her head onto his chest.

"Just let me hold you then," he pleaded tiredly, "at least for tonight."

Eurydice started to refuse. She had placed her hand on his chest with the intention of pushing away from him. In the end, she stayed where she was. He had yet again made her feel guilty for refusing him. She still didn't think he was doing it on purpose, which was what made it even worse. She didn't know why it was so hard for him to understand that she wouldn't share, or why it was wrong for him to think she would want to.

She heard him sigh and begin to relax when he saw that she was going to let him hold her, and she felt him tighten his arm around her carefully. Eurydice listened to his heart beating beneath her ear as he drifted off to sleep, and she felt unexpected tears sting her eyes.

If she had never seen the woman leaving their house, if he hadn't made the mistake of coming to their bed smelling like her, Eurydice might never have known about her. She would have been oblivious, still believing they had managed to make their marriage more than just an arrangement. Because despite what she had said, Eurydice did care about him—a great deal. Her upset over finding he had a mistress wasn't due to jealousy; she was hurt to discover he cared so little for her in return that he would go to another woman. And, all the while, he had made her believe he *did* care…still made her believe he cared, and it was beginning to make her feel that she was in the wrong for not letting him have a mistress and her as well. She was beginning to feel like she was being prideful and vain for not giving in. That had to be wrong.

If he would just stop seeing the other woman, she would let it go. It might take her awhile to forget about it, but she would forgive him. He must surely realize that. She had not outright asked him to stop seeing the other woman, but he had to know that was what she wanted. She couldn't *ask* him to stop seeing his mistress, and Eurydice hated what she had promised him when they married. It had all sounded so simple and reasonable at the time, but now she realized it was impossible.

Chapter Twenty Five

Eurydice's performance at the Theater an der Wien the next week proved to be even more popular than the first. At the first one, there had been several empty seats, but at the second one, all the seats were full. There were even people standing along the walls. She discovered afterward that people had to be turned away at the door because there had been no room for them. She had been astonished by her reception, and at the time, she couldn't help wondering how it had happened.

The thing that pleased her most, however, was that Beethoven had come. She didn't get to speak to him, but she had seen him, sitting in a box not far from Leilah's, and he had given her a small, friendly wave and a smile when he saw that she realized he was there. When she saw him, in that moment, she knew if she never performed for the public again, she would feel she had accomplished all she had ever wanted.

There had been dozens of people clamoring to see her, both before and after the performance—journalists, nobility, managers of other theaters, and just people who had enjoyed hearing her play, both outside the theater and at the side of the stage. And it hadn't been just people from Vienna. There were people from several different cities within the Austrian empire, including Graz, Salzburg, Laibach, Pest, and Leipzig, but also—to her amazement—there were people from Warsaw, Kiev, St. Petersburg, and several other cities. She didn't think they had all come to Vienna specifically to see her, but they had made a point of doing so. Not only had some of them come to see her perform, but those from other places wanted to request she come to their cities. She wasn't sure she wanted to do that…yet, but it was something to consider.

Eurydice had been left feeling overwhelmed by all the adulation, and she had been relieved when she was able to step into the coach to go home. She had never thought she would enjoy the sound of silence so much. She had thought the reaction the previous week had been enough, and she found it a bit disconcerting to see it had only been the beginning. She wasn't so sure she was going to like all the attention.

She eventually learned that part of the reason for her swift rise in popularity was due to publicity. Herr Bakkeman had written the two reviews for the *Wiener Zeitung*, not to mention Count Palffy had seen to it that a schedule of her performances was published there as well. There had been articles in the *Österreichischer Beobachter*, another daily newspaper, and *Das Sonntagsblatt*, a weekly that came out every Sunday. The articles, she suspected, that had brought her the attention from other cities, however, were those that had appeared in the *Allgemeine Musikalische Zeitung*, *Der Wanderer, Der Sammler,* and the *Wiener Theater-Zeitung*. She suspected she had been mentioned in other periodicals, but those were the only ones she had managed to acquire copies of to put into her keepsake chest. Some of the articles had been written by friends of Cora, but others had been written by journalists who had been at the theater for her first performance.

She went to meet with Herr Hohler and provided him with copies of the four sonatas she had performed at the Theater an der Wien as well as copies of the pieces she would be performing at the Burgtheater. When they discussed fees, she told him the same thing she had told Count Palffy: if there was any money earned for her from their publication and sale, she wanted to have it donated to the Taubstummen Institut. When he asked her if it was because of her admiration for Beethoven, Eurydice had to explain it was entirely due to her having a brother who was deaf. He had the compositions printed and in the shops for sale by Friday. Eurydice had been astounded.

Herr Hohler also asked her if she would like him to oversee the publishing of her music in other places, such as London. Eurydice hadn't thought about that. She hadn't really thought about having her music published anywhere, let alone London. After some consideration, she thought that would be fine. She could only imagine what the *ton* was going to think when it discovered she was a published musician and composer, but it wasn't as if she really cared. They were there, she was in Vienna, and she didn't know how long it would be before she was able to go back to Britain at all, let alone for a Season.

She began her rehearsal with the orchestra at the Burgtheater on Wednesday morning, and she understood why Salieri said they would need to practice. The copyists had done well transcribing the scores, but with that number of musicians, it took time to learn a piece and to play it as a single body. Salieri was going to conduct, she discovered, and while she knew she couldn't do it herself, it surprised her that *he* wanted to do so personally. Luckily, the orchestra was an excellent group of musicians, and by Monday, Eurydice thought things were going well.

She met the artistic director of the Burgtheater, Herr Schreyvogel, at one of the practices with the orchestra, and she learned Count Palffy had hired him to oversee what was performed there. He was honest enough to tell her that he had been reluctant to let her give an evening performance, even at the request of Salieri, especially so near to the beginning of the season. He then told her that his opinion had improved after hearing how pleased Count Palffy had been with her premier performance at the Theater an der Wien and reading some of the complimentary critical reviews. Once he heard one or two of the rehearsals for the Burgtheater, he told her he was actually looking forward to it. She liked Herr Schreyvogel.

Eurydice reduced her rehearsals with Schubert to every other day for only two hours. They had become familiar with playing together, and Eurydice had decided they wouldn't play any new pieces for their remaining performances at the Theater an der Wien. Other than one or two things that had needed adjustment, there wasn't anything more that needed to be done. Their playing together was as perfect as it could be. That allowed both of them more time for composing, and while Eurydice couldn't speak for him, her own time had become severely depleted by all the rehearsing she had been doing.

After her second performance at the Theater an der Wien, Eurydice took the following Tuesday to rest. It was Halloween, and she wouldn't be rehearsing with the orchestra at the Burgtheater on the Wednesday following either because it was All Saints' Day. Things were progressing well enough she didn't think anything would suffer from her not being there for three days. She didn't know if she would use the free time to work on her symphony, but she was looking forward to not having anything to do.

Actually, Eurydice needed the time to contemplate her situation. She had received letters from both her father and Sheerness among the many that had slowly begun to arrive for her. She had known there had to be news about Agniezka's divorce when her maid received a letter as well. But the news wasn't good. After looking into it and doing what they could, the only way Agniezka could obtain the divorce was to go to St. Petersburg and appear before the judge herself. Sheerness provided her the name of a lawyer to contact once they were in the city, who would assist them with completing the process, but there was nothing further he could do. Agniezka *had* to be there. The only consolation both Aberdare and Sheerness could give her was that they didn't think there would be any difficulty in having the divorce granted because of the length of separation in both time and distance from her spouse.

The news left Eurydice in a dilemma. She couldn't let Agniezka go all the way to St. Petersburg to face her husband alone, but she didn't believe for an instant that Ellsworth would let the two of them go without him. That meant Eurydice would have to tell him about Felton and Agniezka and the baby. Agniezka gave her permission, but Eurydice was hesitant. She would have to decide soon, though, because Agniezka didn't have much time. Maybe if she showed up in the courtroom blatantly pregnant by another man it would prompt the judge to give her the divorce without a qualm, but both Eurydice and Agniezka would rather not find out.

Cora confirmed she was having a Halloween party. Most people joining them would be expatriates from Britain, and they would bring their children.

Cora had hired a quartet, should anyone feel the need to dance, and Eurydice was pleased she wasn't expected to play one note. There would not be a sit-down meal, but there would be tables with food and beverages. It seemed it was going to be very informal, and Eurydice was looking forward to it.

She went to the nursery to visit the children that afternoon after dinner, and they informed her that their Uncle Gareth was going to help them and the other children at the party make masks. There wasn't going to be any guising, but it would be something to keep them entertained. Eurydice spent her time with them helping Simon learn how to play the tin whistle he'd received for his birthday, Corinna sitting on her lap in a chair by the window. Cassie and Mary Kate preferred to play with their dolls near Nanny Rigsby.

That evening for the party, Agniezka dressed her in a simple but elegant ball gown made of silvery gray velvet with long puffed sleeves, the bodice decorated with lace and tiny pearls. She twisted most of Eurydice's hair into a knot at her nape, but then she braided the remainder and wove it through the knot. She added some jewelry made of platinum and marcasite, and Eurydice was ready. Surprisingly, the silver of the gown complimented her coloring, and Agniezka thought she looked very beautiful.

Agniezka considered for a time putting Eurydice in a morning gown and pelisse, but it was a party, after all. She would have to take Eurydice to the dressmakers for more clothes if she was going to continue to perform on a regular basis. She couldn't wear the same dress every time. It wouldn't be easy to get her to the store; not only did she not care for shopping, but she was very busy. Maybe next week Agniezka would be able to arrange something.

Leilah had already arrived when Eurydice reached the drawing room, but none of the other guests were there yet. The curtains and doors between the drawing room and music room had been opened, and the musicians Cora had hired were setting up near the piano. The servants were arranging the platters of food and the punch bowls on the tables, and extra chairs had been placed along the walls. Eurydice didn't know how many people Cora had invited, but she didn't think it would be able to hold more than thirty, even with the partition open between the two rooms.

Not long after Eurydice entered the room and chatted with Leilah, Nanny Rigsby came in with the children. They looked around themselves with round-eyed awe, and Eurydice did suppose it was unusual for them. They sometimes ate in the great room at the palazzo in Venice, but since arriving in Vienna, most of their time had been spent in the nursery. They did occasionally go out to the park, but most of their time was spent indoors and out of sight. She was sure they would have no difficulty behaving, though.

Simon walked over to her and looked up at her with a studious frown.

"Where's Uncle Gareth?" he asked perplexedly.

"I don't know, Simon," said Eurydice evenly. Where was he indeed?

"But, Aunt Rissy, he said he was going to help us make masks," said the little boy disappointedly.

Eurydice reached down to brush his hair out of his eyes and gave him a soothing smile.

"Well, if he said he was going to be here, then I'm sure he will be. There's still plenty of time."

She had no idea where her husband was. He had been, as usual, gone from their room before she was awake. After Monday night, they weren't speaking to each other as much as before and seeing each other even less. He hadn't been with her to the Burgtheater while she rehearsed. He didn't come to the music room while she practiced with Franz. Sometimes she was awake when he came to bed, sometimes not. After Monday, there had only been one night that she knew of when he had held her again. He had spooned behind her and pulled her close, and Eurydice knew he wouldn't have done it if he had known she was awake. It had left Eurydice feeling confused and unhappy—confused because she didn't want him to touch her but wanted to be held, unhappy because she could tell he had been unable to stop himself, and it seemed he was more determined than ever to see his mistress regardless.

Eurydice could accept and understand that he had to be away from home because of his job, but being gone to spend time with his mistress was purely selfish, and it wasn't something she felt she could tolerate for much longer. She had said she would be as undemanding as possible, but she was beginning to feel she had let this go on much longer than he had any right to expect, regardless of any promises she had made.

Guests for the party began to arrive. Most of them were people Eurydice had met before, and Leilah introduced her to the ones she hadn't. The quartet began to play after enough people were present, and the Windham children were joined by about a dozen others, excitedly running in and out of the groups of adults scattered around the room conversing. Cora eventually joined them from greeting arrivals at the door, and still there was no sign of Ellsworth.

When an hour passed and Ellsworth had still not arrived, Eurydice decided she would help the children make their masks. She didn't know what he had intended to use, but she had Nanny Rigsby go to the nursery to bring her paper, paint, scissors, and string. She knew she was a poor substitute for her husband, but she did her best to help them make masks with the faces of goblins, vampires, werewolves, and even one rabbit for a child who thought there was nothing more frightening. Simon, Cassie, Mary Kate, and Corinna were all disappointed their uncle hadn't been the one to help them, and Eurydice was angry he had broken his word. She could only imagine what had kept him away, but she had a fairly good idea, and that only added fuel to her irritation.

With their masks made, the children resumed their running around the room, occasionally stopping to eat or drink but never slowing down for long. The room was filled with their giggles and shrieks, and Eurydice didn't mind it. Halloween was an occasion most enjoyed by the young. She envied their seemingly endless energy and wished she could borrow some. She wasn't exactly tired, but she didn't think she would have a difficult time falling asleep.

She hadn't been sleeping well lately. Besides her performance anxiety, her husband's infidelity, and Agniezka's divorce, the number of dreams she was having had increased. Most were just dreams, but there were so many. She had reached the end of her diary and started a new one. She had the Dark Dream again, and she still didn't see the entire thing. She did see more of the beginning but was no closer to seeing the end. She didn't believe what she was seeing was the end. There *had* to be more. It was only a sense she had that it continued to a much different conclusion, and she was desperate to know.

And she still could not see the man's face. She didn't know what good it would do to see it, but at least then she would have some warning of when it would come true. Until she met him, it wouldn't happen. That much she knew. She was actually hoping she never met him. That was unlikely, especially since she'd had the dream three times already. She had to wonder why she couldn't see the end. Was it so terrible her mind simply didn't want her to remember? If that were so, what she had seen was bad enough perhaps she should be wishing she *never* saw the end of it.

One of the women had a deck of cards to tell fortunes, and Eurydice had to laugh at some of them. But then Leilah convinced her to let the woman, Mrs. Guines, tell hers. When she was done, Eurydice tried to laugh it off, but she wasn't sure she could. Mrs. Guines said she would begin a long journey before the end of the year and that she would meet a mysterious stranger who would have a profound impact on her future. It was no more specific than anything she had told the other guests she had read for, but considering the things currently preying on her mind, it left Eurydice feeling uneasy. She had never liked having her fortune told.

The servants eventually brought in a large tin tub filled with water and added several apples. Eurydice avoided participating for as long as possible before the children pulled her toward it, all of them dripping wet from having their own go. She wasn't the only adult—or woman—to make an attempt, but hers was probably the least successful. She fished around with her face in the water for several minutes before she was able to sink her teeth into a piece of fruit. Her head and bodice were soaked when she was done, and Leilah had a towel ready for her to dry off. At least Leilah didn't look any less bedraggled from having her own dunk.

As the hour drew closer to midnight, the guests began to leave. Nanny Rigsby took the Windham children up the stairs for bed even before eleven, and Eurydice could see their energy had dwindled. By the time the clock struck midnight, it was only Cora, Leilah, and Eurydice. The servants had already cleared away most of the remnants from the party, and the musicians had packed their instruments away to leave. Once Cora paid them, they were gone as well. Through it all, from start to end, there had been no sign of Ellsworth. Eurydice was torn between waiting for him to come home to give him a talking to for disappointing the children or going to bed. She was leaning toward going to bed.

Leilah and Eurydice sat on the couch the servants had moved back to its proper location, and Cora was just returning from seeing to the musicians. All-in-all, it was a safe assumption that the party had been a success.

"That was a splendid party," said Leilah appreciatively, "but I'm not ready to go home yet. Something is missing."

"Oh?" said Cora curiously.

"I'm thinking there still needs to be more."

"What more could there be?" asked Cora doubtfully. "There was food, dancing, fortune telling, bobbing for apples...." She shrugged.

Leilah sat forward to roll a pair of dice that were left lying on the table, giving Cora an amused smile. Cora's eyes widened, and she shook her head.

"Oh, no, absolutely not," she said firmly.

"Come on," coaxed Leilah with a teasing pout. "It's been so long, and it's quite a lot of fun."

"We're not young girls anymore," said Cora dryly.

"What's going on?" asked Eurydice confusedly.

"Don't you remember when we used to play? You? Me? Julia? When we were in finishing school? As I seem to recall, you were very good at it," teased Leilah with a smile.

"And I say again, we are not young girls anymore," said Cora, but Eurydice could see she was starting to relent.

"Come on!" chortled Leilah. "It's not a complete Halloween without a little high jinks! We won't play for hours like we used to. Frankly, I don't think I would be up to it."

"What is high jinks?" asked Eurydice.

"It's a game your mother, Leilah, and I used to play when we were your age...and younger. It's a most unladylike entertainment, involving gambling and alcohol," said Cora. She and Leilah were smiling at each other. "Oh, very well," she finally said in amused exasperation, "but not for more than an hour." She stood up from the chair and rubbed her hands together. "I should have some whisky hidden away somewhere."

Eurydice still had a lost expression, but she wasn't sure she wanted to do something that involved drinking, especially not whisky. Cora came back with a bottle and a small glass, and she set them on the table.

"I don't know if I want to play," said Eurydice hesitantly.

"Sure you do," assured Leilah. "It's very easy. High roll chooses, low roll does, and the middle starts the next round."

"Chooses what and does what, exactly?" asked Eurydice nervously.

"Low will drink, dare, or divulge, depending on the whim of the high roller. Cora was always good at rolling high, but your mother could handle her liquor," chortled Leilah.

"But I can't do either," said Eurydice dully.

"You have to play," pleaded Leilah. "It's no fun with just two, and you will be carrying on a tradition."

Eurydice thought about it for several minutes. This could not possibly end well, but both women were looking at her hopefully. It would be fun to see what sort of mischief her mother got into when she was young. Eurydice would be going to bed soon, and it would be something relaxing…probably *very* relaxing if she couldn't roll well.

"A-all right," she said finally.

"Huzzah!" said Leilah excitedly.

Leilah began by rolling the dice, then Cora, then Eurydice. Leilah rolled the lowest, and Cora made her take a drink of whisky. She gasped and her eyes watered, and she laughed as she put the glass on the table. Eurydice rolled first the next time, and she rolled lowest while Cora rolled highest again. Cora had her drink as well. Eurydice's reaction wasn't any more stoic than Leilah's.

"My God, that's harsh!" wheezed Eurydice.

And so the game continued for quite some time, with Cora more often than not rolling highest and Eurydice and Leilah drinking. She did occasionally have them perform some feat, like playing the piano with her back turned for Eurydice or performing a somersault for Leilah. Cora would sometimes ask a question, such as whether she had ever snuck out of the house without her parents' permission for Eurydice (no) or whether she had ever danced on a table in a public house for Leilah (yes). For the most part, though, Cora had them drink. All three women were soused. The fortunate thing was that Eurydice was soon so drunk she didn't *care*. After another round, she again rolled lowest, and she lifted the glass and drained it before Cora could speak.

"I was going to ask a question," said Cora amusedly.

"Oh. Well, ask then," giggled Eurydice.

Cora and Leilah both joined her in laughing, and they all laughed even louder when Leilah toppled off the end of the couch to the floor.

"All right, now, this is serious!" said Cora blearily, raising a commanding finger in the air.

"Shh…shh…s-serious," said Leilah, putting a wavering finger to her lips before snorting and giggling as she tried to get off the floor.

"Leilah, you're drunk!" accused Cora with a pout.

"We all are, so no harm done," chortled Leilah after she managed to crawl back onto the couch.

"Ask the question before I fall asleep," said Eurydice with a hiccup. Just then, the clock struck the hour.

"It's 1:00 in the morning, do you know where your husband is?" slurred Cora.

"Yes," said Eurydice flatly with a definite nod and an owlish blink.

"Well? Where is he?" asked Cora expectantly after a few minutes when Eurydice didn't expand on her answer.

"He's with that carrotty, bedizened…*bitch*," hissed Eurydice darkly.

"Could you be more specific?" asked Leilah. "There are a lot of those in this city, and not all of them are screwing your husband." She hiccupped and frowned, and a hand flew to her mouth. "Did I just say that out loud?" she asked rhetorically.

"I don't know. She came here, though. Rusty hair, green eyes, smells foul," said Eurydice dully.

"Ah, *that* bitch," said Cora with a knowing nod. "Anneliese Rathmueller."

"Why are you here?" asked Leilah simply. "If he's with another woman and you don't want him there, make him come home. He's *your* husband."

"Oh, I can't do that," said Eurydice abashedly.

"Yes, you can," said Cora firmly. "He needs to know how lucky he is to have you. It would be one thing if you were a shrew or unpleasant in some way, but you're a good, sweet girl. If you don't bring him to heel now, he will *always* do it. Believe you me." She took a swallow of whisky and tapped the glass loudly on the table. "Nip it in the bud."

"But I don't know where he is. I mean, I *know* where he is, but I don't know *where* he is," said Eurydice uncertainly.

"I know," chirped Leilah helpfully. "I can drop you on my way home."

"There you go," said Cora, waving a hand in the air.

Eurydice looked from one to the other uncertainly. She knew they were right, and she had already decided on her own that she needed to do something, but she wasn't so sure confronting him at the woman's house was the proper way to do it. But she was drunk…and angry, and they combined to dull her common sense enough that it all sounded perfectly reasonable.

It sounded so reasonable, in fact, that less than twenty minutes later she was bundled into a warm pelisse and cloak with a fur muff for her hands and was riding with Leilah in her carriage to be deposited at Rathmueller's on Juden Gasse. Agniezka had looked at her oddly when she went to get her things for going out, knowing she was drunk but thinking Eurydice confronting her husband might not be so terrible. She told Eurydice that she wouldn't wait up, but Eurydice had already turned and weaved her way out of the room.

Eurydice began to sober somewhat as she traveled toward the brothel, wondering what she was going to do if he wasn't there. How was she going to find her way home? Not only was it cold and dark, but she didn't know her way around the city very well, she wouldn't find a hack at this hour, and she was drunk. She brushed her concerns aside because she *knew* he was there. Being inebriated made it easy for her to believe everything was going to be fine and that this was exactly the way to get him to stay away from Anneliese.

Leilah's carriage came to a stop in front of a tall, narrow building, and Eurydice peeked out the window to look at it. There were lamps lit to either side of the door at the top of a short flight of stairs, but it seemed very dark and gloomy. There were no windows on the first floor. She began to have second thoughts and almost changed her mind.

"Remember what I said about gumption," said Leilah gently, sensing her hesitation. "If you aren't willing to fight for what's yours, then you didn't really want it in the first place."

Eurydice nodded slightly as Leilah leaned past her to open the door of the carriage. Leilah looked at her soberly and patted her knee.

"Do you want me to wait for you?" she asked quietly.

Eurydice shook her head. "No, I'll be fine."

"That's the stuff," said Leilah with an affectionate smile.

Eurydice stepped out onto the sidewalk and looked up at the door. She took a deep breath and walked to the top of the stairs. She looked back at Leilah's carriage as Leilah closed the door, and Eurydice gave her a small wave as it pulled away. Eurydice looked back to the door for a few seconds, and then she knocked briefly.

It was answered by a man who was by far the largest she had ever seen, standing well over six-and-a-half feet tall with a muscular build. Even their driver, Jim, and several other of the male employees who worked for her family were dwarfed by him. In her drunken state, she couldn't tell if he seemed large because he actually was or if it was because he had squeezed it all into clothes that were obviously too small. Despite feeling intimidated, she tilted up her chin with determination and looked at him calmly.

"*Ja?*" he enquired.

"I am here to see Mr. Gareth Ellsworth. Could you show me to him, please?" she asked politely in German.

"No women allowed," he said flatly.

"I'm sorry, you don't understand," said Eurydice evenly. "I am his wife, and he needs to come home, so if you could just direct me to him?"

"No women allowed," he repeated.

"Could you at least go tell him that I am here? I will wait just inside the door, quiet as a mouse," she cajoled.

"No women allowed," he reiterated slowly, as if he were talking to someone who might not be all there.

Eurydice took a deep breath as she grew impatient. "Now, there's no need to be rude," she said calmly, giving him a charming smile. "It will only take me a moment. You won't even know I'm here."

"No women allowed," he said darkly with a glower.

"I'm not leaving without my husband, if only because I don't know my way home from here, so you may as well show me to him," she said resolutely, shifting her feet.

"No—" he started, but Eurydice thought if she had to hear him say that one more time she would pop.

"Women allowed," she finished flatly as she reached out to grab him by the wrist in a pressure grip. "Yes, you've said that already...repeatedly," she said with a grunt as she maneuvered his arm into a hold behind his back. "However, I'm not just a woman, I'm a *wife*, and you will show me to my *husband*...now," she said irritatedly, lifting up on his arm for emphasis. "I've tried being polite, which is obviously lost on you, so now we will try things this way."

The hold she had on his arm was highly effective. He could either do as she said, or she could quite easily break his arm. He seemed to realize that. Despite the difference in their sizes, she had him completely at her mercy, and he tried to crane his neck to look back at her over his shoulder. She was smiling politely, but her eyes glittered dangerously. He couldn't decide whether or not she was insane, but it would be something he could think about later, once she let go of his arm. He finally gave her a nod.

"I'll just hold onto this until you take me where I need to go," she said obligingly with a smile as she lifted up on his arm again.

He began to walk in the direction she already had him facing, and Eurydice gently kicked the door behind her to close it. There was no sense letting out all the heat. She clamped her muff beneath her free arm, her reticule dangling from her wrist, as he led her toward a door to the right. She could vaguely hear men and women laughing and music coming from behind the closed door to the left. The footman (or flash man—whatever he liked to call himself) opened the door, and Eurydice lifted up on his arm to make him continue in front of her.

The first thing she noticed was all the red. The walls were painted a bright red. The floor was covered in a carpet made in a darker shade of red. There were red brocade curtains hanging on the walls to frame fake windows that provided views onto fake desert landscapes. The ceiling was painted with a lush mural of a sylvan mythological scene filled with frolicking satyrs and nymphs. Sparkling gold chandeliers hung down to light the room brightly. There were several tables where men sat playing cards, dice, and roulette. There were a few women in the room, standing near some of the men at the tables, and their attire left no question of their profession. The room was hazy from tobacco smoke curling and swirling through the air. The stench of it made Eurydice's upper lip want to curl disgustedly, and she had to fight a sneeze.

Once she got past the disorientation she felt on seeing so much red in such bright light after being in near darkness, Eurydice found Ellsworth sitting on a couch in front of a fake window with Anneliese draped cozily against him. Eurydice tightened her jaw angrily and lifted up on the footman's arm, and he meekly walked with her toward the couch.

Anneliese noticed her arrival before Ellsworth did, or so it seemed, and that was possibly because the bulk of the footman hid her from his view. Anneliese stiffened but didn't move from her position against Ellsworth, and she even wrapped her arm more tightly around his possessively. She gave a hard look first to her footman and then to Eurydice.

Ellsworth realized she was there as soon as the door had opened, and there was only a fleeting look of surprise on his face that was quickly covered by a lazy expression. Eurydice had missed it. To her, he sat with the bawd looking unconcerned, apparently not even realizing she was there until she was only a few feet away from the couch.

Ellsworth's mind was racing as he watched her walk across the room with Bruno. He could see the way she walked beside the giant, his tight expression, the way his right arm was folded behind him. It wasn't obvious to anyone else, but she was forcing the man to do what she wanted by the hold she had on his arm. She was doing it calmly and effortlessly, which meant she knew *exactly* how to do it. Part of Bruno's duties included stopping disgruntled spouses from coming into the club to make trouble, and his size was enough to deter most of them. For those that it wasn't, he was of a size that made an average woman no match for him. Yet somehow, Eurydice had gotten the upper hand.

Ellsworth remembered the way she had flipped him over on the bed in Sacile, the same effortless skill, and he wondered if this was one of the other one or two things her brother had taught her. His feelings about the matter were divided. He was glad Dorian had taught her things to help her defend herself, but he was also angry, because knowing only a few things could leave her feeling as if she were capable of taking care of herself when it could make her put herself into a situation that was beyond her control. Like now.

Added to his concern about what Eurydice was doing to the footman was why she could possibly be there. How had she even known where he was or how to find it? And he was angry with her because she had given her word that she wouldn't question him about anything or anyone. Yet here she was. He could only hope she wasn't going to do something foolish. His curiosity about why she was there was soon satisfied.

Eurydice released the giant's arm once she was close enough to the couch, and he gingerly rubbed at his elbow. She looked up at him with a pleasant smile, and wiped an imaginary speck or two of dust from his sleeve.

"Thank you for your assistance," she said kindly in English, "you've been most helpful."

Anneliese gave Bruno a silent look and a slight nod of her head, and he left the room. She would deal with him later. Eurydice looked at her husband.

"I want you to come home now," she said calmly.

It was then that Ellsworth detected the slight slur, and he realized she was drunk. He wasn't sure how drunk because she had walked across the room with her usual grace. If he hadn't heard it when she spoke, he might never have known. To someone else—someone who didn't know her—she seemed perfectly sober. She might be very drunk, considering how out of character her coming to Rathmueller's was. It would more than account for it, but knowing she was drunk made him concerned she might say something she shouldn't.

"You shouldn't be here," he said mildly, giving her a slight smile.

"No, I agree," said Eurydice dryly as she looked around herself distastefully, "and I will leave as soon as you come with me."

"I will come home when I am ready, but you should leave now."

"You have been here long enough. The children were disappointed you weren't there to help them tonight, and it fell on me to explain to them that something *important* must have kept you away," she said stonily, sparing Anneliese a repugnant sneer.

"They'll get over it, and I want you to leave *now*," said Ellsworth coldly.

He was hoping she was drunk enough she wouldn't remember this in the morning. As strained as their relationship already was, if this continued for much longer, he was going to lose her for good because she would never forgive him. If she had only waited a day or two, this wouldn't have happened. He was really hating his job.

Anneliese began to laugh amusedly, and she casually smoothed one of her hands down Ellsworth's thigh to demonstrate her ownership. The action wasn't lost on Eurydice, and her jaw tightened as she looked at the other woman icily.

"Honestly, Gareth, could you not have done better?" chortled Anneliese amusedly in German. "I believe you've wed the Devil's daughter! Not only is she physically ordinary, but she's a shrew to boot!"

Eurydice narrowed her eyes at the woman and took a deep breath in and out through her nose in an effort to calm down. Perhaps Ellsworth should have told Anneliese that his wife was very fluent in German.

"Before you begin spouting insults about me that you don't want me to understand, perhaps you would do well to find a language I don't know, you Holstein cow," said Eurydice pleasantly in the same language.

Ellsworth looked from one to the other of the women with a slight smile. Anneliese was from Neustadt, and it surprised him that Eurydice was able to detect that. Despite his concern about the situation, he was hoping this would remove him from any responsibility for anything that might happen.

"I hope you're not terribly attached to your ewe," said Anneliese to Ellsworth, switching to Italian, "because if she calls me a cow again, I will end her," she said darkly.

Eurydice laughed. "You could try, but it's unlikely," she said amusedly in the same language, "and you have the accent of a common fishwife."

"Tell that moon-eyed hen to leave now," said Anneliese with a glower, switching to French.

"Your French is no better than your Italian. You speak it as if you have something stuck up your arse," said Eurydice mildly. "Perhaps you shouldn't have learnt it while in bed."

Anneliese inhaled sharply as if she'd just been slapped, and she looked at Eurydice with anger and frustration. Ellsworth was watching the exchange between the two women with moderate amusement. He was proud to see his wife was able to hold her own, even drunk, and he was somehow unsurprised Anneliese was as yet unable to find a language Eurydice didn't know. It was doubtful she ever would. It also pleased him to no end to see Anneliese being repaid for her unkindness. She was getting everything she deserved.

"If that filthy sow does not leave here immediately, I *will* hurt her," said Anneliese to Ellsworth in Russian.

Eurydice laughed doubtfully. "And I say again, you can try. As for *me* being a filthy sow, that's the pot calling the kettle black. You, with the quim so rotten with clap you have to bathe yourself in an even ranker perfume to cover the stench." She looked at Ellsworth and gave him a sardonic smile. "I'd be careful hammering with my tools there. They might fall off," she said as she switched to Gaelic.

Ellsworth tried to suppress a laugh. Then his eyes widened in shock and dismay when he caught the glimmer of something shiny at the edge of his vision as Anneliese sprang from the couch toward his wife with a knife in her hand. He knew she kept one in a sheath strapped to her thigh beneath her gown, and he also knew she could be deadly with it. She may not have understood what Eurydice had said to him, but everything else was enough.

When Anneliese lunged at her, Eurydice easily side-stepped the attack with only a small amount of surprise. Anneliese turned and moved in to attack her again. She feinted a move from an overhead direction, only to lower it at the last second, aiming for Eurydice's stomach. Eurydice managed to deflect it aside with her left arm wrapped in the muff. She reached over with her clear hand to grab Anneliese by the wrist, and the bawd struggled to free her arm and stab at Eurydice. Unfortunately, Eurydice's fingers were in the wrong place to apply a pressure grip to make her release the knife, and Anneliese was stronger than she looked. Their faces were close together, and Eurydice butted her forehead into Anneliese's face, hitting her in the nose and shattering it. Anneliese shrieked in pain and fury, and it only grew louder when Eurydice extended the woman's arm behind her and calmly leaned on the joint with her left elbow and lifted up on her wrist to break her arm. The knife clattered from her hand to the floor, and Eurydice stepped back from Anneliese as she crumpled to her knees, cradling her arm and rocking back and forth.

Ellsworth was astonished. The entire exchange had lasted less than a minute and was over before he even had time to react. Eurydice was calmly examining the muff for holes or tears from the knife as she turned to look at him on the couch.

"Are you ready to come home now?" she asked evenly.

Ellsworth rose from the couch bemusedly to walk toward her, and he paused for a moment to look down at Anneliese where she still sat on the floor, a few of the girls gathered around her trying to help. The other men in the room were either gathered closer or watching from their seats, and several of them wore expressions of astonishment and admiration.

"Be seeing you, Liese," he said dryly.

She looked up at him hatefully. "No, you won't," she spat. "You are no longer welcome at this establishment."

Ellsworth raised an eyebrow and gave her an unconcerned shrug. He put a hand to the small of Eurydice's back to direct her toward the door just as Bruno opened it to come in. The bully looked from Anneliese to the two of them and glared angrily.

"I did it," said Eurydice, "and don't make me hurt you, too." She arched an eyebrow at him daringly, and he moved from the doorway to let them pass.

Ellsworth retrieved his coat, hat, and gloves and hurried Eurydice out into the night before Anneliese changed her mind and sent Bruno after them. There had been enough violence for one night. When they hadn't walked very far, Ellsworth stopped her and turned her to face him to examine her worriedly, brushing his hands over her face and arms. Eurydice pushed his hands away and resumed walking.

"I'm fine," she said flatly.

Somewhere between leaving the house on Singer Strasse and their departure from Rathmueller's, Eurydice had mostly sobered, and she didn't feel any better for having gone to collect Ellsworth. If anything, she felt worse. She was even angrier with him to know he had preferred to be in the company of a woman who behaved like that more than hers, that he would abandon his responsibilities to her and his family to be with such a common doxy.

"What were you thinking coming there? Boozy no less! She could have killed you," said Ellsworth angrily.

"No, she couldn't have," said Eurydice dully, keeping her eyes on her feet as she continued to think.

"You broke your word," he said coldly.

"No, I didn't. I never questioned you about anything. I found it out all on my own. I simply decided I'd had enough," she said absently as she went over the last several minutes again, and when realization came to her of what the only logical answer could be, she stopped dead still, the breath catching in her throat and her face going pale.

"What's wrong?" asked Ellsworth as he turned to walk back to her with a concerned frown.

"You should have told me," she whispered brokenly, and then she tilted her head sideways with a thoughtful frown. "But you were sleeping with her," she said in a reasoning tone, almost to herself. He put a soothing hand to her cheek, and Eurydice pushed it away and looked up at him confusedly. "You *were* having sex with her."

"I've been going to Rathmueller's nearly every night since we got to Vienna, but I haven't been with Anneliese that way since I left for London in March. I ended that with her well before I saw you in Rotherhithe, and it has never entered my mind to start it again," he said quietly.

Eurydice's eyes widened as tears stung them, and she pushed past him to begin walking away quickly, in what she hoped was the direction of home. She began to run as she got to a large market, and when she reached the other side of it, she turned left because there was no other way to go. Ellsworth caught up to her just as she reached a larger intersection, and he spun her around to face him. Her cheeks were wet with tears, and she began to pound at his chest with her fist.

"You should have told me," she said dejectedly.

Ellsworth wrapped his arms around her and pulled her close, and he could feel her shaking as she cried quietly.

"I couldn't tell you," he sighed, "and if you hadn't realized it on your own, I wouldn't be telling you now."

"You let me think.... You made me feel.... Oh, God!" she gasped tormentedly.

"I'm sorry," he whispered somberly. "I've never been unfaithful, and I'm sorry I hurt you."

Eurydice lifted her head to look at him and wiped the back of a hand across her cheek.

"Would you? For your job, would you be unfaithful? You let me believe that you were, but would you really?" she asked earnestly.

"No," he said evenly.

He couldn't bring himself to tell her that he wouldn't be faced with that decision. This was going to be his last assignment, and he could not see that anything like that would be required of him in order for it to be completed. His heart wanted him to say he never would, so that is what he *would* say, but in his head, he knew from past experience, if the situation ever arose, he would do what needed to be done. Fortunately, neither one of them would ever have to find out how far he would go.

Eurydice looked at him searchingly for a moment before she gave him a brief nod and the ghost of a smile. Ellsworth kissed her forehead, and then he draped his arm over her shoulders for them to begin walking again. Eurydice absently wondered how far it was to the house. She couldn't recall how long the ride had been when Leilah had taken her to the brothel by carriage.

"I'm sorry I thrashed Anneliese," she said quietly after a few minutes.

Ellsworth smiled and shook his head with shrug. "She had it coming."

Eurydice frowned. "But she won't help you anymore, will she?"

"No, I expect not, but she hadn't been very helpful of late anyhow," he said as he kissed the side of her head. "If you had waited a day or two, I wouldn't have been there. I would have been at home...with you."

"Oh," said Eurydice dully, and her cheeks colored.

"I would have quit going to see her ages ago, but she kept dangling this one piece of information that I need, and she would always have some excuse for why she couldn't give it yet. I was going to give her one more day to tell me before I tried to find it another way because I couldn't decide if she was stringing me along hoping I would start swiving her again, or if she didn't actually have it, or if she was trying to keep me distracted long enough for the enemy to do something."

Eurydice looked up at him with a frown. "She works for both sides?"

"Anneliese works for whoever is capable of giving her whatever she wants at any given moment. In her profession, it doesn't matter who runs the country. There will always be a need for whores."

"I see," said Eurydice thoughtfully. "Who is the enemy—exactly—these days?" she asked casually.

Ellsworth looked askance at her. "Eurydice," he sighed patiently.

"It's only that if I knew what you were doing, perhaps I wouldn't be so suspicious. I never know if what you're doing is because of your job or if it's for something else, and if I understood *why* you were doing something, I would worry less."

"You worry about me?" asked Ellsworth with amused curiosity.

"All the time," said Eurydice solemnly.

Ellsworth gave her shoulders a squeeze. "I can take care of myself."

"Believing you can take care of yourself only makes it more likely you will put yourself into a situation that requires you to prove it," said Eurydice dryly.

"Like you did tonight?" he hooted.

"Oh, I never saw that coming, and if I had known it would happen, I probably wouldn't have gone, no matter what your mother and Leilah said."

"You played high jinks with them, didn't you?" he asked knowingly after it occurred to him that it would perfectly explain why she had gotten drunk and been foolhardy enough to confront him in a brothel.

"How did you know?" she asked perplexedly.

"Never play high jinks with those two. They get you drunk, and then they take advantage of you. They're like phoukas or leprechauns."

Eurydice's shoulders shook with silent laughter. "You speak as one who knows from experience."

"Oh, aye, I do."

"Are you going to tell me what you're doing?" she finally asked quietly.

Ellsworth rubbed at his chin thoughtfully before he sighed resignedly. "All right. Here it is: someone wants to help Napoleon escape from Saint Helena."

Eurydice raised an eyebrow. "That's it?" she asked doubtfully. "He's only just got there."

"True," agreed Ellsworth.

"It's in the middle of the Atlantic."

"Also true."

"That's why you've been away from home so much?"

"Well, there is more than one someone with this idea in mind, so I have to get the ones sorted out that I know about and find out if any of them are actually capable of doing it. As difficult as it was to get him there, it cannot be allowed, even if they don't intend to help him attempt to rule the world again."

Eurydice looked at him with disbelieving amusement for a moment, finding it difficult to believe something so simple could be so complicated, but then her expression grew serious and her step slowed somewhat as she began to think.

"What is it?" he asked concernedly.

"I can think of one person who might at least be very determined to try."

"Who?"

"Whoever it was that killed Signor Merletto and tried to make you take the blame for it. Whatever Merletto had to tell you must have been important. You must have been very close to finding answers for the person to kill him. Either that, or the man is so insane that killing Merletto was of no consequence to achieving his goal as long as it stopped you, which makes him dangerous, even if he never gets Napoleon off that island."

Ellsworth tapped the end of his nose. "A name was what Anneliese was dangling in front of me. I've been trying to get her to tell me since I got back."

"Oh, Gareth, if she's working for him, that means he knows who you are, if he didn't already know after Venice," said Eurydice anxiously.

Ellsworth gave her shoulders a squeeze and kissed the top of her head. "You let me worry about that. It's part of my job," he soothed.

≪ ≫

Anneliese lay on the couch in the drawing room of her private apartments. A doctor had been to set her arm and to do what he could for her nose. It was unlikely her nose would heal to the perfect straightness it had before being broken, and Anneliese was enraged and feeling vengeful against the woman who had done it. The doctor had given her laudanum, but every breath she took made her nose throb.

"What do you know about his wife?" asked the man sitting at the end of the couch with her feet in his lap.

"I hate the bitch," spat Anneliese darkly.

"Not helpful," said the man pleasantly.

Anneliese rolled her eyes and shrugged. "Not much. Her father is a duke or something in Britain, and she came to Vienna for the music. She's become Salieri's pet, performed at the Theater an der Wien a time or two, and will be performing at the Burg. She's also apparently well-to-do because all the money she's made is being given to the Taubstummen Institut."

"Hmm," said the man thoughtfully. "Anything else?"

"That's about it," said Anneliese flatly, "other than I get the impression their marriage was not a love match."

"No?"

"He wouldn't talk about her much, but I think he was forced to marry her."

"Are you sure they *are* married?"

"Why would you doubt it, Cesaire?"

"I just find it very convenient a man like him would marry a woman like her...someone who could do...this," he said as he waved a hand in her direction.

Anneliese started to snort through her nose derisively and winced at the pain it caused.

"I've not seen or heard anything to indicate otherwise, but it took more than luck for her to do this," said Anneliese as she gingerly lifted her arm. "Bruno said she would have broken his arm if he hadn't done as she told him."

"Do we know her name?"

"Lady Eurydice Ellsworth, formerly Savage."

"On the contrary, my love, I would say she is *still* savage," said Cesaire thoughtfully, "and will need to be dealt with just like...her husband."

Chapter Twenty Six

The walk from Juden Gasse to Singer Strasse wasn't as far as Eurydice had feared it would be, but her toes and the tip of her nose were still numb by the time they reached home. Agniezka had left a shift and dressing gown lying at the foot of the bed, and Eurydice quickly changed into them, carefully draping the clothes she removed onto the bench at her dressing table. The thin silk of her night clothes did nothing to protect her against the cold, but she couldn't bear the thought of wearing something thicker to sleep. She would be too uncomfortable. Besides, until recently, she didn't keep her shift on for long once she got into bed anyhow, and she had the feeling that was about to resume. She washed her face and brushed her teeth and nearly ran across the room to climb into bed under the blankets. Ellsworth had added more wood to the fire, but the floor made her already chilly toes even colder.

Ellsworth was already in the bed warming it, and he didn't hesitate to pull her toward him to kiss her once she got there. He moaned softly at the back of his throat as he pulled her even tighter against him, delighted that she returned his kisses enthusiastically, almost with impatience. Now that she knew the truth, all was forgiven, and he had never doubted it would be. For several minutes, he simply enjoyed having her close to him, kissing her, becoming lost in the smell and feel of her. He finally lifted his head to look at her amusedly.

"Your feet are like ice," he chortled.

Eurydice smiled impudently and ran one of them up his bare leg, and she felt him cringe from the coldness. She had noticed he became cold easily, almost like Psyche, even if he bore it without complaining.

"So do something to warm them up," she purred seductively.

Ellsworth tugged at the front of her shift. "This is in my way."

Rather than sitting up and exposing herself to the cold, Eurydice slid herself further under the blankets and pulled the shift over her head. She put her hand out from under the blankets, holding the shift, and tossed it in what she hoped was the direction of the floor. She moved closer to Ellsworth and began to place kisses up his stomach as she slowly moved her way back to the top of the bed. He jumped at the contact, not able to see what she was doing under the blankets, and he sighed at the back of his throat when she smoothed a hand down his side to his hip as she toyed at one of his nipples with her teeth. Her head finally emerged, and she kissed him temptingly on the lips.

"Hi," she said with a grin.

"Hallo," drawled Ellsworth warmly, and he wrapped an arm around her waist to pull her against him as he began to kiss her neck.

Eurydice wound her fingers in his hair as he laved one of her nipples with his tongue, and she put her leg over his waist to press herself even closer against him. She was already quivering just from being near him; she had missed him so much. He rolled her onto her back and kissed his way down her stomach to begin playing her with his mouth, and Eurydice choked out his name on a whisper. He had one of her legs draped over his shoulder, and her heel dug into his back as she began to orgasm, her back arching off the bed. He took his time kissing his way back up her body to her lips, his touch gentle, almost reverent, and Eurydice felt tears sting her eyes and she inhaled emotionally as he kissed her.

She put a hand to his cheek and wound herself around him to cling to him as he slowly glided into her. He stayed unmoving inside her for a few minutes as they kissed and nuzzled, and Eurydice thought her heart was going to burst simply because it couldn't possibly hold the things she felt at that moment. She was astonished she could care for him so much so soon. He began to steadily plunge in and out of her, and she loved watching his face, seeing the pleasure and need, the intentness and care. There was more involved than just the satisfaction of a physical craving for her, and seeing the expression on his face, she could believe it was the same for him.

"Oh, I missed you," he sighed longingly as he lowered his head to kiss her. "You are so wet, so…sublime."

Eurydice moaned and clung to him helplessly as she began to orgasm, and she smiled tenderly and put a hand to his cheek when Ellsworth came with her. They trembled and sighed together, and when it was over, Ellsworth wrapped his arms around her and rested his head onto the pillow beside hers, his breathing ragged. Eurydice kept him cradled against her, oblivious to his weight bearing down on her.

"My feet aren't cold anymore," she said tiredly after a time, once she was able to breathe somewhat normally again.

Ellsworth chuckled and kissed the side of her neck, and then he moved off of her and pulled her close to his side. Eurydice settled her head onto his chest and smoothed her hand down his side to rest it at his hip with a contented sigh. She placed one of her legs over his and snuggled against him. It was so good to be back where she belonged.

"I have to go to St. Petersburg," he said quietly after a few minutes.

Eurydice had been just on the point of dozing off when he spoke, and her eyes sprang open. She lifted her head to look at him.

"What? Why?" she asked with a frown.

"Your father sent me a letter and said I had to go."

Eurydice started to ask him why her father had told him to go, but she had been pushing matters just getting him to tell her his assignment. Whatever the reason, it was connected to his mission, and that was all she needed to know. She smoothed a hand over his chest contemplatively.

"When?"

"I'm not going at least until after you play at the Burg, but as soon as can be arranged after that," he said evenly, and he bent down to kiss her forehead where it was etched with a frown.

"Then I'm going, too," she said decisively.

"Eurydice," he sighed tiredly.

"I've been invited to perform there and other places, too—some on the way, some not. I have nothing else to do once I play the Burg," she said reasonably. "There is nothing to stop me from going."

"I don't think it would be a good idea," said Ellsworth hesitantly. He had not been looking forward to being away from her, and he disliked the thought of it even more now that they had reconciled.

"Why not? You'll have to sneak there, won't you?" she asked logically.

"Ye-es," he said slowly, "somewhat."

"If I'm going to perform, it makes it unnecessary to sneak. It gives you a perfectly valid reason for going, which might make certain parties less likely to be suspicious and more likely to give something away. Don't you think?"

Ellsworth looked at her consideringly. She did have a point...a very good point. It would provide him with an alibi, so to speak, and she would be with him. Not only did he emotionally not want to be away from her, but after reading her diary, he wanted to be with her to protect her. The weather was turning very cold, and he couldn't escape the feeling he didn't have much time.

"But how could that be arranged?" he asked thoughtfully. "His grace didn't give me a specific time, but I'm sure he intended it to happen before the end of the year, not to mention *I* want to have it done before then."

"That is the difficulty," said Eurydice with a deep sigh, "but I do have almost two weeks before the performance at the Burgtheater." She covered a yawn with the back of her hand, and then she leaned forward to kiss him languidly. "We can talk about it tomorrow. I won't be able to do much until Thursday in any case," she said as she settled herself back into her comfortable position and made sure they were covered by the blankets.

Ellsworth smoothed his hand down her back in a caress and kissed the top of her head affectionately. He really loved his wife.

By sunset on Thursday, Eurydice was well on her way to arranging what could be considered her Grand Tour. She had discussed it with Ellsworth on

Wednesday, and the only part of it that he would need to help with (for the most part) would be finding a suitable coach—meaning the seats would have to be well-cushioned and it would have to be well-sprung, if not for Eurydice then definitely for Agniezka. They would be going to St. Petersburg, but she had accepted other invitations as well. She felt—and he agreed—that it would only provide better cover for Ellsworth if she went to more places than just St. Petersburg. And then she wouldn't have to go one place, come home, only to leave again for another. As much as she disliked riding in a coach, this would take care of all of it at once…at least, until she received more invitations.

The journey to St. Petersburg for Ellsworth to do whatever he needed to do and for her to perform would also give Agniezka the opportunity to tend to her divorce without making it necessary for Eurydice to tell Ellsworth anything. Agniezka had given her permission to discuss it with him, but she still didn't feel comfortable doing so. Now, she wouldn't have to. That had only occurred to her on Wednesday when she was talking to Ellsworth, and it made her more determined than ever to arrange this as quickly as possible.

The only difficulty to that would be exactly how long it would take for the judge to see Agniezka (if that's who she had to see) and if Sergei could be found to be at the proceedings. Agniezka said he was still living in the same house as when they were married…at least, that was what her father had told her. Locating him shouldn't be difficult. The judge, though. That was the tricky part. Eurydice didn't know how the legal system worked in Russia, but things like that could take months in Britain…years. They wouldn't have that long. They would have only days, not weeks.

Eurydice wrote a letter to the lawyer whose name Sheerness had given her, Valentin Srdanov, asking that he move things along as much as he could without Agniezka being there because they wouldn't be able to stay in the city for long. If he could get the preliminaries taken care of before they arrived, appearing before the judge would be all that remained…in theory. She gave him an estimate of when they would arrive—close to the start of December, but she had yet to determine their accommodations. As soon as she knew what those were, she would give him a more exact date for their arrival.

As the time approached for her final performance at the Theater an der Wien on Monday, Eurydice had almost finalized her itinerary. There were a few more details to decide, but it was, for the most part, set. Before she spoke to the people who had invited her to perform, she asked Ellsworth if there were any places he "wanted" to go. What she had meant was if there were any he thought going to would put him nearer to finishing his assignment. There were one or two, Venice included, and Eurydice was excited at the prospect of going back. The tour would take them in a wide loop across the continent that would end close enough to Britain that she would be able to go visit her family, which was also something that made her very happy.

But she didn't intend this trip to take months. She was planning to be with her family by the beginning of February. Considering how the weather was likely to be, and the distances involved, there were only a few places she would give more than one performance, and it would be unlikely that any of the performances would involve concertos or a symphony. She made sure that was understood by the people who had invited her. She did tell them that if they wanted her to perform a concerto or one of the sonatas for piano and violin, they would be responsible for rehearsing the orchestra or pianist prior to her arrival. Now that Herr Hohler had published some of her music, it was available for them to learn, but she wasn't requesting it. If they did want her to perform a concerto, the amount of time she would have to rehearse with the orchestra would be very limited. If she didn't like the way it sounded after a rehearsal, she wouldn't do it.

Her third—and final—performance at the Theater an der Wien was once again successful. She was pleased the run had gone so well, but she was glad it was over. She invited Franz and Salieri to dine with them at Palais Crantzdorf that evening, and for a change, Franz provided the entertainment after the meal by playing one of his own sonatas rather than Eurydice needing to. She found it peculiar to be part of the audience, but she enjoyed sitting on the couch beside Ellsworth holding hands, leaning her head against his shoulder.

Once he had quit going to Rathmueller's, Ellsworth was home more often. He had gone out on Friday and Saturday, but that had been it. He was gone frequently during the day, still, but part of that was because he had to make arrangements for a coach for the tour in addition to whatever else he was doing.

Eurydice did finally ask him on Sunday where he went during the day, feeling emboldened after what had happened on Halloween. She was surprised when he said he usually spent an hour or so with the children in the nursery every day after breakfast, and then he spent about the same amount of time in the library reading the papers. Then he would go to a coffee house for dinner and just listen to the conversations around him. After that he would go to an apartment he had let to exercise for a few hours. Eurydice was curious about what the apartment might look like, but she wasn't going to ask him to take her there. Knowing what he was doing was enough to help set her mind at ease.

She had let him watch her practice *t'ai chi*. He was fascinated, and after the second time, he asked her to teach him. Eurydice was a bit disconcerted by that. Keung had taught her, and everyone else in her family, but she wasn't sure that she was capable of teaching anyone else. Considering what he already knew, she couldn't understand why he would see the need. On Sunday, she had him follow her movements, explaining what they were called as she did them. She was unsurprised to see he would have no difficulty learning it, no matter how inept she might be as a teacher. The key to the exercises was performing them slowly, but she was sure he could see that doing them at a faster speed made them not very dissimilar from some of the *kata* in *jujutsu*.

The ball season officially began the Saturday following her last performance at the Theater an der Wien, but neither Cora or Leilah could convince Eurydice she needed to go to the first event. She did promise she would go to at least one before she and Ellsworth left for St. Petersburg, but it would have to be after she performed at the Burgtheater. Since it would be the only one she would attend, she asked that they try to find a redoute. She had never been to a masked ball before, and she would like to go to one. Cora was pleased to tell her there would be one at the Redoutensaal on the sixteenth.

On the Monday Eurydice was to perform at the Burgtheater, she spent the morning doing a final rehearsal with Salieri and the orchestra. They'd had a month to prepare, and she anticipated it would go well. Even Herr Schreyvogel had smiled with satisfaction after sitting in on the rehearsal. Not only was he the theater's artistic director, he was also a music critic, a much harder to please critic than Herr Bakkeman was Eurydice's impression. When Eurydice saw him smile, it gave her even more confidence things would go well.

The Burgtheater had a deceptive appearance from the outside. Looking at it from the front, it was very narrow and small compared to other parts of the imperial palace that adjoined it as it jutted out into the Michaeler Platz. The Theater an der Wien seemed much larger, but the Burg was able to hold more than eleven hundred guests. Tickets had been available for purchase almost a fortnight beforehand, and by that morning they had all been sold. Eurydice had made sure to reserve a box for her family before there were no more available.

Agniezka dressed her in a light green silk gown embroidered with a darker green thread and gold tinsel. The edge of the bodice was trimmed with a thick gold braid, and the sleeves were fitted to just above her elbow then widened into a soft, flowing triangle that extended just beyond her hand in length. Her hair was braided and coiled, but Agniezka had wound through it with a piece of gold silk, which she tied into a small bow at the side of her head. She looked radiant, her cheeks pink, her eyes bright with excitement and nerves, and it only helped that the sadness that had been there until recently was gone.

They arrived at the theater almost thirty minutes before time for the performance. Cora, Leilah, and Agniezka all went to take their seats in the box Eurydice had reserved, but Ellsworth walked with her to the back of the stage. Now that she was there and could hear the noise from the many conversations of the audience, Eurydice was becoming nervous. She had a strange taste in her mouth, as if she had eaten something that didn't agree with her, and her stomach was in a knot. She had the very distinct feeling she was going to be sick. Even after the three performances at the Theater an der Wien, she had still not grown accustomed to being in front of that many people.

Salieri, Herr Schreyvogel, and Count Palffy all stood at the edge of the stage waiting for her when she arrived. The piano she would be using was in the center of the stage, not far from the edge near the orchestra pit. She could hear the musicians tuning their instruments, blending with the sounds of the audience, and she put a hand to her stomach in an effort to calm the butterflies she felt flittering around in it and took a deep breath. She didn't know what she had been thinking to believe she would want to do this in strange cities all across Europe. At least in Vienna, she had grown accustomed to things.

The three men all kissed her hand when she arrived, and Palffy and Schreyvogel both soon left after wishing her luck. At one point while she tuned her violin, she heard the audience grow still. The conversations soon resumed, but not with the same loudness as before. She was puzzled by it, but she was too nervous to wonder for long. Salieri kissed both her cheeks, and then he made his way to the stand in the orchestra pit where he would conduct.

"You can do this," encouraged Ellsworth after Salieri left. "It's not as if you haven't done this before, right?"

Eurydice took a deep breath and nodded in an effort to calm herself, but he could see she was still anxious. He gave her a warm kiss on the lips, and it didn't help as much as he had hoped it would, but thankfully it didn't make things worse. They could hear applause as Salieri mounted the stand, and Eurydice knew it was time for her to go as well. She felt clammy, and she couldn't understand why she was feeling so nauseous. Ellsworth was right: she had done this before, and the audience wasn't much larger than it had been at the Theater an der Wien. Salieri had said it was a more "intimate" venue, but it hadn't been intimate at all.

"Do you want me to stay here or go to my seat?" asked Ellsworth as he smoothed a calming hand down her cheek.

"Stay...no, go," she said as she rubbed her forehead anxiously. She moaned and put her forehead against his shoulder.

Ellsworth smiled amusedly and put an arm around her. "I'll stay," he said soothingly.

Eurydice lifted her head and nodded, and then after taking a deep, calming breath, she walked onto the stage. The audience erupted with loud applause, and she smiled hesitantly as she went to stand in front of the piano. It was a Broadwood, while the one in the pit was a Streicher. Both instruments were very fine, but she was accustomed to playing Broadwoods. She had requested that one be found for her use, and if nothing else could have been found, she would have arranged for the one from Palais Crantzdorf to be taken to the theater. She settled the Stradivarius beneath her chin and looked to Salieri. He raised his hands, and the first concerto began.

As Eurydice lost herself in the music, she was able to dispel some of the anxiety she felt, especially when she looked to the box where Cora, Leilah, and Agniezka sat or to the side of the stage where Ellsworth stood watching her. That was until she looked to the left of the stage and realized the Imperial boxes were occupied by several people. She couldn't see how many or who they were, but it was enough for her to know they were there.

She tried to forget. She tried to calm herself by reasoning that royalty were people who enjoyed music, just the same as anyone else, but it only marginally helped. She did get through the concerto without any mistakes, but her stomach was even more twisted when it was finished thirty minutes later. The audience applauded, and she gave a graceful curtsy and a hesitant smile, but she was relieved to walk off the stage to Ellsworth where he stood waiting.

Salieri would conduct the orchestra through the symphony, and then she would return to the stage for the piano concerto. Salieri had suggested she play first violin for the symphony, but she hadn't wanted to usurp that right from the musician who normally had the honor. After seeing the Imperial family, at least in some fashion, was attending, she needed the time to compose herself.

Ellsworth pulled her toward him to give her a proud hug and a kiss, and then she put her violin into its case.

"There are people in the Imperial boxes!" she whispered perturbedly.

Ellsworth gave her an amused smile. "Of course there are. What did you think Salieri meant when he said he wanted you to perform for the Court?"

Eurydice frowned and shrugged. "I don't know. I suppose I thought he meant the courtiers, hangers-on, officials, and whatnot. I didn't think he actually meant *the* Court. Do you think the emperor is up there?"

Ellsworth cautiously peeked around the side of the stage as the symphony began, and then he turned back to look at her.

"I would say yes, and his wife, a few children, his brother...," he trailed off with a grin. "Now, hush. I haven't heard this, remember?"

Eurydice snapped her teeth together on further comments because it was true. He had heard her practice for the Theater an der Wien, but he hadn't been to the Burgtheater with her for any of those rehearsals. During the whole time, they had either not been speaking, or he had been busy making arrangements for St. Petersburg and elsewhere. Ellsworth had found two chairs for them, and they sat down as the first movement continued. Ellsworth put an arm around her shoulders, and Eurydice relaxed against him with a slightly shuddering sigh. Her stomach began to feel a little better once she sat down, but it still seemed to have a ball of tension wound in it that wouldn't quite go away.

Eurydice and Ellsworth sat listening to the symphony, but she couldn't quite relax. She should have known Salieri had meant he wanted her to perform for the Imperial family, but why not at a private performance? She wouldn't have been any less anxious, but at least then she would have had no misunderstanding about who her audience would be. She had no doubt he was being paid for this performance, and he might have been given a share of the proceeds from the Theater an der Wien as well, but she didn't think he needed the money so bad as that.

The symphony didn't last nearly as long as Eurydice had hoped it would, but she only had to get through the piano concerto and it would be over. Despite her nervousness, the performance was going well. Ellsworth kissed her cheek, and the audience applauded as she walked back onto the stage to take her seat at the piano. She did her best not to look at the Imperial boxes, and once she had to concentrate on the music, that became easier despite their being directly in her line of vision when her head was raised.

At the end of the concerto, she rose from her seat at the piano and curtsied, and then she waved her hand in the direction of the orchestra with an appreciative smile, as much in thanks as to have the audience applaud for them as well. They had done an outstanding job. Salieri joined her on the stage, and they both bowed and curtsied to the enthusiastic applause of the audience before he escorted her off the stage to the left. Eurydice looked back over her shoulder disconcertedly to the right of the stage where she had left Ellsworth, and then she looked at Salieri with a slight frown of confusion.

"Where are we going?" she asked nervously.

"There are some people who would like to meet you," said Salieri with a proud smile.

Eurydice didn't need to wonder who he meant. "Oh, but my husband and my family...," she trailed off concernedly.

"They will completely understand, my dear," said Salieri with a chuckle of amusement.

He led her first through one doorway then another, up a flight of stairs to a hallway that ended in still more doors, but these were barred by two guards in Imperial livery. Eurydice wasn't sure if they were still in the theater, and she also wasn't sure she was prepared for this. Her stomach didn't feel right. She wasn't sure if it was upset from the concert or if she was truly that nervous to be meeting the emperor or if she had actually eaten something disagreeable. As it had just started before she arrived at the theater, it was likely it was just anxiety, but whatever the cause, she had the inescapable feeling she was going to be sick. She put a fluttery hand to her stomach as the doors were opened, and the guards stood aside for them to enter the room beyond.

Several people were there, but Eurydice didn't recognize most of them. Count Palffy and Herr Schreyvogel were there, but those were the only ones she knew. She couldn't tell who was a member of the Imperial family and who was not. Some of the men wore medals or badges, but she didn't know what any of them signified. She quickly determined none of the younger men were the emperor, but that still left three or four to choose from. The men and women all stood around talking, and Eurydice put a hand to her stomach as she felt queasy. She wanted to sit down. As she entered the room with Salieri, everyone stopped talking and turned to look at her. She wished Ellsworth was with her...or Agniezka. When everyone began to applaud, her cheeks turned a bright pink, and she held on even tighter to Salieri's arm.

Salieri began to introduce her to the people as he led her among them. The first was Prince Albert of Saxony, by far the oldest man in the room, and an uncle by marriage to the emperor. He was very nice, and he told her she played beautifully. Eurydice blushed a brighter shade and told him thank you. He then told her that she reminded him of a Russian countess he had once met when he was younger, a Countess Alexa Goydanova, who had also played the violin. Eurydice was astonished and explained the countess was her grandmother. That prompted him to give a brief chuckle and say that would be the perfect explanation of the resemblance.

She was next introduced to the Archduchesses Leopoldina and Clementina, two of the emperor's daughters. Both were about the same age as Eurydice, perhaps a little younger, one blond, the other with light brown hair, but they both had the same blue eyes, soft features, and similar mouths. They were also very kind, and Eurydice became a bit flustered when they asked her where she had gotten her gown. Of all the things she thought they would ask about, her dress was not among them. She explained it had been made by her family's dressmaker in Wales, and they both seemed genuinely disappointed to discover they would be unable to acquire their own.

Then she was introduced to another daughter, the Empress Marie Louise, Duchess of Parma. She was Napoleon's wife, and until the Congress of Vienna, she had been Empress of the French. She had the same blue eyes and mouth of her sisters, but her hair was more of a russet than brown. She had flawless pale skin, and she shared the same elegance and regality of carriage as her younger sisters. She also told Eurydice how much she enjoyed listening to her play. Eurydice tried not to stare, knowing who her husband was, and she had to wonder how the woman felt about all the things that had happened over the last two years since she had been separated from him. It was true the marriage had been one of state, but he *was* her husband.

She was then introduced to the emperor's brother, the Archduke Karl, and his new wife, Henrietta. He had interesting features, but he wasn't what Eurydice would call traditionally handsome, and his wife was less than half his age. Despite the age difference, they seemed very happy together and made a very striking couple. Eurydice thought Henrietta was very beautiful with pale skin, black hair, and dark eyes. To her surprise, Eurydice learned they were married within only a few days of when she had married Ellsworth. She idly wondered if they'd had a honeymoon and if so where they had gone. Like everyone else she had met so far, both of them were very kind and gracious, telling her how much they had enjoyed her performance.

Then she was introduced to Prince von Metternich. She didn't remember her Grandfather Sanders. She only knew of him what her mother, father, and *babushka* had told her, but she felt the man standing in front of her and her grandfather would probably be very similar in personality. While she wouldn't say he had charisma, there was something charming and magnetic about him. There was nothing unassuming about him, but she wouldn't say he was arrogant, just *very* self-assured. And really, as Salieri had been introducing her to the people in the room, of all of them, she had actually thought *he* was the emperor. To her surprise, he spoke to her in excellent English. What surprised her even more was when he told her that he had met her parents and her grandmother years before when he had been to England and that he still maintained a correspondence with her father. He had to agree with Prince Albert that she bore a striking resemblance to her grandmother.

Salieri next introduced her to Graf von Stackelberg, who she might have thought from his title was Germanic, but she discovered he was from Estonia, and an ambassador for Russia. He was very polite and soft-spoken, with blue eyes and gray hair. He thanked her for her performance and mentioned that he felt the violin concerto had a bit of a Russian theme. She confirmed that it did. He then asked her if she would be willing to compose something for a smaller group of instruments, such as a quartet or duet, on commission, and Eurydice had to politely refuse. She couldn't bring herself to tell him she was incapable of composing something by request, so she instead told him she didn't compose for financial gain, which was true but not the entire truth.

When Salieri introduced her to the emperor and empress, after meeting his brother, it was obvious that he had to be. They bore a strong resemblance to one another. The main differences were that Franz had blond hair that was already turning white and receding. Karl had dark brown, curly hair that showed no gray. Eurydice didn't think there was that much difference between their ages. The empress, Maria Ludovika, was very beautiful, and Eurydice knew she could not possibly be the mother of his children because she didn't look much older than Marie Louise, his eldest daughter. She had dark hair and eyes, with delicate features. She seemed very fragile to Eurydice, but she appeared to be happy.

"Your majesties," said Eurydice quietly as she gave her most graceful curtsy once she was introduced. She felt slightly dizzy once she straightened, and she realized she hadn't eaten since that morning.

"A beautiful performance, Lady Eurydice," said the emperor with a kind smile.

"Thank you, your majesty," said Eurydice, and she thought if her cheeks turned any pinker her face was going to start tingling.

"I understand you've been donating all the money you are making to the Taubstummen Institut?"

"Yes, your majesty," confirmed Eurydice. "I have no need of it, and I have a younger brother who is deaf. Naturally, an institution that assists those affected by deafness holds a special place for me."

He smiled understandingly. "Your generosity is to be commended. There are some who believe too much is not enough," he said thoughtfully, giving a slightly hard look to someone behind her. She was sure he was directing the comment to that person in particular, but she thought better of turning to see who he meant. "You will be performing again soon?"

"I'm afraid not, your majesty," said Eurydice hesitantly. She was sure she shouldn't be disagreeing with the emperor, but it was unavoidable. "At least, I won't be for some time. I leave for a tour on Saturday, and I'm not sure when I'll be returning."

"A tour? Where are you going?" he demanded imperiously.

"First, to Warsaw, followed by Petersburg—"

"You are to play for the tsar, then?"

"No, your majesty, I don't believe so," said Eurydice quietly. She could feel her cheeks beginning to sting from the redness. She didn't think she had ever blushed so much for so long in her life.

"You will play for Alexander," he ordered.

Eurydice frowned disconcertedly, and she opened and closed her mouth a few times as she tried to think of how best to phrase what she needed to say without offending or angering him.

"Forgive me, your majesty, but how am I to do that?"

"Because I say you will," he said firmly.

Eurydice was unwell. She felt queasy and dizzy, and the anxiety the emperor was causing only made it worse. She wished Ellsworth was with her.

"I will send him a letter and Stackelberg and Metternich will also send letters, and it will be all arranged," said Franz finally.

"Oh," sighed Eurydice, and she thought she was going to faint. "Your majesty is most gracious and kind," she said breathlessly, not sure what else she could say. She most certainly couldn't argue and refuse to do it.

"Think nothing of it," he said, waving a dismissive hand through the air. "Where else are you going?"

"Moscow, Kiev, Pest, Laibach, Venice, Milan, Geneva, and Paris. Then I will go home to Britain to spend time with my family before returning here. I don't anticipate that I will be back before April."

"You're not going to any of the Germanic states or Prussia," he said critically.

"No, your majesty. I've not been invited. Perhaps another time."

"Humph," said Franz disdainfully, and Eurydice couldn't decide if it was directed at her or the Prussians and the Germans.

Eurydice felt she had spent enough time with the Imperial family. She had met everyone and talked to them and everyone else in the room, and what she really wanted was her husband. She should be hungry and felt that she *needed* to eat something, but the thought of it didn't appeal to her. She was hopeful that would improve once she was back with her family and on her way home.

"If your majesty will forgive me, I must return to my husband and family," she said quietly.

"Certainly, of course," said Franz understandingly. "The tsar will be expecting you when you arrive in St. Petersburg."

"As your majesty wishes," said Eurydice with a graceful curtsy.

She linked her arm through Salieri's elbow, and she wondered if he noticed she was trembling. She wasn't able to start breathing normally again until they left the room and he led her through the corridors between the palace and the theater. She sighed with relief when they arrived at the lobby, and Ellsworth stood there with Cora, Leilah, and Agniezka waiting for her. Salieri kissed her hand and gave her a warm smile as he gave it a squeeze.

"If I don't see you before you leave, then I will hopefully see you when you return," he said proudly.

"Of course, Herr Kapellmeister," said Eurydice, giving him a weak smile.

After he left, Ellsworth turned her toward him with a concerned frown and smoothed a hand across her forehead and down her cheek. He knew where Salieri had taken her, but she looked unwell. Her eyes were glassy and her complexion was a shade he had never seen it before. Her cheeks were pink, but the underlying tone was very white, quite different from its usual golden color.

"Are you all right?" he asked worriedly.

"Yes…no…I don't know," she said dully, and luckily Ellsworth had his hands on her shoulders and was able to grab her as she weaved on her feet and almost collapsed in a faint.

The other three women gasped in alarm, but the dizziness was only temporary and Eurydice soon righted herself.

"Did he do something to you?" asked Ellsworth tensely.

"No, not really," said Eurydice weakly.

"What does that mean?" demanded Ellsworth.

"I think I just need something to eat," said Eurydice vaguely.

"What…did he…do?" demanded Ellsworth, still holding her by her upper arms.

"He took me to meet the Imperial family, and Metternich, and a Russian ambassador, and then the emperor commanded that I have to play for the tsar in St. Petersburg."

"*Commanded*?" said Ellsworth disbelievingly.

"Yes. He said: 'You will play for the tsar,'" she said in a fair imitation of the emperor, "when I told him I was going to Petersburg, and Franz said he would send Alexander a letter to make sure he knew I was coming," said Eurydice dully.

"And that's all that happened?" asked Ellsworth doubtfully.

"Yes," said Eurydice tiredly. "Can we go now? I need to eat something."

Ellsworth looked at her consideringly. He could understand why the emperor commanding her to perform for the tsar might upset her, but she seemed far more overwrought than he would expect even that to cause. He did know she had been too nervous to eat before the performance; perhaps that really was what made it worse. She did seem to be a little better. For a few minutes he had thought he might need to carry her. He put an arm around her shoulders after Agniezka helped her into her pelisse and cloak, and his concern lessened somewhat when she didn't seem quite so pale.

After they got home and had supper, Eurydice seemed to be back to herself again; although, Ellsworth did notice she didn't eat as much as usual. Until that night, she seemed healthy and fit, and once they were home and she had eaten, despite her mostly picking at her food, she didn't seem to be unwell. He hoped the mental strain of performing all over Europe wasn't going to prove too much for her. He hoped the tour wasn't going to be a bad idea. He thought for a time about looking at her diary to see if she'd had any dreams to account for it, but when she came to bed after having a bath and they made love, there was no lack of enthusiasm, and Ellsworth decided he had been concerned over nothing.

Agniezka dressed Eurydice in a new gown for the redoute. She had managed to get Eurydice to the dressmaker the first Friday in November, and the things she had ordered had been ready and delivered just that morning. It was made of a beautiful velvet that on first glance appeared to be dark green but shifted to burgundy in certain light. The bottom edge was trimmed in a wide band of embroidery in gold, black, and burgundy thread, and a matching, narrower band edged the bottom of the sleeves and bodice. She wore another necklace Psyche had brought back from Greece for her, made of silver with beads of onyx and agate and a beautiful medallion of translucent green amber with an inclusion of a small dragonfly, its wings perfectly spread.

Agniezka had made her mask with assistance from Ottilie. It was made of papier-mâché, covered in velvet that matched her dress, trimmed around the edges and the eyeholes with gold soutache. Both sides at the outer corners were adorned with matching, large, paste brooches with red, green, and purple stones (which were actually a set of earrings purchased at a secondhand shop) with satin ribbons of gold, green, black, and burgundy hanging down from them. To the right edge, there were also several feathers in black, green, and burgundy sticking up from the brooch, almost like a hair adornment. There was no handle; it was held in place by a satin ribbon Agniezka had found that matched the color of Eurydice's hair, and once it was tied behind her head, it would be almost unnoticeable.

Eurydice didn't put on the mask at the house; she would put it on once she reached the Redoutensaal because wearing it in the carriage or trying to walk in it for any distance would be too distracting. Ellsworth came out of Schellen's room carrying a mask of his own, infinitely simpler in design than hers, covered in black satin edged in gold. Eurydice told Agniezka that she wouldn't need to wait up for her, and she took Ellsworth's arm to go downstairs to meet Cora in the entrance hall. Her mask was light cream in color, edged along the top in white feathers, and it had a handle. Eurydice was going to wish hers had one before the night was through, she was sure.

The ride in the carriage to the hall was brief, and Etzel opened the door of the vehicle to let them out. The air was very cold, and Eurydice could feel a frostiness to it. She thought it might snow. Once they were inside, Ellsworth took their coats and wraps to be deposited in the cloak room, and Cora helped Eurydice tie on her mask. When Ellsworth came back, she helped him put his on, and Eurydice felt her heart flutter a little when she looked at him. He looked very dashing.

Just before they entered the room, an attendant gave both women their dance cards. The first two dances were marked through. Apparently, they were late and had already missed them. Ellsworth signed his name to Eurydice's card for two waltzes and an Allemande. As Eurydice examined her dance card, she was relieved to see most of the dances were ones she knew; at least, the names were the same. She hoped the steps weren't different. She marked through those she didn't know, deciding to use them for time to allow herself rest. She didn't know if any other men would ask her to dance, but she thought she should do it, just in case.

Leilah soon found them in the throng of attendees, and Eurydice was glad to see her mask tied as well. She had noticed there was a fairly even amount of those with handles and those without. Some men wore masks, some did not. Most of the masks weren't as elaborate as those worn for Carnival in Venice, but there were a few men and women who wore masks that covered their entire face, some even going so far as to have hats attached to them, but there weren't many. Leilah's was covered in red satin to match her gown and edged in gold with red feathers.

Friends of Leilah and Cora began to come see them, and Eurydice's dance card steadily filled, making her glad she had marked through some. There were very few unclaimed before the end of the song that was playing when they entered. One of the good things about wearing the mask was that it saved her from being accosted by strangers who had seen her perform...for the most part. Those who were within earshot to hear when someone addressed her by name soon came to express their admiration, and it was one of the rare times when Eurydice found herself wishing her name wasn't so distinctive. She bore it politely, but it made her uncomfortable. It was as if they felt her performing on the stage had been the only introduction they needed. Eurydice thought it was bad manners and in poor taste.

As Ellsworth led her onto the floor for a waltz, Eurydice was glad this was to be the only function she would be attending in Vienna that year. Perhaps next year, after she grew accustomed to everything, she would feel more—if not enthusiastic, then at least—willing to attend the Season. She was hoping her husband would be done with his assignment by then and they would move back to Britain. She didn't care for the Season there, either, but at least she was familiar with it. The only thing she would miss would be the accessibility to good music and some of the greatest composers who had ever lived.

She had dared to write a letter to Beethoven, thanking him for playing with her and for attending one of her performances at the Theater an der Wien. She hadn't expected that he would write her back, and she had been utterly surprised when he did. His response had been friendly and encouraging, and he had said he anticipated much more great music from her for years to come. He also asked her to continue to write to him as often as she was able and told her that she should never hesitate to contact him should she require his assistance for anything. She had glowed with excitement and happiness after she read the letter, and her reaction didn't diminish much even after she had read it the *third* time. She had written a reply and put his letter in her keepsake chest, and she would do that with any others he might send.

Both Leilah and Cora were proud she was to make a tour of Europe, and yet they were also sad she would be leaving them so soon after arriving. They were a little concerned that she would be making the journey just as the weather turned so cold, and she would miss Christmas. Eurydice assured them she would be fine. She had every confidence Ellsworth would take care of her, and Agniezka would be there as well. Eurydice had already purchased

Christmas gifts for Cora, Leilah, and the Windhams, but she told them all they could absolutely not open them until the appropriate day. She told them she would write often, and she gave them a copy of her itinerary so if they tried to write back they would have some idea of where to send the letters for her to actually receive them. She was going to miss them just as much as they were going to miss her.

"I like your mask," said Ellsworth softly in her ear while they danced.

"Do you now?" said Eurydice with a teasing smile.

"Mm-hmm. I was thinking maybe later you could wear it to bed."

Eurydice's eyes widened in surprise as she looked at him, and then she laughed amusedly.

"Only if you wear yours," she purred.

"You have yourself a deal, sweetheart," he drawled seductively.

Their relationship had continued to improve since Halloween, and the weeks when she had thought he was having an affair with Anneliese were almost like a bad dream. Eurydice felt more than ever that she could not have chosen a better husband. He was kind and handsome, a more than adequate lover, and he accepted her just as she was. He didn't grow irritated when she played a piece of music repeatedly. He didn't try to make her be more social. He was encouraging and supportive, and she couldn't remember why she had been so unwilling to marry him. There were still secrets, but she didn't care, and he didn't seem to mind hers either. She couldn't quite say for sure that she loved him, but she couldn't imagine being without him.

When their dance was over, Ellsworth escorted her to the edge of the floor and stayed with her until her next partner came for her before he took Leilah out. She enjoyed her dance with Count von Heide, but she found to her surprise that she needed to find a garderobe. She had gone before they left the house, and that was usually sufficient until she got home. Unfortunately, she wasn't free for the next dance, and Herr Bakkeman escorted her out. By the time he took her back to the edge of the floor, she was almost desperate, but she was free for the next dance. Leilah happened to be standing there when she arrived, and Eurydice asked as politely as she could where she might find the facilities. Leilah was free for the dance as well, and she took Eurydice back to the lobby and led her down a short hall, pointing out the cloak room along the way and the room where she might go for refreshment.

The room they entered was the powder room, and Leilah pointed to a door at the other end. Eurydice went to it, and when she opened it she almost turned around and left again. If she hadn't needed to go as bad as she did, she probably would have. The smell didn't sit well with her stomach, and she had to fight a wave of nausea. There were other women in the room, availing themselves of its use, and Eurydice was able to find one space available near the farthest end from the door. She took a deep breath and held it as she went to it. She did what she needed to do, and then she went to the bidet to rinse and dry and left as quickly as she could. She didn't breathe again until she was back to the other room, and she was grateful for how long she was able to go without air.

Leilah was at one of the mirrors in the powder room, carefully removing a few drips of wax that had fallen onto her dress and hair from the chandeliers. When she saw Eurydice, she helped her do the same, including one that had become attached to her mask.

"That room doesn't smell good," said Eurydice, wrinkling her nose.

"Really?" said Leilah in surprise. "I've never noticed it was any worse than others I've been in. At least they have bidets here and water flowing through the latrine. Some don't, and those are the worst."

Eurydice couldn't comment. She'd never used public facilities before, so she didn't know how these compared to elsewhere. She only knew that the water closets in her family's homes did not smell. She hadn't noticed that the garderobe in Palais Crantzdorf had a smell, either. She would imagine water running through to clear things out would reduce the odor. Apparently, it didn't. Either that, or her senses were too sensitive for it or it saw too much use for the water to do its work.

They had a few minutes before the end of the song playing when they returned to the hall, and Leilah spent the time gossiping about the people who were there. Eurydice didn't know how Leilah could recognize them in their masks, but she supposed it came from the many years Leilah had been there. Eurydice would become familiar with them, too, eventually. Her next partner soon came for her, and she went with him for a cotillion.

Ellsworth was waiting for her when she went back to the edge of the floor, and they went out for the Allemande. He was glad to hear she was enjoying herself, and he reminded her that she had promised to wear her mask to bed. Then she was claimed by her next partner when he returned her to the edge of the floor. Once the gavotte ended, to her surprise, she realized she needed to go to the garderobe yet again. Her next dance was free, but she couldn't recall ever needing to use the facilities once, much less twice, ever before. Now that she knew where it was, she wasn't concerned about having Cora or Leilah go with her, but she *was* concerned that she needed to go so often. She hoped she wasn't developing an infection or some other problem. She'd never had one before so she wasn't sure, and she hadn't noticed any difficulties. She just *needed* to go. Perhaps she had drunk too much before she left the house. She didn't think she had, but it had to be the explanation.

She didn't find that the room smelled any better the second time she went, and she didn't stay any longer than necessary. She thought she was going to be sick, and the only thing that helped her manage to keep it under control was the thought that she might have to put her head near something that smelled so foul. That thought actually almost made things worse, but it made her more determined than ever to get out of the room. She stopped in front of a mirror in the powder room to make sure she hadn't acquired any new drips of wax, and then she left.

The song wasn't quite over when she got back to the dance hall. She looked through the people along the edge of the floor where she stood for someone she knew, but she didn't see anyone. After looking through the mass of people on the floor, she was able to spot Cora and Leilah, and after several seconds more, she was able to find Ellsworth dancing with someone on the other side of the room. She thought it might be Countess von Heide, but Eurydice couldn't quite remember what her mask looked like to be sure.

"Have you been deserted, Lady Eurydice?" asked a man standing beside her. He hadn't been there a minute ago.

Eurydice jumped when he spoke because he was standing very close. She turned to look at him, but she didn't think she knew him. And when she turned toward him, either she did it too quickly or her stomach was still upset from the garderobe, but she felt dizzy. She had to blink a few times and take a deep breath to keep herself from weaving. She hoped she wasn't becoming ill, not so close to when she would be leaving for Petersburg. The sensation only lasted a few seconds, and she was then able to give him a full assessment.

He was one of the few wearing a mask to cover their whole face. It was gray with black and silver designs painted over its surface. It also had a black tricorn hat edged in silver braid and trimmed with gray feathers attached to it. Eurydice could only tell that his eyes were brown and he had dark hair. The mask didn't follow the actual contours of his face. He was tall and muscular, but that was the only other thing she could tell. She didn't remember the mask, but he might have not been wearing it when she met him earlier. She was terrible with names and faces, and his wearing the mask ruined any chance she might have of recalling who he was. She gave him a slight smile, hoping she might remember who he was if they spoke a little longer.

"No, I've not been deserted," she said evenly. "My husband will be claiming me for the waltz after the landler is over."

"A beautiful woman like you shouldn't be left alone," he said warmly.

Eurydice frowned slightly. He spoke German, but he wasn't a native. He spoke very well, but she detected another accent mingled with it. She would need to listen a little more before she could decide just what it was. His voice sounded young, and what little of him she could see behind the mask also seemed young. She thought he was in his thirties…not beyond forty. She still didn't recognize him, and asking him would be rude if they had already been introduced. They had to have been; otherwise, he wouldn't know her name.

"I'm in a room full of people; I'm not alone," she said with a dry smile. "Aside from that, here you are with me."

He chuckled, and she saw the corners of his eyes crinkle. "Ah, but perhaps I'm the reason you shouldn't be alone," he teased.

Eurydice blinked. "I'm sorry?" she asked confusedly.

"A woman like you is very tempting for a man like me," he said seductively. "Beautiful, wealthy, intelligent, gifted." He leaned closer and inhaled with his eyes closed. "And you smell intoxicating."

"I beg your pardon," she said stiffly.

"If I could get you alone for just ten minutes…," he trailed off with a slow shake of his head. "The things I would do to you."

Eurydice continued to stiffen and compressed her lips. "Are you drunk?" she asked flatly.

He laughed again. "Only on the sight of you," he purred.

"Sir, I find your comments offensive and unwanted," she said coldly. "I'm a married woman, and even if I weren't, I would still find them so."

"Your mouth says no, but your eyes say yes," he said softly. "I could make you forget your husband."

Eurydice scoffed derisively. "No, you couldn't. Go away."

The song ended then, and she searched for Ellsworth as dancers began to leave the floor. His arrival would either make the man mind his manners or leave. She would prefer his leaving. She would really like to punch him, but that would be socially unacceptable on too many levels.

"We will see each other again, Lady Eurydice," said the man in the silver mask softly, "hopefully, very soon."

"No, we—" she began hotly as she turned to look at him, but he was gone.

She frowned and looked around herself among the people for some sign of him. He had disappeared. She jumped and squeaked in surprise when she felt an arm come around her waist from behind.

"Here I am," purred Ellsworth close to her ear.

She turned in his arms to look at him. "Oh," she said breathlessly.

He noticed her flushed cheeks and frowned worriedly. "What's wrong?"

Eurydice couldn't tell him what had just happened. If she did, he would spend the rest of the night looking for the man in the silver mask. Dueling was frowned on in Vienna, but it wasn't illegal, and they took it far more seriously in Austria than they did even in Britain. She had no concern that Ellsworth would come to any harm from it, but she still didn't want to see something like that happen. It was a burden she didn't want on her conscience. The man was gone, and she would never see him again.

After his crude behavior, Eurydice knew he wasn't one of Leilah or Cora's friends. He might have been one of the people who came to speak with her who had discovered who she was beneath her mask, but there was something about him that made Eurydice think he hadn't even been one of them. She didn't know who he was, yet he knew her, and that concerned her, especially after the things he had said. It didn't worry her enough to tell Ellsworth, though. They would be leaving for St. Petersburg early the morning after tomorrow, and that would be that. She wasn't going to let the incident ruin the rest of the night for her.

"Nothing's wrong," she said softly, giving him a slight smile. "I was just lonely."

Ellsworth threw his head back and laughed amusedly, giving her waist a slight squeeze.

"You're just bamming me," he chortled. "There are very few people I know who are as happy to be left alone as you."

"Well, if you must know, the garderobe here smells vile, and it's upset my stomach."

"Do you want to leave?" he asked concernedly.

"No," she said slowly. "What I want is to waltz with my husband again and then go home to bed."

"In your mask," said Ellsworth.

"Yes, in my mask," sighed Eurydice patiently. Ellsworth grinned boyishly.

Chapter Twenty Seven

There was a thick blanket of snow on the ground when they left Vienna on Saturday morning. It had started to snow on Thursday night while they had been attending the redoute, and it had continued all through Friday until late in the evening. The streets and roads, at least in the city, were clear because the temperature wasn't quite cold enough to keep it from melting, but Eurydice couldn't say how conditions might be further out. It was nearing the end of November, and they would only be traveling north for a while. She imagined there would only be more of the same for quite some time.

Ellsworth had found an excellent coach, much better than the one they had ridden in from Venice. It wasn't as large as the coach had been for Cora and the children, but it was larger than the one she and Ellsworth had used. It was also better sprung, and the seats and walls were nicely padded, covered in soft, cream-colored, squabbed leather. The floor was covered in a lovely wool carpet that matched the leather, and there was even a coach stove filled with coals, which could be replaced with fresh ones when they stopped to change the horses, to keep them warm.

The exterior was painted bright blue and black with gold striping, and the fixtures were all gleaming, polished brass. She almost thought it had been freshly painted, but Ellsworth told her he had purchased it as-is. Eurydice was surprised when she discovered he had bought it outright. The seat for the driver was lower than on some coaches, and it had an overhanging roof to somewhat protect him and his assistant from the elements. There was plenty of room for storing luggage on top and at the rear with leather coverings that could be tied over it to protect it from the elements. It was just as well there was so much room for luggage because Eurydice had a lot. Although it was unintentional, she was carrying with her everything she had arrived with in Vienna, plus the new clothes Agniezka had ordered at the dressmakers…and Casanova.

She had thought for a time to leave the macaw in Vienna, but she couldn't expect Cora's servants to tend to him, although they would try. Even if they didn't speak Italian to understand what he was saying, Eurydice could only imagine what he would be saying while she was gone. That was enough for her to know she couldn't leave him. He had traveled well from Venice to Vienna, and other than his language, he was a well-behaved bird. She anticipated it would be the same this time.

Agniezka had drunk her ginger tea before they left Palais Crantzdorf, and she also carried a small, corked jug with more for while they traveled. Eurydice felt terrible that her maid would have to endure yet more sickness. She had just gotten to the point where her pregnancy was no longer making her nauseous in the past fortnight. There were, fortunately, small windows on the sides in addition to those in the doors, but they weren't very large, and they didn't open. It would make the inside of the coach warmer, especially if the curtains were closed to keep the cold from seeping through the glass. At least having a window to peer out of would make it less likely Agniezka would have traveling sickness. It always helped when she could see where she was going, but she and Schellen would be sharing the rear-facing seat with Casanova between them. Although Eurydice felt bad for her, Agniezka knew the journey was necessary, and then she would be free to marry Felton.

Eurydice felt a little queasy herself while they traveled, and that surprised her. It wasn't bad enough that she thought she was going to be sick, but she had never had traveling sickness before. It in no way compared to what Agniezka might be feeling, and Eurydice felt sure whatever might be causing it was temporary. It was probably her excitement for traveling across Europe that was making her feel that way rather than the actual journey, and she felt more confident that was the cause when she began to feel better as the day progressed, even if it never did quite go away.

The coach was traveling much faster than it had on the journey from Venice to Vienna, and it seemed to be moving at the rate Eurydice was accustomed to going when her family went from Wilderland to London, perhaps even faster. They traveled along the Danube for much of the morning, and by the time they stopped for dinner they had already reached Tirnau, well on the other side of it. The road they traveled was the main route between Vienna and Warsaw, and it was in excellent condition despite the snow that covered the embankments, fields, and forests to either side of it. The coach stove kept them warm, and there was no lack of coaching inns and post houses along the way to exchange horses and replace the coals in the stove. They were just reaching the foothills of the Carpathian Mountains when they stopped for the night in Trentschin in the valley of the Vaag River.

Eurydice was mildly concerned when she woke up the next morning and found her nausea was still there. It actually seemed worse, even if she still didn't quite feel like she was going to vomit. It was as if a blanket of queasiness had settled in the pit of her stomach that didn't want to go away.

Her concern was that she was actually developing some illness, especially when it was combined with the fact that she had needed to relieve herself every time they had stopped the day before. That particular inconvenience hadn't cleared away after the redoute, and while it hadn't grown any worse and she still didn't notice any discomfort when she did so, it was something abnormal for her. She didn't feel feverish or chilled, and once she managed to get past the queasiness and eat, her appetite remained the same. She didn't feel any worse after eating, but she also didn't feel any better.

She didn't want to mention it to anyone just yet. So far, it was more annoyance than worry. She was afraid if she mentioned it to Ellsworth, he would want to send her back to Vienna, and she had to get to St. Petersburg. Agniezka's time was running out, and she couldn't go alone. Eurydice would wait and see, try to decide what was causing it, before she told anyone. As for the nausea, if it didn't improve or got worse, she would use some of Agniezka's ginger tea or try something else. By the time they stopped at Bielitz-Biala that night, it wasn't any worse and had improved for the most part, but again, it wasn't gone, and Eurydice wasn't sure what she was going to do about getting rid of it.

By Tuesday morning, the nausea was bad enough that she was barely able to keep it under control until Ellsworth left their room before she went to the chamber pot to throw up. If he had wanted to make love, she would have needed to refuse, and he would have realized something was wrong. She didn't want him to know. Not until she determined what was causing it. If she could figure that out, then perhaps she could get rid of it before he found out. They were almost to Warsaw, but they were still close enough to Vienna he could send her back. He could also decide to remain at Warsaw longer in order for her to recuperate and delay their reaching Petersburg. She didn't want that.

Since it was starting before she even got in the coach, it was fairly safe to say it wasn't traveling sickness. Although the types of food she was eating had changed as she got further away from Vienna, it was more of a difference in preparation than content. She didn't think she was eating something that disagreed with her. It could be caused by anxiety for performing in front of people in strange cities; it was getting worse as the first date approached, but she didn't feel any more nervous than usual.

That left an infection. Despite her not feeling feverish or chilled, despite her not feeling any discomfort when urinating, and not having any other pains or loss of appetite, needing to go frequently combined with the steadily worsening nausea seemed to indicate that was the cause. She had nothing with her to treat an infection, much less a physician to confirm what she suspected, but they would soon be to Warsaw. She could at least find an apothecary. In the meantime, she would have to do what she could for the nausea.

When Agniezka came in to help her dress, Eurydice asked if she might try some of the ginger tea. She didn't want to worry her maid, so she said she was having mild traveling sickness. Agniezka looked at her suspiciously, knowing

Eurydice had never had it in the eleven years she had been her maid, but anything was possible, and she went back to her room to get some. In the meantime, Eurydice put slight pressure on a spot on one of her wrists, which Keung had shown her how to do, and it helped to keep her from vomiting again until she drank some of the tea. Once she drank the tea, she began to feel better, even if the nausea didn't go away, and she was able to act convincingly enough to make it seem she had only drunk it in preparation for traveling rather than already being sick.

Between drinking the tea and occasionally putting pressure on her wrist, Eurydice felt fine most of the day while they traveled. By the time they reached Warsaw in the late afternoon, she could have almost forgotten she wasn't feeling well. They would stay in Warsaw at least for one day, and that would give her time to find an apothecary. She was hopeful a day without travel might help to make her feel better. She had slept most of the day while they traveled, and that had helped as well.

Once they were settled into their room, she sent a message to Stefan Wróbel, the man who had invited her to perform, to let him know she had arrived. She wasn't sure where he lived or where she would be performing, but she was surprised and pleased when he arrived at the inn where they were staying to speak with her not long after she sent the message. He stayed to have supper with Eurydice and Ellsworth to discuss her performance, which would be the following night.

The theater, the Teatr Nardowy on Krasinskie Square, wasn't as large as the Burgtheater or the Theater an der Wien, capable of only holding a little over five hundred people. Compared to Vienna, it sounded almost cozy and much closer to the size she had anticipated when Salieri had said she would play at a more "intimate" venue.

She asked if it would be possible for her to go to the theater to practice and familiarize herself with the piano, which she learned was a Pleyel, for a few hours tomorrow before the performance. She'd never played an instrument by that particular maker, so it would be best to hear how it sounded beforehand. Pan Wróbel said that would be fine. Eurydice could just practice her violin at the inn, but she didn't know how the proprietor would feel about the noise. When she was practicing, she knew it could sometimes sound like just noise to someone else.

Eurydice asked Wróbel if he intended for her to play a concerto or if he wanted a sonata for violin and piano…the symphony, but all he wanted was her. He had posted notices announcing her concert, and the tickets were made available for purchase the Wednesday of the previous week. They were all sold by Friday. Eurydice was surprised when he told her that, and she couldn't understand how it could have happened. She supposed it was possible a performance by a woman was novel enough to generate that much interest.

Pan Wróbel also asked if she would consider giving a second performance on Thursday night, should the first go well. As tempted as Eurydice was to stay in one place for a day or so longer, she had to politely refuse. With Ellsworth's help, she had given set dates for when she would perform in the other cities, allowing the most time for herself in St. Petersburg and Venice for Ellsworth's benefit. She had given herself a little time for delays (such as carriage wheels falling apart or a snowstorm), but not an entire extra day.

The only other thing they discussed was her payment. It was again something Eurydice hadn't taken into consideration. Tours like the one she was undertaking were often used by other musicians and composers to make money, but Eurydice didn't *need* money. She didn't know what charitable institutions there were in the city, and she had no notion of how much she stood to make. She also didn't know how it would be paid, whether in actual coin or a bank note. When she asked, Wróbel said it would be a bank note. That would be more portable than coins, but she didn't know what she would do with it once she returned to Vienna. Ellsworth would know how to handle it, and so she would leave that to him when they returned home. If nothing else, she could give it to the Taubstummen Institut.

When Eurydice went to bed, she was hopeful she wouldn't be sick in the morning. She felt fine after supper, and she enjoyed having sex with Ellsworth, even if she was tired…especially once they were through. Perhaps the cause of her nausea was clearing away on its own. She was hoping that, but she had the feeling that wasn't going to be the case. She had the feeling she was going to wake up just as unwell as she had been that morning. Even more, she was worried she was going to wake up feeling worse. It had been going that way, so she wouldn't be surprised.

The only thing she was thinking about was how she was going to go to the apothecary without Ellsworth. He was usually awake before her, especially of late, and there was nothing in Warsaw to keep him otherwise occupied. At least in Vienna he had his own schedule. While they were on this tour, unless they were in a city where he needed to go for his assignment, she was the only thing requiring his attention. She liked that…except in this instance when she had something to do that she didn't want him to know about. She needed to think about it more, but she was too tired, and she drifted off to sleep without coming to a decision.

Eurydice woke up the next morning to Ellsworth kissing and nuzzling her neck, one of his hands slowly running from her breastbone to her stomach and back again. After a few passes while she was awake, it felt as if the swarm of butterflies it caused in her stomach was following after his fingers. She didn't know what time it was or how long he had been awake, but it had been long enough for him to shave, even if he wasn't dressed. She could smell the pleasant scent of his shaving lotion, and she inhaled deeply with her eyes closed, a smile playing at the corners of her mouth as she moved a hand to the back of his head to gently twine her fingers in his hair. To her surprise, she didn't feel nauseous.

"Good morning, Mr. Ellsworth," she sighed as his mouth moved to one of her breasts.

"Good morning, Mrs. Ellsworth," he replied with a grin as he licked at her nipple before gently grazing it with his teeth.

Eurydice sucked in air through her teeth and arched her back, finding the lightness of his touch particularly pleasurable, and she tugged at his hair to bring his mouth to hers for a kiss. She smoothed a hand down his cheek to his shoulder and looked at him with an impudent smile.

"You smell so good, I could just eat you up," she purred.

Ellsworth chuckled. "I'll let you."

"What is that?" she asked curiously. "Lime and…?"

"Basil," he supplied as he settled between her thighs and rubbed against her temptingly.

"Really?" she said in surprise. "That would explain why you smell so entirely edible," she sighed as she ran her hands down his back to grab his buttocks.

She had always thought he smelled delicious, but that morning, he smelled uncommonly good, and she moved her mouth to his neck to run her tongue up the side of it to his ear to nip at it with her teeth as she rubbed one of her legs against his. She felt as fit as a fiddle, and it seemed she wouldn't need to worry about going to the apothecary after all. She hadn't felt this well since they left Vienna. She moved against Ellsworth impatiently, and he lifted his head from tasting her breasts to look at her with a chuckle.

"You're not playing this morning, Mrs. Ellsworth," he teased as he slowly pushed into her. "You want me bad."

Eurydice sighed contentedly and wrapped her legs around his waist. "Yes," she gasped as he began to thrust in and out of her.

She couldn't resist his neck, licking and sucking it excitedly as he steadily plunged into her, nuzzling it, nipping at his ear. She bit down on the skin where his neck joined his shoulder as she began to orgasm, her body quivering at the intensity of it. Ellsworth sucked in air through his teeth and groaned as he reached his own release shortly after, and he lowered his head to rest it in the crook of her neck, breathing heavily. He moved his lips to the side of her neck to cover it with teasing nibbles before moving them to her mouth to kiss her passionately. He lifted his head to smooth his fingers down her cheek with an amused smile.

"I thought you were joking when you said you would eat me," he chortled.

"Mm," she said with a satisfied smile. Then she frowned slightly when she looked at his neck. "Oh, no."

"What?" said Ellsworth with a frown of his own.

He had three lovebites on his neck, the biggest one being where she had bit him when she had her orgasm. She didn't know what had come over her; it was as if she had been unable to stop herself.

"You might want to look in the mirror," she said slowly.

"Did you mark my neck?" he asked in amused surprise as he got up from the bed to look in the mirror over the wash basin. He turned his head to look back at her over his shoulder with a wolfish grin. "I've never had a woman do that before."

"I'm sorry," she said softly.

Ellsworth climbed back onto the bed and ran his lips up her body from her hip to her neck before giving her a smacking kiss on the lips.

"No need to apologize, sweetheart. It's not as if they hurt, and my cravat will cover them just fine." He ran a finger down her cheek and gave her a smile. "As long as it made you happy."

"It did," she sighed contentedly, and she lifted her head to give him a soft kiss.

She could feel a beam of sunlight coming between the curtains to warm a spot on her leg, and she looked toward the window. She couldn't tell how late it was and there was no clock in the room.

"What time is it?"

"Almost nine, I think," said Ellsworth casually as he looked down at her, his head propped on one of his hands.

"Agniezka will be coming soon to help me dress and bring my breakfast," she said absently.

"I suppose that means I should get dressed before I embarrass her again," he said with a grin.

"Hmm," said Eurydice with a slight smile. "She thinks you're well put-together."

Ellsworth chuckled. "And what about you?"

"Oh, sweetheart, I *know* you are well put-together," drawled Eurydice as she smoothed a hand down his chest.

Ellsworth shook his head with disbelieving amusement. "You're becoming incorrigible."

"And you like it," said Eurydice impudently, giving him a wink.

"I would show you just how much, but…your maid will be here soon."

"Dang it," sighed Eurydice wistfully.

Ellsworth laughed silently as he got off the bed to get dressed.

"What do you want to do today?" he asked.

"I need to rehearse."

"Not until this afternoon, and the concert isn't until eight," said Ellsworth after he pulled his shirt over his head and began to tuck it into his trousers. "Do you want to shop? Go to a park?"

"It's a bit cold for a park, don't you think?" asked Eurydice amusedly as she pulled her shift over her head. She had to put a steadying hand onto the bed as she felt a slight wave of dizziness.

"Well, now you mention it," said Ellsworth with a chuckle. "I would suggest ice skating, but we've no skates, and I don't think the weather's been cold enough for the ice to be safe yet."

"I'm not one of those women who likes to do nothing more than shop, but that might be entertaining…at least, seeing some of the city would be. I also have some letters to write."

Ellsworth didn't notice her eyes had gone slightly out of focus, but Eurydice did. The sensation quickly passed, but it was more than a little disconcerting, especially when she felt a mild wave of nausea following it. She put pressure on the spot on her wrist, and that cleared it, provided she kept her thumb there, but it appeared she would have to go to the apothecary after all. She couldn't understand it. She had felt fine when she woke up.

She tilted her head sideways as she thought about it, realizing it hadn't started until Ellsworth had been away from her for more than a minute or two and how agreeable she had found his shaving lotion to be. She decided to find out if what she thought was true. She got up from the bed and went to him under the pretense of helping him dress. When she smelled him, the nausea began to go away. After she stood next to him for more than a few minutes, it was completely gone. She didn't think it was because she was standing, and as much as she liked her husband, she didn't think it was him in particular that soothed her stomach. There was something in the lotion.

Ellsworth had put his cravat around his neck to begin tying it, and Eurydice watched with some interest. Persephone could tie all different kinds of configurations, but Eurydice had no notion of how to tie even a simple knot. She'd never watched Ellsworth tie his cravat before, and the way he wound it this way and that soon got too confusing for her to remember. It did completely cover his lovebites, though. When he was done, he pulled her toward him to give her a kiss and rested his arms around her waist.

"If you have letters to write, I have an errand or two that I would like to attend to myself in the meantime," he said finally.

Eurydice looked at him with a slight frown. She didn't know what errands he could possibly have in Warsaw, particularly since it wasn't one of the cities he needed to go to for his assignment. She could ask him; she had realized the reason he had told her she couldn't ask questions was because of his job, but she didn't want to pry. Aside from that, depending on how long he was gone, it might give her time to go to an apothecary. She could send Agniezka, but Agniezka couldn't speak Polish; Eurydice could.

"How long?" asked Eurydice evenly, adjusting the collar of his coat and brushing it with her hand.

"Not long," said Ellsworth with a secretive smile. "I'll be back by dinner, and then we can shop in the Rynek Market before you rehearse."

"All right," said Eurydice agreeably. That would give her plenty of time to go to the apothecary (she hoped) and get her letters written. "You've already had breakfast."

"Yes, I did. You slept like a log, so I had to do something to occupy myself until I just couldn't wait anymore," he said with a grin. "Are you feeling well?"

"Of course," said Eurydice evenly. "Why do you ask?"

"It's just that you slept most of the day in the coach yesterday, and then you slept so late today. I thought you might not be feeling well."

Eurydice shrugged negligibly. "I'm fine, just a little tired, I suppose."

"Well, you should be well-rested for tonight then," he said as he playfully tweaked the end of her nose.

"One would think," she said dryly with a smile.

Agniezka came into the room then carrying a tray with their breakfast, and Ellsworth gave Eurydice a thorough kiss before leaving the room. She looked after him for a few seconds, but then she went to the table where Agniezka had placed their food and began to eat. She wrote her diary entries and began her letters while she did so. The nausea returned soon after Ellsworth left, but it was at a tolerable level and seemed to improve as she ate. It didn't go away, however. Eurydice couldn't put pressure on her wrist to keep it from getting worse while she wrote and ate, and she couldn't have Agniezka bring her some of the ginger tea because she couldn't use the excuse of traveling sickness for needing it.

When Agniezka helped her get dressed, Eurydice decided to wear the cuff bracelet Lady Bardsey had given her for her birthday. It was fairly tight, and she took a piece of paper and rolled it into a ball to fit underneath it and put pressure on her wrist where she would have placed her finger. With that in place, the nausea was manageable. Agniezka had looked at her curiously when she did it, but she didn't ask any questions. She suspected something was wrong, but she would wait until Eurydice told her.

After Eurydice was done writing the letters to her sisters and parents, she wrote letters to Cora and Leilah and the Windhams. She wasn't sure where she should send Psyche's letter. She thought it was likely Psyche and Sheerness had returned to England, so after some consideration, she addressed it to their home on Sheppey. She had already sent letters to her family letting them know she would be touring Europe, giving them a copy of her itinerary and letting them know she would be coming home to Britain hopefully by February. She didn't mention she was unwell. She didn't want them to worry, and she was sure she would get what she needed at the apothecary to take care of it.

Once her letters were done, she had Agniezka help her into a pelisse and cloak, and then she went to ask the innkeeper if he knew where she might find an apothecary. Agniezka went with her to the shop, but Eurydice didn't tell her where they were going. When she got the directions from Pan Pniewski, they left the inn and went only a short distance up the street before arriving at the apothecary. Agniezka had a slight frown as she realized where they had gone, but she didn't ask Eurydice why.

Eurydice got more ginger for Agniezka while they were there. She didn't know if her maid still needed it as much anymore, but her supply had to be getting low. Then she began to describe to the apothecary what she needed for her own ailment. Since she didn't know what it was that was bothering her and what she needed to take care of it, she described her symptoms. He gave her a bottle containing a tincture of dropwort and provided her with instructions for its use. He said it was the best thing he knew of to treat what it sounded like she had. He gave her a vinaigrette and mixed several oils and tinctures together into a little stoppered bottle which he told her to use in the vinaigrette to help control her nausea until the other medicine cured her infection.

The difficult part of the transaction came when Eurydice had to pay for it. She had no Polish money. He at first refused to sell it to her, but when she gave him a sovereign, he bit it, smiled happily, and told her that would be fine. Eurydice was sure the sovereign was more than enough for the cost, but she was to the point she didn't care. If the things he had given her would cure her illness, it was well worth a sovereign.

Agniezka remained silent until they left the apothecary, and then she looked at Eurydice with a thoughtful frown.

"Are you finally going to tell me what's wrong?" she asked quietly.

Eurydice looked at her with an apologetic smile. "I'm sorry, Agniezka. I didn't want to worry you, but it seems I have anyhow."

"Well?" prodded Agniezka with a raised eyebrow.

"I'm not sure what's wrong, really. I seem to have acquired an infection shortly before we left Vienna, and it's only grown worse." She shrugged.

"What kind of infection?"

"I don't know what kind, but it's making me need to pee all the time, and it's gotten bad enough I'm constantly sick to my stomach...sometimes bad enough to vomit." With someone else, Eurydice might have put it more delicately, but with Agniezka, straightforwardness was appreciated.

"Hmm," said Agniezka thoughtfully. "And that's all?"

"That's all." Eurydice gave her a teasing smile. "I'm not dying. I swear."

Agniezka gave her a smile of her own. "You can't say anything to Ellsworth. He'll want to send me home," said Eurydice gravely.

"As if I talk to your husband!" said Agniezka amusedly. "I've only just recently decided I may not need to shoot him after all."

Eurydice laughed. She didn't doubt Agniezka was only partially teasing. Eurydice had told Agniezka that her thinking he was having an affair had only been a misunderstanding, but Agniezka was not so quick to forgive him as Eurydice. Agniezka thought he shouldn't have been doing something to make her think it possible in the first instance. Of course, Eurydice couldn't tell her what had caused the confusion. The only thing that had made Agniezka willing to give him another chance was seeing how happy he and Eurydice were. She would hear Eurydice laugh—a genuine laugh, and Agniezka found it difficult to keep her dislike for him when he was capable of causing that.

Ellsworth was at the inn when they arrived back, and Eurydice caught him mid-pace when she walked into their room. He turned to look at the door with a frown as she entered with Agniezka. After Eurydice gave her the jar containing her ginger, Agniezka left for her own room to put it away. She could see that Ellsworth was upset and thought it would be best if she wasn't there to hear any part of the conversation they might have. She was sure if it were anything serious, Eurydice would tell her. He seemed to be more worried than angry. Aside from that, she needed to get the tray from the kitchen with their dinner. She couldn't say for Eurydice, but she was starving.

"I thought you were going to write letters while I was gone," he said bluntly. "Where did you go?"

Eurydice looked at him with a mild expression, but she found the question unfair when she hadn't asked the same when he went to run his "errands."

"Agniezka needed more ginger for her tea, so we went to an apothecary," said Eurydice evenly. She hadn't done that with the intention of using it as an excuse, but it worked perfectly for it. "She couldn't go by herself because she doesn't speak Polish, and it's unlikely the apothecary would speak Russian, German, Italian, French, or English. I was gone less than an hour."

"Oh," said Ellsworth dully. "Couldn't you have waited until we went shopping after dinner?"

Eurydice shrugged. "I could have, but I had the time before dinner, and I didn't know if we would find one when we went shopping later. I wasn't trying to be a sneak."

"No, no, I know," said Ellsworth hurriedly with a half-smile. He walked toward her and pulled her into his arms for a kiss. "It's just that we're in a strange city, and you're a beautiful woman…. I was worried."

Eurydice gave him a smile and put a hand to his cheek. "I can take care of myself."

"Knowing one or two things from your brother doesn't mean you can take care of yourself."

"I know more than just the one or two things from Dorian."

"*T'ai chi* doesn't count," said Ellsworth softly.

"Ah, but then there's the *wǔshù*," said Eurydice calmly.

"The what?"

"It's the reason I only know one or two things from *jujutsu*. I wouldn't have had the time I needed for my music and other things if I had tried to learn that, too, and *wǔshù* works just as well, so…."

"What is it?"

"It is to the Chinese what *jujutsu* is to the Japanese." Ellsworth looked at her doubtfully. "I don't know all the things you know, and it is a different martial art, but it can be just as lethal."

Eurydice sighed resignedly and gently removed herself from his arms when he continued to look at her disbelievingly. She went to set her reticule on the dressing table and removed her cloak and pelisse to drape them across the bench in front of it. Then she went to stand in front of Ellsworth again. She wouldn't be able to use her lower body very effectively because of the dress, but she would be able to show him enough to get her point across.

"Try to hit me," she said evenly.

"I most certainly will not," he said flatly.

"It's obvious you don't believe me, so try to hit me. Don't try to hit me like you're afraid you might hurt me, either," said Eurydice with a grin. "I will admit I am a bit out of practice, but I'll be fine."

"I'm not going to do it," said Ellsworth, folding his arms across his chest and shaking his head.

"Then you will have to believe me when I tell you I am perfectly capable of taking care of myself," said Eurydice softly. "Agniezka knows. Write to my father. Ask him."

"Aberdare knows?" he asked in surprise.

"Of course, he knows," said Eurydice simply. "He had Keung teach it to my entire family, especially my sisters and myself. I would have to say that, overall, Pandora is the best of everyone in my family, but Persephone is very close. She is frighteningly good with pressure points. There is one she knows that can render someone unconscious with one finger to just the right spot. I've never been able to learn that one. Psyche and Pandora like to do the flashy, impressive things, like break bricks and boards. I was always worried I would hurt my hands, so I'm not as good at it."

Ellsworth looked shocked. "You're serious," he said breathlessly.

"Of course I am."

He raised a hand to strike her across the face, and Eurydice grabbed his wrist and spun his arm to pin it behind his back at an uncomfortable angle, not unlike the hold she had used to make Bruno do what she wanted. Ellsworth bent forward slightly to relieve the pressure on the joint and gasped as she raised up on it slightly before letting it go. He had given her no warning, and she had reacted reflexively and swiftly. That was something that only came from years of practice, and when he combined it with what he had seen her do at Rathmueller's, he had to believe what she told him, despite how fragile she appeared. He turned to look at her.

"I told you so," she said mildly with a slight smile.

Ellsworth pulled her toward him to give her a kiss. "I beg your pardon," he sighed.

After dinner, they went to the Rynek Market, the Old Town Square, which wasn't very far from the inn where they were staying. Eurydice didn't find anything in the stores that appealed to her, but she wasn't fond of shopping. Agniezka, who went with them, convinced her to buy a few things she might need, but if her maid hadn't told her to, Eurydice wouldn't have bought anything.

With the help of the vinaigrette and Ellsworth walking beside her, Eurydice didn't feel at all unwell, and she took some of the tincture she had bought when she had dinner. She wouldn't notice a difference immediately, and it didn't surprise her that she needed to use the chamber pot when they got back to their room from shopping, even though she had used it before they left. She hadn't thought to ask the apothecary how long she should expect it to take before it worked, but she was sure she would know when it happened.

She practiced at the theater for only three hours before she decided she was ready. The Pleyel proved to be an excellent instrument, but she was still very fond of a Broadwood. The Pleyel had a warm sound, and it had a volume comparable to her preferred piano. She would play the two sonatas she had performed at the Theater an der Wien, but she would also play another for each instrument. Ellsworth recommended the piano sonata she had written for her parents and *Le Papillon.* She agreed those would suit. She had to use the chamber pot yet again when they returned from the theater, and she was finding it to be an inconvenient annoyance.

The performance that night was very successful, and she was called back for two encores and received a standing ovation. As pleased as Eurydice was by the reaction of the audience, she was glad they had not called her back yet a third time. She had become dizzy while she played the violin sonatas, and she found herself exhausted when it was over, not to mention that she had actually vomited before the performance. She had been able to excuse it away to nervousness to Ellsworth, but she wasn't sure he believed her. She was feeling nauseous for most of the performance, and she hoped the medicine would start to work soon. She didn't know how she would manage to perform if she had to do it feeling how she felt.

When they got back to the inn, the first thing she did was use the chamber pot. When she had supper, her appetite was fine despite the slight feeling of nausea. She took more of the tincture before she went to bed while Ellsworth wasn't looking and placed the vinaigrette onto the night table. Ellsworth teased her about it, thinking it affectation, and he found it especially amusing when he opened it and smelled it. One of the ingredients was basil. Eurydice didn't think she was going to need it if Ellsworth was still in bed when she got up the next morning, but it wasn't going to help for him to be there unless he had shaved. It certainly hadn't helped on Tuesday.

As exhausted as she was, she and Ellsworth made love, and she enjoyed it as usual. She had wanted to refuse because she was so tired, but if she did, Ellsworth would realize something was wrong. The only time she had ever refused before was when she was having her courses, and she wasn't having them currently. One of the last thoughts she had before she went to sleep was that with the combination of all the things she was using to make herself feel well, she didn't know how she could possibly be feeling so unwell and how it could not possibly have happened at a more inconvenient time.

Chapter Twenty Eight

It took them a week to arrive in St. Petersburg once they left Warsaw. Despite how comfortable the coach was, Eurydice was overjoyed when they arrived in Russia's capital for several reasons. The main one, of course, was that she simply didn't like being in a coach for that long. It was seven days she hadn't been able to practice or compose. Then there was sleeping in a different, unfamiliar bed every night. Having Ellsworth with her was the only thing that made it tolerable.

While it seemed the medicine she had gotten was working for how often she needed to relieve herself, she was still plagued by the nausea. She was using the ginger tea almost as much as Agniezka, in addition to having the bracelet and using the vinaigrette. It had gotten bad enough that she had the bracelet on all the time, even when she went to bed. She vomited at least once a day, sometimes two or three times. It hadn't escaped Ellsworth's attention, but she had been able to convince him that it was traveling sickness. Eurydice didn't know how she was going to make that seem plausible when they were stopped in one place, but perhaps she would be able to conceal it better once he was occupied with other things.

Another thing that made her happy to be there was that Agniezka was finally going to be free of her husband. This return to Russia had been a long journey for Agniezka, but it was going to be so good for her. She would have her divorce, and she would be free to take a new, better husband. Not only that, but while they were there, she would get to see her father. She hadn't seen him since she and Nickolai had left eleven years ago. They wrote to each other often, but it wasn't the same as being able to see each other. Agniezka hadn't told him she was coming, so Eurydice hoped it would be a pleasant surprise.

It was late in the evening on Wednesday when they arrived, and the ground was covered with a thick blanket of snow. The air was very cold and damp, and Eurydice could feel it seeping through her cloak and pelisse, even the short distance from the coach to the door of the hotel. Rather than having to let separate rooms for Agniezka and Schellen, they were given a suite with attached quarters for them. Also, much to Eurydice's pleasure, there was a bathing room and a garderobe. This was by far the best place they had stayed since leaving Vienna. The tub would have to be filled from buckets sent up from the kitchen via a dumbwaiter, but that was well above anything they'd had so far, and the garderobe had a bidet. The room was warm and relatively free of drafts, and the bed was large and seemed like it was going to be very snug.

Eurydice would send a message to Gospodin Trubachev to let him know she had arrived. Her performance wouldn't be until Friday, so she would have one full day—she hoped—before her performance to rest and rehearse. They would be staying in St. Petersburg for almost a full week to give Ellsworth the time he needed for his task. She only intended to give one concert, but she could conceivably do another should Gospodin Trubachev request it. Of course, that might change depending on what the tsar (or his intermediary) had to say once he received her message she intended to send tomorrow. The more she thought about it, the more she began to think the one scheduled performance and whatever might be arranged for the tsar would be enough. Whatever was making her ill also caused her to be tired. Perhaps having a few days of not going anywhere and not performing would help.

She would send a message to Gospodin Srdanov tomorrow along with the other two messages. She was hopeful he'd had the time to arrange things as much as possible before their arrival, but she didn't know how the procedure of being granted a divorce was handled in Russia. She didn't know if it was a civic or a religious matter. Agniezka was Russian Orthodox, and Eurydice didn't know if that made a difference. She did think Srdanov would want to speak to Agniezka beforehand. Under the circumstances, Eurydice would be concerned if he didn't.

When she went to bed that night, Eurydice drank some ginger tea, wore the bracelet, and had the vinaigrette on the night table. Other than being tired, she felt fine. The nausea and exhaustion were starting to worry her, though. There was never a convenient time to be sick, but this definitely had to be the worst possible time. She still had eight more cities to perform in after St. Petersburg and then go home to see her family and return to Vienna. If she didn't get well soon, Ellsworth would send her back to Vienna, even if it meant canceling the rest of her performances. He would go to Venice and Paris without her. Either she had to get well or she would have to become better at hiding she was *un*well. The only comfort she had was knowing that she wasn't going to die from it. Her dreams told her that much.

As for her dreams, they continued much the same as they ever had. They didn't care that she was ill or that she had other things to do. She'd had the Dark Dream again, but she was only able to see a little more of it toward the end. She still couldn't recall the man's face, but she could hear his voice beginning to repeat in her head. It sounded familiar and in French, but it wasn't one she could associate to a specific person. She had just about decided she was never going to see the beginning, what started all of it, so she didn't know when she might expect it to happen. But the end. The more she saw of the end, the less she wanted to see. It was beginning to give her bad dreams, dreams that weren't visions but spawned from what the Dark Dream foretold. She had the feeling it was going to happen soon—not next winter or the one after that. This one…somewhere…before they went back to Vienna. It was all the more reason she needed to get well.

Ellsworth could tell she was exhausted when they went to bed, and he didn't want to make love. Well, he did, but he was more concerned about Eurydice than satisfying a need. He wasn't at all surprised when she fell asleep within minutes of snuggling beside him and laying her head on his chest. She had told him it was traveling sickness, but she'd never had it before; the whole time aboard the *Medea* and traveling from Venice to Vienna, he knew she hadn't been sick once. He thought it was odd that she would be developing it now. He couldn't escape the feeling it might be something more serious, but she didn't want to tell him because she was determined to complete her tour. He would keep an eye on her, and if it started to get worse, or if it didn't go away, something would have to be done.

Ellsworth was gone when Eurydice woke up the next morning. She was disappointed, but she was also relieved because she had to go throw up as soon as she woke. She took the vinaigrette with her, and when she was able to lift her head, she opened it and put it near her nose to smell the contents. She adjusted the bracelet on her wrist, and when she felt her stomach was a little more settled, she relieved herself, washed her face and brushed her teeth, and went back to the bed chamber. She sat on the edge of the bed with her eyes closed, breathing deeply, trying to control the nausea. She eventually went to the desk and began to write her diary entries, pausing occasionally to smell the vinaigrette. She was just finishing the entry in her life diary when Agniezka came in with a tray.

"I have a few things for you to try," said Agniezka excitedly.

"Oh, I'm not really hungry," said Eurydice hesitantly.

"Just try it," coaxed Agniezka as she set the tray on the table near the window. "Getting something into your stomach makes you feel better."

The thought of eating didn't interest Eurydice at all, but she had to eat something. There were poached eggs and ham, but there was also a sweet brown bread made with honey and spices, and a drink made with honey, spices, and fruit juice. Eurydice's stomach churned when she smelled the eggs, and she pushed them away from her as far as she could. The spiced bread, though, she found tolerable, and the drink, called *sbiten,* helped soothe her stomach enough that she was able to eat the ham as well. She also found the more she ate, the better she felt, but she couldn't eat the eggs. It was as if her body refused to let her even try. She couldn't understand it. She loved eggs. But as her body seemed to be rebelling against her more and more lately, she didn't know why she was surprised.

She worked on the messages she needed to send while she ate. All three were very brief, simply letting the men know she had arrived and where she was staying. She wanted to see Gospodin Trubachev as soon as possible to discuss where she would be performing and what he expected, whether a concerto or simple violin and piano sonatas. If he had arranged an orchestra for a concerto or two, she would need to spend as much time as possible rehearsing with them. Even if they weren't her own pieces (and she would prefer if they were), depending on whose they were, she and the orchestra would still need the time. As for Gospodin Srdanov, he had to know that she and Agniezka would only be there a week, and Agniezka needed to know what had to be done. Eurydice wasn't even sure how to send the message to the tsar, so she addressed it rather generically to his secretary (assuming he had one), and she mentioned in it that the Austrian emperor, Metternich, and Stackelberg were all to have sent letters on her behalf. She was actually hoping she never heard anything back; performing for Emperor Franz had been nerve-racking enough. While she was honored to play for royalty, she wasn't sure her health was up to the strain.

Eurydice had Agniezka arrange for the messages to be delivered once she was done writing them. After she finished eating what she could of breakfast, Agniezka helped her dress. Until she had responses from any of the messages, all she could do was wait. Agniezka wanted to go visit her father, Gennadiy, but she didn't want to go alone. Today wouldn't be good for Eurydice, and probably not tomorrow either. Perhaps on Saturday or Sunday, once Eurydice had rehearsed and given her concert, they would have the time. It was unlikely anything would be done with Agniezka's divorce until Monday. Hopefully it *would* be done on Monday; they would be leaving the city on Wednesday morning. Eurydice would rather it be over and done as soon as possible.

"Are you feeling better?" asked Agniezka sympathetically.

"For the moment," said Eurydice dryly. "I think the traveling is making it worse. It has made me very tired. Now that we're in one place for a while, I'm sure I'll be back to myself in no time," assured Eurydice.

"You know you don't *have* to give all of these performances."

"Oh, but I want to. I've already scheduled them, and if I cancel, what might it do to my reputation?"

"Your reputation will matter for naught if giving them kills you," said Agniezka flatly.

Eurydice gave her a wry smile. "It's not going to kill me. I know that much," she said dully, and some of the humor left her expression.

Agniezka looked at her with a concerned frown. She didn't think Eurydice was lying about how serious her illness was, and Agniezka was beginning to have suspicions. But the tone Eurydice had used was one Agniezka had heard before, and the expression on her face.... She knew Eurydice had had a dream, and whatever it had been, it worried the younger woman. That worried Agniezka.

"Perhaps you're right," she said with an even smile. "Although, Petersburg is very damp, and in the winter it makes the cold sink into your bones until they thaw in the spring."

Eurydice chuckled. "That's why there are fireplaces, hot drinks, and husbands to cuddle with."

Agniezka snorted amusedly. "Provided the husband is one you *want* to cuddle with."

"Just think, by this time next week, you will be a woman free to have one of those."

Agniezka looked at her with a thoughtful frown. "Have you...have you seen anything?" she asked hesitantly.

"No, Agniezka, I'm sorry, I haven't," said Eurydice softly. "But I am sure everything is going to be fine," she said with a soothing smile.

"I hope so," sighed Agniezka.

Eurydice spent her time while she waited working on her symphony. She was only a third of the way through it, she thought, and it had been set aside for almost two weeks while they had been traveling. The music in her head wasn't going anywhere until she put it onto the page, but it would be nice to have it there. By mid-morning, she was able to make a fair amount of progress despite her nausea, when there was a knock at the door to their suite. Agniezka rose from her seat where she was knitting by the fireplace and went to answer it while Eurydice worked. She came to the desk to hand Eurydice a message delivered by one of the maids. There was no address or seal. Eurydice opened it and read, and then she looked at Agniezka.

"Gospodin Srdanov is downstairs. Are you ready?"

Agniezka gave her a dull smile. "As ready as I'll ever be."

The two of them left the room and walked down the hall to the stairs. When they reached the ground floor, they went to the lobby. There were a few people there, several of them men, and Eurydice wasn't sure which one would be Gospodin Srdanov. She couldn't determine it by looking for a man with an expectant expression, as if he were waiting for someone, because several of them looked like that. After a minute or two of indecision, she went to the desk and asked the attendant. He nodded his head in the direction of one of the men, standing alone and examining his watch, and after Eurydice thanked the man behind the desk, she asked if there was a room where they might converse in private and asked that tea and *sbiten* be brought. He said they could take their guest down the short hall just to the right of the desk and use the second room on the right. Tea would be brought shortly. Eurydice thanked him again, and she and Agniezka went to meet the lawyer.

"Gospodin Srdanov?" said Eurydice when she neared him.

He looked at her and nodded. "*Da,*" he said evenly. "You are Lady Eurydice Ellsworth?"

"*Da,*" confirmed Eurydice, and she held out her hand. He kissed the air just above it politely and released it.

"And you would be Agniezka Skryabina Sheremetevskaya?"

"*Da,*" said Agniezka dully. She hadn't used her married name since she had left Russia.

"Please, Gospodin Srdanov," said Eurydice politely, gesturing toward the hall with her hand. "If you'll come this way, there's a room where we may talk privately. I've also sent for tea."

"Excellent," said Gospodin Srdanov with a happy smile.

Eurydice thought he was somewhere in his fifties, with dark, graying hair, brown eyes, and a swarthy complexion. He was just above her in height, his girth slightly starting to thicken because of age. He seemed kind, and Eurydice hoped that would prove to be the case. He was well-dressed and carried a small portfolio, and Eurydice supposed he looked just as a lawyer should.

They went to the room the man at the desk had directed them to use, and she found that it was a small parlor. A maid was just starting a fire on the grate, and she had opened the curtains to allow the light to enter. There was a settee and two chairs near a small, low table, and there was also a small dining table where a meal could be served. The maid smiled briefly once she completed her work and left the room.

"Your journey from Vienna went well?" asked Sdranov politely as they took seats on the settee and chairs.

"Yes, it did," said Eurydice with a smile. "I was surprised it went so quickly. We hadn't anticipated we would be here from Warsaw until sometime today; we arrived last night."

"Good, good," said Srdanov with a smile. "You are a…composer?"

"Yes, and a musician. I am on a tour of Europe at the moment."

"Really? You are to perform in Petersburg?" he asked with surprise.

"Yes, although I'm not sure where at the moment. I was invited by Gospodin Rolan Trubachev with the Philharmonic Society, and then I've received a request to perform by Imperial command for his majesty." Eurydice gave him a slightly embarrassed smile. "As I've never been here before and only just arrived, I'm afraid I don't know where either will take place."

Srdanov smiled widely. "Ah, you are the one Bullant has been in such a flurry over."

"I'm sorry?" said Eurydice confusedly.

"Antoine Bullant is the director of the Philharmonic Society. He has been busily rehearsing his orchestra for some weeks." Srdanov set his case flat onto the table in preparation for opening it. "I am sure we will be going to your performance, wherever it may be, but my wife attends to things like that."

"Oh," said Eurydice with a slight blush.

"As for the tsar, I can only say it will be given at his private theater at the Hermitage. No one will be able to buy tickets for that," he said with a smile.

"Hmm," said Eurydice, wondering how big his private theater might be.

A maid entered with their tea and *sbiten* and set the tray on the table and quietly left. Eurydice poured tea for Srdanov and Agniezka, but she had some of the *sbiten* for herself. It settled her stomach better than the ginger tea, and she didn't care for regular tea if she had a choice. She could have had the maid bring coffee, but Russian coffee was too strong for her and seemed to upset her stomach even more lately. There was also a small plate with biscuits and cake, but Eurydice wasn't interested in food. She would leave it to the others to serve themselves should they want it.

"Now," said Srdanov after they had their cups, "to the matter at hand. I was contacted by both your father and the Earl of Sheerness, Lady Eurydice, to attend to Gospoda Sheremetevskaya's divorce. Under normal circumstances, it would be a simple matter of submitting a petition to the Synod and letting them decide. It should have been made even simpler because of the length of time you and your husband, uh, Sergei Sheremetev, have lived apart," he said as he removed some papers from his portfolio and glanced up at Agniezka. "However, both of you are nobles and of the Orthodox faith, which complicates things somewhat."

Eurydice and Agniezka both looked at him worriedly.

"But neither of us are titled," said Agniezka softly.

"No, but you are of the hereditary nobility, and your husband has heritable property," said Srdanov. "I said it complicates the situation, but it doesn't make the divorce impossible. Were both of you serfs or simply freeborn, as I said, a petition would be sent to the Synod, they would decide the matter, and that would be that. The divorce could have been given for the cause of desertion, which is still the reason I intend to use unless you can give another one, but because you are nobility, and because the desertion was yours and you are submitting the petition, the Synod will not grant the divorce or make a decision without a hearing, attended by both you and Gospodin Sheremetev."

Agniezka took Eurydice's hand and squeezed it tightly. She hadn't seen her husband since she left Russia and had no desire to do so now, but if it was the only way to be completely free of him, she would do it. He couldn't abuse her in front of witnesses. She would be safe from him.

"H-how…how is this to be done?" she asked nervously.

"Once I received Lady Eurydice's letter telling me you would be coming, I filed the papers necessary and contacted your husband. The hearing will be this Monday at two, and he has agreed to be there."

Eurydice felt Agniezka's grip on her hand tighten. "Will it take long for them to decide?" asked Eurydice calmly.

Srdanov shrugged negligibly. "They will hear the evidence, and you should have their decision before you leave the room." He could see both women were anxious. "I am sure the hearing is only a formality," he soothed.

Both Eurydice and Agniezka hoped he was right. Gospodin Srdanov stayed for a little while longer to give them details of where the hearing would be held and had Agniezka sign some papers he had brought with him and had

Eurydice sign as a witness. He said those, too, were just a formality, but Eurydice made sure Agniezka read them and understood them before she put her name on. They thanked Gospodin Srdanov for coming and assured him they would be on time for the hearing on Monday. Eurydice wouldn't be able to go into the room with Agniezka, but she would wait outside for her.

After Gospodin Srdanov left, Agniezka stood up and began to pace, a hand to her stomach. When she did that, it smoothed the fabric of her dress against her body, and it made the gentle swell of her growing abdomen obvious. It was only when Agniezka did that it was noticeable, and Eurydice could understand her anxiety. This hearing was going to take place not a day too soon. If it were delayed any longer, there would be no way to disguise that she was pregnant.

Eurydice wanted to believe Srdanov was right that the hearing was only a formality. After eleven years, Eurydice was surprised Sergei hadn't initiated a divorce himself. He was still young, and he had property. Surely he would want to remarry to produce an heir to leave it to. She couldn't say. Other than knowing he had been criminally abusive toward Agniezka, Eurydice didn't know anything else. She had the impression from things Agniezka had said that he was handsome and capable of being charming, that he was wealthy, and slightly above Agniezka in station, but she knew nothing else. She wouldn't even recognize him if she saw him.

Eurydice finally convinced Agniezka that they should leave the parlor and go back to their suite. Her pacing there wasn't going to solve anything, and Eurydice was sure the anxiety wasn't good for the baby. When they went to the desk for Eurydice to thank the attendant for allowing them to use the room for their meeting, he pointed out that two more gentlemen had arrived to see her. Eurydice looked from him, to the men, and then to Agniezka. It was almost time for dinner, and while the *sbiten* had helped to soothe her stomach, and she had the vinaigrette with her and wore the bracelet, she knew if she didn't eat, her nausea would grow worse. She looked back at the attendant again.

"I trust we can continue to use the parlor?" she enquired dryly. He nodded. She turned to look at Agniezka. "Can you arrange for something to be brought to our room for dinner? I don't know how long this will take, but I'm sure I will need food immediately after."

"Of course," said Agniezka, rubbing her shoulder soothingly.

Eurydice went to meet the two gentlemen. One was Gospodin Trubachev, who had invited her, and the other was Antoine Bullant, who Srdanov had mentioned. She invited them to the parlor she had just left, and the tea service was still there. She offered them tea, but they declined. Eurydice was relieved because she was sure it was cold by that point. She also hoped it meant they didn't intend to stay long.

They informed her that the performance would be the following evening at nine in a hall frequently rented by the Philharmonic Society. It wasn't large, capable of holding only four hundred or so guests, but the acoustics were excellent. She would perform both concertos from the Burgtheater, and they asked that she play two or three additional sonatas. When Eurydice heard they intended her to play both pieces accompanied by orchestra, she knew she would need most of that day and possibly the next to prepare. Gospodin Trubachev assured her the orchestra had been rehearsing diligently without her, and that the first violinist and a pianist had been playing the parts she would perform while they did so. She was sure the musicians were proficient, but performing the concertos with so little practice made her anxious.

Both men were nice, but they couldn't tell her anything regarding ticket sales or how much she could expect to be paid. It would be given to her in a bank note and she wasn't doing the performance for money, but it was obvious from the conversation she had with them that the musical world of St. Petersburg was not as well-organized as that of Vienna. They assured her that expectations on attendance could not be based solely on how well tickets were selling; some of the nobility did not buy tickets. With everything they said, the knot of anxiety in Eurydice's stomach only began to grow, and she could feel her nausea threatening to overwhelm her.

She conducted her business with them as quickly as she could without being rude and assured them that she would be to the hall to rehearse with the orchestra as soon as she finished eating her dinner. She needed them to leave so she could go to her room and throw up. Luckily, the meeting was as brief as she had hoped it would be, and she left the parlor with them. She shook their hands in the lobby, again assuring them she would be to rehearsal very soon, and then she quickly walked up the stairs to her suite, knowing that running would only make it more likely she would be sick. She kept the vinaigrette near her nose, breathing in and out deeply, and she was able to make it to her room and the garderobe before she lost the contents of her stomach.

When she was through, she rested her forehead against the cold stone on the floor for a few minutes, waiting for the wave of dizziness that accompanied the vomiting to subside. Eurydice didn't know how she could possibly perform feeling like this. Knowing the illness wasn't fatal did nothing to make her feel better about it. She couldn't understand why the dropwort may have worked on the needing to relieve herself (for the most part) but not the vomiting. She didn't think she could be suffering from two different illnesses; like everyone else in her family, she wasn't prone to sickliness, and she didn't want to believe it might be caused by some mental incapacity. She stood up, went to the washstand to splash cold water onto her face and rinsed her mouth, and then she went to the main room of the suite. Agniezka had dinner waiting for her.

"I'm sure you'll start to feel better soon," said Agniezka softly.

"Oh, I hope so. I will be absolutely mortified if I have to stop in the middle of a concert to shoot the cat."

Agniezka gave her a dry smile. "It seems to be better when you have food in your stomach. We'll just have to make sure you have food in your stomach all the time. I'll bring your breakfast to you in bed, make sure you have a snack before you go to sleep, and see that you eat when you need to."

"Oh, Agniezka, I can't ask you to do that. That's too much work, and you need to be well more than I do."

"Nonsense. I am fine these days. I haven't needed the ginger tea since we left Warsaw, not even in the coach."

"But—"

"Not another word," cut in Agniezka with a smile. "I haven't had this much energy in a very long time, and I don't know how long it will last. You might want to take advantage of it while you can," she chortled. "Now, eat."

Eurydice did as she was told. It wasn't easy at first. She did manage to eat at least a little of everything Agniezka had brought. There was roast chicken, which Eurydice practically devoured, and she couldn't recall ever having chicken that tasted quite so well-cooked. There was a dish made with sliced beef, noodles, and cream, seasoned with a little lemon and parsley that she'd never had before. Agniezka couldn't recall ever having it before either, but both of them thought it was absolutely divine. There was paprikash, which was one of Eurydice's favorite foods, and she was glad she was going to be in Russia for a while because it was a fairly common dish she would get to have several more times. For dessert, there was ice cream served with thin biscuits, peach preserves, and whipped cream. Eurydice liked it so much that she was quite rude and ran her finger around the bowl to get the very last bit of it. And it wasn't the ice cream that she had enjoyed so much as the peach preserves. They had been very tasty preserves.

She felt much better once she had food in her stomach, and after Agniezka tidied her hair, Eurydice made sure she had all her necessities for controlling her nausea to take with her to the hall for rehearsal. Agniezka had gone down to arrange for their transportation while Eurydice finished eating. When they went outside, there was a pretty sleigh drawn by a single black horse waiting for them. It was obvious the sleigh was intended for a woman to drive, painted white with gilded fittings and trim, the cushions of the seat covered in burgundy velvet. It had a leather bonnet that could be pulled up, but that was folded down. There was a throw made of bear fur for them to put over their laps, which they did once they were seated and Eurydice had safely stored her violin.

Eurydice let Agniezka drive, partly because she wasn't familiar with driving a sleigh and partly because she didn't know her way around the city. Agniezka pointed things out as they traveled, showing her several cathedrals, palaces, and government buildings. There were a lot of things that were new, built in the eleven years Agniezka had been gone. Still, the main streets hadn't changed, and she was able to find the hall on Nevsky Prospekt without any difficulty. It really wasn't that far from their hotel.

When Eurydice first looked at it, she thought Gospodin Trubachev had directed her wrongly because it looked like someone's residence, albeit a very *large* one. If Trubachev hadn't told her which entrance to use, she might have gone to the front door and knocked. She could hear an orchestra playing, and it didn't take her long to recognize one of her own concertos. She stood for a few seconds on the sidewalk, listening with her head tilted sideways observantly, while Agniezka secured the horse to a nearby hitching post. From outside at a distance, Eurydice thought they sounded very good.

There was an entrance to a narrow colonnade near one end of the building, and Eurydice and Agniezka went to that. Not far inside, there was a staircase that led upward. The doors were open when they reached the top, and the sound of music was louder. They entered what might have been a reception room or even a drawing room at one point, but it was obviously intended now to be a foyer for the hall, its cream-colored walls covered in mirrors and lined with columns to give the illusion of a larger space, large chandeliers (currently unlit) hanging from the high, plaster-adorned ceiling. The doors to the hall were open as well, and Eurydice and Agniezka hesitantly walked through them.

The hall was not what Eurydice had anticipated, but Trubachev had been accurate about the acoustics. It sounded wonderful. Looking at it, Eurydice thought it resembled a ball room. The ceiling was very high, easily twenty feet, coffered and adorned with plaster and gilding, a single, giant chandelier hanging from the center. There were sconces along the walls at a lower height between the windows. There were no boxes or loges, and the floor was all one level. Seating was simply chairs arranged in rows with a central aisle. The stage rose above the height of the floor by only two or three feet, and it was small. The very large orchestra was arranged onto it, a piano in the middle. The stand for the conductor was at the very edge. Looking at it, Eurydice could imagine it was going to feel like she was performing in a large drawing room. She couldn't help wondering why she couldn't have given her first performance in Vienna at a place like this. It would have been much less traumatic.

As Eurydice and Agniezka walked up the aisle in the center, Gospodin Trubachev got up from his seat in one of the chairs near the stage and came to greet them with a huge smile when he realized they were there.

"Lady Eurydice, we weren't expecting you for another hour," he said happily as he took one of her hands to kiss the air above it. He turned toward the stage and whistled shrilly between his teeth. The musicians stopped playing, and the conductor turned to look at them. "Everyone, this is Lady Eurydice Ellsworth," he called proudly.

Much to Eurydice's surprise, they all began to applaud, and she colored profusely. They walked with Trubachev the rest of the way to the stage, and Agniezka helped Eurydice remove her cloak and pelisse and draped them over a nearby chair. Trubachev introduced her to the conductor, a Belgian named Paris, which Eurydice found mildly humorous. He also introduced the pianist and the first violinist. All of them were very happy to meet her and told her how much they were enjoying the opportunity to play her music. Eurydice didn't know what to say. She was flattered by their compliments, and her cheeks were a bright shade of pink.

It was dark outside when she and Agniezka left after the rehearsal, but Eurydice thought it had gone very well. There were a few things that had needed adjustment, but overall, she was well-pleased. She had at first been hesitant to say anything, not wanting to insult Monsieur Paris, but who could there have possibly been who was better at offering suggestions than the composer? No one besides Eurydice would know exactly how the concertos were meant to be played. There really hadn't been many things that needed improvement, but Paris had to agree they *were* improvements. The rehearsal set her mind at ease that the concert the following night would go well.

Eurydice went to their suite once they reached the hotel while Agniezka went to arrange for supper and have water brought up for the bath. When Eurydice reached the room, Ellsworth wasn't there. She was disappointed. She had missed him all day. She didn't know if he would be back before she went to bed, either. He had to tend to his assignment, but she couldn't believe it would require him to be gone all day. Of course, he may have come back while she was at rehearsal, but he hadn't gone to see her at the hall.

When Agniezka came to the room with the tray carrying their supper, she also had a letter that had been given to her by the attendant at the desk. Eurydice opened it and read, finding that it was a message from the tsar's chamberlain, Aleksandr Naryshkin. He had been expecting her letter, and she would perform for the tsar at the Hermitage Theater on Saturday evening at nine. She would be allowed two hours at the theater to rehearse on Saturday afternoon before the performance, should she require it. Eurydice decided she would most definitely require it, if for nothing other than to have a feel for where she would be performing. Since it wouldn't be until the afternoon, she and Agniezka would have plenty of time to go see her father in the morning and spend most of the day should Agniezka wish to do so.

Several maids came into the suite to go to the bathing room and fill the tub while the two women ate their solitary supper. When Eurydice heard the door open, she looked toward it expectantly, hoping it was her husband, and she tried to contain her disappointment when she saw that it wasn't.

The women were done with their chore by the time Agniezka finished eating, and Eurydice let her go take a bath while she finished eating her own food. She was very tired, which was one of the reasons she was taking so long to eat. She was almost tempted to forego having a bath, but she needed one, and she needed to use her depilatory. She'd delayed as long as she could, and the only reason she had done so was that she was concerned the fumes were going to upset her stomach. By the time she was done eating and changed into a dressing gown, Agniezka was through with the tub.

Eurydice let Agniezka go to bed, and she went to the bathing room with the jar of depilatory. She opened the windows in the room, and then she removed her dressing gown and put on the depilatory after dipping one of the buckets into the tub. The chemicals in the cream smelled very harsh, and Eurydice held her breath for the few minutes it required for it to do its job before she quickly rinsed it off. When she was done, she closed the windows after the fumes had cleared from the room somewhat, and then she gratefully stepped into the tub and sank into the hot water up to her chin with a tired sigh. She sat for a minute or two before she quickly washed, and then she leaned back against the edge again and closed her eyes, intending to soak and relax, enjoying the heat of the water as it swirled around her limbs.

Eurydice woke with surprise when she was lifted out of the tub. She felt very cold, and that was when she realized she must have fallen asleep and had been that way for quite some time. She looked up to see Ellsworth looking down at her worriedly as he carried her to the bed, and she fought back a shiver as the cool air began to dry the water on her already numb skin. He settled her under the blankets, and then he quickly undressed and climbed into the bed and pulled her toward him. He felt very warm compared to her, and she snuggled against him relievedly as the heat of his body began to ease the chill she felt. The room began to grow brighter, and she realized he must have added wood to the fire before he went into the bathing room and found her. She had to wonder what time it was.

"Why didn't you have Agniezka help you bathe?" he asked shortly.

"Because I am perfectly capable of washing myself," said Eurydice dryly.

"You could have frozen to death…or drowned," he said stiffly.

Eurydice smoothed a soothing hand over his chest and kissed the skin beneath her cheek, but she couldn't argue with what he said. She had been known to doze off in the tub before, but she'd never fallen asleep so soundly that the water went cold without waking her. She had been there long enough that her hair had completely dried, so she estimated she had been there asleep for at least an hour, perhaps longer. She felt him shiver slightly from her cold body sapping the warmth out of his, and her toes and fingers began to tingle slightly as she felt them grow warmer.

"I'm sorry," she said quietly. "I guess I was more tired than I thought."

Ellsworth put a finger under her chin and raised her face to give her a soft kiss on the lips.

"Are you sure that's all it was?" he asked her searchingly.

Eurydice put a hand to his cheek and gave him a soothing smile. "Of course. What else would it be?"

"Sometimes…sometimes I feel like you aren't well, and you don't want to tell me."

Eurydice settled on top of him and lifted up on her elbows to either side of his head to look down at him with a wry smile before kissing him warmly.

"I'm fine," she sighed as she moved her lips along his jaw toward his ear. "Perhaps spread a bit thinly from traveling and performance anxiety," she said softly as she began to tease his earlobe with her teeth, "but I am absolutely…fine."

Ellsworth moved his hands to her hips and sighed longingly as she began to kiss her way down his neck to his chest. He wasn't convinced she was telling the truth, but the things she was doing were making it harder for him to concentrate on his worry. That was Eurydice's intention. She was tired, but she would do what she had to to keep him from finding out how sick she was.

"My concert is tomorrow night at nine at the Sâle Lyon on Nevsky," she said as she began to toy with one of his nipples. "Will you be there?"

"Of course," he gasped as she moved one of her hands to his erection and began to stroke him.

"I play for the tsar at the Hermitage at nine on Saturday night."

"I wouldn't dream of missing it," he managed to get out as she began to kiss her way down his stomach to his navel.

He lifted his head to look at her as she began to play him with her mouth, and she gave him an impudent wink. He smiled sardonically and let his head drop back to the pillows with his eyes closed as he felt his heart begin to thud in his chest excitedly.

"Nah, you're fine as frog hair," he sighed.

Ellsworth was gone when Eurydice woke up the next morning, and again her feelings were mixed. She managed to avoid being sick because Agniezka brought her some of the spiced bread and *sbiten* before she got out of bed. It was a good thing because she had neither her vinaigrette nor her bracelet. Once she was sure she would be able to move without vomiting, she got up and went to the garderobe, and then she went to the table to eat the rest of her breakfast. There were eggs again, but they were scrambled and mixed with a soft cheese and ham in an omelet. Eurydice was able to eat them prepared that way. There was also bacon, and Eurydice devoured it and wanted more. Unfortunately, there wasn't any more unless Agniezka went to the kitchen to get it.

Eurydice worked on her symphony until mid-morning, and then she and Agniezka went to the hall on Nevsky Prospekt for a few more hours of rehearsal before that night. While she was there, she talked to Trubachev and Monsieur Paris about the orchestra performing with her the following night at the Hermitage. Both men agreed they would like to do it, but they would have to discuss it with the rest of the musicians. They didn't think it would be a problem, but they would give her a firm answer that night at the concert.

After rehearsal, Eurydice and Agniezka went back to the hotel for dinner. Then Eurydice spent the remainder of the afternoon and well into the evening working on her symphony while Agniezka embroidered and knitted. She left at one point to go get a tray with a small mid-afternoon meal for Eurydice and herself, but they spent most of the time in companionable silence working on their own projects. To Eurydice's relief, she only felt occasional nausea, which was managed completely when she put on her bracelet with the piece of paper beneath it. She didn't have to use the vinaigrette once. When it was close to seven, Agniezka left again to get another tray. Eurydice might become sick if she couldn't eat something until after the performance.

Agniezka went to change clothes while Eurydice finished eating her food, and then she helped Eurydice dress for the concert, putting her into an evening gown of soft, myrtle green velvet that complimented her hair and complexion. The sleeves were long and slashed, exposing an undersleeve of white mull. The bodice was low, but there was a high, pointed lace collar at the neck. For a time, they thought Eurydice might need to wear something else because the collar would be in the way of her violin, but when she removed the instrument from its case to try it, she found that it would be fine. They put a strand of pearls around her neck and a pair of filigreed gold earrings with pearl accents in her ears. Her hair was a bit more wavy and unruly than usual, so Agniezka gathered it onto her head and wound through it with a green velvet ribbon that matched her dress rather than trying to wind it into its usual coil. Agniezka was just finishing Eurydice's hair when Ellsworth came in from Schellen's room in evening dress, adjusting his sleeves and waistcoat, an outer coat draped over his arm and a hat and gloves in his hand. It was almost 8:30.

"I bet you thought I forgot," he said with a grin when he saw Eurydice's relieved expression.

"I was beginning to wonder," she said with a dry smile as she rose from the dressing table and went to give him a quick peck on the lips.

"I would never miss one of your performances," he said warmly as he wrapped his arms around her waist to give her a more thorough kiss. "Mrs. Ellsworth, you are looking absolutely lovely tonight."

Eurydice blushed, and she jumped when Agniezka cleared her throat behind them to get Eurydice's attention and help her into her coat and cloak. Ellsworth chuckled amusedly as he put on his own outer clothing, and then he linked his arms through those of both women and they left the room.

There was an enclosed sleigh when they left the hotel, a driver waiting to open the door for them. Eurydice didn't know if that was what Ellsworth had been using both the day before and that one while he tended to business or if he had arranged for it specifically for that night. Either way, Eurydice was glad for it. There was a flurry of snow drifting from the sky. They made it to the theater well before time for the performance.

Instead of going to the foyer, the three of them went to a different entrance that took them to the rooms behind the stage. Trubachev, Bullant, and Paris were all there. Eurydice could hear the orchestra tuning its instruments, and she could hear muted conversations as well. She felt the same nervous anxiety she usually felt before a performance, but the nausea was at a tolerable level. Trubechev and Bullant wished Eurydice and Paris luck before they went to take their seats in the audience. Agniezka and Ellsworth stayed a little longer while Eurydice made sure her violin was tuned and tightened her bow, and then they both went to take their seats.

Paris went out through a door to the stage, and then after the applause for him slowed somewhat, Eurydice went out. She was a bit disconcerted when the audience erupted with loud applause. She wasn't aware she was that well-known to the audience in St. Petersburg...or that well-liked anywhere. Her cheeks colored, and she gave a brief curtsy and smile before she took her seat at the piano. Once she was seated, the audience went so silent, Eurydice had to turn her head away from the keyboard to make sure they were still there. Ellsworth and Agniezka sat in chairs in the front row to the right of the aisle, and Ellsworth gave her an amused smile and a wink when he saw her slightly awed expression.

The orchestra began the first strains of the concerto, and Eurydice became lost in the music. The piece was very energetic, with several runs up and down the scales. She was again amazed by the acoustics of the small hall, and the piano—another Pleyel—had a beautiful sound. As she played, she thought she might have to look into getting one of her own. She still much preferred Broadwoods, but she was beginning to think a Pleyel was just as excellent in a completely different way.

When the concerto was finished, the audience was completely silent for several seconds, and Eurydice turned to look at them uncertainly. She couldn't tell if they were silent because they hadn't liked it, or if they were silent because they didn't realize it was finished. She was astounded when they began to applaud raucously with shouts of "bravo!" It was then that she realized they were silent because of how much they had liked it. She stood up from the piano and curtsied with a hesitant smile, and then she reseated herself to play the piano sonata, the one she had written for her parents.

When the concert was finished, Eurydice thought the St. Petersburg audience was perhaps the best she had performed for so far. They were very polite all through it, remaining utterly silent while the songs were played and providing overwhelmingly enthusiastic applause when they ended. They called her back for two encores, and probably would have called her back for another, but she was glad when they didn't because it was nearing midnight and time for her to eat something.

Members of the audience came to meet her when the concert was over, and to her surprise, she found several people from England and Austria among them. Many of those from Britain knew her father or at least of him. Several of those from Austria had heard of her skill from friends and family, and they were pleased to find it had not been exaggerated. Eurydice was flustered by all of the compliments, and she also began to feel dizzy from standing so long. She couldn't decide if it was because she was tired, or hungry, or a combination of both. She gratefully leaned on Ellsworth's arm as he stood beside her while the people came to meet her.

There was a bit of an anxious moment when Gospodin Srdanov and his wife, Ekaterina, came to talk to her, and she politely introduced them to Ellsworth. Ellsworth was curious how she might know the lawyer, but he didn't ask, much to Eurydice's relief. She was hopeful that he would forget about it completely before they reached the hotel, and she supposed she could tell him they were acquainted with one another because of her father, if necessary. It wouldn't be a complete lie, but she hoped she wouldn't have to say anything at all.

Gospodin Trubachev eventually came to her and pressed an envelope containing the bank note for her performance into her hands. He assured her the orchestra and Monsieur Paris would be at the Hermitage for the performance the following evening. In fact, he would see that everything was organized for her rehearsal there the following afternoon. Eurydice was grateful, and she thanked him happily. She was relieved to find all the anxiety and uncertainty she had felt about the city were unwarranted. She still thought things were a disorganized, but the end result proved to be exceptional.

Eurydice, Ellsworth, and Agniezka were eventually able to leave for the hotel, and Eurydice thought it wasn't going to be a moment too soon. She could feel her nausea begin to grow worse as they traveled, and she put pressure on her other wrist without the bracelet in an effort to control it. She was trying to curtail her use of the vinaigrette in front of Ellsworth to keep him from growing suspicious. When they reached the hotel, Agniezka went directly to arrange for a meal to be delivered to their rooms. Despite the lateness of the hour, two maids soon arrived in their suite with trays bearing their food.

Eurydice started slowly, letting the small amount of food settle her stomach before she ate more. There was more of the wonderful roast chicken, and paprikash, and much to Eurydice's delight, broiled lobster. At one point, Ellsworth looked at her speculatively as she ate, finding the way she seemed to inhale her food just the least bit peculiar. For dessert, there was a dish almost like streusel, the filling made of dried fruit and preserves mixed with a sweet wine, topped with whipped cream. If it had been just Eurydice and Agniezka in the room, she would have licked the plate, but Ellsworth was already looking at her oddly enough. By the time they were through with their meal, Eurydice was full to satisfaction…and very sleepy.

Agniezka helped her dress for bed and said good night. Eurydice barely had the energy to wash her face and brush her teeth before climbing into bed and snuggling beneath the blankets. She was almost asleep when Ellsworth got into bed and spooned behind her, putting an arm around her waist. Eurydice smiled contentedly and snuggled against him.

"I'll be going with Agniezka to see her father tomorrow morning," she said sleepily.

"Her father?" blurted Ellsworth in surprise.

"Yes, he lives not far from here, near Tsarskoye Selo. She hasn't seen him since she left Russia, so since we're here…." Eurydice yawned.

"I didn't even realize she had any family."

"Of course she does. Her brother, Nickolai, used to be Myron's valet, so he's been a bit at ends. I think my parents may appoint him valet for Cosmo and Christopher, but since they'll be going off to Harrow, that may not happen." She shrugged and smoothed a hand over his arm at her waist. "I'm sure they'll find something for him, if he wants it."

"She has a brother, too?"

"Why are you so surprised she has family?" asked Eurydice sleepily.

Ellsworth smoothed his hand over her stomach and placed a kiss on her neck.

"I don't know. It just never occurred to me that she might have any…for her to be so far away from them."

"If we move to Scotland, she won't be so far away from her brother, and it's possible she could convince her father to move there without much difficulty. Life here isn't easy when you're poor, even if you are nobility."

"Wait…she's a *noble*?"

"Not titled, but noble, yes…like you," sighed Eurydice blearily.

"Why is she a lady's maid then?"

"Oh, I can't tell you that," said Eurydice slowly as she drifted off.

Ellsworth began to place kisses along her shoulder to her neck, and he smoothed one of his hands up her stomach to cup one of her breasts. He frowned slightly as he squeezed it gently, and then he moved his hand over it before cupping it again.

"Am I being sapheaded, or have your bubbies grown?" he asked amazedly.

Eurydice's only response was to say something unintelligible in her sleep and snuggle against him. Ellsworth sighed resignedly and kept his hand on her breast. Perhaps it was silly, but he could swear they were larger than they used to be. As many times as he had played with them, felt them, looked at them—he would have sworn he was quite familiar with her breasts. It wasn't as if they had grown enormous, but the way they fit into his palm just felt different somehow. He would have to try to remember to examine them closer the next time he actually looked at them.

Chapter Twenty Nine

Eurydice let Agniezka drive the sleigh as they traveled out of St. Petersburg to see her father. They were in the same sleigh they had used to go to the Sâle Lyon on Thursday, and the bonnet was still down, letting the morning sunlight bathe them with its warmth in counterpoint to the chill of the wind blowing against their skin as the horse trotted along briskly. The snow that had been falling on the way to the theater the previous evening had continued to fall through the night, and everything was covered thickly, the sun causing it to glare blindingly into their eyes at times, but the country outside the city was beautiful and for the most part free of trees, just a wide open expanse of unbroken white, only dotted occasionally by houses.

The place where Gennadiy lived was slightly beyond Tsarskoye Selo but not by much, and definitely not as far as Gatchina. The nearest town was a small village called Sophia, built around a cathedral there that bore the name of the saint, a planned village created by Catherine. The area was dotted with Imperial and noble palaces, but Gennadiy didn't live in anything so grand. He did own it, though, which was more than could be said for some of the people who lived there. Eurydice was looking forward to meeting him, and she hoped he was as happy to see Agniezka as she was excited to see him.

Agniezka had woken Eurydice very early. Ellsworth had still been in the suite when she got up, if not in their room, and Eurydice had been happy to see him, despite having to fight her nausea until he left. She and Agniezka had needed to leave early in order to get to Gennadiy's with plenty of time for her to visit with her father before Eurydice went to the Hermitage Theater to rehearse that afternoon. For a time, Eurydice had wondered if waiting until Sunday to go see him might not have been better, but Agniezka was impatient to see her father, and she had already waited so long.

They passed by the fence and gates surrounding the Catherine Palace, and Eurydice's eyes rounded with awe when she looked at it. She didn't think she had ever seen a palace so big. Wilderland was a large castle—one of the largest in Britain aside from those belonging to the king, but this palace made it seem puny in comparison. As she looked at it with her head tilted sideways, she wondered if it were only an illusion, though. Wilderland covered a smaller area of land, but it had several more floors. She wasn't as good with mathematics as Pandora, but Eurydice was willing to bet her sister would be able to tell which was bigger. For her part, Eurydice thought the Catherine Palace was *much* bigger.

"I was married to Sergei there," said Agniezka quietly as she pointed to the cathedral when they traveled past it.

It was a beautiful building, composed mostly of white, with a large dome in the center surrounded by four smaller ones and lots of columns, the dark doorways and windows standing out in stark contrast. Eurydice thought it looked oddly familiar, almost Byzantine, and she imagined it had been a beautiful wedding. It was only unfortunate what had happened afterward. A marriage that began in such a beautiful place should not have been so unhappy.

"Down that lane is where Sergei lives," said Agniezka as she pointed to a track to the left that turned off the road they traveled into the growing woods.

Eurydice didn't strain her neck to see the house. Just knowing it was there was enough. She hadn't realized going to see her father would put Agniezka in such close proximity to her husband, and Eurydice grew anxious that being there might risk Sergei seeing his wife and what might happen if he did. It was doubtful Sergei wouldn't recognize Agniezka; she hadn't changed much in the eleven years Eurydice had known her. Eurydice didn't know how big Sergei was, so she didn't know if she would be able to protect Agniezka from him or not. She was hopeful that wouldn't be something she would need to find out.

It was mid-morning when they turned down another lane to the right. It curved through the forest for only a short distance before the trees thinned somewhat, and Eurydice could see a house. It was of a modest size, with only two floors, the ground floor with rooms that extended just beyond the top on either side. It was covered in golden stucco, the trim and shutters white. There was a balcony on the front, where a set of doors on the top floor opened onto it, and it made a covered porch beneath. Not far from the house was a stable and carriage house covered in the same golden stucco. As they neared it, Eurydice could see it was in need of repairs, but it was well-tended and tidy, and she imagined it had been a lovely place to grow up. There were curls of smoke rising from the two chimneys to either side of the central wing, so it appeared that someone was home.

Agniezka pulled the sleigh to a stop in front of the house and secured the reins to a nearby post. Eurydice could see she was nervous as they stepped onto the porch, and Agniezka pulled the rope to ring the bell near the door. It was shortly answered by an older gentleman in his shirt sleeves.

He was tall, and despite being in his early sixties, he still had a powerful build that was only just beginning to thicken around the middle. His hair was a dark brown, graying at the temples, and he had the same blue eyes of his children. Eurydice could see the resemblance Nickolai bore to his father immediately. Despite his age, he was still very handsome, and despite his straitened circumstances, there was no doubt he was a nobleman, his air commanding and self-assured. He reminded Eurydice of her father.

For a moment, he looked at them in stunned silence, and then he pulled Agniezka toward him to hug her tightly, laughing and crying emotionally.

"Agniezka, *lubova,*" he sighed.

"Papa," she whispered, and Eurydice felt tears sting her eyes at seeing their happiness.

"Come in, come in," said Gennadiy enthusiastically after a minute or two of holding his daughter. "Zenaida!" he called after they were inside and he had closed the door.

Before long, an older woman, much older than Gennadiy, came bustling in, dressed all in black except for the white work apron she wore. She was very short, possibly not even five feet tall, her figure rounded, and her face wizened with age. Her hair was stark white, put into a tight coil low on her neck, and she had piercing blue eyes, making her seem very stern and imperious despite her size. The irritated expression she had on being called away from her chores disappeared when she saw Agniezka, and she threw her apron over her face emotionally before going toward the younger woman to hug her.

"Agniezka, *malutka!*" she cried. After a moment, she patted Agniezka's arm affectionately. "I will go make tea," she said happily.

Gennadiy directed them into a room that opened off the central hall in one of the side wings. It was a small parlor, filled with furnishings that might once have been very plush but were now becoming worn with age. The wood was all polished to a high sheen, and Eurydice didn't think she saw a speck of dust anywhere, but the upholstery on the couch and chairs was faded and becoming threadbare in places. Eurydice thought it was just lovely and very cozy.

"Papa, this is Lady Eurydice Ellsworth, Aberdare's daughter," said Agniezka quietly.

Gennadiy looked at her and smiled widely before taking her by the shoulders and kissing both her cheeks.

"Welcome, Lady Eurydice," he said warmly. "You look just like your *babushka.*"

"Thank you," said Eurydice quietly. "You knew her?"

"I met her several times," he said with a nod. "A lovely woman, both inside and out. Her death was unfortunate."

"Yes, it was," agreed Eurydice softly.

Zenaida soon came in with a cart bearing a tray with tea and biscuits. She stayed only a moment to see they were all served before leaving after brushing an affectionate hand down Agniezka's cheek.

Agniezka and her father spent some time catching up on things that had happened in the eleven years they had been apart. Most of it had been covered in the letters they had sent to each other, but talking face to face gave everything a different perspective. Agniezka assured him that Nickolai was well and happy. Eurydice confirmed that everyone in her family, despite the loss of her two brothers, was well and the number of family members was steadily increasing, the most recent addition being her own husband.

Then the moment came when Gennadiy asked Agniezka how and why she and Eurydice were in Petersburg. The two women looked at each other uncertainly for a few seconds.

"I'm here because I'm touring for my music. Gospodin Trubachev from the Philharmonic Society invited me to come here from Vienna to perform, which I did last night. I'll also be performing for Alexander at the Hermitage Theater tonight," said Eurydice evenly.

"You are a musician?" asked Gennadiy in amazement. "You play the violin like your *babushka*?"

"I do," said Eurydice with a nod.

"Your family must be very proud," he said with a smile.

"They are," confirmed Eurydice with a smile of her own.

"Papa, I'm here to divorce Sergei," blurted Agniezka quietly.

Gennadiy turned to look at her in shock, his smile fading. "What?"

"I should have done it so long ago, but now there are reasons why I have to," she said somberly.

"What reasons?" asked Gennadiy stiffly.

"I have met another man, the man I *thought* Sergei was." Gennadiy continued to look at his daughter stonily. "You would like him, Papa. He is kind and intelligent and honorable...and he loves me," she finished softly.

"I cannot pretend I have anything but a keen dislike for your husband," said Gennadiy evenly. "After what he did to you and then to have my family taken away from me...." He lifted his hands from his sides. "But *divorce*?"

"It's been eleven years, Papa. Nickolai still cannot come back to this country, and it is what keeps you here living as little better than a serf. You have been here paying *him* for the privilege of beating me."

It was true. Gennadiy had been paying Sergei the dowry he had promised for marrying Agniezka in installments. Gennadiy had only given him the last of it the previous year. Despite Agniezka leaving Sergei after less than a year of marriage, despite Sergei's reprehensible treatment of his wife, Gennadiy had been obligated by honor to pay the dowry regardless. It had caused hardship to Gennadiy, both to his pride and his finances, but it was finally done.

"Simon is a good man, and I cannot allow Sergei to continue to have the power to make my family unhappy any longer," said Agniezka resolutely after her father continued to look at her silently.

"Simon, hmm?" said Gennadiy, relenting somewhat.

"He's a physician," said Agniezka proudly, giving him a coaxing smile.

"A respectable occupation," said Gennadiy with a slight smile of his own. "Will I be able to meet him?"

"I hope so, Papa," said Agniezka wistfully. "He's in Britain."

"And you cannot convince him to move here?" Agniezka smiled amusedly and shook her head negatively. "Then I suppose I will have to move there," sighed Gennadiy with pretended long-suffering.

"Really?" said Agniezka hopefully.

"Eh, the winters here are very cold, and age is making my joints begin to feel them much more. I am sure Zenaida would not be sad to see the last of this place. It is becoming too much work for her, but she would deny that to her very grave." He took one of Agniezka's hands in his and patted it soothingly. "I should have left with you and Nickolai, but I am proud. Now I want to be there to enjoy my *vnuki*."

Agniezka's happy expression faded somewhat, and she knew she had to tell her father everything. "That day is not so very far away," she said softly.

"What do you mean?" asked Gennadiy with a frown.

"I will have your first grandchild in the spring."

Gennadiy's jaw dropped in shock. "What is this?" he asked as he stood up from the couch to look down at his daughter.

"Simon and I had intended to marry before it happened, but then it did happen, and now it is all the more urgent that I rid myself of Sergei to give my child the name of its father."

"*Lubova*, what have you done?" gasped her father in dismay.

Agniezka stood up to look at her father. "I have done nothing wrong," she said plaintively. "My marriage to Sergei ended the day I left him."

Gennadiy looked at her with conflicting emotions in his expression. There was disappointment and sadness and compassion and love, but there was no shame...no contempt. He lifted a hand to gently brush it down her cheek.

"There is so much of your mother in you," he said softly. He moved his hand to her shoulder and patted it with a slight, decisive nod. "Then I suppose I will have to begin making arrangements to move to Britain very soon."

Agniezka smiled relievedly, and she wrapped her arms around her father's neck to hug him tightly.

"I love you, Papa," she whispered.

Agniezka and Eurydice stayed at Gennadiy's house for dinner and for an hour or so after discussing many things—plans for Gennadiy's move to Britain, Eurydice's tour, the anticipated birth of Agniezka's child. Eurydice liked Gennadiy very much, and she was glad she got to meet him. He had a wonderful sense of humor, and he was a great story teller.

She hadn't mentioned to Agniezka that she and Ellsworth intended to move to Scotland once he was finished with his assignment because Eurydice wasn't allowed to tell her that. Another thing that made Eurydice hesitate to mention it was that she didn't know when the day would come that Ellsworth *would* finish his assignment. She was hopeful it would be soon, but as things currently stood, Agniezka would leave Eurydice when they went to Britain to visit her family and stay there at least until after the birth of her child and probably for far longer if Ellsworth couldn't finish his assignment for them to move back.

They returned to St. Petersburg with the promise they would come visit Gennadiy again before leaving for Moscow. Agniezka was more cheerful than she had been for some time, and she was optimistic things would go well with her hearing. She was overjoyed her father had decided to move to Britain, and she couldn't wait to write a letter to her brother to tell him. Nickolai would be just as pleased as she was. They might have been forced to leave Russia under unfortunate circumstances, but neither of them had any desire to move back. The only thing that might have urged them to return would have been their father, and once he was settled in Britain, there would be nothing.

When they reached the hotel, Agniezka arranged to have a tray with a small meal brought to their room for Eurydice to eat before going to rehearse at the Hermitage. Unsurprisingly, Ellsworth wasn't in their room, and Eurydice wasn't going to concern herself with where he might be. As long as he was working on his assignment, that was all she needed to know. She ate as quickly as she could, and then she and Agniezka left the hotel again for the Hermitage.

Agniezka turned the sleigh to go across the Admiralty Plaza toward the Neva. There was a skin of ice covering most of the river's surface as they approached, but it wasn't very thick and there were still patches where the water beneath could be seen. Agniezka told Eurydice that by the end of the month it would have ice several feet thick, thick enough for horse races and sleigh races and a frost fair. It happened every year without fail. The Thames only froze that solid occasionally and hadn't done so for a year or two. Eurydice's family was always at Wilderland for the winter, so she had never actually seen the Thames freeze, and it appeared she wouldn't be to a frost fair in Petersburg either.

They could look across the river to the tip of Vasilievsky Island, and Agniezka pointed out they were on the Palace Embankment then and that anything they passed until they reached the theater was part of the Winter Palace and Hermitage. When Agniezka said that, Eurydice thought they were almost there. She was astounded when they continued down the quay for what seemed like an eternity, the façade of the building changing occasionally but never showing a gap, not even when they crossed a narrow canal and finally came to a stop.

"Wow," said Eurydice in amazement. "That is impressive."

Agniezka chuckled as she and Eurydice stepped out of the sleigh. "That's one way of putting it," she said dryly.

They went to what was a fairly small door on the front of the building, the only door Eurydice could see, and went inside. They took a flight of stairs to the next floor. Eurydice was sure there was another way, but she hadn't seen it, and she didn't think she should open doors if she wasn't sure where they would lead. The hallway curved around, and they found themselves in a large foyer. When she looked out a window, she realized it was the arch over the canal between the theater and the rest of the palace. She was a bit awed by the enormity and *grandness* of everything. She'd never seen anything like it. Not that she would want it for herself, but she had to wonder what it was like to have that much wealth and power, to have the resources available to have something made on that scale.

They went through a set of doors and found themselves in a room designed very much like an ancient amphitheater…except it was enclosed, the benches were covered in red velvet cushions, and there was lots of wooden railing and molded plasterwork everywhere. Eurydice and Agniezka walked down the central aisle to the floor where the orchestra was arranged, tuning their instruments. Agniezka quietly took a seat on the front row, and Eurydice removed her pelisse and cloak to set them beside her on the bench.

Trubachev and Paris were there with a man Eurydice didn't know, and he was dressed too finely to be one of the musicians. Trubachev introduced him as Aleksandr Naryshkin, not only the tsar's chamberlain, but also the director of the Imperial theaters. He was much nicer than the abrupt tone of his letter had led her to think he would be. He was slightly older than her father, and when they got into (somehow) a discussion of her lineage, he said his father had known her grandfather while he had served with the English embassy. He also said the Goydanovs were a well-respected and well-known princely family. It was likely some of her relations would be at the performance that night. Eurydice didn't know if she should be excited or not. He left to tend to his other duties shortly after that, but not before he said he was looking forward to her concert after hearing good things about her from Vienna.

The piano had been placed on the stage, and Eurydice was disappointed she would have to play apart from the orchestra. The previous night, having herself in their midst had helped with her anxiety. The Hermitage was much smaller than the Sâle Lyon had been, but she didn't think that was going to help matters much, especially since the audience would be royalty, princes, and nobility. Performing for just one of the three would be bad enough.

The rehearsal went well, and Eurydice had no doubt the performance would go splendidly. As it was, she and Agniezka had just enough time after rehearsal to go back to the hotel, have supper, and begin to dress for the performance. Eurydice would have liked it if she would have had time for a short nap—she was that tired, but there wasn't any time. The only consolation she had was that she wasn't intending for this performance to be as long as that the previous night. She would perform the two concertos and one sonata, barring any encores requested.

Eurydice was growing impatient and anxious by the time she was dressed. Ellsworth was still not there. She didn't know if he was in Schellen's room getting ready or not, and she didn't think she should knock to find out. She had almost decided she and Agniezka would need to leave without him when Ellsworth came into the suite from the hallway. He wasn't dressed for the theater.

"I know, I'm late," he said as he hurried through the suite to Schellen's room. "I'll just change my waistcoat and coat. I won't be five minutes."

Agniezka looked at Eurydice sardonically. "He knows he is late, but *why* is he late?"

Eurydice shrugged noncommittally. She knew the overall reason, but not the specific reason. Only Ellsworth knew that, and he most likely wouldn't tell her, even if she asked. She did have to wonder why whatever it was he was doing was taking him *all* day to accomplish, though.

He came out of Schellen's room in less than five minutes. His cravat wasn't done in a complicated style, and his hair was a bit windblown, but he was presentable. They were just barely going to make it to the theater on time. The closed sleigh was waiting for them when they left the hotel. They went to the theater by the same route Eurydice had taken with Agniezka earlier, and there really was no faster way to get there. Fortunately for Eurydice, being late only meant she would have less time to spend tuning her violin and growing anxious about performing.

When they reached the theater, they used the same door Eurydice and Agniezka had used earlier, but rather than taking the stairs to the auditorium entrance, they took a door to the left that led them behind the stage. Both Trubachev and Paris were there, and they turned to look at her with relief when Eurydice arrived. She apologized for being late and quickly removed her outer clothes to give to Agniezka and began tuning her violin. Luckily, it wasn't out of tune and didn't need adjustment. She tightened and rosined her bow, and then she was ready to perform.

Ellsworth and Agniezka wished her luck, and they left her to use one of the side doors to enter the auditorium. Eurydice asked Monsieur Paris if he knew how many people were there. The only thing he could tell her was that the theater wasn't full. Considering the theater would only hold about two hundred fifty people when every seat was taken, this would be her smallest audience since leaving the drawing room. She would have been even more comfortable with it if the people who *were* filling the seats weren't royalty…or strangers.

The performance went well, but Eurydice could tell her audience was unlike any other she had ever played for. She thought they had enjoyed it, but their applause had only been polite, not enthusiastic. There were no standing ovations and certainly no requests for an encore. Their reaction was so understated that Eurydice was at first concerned they hadn't liked it. Then she realized that they—as nobility and royalty—felt that displaying too much exuberance was beneath them. Eurydice had enjoyed the performance at the Sâle Lyon much, much more.

In light of their underwhelming response, Eurydice was disconcerted when Naryshkin came toward the stage with several people. They had been seated in a box to the right, and Eurydice suspected one of them was the tsar. She helplessly looked toward Ellsworth and Agniezka where they sat near the door at the top of the aisle the people were walking down. She would like it if they were there with her. She would have also preferred to not be doing this on the stage in front of the entire audience. Despite the brevity of her performance, the hour was growing late; she was tired and hungry, and she could feel her nausea building. She tried to surreptitiously signal to her husband and her maid that she wanted them to join her on the stage.

The cluster of people paused to speak with Paris while she continued to signal, and she sighed with relief when the two of them began to walk down the aisle. While they were doing that, Eurydice tried to determine who the people were with Naryshkin. Forewarned would be forearmed, and she didn't want to make some type of social *faux pas*. It was hard enough to maintain her equilibrium just trying to control her nausea and dizziness.

There were three men and three women with Naryshkin, but Paris only bowed deeply to one of them. He had to be the tsar. He was young, with blond hair and light-colored eyes, and the left breast of his black coat was crossed by a light blue sash while the right was covered with medals. She suspected the two other, younger men were his brothers; they all bore a resemblance to one another. The women, however, she wasn't so sure about. One, she assumed, was his wife. The older woman…was his mother? Eurydice could only guess, and she didn't know which of the two younger women was the tsarina.

Ellsworth and Agniezka joined her, and Eurydice began to feel better when her husband put a comforting arm around her waist. Just smelling him began to soothe her stomach. Agniezka took her bow and violin and began to whisper to her about the people below talking with Paris. The two younger men were the tsar's brothers, Constantine and Nicholas. He had one more, Mikhail, but he wasn't there. Of the two younger women, the pretty one with dark blond hair and blue eyes was the tsarina, Elizabeth Alexeievna. The older woman dressed in black was the tsar's mother, Maria Feodorovna, but Agniezka wasn't sure about the other young woman. She thought it might be his sister Ekaterina, but she couldn't say. She finished providing the information not a moment too soon because they ascended the stairs and stood in front of Eurydice.

"Your majesty, may I present Lady Eurydice Ellsworth, her husband, Mr. Gareth Ellsworth, and Gospoda Agniezka Gennadiovna Skryabina-Sheremetevskaya?" said Naryshkin.

"Your majesty," they all said quietly, giving their most courtly bow and curtsies.

Eurydice heard Ellsworth's breath hitch slightly as he bowed, and she tried very hard not to turn her head to look at him with concern. She also had to try not to wobble because the curtsy was making her dizzy. After a respectable amount of time, they straightened, and Eurydice gratefully leaned on her husband and finally gave him a sidelong glance. He seemed (outwardly) to be perfectly fine. The tsar took her hand and respectfully kissed the air above it, and Eurydice's cheeks began to turn pink even as she was sure her skin had to be changing to a shade of green from her nausea. She could only hope this meeting would be as brief as the one had been with Franz.

"Wonderful music, wonderful performance," he said grandly. "I am very pleased Franz had not exaggerated your skill. I am also surprised he was willing to let you come."

"Thank you, your majesty, you are most kind," said Eurydice politely. She wasn't going to argue and tell him that as a citizen of the United Kingdom, the Emperor of Austria had no control over where she might or might not go. The fact that she was standing in front of the Tsar of Russia belied that point.

He waved a hand through the air. "Actually, I am surprised you did not play for me on our last meeting."

Eurydice frowned slightly. "But I have not met your majesty before," she said hesitantly.

"Of course, you have," he said amusedly. "I never forget a beautiful woman."

"I'm sorry, but your majesty is mistaken," said Eurydice softly. She heard a collective gasp from nearly everyone in the room. "I am sure I would remember meeting such a grand personage as the Tsar of All the Russias."

"Perhaps it was in Vienna," said the tsar, beginning to frown slightly himself. "I am sure I have seen you somewhere before."

"No, your majesty, I have not seen you before," insisted Eurydice. "I had never left Britain before August of this year, and I only arrived in Vienna at the beginning of October."

"I was in Britain not so very long ago, perhaps there?"

Eurydice shook her head. "No, your majesty."

She disliked disagreeing with him, and his mother looked at her as if she thought Eurydice was simply being coy, as if she were attempting to pique his interest. She truly had never met him before; it would be difficult to forget. She did remember when he had been in London to meet the Prince Regent, but she hadn't attended any of the social functions where he had been present. Her family didn't usually gather with the same set as the prince. She was curious why he seemed so sure he had met her, and she could see that it bothered him when she continued to insist he hadn't.

"You speak Russian very well, like a native born. How is that possible if you had never left Britain before this year?" He asked it in a slightly accusatory tone.

"My *babushka* was the Countess Alexa Feodorovna Goydanova. She was a lady-in-waiting to the Tsarina Catherine until she permanently moved to Britain with my grandfather in 1765. Although she spoke English very well, she preferred to speak—and made all her grandchildren learn—Russian."

While she was speaking, an expression of realization came onto his face, and he began to smile and nod. Eurydice was alarmed when he grabbed her by the wrist and led her down the stairs from the stage.

"Come with me!" he said excitedly.

Eurydice helplessly looked over her shoulder to Ellsworth and Agniezka, not really seeing that she had any choice *but* to go with him. She was only marginally relieved to see that his family and hers, along with Naryshkin and several other people, were following them. She put a hand to her stomach and began to breathe in and out through her nose slowly as she tried to control her nausea. She didn't know where he was taking her or how long it was going to take, but she was going to be sick or faint if she didn't get to sit down and eat soon.

Alexander first took her to the foyer and led her to the other side where guards stood watch. They opened the doors and saluted as they saw him approach. Eurydice had to wonder what they were thinking to see him pulling her along by the wrist almost at a jog. When they entered the small vestibule on the other side with stairs leading down, the tsar turned to the left, taking Eurydice down a hall that quite took her breath away. There were servants who hurried along with them carrying lanterns because there were no lights in the long, narrow hall, but even in the darkness, what Eurydice could see astounded her. If she could have paused to take a longer look, she would have.

When they were midway down the hall, the tsar suddenly turned to the right, nearly losing the servants with the lanterns. Luckily, this hall (or were they rooms?) was lit by chandeliers. Judging from the breathless expressions on the faces of a few servants they passed, they had just recently and speedily been made that way. Eurydice felt sorry for them and didn't envy their job.

When they reached the end of that hall, the tsar made another turn to the right. Everywhere they passed, she saw paintings and sculptures, cases filled with various objects, some fairly recent, some obviously ancient. She felt like she was in a museum rather than a palace, and she found it difficult to believe that all the things she was seeing had been amassed for private enjoyment…like a dragon's horde of gold and jewels hidden in a cave. She wasn't as familiar with antiquities as Psyche and her father—or her mother, but even Eurydice could tell it was an impressive collection.

Again, when they reached the end of the hall, they made a turn, only this time to the left, passing through what seemed to be a greenhouse. It was peculiar to her to smell roses and other flowers when there was snow at least a foot thick on the ground outside, but the smell calmed her stomach somewhat. That was short-lived, however, when they went through another doorway to the left, and by that point, Eurydice was completely lost. Luckily, it seemed they had arrived at their intended destination because the tsar's pace slowed, and he began to look over the paintings hanging on the wall.

The paintings were all on the right because the wall on the left was nothing but windows facing onto a narrow courtyard. The paintings all seemed to be portraits in various mediums, some large, some small, some of men, some of women. There were even a few of families or couples, but Eurydice didn't recognize any of the people…so far. Some of them seemed to be fairly recent, but some of them—judging from the clothing worn by the subjects—were older by at least a century or more. They went through a small room for which Eurydice could discern no useful purpose other than to break the monotony of the hall and separate off the doors inside it, but the hall continued on the other side. They were almost to the other end of it when it seemed the tsar had found what he was looking for. He smiled widely and waved his hand at it to direct Eurydice's attention to it, and she gasped in amazement.

"I told you, I *never* forget a beautiful woman," he said amusedly.

The portrait was not of Eurydice, but it very easily could have been. It was a picture of her grandmother when she was about the age Eurydice currently was. She was dressed in a gown popular more than fifty years before, but her hair was left its natural color rather than being powdered. Also, rather than having her hair in a formal, tight style that was typical for the time, it was quite simple, with the natural waves loosely coiled at the back of her head, some of them framing her face and falling to her shoulders. She sat comfortably in a chair, her left elbow propped onto a small table beside her strewn with pages of sheet music. Her left hand held the neck of a violin which rested in her lap, and her right held a bow balanced jauntily against her shoulder. The violin was *La Ragazza Dolce*. Alexa had a slight smile, one eyebrow arched sardonically. She looked very beautiful and uncannily like Eurydice.

"Oh," said Eurydice softly.

"I've seen that very look on your face," whispered Ellsworth in her ear amusedly.

Eurydice turned to look at the tsar. "That's my *babushka*," she said quietly.

"Yes, I realize that now," he said with a chuckle. "You must have it," he said decisively.

"Oh, your majesty, I couldn't possibly!" said Eurydice in astonishment.

"Nonsense. It is my gift to you for playing so beautifully," he said dismissively. "Where are you staying? I shall have it packed and delivered there immediately."

"I am staying at the Hotel Tverskaya, but—"

Alexander snapped his fingers and pointed at the painting, and two servants quickly came to begin removing the large canvas in its frame from the wall. Eurydice looked at Agniezka, and she shrugged with a dry smile and quietly gave Eurydice her vinaigrette. She didn't want to use it in front of Ellsworth, but Agniezka had noticed her pallor. It was past time for Eurydice to eat. Their meal once they had arrived back from the rehearsal had not been very large. Eurydice didn't want to use the vinaigrette in front of the tsar and possibly risk insulting him, but she would be absolutely mortified if she got sick in front of him. Agniezka wisely realized that.

"Your majesty is the most generous of princes," said Eurydice weakly, unable to think of anything else to say.

He looked most pleased with himself, and he tucked her hand into the crook of his elbow as they walked back to the theater at a more sedate pace than they had left it. Eurydice did like the painting, but like the portrait Isabey had made of her, she had no notion of what she was going to do with it. Unlike the painting Isabey had made of her, which was only about two feet high by a little less in width, the one of her *babushka* was large, measuring easily four feet in height by three feet in width. It was possibly even larger. Until she had a home of her own, they would both have to be kept stored. She didn't know the artist, possibly de La Tour, but the work had been done in pastels. Whoever he had been, his skill at realistically portraying his subjects had been incredible.

While she was walking with the tsar, she was able to occasionally put the vinaigrette to her nose surreptitiously, just often enough that her nausea didn't overwhelm her and make her vomit. He would point things out to her here and there as they walked back to the theater, now that they were taking their time, and Eurydice was amazed by all the treasures. She occasionally felt that was his intention, but she wasn't sure why he wanted her to be. When they returned to the hall they had first entered on crossing the canal, Eurydice commented on how beautiful she thought it was. Alexander informed her it was called the Raphael Loggia and that it had been commissioned by his grandmother as a faithful reproduction of a hall in the Vatican created by that painter. Eurydice was sure Arachne would be impressed. Eurydice wasn't much interested in art or painting, and even *she* was impressed.

When they returned to the theater, the remaining time Eurydice had to stay was brief. She was finally, formally introduced to the tsar's family, and several of the members of the audience also introduced themselves. Some were members of the French and British embassies. Others were nobility. She did meet a Prince Goydanov who was the son of her grandmother's second cousin. Eurydice didn't know how that made them related, but they *were* apparently related. Everyone was nice, but she would forget most of their names by the time she returned to the hotel. She was terrible at remembering names even under the best of circumstances; this was *not* the best of circumstances.

The tsar took his leave with his family and the majority of the audience. Naryshkin was preparing to go as well, but not before pressing envelopes into the hands of Trubachev, Paris, and Eurydice. She was a bit disconcerted, but she would look at it when she got back to the hotel. It was her fee for the performance, which she hadn't expected to receive. As it was by Imperial command, and the tsar had been generous enough to give her the painting of her *babushka*, to receive money on top of it discomfited her.

Agniezka helped her into her pelisse and cloak, and the three of them left. Before Eurydice got into the sleigh, she went to the quay and was sick. She had tried to keep it controlled, but they had been there too long. If they had left even twenty minutes earlier, she would have been fine. If she didn't do it now, it would happen in the sleigh, and that would be worse. Once she got it out of the way, she would make it back to the hotel, and once there, she would eat. That would keep her from getting sick again…at least until morning.

Ellsworth was standing beside her when she lifted her head, and she removed a handkerchief from her reticule to wipe her mouth as he looked at her worriedly.

"I'm fine," she said quietly.

"I don't believe that," he said shortly.

"Truly, I'm fine," she said evenly. "I'm just tired and hungry...and a bit overwhelmed."

"You're lying," bit out Ellsworth, "and you've been lying to me about being unwell for days."

"I am not lying about being unwell," she said patiently. She shrugged and frowned. "Well, yes, I'm not feeling well, but I am not *un*well. I'm not going to die from whatever this is."

"How do you know?"

Eurydice raised an eyebrow wryly, and Ellsworth tightened his jaw.

"I don't want to discuss this here," she said evenly. "I want to go back to the hotel, eat, have a bath, and go to bed, so can we go now, please?"

Ellsworth compressed his lips. "Fine," he said stiffly.

The two of them went to the sleigh and got in. The ride back to the hotel was a quiet one. Eurydice had been afraid Ellsworth would discover she wasn't well, and he had. Now she was concerned he might want to send her back to Vienna. He hadn't said that he would, but she hadn't given him the chance to do so yet. If he did say he wanted to, she would argue against it.

She didn't feel unwell...not really. Yes, she was nauseous from the moment she woke until she went to bed, but after a week or two of bearing it, she had grown accustomed to it, even if she didn't like it. She was even able to keep it to a manageable level...usually. As for being tired, that wasn't constant, and she couldn't tell how much of the tiredness was caused by the nausea and what of it might be a separate symptom. She had quit taking the dropwort when they arrived in St. Petersburg. The need to relieve herself had returned to a bearable level, and it hadn't grown worse when she quit taking the medicine. She was yet to run a fever or have chills, and her appetite, once she was able to eat, actually seemed to have grown. Other than the tiredness and nausea, she felt perfectly fine. She truly didn't feel that her illness warranted sending her back to Vienna.

When they arrived at the hotel, true to his word, Eurydice found the painting of her grandmother from the tsar sitting at the desk. It had been secured in a wooden frame and wrapped in cloth overlaid with waxed paper bound with twine. Packaged as it was, the painting was almost as tall as Eurydice. Agniezka went to make arrangements for their supper and to have the maids come up to prepare the bath. Eurydice was going to help Ellsworth carry the painting to their suite, but he wouldn't let her. However, when he attempted to pick it up and carry it by himself, she watched a brief look of pain pass over his features before he set it back down and asked the attendant to have servants deliver it to their suite. Eurydice's eyes narrowed as she looked at Ellsworth.

Once they reached their room, she removed her outer clothing while Ellsworth added wood to the fire, and then she turned to look at him.

"Why were you late this evening?" she asked calmly.

Ellsworth straightened from bending to put on the wood and turned to look at her. When he did, she could see that first breath pained him.

"You know I can't tell you that," he said calmly.

Eurydice walked toward him, and before he had a chance to stop her, she put her hands to either side of his chest and squeezed it. He gasped, and his face paled, and he pushed her hands away.

"I bruised a few ribs, but I'll be fine. I just slipped and fell," said Ellsworth evenly when he saw her worried look.

"Slipped and fell? On what? The ice? The snow?" asked Eurydice flatly. She couldn't believe he had slipped and fallen; he was too surefooted for that.

"You could say that," said Ellsworth vaguely.

"Now who's lying?" said Eurydice sarcastically.

"I'm not lying," said Ellsworth patiently. "I did slip and fall because of some ice. It just happens that I slipped and fell off the side of a building," he said lamely.

"Oh, Gareth," gasped Eurydice concernedly, putting a hand to his cheek.

He gave her a sardonic grin and shrugged. "I'm fine, really. A snowdrift kept me from doing any serious damage." Eurydice continued to look at him doubtfully, and he gave her a gentle kiss. "I'm fine," he sighed.

Eurydice carefully put her arms around his waist and rested her head against his chest, listening to the comforting, steady beat of his heart. If the snowdrift hadn't been there, what would have happened? That was something that just occurred to her. What would have happened if he had been killed? The thought of something like that happening disturbed her to even contemplate, but how would it reflect on him? Would anyone besides her and her father know it had happened in service to his country? Even if he didn't die, once his services were no longer required, would he receive any recognition for the things he had done for Britain? She tried to put the thoughts from her mind, but they didn't want to go away.

Agniezka soon returned, followed by two footmen bearing the painting and two maids with their supper. Once the maids put their food on the table, they went to the bathing room to begin filling the tub.

Eurydice idly wondered why Schellen never joined them for their meals. He ate with them while they were traveling, at least in the common room, but Eurydice rarely saw him otherwise. He seemed nice, about the same age as Ellsworth, not unattractive, but he wasn't sociable. She could only assume he was a good valet. Ellsworth didn't complain; she never saw him with cuts from being shaved; his clothes were always presentable. She was sure Ellsworth would have left him in Vienna if he were doing his job inadequately.

Eurydice asked Agniezka if she wanted to bathe once she was done eating and the maids had filled the tub, but Agniezka said she was fine. Eurydice gave her a smile and told her she could go to bed then. Ellsworth narrowed his eyes as he looked at Eurydice, but he didn't say anything. Eurydice finished eating a few minutes after Agniezka had gone to bed, and she went to the bathing room to get in the tub before the water turned cold. She wasn't there long when Ellsworth came to join her. She gave him a wry smile as he sank into the water with his back at the other end.

"Are you here to make sure I don't drown?"

"Can't I bathe with my wife?" he retorted with his own wry smile.

Eurydice could see the bruises along his right side, and she shifted in the tub to lean toward him and balance herself on her hands to either side of his hips. She gave him a teasing kiss before she began to trail her lips down his neck to his chest.

"You're not going to distract me," he said softly.

"Why would I need to distract you?" she asked absently as she toyed with one of his nipples.

"Because you don't want to talk about being sick," he sighed as she continued to tease him.

Eurydice lifted her head to look at him calmly. "It's nothing to worry about. I have some sort of stomach ailment, I expect. Nervous indigestion or something like."

"And you know this because you've been examined by a physician?" he asked dryly.

"No, I haven't, but that's because I don't need to," said Eurydice as she began to kiss his chest again. "As long as I eat frequently and get plenty of rest, I'm fine."

Ellsworth lifted her face by the chin to look at him. "Dicy, you're traveling all over Europe in a coach. How do you expect to accomplish that?" He frowned slightly. "Maybe you should go back to Vienna."

"No," she said flatly, "and every time you ask it or suggest it, I will give you the same answer."

She moved away from him and leaned her back against the other end of the tub to begin washing. She knew it had been coming, and she would continue to refuse until he tied her up and put her in a coach to forcibly *make* her go back.

"I don't want you to come to any harm," he said quietly as he watched her.

She lifted an eyebrow and gave him a dry smile. "Honestly, do I look sick?"

"No, actually," he said evenly, "but throwing up all the time isn't normal, and it can't be good for you."

"Who's to say that going back to Vienna would make me better? And I don't throw up *all* the time, only when I haven't had anything to eat for a while or when something happens that is particularly stressful."

Ellsworth could see he wasn't going to win this argument. Every time he tried to tell her something reasonable, she would find a response to counter with that was also reasonable. She truly didn't look sick; she looked as beautiful and as healthy as ever. But he had promised her father he would take care of her, that he wouldn't let her come to any harm. While an illness was something beyond his control, preventing it from becoming worse by not letting her travel across Europe in a coach, sleeping in a strange city practically every night, in winter, was something he *could* control.

"I still think you should go back to Vienna," he finally said.

"And I still say I'm not going," she countered. "If I begin to actually *feel* like I am sick, I'll go back, but I don't." She shrugged. "At the moment, I'm feeling more inconvenienced than anything."

"I can't do my job if I'm worrying about you."

Eurydice put down the flannel and leaned toward him again to kiss him softly on the lips.

"I'm fine," she whispered. "Truly. I'm no ninny—you know that. I'm also not so pigheaded that I would continue on even if I thought it might risk my health. So don't worry. I would feel terrible if something happened to you because of me."

Ellsworth gave her a slight smile and put his arms around her waist.

"You would?"

"I would," sighed Eurydice as she began to nibble at his ear.

Chapter Thirty

Eurydice and Agniezka went to see Gennadiy again the following day and didn't return to St. Petersburg until late in the evening. Eurydice tried to convince Ellsworth to come with them, but he said he had things to do. She was unsurprised. She thought bruising his ribs would make him want to take one day off to rest and recuperate, but apparently not. Her performances were done, and other than Agniezka's divorce hearing on Monday, there was nothing more to occupy her than to visit Gennadiy, compose…and shop.

Shopping was not very high on her list of priorities. She had no house to purchase goods for. She didn't need any clothing or accessories. Most of the things she bought when she and Agniezka went shopping on Monday morning were things for Agniezka and her baby. Agniezka had tried to stop her, but Eurydice insisted, and it wasn't as if she bought a lot. Aside from not knowing what things to buy, the space they would have to carry anything was limited. She had Agniezka help her buy presents for her family, but she didn't know how she was going to have them delivered. She wasn't even sure they would reach Britain in time for Christmas. She would have to ask Ellsworth to help her send them. He would know what to do.

Eurydice also tried to decide what to buy Ellsworth as a gift for Christmas. She didn't have a clue. She still knew next to nothing about the things he liked and didn't like. She had learned that he liked coffee and that he occasionally liked to smoke a cigar, but not often. He preferred whisky from Islay to that produced just about anywhere else in Scotland. He liked Irish whiskey, but only if it was Jameson's. He wasn't a dandy; as long as he had on clothes, that was all that mattered to him, and he was just as comfortable not wearing any. She had only recently discovered his birthday was in February, and he was thirty. He didn't have a sweet tooth. She didn't know his favorite color or favorite food. He was a man, so she couldn't just buy a piece of jewelry and be done with it. She hadn't noticed that he wore any kind of jewelry in any case, other than his wedding ring. She needed to buy him a gift, but she didn't know what she was going to get.

After their brief expedition to shop, Eurydice and Agniezka went back to the hotel for dinner. With Agniezka making sure that she was eating at frequent intervals, Eurydice had managed to get through all of Sunday and Monday morning without getting sick, even if she did feel nauseous. Eurydice was determined to prove to Ellsworth that she was fine and that sending her back to Vienna was unnecessary. It would take more than a few days to convince him, but she *would* convince him.

By the time they finished dinner, it was time for Agniezka to go to the Consistory for her divorce hearing. When Gospodin Srdanov said the Synod wouldn't grant the divorce without a hearing, it wasn't going to hear the case itself. With all the things it was responsible for overseeing for the Russian Orthodox Church, it entrusted such matters to lower bodies. The Synod itself would only be required to offer a decision if the Consistory was unable to reach its own. That would be unlikely, but whether or not the decision the Consistory made was the one Agniezka wanted would be anyone's guess. Both women anticipated it would be.

The route they took was one they hadn't used before, and there was a light snow falling when they left the hotel. They again started across the Admiralty Plaza, but instead of going to the right of the building, they went to the left. Agniezka took them across a pontoon bridge on the Neva—one of only two over the river in the entire city, neither of which was permanent—to Vasilievsky Island. They turned to the right once they crossed the bridge, and after traveling a short distance they turned to the left. That took them down a long row of interconnected buildings. Agniezka said they were called the Twelve Colleges, each of them housing different departments of the government, including the Senate and the Synod. It might have all appeared to be one very long building if not for the part of each one that jutted out slightly from the façade where the entrance was located to the different departments. The Synod was at the very end, and while the Synod wouldn't be hearing the case, that's where the Consistory was found.

Agniezka pulled the sleigh to a stop and tied the reins to a post. Both women were hopeful the hearing wouldn't take long. The snow had begun to fall even heavier, and they were concerned it might be necessary to shovel it out of the sleigh when they came out. As it was, they lifted the bonnet and hoped it would be enough to protect it at least temporarily.

They had arrived only a few minutes early, unsure whether or not the Consistory had a docket of cases. If they were behind schedule, neither woman wanted to extend the amount of time they would have to wait by arriving too early. If there was no delay, it was so much the better that they had the few minutes beforehand to discuss things with Gospodin Srdanov. They went to the first floor, where Srdanov had told them they should go when they arrived, and found him waiting outside a set of double doors. There was a younger man waiting there as well, and when she looked at Agniezka and saw the way her face paled at the sight of him, Eurydice knew it had to be Sergei.

He was in his thirties, with dark hair and eyes. He was tall and strongly built, and Eurydice could see that next to him, Agniezka would have been unable to defend herself, especially when she had been only a girl of fifteen or sixteen years old. He was very handsome, with refined bone structure, a strong jaw, and chiseled lips, but Eurydice could also see from the way he carried himself that he was vain and arrogant. His clothing was expensive, a black morning coat and breeches with a blue satin, brocaded waistcoat, his shirt and cravat of very fine linen. He had a thick fur coat draped over his arm, which Eurydice thought might be lynx, and an ushanka in his hand made of sealskin.

Agniezka gave him a slight nod, but she did not and would not speak to him unless she had to. Instead, she moved a little away from him to speak quietly with Eurydice and Srdanov. Srdanov would go in with her, but she would have to speak for herself, answering any questions the committee might have for her. He would be with her to explain things, should she require it. It was being allowed because of the perfectly plausible—if inaccurate—reason that Agniezka was a woman and had been out of the country for eleven years. She might not be able to understand things on her own. Srdanov assured her that he expected the Consistory to grant the divorce, but should they not, he would appeal it to the Synod.

Agniezka's face grew alarmed when he said that, but he again stated he fully expected things to go well. Eurydice believed that, too. She couldn't bear to think of it any other way. Eurydice took Agniezka's pelisse and cloak, and she gave her arm a reassuring squeeze just as the doors opened.

"Sheremetev and Sheremetevskaya," said the clerk who had opened the doors.

"I'll be right here," assured Eurydice quietly as Agniezka went into the room with Srdanov.

Sergei looked at Eurydice before he went into the room and started to say something, but then he shook his head slightly and gave her a secretive smile before he turned to enter the room. The clerk closed the doors, and Eurydice frowned, wondering what it had meant.

She went to a nearby window to look outside, and the snow was falling even heavier. It was thick enough that it was difficult for her to see the other buildings around the plaza. Sleighs and coaches were traveling through it, but slowly, and Eurydice became concerned she and Agniezka might have trouble returning to the hotel if it didn't let up.

Eurydice walked to the thick doors of the room, but she could hear nothing on the other side of them. She thought about putting her ear to them to listen, but that would be rude, not to mention unnecessary. Agniezka and Srdanov would come out soon enough, and then they would return to the hotel. Agniezka could tell her how things went once they got there…after she wrote a letter to Felton to let him know it was done.

After it seemed the doors had been closed a long time, Eurydice retrieved her watch from her reticule and looked at it. It was almost three. She frowned and began to pace from the doors to the window. The snow was still falling, and the sun was starting to set. It was taking an eternity. She began to grow concerned. What could they be discussing in there? It should be simple. Agniezka left her husband eleven years ago because he beat her…constantly, and she hadn't even been living in the same country for the same amount of time. There should be no question the two of them needed to be divorced.

Eurydice had just made another circuit a half hour later when the doors opened, and she turned to look at them expectantly with a slight smile. What she saw made the smile disappear along with much of the color from her face. Agniezka was walking out with Sergei, her hand tucked into his elbow. The expression she wore—or rather the lack of any at all—disturbed Eurydice. Her eyes had a hollow look, and her skin was so pale she might have been dead. Sergei gave Eurydice a purely malicious smile and led his wife toward the stairs without pausing.

"Agniezka!" called Eurydice worriedly, and she hurried after them to grab Agniezka by the arm.

"They said I have to go home with my husband now," said Agniezka dully, not looking at her.

"What?" gasped Eurydice breathlessly.

"He said he does not wish to divorce me because he still loves me, so they have told me I must go home with him."

"Oh, no," sighed Eurydice, aghast.

"Oh, yes," said Sergei victoriously. He tugged on Agniezka's arm to start her walking again. "Come along, *lubova*. The house has been so lonely these eleven years without you. We'll have to make sure your homecoming is extra special, eh?"

Eurydice put a hand to her stomach as she helplessly watched them go, and she thought she was going to be sick.

"It will be all right, Agniezka," she called as Agniezka reached the bottom of the stairs with Sergei pulling her along. "I'll make it all right," Eurydice said softly, putting a hand out to the wall as she felt a wave of dizziness overwhelm her.

"Lady Eurydice, are you all right?" asked Gospodin Srdanov worriedly as he put out his hands to steady her.

"No, I'm not," she said faintly. "What happened? Why is she with him? You said there wouldn't be any problem, that this would only be a formality."

"I couldn't argue for her, and she plead her case well, but in Russia—"he shrugged—"the man, unfortunately, has the final say. When I met with Gospodin Sheremetev to discuss the divorce, he assured me that he wouldn't argue against it. What he said in there, however, was the exact opposite. He told them he still loved her, that all this time he had thought she was dead, not realizing she had simply run away. If he had been the one to abandon her, if he had been the one to petition for the divorce instead of her, she would not be with him. But, because he is the man, and he did not want the divorce, the Consistory wouldn't give it. They did not view *her* abandonment of *him* as a valid reason for Gospoda Sheremetevskaya to have a divorce. In their eyes, Gospodin Sheremetev was the one who had been wronged. If he was willing to forgive her and take her back, who are they to keep them apart?"

"Oh, no," said Eurydice weakly, removing her vinaigrette from her reticule and placing it to her nose.

"I will apply to the Synod, but if he continues in the same vein, I do not hold out much hope the outcome will be any different," said Srdanov. "I am truly sorry. I honestly did not think it would come to this."

"Thank you, Gospodin Srdanov, for everything," said Eurydice softly, and she adjusted the things she held in her arms to put on her own pelisse and cloak. "If you could start the proceedings for the Synod to hear the case, I would be most grateful. I've got to find my husband."

Eurydice hurried down the stairs and outside to the waiting sleigh. The snow was still falling, and the sun had mostly set. She had no flint to light the lanterns on the sleigh, and the seat was covered with snow. She quickly dusted it off as best she could and untied the horse. She got on the seat and turned the horse in the opposite direction, clicking to him to go faster. Most of the other traffic had gone with the oncoming darkness and heavily falling snow, and Eurydice turned onto the embankment without slowing. She felt the runners skid a little as she made the turn onto the bridge, but she didn't slow down and urged the horse to go even faster. Eurydice only hoped she could remember the way back to the hotel.

When she reached the plaza on the opposite bank, she hurtled across it quickly, causing passersby to look at her in shock and astonishment, some shouting at her to slow down in several different languages. There was more traffic on this side of the river, both vehicle and pedestrian, and it was becoming too dark to see, especially because of the snow. She was breathing in and out quickly, her heart beating at a panicked pace. She almost missed the street she needed to turn down behind the Admiralty in the darkness, and she felt the back end of the sleigh wobble and lurch as she bumped into a curb. Then Eurydice crossed another bridge, and she knew she'd gone too far. She was almost sobbing as she found a place on the busy street to turn around, and she made herself slow down and take her time as she headed back the way she had come. It would do neither her nor Agniezka any good if she got lost.

She crossed back over the Moika, and then she turned left onto what she hoped was the correct street. She almost began to cry when she recognized the hotel. She carefully eased the sleigh to a stop and tied the horse to a post. She tried not to run across the lobby to the stairs, and she didn't even pause at the desk to tell them she had returned the sleigh or find if there had been any messages before going to their suite. When she got there, the rooms were dark.

"Ellsworth?" she called hopefully.

She was answered by silence until Casanova made his presence known. She went to his cage and put the cloth over it after making sure he still had food and water. Listening to his nonsense was not something she could tolerate at the moment, and it would certainly do nothing to cheer her.

She didn't know why it surprised her to find Ellsworth wasn't there, but of all the times when she truly needed him to be there, he was gone. She went to add more wood to the fire and got a rush to light a few of the lamps. Then she began to pace, alternating between shaking her hands to thaw them and scratching her forehead nervously. She needed to be doing something to get Agniezka back, but she couldn't do it without Ellsworth. She didn't know what she was going to do. She needed her husband, but she didn't know how to find him. How could she possibly find him when he never told her where he was going or what he was doing? They had never discussed what she should do to find him in an emergency—like right then.

She only paced for a few more minutes before she had to go to the garderobe and vomit. It was time for her to eat something. It was nearing five in the evening. If Agniezka were there, it would have already been seen to. She rinsed her face and mouth, and then she put her thumb to her wrist and began to pace again. She needed food, but to get it she would have to go downstairs. If she went downstairs, she might miss Ellsworth if he came back. If he came back soon after she ordered the food to be brought to the room, then she wouldn't have time to eat it, and she would still be without it. She didn't think she could eat, but she wouldn't be able to think if she was spending all of her time throwing up.

She finally groaned under her breath and left the room to go downstairs to the common room. She asked for a tray with whatever was readily available, except for *borscht* or anything with pickled herring, and a large pot of *sbiten*. When she got back to the suite, Ellsworth was still not there (of course). Her stomach felt terrible. Part of it was from needing to eat, but she was becoming almost hysterical with panic as she tried to think of what she was going to do.

Agniezka could not stay with Sergei. Eurydice was terrified that if they didn't get her away from him tonight, he would kill her, especially if he found out she was with child by another man. Agniezka should have never come back to Russia. They should have found another way to resolve this without her ever needing to, but it had seemed like it would be so simple. That should have been the first indication that everything would go terribly wrong.

Eurydice jumped when there was a knock at the door. She went to open it, and a maid came in with her tray. Eurydice tipped her and thanked her after she put the tray on the table, and then she left. Eurydice poured herself a cup of *sbiten*, and she rolled the hot glass in her hands to thaw her fingers the rest of the way before taking a small sip. The liquid began to settle her stomach as she continued to drink, and once she finished the first cup, she poured another and set it on the table to cool a little. She removed a piece of the roasted chicken from the tray and began to pick off strips of the meat as she paced.

She went to the window at one point to look out, and she was astonished at how dark it was outside. There were a few lights here and there, but the snow was falling so heavily they were very dim, and Eurydice couldn't even be sure of their distance. She put the chicken down on the table and wiped her hands on a napkin, and then she went to the door to Schellen's room and knocked. He answered it before long, looking at her with a guarded expression.

"Yes, my lady?" he said politely.

"Did Ellsworth tell you what time to expect him back?"

"No, my lady," he said slowly, his expression not changing.

"Did he tell you where he has gone?"

"No, my lady," he said evenly.

Eurydice shook her head and rolled her eyes with a self-deprecating laugh. "Of course not," she said tartly, "because *I* couldn't possibly need his help," she finished brokenly. She waved a hand in the air defeatedly. "Thank you, Schellen," she said quietly, giving him an apologetic smile. It wasn't his fault.

He nodded and closed his door, giving her an odd look as he did so. Eurydice went back to the table and looked at the chicken. After a moment of indecision, she picked it back up and began to eat some more. Until Ellsworth returned, there was nothing else she could do except eat…and worry. She finally sat down to eat the other things the maid had brought that weren't as portable as the chicken. There were lamb dumplings, a stew made with beef and vegetables, another dish made from potatoes called *kartoshnik*, and a custard-like dish made with peaches for dessert. Eurydice was full when she was done, eating nearly everything that had been brought. It eased the nausea she had felt, but she could still feel a nervous ball in the pit of her stomach.

She went to her reticule to look at her watch, and she grew even more anxious when she saw that it was nearly six in the evening. Agniezka was to Sergei's house by now, and Eurydice tried not to think about what he might be doing to his wife. She needed Ellsworth to come back, but if he followed his normal pattern, she might not see him for several more hours. She began to pace again, and she tried to breathe in and out deeply to keep herself calm. Becoming hysterical wouldn't solve anything.

She was on another circuit from one end of the room to the other when the door to the hall opened. Ellsworth came in carrying his coat draped over his arm, several letters in his hand. He grinned when he saw Eurydice.

"Considering all of these are yours, I'm surprised you left them at the desk," he chortled as he closed the door. He lifted the top one. "There's one for Agniezka, too." Then he looked around the suite. "Is she in her room?"

"No," said Eurydice quickly. She went to the chair where she had placed her pelisse and cloak and began to put them on. "We have to go."

"Go?" he said with an amused half-smile, and then he noticed what she was doing and her almost frantic behavior. "What's wrong?"

"The hearing didn't go well, and now she's with him, and she doesn't have her cloak, and I…and it…oh!" said Eurydice, and she put a hand to her stomach and waved the other in front of her face in an effort to keep herself from becoming sick again. She took a deep breath before she picked up Agniezka's cloak and pelisse and draped them over her arm.

Ellsworth walked toward her and put one hand to her shoulder and the other to her cheek. He was frowning concernedly as he looked at her. She was almost hysterical, and he knew whatever had happened must be extremely bad for her to look that way. When Schellen found him, telling him he should go see his wife, Ellsworth thought the man was worrying over nothing, but now he could see his valet had not been exaggerating.

"Shh," he whispered soothingly. "What hearing?"

"I can't explain now," said Eurydice as she tugged at his arm to pull him toward the door. "We have to go to Sophia."

"Who's Sophia?"

"It's not a who; it's a where," said Eurydice as she pulled him to the door and opened it. "It's on the other side of Tsarskoye Selo. It's where he lives. We have to hurry."

"Who is *he*?" asked Ellsworth as he let her continue to pull him along by the arm down the hall.

"I'll tell you while we're on the way there, but for now, will you move your bloody arse?" she said frustratedly.

Ellsworth raised a sardonic eyebrow at her tone and language, but he began to walk faster. They went down the stairs, and he stopped at the desk to find out if a sleigh was available. The closed sleigh they used at night was not, but the one Eurydice and Agniezka normally used was. It would have to do. The attendant tried to dissuade them from going out because of the snowstorm, but Eurydice was having none of it. When they went out, the lanterns had been lit on the sleigh. The bonnet was still up, and the bear fur throw was there. Ellsworth turned to look at her after he looked around himself at the weather.

"Dicy, are you sure we need to do this now?" he asked softly.

"Yes, she can't stay with him," said Eurydice gravely.

Ellsworth gave her a brief nod and started the horse on its way. As they traveled through the city, there were street lamps to help them see, but the snow was falling so heavily, their light did little better than keep them on the street rather than the sidewalk. They had crossed the Moika and were almost to the Griboyedova when Ellsworth spoke.

"You need to start telling me what's happened," he said evenly, keeping his eyes ahead of him.

Eurydice looked at him. "You came to Petersburg because of your assignment. I came because of my music. Agniezka came to get a divorce," she said slowly.

He looked at her in shock. "What?"

"My father and Sheerness had been sending letters here on her behalf before we even left Venice to have it arranged, but she had to come appear before the Consistory because she's nobility."

"That's what Sheerness was doing for you?" Eurydice nodded. "Is that why you came?"

"No, I came to perform…and to be with you, but it provided Agniezka with the opportunity to take care of her own matter."

"The hearing?"

"Yes, but the Consistory wouldn't give her the divorce. Her husband, Sergei, told them that he still loved her, even though she abandoned him, and they made her go home with him," said Eurydice brokenly.

"I'm not seeing the problem," said Ellsworth flatly.

"But he *doesn't* love her," said Eurydice earnestly, "and she certainly doesn't love him."

"But he *is* her husband," said Ellsworth stiffly, and he began to slow the pace of the horse.

"Don't you slow down, or so help me, I'll take over the reins myself," said Eurydice coldly. Ellsworth tightened his jaw, and he kept the horse to its pace. "He's the reason she works for my family…*and* her brother, too. If Nickolai ever comes back here, he will be sent to Siberia." Ellsworth looked at her with a doubtfully raised eyebrow, thinking it all sounded a bit melodramatic, and Eurydice could see she would have to tell him more than she had thought would be necessary. "Sergei is the reason Agniezka's back was broken."

"How so?"

"He did it with his own hands! Agniezka left him because he abused her. She married him when she was fifteen, almost sixteen, and things went well for about a month. At least, he didn't start to abuse her until then. He would get drunk and fly into rages even before that, but it grew worse. At first it was only an occasional slap across the face, sending her to her room without food, calling her names that weren't very nice. Then it escalated to raping, beating, starving…locking her in the cellar without clothes or a candle for days. He treated her worse than an animal."

"Bloody hell," gasped Ellsworth, and he flicked the reins to make the horse go faster.

"The last time it happened, he beat her senseless after he raped her and threw her down the stairs to break her back. Then he went to sleep from being drunk. Agniezka managed to escape while he was unconscious, and she had to crawl on her hands and knees through the snow on a night not unlike this one to her father's house. When Nickolai saw her, he went to Sergei's house and nearly beat him to death. He would have if Gennadiy hadn't stopped him."

They had crossed the Fontanka and were almost out of the city. The street lights were growing fewer, and it was becoming harder to see. Eurydice was anxious because she knew it would be more than an hour—almost two—before they reached Agniezka, even if they were driving in daylight and fine weather. Now, she could only hope they would make it by midnight, and every minute it took them to get there was another that something could go horribly wrong.

"Why didn't Gennadiy let Nickolai kill him?"

"It wasn't because he liked his son-in-law," said Eurydice dryly. She only felt slightly calmer after telling Ellsworth the truth. "He simply didn't want his son to have that on his conscience." She shrugged. "He probably should have, though. The punishment would have been no less harsh either way; getting sent to Siberia for thrashing someone…killing someone. There is no death penalty in Russia. In Sergei's case, death was—is—far more deserved."

"You don't think he's changed in eleven years?"

Eurydice scoffed derisively. "He hasn't changed. This afternoon when he came out of the hearing with Agniezka, he was *gloating*, as good as saying he intended to pick up right where he left off."

"You should have told me about this," said Ellsworth in an even tone, but Eurydice could tell he was angry.

"It wasn't my place to tell you, and if things had gone well at the hearing, I still wouldn't have told you."

"But things *didn't* go well. Did you not realize they might not and plan for that? If I had known about this, I could have been there with you, and he would have never left the building with her."

"You didn't need to know before things went wrong," defended Eurydice patiently, "and it wasn't my place to tell you," she repeated with a shrug. "Now, you need to know."

Ellsworth clenched his jaw and looked away from her. She was right, and yet she wasn't. He could understand her desire to keep a confidence, but she had taken it too far. At least now he knew most of the things she had been keeping from him, and he hadn't needed to read her Arabic diary to learn them. He was sure there was more, but the answers he now had took care of the ones that had been bothering him…except one.

"Does Felton have anything to do with Agniezka wanting a divorce?" he asked calmly. Eurydice turned her head to look at him levelly. "It just seems strange she would decide after *eleven* years that she needs a divorce, and the one letter she's received here came from him."

Eurydice took a deep breath and adjusted her hands inside her muff and put it up to her nose to thaw her face a little. She would have to tell him eventually because it would soon be obvious…provided nothing happened tonight. There was no point to delaying it any further.

"Yes, he has everything to do with it," she said softly. "Agniezka and Felton wish to marry."

"Ah," said Ellsworth mildly with a slight smile.

"And she's also carrying his child," finished Eurydice calmly.

"What?" he blurted dumbly.

"That day you saw Felton coming out of my room at the palazzo, Agniezka had sent him to tell me that and to enlist my help in getting Agniezka divorced from Sergei for them to be married before the baby was born." Eurydice's expression grew thoughtful. "I don't know if they'll be married by May or not. They certainly won't be married before it's obvious she's pregnant."

"Bloody hell, woman! That was something I needed to know!" said Ellsworth angrily.

"Not until now you didn't," said Eurydice exasperatedly. "She's not your servant, and it's not as if it's *your* child. So, why did you need to know?"

"You should have told me," he said through clenched teeth, "all of it. If I had been there with you, Agniezka wouldn't be with Sergei—a man who has in the past beat his wife with no provocation, and you sent her to him pregnant by another man."

"I didn't send her to him!" said Eurydice breathlessly. "If I had known this would happen, I never would have let her leave Vienna."

"If you had trusted me and told me about all of this, we wouldn't be doing what we're doing right now."

"Very well, if you think you could have stopped Sergei from taking her, what would you have done? It's not as if you could have beat him senseless or conked him one."

"You know as well as I do that I could have managed the situation very discreetly. It's all part of the service I provide," he said sarcastically. Eurydice chose not to say anything because she knew he was right. "Is there anything else I should know?"

"Nothing is coming to mind," said Eurydice flatly.

They had left the city far behind, and despite the snow and darkness, Ellsworth kept the sleigh moving at a fast pace. They would be fairly safe from accidents because the way was mostly flat, and the weather was cold enough that any lakes or streams hidden beneath the snow were frozen solid. The only thing they would need to worry about would be trees…or buildings, neither of which would be a problem provided they stayed on the road.

After they had been traveling for a little more than an hour, the snow began to taper off, but it didn't stop completely. It made it easier to see where they were going, which was good because it was about to change from a fairly straight path to requiring a few turns. The moon would only appear as an occasional sliver between the clouds and provided no light. When the snow lessened, the air began to grow even colder, and Eurydice wished they had the closed sleigh. Her face was so cold she couldn't feel her nose.

They didn't talk very much after Eurydice explained everything, partly because there was nothing more to say, partly because it was so cold. Eurydice wasn't even sure she could make her lips move anymore. Perhaps she should have told Ellsworth everything before they left Vienna, but she honestly hadn't seen a reason why he needed to know. Aside from that, there were so many other things that required his attention, she hadn't wanted to burden him with even more. She hadn't foreseen the possibility things would go as terribly wrong as they had. If anything happened to Agniezka because of all this, Eurydice would never forgive herself.

"You do know where he lives?" asked Ellsworth after they passed Sophia Cathedral.

"I think so," said Eurydice in a slurred voice. Her face was so cold she could scarcely make her lips move.

"What does that mean?" asked Ellsworth sharply. His fingers had long since gone numb inside his gloves, and it was making him testy.

"Agniezka pointed out the lane to go to his house the first time we went to see Gennadiy, but that was in daylight, and we didn't actually go to his house." Ellsworth muttered a curse under his breath. "It's to the left in those woods just ahead. There are no gate posts to mark it, and it's very narrow. You may want to slow down a little once we're about a quarter of a mile in."

Ellsworth looked at her doubtfully. In weather like this, they could ill-afford to get lost. As late as it was and as remote as everything was, freezing to death was not impossible. He could perfectly understand why she hadn't wanted to wait until morning, now that she had told him everything, but the conditions could have been better.

He slowed the horse to a walk after they had gone the distance she suggested. Eurydice scooted closer to him and leaned forward slightly to look past him at the left side of the road. Looking for tracks would be pointless. The trees had stopped the snow, but only the slight flurry it had been; there was still a new layer several inches thick from the heavier snow falling earlier.

"Here!" said Eurydice quickly.

"Are you sure?" asked Ellsworth doubtfully. He could see nothing but darkness in the trees, and the space between them was indeed very narrow— wide enough for one vehicle but definitely not two.

"Yes, I'm sure," said Eurydice with a nod of her head. "I recognize that tree with the odd limb there," she said as she pointed to a nearby oak with a limb bent at an almost perfect right angle pointing downward.

Ellsworth clicked to the horse and got him to turn down the lane. He kept the animal to a walk for several reasons, not the least of which being that he didn't want to make any undue sound and alert Sergei to their arrival. The lane had a slight verge from years of use, and it helped Ellsworth keep the sleigh where it belonged, especially when there were a few curves. They went around one that turned to the left, and Ellsworth could see lights through the trees. They hadn't gone very much farther when they arrived at a large clearing, and the house loomed in front of them.

From the angle they were looking, it didn't seem very large. It was bigger than Gennadiy's house, but not as large as the country houses of some of the nobility. It was two floors with a cellar beneath, having a central wing and others to either side at right angles. There was a balcony on the top floor of the central wing, creating a covered porch over the main entrance, very much like Gennadiy's. Sergei's house, however, was made of wood, and the trim around the windows and doors, along the eaves, and the balustrade on the balcony and porch were all very ornately carved with tracery, ogees, and turned pilasters.

As Eurydice stepped into the snow, at least her feet were warm. Agniezka had convinced her to buy a pair of fur-lined felt boots. They came up her leg to just below her knee and were very comfortable to wear. As it was, the snow was just below the fur at the top of them. She lifted the bottom edge of her clothes to keep them from dragging through the snow and getting wet, and she had Agniezka's cloak and pelisse draped over her arm. She removed one of the lanterns from the sleigh and carried it with her. Ellsworth started for the porch, but Eurydice stopped him.

"She's not going to be in the house," she said quietly.

She lifted the lantern and began to walk around the side of the house, looking for an entrance to the cellar. Ellsworth was following her, looking into the windows on the ground floor for any signs of movement. Most of the curtains were drawn, and most of the rooms were dark, but he decided the rooms on the ground floor were empty. There were a few windows with light in them on the top floor, but he wasn't sure if anyone was there.

When they went around the back, they could see the central wing extended further beyond the side wings, giving the house the shape of a large cross. The kitchen was in a separate building, and the servants' quarters were separate as well. There was a barn and what might be a smokehouse, but that was the extent of the outbuildings. They were to the very back of the house when they found the entrance to the cellar. At least, they were fairly sure it was the entrance. It was covered with snow they had to dust off to make sure.

They were about to open the doors when something blue hanging on the side of the house caught Eurydice's attention. She moved closer to shake the snow off of it, and she recognized it as the dress Agniezka had been wearing. She pulled it off the hook where it was hanging and found her chemise there as well. Sifting her fingers through a small drift of snow on the ground beneath them revealed Agniezka's boots. Eurydice felt the blood drain from her face, and she turned to look at Ellsworth.

"These are Agniezka's clothes. I think he's put her down there naked," she whispered worriedly, her lower lip trembling.

Ellsworth opened the doors as quietly as he could, and Eurydice started down the stairs before he could stop her. Ellsworth clenched his jaw and shook his head then quickly followed behind her after having a brief look around.

"Agniezka?" Eurydice whispered loudly once she stood on the floor. She lifted the lantern above her head to give more light. "Agniezka?" she called again worriedly.

The cellar only covered the area beneath the central part of the house. It was a large, unfinished room with a dirt floor. There was a place closed off in one corner for storing coal, and shelves lined most of another wall for storing vegetables, wine, and other items, but it was otherwise empty. There was no set of stairs to go into the house; the only way in was through the doors Eurydice and Ellsworth had taken. Eurydice walked a little further in. It was warmer in the cellar than it was outside, but it was still very cold, much too cold to survive for long without clothes.

"Agniezka?"

Eurydice saw movement out the corner of her eye, and she turned the lantern in that direction. She stifled a scream when she saw a large rat scurrying away, its beady eyes glowing red in the light, and she moved closer to Ellsworth and probably would have jumped into his arms if she'd had her hands free to hold on to him.

"You're afraid of rats?" he asked amusedly.

Eurydice shuddered. "They're nasty, vicious, smelly.... Even Psyche doesn't like rats."

She jumped when she heard another noise, and she swiveled to turn the lantern in the direction where she thought it originated. She also heard the muffled sound of metal clinking, and then she saw Agniezka crouched and curled up in a ball in a corner on the far end of the room near the front of the house, her arms wrapped around her legs.

"Agniezka?" called Eurydice, her voice a mixture of relief and concern when she saw her maid, her bare skin a pale white in the light.

"Eurydice?" called Agniezka weakly.

She slowly stood and tried to walk to her friend, but there was a fetter around her ankle attached to a chain fastened to the wall. It kept her from going more than a few feet. Eurydice hurried toward her after she gave the lantern to Ellsworth and quickly wrapped Agniezka in her cloak.

"What are you doing here?" asked Agniezka confusedly.

"As if I'd leave you like this," said Eurydice dryly with a soft smile. "We got here as quickly as we could."

Both women looked as Ellsworth bent down to undo the fetter. He removed a pouch from his coat pocket and selected a small metal tool from it. He had the shackle unfastened and removed in a matter of seconds. Eurydice was unsurprised, but Agniezka looked at him in puzzlement, wondering what he would be doing with something like that.

"Now, I found your clothes where Sergei left them, but I'm afraid they might be wet from the snow," said Eurydice once Ellsworth was done. She couldn't tell if they were wet because she hadn't removed her gloves. "I have your pelisse and cloak, but you will still be shoeless."

"You found my *valenki*?" asked Agniezka hopefully.

"Yes, but they were buried under a foot of snow. They're probably soaking wet," said Eurydice as she held them out.

"They'll be fine," said Agniezka as she took them and removed her woolen hose from inside to put them on. Then she put on the boots, and Eurydice heard her audible sigh of relief. "You shook the snow off my clothes?"

"Yes, but—" began Eurydice as Agniezka took her chemise and gown to begin putting them on as well.

"It's too cold for the snow to melt just from the air. If you shook them off before you put them close to your body, they should be dry."

Agniezka's lip was split, and her nose had been bleeding. She had a large bruise on one cheek, and her eye was nearly swollen shut on the same side.

Eurydice didn't see any bruises on the rest of Agniezka's body, and she hoped Sergei didn't notice the roundness of Agniezka's stomach when he made her remove her clothes.

"He didn't do anything else, did he?" asked Eurydice hesitantly as she fastened the back of Agniezka's gown.

"No. He said he would save the *festivities* until after he had some sleep." She scoffed as she put on her pelisse and fastened the buttons. "It is more likely he is saving it until after he is drunk."

"I don't think there's anyone in the house," said Ellsworth as he looked up at the ceiling.

"He does his drinking in his study," said Agniezka, tilting her head in the direction of the wing on the other side of the house. "He told the servants they could go to their quarters for the night—fewer witnesses that way."

"Are you all right? Do you need a doctor?" asked Ellsworth solicitously.

"I'll be fine. I've had much worse," said Agniezka with a tight smile. "Thank you for asking." Ellsworth nodded.

"Let's get you back to the hotel," said Eurydice as she put an arm around Agniezka's shoulders. "I don't know what can be done legally or how quickly, but if nothing else, we can get you on a ship to Britain until it's arranged for the Synod to hear your case."

"But I can't leave you," said Agniezka concernedly as they began to make their way to the stairs.

"Tush," said Eurydice dismissively. "I am perfectly capable of dressing myself, and I would sooner walk around naked than I would risk something happening to you if you stayed."

They stood outside the cellar, and Ellsworth closed the doors. The snow had stopped, but the wind would blow and lift some of that which had fallen to swirl it through the air in biting whirlwinds. Looking at the sky, the clouds still billowed there, and it was likely more snow would fall before morning.

"Sergei told me that my room was exactly as I'd left it eleven years ago," said Agniezka dully. "If that's so, I would like to get my things, such as my mother's jewelry."

Eurydice and Ellsworth looked at each other. It would be risky. Ellsworth hadn't seen any signs of someone in the house, but Agniezka said Sergei was in his study in the other wing, where Ellsworth hadn't been able to look. If Sergei had drank himself unconscious, they would probably be safe. If not, he might discover Eurydice and Ellsworth were there to help Agniezka. Ellsworth would restrain the man if necessary, but it would ruin Agniezka's chances of being granted a divorce. It was unlikely Agniezka would ever have another opportunity to get the things she had been forced to leave behind, and Eurydice could understand her not wanting to leave her heirlooms and personal belongings to Sergei. She gave Ellsworth a shrug to let him know she would abide by whatever he decided. They walked around to the front of the house, but Ellsworth had the two women stop before going onto the porch.

"Wait here," he said quietly, and he went around the other side of the house. He came back a few minutes later. "He appears to be asleep in a chair in his study, but I don't know how deeply or how long he will stay that way. You need to do this as quickly and as quietly as you can."

Agniezka and Eurydice nodded, and the three of them went onto the porch. The door wasn't locked, and Agniezka opened it carefully. The hinges were nicely oiled, and it made no sound as they went into the house and closed it behind them. The landing for the stairs wasn't far from the door, and they began to climb them with Agniezka leading the way. Eurydice and Ellsworth stepped on the treads where she did to avoid any squeaks they might have, and they all made it safely to the top.

Agniezka's room was in the wing opposite from the study, and that was fortuitous. The sound of them moving around directly over his head might wake Sergei, and Ellsworth wanted to avoid that if at all possible. The door to the room was closed but not locked, and in contrast to the well-oiled front door, it made a harsh creaking noise when Agniezka opened it. She managed to reduce it by opening the door quickly once the noise started, but it echoed in the silence of the house.

"I'll keep watch at the door," whispered Ellsworth. "Make this quick."

When Sergei said her room was exactly as Agniezka had left it, he meant it literally. There was a thick layer of dust covering all the exposed surfaces. He had not even allowed the servants in to clean, which explained the unoiled hinges. Eurydice had the lantern from the sleigh, and it provided enough light for them to see what they were doing in the otherwise pitch black room.

Agniezka went to a closet and carefully opened the door to retrieve a trunk.

"Lacquered birchwood," said Agniezka when she saw Eurydice's concerned look at her carrying something that large. "It's very light, but it's also very sturdy and waterproof."

She opened it, and then she went to the dressing table for her jewel box and the few other items sitting there. There were small paintings of her mother, father, and Nickolai that she added, a Bible and two other books, and a few items of bric-a-brac that she wrapped in clothes from a drawer to protect. She stood for a minute with her hands on her hips as she tried to decide if there was anything else that she wanted.

Several times, Eurydice needed to rub her nose to stifle sneezes as Agniezka's moving things in the room stirred up dust. Her eyes were watering, and she was trying to control the urge. It was difficult, and she hoped they would leave soon.

Agniezka went to the closet and came out with several items of clothing that she added to the trunk. Eurydice might have complained, but they appeared to be something other than regular dresses, or even ball gowns. She went in and came back out to place a snug-fitting hat made from fox fur on Eurydice's head before she put one made from lynx on her own. She made one more trip for a few more items of clothing and furs before she came back out to add them to the trunk. She gave the room another once-over and decided that was everything she wanted. Sergei could burn the rest for all she cared.

She closed the lid on the almost-full trunk, and then she was ready to leave. Eurydice set the lantern on top of the trunk and grabbed the leather handle at one end to help Agniezka carry it. It was surprisingly light. They were almost to the door when Eurydice sneezed, and then she sneezed again, and again, and she probably would have done it at least once more if Ellsworth hadn't come behind her and squeezed her nose. She didn't have a free hand to do it herself, and once she had started, she had been powerless to stop it. All of them stood silently and listened, and then Eurydice and Agniezka's eyes widened in alarm when they heard booted feet thundering up the stairs. Sergei was awake.

Ellsworth turned to face the doorway and was able to take a few steps into the hall before Sergei reached the top of the stairs. Needless to say, Sergei was surprised to see a man standing there.

"Who the hell are you?" asked Sergei angrily.

"A concerned citizen," said Ellsworth mildly, slowly walking toward Sergei. "It's not very nice to chain your wife in the cellar."

Sergei sneered. "That is what one does with a *sooka* that will not stay home," he said arrogantly.

Ellsworth couldn't tell if Sergei was drunk or not. His speech wasn't slurred, and he seemed steady on his feet, but Ellsworth could smell alcohol, probably vodka. He could also see the man was just plain mean, and it was going to be impossible for him to reason with Sergei to make him let Agniezka go peacefully. He would try, if given the choice, but Ellsworth wasn't going to let Agniezka stay, no matter what he had to do to make it possible for her to leave. He took a few more steps toward Sergei and was within arm's reach of him. He would need to get him to move out of the way of the stairs so the two women could go down.

"She's not a dog; she's a person—your wife," said Ellsworth tightly, clenching his jaw. He had no tolerance for men who abused women.

"Yes, she is, and I can do anything I want to her. I could even kill her, and nothing would happen," said Sergei malevolently, smiling darkly.

"You won't get to find out," said Ellsworth softly.

He reached out to grab one of Sergei's wrists and bent his arm behind him while he put the other hand to his shoulder. Sergei roared angrily and immediately began to struggle, but Ellsworth was able to move him out of the way of the stairs to the other side of the landing.

"Go to the sleigh," Ellsworth ordered the two women as he tried to keep his hold on Sergei.

The Russian was strong, and Ellsworth's ribs were still sore from falling off a building on Saturday. He wasn't sure how long he would be able to hold Sergei, and while he would restrain him again should he need to, it would be best not to let Sergei get loose in the first instance. It would only take one well-placed punch or kick to make something very bad happen.

Eurydice and Agniezka quickly did as they were told. The trunk was light enough that Eurydice was able to hold the handle with one hand and grab the lantern with the other as they went down the stairs. Sergei thrashed out with his legs and tried to kick Agniezka as she went by, but she was just out of his reach. Sergei roared furiously and struggled even more to get loose. Agniezka and Eurydice were to the bottom of the stairs and heading out the door.

"Get back here, you bitch!" yelled Sergei. "You can't leave me! You have to do what I say! The Bible and the Church command it! I am your husband!"

"Not for very much longer," said Ellsworth stilly.

≪　≫

Agniezka and Eurydice had just placed the trunk onto the shelf at the back of the sleigh when they heard a commotion inside the house, and then it went suddenly quiet. There was no yelling or cursing—just silence. They looked at each other worriedly, and then they looked at the house.

"Wait here," said Eurydice, and she hurried up the steps to the porch. She didn't think Sergei would get the upper hand over Ellsworth, but just in case, she needed Agniezka somewhere safe.

When she got inside, Eurydice could see that something happening to Ellsworth was not the case. Sergei wouldn't be getting the upper hand over anyone ever again. He was lying sprawled at the bottom of the stairs, and Eurydice didn't need to be a doctor to know his neck was broken. One of his arms was broken in at least two places, and one of his legs was broken as well. His eyes were open but unseeing, and Eurydice looked away from the vacant, glassy stare to Ellsworth where he stood at the top of the stairs.

"He was drunk. He fell down the stairs, and he broke his neck," said Ellsworth calmly as he walked down to join her.

Eurydice frowned uncertainly as she looked at him. She wouldn't ask, but in her heart she knew Sergei's death had been no accident. There had been no witnesses, so there would be no way to prove otherwise, but Eurydice didn't need proof. Ellsworth had killed him.

As he reached her and put his arms around her, Eurydice couldn't decide how she should feel about it. A part of her knew she should be horrified, but she couldn't help feeling overwhelming relief. Agniezka was finally free of her husband, and there would be no more worry over a divorce. He had been repaid for all the cruelty he had ever inflicted on his wife and her family. Eurydice couldn't think any less of Ellsworth for doing what he had done. She didn't know if he had done it intentionally, and she didn't need to know; the end result would have been the same.

"Eurydice, are you—?" began Agniezka as she came through the doorway, and her words faded as she saw her husband lying obviously dead on the floor.

Eurydice turned in her husband's arms to look at Agniezka. "He was drunk. He fell down the stairs, and he broke his neck," she said quietly.

Chapter Thirty One

As tempted as the three of them had been to simply leave and let Sergei rot where he lay, they all realized the first person the police would come searching for would be Agniezka. The servants had seen her arrive. For Sergei to be found dead and her gone with many of her belongings, it would be very difficult for them not to think she had been responsible, especially if the servants told the police of Sergei's history of abusing her.

By the time the authorities had arrived and completed their questioning, it was very late. They had at first been determined that someone should go to jail for Sergei's death, but when no one gave them a statement to contradict what had allegedly happened, when all the statements only seemed to provide evidence for Sergei being drunk and having an accident, they had to believe that was what it had been. When they discovered Eurydice had performed for the tsar by Imperial command and that Alexander had liked it so much he had given her a portrait of her *babushka* that had been hanging in the Hermitage, the police apologized for taking so much of their time and hoped the Ellsworths enjoyed the rest of their stay in Russia.

None of the three wanted to stay in Sergei's house, but they were too tired to drive back to St. Petersburg. Agniezka suggested they go to her father's house. It was small, but it was close, and she wanted to tell him what had happened as soon as she could. They would be leaving the city for Moscow on Wednesday morning, and she might not have another chance. As for her reaction to her husband's death, when she realized she was forever rid of him, she had started crying with relief.

Gennadiy was surprised when they arrived on his doorstep at nearly three in the morning, but when he saw his daughter's face and how exhausted all three of them looked, he quickly asked them to come in. Agniezka told him she would talk to him more after they had some sleep, but she briefly explained what had happened since she had seen him on Sunday. At first, all he could do was look at her in open-mouthed astonishment. Then he pulled her to him in a tight hug and smoothed a hand across her hair.

"You will sleep now. We will talk in the morning," he said quietly. He looked to the doorway. "Zenaida, I know you're listening," he said mildly, his eyes twinkling with humor. The little old woman came in with her chin tilted defiantly. "Please, show our guests to their rooms. You can put the Ellsworths in Nickolai's old room, and Agniezka, of course, can sleep in her own."

Agniezka kissed her father's cheek, and the three of them followed Zenaida up the stairs. She took them down a short hall that led to the back of the house and opened the door on a respectably-sized bedroom that she told Eurydice and Ellsworth would be theirs. Eurydice hugged Agniezka good night, and then she went into the room with her husband and closed the door.

They didn't have a light, and there was no fire in the fireplace. Ellsworth went to the hearth and soon had a nice blaze going while Eurydice felt around and turned down the blankets on the bed. They both got undressed and climbed in. They had managed to thaw somewhat sitting in Gennadiy's parlor, but they had been in the cold for so long that it would take until morning to feel warm again. Eurydice snuggled close to Ellsworth, and she rested her chin on the back of her hand where it lay on his chest to look up at him.

"I'm sorry I sneezed," she said quietly.

Ellsworth brushed a gentle finger down her cheek and leaned forward to kiss her forehead, grunting slightly at the pain it caused in his ribs.

"It wasn't your fault," he said softly.

"But if I hadn't sneezed, he wouldn't have woke, and he wouldn't have—"

Ellsworth put a finger to her lips, and then he rolled over so they were facing each other on their sides.

"It wasn't your fault," he said again slowly. "I could have said no to going in the house. I had accepted that he might wake up and what might happen if he did before we ever walked through the door."

"But—" she started again.

"Shh, Dicy. It's part of my job," he sighed. "It's part of what I do." He gave her a kiss and rested his forehead against hers. "It's part of who I am," he whispered.

Eurydice frowned as she looked at him. She had the impression that he didn't think he was a very nice man, because of what he was it somehow made him *bad*. She didn't believe that.

"You're a good man, Gareth Sinclair Ellsworth, and you will never make me think anything else," she whispered determinedly.

Ellsworth looked at her searchingly. She said that as if she believed it, but if she knew half the things he had done, she might change her mind. That's why he wasn't going to tell her—because he wanted to be the man she thought he was. She hadn't asked him if he had killed Sergei, either accidentally or purposely, and she wouldn't…because she already knew the truth, and it didn't matter to her one way or the other.

Eurydice leaned closer and kissed him gently on the lips, and then she put her leg over his thigh. She adjusted herself so that she was turned almost onto her back, and then she pulled him toward her and settled his head against her chest, wrapping her arms around his shoulders after making sure they were both well-covered by the blankets. He was more than happy to put his arms around her waist and snuggle against her. They were both exhausted after the long day and soon drifted off to sleep.

They left Gennadiy's house shortly after dinner on Tuesday. Sergei had been deeply in debt, and it didn't take long for his creditors to begin circling like vultures. Agniezka was lucky she had gotten her things when she did; otherwise, she wouldn't have been able to get them at all. The local priest would see that Sergei was given a proper burial, but neither Agniezka nor Gennadiy planned to attend the funeral. It wouldn't be held until Thursday, by which time Agniezka would be on her way to Moscow with Eurydice and Ellsworth. Gennadiy had loathed his son-in-law, for everything Sergei had done to his family, and the only thing he would want to do is spit on Sergei's coffin, of which he was sure the priest would disapprove.

Eurydice spent the rest of the day tending to correspondence. She had received a handful of letters from her family and other people, and it took her the rest of the evening once they were to the hotel to respond. She also made sure to send a note to Gospodin Srdanov to let him know appealing to the Synod would no longer be necessary. She didn't go into exact detail on what had happened. She only told him Sergei had died in an unfortunate accident, so Agniezka was now a widow and no longer needed a divorce. She wrote letters to her father and Sheerness explaining the same thing. She would never tell them what had really happened (as she understood it) unless they asked.

Eurydice woke up terribly sick that morning. She had been too tired and hungry, and she had none of the things with her that she normally used to control the nausea. It had started Ellsworth into suggesting she should go back to Vienna again, and her refusing to do so…again. She was much better after breakfast, but Ellsworth was unhappy she wouldn't even consider returning. She felt guilty that she was causing him worry, and she didn't know what she could do to make him believe she would be fine.

Once they returned to St. Petersburg, after Eurydice asked him to attend to sending the packages with her family's presents to Britain, Ellsworth spent most of the day and much of the night away from the hotel. He had to finish what he was sent there to do, and he would have been done the night before had it not been for Sergei. The fortunate thing was that darkness came to Petersburg early, which allowed him to begin what he needed to do earlier than he might elsewhere.

Before he left, he told Eurydice that if she ever needed him for an emergency to tell Schellen. That surprised Eurydice, but after he said it, she did realize he had arrived at the hotel shortly after she had asked Schellen her questions. She didn't think Schellen shared Ellsworth's occupation, but she suspected the valet might be an "assistant," possibly even a sparring partner. It cast the Austrian into a whole new light for Eurydice. Ellsworth did make sure she understood it really was *only* for an emergency. She couldn't tell Schellen to find him just because she was lonely. Eurydice had sniffed at him insultedly. As if she would ever be so silly.

Eurydice and Agniezka had baths before going to bed. They both needed them, and they didn't know when they would next be able to have one…at least not until they arrived in Moscow. Eurydice was sure Ellsworth had made suitable arrangements for where they would stay along the way and once they arrived, but bathing when one had the chance was always wise.

Agniezka was happier than Eurydice could ever recall seeing her. She had written a letter to Felton telling him the good news, but she, too, did not go into detail about Sergei's end. She also wrote a letter to her brother, telling him that their father would be moving to Great Britain before the end of the following year and that he would probably be safe from Siberia should he decide to return to Russia. She didn't expect that he would, but it was worth knowing.

Eurydice had been concerned about Agniezka's baby after her ordeal the previous day, but Agniezka assured her the baby was fine. Not long after she finished her bath, her maid had smiled excitedly and put Eurydice's hand to her stomach. Eurydice had frowned confusedly for a moment, but then she felt a few light taps against her palm that she almost mistook for a muscle twitching. She had looked at Agniezka in amazement when she realized what it was. Agniezka told her the coolness of the air against her stomach after the warm bath was making the baby move around more than usual. Once she felt that, Eurydice was relieved and felt almost giddy.

She went to bed after her own bath and snuggled beneath the covers in the middle, hugging a pillow to her and missing her husband. She wanted to wait up for Ellsworth to come back, but she was so tired she fell asleep after only a short time. One of her last thoughts as she nodded off was that she hoped whatever Ellsworth had come to Petersburg to do, he had been successful.

Wednesday morning came brittlely cold. They were awake before sunrise, and Agniezka brought Eurydice some spiced bread and *sbiten* before she moved from the bed. Ellsworth had already gone to arrange for the coach to be prepared, and Eurydice only had about thirty minutes until she had to be out of the bed and dressed before the servants arrived to begin taking their belongings down to be loaded. She managed it, barely, but her stomach didn't agree with the speed at which she needed to move. Agniezka coaxed Eurydice into moving as quickly as she could to get her dressed, and then she left her be to sit at the table and eat the rest of her breakfast in an attempt to let her body catch up. If it didn't, she would be sick for much of the morning.

It wasn't sunrise yet when they left St. Petersburg. Once they were on their way, Eurydice promptly went back to sleep, her feet propped in Ellsworth's lap, her head resting on a pillow wedged into the corner of the seat near the window. She stayed that way until they stopped for dinner in Luban, and she woke up with a terrible crick in her neck and feeling nauseous. She felt better once she ate dinner, and she decided against going back to sleep when they resumed their journey. She was exhausted when they stopped in Novgorod.

She did the same thing the following day, going back to sleep until they stopped for dinner in Krestzi then staying awake until they stopped for the night in Edrovo, but she arranged herself differently on the seat: she slept with her head and torso across Ellsworth while he had his back wedged into the corner. She still woke up with a crick in her neck, and she didn't get as much sleep because he had to get out whenever they changed horses and woke her up. But, she wasn't nauseous because of his shaving lotion. He was somewhat stiff and exhausted when they stopped for the night, too, and Eurydice was disappointed she wouldn't be able to sleep that way the following day.

On Friday, she tried a different pillow wedged into the corner by the window and placed another behind her back. When she woke up for dinner, she felt rested and had no crick in her neck, but she was nauseous. At that point, she decided it was impossible to sleep comfortably in a coach, but she would only become more exhausted if she didn't.

She tried to stay awake when they got back in the coach after dinner, but once the sun went down, she began to have trouble keeping her eyes open. After her head drooped sideways onto his shoulder for the tenth time, Ellsworth sighed resignedly and wedged himself into the corner to settle her against his chest and let her sleep. She woke up at one point to realize he was carrying her in his arms, but she was too tired to care.

The next time Eurydice woke, there was a bright beam of sunlight shining into her eyes. When she realized she was sleeping in a snug, comfortable bed and it was well past the time they usually left in the morning, she began to sit up in alarm, but then her head started to hurt and she began to sneeze. Trying to stop sneezing even as she fought the nausea she usually felt on waking wasn't easy, and she grimaced as she put her hands over her face.

"Ugh," she muttered through her hands.

"Are you all right?" asked Ellsworth, his tone a mixture of concern and amusement.

"No," mumbled Eurydice, still keeping her hands over her face. Ellsworth lifted one of them away to look at her, and she squinted her eye open. "Why haven't we left yet?"

Ellsworth raised a disbelieving eyebrow. "It's nine in the morning, and you're still in bed asleep. I think the reason speaks for itself."

Eurydice moved her other hand away and looked at him. He was in bed beside her propped up on one of his elbows. Her outer clothes had been removed (and she wasn't sure if he or Agniezka had done it, or if they had colluded together), but she was still in her chemise. After she was awake for a few minutes, and she was able to control her nausea somewhat, it wasn't hard for her to determine she had developed a cold at some point. That would explain why she had been so tired the previous day, but she didn't think she had a fever. She would be fine.

"I have a cold," she said calmly.

"Is that what it is?" asked Ellsworth amusedly.

He lay across her slightly to reach for something on the table on her side of the bed, and Eurydice thought she was going to be sick from the pressure it put on her stomach. Added to that was an intense pain she felt in her left breast where it was flattened by his chest. He wasn't putting that much weight on it, but it felt incredibly tender. She closed her eyes and inhaled slowly to keep herself from crying out. By the time he straightened back up, she was able to keep her features composed, but she was fairly sure her eyes were watering.

"Well, I'm awake. Can we go now?" she asked evenly.

"No," he drew out slowly. "I don't think so. Here."

He was holding a cup of *sbiten*, and she sat up slightly and took it from him. She looked at the night table, and she saw a tray with a pot and some of the spiced bread. She gave Ellsworth a questioning look as she took a sip from the cup. It was fairly hot, but not as hot as she was accustomed to having it.

"Agniezka brought that in for you an hour ago," he explained.

"Why can't we go?"

"I think I've already explained this," he said with a grin.

"I only have a cold," said Eurydice stiffly.

"And you are going to stay in a cozy bed for the day rather than traveling across the countryside in a coach and risk it becoming something worse."

"Oh, but I don—" began Eurydice stubbornly.

"No," interrupted Ellsworth with a grin.

"But—"

"Shh," he cut in again.

"I—"

"Hush," he said. She started to speak again, but before she even got out a syllable, he stopped her again. "No means no," he chortled. "The coach won't go anywhere without my say-so, and I'm not saying so."

Eurydice groaned frustratedly. "Fine," she said finally. "So, where am I getting to spend the day in bed?"

"Tver."

Eurydice's eyes widened in surprise. "Oh, that's not fair," she said disappointedly.

Ellsworth frowned slightly in puzzlement, and then it cleared as realization dawned on him.

"Oh, I'm sorry, Dicy. I truly wasn't thinking about your grandmother being from here," he said softly.

She sighed resignedly. "Yes, well, it's not the same as it was when my *babushka* grew up here in any event. It nearly all burned down the same year my father was born."

Ellsworth brushed a finger down her cheek and kissed her forehead.

"Even still," he said softly. "I truly am sorry."

Eurydice looked at him and gave him a smile. "I know."

"Hmm. Perhaps I should rephrase that. I'm sorry it is Tver, but I'm tickled to death you have to spend the day in bed."

"Oh?"

"You can't go anywhere. I have nowhere to go." He snuggled closer to her and lowered his head to kiss her. "I think I'll just stay right here with you all day…in commiseration, of course."

"Oh, of course," she said amusedly.

Eurydice felt better for having spent the day in bed. They left at their usual time the following morning, and she managed to stay awake in the interim between their departure and stopping for dinner in Klin. Of course, she was ready for bed when they arrived in Moscow that night, but she had been feeling that way over the last few days even with a nap. It was an improvement.

It was very late when they arrived in Moscow, and Eurydice had been unable to see anything of the city as they approached it. She did notice there weren't a lot of lights along the streets. Many of the buildings were eerily dark, too. Some of it could be due to the lateness of the hour, but the city seemed to be strangely empty.

When she mentioned that to Ellsworth, he told her it would be awhile before the city was full again. The majority of it had burned to the ground three years earlier. Whether it was Napoleon's army or someone else who had caused it was questioned at first, but the blame couldn't be given to any one person or people. Maybe some of it burned by accident, perhaps some on purpose. Either way, the end result was the same: Moscow had to be rebuilt.

After Eurydice heard that, she was surprised Ellsworth had been able to find a place for them to stay and even more surprised Gospodin Bukeavich would invite her to perform. How was she to play for an audience that wasn't there in a building that didn't exist? She was sure he wouldn't have asked her to come if there was nowhere for her to perform, and it would all be explained when she sent him a message the next day to let him know she had arrived.

The hotel Ellsworth had found was very nice. It was located on Kuznetsky Most, in one of the few places in the city that hadn't burned. The style of it, though, led Eurydice to believe it wasn't very old. As long as the room was warm, the bed was clean and comfortable, and she could have a bath, she didn't care how old it was.

They had a suite on the second floor, designed much the same as the one had been at the Hotel Tverskaya in St. Petersburg, but there was no bathing room. Instead, there was a *banya* on the ground floor. Eurydice thought that would do nicely, but the only part she was interested in was the baths *before* going into the heat. She had never become accustomed to that part, despite how hot she enjoyed her bath water.

There was nothing to see out the windows of their rooms, partly because it was dark and partly because there was a taller building across the street from it, but at least there were windows. Eurydice wanted a bath, but she was too tired, and she decided she would have one the following day. She got undressed and curled up beside Ellsworth under the blankets with an exhausted sigh. At least she had arrived early enough to be well-rested before she performed.

Eurydice met with Gospodin Bukeavich shortly before dinner the following day. He allayed her worries about where she was going to perform and who was to be the audience. The French had managed to save the theater built by their people, and that would be her venue. As for her audience, since the fire, entertainment in the city was scarce. When broadsheets were distributed for her upcoming performances on Thursday and tickets became available for purchase on Friday, all of them had sold by that morning before he came to see her. Word of her talent combined with the lack of other options had made the demand very high. There were some seats reserved for the nobility still in the area, but Bukeavich anticipated those would be filled as well.

She would give three performances beginning Wednesday. Bukeavich asked if she would consider performing afternoon concerts as well on Thursday and Friday, increasing the number altogether to five, due to the overwhelming interest of the public. Eurydice said she would consider it, but she also said she would give him a definite answer after she had been to the theater and rehearsed. Agreeing to something like that blindly would be downright silly.

Bukeavich told her an orchestra had been practicing the concertos. She asked him how they were with Beethoven. She would perform her own pieces gladly, but she had been playing the same ones at every performance. She was craving some variety. If they were familiar with a few pieces by Beethoven— or Haydn, for that matter—she could perform her concertos and something by another composer rather than one of her sonatas. She only had so many of those. She didn't want to make a firm decision on that yet, either, and she didn't want to make any difficult demands. She still had to hear the orchestra; if worse came to worst, she could be performing the entire concert by herself from start to finish. She hadn't needed to do that yet after having an orchestra rehearsed to perform with her, but it could happen.

When Ellsworth heard how many performances she had committed to giving and that more were requested, he was concerned it might be too much strain for her. Eurydice did think about that, but provided rehearsal went well and all other things were equal, she would manage. He reminded her that she was getting over a cold and still had a stomach ailment to contend with, but she felt confident she would be fine. She promised she wouldn't overtax herself.

After dinner, he arranged for a sleigh to take Eurydice to rehearse. Agniezka would go with her tomorrow, but she wanted to stay at the hotel that afternoon. Rather than taking her directly to the theater, though, he went a circuitous route, going south to the embankment along the river before going north again to take her past the Kremlin and St. Basil's Cathedral. When Eurydice saw the church, her jaw dropped in amazement. She had never seen anything like it.

"Oh, my goodness!" she gasped.

Ellsworth chuckled at her reaction. On first seeing it, it tended to awe most everyone. The size of it, all of the colors and domes—it was a bit unexpected. St. Stephen's in Vienna was astonishing as well, but in a completely different way. It was unlikely she would ever see anything like it anywhere else. There were several more cathedrals in Russia built in the same style, with the onion domes and spires—some of them in Moscow and its outlying areas, but none were decorated quite as colorfully as St. Basil's. It was unique, and one either loved it or hated it. Eurydice loved it.

Ellsworth showed her a few other things as they crossed Red Square. The Kremlin was obvious, but he told her the last time he had been there, it had a moat. Now it was level with the rest of the square up to the wall and planted with trees. He also pointed out that most of the buildings on the opposite side of the square from it were the Trading Rows, and the Gostiny Dvor was on the block behind the Middle Trading Rows between Ilyinsky and Varvarka. She could see the buildings were new; some of them were still under construction.

There was a raised, round platform made of white stone just past St. Basil's that was known as the Place of Skulls. It wasn't as morbid as its name led one to believe. It was used as a place for announcements, such as the tsar's *ukazes* or religious ceremonies. Eurydice wondered why it had such a gloomy name if no one had even been executed there. After some consideration, she thought it might be appropriate after all, depending on the announcement.

There was another cathedral at the other end of the square, but not as large as St. Basil's. It was colorful, too, and just as beautiful. They reminded Eurydice of marzipan. Across the square from that was the state apothecary building. Eurydice didn't think she'd ever seen one so large. The Provincial Board was to the right just before they left the square, and then they went through the Resurrection Gate into yet another square. They crossed it at an angle to the left, and then they arrived at the theater after a short drive up a street heading north. Even with the detour across Red Square, it was a short trip from the hotel.

Eurydice wasn't going to ask Ellsworth how he knew so much about Moscow. She doubted he would tell her because he had probably been there at some point because of his job. But one nice thing from his brief tour was that she learned where she could go to find a Christmas present for him. They would be in Kiev for the holiday, but she didn't know what the options would be for finding him one there. She didn't want to wait to the last minute, as hard as she was finding it to decide what to get him. The only trick would be having the opportunity to look without him there. He had a tendency to go with her when she went out if he didn't have something to do for his assignment. That was going to make it difficult.

The theater was small, only capable of holding an audience of about three hundred. The acoustics could use improvement, but they had a Broadwood that was decent. After having nearly a month to rehearse before her arrival, the orchestra sounded almost perfect, and Eurydice only had to make one or two adjustments before she felt their accompaniment would be suitable. The pianist was excellent, and much to her pleasure, she discovered he had rehearsed the parts for the violin-piano sonatas. It wasn't quite the same as when she had played them with Schubert, but it would suffice. After the rehearsal, she told Bukeavich she would be willing to perform the two matinees he had mentioned, which pleased him and worried Ellsworth.

It had been dark for quite a while when Eurydice and Ellsworth left the theater. She would go back to to rehearse the following afternoon and again on Wednesday before the first performance. That would leave her the morning hours for her own purposes. She would like to work more on her symphony, which was coming along nicely, but it would also give her the time to find Ellsworth a present...if she could find something else for him to do while she did that. Before she went shopping, though, she would need to find out what he liked, and she wasn't sure how she could do that without him becoming suspicious. If she were still in Vienna, she could ask Cora or Leilah. She doubted Schellen would know, and Eurydice wasn't sure how she would approach him about it in any case.

After supper, Eurydice and Agniezka gathered their things to go have a bath. Eurydice's nausea had remained at a tolerable level all day, and while it wasn't completely gone, she at least felt functional. She suspected that spending the day in bed in Tver and Agniezka making sure she was regularly fed was helping. It still bothered her that she couldn't find out what was causing it in the first instance or what she could do to make it stop. She didn't want to believe she would have to suffer with it for the rest of her life. Perhaps if it hadn't stopped by the time they got to Britain, she would have Dr. Hinton, Felton, or Keung examine her.

The hotel was built around a large inner courtyard with a smaller courtyard behind, where the mews was located. There were arched openings on the ground floor to either side of the main part of the hotel, where coaches and horses could be led behind it for stabling. To get to the *banya*, they had to take a hall on the first floor over the arch on the right to the side wing and take the set of stairs there to the ground floor. It was a bit inconvenient, but Eurydice was willing to go through a little inconvenience for a hot bath.

She could feel the heat and moisture in the air as soon as they went through the doors at the bottom of the stairs. There was an attendant waiting there who asked them if they wanted the public baths or private. It didn't take much consideration for Eurydice to ask for private. Being naked in front of her family was one thing; being naked in front of strangers was quite another. There was a pool in the public part of the baths, but Eurydice wasn't interested in swimming...at least, not at that moment.

The baths were beautiful, decorated with tile and marble with lots of columns and statues and open spaces. The attendant led them along the edge of the pool, where there were a few people swimming, and Eurydice tried not to stare. It was best not to know what some people looked like naked. The attendant opened one of the sets of doors almost at the far end of the pool and showed them into a suite decorated in pale blues, pinks, and white. He asked if they would require any assistance, but both thought they would manage well enough on their own. With that, he left them to enjoy their bath.

There was an anteroom to the suite with benches and mirrors where they could remove their things, with stacks of towels for drying off when they were through. Beyond that was a larger room with four smaller tubs along the walls and a larger one able to accommodate several people at once in the center, almost like a small pool. Beyond that was a door in the far wall that would lead—they assumed—to the heat room. All of the tubs were already filled with water, and they found that the ones along the sides were hot, while the one in the middle was ice cold. Eurydice was looking forward to her bath.

She and Agniezka selected their tubs and stepped in. Eurydice sighed contentedly as she settled into the water up to her neck and closed her eyes. It was at just the right temperature for her—hot enough that her skin tingled slightly when she first got in, and swirling her arms beneath the surface caused waves of heat to curl across her skin. Agniezka got a bucket that had been placed on a table between the two tubs and used it to add some of the cold water from the central tub into her own until she had it at a more tolerable temperature for her. She had never enjoyed an extremely hot bath and cared for them even less the further along she got in her pregnancy.

They relaxed and talked while they washed, and Eurydice mentioned she had still not decided what to get Ellsworth for Christmas. Agniezka laughed and said she could offer no suggestions. Eurydice hadn't really thought she could. She mentioned a few things Eurydice might think of buying, but she couldn't tell her what Ellsworth might like. Eurydice was beginning to wonder if she absolutely *had* to get him a gift. Yes, she had to, said Agniezka.

They were still washing and talking when Eurydice looked at the doorway to the anteroom and jumped in surprise. Ellsworth was there wrapping a towel around his waist in preparation for walking across the room for a bath of his own. Agniezka didn't know he was there because she was sitting with her back turned to the door to face Eurydice in her own tub while they talked. If Eurydice hadn't looked at the doorway, she wouldn't have known he was there either. She narrowed her eyes as she looked at him when he realized she had seen him, and he gave her a mischievous grin. Agniezka had been embarrassed when she had walked into the bathing room in Venice and saw him naked, so Eurydice wasn't sure how she was going to react now, whether he was well put-together or not. It was typical for men and women to bathe together in Russia, and Eurydice always enjoyed having a bath with her husband, but she didn't want to make Agniezka uncomfortable.

"What's wrong?" asked Agniezka with a frown when she saw her expression, and then she turned to look at the doorway as well. "Oh," she said mildly when she saw Ellsworth. She looked back at Eurydice and shrugged indifferently.

Ellsworth's grin widened at Eurydice's uncertain look between him and Agniezka, and then he draped his towel on the table with the bucket and climbed in the tub with her, his back turned to Agniezka.

Agniezka's eyes did widen when she saw the tattoo on his back; she had never seen it until then. She gave Eurydice a questioning look, and it was Eurydice's turn to shrug. How could she explain it? She couldn't, really, without telling Agniezka more than she should know.

When Ellsworth saw the look Eurydice gave her maid, he realized what had caused it, and he mouthed "sorry" to his wife. He had forgotten Agniezka hadn't been with them on the beach in Pantelleria. If she had been, she wouldn't have any reason to question the tattoo now. What he said then would have been an explanation, even if it wasn't true. He would have to remember to tell Eurydice to give Agniezka the fib he had used then should she ask about it at some point. Hopefully, Eurydice would feel comfortable doing that.

"This water is hot," said Ellsworth after only a few seconds.

"Yes," purred Eurydice with a smile, "just the way I like it."

Ellsworth chuckled. "I feel like I'm back in Japan."

Eurydice gave him a dry smile. "There aren't any *geisha* here."

Ellsworth lifted an eyebrow. "You know about those?"

"Do you really need to ask?" she chortled.

"Hmm. No, I probably don't," he said dryly. "You can be my *geisha*," he said with a teasing wink and a wolfish grin.

"Hah!" hooted Eurydice amusedly. "I have none of the qualifications necessary for that occupation."

"Oh, yes, you do," drawled Ellsworth, and Eurydice gave him a wry smirk and splashed water at him.

Agniezka finished washing, and then she got out of her tub and went to the one in the middle and settled into it. She rested her arms on the edge of the pool and relaxed her chin on them to look at Eurydice and Ellsworth as they bantered with one another. It made her happy to see the two of them getting on so well together. She could never thank them enough for coming to rescue her from Sergei, and she was going to miss Eurydice so much when she stayed behind in Britain and Eurydice went back to Vienna.

Who was going to take care of her then? After eleven years, Agniezka knew all the things Eurydice liked and disliked. She tended to all the little things that needed to be done so Eurydice wouldn't have to worry about them. Who was going to do that for her when Agniezka wasn't with her? In all her years of service, Agniezka had never felt like a maid, had never been treated like one. She had been a companion and a friend, and she felt almost like an older sister caring for a younger one. It was going to be a similar kind of loss she would feel when they were no longer together. She hoped they would be together again at some point, but she couldn't say if they would.

At least it seemed her marriage to Ellsworth was a success after all. It had been a bit uncertain at first, and there were still occasions when they disagreed with one another, but after almost three months, they seemed very happy. She had never seen Eurydice laugh or cry so much. The crying was not so good, but Agniezka thought the overall effect was wonderful. Eurydice's personality had blossomed since her marriage. It at least gave Agniezka some hope that Eurydice would not be lonely without her.

After soaking in the cold water for a few minutes, she stepped out to get a towel and begin drying off. Watching the two of them together made her lonely for Simon, and she thought they might like to be alone. Once Ellsworth came in, she might as well not have been there in any case. It didn't hurt her feelings to have seemingly disappeared; it did her heart good to see Eurydice so easily distracted.

"I'm going to bed now," she called.

"Oh," said Eurydice in surprise. "Good night, Agniezka. Sleep well."

"I usually do," said Agniezka amusedly. "I won't wait up."

Ellsworth convinced Eurydice to go ice skating the following morning after breakfast. He had first needed to find skates for them, which took an hour or two. If Eurydice had known it was going to take him that long, she might have chanced shopping for his present. He might have seen her, though, depending on where he went, so perhaps it was just as well she didn't. As it was, she spent the time composing…and questioning Schellen on suggestions he might have for presents for her husband. He didn't have any, just as Eurydice suspected he wouldn't, and he gave her an odd look when she asked him.

Ellsworth took her to a place called Christye Prudy to skate, quite a distance from the center of the city. It seemed to be a very popular place for ice skating, and she did enjoy the exercise. Eurydice noticed the way he cautiously stepped onto the ice, as if he expected it to break beneath his feet, and she suspected it was a lasting effect from what had happened to William. Once he was on the ice, though, and he saw the way everyone else was carelessly skating, he was able to relax. At least, he appeared to relax.

She had noticed that about him. Despite how disagreeable he might find something, whether it inconvenienced him or caused him pain, he would do whatever was necessary. She suspected he had a phobia about the ice breaking, but he *made* himself do it. When he was shot in the leg, it might have hurt, but he acted as if it didn't. The same with his ribs, which were only beginning to mend. He hadn't wanted to marry her, but he did it because it was necessary. She was sure part of it was due to his job, where it might be a matter of life or death if something was noticeably wrong, but he had a tendency to always do it, as if he *needed* to always have everything seem perfectly normal, even when things were far from it.

They went back to the hotel for dinner afterward, and then they and Agniezka went to the theater for Eurydice's rehearsal. Everything went just as smoothly as it had the day before, and Eurydice didn't feel they needed to spend quite as long at it. She was tempted not to rehearse the following afternoon, but it would be better to do it and not need it.

The next morning, Eurydice and Ellsworth went skating again. They tried to get Agniezka to go with them, but she was content to stay at the hotel and work on her knitting and embroidery. She was also reading one of the books she had retrieved from Sergei's house, a collection of Russian folk tales and poetry that had belonged to her mother. She told Eurydice she would let her read it when she was done, if Eurydice would like.

After dinner, Ellsworth surprised Eurydice when he said he wouldn't be going with her for the rehearsal. He told her there was someone he wanted to call on in nearby Ostankino, but he wasn't sure if the man was there. Eurydice started to ask him about it, but then she realized his going to Ostankino rather than going with her and Agniezka to the rehearsal would give her the perfect opportunity to find him a present. He wouldn't be in town, and he would think she had just gone to rehearse. He said he would be back in plenty of time to go with her to the performance at nine. If she rehearsed one or two hours, that would give her the same amount of time to shop.

She told Agniezka her plan after they were in the sleigh going to the theater. Agniezka smiled amusedly and told her she could simply tell her husband she needed to buy his present, but Eurydice explained that she didn't want Ellsworth to know she hadn't already found one for him. She just knew he had already gotten one for her, and she didn't want him to think she had no ideas. She did manage to discover that his favorite color was indigo and his favorite animal was a monkey. She thought both were unusual, and she didn't know how either would help her find him a Christmas gift. Still, it was more than she had before.

The rehearsal went well, as Eurydice had no doubt it would, and they went through each piece once. After she told Gospodin Bukeavich that she would be back that evening for the concert, Eurydice and Agniezka left for Eurydice's quest to find a present. When they left the theater, the sun was starting to set, but Eurydice was hopeful she would have an hour or two to shop.

When they got to Red Square, Eurydice didn't know where to begin. She decided to start with the Upper Trading Rows, since they were closest to that end of the square. When she and Agniezka went inside, Eurydice was overwhelmed. It was enormous. There were stalls several rows deep, and it was crowded with other people shopping. There were lanterns hanging from the ceiling above each row and skylights, so it was at least not dark, but there was no organization to the different wares—a vendor selling leather goods could be situated by one selling fruit and vegetables. There was no end to the variety available, however, and some merchants were selling new items, others selling secondhand or antiques. As Eurydice and Agniezka walked up and down the rows, Eurydice was a bit dazed by the choices, but she wasn't seeing anything that she thought Ellsworth might like.

One thing she did purchase not long after they went in was a small basket of peaches. They were outrageously expensive, and no amount of bargaining with the vendor would get him to lower his price. Eurydice couldn't blame him; having peaches in winter fairly well gave him the right to demand whatever price he wanted. He lived in a small town between Moscow and Kiev, growing his wares in hothouses, one for the warm months, another for the cold, so that he had peaches and other rare produce to sell year-round. For someone who really wanted peaches, like Eurydice, no price was too high. Agniezka shook her head, but Eurydice couldn't help it. She saw the peaches, and she *had* to have them. She shared them with Agniezka as the two of them walked up and down the rows, and Agniezka had to admit they were good.

The more Eurydice looked, the less able she was to decide. Perhaps if she had fewer choices, the decision would be easier. She looked at watches, clothing, books—none of it struck her as something Ellsworth might like. She did buy a very nice picture of St. Basil's for herself, but her husband wouldn't appreciate it. At one point, she found a haberdashery, but she left with nothing. She thought it likely that she would buy him something he didn't need or want, and she began to frown frustratedly as they walked up and down the rows.

They were to the row at the very back when they came to a furrier. There was a display of *ushankas* made from various furs, and Eurydice began to look them over thoughtfully. She gently ran her fingers over them, and she found one that she liked, made of sable and sealskin. She lifted it off the stand to look at the diameter of it, and she thought it might be the right size. Of course, she had no way to tell for certain, but they were supposed to be fairly tight-fitting. She removed her own hat, the one made of fox that Agniezka had given her, and put the *ushanka* on her own head. It fell down to the bridge of her nose and covered her eyes. She pulled it off and put her own hat back.

"What do you think?" she asked Agniezka.

"It's a good color for you," said Agniezka amusedly. Eurydice gave her a wry smile. "The quality is excellent, and sealskin is very warm, especially with the sable lining." She shrugged. "He would look very handsome in it."

Eurydice decided to get it. It would at least be something useful, and she had to agree with Agniezka that he would look handsome. A little further into the stall, she found coats, but she couldn't find one that she thought would be the right size for Ellsworth. She had almost decided against buying one when the vendor came to ask her if she needed assistance. She explained she wanted to buy a coat for her husband, but she didn't know his measurements. The man smiled amusedly and asked her to describe him, which she did as best she could with help from Agniezka. He sorted through the coats and found one made of sealskin and sable, which would match the *ushanka*. He thought it would be the right size, perhaps a little wide through the shoulders but not by much.

She bargained with him on the price for the hat and the coat and arrived at one she thought was reasonable. She paid him, and then he took the items to the back to put into boxes and brought them out to her. Eurydice felt almost giddy. She had successfully bought her first Christmas gift for her husband.

They were about to leave the stall, when she spied some beautiful velvet, fur-lined cloaks. She looked at Agniezka, and then she went to look at them, finding one with lynx and one with fox to match their hats. Agniezka tried to discourage her from buying them, but the prices for the garments the man was selling were very reasonable, far cheaper than she would ever be able to buy them in Britain, or anywhere else for that matter. The only unfortunate thing, Eurydice thought as he took them to the back to put them in boxes as well, was that she and Agniezka would have to wait until after she gave Ellsworth his gift at Christmas before they could wear them; otherwise, he would know she had been to the Trading Rows, or at least that she had been shopping without him.

Eurydice and Agniezka thought the easiest way for them to get back to where they had left the sleigh would be to go to the end of the row, leave the building, and walk around the outside of it. They were almost to the doors to go outside when the wares in another stall caught Eurydice's eye. She hesitated for a moment, knowing she and Agniezka needed to go, but she decided to look at the one thing in particular that drew her attention.

She walked in and went directly to the display. She gave the boxes holding the *ushanka* and coat to Agniezka to hold, not taking her eyes off the sword, and she carefully lifted it from the stand. It was beautiful. She turned it to examine the blade, and then she raised it to examine the soundness of it before looking down the blade for any signs of warping. It was in perfect condition. She put it back on the stand, and then she picked up the scabbard. It was the original made for the sword. There was a smaller sword and scabbard to complete the set, and after examining all of it, she just knew she had to get it for Ellsworth. It was completely useless, and he didn't need it, but she thought he would like it nevertheless.

A loud, mewling howl from a cage at the back of the stall made her jump and look at it in astonishment as she thought it sounded almost like a crying baby. She had noticed the cage, but she hadn't realized it was occupied. She went toward it and peered in curiously. It was a monkey, a very young one. He looked at her with inquisitive green eyes, his fur a soft golden color. She'd never seen a live monkey before. She cautiously put a finger through the bars, and he just as cautiously reached toward her finger to wrap his hand around it.

"Can I help you?" asked a man from behind her.

Eurydice removed her finger from the cage and turned to look at the man. He spoke Russian without an accent, but Eurydice wasn't quite sure he was a native. His features were Asian, but she couldn't place what part of Asia he might be from. After some thought, she realized he was probably from the far east of Russia, bordering Mongolia and China. It would explain how he had come by the swords.

"Is the monkey for sale?" she asked curiously as she looked back over her shoulder at the cage.

The man gave her a slight smile. "He was, but I'm afraid he's been sold already."

"Oh," said Eurydice disappointedly.

She didn't know what she or Ellsworth would do with a monkey anyhow, and baby monkeys did not stay baby monkeys forever. At some point, they grew big...and mean, she suspected. She had only thought it would be something to consider as a gift for Ellsworth, since it was his favorite animal, but what she was intending to buy was going to be much better in the long run.

"In that case, I'm interested in the sword set you have there," she said, pointing to what had originally drew her into the shop.

When he told her the price, Eurydice wasn't surprised, but she wasn't going to pay it, either. She began to bargain with him, and when she finally walked out of the store with both swords in their scabbards carefully wrapped in cloth and stored in another box, she had managed to bring it down to something that was still exorbitant but tolerable. The baby monkey had watched her the entire time she bargained with the stall keeper, one of his little hands holding onto the bars on his cage, and she was oddly sad to leave him there. She hoped whoever bought the little thing would treat him well. What would have been ideal would have been someone not removing him from his mother in the first instance. A child needed its mother.

Ellsworth had not returned to the hotel when Eurydice and Agniezka made it back to their suite, and Eurydice breathed a sigh of relief. She found a place to put the boxes in one of her trunks, where they could be kept until the appointed day. She felt very accomplished, knowing she had found several things. Agniezka arranged for their supper while she put away Ellsworth's presents and their cloaks, and by the time Eurydice returned from using the garderobe, their food had arrived.

Ellsworth returned just as Agniezka was helping Eurydice dress.

"Was your friend in town?" asked Eurydice after he came to give her a kiss on the cheek.

"Yes, he was, which is why I'm so late. Luckily, he fed me, or I would be starving by now," he said amusedly. "How was rehearsal?"

"Excellent, as usual, and I was starving by the time we were through," chortled Eurydice. "I couldn't wait to get back here to eat."

"Hmm," said Ellsworth, thinking Eurydice's appetite had grown recently, and he wondered if it was due to her vomiting or if the vomiting was caused by the eating. She still seemed to be in excellent health otherwise. "I had better get dressed."

Eurydice watched him leave, and she sighed contentedly as she went back to the dressing table and took her seat to let Agniezka resume styling her hair.

They were all dressed and ready to leave in plenty of time before the concert. The reaction of the audience reminded Eurydice of that at the Sâle

Lyon—polite quietness during the performance followed by exuberant applause. Bukeavich had told her they were desperate for entertainment, but Eurydice liked to think the applause was caused by genuine appreciation rather than by relief from monotony. Eurydice had decided that the Russian audience was by far the best she had played for. She still had several countries to go to, but it would be difficult to find one better.

She was ready for sleep by the time they returned to the hotel. It had been a long day. Between ice skating that morning and spending almost two hours walking through the Trading Rows, Eurydice had gotten more exercise than she had been accustomed to for quite some time. She wasn't complaining; she thought she could use more and hadn't been getting a decent amount since they left Vienna. But, that didn't mean it wasn't making her tired, and she was having enough difficulty not feeling that way without over-exerting herself.

Eurydice climbed into bed after washing her face and brushing her teeth. She stretched and snuggled beside Ellsworth, and then she yawned tiredly. She would make love if he wanted to, but she would be perfectly happy to go to sleep. He had been quiet most of the evening, but he was never very talkative. Tonight, though, he seemed more reticent than usual. He put his arm around her and rested his hand at her hip as she settled her head onto his chest.

"Is anything wrong?" she asked hesitantly after a few minutes. Something just did not seem right.

"No," said Ellsworth negligibly, smoothing his hand up her waist.

"Oh, all right," said Eurydice acceptingly.

"I hadn't intended to be gone so long this afternoon," he said quietly.

Eurydice rested her cheek on the back of her hand to look up at him. "It was fine. I had rehearsal, so it wasn't as if I were left alone, pining for you," she said with a slight smile.

"Yes, I'm sure you found other things to occupy yourself while I was gone," he said amusedly.

"It wasn't necessary to find anything," said Eurydice simply with a tilting of her head. "When rehearsal was over, I had just enough time to come back here to eat and dress for the concert before you were back."

"And that's all you did?" he asked doubtfully.

Eurydice gave him a slightly exasperated smile. "Of course." Eurydice saw his expression change from one of relaxed amusement to suspicion. "What? What's wrong?"

"You're lying to me," he said stiffly, and the rigidity in his face radiated throughout his whole body.

"Why would you think I am lying?" scoffed Eurydice.

"Because I *know* you are lying," he said coldly. "You went to Red Square after rehearsal, before you came back to the hotel."

Eurydice sat up and away from Ellsworth, curling her knees to her chest and wrapping her arms around them. She looked at him with a puzzled frown.

"How would you know? Were you *following* me?" she asked breathlessly.

"No, I wasn't," denied Ellsworth firmly.

"Then how do you know where I went? You weren't even here when I got back." Eurydice could feel a knot forming in her stomach. "Unless…unless you had *Schellen* follow me?" she gasped sickenedly. Ellsworth didn't answer her and set his jaw, and one of her hands went to her mouth in dismay. "All the time?" she whispered weakly.

"Only when you go somewhere without me," he said evenly.

"How long? How long have you had your spy following me?"

"Since we arrived in Vienna, and Schellen is *not* a spy," he said tightly.

"No? He tells you everywhere I go, everyone I see, everything I do, and he's been doing it without my knowledge or consent. That is *spying*!" hissed Eurydice angrily. "You trust me so little, you think so little of me, that you cannot leave me alone." She looked away from him and wiped at the wetness on her cheeks with one of her hands.

"That's not the point. The point is you lied," said Ellsworth flatly.

Eurydice looked at him over her shoulder. "Yes, I lied to you," she whispered unevenly, "because I didn't want you to know I had been to buy your Christmas present."

Ellsworth paled and felt a bit sickened himself. He had been so suspicious, so quick to assume she was doing something she shouldn't, and the reason had been completely innocent and selfless. It also explained why Schellen had only told him she went to the Trading Rows to shop; he must have realized she was buying a present for Ellsworth and hadn't wanted to ruin the surprise. Ellsworth was feeling mortified.

"I don't want him following me anymore," said Eurydice dully.

"I'm sorry, but it's for your own good," said Ellsworth gently. Eurydice's eyes widened and her lower lip trembled. "It's for your protection."

"Protection? From *what*?" gasped Eurydice.

"You know more than what's good for you about my job," he said evenly.

"But I don't know anything!" she said exasperatedly. "You don't trust me enough to tell me anything. You don't trust me at all," she said flatly. "And I can take care of myself."

"You know more than you think you do, and I *do* trust you. I promised your father I wouldn't let anything happen to you, so Schellen will follow you until I decide it's no longer necessary."

Eurydice wanted to argue further, but she could see he wasn't going to change his mind. He said Schellen was following her for her protection. Maybe that was so, but if it were, it shouldn't matter where she went and what she did as long as she came back. He shouldn't be using the information Schellen gave him to confront her and accuse her of lying. It only proved he *didn't* trust her. And he still thought she couldn't protect herself. Just because she didn't flaunt it didn't mean she was incapable.

"Fine," she said tiredly. It was an argument she wouldn't win…at least, not yet.

She lay back down on her side facing away from him and pulled the blankets up to her neck. She heard Ellsworth sigh gustily, and then he rolled over on his side to spoon behind her and pull her close. She began to struggle to move away from him, but he wouldn't let her go. She finally quit fighting and sighed frustratedly.

"I'm sorry," whispered Ellsworth sadly. He knew she would take it exactly the way she did. He shouldn't have said anything.

Eurydice put her arm over his at her waist and let him snuggle closer against her. She wasn't ready to accept his apology, but she would eventually, especially once she found a way to get Schellen to quit following her.

Chapter Thirty Two

All of Eurydice's performances at the French Theater were given to packed audiences. She was sure more tickets were sold—or at least more people had attended—than the building could safely hold. Bukeavich tried to convince her to stay for even more performances, but she told him she had made a commitment to be elsewhere. She might consider coming back later, possibly the following year. He was disappointed but understanding.

Bukeavich waited until after the last performance to give Eurydice one bank note for all five. It was an astonishing amount of money, and Eurydice tried not to think about it. She put it in the strongbox Ellsworth had purchased for her in Warsaw with all the other bank notes. She would decide what to do with the money after she finished the tour. There was no point until she saw the final tally, but she was beginning to think it was going to be unbelievable. She could understand why so many composers toured to earn money.

Eurydice and Ellsworth were speaking to each other, they even had sex, but Eurydice was still keeping herself distant from him. He remained firm on having Schellen follow her when he couldn't be with her himself, and that rankled her. Before she had discovered Schellen was following her, she had never suspected. He was so skillful at seeming invisible, she had never once caught him. Even after Ellsworth had told her, on the two occasions she had gone somewhere without him, even trying her best to spy him out, she never saw Schellen. She could almost believe Ellsworth had been lying, but she knew he wasn't. Knowing Schellen was there made her self-conscious, despite her best efforts to pretend he wasn't. She was beginning to feel like a dog on a leash...even if it was a long one.

They left from Moscow for Kiev early on Saturday morning. Eurydice was very tired from the late night she'd had because of her last concert, and as hard as she tried to stay awake, she went to sleep in the coach before the sun was even up, waking up at dinner with a very bad crick...again.

The weather on the way to Kiev was a mixture of good and bad, but the worst of it fortuitously seemed to wait until they were stopped for the night. At one point, Ellsworth considered looking for a sleigh, but he decided against it when he realized that some of the places they would be going would not have snow, or not enough to be suitable for a sleigh. The roads were traveled frequently enough that they were in good condition, and while the coach had to go slow occasionally, a sleigh would have most likely done no better.

They arrived in Kiev around midday on Wednesday, and they crossed the Dnieper into the city using a pontoon bridge. The river was mostly iced over, but it wasn't quite frozen enough to support traffic yet. The city was beautiful. Eurydice could see the domes and spires of several churches and monasteries, and it was going to be a lovely place to spend Christmas, since she couldn't be home with her family.

The Hotel Zhuliany, where they would be staying, was large, bigger than the Oktiabrskaya where they had stayed in Moscow but not quite as big as the Tverskaya had been in St. Petersburg. The suite where they would be living for almost a week, however, was by far the most spacious and luxurious they had been in yet. The only thing to dislike was that it was on the top floor of a four-storied hotel, but it was worth the effort it took to climb all the stairs. Eurydice loved it. The Zhuliany was on a corner on a hill, where the surroundings were lower in two directions. Their suite was in the corner of the top floor, giving them a marvelous view of the city.

The door opened onto a large parlor decorated with comfortable furniture in cream, burgundy, and dark blue. A set of glass doors opened onto a covered loggia for them to take advantage of the view. Also in the room was a beautiful Broadwood piano, which Ellsworth swore he didn't know would be in the suite when he was making arrangements for their stay. There was a large skylight to brighten the room during the day, but there were several oil lamps for night. There was a water closet and a bathing room, rooms for Agniezka and Schellen, a dining room, and a very large room for Eurydice and Ellsworth. It was more like an apartment than a suite.

Eurydice really liked the room that was to be hers and Ellsworth's. The overall color was white, with gilding and a dark blue-green. It had its own fireplace, with a rug made from bearskin on the floor in front of it. It was very light and airy, with several windows and its own balcony, but it didn't feel at all drafty. She didn't know if Ellsworth had been familiar with the hotel prior to making arrangements for their stay, but he couldn't have made a better choice had he tried.

Once they were settled into their rooms, Agniezka went down to arrange for dinner to be sent to their suite. Eurydice wrote a message for Dobran Stelmakh, the man who had invited her to perform in Kiev. She knew he wanted her to perform on Friday and Saturday before Christmas. Actually, for him, Christmas was still more than two weeks away rather than only five days. That had been one of the things she had needed to keep in mind when she scheduled her performances in Russia: they still used the Julian calendar. By the time they had finished dinner, she received a response from Stelmakh letting her know he would come to see her at four that afternoon. That would only be two hours away.

Eurydice spent the time working on her symphony. Despite how little time she had been able to devote to working on it, she was more than halfway done. If she had a week or two of uninterrupted time to give to it, she would be completely finished. As it was, she might be done by the time they reached Paris. She still didn't think it would ever be performed in public, simply because it was so unusual, but she had to write what she was hearing.

A maid came to the door of their suite shortly after four. Eurydice thought about it for a moment before she decided she would go downstairs to meet with Stelmakh. She couldn't make the maid walk down and then back up again to show him to the suite. She left the symphony on the desk to work on it more when she came back. Ellsworth said he would go with her, and she shrugged indifferently. At least it wouldn't be Schellen sneaking after her. Casanova called after her as she was leaving the suite, and Eurydice paused to ask Agniezka to make sure he had food and water…before covering his cage.

He really was a well-behaved bird, his vocabulary notwithstanding, and he was tolerating traveling across the continent well. She took him out of the cage when it needed to be cleaned, and he never tried to fly away. Ellsworth could even get him to take pieces of fruit and nuts held in his mouth without coming out of the experience lipless. She supposed the parrot was happy. Despite his ability to talk, she knew his vocabulary had been learned; he couldn't actually *tell* her what he was feeling. Ellsworth paid him more attention than she did, not to imply that she neglected him, and she did like the bird. She had grown quite fond of him and would miss it if she didn't have him to proposition her sexually at least once a day.

Stelmakh was just as enthusiastic about having her perform in Kiev when she met him in the common room downstairs as he had originally been when he invited her in Vienna. He was very young to be an theater artistic director, with sandy blond hair and blue eyes behind bi-focal spectacles. Eurydice only realized they were that way when she noticed how the size of his eye changed shape, depending on which portion of the lenses he looked through. They were very unusual. He seemed to be knowledgeable and capable despite his age. The City Theater, as it was called, was on a square not far from the Hotel Zhuliany, very easily within walking distance. He told her the theater was of a modest size, capable of holding an audience of almost five hundred, and it was less than fifteen years old. After confirming that her performances would be on Friday and Saturday night, she left him with the assurance that she would be to the theater to rehearse the following morning. She thought he was going to skip as he walked across the lobby to the exit.

"He's very exuberant, isn't he?" commented Ellsworth casually as they started up the stairs back to the suite.

Eurydice shrugged. "I suppose it is because he enjoys what he does. That cannot be a bad thing," she said evenly.

"No, probably not," said Ellsworth with a slight smile.

They had only walked to the landing on the first floor when Eurydice stopped and looked back the way they had come.

"Oh, phoo!" she said vexedly.

"What?"

"Oh, I want a bath, and I meant to tell the clerk at the desk while I was downstairs rather than Agniezka having to walk down and back up again."

He smiled amusedly. "You go on up to the room; I'll take care of it," he said agreeably.

"Thank you," said Eurydice gratefully. Agniezka was in good health, but it was unnecessary to make her go up and down so many stairs when she was there to do it herself.

"You're welcome," said Ellsworth, giving her a light kiss on the cheek before he started back down the stairs.

Eurydice started up, but she only made it a step before she stopped again and turned to look at him.

"Oh, go ahead and arrange for supper to be brought up around eight as well," she called as an afterthought.

"All right," said Ellsworth as he looked back up the stairs at her. "Anything else?" he asked dryly.

"Peaches," said Eurydice decidedly. "I would really like some peaches in the suite to snack on."

"Dicy, it's winter…in Kiev. It's unlikely they will have any peaches," he said with an amused chuckle.

"It won't hurt to ask," she said practically. "I would *really* like some peaches," she repeated earnestly.

"All right, I'll ask," he chortled as he turned to go down the stairs.

"Thank you," called Eurydice happily, and she could see him shaking his head as he disappeared from sight.

Eurydice reached the next landing with a gusty sigh and walked down the hall she had to take to get to the stairs for the top floor. She was a little winded, but she would be fine after walking the hall in preparation for the final set.

A man was walking toward her from the other direction as she approached the stairs, and she kept to the right as he came nearer. She smiled politely when he smiled warmly at her, but he made her feel uncomfortable. There was something about the way he smiled that was too familiar and appreciative for her liking. He was tall and well built, with dark hair and brown eyes. He was attractive in a sensual way, and Eurydice sensed that he knew it and wasn't beyond trying to use it. It would be best if she walked past him as quickly as possible and got up the stairs.

Then, to her dismay, she started to feel dizzy and had to put her hand up to the wall to maintain her balance as her eyes started to lose their focus. She did her best to keep walking, but she was weaving on her feet, and her heart was palpitating anxiously because she was sure she was going to faint in front of this strange, strange man. She felt him put his hands out to grab her by the shoulders, and Eurydice shrank away from him. She couldn't focus her eyes.

"Are you all right?" he asked solicitously.

"I'm fine, thank you," said Eurydice weakly as she tried to move out of his grasp.

"Are you sure you don't need any help?" he asked softly.

There was something oddly familiar about his voice. It was a silky tenor, almost sinuous and hypnotic, but she hadn't met him before. He was speaking Russian, but she could detect an underlying accent, which led her to believe it wasn't his native tongue. The only thing she did know was there was something about him that she instantly did not like.

"No, no, I'm fine," said Eurydice, trying to give him a smile. "Thank you for your concern."

"Are you sure you don't need me to help you to your room, Lady Eurydice?" he asked smoothly.

"How did you—?" she began with a frown, but she didn't get to finish.

"Oi! What is this?" called Ellsworth as he reached the top of the stairs and began to walk down the hall toward them quickly.

"I beg your pardon," said the man calmly, "but this woman appears to be in some distress. I was simply offering my assistance."

Eurydice blindly reached out a hand toward Ellsworth and grabbed his sleeve, relieved that he had arrived when he did.

"This *woman* is my wife," said Ellsworth stiffly.

"I'm fine," said Eurydice dully, patting his arm reassuringly, even as she continued to weave on her feet and struggled to focus. "That is just what I was telling Mr....um...Mr....." She tried to focus on his face, but her body continued to refuse to obey.

"Arontsov. Istvan Arontsov," he supplied smoothly.

Eurydice continued to frown. He wasn't Russian. He had also known her name. Something about him, this whole thing, was quite simply *off.*

"Thank you for your concern, Gospodin Arontsov," said Ellsworth evenly before lifting Eurydice in his arms.

"I'm fine," repeated Eurydice. "Really, I'm fine, Gareth," she said vacantly. "Thank you, Gospodin Arontsov," she called vaguely over his shoulder as Ellsworth began to walk away from the man down the hall.

"Think nothing of it," said Arontsov gallantly.

Eurydice was able to get her eyes to focus again by the time Ellsworth reached the bottom of the stairs. By the time he reached the top of them, she wasn't dizzy anymore.

"You don't have to carry me," she said evenly. "I'm fine."

Ellsworth looked down at her. The color had returned to her cheeks, and she no longer had that disturbing blind stare, but he wasn't going to let her walk. Anyone who looked like she did when he first saw her after he reached the top of the stairs was far from fine. She continued to refuse to believe there was something seriously wrong with her.

"I want you to see a physician," he said firmly.

"Why? I don't need one," she said calmly, "and will you put me down?"

"No, I'm not putting you down, and you *do* need to see a doctor."

"I was only a little winded from walking up the stairs," she said exasperatedly. "I am perfectly fine, so put me down. Now."

"No."

Eurydice groaned frustratedly. "I won't see a doctor."

"Yes, you will, and I want you to cancel your performances, too," said Ellsworth firmly.

"The hell you say!" shouted Eurydice. "I will not! Now, put me down!"

Ellsworth opened the door to the suite then kicked it closed with his foot when they were through. Agniezka watched them go by from her seat by the fire in the parlor with her jaw slack in disbelief. Ellsworth carried Eurydice to the bed and gently laid her onto it.

"There, now I've put you down," he said calmly. Eurydice started to get up, and Ellsworth put a hand to her shoulder and held her down. "Stay."

"I am not a dog," she said angrily, and she grabbed his wrist in a pressure grip to forcefully remove it from her shoulder. He put his other hand to her other shoulder, and she did the same thing and sat up. "I don't need to be in bed," she grated through clenched teeth, and she swung her legs over the side of it to stand before letting go of his wrists.

Ellsworth looked at her aggravatedly. She did seem to be perfectly healthy at that moment, but she hadn't been in the hall, and all the other things he had seen over the last few weeks gave him no choice but to believe she wasn't well. Either she didn't want to think she was ill, or she knew she was and was simply being stubborn. He wouldn't be able to bear it if something happened to her. He finally looked at her pleadingly and put a hand to her cheek.

"Dicy, please, let a doctor examine you. For me? If he says you are well, then I won't say another word," he said somberly.

Eurydice thought about refusing again, but she had to admit—if only to herself—that she was worried, too. She still believed she wasn't going to die from it, but if a doctor could tell her what was wrong and how to make it go away, it would be so much better. Having a doctor tell Ellsworth she was fine would make him leave off about Vienna, and that would be a relief.

"Very well, I'll see a doctor," she finally said quietly.

Ellsworth's expression changed to one of relief, and he kissed her softly on the lips.

"Thank you," he sighed, putting his arms around her. "Before rehearsal tomorrow morning," he said evenly.

Eurydice leaned her head back from where it had been resting against his chest to look up at him with a slight frown.

"But I'm to be there at ten," she said disconcertedly.

"Then we'll have to make sure you see him before ten," said Ellsworth with a slightly amused smile. He ran a finger down her nose before gently tweaking it. "Stelmakh will understand if you're a few minutes late."

"That's very unprofessional," said Eurydice primly.

Ellsworth snorted amusedly. "Five or ten minutes will be fine." Eurydice started to disagree when there was a muffled knock at the door of the suite. "That would be your peaches."

"You found me peaches?" asked Eurydice joyfully.

"Yes. It seems there is a man with a hothouse. Needless to say, they were not cheap."

Eurydice stood on her tiptoes to kiss him appreciatively before nipping at his bottom lip and giving him a smile. "Thank you."

"Hmm," he said thoughtfully. "That was very nice, but I bet it will be even better peach-flavored."

Eurydice was nervous. She was sure she was going to be fine, but as she sat eating her breakfast while she waited for the doctor to arrive, she couldn't help wondering what would happen if she was wrong. Ellsworth would force her to go back to Vienna (or try to), and he would be angry with her for not seeing a doctor sooner. She had been nauseous when she woke up, as usual, but it didn't seem to be quite as bad. She wasn't sure if that was because she might be getting better or if the thought of seeing a doctor was somehow making her body behave more like it should. Either way, she didn't have much of an appetite because of her anxiety.

Dr. Herzen arrived shortly before nine and knocked at the door to their suite. Eurydice jumped at the sound and tried to remain calm, but she could feel a tense ball forming in her stomach. Ellsworth went to the door and invited the doctor to come in. He was older, short and rotund, with spectacles and white hair. His face was kindly with an intelligent light to his blue eyes. Eurydice supposed if she couldn't be examined by Keung or Hinton, this doctor would do well enough.

Eurydice had already told Ellsworth she didn't want him there while the doctor examined her. He had balked at first, but Eurydice said she wouldn't do it if he was there. She would have Agniezka with her, but Ellsworth would have to wait until afterward to find out the results. She would even let him question the doctor if he liked, but she didn't want him there for the examination. She didn't tell him, but the reason she would rather not have him there was that he might become angry if he discovered the full extent of things and how long it had been happening. She didn't want him to know.

Eurydice went with Dr. Herzen and Agniezka into her room and closed the door. She invited him to take a seat in the chair near the fire while she and Agniezka sat on the settee. Then he asked her to explain for him the problem she was having. She was slightly uncomfortable at first, but she told him about the nausea and vomiting, the frequent need to urinate, the dizziness, tiredness, breast tenderness, and the heightened sensitivity to some smells and flavors. He nodded attentively while she talked, and then Eurydice looked at him expectantly when she was through.

"Have you had any fever, any chills?"

"No, not at all," said Eurydice calmly.

"And you say the urination has lessened, the nausea and vomiting improve when you eat and have enough rest?"

"Yes."

"How long has this been happening?"

Eurydice thought about it. "Since about mid-November…well, the beginning of November, by Julian."

"Hmm," he said thoughtfully. "And when did you last have your courses?"

Eurydice blinked at the question, but then she frowned as she began to think about it. When *had* she last had them? Her cheeks began to tingle as the blood drained out of them when she realized she'd not had them since Vienna, before Halloween. She felt as if her heart had stopped beating when she began to realize the only thing it could mean. Everything began to make perfect sense, and she couldn't believe she had been so blind not to recognize it.

"The middle of October…um…the ninth, I believe, by your calendar," she said weakly. "I'm pregnant, aren't I?" she asked breathlessly.

"Yes, I believe you are," said Dr. Herzen mildly, "but I would like to do one thing to be sure?" Eurydice nodded dumbly. "I want to palp your womb, so if you could just lie down on the bed for me, please." Eurydice stood up and went to do as she was told. "No pillows, flat on your back, please," said Dr. Herzen gently. "That's it. Now, if I can get you to bend your knees and move your legs apart." Eurydice blushed but did as he requested. "I apologize for this. I know this is undignified and invasive. I'll try to be as quick as I can. The best thing you can do is try to relax."

She had to agree with his description, but he was careful and quick, and it was over in only a minute. He patted her knee soothingly when he was done, and then he went to the washstand to wash his hands and dry them. Eurydice went to take her seat beside Agniezka on the settee.

"Did you know?" she asked Agniezka quietly.

Agniezka shrugged and gave her a slight smile. "I thought you might be, but I was waiting to see if you figured it out for yourself before I said anything. I did have other things on my mind, and you did, too, so…."

Both women stood as Dr. Herzen retrieved his small valise from where he had placed it beside the chair and didn't retake his seat.

"Everything seems perfectly normal," he said mildly. "You should deliver, based on your dates, probably sometime in July. Congratulations," he said with a kind smile.

"Thank you, Dr. Herzen," said Eurydice evenly. It was pointless to ask if anything could be done for the nausea. From watching Agniezka, she knew she would simply have to wait for it to get better, but at least it *would* get better. "Doctor, if you could, please don't tell my husband." He raised a dubious eyebrow as he looked at her. "It's just that this will be our first child and with Christmas so close, I thought it would be a nice surprise," she said hopefully.

"Of course," he said with an amused smile.

"Thank you so much," said Eurydice relievedly.

Eurydice, Agniezka, and Dr. Herzen left the bedroom and entered the parlor. Ellsworth was standing by the fireplace looking down at the flames with a contemplative expression when the door opened, and he looked up at them expectantly when he realized they were there.

"Well?"

"She's fine," assured the doctor dismissively.

"Fine?" blurted Ellsworth disbelievingly. "She told you about the nausea and vomiting? The dizziness?"

"Of course," said Dr. Herzen. "That should be better in another, oh, two or three weeks, I expect."

"She said she has a stomach ailment. Is that true?" asked Ellsworth suspiciously.

"Humph. More or less," said Herzen dryly.

"She's not going to die?" asked Ellsworth earnestly.

The doctor gave him an amused smile. "Oh, no, I don't think so," he said with his eyes twinkling. "She's young and healthy. Let her eat what she wants when she wants. Let her get all the rest she wants…or doesn't. Don't try to limit her activities, but she doesn't need to begin ice swimming if she isn't doing it already. She's perfectly fine," he said with an assuring smile.

"You're sure?" asked Ellsworth hopefully.

"Absolutely," confirmed Herzen.

Ellsworth walked him to the door and thanked him again, and then he went to Eurydice and pulled her toward him to kiss her warmly. She looked up at him when the kiss ended, and she knew she couldn't tell him, not even at Christmas. He would want to make her go home to Vienna. He was already so concerned about her that he had Schellen following her wherever she went. If he knew she was pregnant, he would never let her go anywhere. Added to all that was the knowledge that he still had an assignment to finish. He had already told her that he couldn't do his job properly if he was worried about her. Knowing they were going to have a child would only make it that much worse. She didn't want to make his life more complicated. So, she would wait to tell him, either until he was done with his assignment or until she couldn't hide it anymore. She didn't know how long either would take.

"Feel better now?" she asked him softly.

"Much," he sighed with a smile.

Eurydice's performances at the City Theater went well, and she had to decline when Stelmakh asked her to consider giving more. Sunday was

Christmas Eve, Monday was Christmas, and they would be leaving for Buda-Pest on Tuesday. Just as she had told Bukeavich in Moscow, she would consider coming back at another time. Russian audiences were the best, and if she never went back to perform anywhere else, she did hope she would be able to go back to Russia…except, perhaps next time she could go back when the weather wasn't so cold.

Ellsworth somehow managed to arrange for a Christmas tree to be placed in their suite. It wasn't large, but it was a tree, and it was very pretty. Eurydice hadn't expected they would have one, and while they weren't home with the rest of their family, it would suffice.

Now that Eurydice knew what was wrong with her, it made it more bearable. Her feelings about it, however, were ambivalent. She had expected she would have a child at some point, but she hadn't anticipated it would be so soon. She had the impression Ellsworth hadn't either, which only made her all the more hesitant to tell him. She had told Agniezka that she wasn't going to tell him at Christmas as she had told Dr. Herzen she would. Agniezka had frowned confusedly, but she trusted Eurydice had a perfectly good reason for it. Eurydice frequently found herself with her hand resting on her still flat stomach, wondering about the little person growing there and whether or not she was going to be prepared for his (or her) arrival. She suspected not, but she would have to make the best of it.

And yet a part of her was overjoyed to know she was going to have a child, and it wasn't due to some feminine pride in being capable of creating life. It was because she knew it was Ellsworth's child. It was knowing there was a part of him growing inside her that made her occasionally smile for no particular reason and made her heart flutter when she looked at him. She couldn't imagine she would feel that way if the child belonged to any other man. It wasn't because she knew it would be fulfilling the promise she had made to provide him with an heir; there was no guarantee it would be a boy. It was simply that she was going to have the child of the man she loved. She had often thought she wouldn't care to have children, but being married to Ellsworth had changed her opinion on the matter.

When Christmas Eve arrived, Eurydice was impatient for sunset. Her family never waited until Christmas Day to open their presents, but they did at least wait for sunset on the Eve. Ellsworth had laughed when he saw her bristling with excitement and said he wouldn't dare go against tradition. His mother had always made him and his siblings wait until *the* day, and the sun had to be up, and everyone had to be there before a single gift could be unwrapped. He liked the Aberdares' tradition better. They still waited for everyone to be there, but after sunset on Christmas Eve suited him much better.

It started snowing around dinner, and as the sun began to set, it continued to fall in large, wet flakes. Eurydice tried to forget by working on her symphony. She was feeling better than she had for quite some time. Her nausea had been at a bearable level that morning, and she didn't need to wear the bracelet on her wrist to control it throughout the day. She still had *sbiten* and the spiced bread before she got up, but while she had been nauseous, it hadn't gotten to the point that she felt she was going to vomit. Dr. Herzen had said it would be another two or three weeks, and Agniezka confirmed he was probably right. Eurydice was relieved it was almost over, and she was happy it had decided to be mild for Christmas. It could be bad again the next day or the day after, but she would have been disappointed to feel sick on Christmas Eve.

By six in the evening, twilight had gone, and the snow was still falling. When Eurydice looked out the glass doors of the balcony onto Kiev, she thought it looked perfect, with parts of the city glowing in haloed pools of lamplight, sleighs pulled by horses, their passengers wrapped in furs and blankets, traveling the streets. For them, Christmas was still more than a week away, and she was sure being out in the cold did not make them appreciate how picturesque they made things.

Ellsworth came behind her to put his arms around her waist and look out the window as well. Eurydice leaned her head back against his chest and sighed contentedly. She was very happy. She didn't think she could remember a time when she had ever felt so at peace. Everything was perfect.

"Agniezka has gone down to arrange for supper," he stated mildly.

"Schellen knows he's expected to join us?" she asked as she continued to watch the snow fall.

"Oh, yes, he knows," said Ellsworth in mild amusement, "and he's not happy about it."

Eurydice looked up at him. "Why not?" she asked with a frown.

"He's not very sociable, or haven't you noticed that?"

"Humph," said Eurydice affrontedly.

"He's a valet, a proper one," said Ellsworth evenly.

Eurydice turned in his arms to look up at him. "But he's more than that. You know it; I know it," she said flatly. Ellsworth sighed fitfully. "He does more than shave you and tie your cravat…make sure your socks match. You trust him…a lot."

"I do," said Ellsworth softly, running a finger down her cheek.

"Then he needs to have supper with us and open gifts."

"Gifts? You bought him a *gift?*" asked Ellsworth disbelievingly.

Eurydice smiled. "Yes, but I don't know if he's going to like it."

"Dicy, don't be mean to him," reproved Ellsworth. "If you must be angry with someone for him following you, it should be me. He is only doing what I asked him to do."

"I would never be mean to him," said Eurydice, her eyes widening.

"Hmm," said Ellsworth as he looked at her through narrowed eyes.

The maids came up with supper shortly before eight, and there was more food than four people could possibly eat. There was *vushka*—a soup with dumplings containing mushrooms and veal, a fish soup called *yushka*, pickled cucumbers and tomatoes, a goose stuffed with apples and raisins, roast lamb, cabbage rolls, and a torte made with dried fruit, nuts, and chocolate, as well as a compote with cherries and peaches, for dessert. They brought mead, claret, and a sweet white wine to drink. It was a feast, entirely suitable for Christmas.

Schellen came into the dining room shortly after the maids brought the meal, and Eurydice could see he was self-conscious. She hadn't intended to make him feel uncomfortable by inviting him, and she did her best to put him at ease. She refrained from asking him anything about his job, either the services he actually provided as a valet or others, and instead asked him things about where he was from in Austria. He really was nice and polite, if reticent, and she had to wonder what had led him to his occupation.

Eurydice was quite full when supper was finished. She had especially enjoyed the *vushka*, pickled cucumbers, cabbage rolls and roast lamb, and she would have eaten most of the compote by herself if she had thought she could find room for one more bite. There was still food left when they were through, and no one was hungry. The maids would clear everything away in the morning when they came with breakfast.

Eurydice was impatient to open gifts, but she made herself wait. Instead, she went to the piano and played a few carols. After only three or four, it was obvious none of them were gifted singers. It wasn't even that, really, because Eurydice thought Ellsworth had a nice voice; none of them knew the words.

She asked Ellsworth to play the piano for her after her turn with the carols. He was unwilling at first, but when he saw Eurydice looking at him hopefully, he shook his head and sat on the bench. She hadn't heard him since they had played the duet together in Vienna. The piece he chose was one she'd never heard before, but she instantly liked it. It was a rondo of moderate tempo with several arpeggios, and she enjoyed watching his fingers gracefully move across the keys. She couldn't help thinking again that he could have been a great pianist, and it saddened her somewhat that he didn't play more often. When he was finished, she asked him about the piece, but the only thing he would tell her was that he had not written it.

After the song, Eurydice couldn't wait for gifts anymore. It was nearing 10:00, and her family would have long since opened them. She went to the bedroom to bring out the gifts she had bought. She missed a step when she saw something large and covered with cloth sitting on the floor near the tree, remembering the last time she had seen something like that. It was at least as tall as Casanova's cage and somewhat larger in width, and she eyed it with trepidation. She distributed the presents she had—one for Schellen, two for Agniezka, and four for Ellsworth. Schellen looked at her in surprise when she held his out to him, and she could see he was flustered because he hadn't expected one and had none to give.

Eurydice was startled by the number for her, and it seemed Ellsworth had followed her own thinking: buy more than one, and there was bound to be something among them that he would like. Only he had taken it even further.

Agniezka went to her room to retrieve gifts and had to come and go several times before she was through. Their families had all sent packages to Kiev, knowing they would be there for the holiday, and had entrusted them to Agniezka for the appointed day. Eurydice was alarmed by the number, wondering how they were going to carry them all on the coach, especially the very large, square one Ellsworth had gotten for her. She didn't imagine it was simply a box to be discarded.

Eurydice had the most to open, some of them quite large, and Ellsworth and Agniezka told her that she should start. All her gifts were piled around her where she sat on one of the couches—except for the large one, and she didn't know where to begin. She finally closed her eyes and picked. The one she chose was large but fairly light, wrapped in a shimmery blue silk. She untied the ribbon to remove the cloth and revealed a lacquered wooden box. When she opened the lid, she found a beautiful lute, decoratively inlaid with different woods and mother of pearl. The note inside with the instrument told her it was from Psyche and Sheerness, the simple message, *'Learn to play this!'* She didn't know when she would have time, but she would do her best to comply.

Ellsworth went next, and he did the same thing Eurydice had, closing his eyes and choosing. It wasn't one from Eurydice. When he opened it, he found a box with cigars from Pandora and Islington. He lifted one and held it to his nose to smell it with an appreciative smile. They were of very good quality. Eurydice wasn't sure how many were in the wooden box, but it looked like at least two dozen. In two small compartments to the sides of the cigars, there was a tool for clipping the ends and a small glass lamp. At least, that was what they thought at first. Pandora had sent an instructional diagram, and when Ellsworth followed the directions, he discovered it was a lighter for the cigars.

"That's amazing," he said with a boyish grin as he snuffed it and lit it again. "She made this?" he asked Eurydice in wonder.

"I'm sure she did," said Eurydice dryly. She suspected the entire point behind sending the cigars was for Pandora to give him the lighter.

"Did she patent it?"

"Oh, Pandora has never patented anything she's done and probably never will. She likes to make things for her family and friends, and she says the entire patenting business is too much hassle to be worth the effort for her," said Eurydice with a slight smile. "Besides, some of the things she's invented are far too impractical to be reproduced very easily or cheaply despite their usefulness or how fabulous they are."

Next, Agniezka selected a gift to open, one sent by Felton. It was small, as most of her gifts were, and when she opened it, she put a hand to her chest and sighed. It was a gold ring, set with four diamonds and a single blue topaz. She took it out of the box and put it on her left ring finger before showing it to Eurydice and Ellsworth. It was beautiful and perfect for a promise ring.

They all looked at Schellen expectantly, but he said he would wait a little longer. Eurydice was curious to see his reaction, but she could understand his hesitation. Eurydice closed her eyes and selected another gift. It was the one sent by her parents, and while she appreciated the beautiful pendant of carved and filigreed gold in the shape of a lute (which turned out to be a vinaigrette), she was disappointed it wasn't one from Ellsworth. He selected another gift, and it was a book of works by Friedrich Schiller from his mother. Agniezka opened another of hers, one sent from Chrissoula and Stockbridge, and it was a beautifully embroidered silk shawl. Schellen again declined to open his gift.

The three of them went around again several more times, and they were yet to open the ones from each other. Eurydice received a bow from Persephone, more composition paper from Arachne, a pretty set of earrings from Dorian and Selena, a shawl from Annabelle, and a book with descriptions and prints of different birds from her younger brothers. Ellsworth got a new pocket watch from the Aberdares, embroidered and monogrammed handkerchiefs from Arachne, an interesting Japanese print from Psyche and Sheerness, a pocketknife from Persephone, and a gold and citrine fob from Leilah. Agniezka received a book of poetry from her brother, jars containing hand lotion and face cream from Maiyin and Keung, a fabulous knitted shawl from Psyche, and a beautiful set of earrings and a necklace made with amethysts from Felton. The only ones that remained for her were those from Eurydice and one from Ellsworth.

"Come on, Schellen, it's your turn now," cajoled Eurydice. "It won't explode, I swear," she teased.

He finally untied the ribbon holding on the dark blue silk (which happened to be a handkerchief) and opened the box. Eurydice had gotten him a pocket watch, but it was the fob that had prompted her to get it. It was in the shape of a small shield with a sword behind it, rows of garnets going top to bottom and left to right in the shape of a cross. She thought if he was to be her knight protector, he should have a sword and shield. She was wondering if he would understand the significance, but when he looked up at her from the box, she could see that he did.

"Thank you," he said quietly, "it's very nice."

"You're quite welcome," said Eurydice with a smile.

Eurydice adjusted the remaining gifts she had. She still had several to go, and she was impatient to open one from Ellsworth. She dispensed with closing her eyes. She chose the smallest one first and untied the ribbon…with some effort. Obviously, tying bows was not his strong suit, but she appreciated that he had done it himself. It was a jeweler's box, and she looked up at Ellsworth in surprise before she looked back down at what was in it and blinked her eyes emotionally.

It was a pendant made of gold, exquisitely etched and filigreed to look like a koi. Its eyes were made of marcasite, and as she lifted it out of the box, she saw the body was articulated along its two-inch length to undulate as if it were swimming. It was beautiful, and she loved it immediately.

"Help me put it on," she said as she held it out and turned her back.

The chain was longer than she expected, and it slid beneath the edge of her bodice to settle directly between her breasts just above her heart. She lifted it out and settled it on top of her gown, and then she turned to look at Ellsworth and leaned toward him to give him a soft kiss.

"It's lovely," she said fondly. She was never going to take it off.

Ellsworth chose to open one from her as well, and Eurydice held her breath in anticipation. He opened the box to reveal the sable and sealskin coat. He pulled it out, and then he stood up to try it on. The man at the Trading Rows had been wrong—it fit him perfectly. Eurydice had underestimated how broad his shoulders were. He smoothed his hands over the fur and adjusted the front of it, and then he looked at her with a pleased grin.

"I like this," he almost purred, and then he leaned down to give her a smacking kiss on the lips before sitting down without removing the coat.

Eurydice was happy he liked it. He wasn't fond of the cold, and there would still be more of it for him to tolerate. It would be something he could use for years, and he looked very handsome wearing it. She couldn't wait to see what he looked like with the *ushanka*.

Agniezka opened one of the gifts from Eurydice, a chatelaine of gold vermeil with scissors, needlecase, thimble, and magnifying glass. She had a sewing box, but this would save her from getting it when she only needed to make a quick repair. It was ornately decorated with flowers and vines, making it like jewelry rather than something practical. Agniezka appreciated it.

Eurydice opened the next gift from Ellsworth. She was going to save the largest one for last simply because she wasn't sure she wanted to know what was in it. The one she was opening was fairly large, but not heavy, and she gave him an amused glance when she again had to struggle with the bow. It was a simple, unfinished wooden box, but she gasped when she opened it to reveal a beautiful violin. She looked up at him wonderingly.

"It was made by Ivan Batov in Petersburg," he supplied.

Eurydice carefully lifted the instrument to examine it. It was fantastic, and she could smell a faint hint of the varnish used to finish it.

"It's new?" she asked in surprise. She'd never had a new violin, not one that had never been played by anyone else.

"Made just for you," said Ellsworth with a grin.

Eurydice put it back in the box and closed the lid, and then she reached out to brush a hand down his cheek. She would tune it and play it tomorrow. She was excited to hear how it sounded.

"Thank you," she said softly.

He opened the box with the *ushanka*, and he chuckled as he lifted it out and put it on. He was dashing with the coat and hat, and Eurydice's heart fluttered as she looked at him. He took them off after a short while because they made him too hot, and Eurydice found that amusing.

Agniezka opened the gift from Ellsworth, a box with knitting needles of various sizes with pins and specialty hoops for making different stitches. It had a handle, and it was large enough to hold her other knitting and sewing items as well as several skeins of yarn. It was very thoughtful, and Agniezka thanked him with a kind smile. Eurydice was proud of him for finding something useful and for getting a gift at all. Someone else might not have.

Eurydice opened the next small present from Ellsworth, revealing another jeweler's box. She looked up at him with a raised eyebrow before she opened it, and her eyes widened when she did. It was a gold, heart-shaped locket, but it was by far the most extravagant one she had ever seen. The heart itself was about three-quarters of an inch in size, but it was edged with lacy filigree and wirework with two arrows crossed behind it, making the piece three times larger. When she opened the heart, one side had a miniature of Ellsworth, the other a lock of his hair. She wanted to wear it, too, but she didn't want to take off the koi. Perhaps she could wear them on alternating days. She lifted it by the chain, and she thought it might be longer than the one for the koi. She was easily able to put it over her head without unfastening the clasp, and she smiled happily when it rested just beneath the koi. She could wear them both.

"Thank you," she said warmly as she lifted her head to look at Ellsworth. Both necklaces were thoughtful and sentimental, and she wouldn't have thought she would like them so much until he had given them to her.

Ellsworth opened the smallest gift from Eurydice, one she had purchased at the Trading Rows on a second trip she made while they were in Moscow, from the same man she had bought the swords. She had gone back to his stall because she had noticed the monkey was still there, which she thought was curious after he had said it was sold. She had asked him about his wares, and he told her that he was from Okhotsk. Six months of the year, when it was warmer, he was there, trading with the Chinese and Japanese, and then he would travel across the empire to Moscow to sell the things he acquired and get things from the western part of the empire to trade in the east. Eurydice had the impression it was a very good business.

What she got for Ellsworth the second time was very small, and she had overlooked it the first time because she was distracted by the swords and the monkey. Inside the box was a small, green jade pendant, almost two inches in length and a little over an inch wide, in the shape of a koi. It was carved with detailed scales and fins on both sides, and the craftsmanship was remarkable. He was curled around a marsh reed, which curved over his head to form an open loop, where the pendant could be attached to a chain to go around the neck. Eurydice had replaced the gold chain it had come with and used a thin leather thong, thinking it made it more masculine and suitable for Ellsworth. She didn't know if he would wear it, but she had wanted to get it anyhow. Ellsworth ran his finger over it, and then he looked up at Eurydice.

"Thank you," he said warmly.

Agniezka opened her second gift from Eurydice, a set of combs made from gold and tortoise shell. They were meant to be decorative and useful, and Agniezka was proud of Eurydice for choosing so well. She apparently paid more attention to things like that than Agniezka thought. She got up from her seat to give Eurydice a hug. They were very pretty.

Eurydice and Ellsworth opened their remaining gifts. She got more perfume and toiletries from Maiyin and Keung, a *yangqin*—a Chinese hammered dulcimer—from Pandora and Islington, a fan from the Windham children, a cashmere shawl from Leilah, and a set of earrings made with yellow topaz from Cora. He got a print of hunting dogs from his nieces and nephew and a book of John Donne's poetry from Dorian and Selena. He had Eurydice open all of her gifts except for the last, large one from him before he opened the last one from her.

He lifted the box to put it on his lap, and he looked at her with a raised eyebrow when he noted the weight of it. He unfastened the bow and removed the cloth on the oblong box, which was about three feet long by a foot wide and a mere six inches tall. He opened it and folded back the cloth, and then he looked at Eurydice in astonishment. Of all the things he thought she might buy for him, this was not one of them.

They were Japanese swords, a matched *katana* and *wakizashi* with the *koshirae* mountings, and they were beautiful to behold. He lifted the longer *katana* from the box and gently eased it out of the scabbard about six inches to examine the blade. The craftsmanship bordered on artistry, and his hands shook slightly as he held it. He couldn't see the maker's mark because of the hilt, but he didn't think they were freshly forged. The blade was in excellent condition, but it wasn't new. He had "new" ones, which he had acquired when he was in Japan. He could tell the difference.

"Oh, Eurydice, you shouldn't have," he said breathlessly.

"Do you not like them?" she asked with a concerned frown. She was sure he would like them.

"No, no, I absolutely *love* them," he said feelingly, "but, my God...." He looked up at her. "You could not have come by them cheaply."

"I'm gifted at negotiating," she said with a smile and a wink.

"But still...," he said slowly.

"It's rude to discuss the price of a gift," she said gently, "and I felt no twinge over what I spent. That should be good enough."

Ellsworth reseated the sword in its scabbard before putting it back in the box, and then he leaned toward her to kiss her warmly. "Thank you."

Eurydice blushed with pleasure. She had hoped he would like them. She didn't think he would need to use them, even if he knew *how*, so she would send a letter home to the Ashikaga to arrange for *shirasaya* mountings and a stand. She was sure the man from Okhotsk had no knowledge of their proper care, and she didn't know how he had convinced a swordsmith or *samurai* to part with them. Men who named their swords wouldn't easily let them go, especially not to a *gaijin*, no matter how Oriental he looked.

Then it was Eurydice's turn to open her final present. The cloth was draped over it rather than wrapping it, and she took a deep preparatory breath before she lifted it off. She exhaled in a sigh of relief when there wasn't a cage hidden underneath. Casanova was hard enough to care for; she didn't know how she would manage anything else. Besides, she had a baby coming that was going to take up any time she might have. She tilted her head sideways with a frown as she tried to decide what the gift was.

She opened the box, and inside it she found another box, about two feet square. Eurydice looked back over her shoulder at Ellsworth through narrowed eyes, and then she removed the smaller box and opened it to reveal yet another box, about one foot square on each side. She opened that box to reveal an even smaller one, about six inches square. She lifted it out, and before she opened it, she looked at Ellsworth.

"So help me, if there's another box in here…," she threatened mildly with a wry smile. Ellsworth gave her a grin.

She opened the final box and found something wrapped in a delicately woven white shawl that she would have been glad to receive on its own. When she folded back the cloth, she found a set of beautiful *matryoshka*. They were dressed in dark blue and white, holding flowers in their hands, and they all had dark red hair and amber-colored eyes. The reasoning behind the nested boxes became clear when she saw the dolls, and she looked up at Ellsworth, shaking her head with mild exasperation as her shoulders shook with silent laughter.

"I scared you didn't I, with that big box?" he chortled.

"I was nervous," she conceded with a smile, "and I am relieved that we will not have to find a place to put that large box on the coach."

"You and me both," he chuckled.

With her last present opened, the evening drew to a close. It was already past midnight, and Eurydice could tell; she was very tired. She fit all the boxes she would no longer need into the largest one. She set the *yangqin,* lute, and violin in their boxes on the table in the parlor; she would put the violin into her traveling case tomorrow, and the boxes for the other two instruments were meant to be kept. She was able to carry everything else, including all the cloth in which her gifts had been wrapped. She wished Schellen a happy Christmas, and then she told Agniezka she wouldn't need help getting ready for bed. She gave her a hug and wished her a happy Christmas before going to the bedroom.

She packed away her gifts, and then she got dressed for bed. She had just finished washing her face and brushing her teeth when Ellsworth came into the bedroom carrying his own presents. She pulled back the blankets on the bed while he put them away, and then she began to walk around the room turning off the lamps as he got ready for bed. He came behind her to put his arms around her waist and kiss her neck.

"Happy Christmas, sweetheart," he purred.

Eurydice turned in his arms to put hers around his neck and looked up at him. "Happy Christmas."

He held up his hand, showing her the jade pendant. "Help me tie this on." She took it from him and tried to tie it around his neck, but he was too tall for her to reach and do it properly. He made a fake choking sound at one point. "Are you trying to throttle me?" he asked dryly.

"You're too tall for me to do this standing up," said Eurydice patiently.

He went to the edge of the bed and sat, and then she could tie it. The knot would not easily come loose. It rested just below the hollow at the base of his neck, and Eurydice thought it looked perfect.

"There," she said with satisfaction.

Ellsworth grabbed her around the waist to nuzzle her stomach, and she whooped in surprise when he lifted her and tossed her onto the bed with a low, playful growl. He began to kiss her ravenously as he untied her dressing gown, and Eurydice weakly put a hand to the back of his head and sighed at the back of her throat. He moved his lips down her neck to the edge of her shift, and then he lifted his head to look down at her and tug at her clothes.

"Yet another gift to unwrap," he panted with a grin.

Eurydice chuckled and slid out from under him to sit up on her knees. She removed her robe and tossed it toward the bench at the foot of the bed, and then she pulled her shift over her head and tossed it there as well. Ellsworth began to place kisses up one of her thighs to her hip, and Eurydice gasped when he grabbed her other hip to make her pivot and straddle his face. He began to play her with his mouth, and Eurydice dug her fingers into his hair and quivered with a soft moan of pleasure.

She looked down to see him watching her, and she gave him a saucy smile as she reached behind her to begin stroking his semi-erect member. Her grin widened when she felt him jump and lose his concentration for a moment, but it was only for a moment, and Eurydice soon lost her own as she began to orgasm, her body spasming as her back arched. She moved off of him and bent down to kiss him appreciatively, and then she placed kisses down his neck to his chest as her hand glided down his stomach to start stroking him again.

She teased one of his nipples with her teeth as she continued to stroke him, and she loved the way he gasped and sighed as he arched slightly off the bed. She continued to kiss down his torso, and she felt him clench his fingers in the hair at the back of her head as she ran her tongue up his erection.

"Alleluia," he gasped, and Eurydice laughed softly.

She loved the feel of him growing harder as she teased him, the way he sighed and whispered her name, and the expression on his face of utter bliss. She enjoyed pleasing him and reveled in her ability to make him quiver, the power she had to reduce him to a helpless, trembling mass. She could feel him almost throbbing in her hand as she stroked him, and it wouldn't be long before he climaxed. She had become so attuned to pleasing him and his responses that she knew he was already fighting it. She put a steadying hand to his hip as he began to come, and his back arched off the bed as he released a low groan of satisfaction.

Eurydice slowly stopped what she was doing, and then she casually began to kiss her way back up his body, smiling slightly at the way he still quivered as he gasped for air. She ran her tongue up his neck to his lips before kissing him hungrily, and she felt him weakly lift a hand to smooth it down her back.

"Oh, happy Christmas," he sighed softly.

Eurydice smiled affectionately, and she tugged at his shoulder to get him to move on the bed and lay on it properly. She put them under the blankets before she snuggled against him and settled her head onto his chest. She kissed the skin beneath her cheek and drifted off to sleep with a contented smile.

Sometime later, Eurydice woke up with a slight shiver. She was in the bed alone, and when she raised herself up on her elbows to look around the room with a slight frown, she saw the door to the balcony ajar. The fire was burning well, but the air outside was cold, causing a draft to flow through the room. She could smell cigar smoke, and she put a hand to her stomach and breathed shallowly in an effort to control the nausea it provoked. She had never been overly fond of the smell, and now that she was pregnant, she found she could tolerate it even less.

She got out of bed and slipped on her dressing gown, and then she left the room to go to the water closet, since she was awake. She passed into the dining room to grab a piece of bread left over from their supper, a peach, a pickled cucumber, and a glass of wine on her way back to the bedroom, and by the time she returned there, the nausea had lessened to a bearable level. She thought about getting back in bed under the covers, but she didn't want to get crumbs from the bread in the blankets, so she went to sit on the rug in front of the fire while she consumed her snack. She was only there for a minute or two before Ellsworth came in from the balcony, wearing nothing but his fur coat and hat.

He looked around the room with a concerned frown when he didn't see her on the bed after he closed the door, and then he sauntered toward her with a grin when he saw her sitting on the rug. Eurydice felt her mouth go dry as he came nearer. The front of his coat was open, and the picture he made with the fur and bare skin, with that sensual smile and the animal grace, made it very difficult for her to swallow the piece of bread she had been eating. He lounged on his side on the rug beside her and looked at her with a raised eyebrow.

"What are you doing awake?"

"I got cold, and then I needed to pee, and then I decided I was hungry, so...," she trailed off as she finished her bread.

She had already eaten her cucumber and the last of the small piece of bread. She rubbed some of the fuzz from the peach before taking a bite, and she moaned pleasurably at the taste. It was a very good peach. Ellsworth shook his head with a silent laugh at her reaction. She held it out to him to take a bite, which he did. The juice began to run down his chin, and Eurydice leaned toward him to catch it with her tongue, tracing it from where it had just started to go beneath his chin onto his neck up to his bottom lip, which she nipped at playfully with her teeth.

"Oh, that gets me hot," he sighed.

Eurydice pulled off his hat and tossed it onto the nearby settee, and then she pushed at his shoulder to make him turn onto his back, propped up on his elbows. She straddled his lap and took another bite of the peach, and then she held it up to his mouth for him to have another bite as well. She reached beyond him to pick up the glass of wine from where she had placed it on the bare floor nearby, and Ellsworth sighed and closed his eyes as she rubbed against him.

He untied the sash on her dressing gown and flipped the material out of the way to expose her breasts when she straightened up, and Eurydice gave him a wanton glance as she took a sip from the glass. She held it up to his mouth as she took another bite from the peach, and she purposely let some of it spill out to run down his neck. She leaned toward him to lick it off, and Ellsworth straightened up and shifted her slightly to remove his coat. Once she had cleaned off the wine, he held onto her while he worked it loose from beneath him and tossed it onto the settee with his hat. She rubbed against him while he moved, and Ellsworth had difficulty breathing by the time he was through.

He leaned toward her to suckle at one of her breasts, and Eurydice sighed pleasurably and almost dropped the glass and the peach. Her nipples had become very sensitive, and his gentle touch made her quiver with delight. She took another bite from the peach and rubbed against him excitedly as he continued to tease her breast, and when he lifted his head to look up at her, she lowered hers to kiss him warmly.

"Mm," purred Ellsworth happily, "there cannot be anything better than peach-flavored kisses."

Eurydice gave him the last of the wine, and she set the glass back on the floor. She moved her hand between them to begin stroking him as she kissed along his neck to his ear, and Ellsworth sighed and wrapped his arms around her waist beneath her dressing gown. She took one last bite of the peach before letting him have the rest, and then she tossed the pit into the fire. She started to put her fingers in her mouth to clean off the juice and pith, and Ellsworth grabbed her hand to bring it to his own mouth. Her heart beat excitedly as he sucked and licked at her fingers, and she rubbed against him as she continued to stroke him with her other hand.

With both of her hands free, Ellsworth slid her dressing gown off and threw it onto the settee with his things. He cradled a hand to the back of her head and wrapped an arm around her waist as he began to kiss his way down her neck to her breasts. Eurydice whimpered as he teased one of her nipples, and she couldn't wait anymore.

"I want you inside me now," she gasped breathlessly, and she raised herself up on her knees to slowly settle onto his erection with a sigh.

Ellsworth watched her face as she slowly began to move up and down, her expression one of pleasure and almost desperation. He ran his fingers down her cheek to her neck before cupping one of her breasts and lowering his head to worry the nipple with his teeth. Eurydice cried out and wrapped her fingers in his hair to pull his mouth to hers and kiss him heatedly. That was something that had previously been pleasurable to her but now was painful.

She began to move quicker and less rhythmically as she neared her orgasm, and Ellsworth grabbed her hips to lower her onto her back on the rug. She made a sound of frustration when he did it, and Ellsworth raised one of her legs to place it over his shoulder as she wrapped the other one around his waist, and he began to thrust into her with a soft moan. She dug her fingers into the rug as he began to tease her button, and she cried out his name disjointedly as she began to orgasm. She felt herself quivering as the spasms worked through her body, and her leg slid off his shoulder as Ellsworth began to come as well with a low groan. Eurydice lifted herself to wrap her arms around his neck and kiss him passionately as she moved against him.

She weakly rested her forehead against his cheek as she struggled to get her breathing under control, and she could feel her heart palpitating. Ellsworth smoothed a hand down her back and kissed her neck as he cradled her against him. He would have been content if the only thing he had received for Christmas was Eurydice wrapped in a bow. She was the perfect gift—she provided hours of enjoyment, continued to amaze, and kept on giving.

Eurydice nestled her forehead into the crook of his neck and shoulder tiredly as she sat straddled across his lap, and after a few minutes, once he had regained some of his strength, he lifted her in his arms and carried her to the bed. She snuggled against him beneath the blankets and lifted her head to kiss him softly and nuzzle his nose before resting her head on his chest. Ellsworth wrapped his arms around her with a tired sigh, and both soon fell asleep.

Cesaire Dubonnet stood watching the two of them through a slit in the curtains from the balcony. His intention had not been to watch them when he went there. From his room on the floor below, he knew Ellsworth had been there, and his plan had been to climb onto the balcony and deal with him. But he had missed his opportunity when the man had gone inside before Cesaire's arrival. This furtive, Peeping Tom behavior was something Cesaire considered beneath him…usually.

Then he saw it as an opportunity to observe his enemy and learn something more to use against him. In that respect, he had succeeded. Cesaire had to admire their athletics. She was exceptionally talented, and Cesaire had felt a stab of envy as he watched them. The thing that had been useful, however, was seeing that Ellsworth was completely besotted. Cesaire had suspected as much the other day, but tonight confirmed it. If something happened to his wife, Ellsworth would be destroyed.

Cesaire had been suspicious of whether or not the two were married, but he could see that they were after watching them together. Whatever else, they were man and wife. Cesaire was disappointed in Ellsworth by that. Cesaire had thought the man was smarter, to know that having a wife, especially one he truly cared for, was a weakness in their occupation.

There was something peculiar about her, though. He wasn't sure what or whether it would be useful, but he was beginning to shift his focus toward her. Ellsworth would still be the final objective, but his wife, this Eurydice, would be a challenge Cesaire was very much looking forward to undertaking. Cesaire still wasn't convinced she didn't share Ellsworth's occupation, but in the end it would be irrelevant. She was more than a pawn in this game, possibly a rook, but she would still be removed from the board. Soon.

Chapter Thirty Three

The New Year came with an inauspicious beginning. They were supposed to arrive in Buda-Pest on New Year's Eve, but the weather and terrain had made that impossible. Traveling across the Ukraine had gone well enough, but a snowstorm struck just as they were to go through the Carpathian Mountains taking the Borgo Pass. It never got bad enough that they had to completely stop, but it slowed them enough that they stayed in Torok on New Year's Eve and arrived in Buda-Pest on New Year's Day, behind schedule.

Eurydice had committed to perform in Pest on the night of the second. Arriving there late in the afternoon on the first gave her limited opportunity to rehearse with the orchestra. She was not pleased when she arrived. The conductor had rearranged some of the music, ostensibly to make it easier for the orchestra to play, before letting them attempt to learn it as originally written and without the knowledge of Herr Gergely, who had invited Eurydice to Pest. Eurydice didn't discover the conductor had done this until she arrived for rehearsal on Tuesday morning, suffering from pregnancy sickness and road weary. For the first time in her life, Eurydice lost her temper and had a tantrum of unbelievable volume. She was as shocked by it as her audience had been, and she felt mortified after it was over. She didn't hold the orchestra at fault, and she should have reserved her outrage for Herr Farkas, the conductor, in private. As it was, she apologized and did her best to rearrange her own parts before the evening. Sadly, it had been passable but not great, and she had the impression she would not be invited back to perform in Pest.

While they were there, after her outburst and the less than stellar performance, Ellsworth asked if she wanted to go back to Vienna. They could be there in less than two days. She was tired, and while the nausea and vomiting were improving, they hadn't completely gone. Dr. Herzen had told him she would be fine, but they wouldn't be getting any closer to Vienna after this. He only suggested it. He didn't demand it or tell her she needed to. She sincerely told him she would sleep on it, and she did. But in the morning, she decided to continue on. They would soon be in Venice, and it would give her the chance to rest. She should have expected not all of her performances would go well. She should have been amazed they had gone as well as they had. Before they left Pest, though, Ellsworth asked her to promise she would let him know if she felt like she couldn't continue. She promised.

When they left Pest on Wednesday, the weather looked promising, but shortly after they stopped for dinner in Fok, the coach hit a hole in the road, hidden beneath the snow, and damaged a wheel. It didn't break, but the strake was warped. The coach had to barely move along until they arrived at the next village, where a blacksmith was able to give them a new one. It didn't put them too far behind, and they arrived in Laibach by mid-day on Friday.

After they settled in at the inn and had dinner, Eurydice sent a message to Herr Kovach to let him know she had arrived. Their accommodations weren't the best, but they could be worse. There was a draft circulating through the room Eurydice shared with Ellsworth, but she would only have to tolerate it for two nights. Another night or two in other hotels or inns, then she would be at the palazzo in Venice for a week. Just the thought of it made lots of things more tolerable.

Laibach was a pretty city, built around three rivers, and some of it had a Venetian air to it…except it was cold. Eurydice was sure Venice wouldn't be balmy in January, but it was unlikely there would be snow or ice, and the palazzo would be comfortable. All she had to do was get through a few more days. She began to grow impatient to be there, and she wasn't sure how she would be able to concentrate on her performance in Laibach.

Herr Kovach came to speak with her not long after she sent her message. She would perform the following night, and she made arrangements to rehearse with the orchestra that evening. She did not want another Pest, and after that fiasco, she had firmly decided if the conductor rearranged her music, she would perform her sonatas with no accompaniment. She would dislike having to do that to the orchestra, but she would if necessary. When she said that to Ellsworth, he chuckled and said she was becoming tetchy in her fame.

The rehearsal went well. The conductor left her music exactly as she had written it, and after having almost two months to rehearse, the orchestra sounded wonderful. They had even learned the symphony. The playbill would follow the same pattern as it had at the Burgtheater. A concerto followed by the symphony, and then she would play the final concerto. They practiced until shortly before seven, when the orchestra had to prepare for that night's performance, and she arranged to rehearse with them again for a few hours the following morning.

Eurydice went back to the hotel with Ellsworth, and they had an early supper. She arranged for a bath to be brought up, and she let Agniezka use it before she did, as usual. Her maid was looking more pregnant every day, and Agniezka said the little flutters had become acrobatics that usually happened when she was trying to rest. She was also developing constant heartburn, and nothing she did would relieve it for long. Eurydice wasn't enthusiastic about the things she would have to look forward to in the coming months.

Ellsworth had wanted to share Eurydice's bath, but the tub they brought was too small. There was simply no room for the two of them to be in it together. Instead, he sat outside the tub and talked with her while she washed and then he helped her wash her back. The water was quite a bit cooler when it was his turn to get in, but it was warm enough.

"What does Schellen do for a bath?" asked Eurydice curiously, and then she colored slightly. "I probably shouldn't be asking that."

Ellsworth looked at her with a grin and shrugged. "If there's a public bathing house, he goes there. Otherwise, he goes to a river or lake…if he feels like he needs to bathe badly enough."

"Even in the winter?" blurted Eurydice in surprise.

Ellsworth chuckled. "He doesn't stay in very long."

"But still…," said Eurydice with a shake of her head. "*I* wouldn't want to have it necessary to chip away ice to have a bath."

"Me either, but Schellen has iron skin," he said with an amused smile.

Eurydice had an extra blanket placed on the bed that night. The inn brought to mind the one they had stayed at on the way from Venice to Vienna, where the room would be quite warm, until a wind found one of the chinks in the wall to blow a draft through the room. With the extra blanket and Ellsworth to snuggle beside, she was quite warm, and she had no trouble falling asleep.

Agniezka brought Eurydice some ginger tea the following morning. After leaving Russia, she no longer had access to *sbiten*, and the ginger tea was her only option. The nausea was improving, and the tea settled her stomach quite well. The need to relieve herself was back to what it had been before she became pregnant. She was still occasionally dizzy, but only if she stood up too quickly or for too long. For Eurydice, she was almost vivacious that morning because she hadn't felt so well for some time.

The rehearsal went well, putting Eurydice into an even better mood, and Ellsworth looked at her occasionally throughout the day with uncertainty, wondering what could have brought about the change. If he didn't know better, he might think she was pretending for his benefit. But he did know better, and he was relieved she seemed to be on the mend. It freed his mind to think about other things, like what he needed to do when he arrived in Venice.

Eurydice's concert, while not heavily attended, was at least performed capably, and she was satisfied. Herr Kovach gave her a bank note, which she added to the others in the strong-box. She had not yet looked at the amounts on most of them. It would only make her nervous. Ellsworth was still amazed at her almost frolicsome disposition, which increased after her performance. It wasn't a good idea to look a gift horse in the mouth, but he had to know.

"You are certainly in a good mood," he said mildly when they were settling down for bed.

Eurydice rolled over to settle on top of him and propped herself up on her elbows to either side of his head. She looked down with a grin before nuzzling his neck.

"I am absolutely in a *wonderful* mood," she averred softly as she began to kiss from his shoulder up to his ear.

"Why?" he asked slowly on a sigh. He wanted to know, but he was beginning not to care.

"Because I am starting to feel better, my concert went well, and we leave for Venice tomorrow," she said, punctuating each reason with a kiss to a different part of his face.

Ellsworth rolled over to place her beneath him and kissed her soundly before looking at her with a grin.

"Hurray," he purred as he lowered his lips to her neck.

Eurydice woke up with a start, her eyes wide open, and her heart was pounding anxiously. She put a hand to one of her cheeks, and she could feel the dampness of tears. She didn't know what time it was, but it was dark. The fire had died down to little more than embers, and the only warmth she had was the blankets and Ellsworth spooned behind her, cradling her close. She felt cold, chilled to the bone, and she had to fight to suppress a shiver.

She had seen the end of the Dark Dream, and she wasn't going to forget it, even if she never wrote it down. She'd not had any part of it since they were in St. Petersburg, not even the nightmares the part of it she had repeatedly dreamt had caused. She hadn't forgotten, but she had begun to think of other things, to put it to the back of her mind, hoping since she wasn't having it as much it meant she would have more time. Now that she had seen the end, she knew that wasn't so. She wasn't going to have much more time at all.

She put a hand up to her eyes and pressed it against them in an effort to stop the tears, and she could feel them leaking between her fingers. She inhaled slowly through her nose to keep a sob from escaping. She wished she hadn't seen. She didn't want to know, and now that she did, she couldn't forget. There were still pieces missing, particularly the face of the man who would cause it, but she couldn't decide if it mattered anymore. She wouldn't be able to stop it.

"Are you awake?" mumbled Ellsworth sleepily, tightening his arm around her waist and snuggling closer against her.

Eurydice jumped at the sound of his voice, and her eyes widened in alarm as she tried to think of what to do. For the moment, she couldn't trust her voice to speak, but she couldn't pretend she was sleeping.

"Mm-hmm," she said softly.

He nuzzled her neck before giving it a soft kiss, and Eurydice could tell he was still more asleep than awake.

"You should be sleeping," he sighed. "We'll be leaving early...for Venice," he said amusedly.

She couldn't tell him about the dream. She knew he wondered about it, although he never asked her, and she knew she couldn't tell him. Even if she could tell someone else, he could *not* know. She turned in his arms to face him, and she put a gentle hand to his cheek before she kissed him desperately.

"I love you," she whispered brokenly.

"Eurydice?" he said confusedly.

"I love you, Gareth," she said again, and she began to place feverish kisses on his face.

"Dicy, what—?" he started bemusedly.

"I love you," she sighed.

Ellsworth frowned as she continued to kiss him, telling him over and over that she loved him. As moved as he was to hear her say it, her actions left him confused and concerned. Something was not right. He didn't know what had prompted her to profess her feelings, but it came as unexpected. At first he wasn't even sure she was awake, but it only took him a moment to realize she was. She seemed almost desperate as she kissed him and touched him, and he could tell she had been crying.

"Eurydice, what's wrong?" he asked soothingly, attempting to calm her. He clenched his jaw and sucked in air through his teeth as she wrapped her fingers around him and began to stroke him. "Dicy, slow down," he sighed. "I'm not going anywhere."

Eurydice gasped as if she'd been struck, and she stilled for a moment, brushing a gentle hand down his cheek. He cursed that there was no light to see her face, and he almost thought of getting up to put more wood on the fire. She started kissing him again—slower, deeper, and Ellsworth didn't really think these kisses showed any less desperation. It was obvious something was wrong, and she didn't intend to tell him what it was. He couldn't understand. Everything had been better than fine before they went to sleep.

She continued to kiss him and touch him, and despite his concern, despite his wanting her to talk to him, he couldn't help but respond. He let her lead, lying passively for the most part as she made love to him, and he found this reversal to be erotic by itself. She kissed him and caressed him, stroked and teased him, and his heart pounded in his chest excitedly. He hoped this would help her, but he was willing to let her have her way with him even if it didn't.

Eurydice climbed on top of him and settled herself onto his erection with a soft moan, digging her nails into his chest. Ellsworth inhaled sharply, and she leaned forward to kiss him hungrily as she began to ride him. She straightened and tossed her head back in abandon, her back arching, bracing her hands against his chest. Ellsworth smoothed his hands up her hips to cup her breasts, and she put her hands over his to get him to loosen his hold somewhat as she looked down at him. She leaned forward to suck on his neck as she began to orgasm, and Ellsworth was sure there would be a mark. He didn't care.

He put a hand behind her neck and another around her waist, and he rolled over to place her beneath him. He drove into her with long, deep strokes as

Eurydice wrapped her legs around his waist, and he shuddered slightly with a low moan as he began to come. He rested his head onto her chest as he slowly stopped moving, and Eurydice cradled him against her, making sure they were covered by the blankets. She smoothed a gentle hand across his back, and Ellsworth began to drift back to sleep. Eurydice could feel him settle heavier against her and kissed the top of his head as she blinked away her tears.

"I will *always* love you," she whispered fiercely.

Eurydice wouldn't tell Ellsworth what was troubling her. He asked her in the morning, but she would only look at him and tell him she couldn't say. All of her cheerfulness of the previous day had gone as if it had never been there and seemed to have taken more of her good spirits with it. She had only picked at her breakfast, eating very little of it, and her face was so sad. It had been a long time since he had seen her look that way, and she wouldn't tell him *why*. She insisted it was nothing he had done, that her health was still improving, that there was nothing wrong. No one had done anything to upset her. Nothing had happened to worry her. She insisted she was fine. If that were so, then why did Ellsworth feel more concerned about her than ever?

They left from Laibach very early, and the coach traveled over the roads at an excellent pace, especially when the snow began to disappear. As much as Eurydice was hopeful they would be to Venice that night, it was physically impossible. After stopping in Gorizia for dinner, they were only able to make it as far as Treviso before it was too late to continue. Their journey over the plain took far less time than it had when they had traveled to Vienna, but it simply couldn't be done.

As it was, they reached the palazzo before midday on Monday. Ellsworth made arrangements for the keeping of their coach in Mestre, and then he arranged for boats to ferry them and their belongings across the lagoon to the city. Eurydice had been excited to be going, not because she would perform, but because she would be at the palazzo. Ellsworth was hopeful it might lift her from her doldrums.

Signor Montenegro was happy to see them when they arrived. Eurydice was happy to see him, too, and his presence began to calm her.

"*Buon giorno!*" he said with a smile when he opened the door. "*Entrato! Entrato!* We weren't expecting you until evening, but we are ready."

He turned slightly to whistle sharply through his teeth, and only a minute later two servants came running. He began giving them instructions to unload the trunks and belongings, and he paused for a moment to look at Eurydice and Ellsworth.

"We have prepared the room where you stayed in September. That will be fine?"

"Of course, Signor Montenegro," said Eurydice with an agreeable smile. She was happy he had put them back in the gold room. She would feel odd sleeping in the room that was usually her parents', and it was much too large.

"*Bene*," he said with a smile, and he began to issue further orders.

Schellen said he would stay to make sure the trunks went to the proper rooms, and Ellsworth, Eurydice, and Agniezka went with Signor Montenegro. Eurydice wanted to see the courtyard before they went upstairs, and she went to the gate and opened it. Despite the absence of flowers and the leaves having fallen from the trees, it was still beautiful and peaceful, and she would come back once she was settled in. There were a few things she wanted to do before she came back, but she *would* be back before the end of the day.

Signor Montenegro walked with them to their suite, and he told them he would arrange for dinner to be prepared. There were a few maids in the room tending to the last-minute preparations, like starting the fires, turning down the blankets, and making sure there were linens in the bathing room. Eurydice was glad they were tending to that because she wanted to have a nice long soak in a tub of hot water.

One of the men came in carrying Casanova's cage, and she had him set it on the table near the loggia. She had covered the cage while they were on the boat to avoid any embarrassing offensive outbursts, but once he was on the table, she removed the cloth and folded it to put on the table beside the cage.

"*Porca!*" he squawked.

Eurydice clicked her tongue at him. "Now, now, Casanova. If you're going to be like that, I'll put the cover back on," she said mildly.

He lifted one of his feet to scratch the side of his head before sidling closer to the side of the cage near her.

"*Innamorata mia, amo i vostra occhi,*" he crooned.

"That's better," said Eurydice dryly. She would arrange for him to have some fruit and nuts.

She went out to the loggia, and Ellsworth came out behind her to put his arms around her waist. She leaned against him with a fitful sigh as she looked over the roofs of the nearby buildings. She would have to send a message to Signor Duchesi. She didn't want to rehearse today. Her first performance wouldn't be until Thursday. It would give her Tuesday and Wednesday, maybe even Thursday morning, to prepare. Provided the orchestra had rehearsed, that would be plenty.

"I missed this place," said Ellsworth quietly.

"Me, too," said Eurydice absently. She almost felt like she was home. "Can't we just stay here until spring?"

Ellsworth scoffed softly with amusement. "I suppose we could," he said agreeably, "but what about your family?"

"Eh, they could come visit," said Eurydice dismissively. "It's a big house."

Ellsworth kissed the side of her neck and rested his chin on her head. "I would still have to go to Paris, but after that, I would be all yours," he sighed.

Eurydice turned in his arms to look up at him. "You don't *have* to go," she said somberly. "Couldn't someone else go?"

"No, I'm afraid not," he said gently. "It's *my* job."

Eurydice reached up a hand to brush her fingers down his cheek, and then she moved out of his arms to go back inside.

"Dicy, why won't you tell me what's wrong?" he asked quietly after he came back in and closed the door.

"Nothing is wrong," she said evenly. "Everything is perfectly…perfect," she said with a brittle smile and a shrug.

"Then why are you so sad?"

"Because everything changes," she said softly, "and I don't want this to change."

Ellsworth frowned and walked toward her. "It doesn't have to change."

Eurydice gave him a bitter smile, and she blinked several times before looking away from him. "*Everything* changes," she whispered.

"I won't let anything happen to you," said Ellsworth determinedly as he pulled her close in a tight hug.

"I know," she said softly around the lump in her throat, resting her ear against his chest to listen to his heartbeat. It sounded so strong and steady, and it helped to soothe her a little. She cleared her throat and looked up at him with a self-deprecating smile. "In any event, there is nothing wrong."

Eurydice had a long soak in the tub after dinner, and she felt a little better. Ellsworth needed to go out, and she tried not to be disappointed. He said he would be back before supper, but knowing he would be gone from the palazzo much of the time they were in Venice was the only thing disappointing about their being there. He would go out at night as well, after he thought she was asleep. He would be safe, but he was fitting another piece into the puzzle. She couldn't stop him, and that was the part that was so hard to accept.

She received a response back from the message she sent to Signor Duchesi, telling her that he would like to see her at the theater the following morning at ten. She didn't know where it was, but she could ask Ellsworth or Signor Montenegro. She didn't know how far it was and whether or not she would be able to walk. She wasn't sure if she would *want* to walk there, but if it were close enough, the exercise would do her good.

When it was time for supper, Ellsworth had not returned to the palazzo. Eurydice wasn't worried, but she was disappointed. He had said he would be back. After she'd had her bath, she had gone to the courtyard and spent a long time standing on the bridge watching the fish swim around in their pool. She stayed until it began to grow too dark to see, and then she went to the sitting room in their suite to work on her symphony. She had expected Ellsworth to arrive at any time, but in the end, she and Agniezka dined alone.

Eurydice was tired after supper, and she went back to their suite and got ready for bed. Once Agniezka helped her into her shift and braided her hair, Eurydice washed her face and brushed her teeth, and then she climbed into bed and curled up in the middle of it, hugging a pillow close. She wanted to stay awake and wait for Ellsworth, but she couldn't keep her eyes open. She was entirely unhappy that he hadn't returned when he said he would, and she could only grudgingly hope it was for a good reason.

She didn't know what time it was when Ellsworth did finally get home, but she woke up slightly when he got into the bed and removed the pillow she had been holding and spooned behind her. She started to turn her head to speak to him, but he shushed her and soothed her back to sleep, cradling her close.

When she woke up in the morning, he was still there, sound asleep, and that was when she knew he had returned very late. If it had only been an hour or two after she went to bed herself, he would be awake before her. For several minutes, she enjoyed lying there being held by him, but she eventually, carefully, got out of the bed. Her watch had chimed shortly after she woke, and the sun was up. If she was going to have time to eat breakfast before walking to the theater to rehearse, she had to get out of bed.

She decided to walk after she had asked Signor Montenegro where it was. He assured her it was very close, easy to find, and very easy to get to on foot. When he provided her with the directions, Eurydice had to agree that it was. She thought it might take longer to go by gondola. She might arrive there at night by water, but there was nothing wrong with walking during the day.

Agniezka was coming out of her room just as Eurydice finished in the water closet. She started to speak, and Eurydice put a finger up to her lips and pointed at Ellsworth still sleeping on the bed. Agniezka raised an eyebrow, but she shrugged and went to the water closet. When she came back out, she went to the wardrobe for Eurydice's clothes and helped her dress. Ellsworth didn't stir the entire time, and Agniezka thought that was odd.

Eurydice wanted to remove the cover from Casanova's cage for him to enjoy the sunlight, but she was afraid his squawking and chattering might wake Ellsworth. She and Agniezka would be back to the palazzo for dinner; she would remove it then. Before they left the room to go to the great hall, Eurydice quietly went to the side of the bed to give Ellsworth a soft kiss on the cheek after she ran a gentle hand across his hair.

"Have you told him that you're going to have his child yet?" asked Agniezka softly as they walked down the stairs.

Eurydice looked at her pensively. "No, I haven't," she said dully.

"You should tell him," said Agniezka firmly.

"I can't," said Eurydice sadly with a shake of her head. Agniezka looked at her with a confused frown. "I was going to tell him...eventually, but I can't...not now," she said brokenly, her voice barely above a whisper.

"*Malutka,* what's wrong?" asked Agniezka concernedly, and she put a gentle hand to Eurydice's arm to stop her. Eurydice's face was sad, and her eyes glistened with tears. "What's wrong?" repeated Agniezka, rubbing Eurydice's shoulder soothingly.

"Oh, Agniezka, something terrible is going to happen, and I can't tell him...any of it. I can't tell him, and I can't change it, and...oh!" she gasped, and she put a hand to her mouth to stifle a sob.

Agniezka looked at her sympathetically and pulled her close. Eurydice buried her face in Agniezka's shoulder, and the older woman could feel her trembling. From what Eurydice said, Agniezka knew she'd had a dream...of something awful, and from the way it was troubling her, Agniezka could tell it was going to happen soon. She hadn't been this way when her *babushka* and Myron had died until her grandmother had contracted her infection and her brother had arranged the duel. Eurydice straightened up and cleared her throat, and she bravely wiped the tears from her cheeks.

"He can't know," said Eurydice with husky firmness, giving Agniezka a determined look. "He can't know about the baby or that anything is wrong. Promise me you won't say anything, no matter what happens."

Agniezka reluctantly nodded her head. She wasn't sure what she could tell him even if she did say something. She knew from past experience that Eurydice wouldn't tell Agniezka what she had seen, not unless she asked, and Agniezka would not look in her dream diary. There were some things she would rather not know. She could see Eurydice wanted to talk about it, but that she also did *not* want to.

"Is it about the baby?" she asked worriedly.

"No, it's going to be much worse than that," whispered Eurydice.

Eurydice had enjoyed the walk to Teatro La Fenice, the theater where she would perform, and it did much to clear her head. Once she began to rehearse, she was able to lose herself in her music and forget everything else for at least a little while. It was a blessed relief. The theater was slightly larger than the Burgtheater, but not by much, and it would be the largest venue she had played since leaving Vienna. They didn't rehearse in the auditorium itself but instead used one of the rooms for that at the rear of the building. Signor Duchesi did show her the grand auditorium where she would be performing. The acoustics were good, but she wouldn't say they were the best. The auditorium itself was very pretty, easily comparable to the Burgtheater and Theater an der Wien with its many tiers of loges. She was surprised Signor Duchesi wanted her to perform at a place so large for three nights, but apparently her reputation had grown, and he was confident that it would be a successful (and profitable) run.

Eurydice and Agniezka had to cross two small bridges to get to and from the theater, and they were crowded both on the way to the theater and back. The Campo San Fantin at the rear of the theater, named after the nearby church, was full with people shopping at the stalls of a small market there. The bridges were little more than narrow planks between two alleys, and Eurydice kept a firm grip on her violin when she was jostled as they crossed the Ponte dei Fuseri, which crossed the canal that went down the side of the palazzo.

When they returned to the palazzo, Eurydice was unsurprised to find that Ellsworth had gone. She was hopeful he would be back for supper, but she didn't expect it. She would have to accept that while they were in Venice, it would be unlikely she would see him at all...except perhaps for her performances. She hated that, and she hated there was nothing she could do about it. She would have to find things to occupy herself while he was gone and try to be happy when she did see him.

So, after dinner, she worked on her symphony, and she was amazed at how close she was to being done. She thought it would take her until she reached Paris to get to that point, but with nothing else requiring her attention, the notes seemed to place themselves onto the paper with little effort from her. She filled sheet after sheet, and it seemed to flow out so quickly she was sure there had to be numerous mistakes. When she put down her pen shortly before supper and looked over what she had transcribed, however, she was unable to see any.

She and Agniezka again had supper alone. The food was excellent, and they talked, but the palazzo was so quiet and empty. She missed the sounds of the children and many conversations of when her family had been there. It just didn't feel like the same house without them. The same sense of peace she had experienced before was not there. She didn't know if that was because of its emptiness or because she knew of the things to come that she hadn't before.

After supper, she got ready for bed and climbed under the blankets once she covered Casanova's cage and added wood to the fire. She put a hand to her stomach and smoothed it across the still-flat surface thoughtfully. She still had a few more weeks before she would no longer be able to hide it, but by then it wouldn't matter. There were so many things that were no longer going to matter. Her pregnancy sickness was going away, and she expected it would be completely gone by the time they reached Paris. Eurydice was relieved, but it wasn't going to matter either. Ellsworth wouldn't even notice.

Her eyelids were beginning to droop as she started to drift off to sleep, watching the shadows from the fire flicker on the wall, but they sprang back open again when she thought she heard something on the loggia. She had lifted her head from the pillow to look at the glass doors there when she heard the door open to their suite and Ellsworth came in. She frowned as she looked from the loggia back to her husband. She had been almost asleep; perhaps she had mistaken which direction she thought the noise was coming from.

When he saw she was awake, Ellsworth came over to the bed and crawled across it to kiss her before he started to undress.

"You're awake," he said warmly.

"You're home early."

"I made progress," he said happily as he got off the bed to undress.

"What kind of progress?" asked Eurydice dully. She honestly couldn't be excited.

"I think I found a name," said Ellsworth proudly.

"*The* name?"

"Oh, yes," said Ellsworth with a grin as he removed his pants. "It's only taken me four months," he said wryly, "but I think I finally have it."

"And now that you have it, what will you do with it?" asked Eurydice to his back as he went into the bathing room to wash his face and brush his teeth.

"I don't know," said Ellsworth when he came back. He climbed under the blankets and moved toward her to pull her close. "Mm," he sighed as he kissed her neck, "I don't want to talk about that right now."

Eurydice weakly put a hand to his shoulder and sighed as he kissed her hungrily.

"Wouldn't it be more helpful if you knew what he looked like?" she said softly as he began to run his hand up her thigh beneath her shift as his lips trailed down her neck.

"One step at a time," he said distractedly. "This needs to go," he said as he grabbed at her shift.

Eurydice sat up to remove it, and Ellsworth sat up slightly to nuzzle his face between her breasts. Eurydice smiled softly at his impatience and curled her fingers into his hair. She wasn't as tired these days; otherwise, she might have told him no, especially since she had almost been asleep. She had missed him, and she would have to take advantage of the opportunities when they came to her, whether she felt like it or not.

She cut her eyes to the doors of the loggia with a thoughtful frown as he took one of her breasts into his mouth and grazed the nipple with his teeth. She had been so sure she heard a noise coming from there before he came in. Perhaps it had been an animal…a bird. The moon was almost full, and while she could see its light coming through the windows and doors, she could see no unusual shadows. She had very acute hearing, and she simply couldn't believe she had been mistaken.

Ellsworth was soon able to distract her from her thoughts and worries, and she lay back against the pillows as he began to kiss his way down her stomach. It was probably nothing to be concerned about.

Ellsworth was still there when she woke up, but he wouldn't be able to go with her to rehearsal. Now that he had the man's name (which he wouldn't tell her), he agreed that knowing what he looked like would be more helpful. A name was an easy enough thing to change, but it wasn't so easy to change his appearance. Disguises could be worn, some of them quite good, but Ellsworth felt it would be less likely. She watched him go to Schellen's room with his things to dress, and she lay in the bed for a moment with a frown.

Ellsworth said he needed to find the man to keep him from helping Napoleon escape, but after her dreams, Eurydice wasn't so confident that was the man's objective. Perhaps as a final one, it would be, but she had the feeling he had found another one to occupy him in the meantime: doing away with Ellsworth. Everything her husband did that put him closer to finding his enemy moved him toward the terrible things she saw in her dream. She believed that, knew that without question.

Agniezka soon came in to help her dress and asked if she needed any of the ginger tea. Surprisingly enough, Eurydice didn't think she would. She did feel a little nauseous, but when she put on the cuff bracelet, it went away. The weather was mild, sunny and warm enough she thought she would be fine with just a warm pelisse rather than needing a cloak as well. Once Agniezka styled her hair, Eurydice went to the sitting room to put her Batov into a carrying case, and they went down for breakfast, where Ellsworth soon joined them.

Eurydice enjoyed her breakfast of coffee, an omelet with peppers and cheese, ham, and crusty bread with butter and lime curd. She tried to act as if nothing was wrong—if not smiling and laughing, then at least not as if she would burst into tears. For Ellsworth's sake, she would pretend. After they finished, Eurydice gave him a kiss, and she and Agniezka left for the theater.

The air was somewhat cool in the shadows of the alleys they walked through, but then they would walk into a place where the sun was shining, and it would feel glorious. Unfortunately, the only places they encountered an opening that large after they left the courtyard at the rear of the palazzo was on the two bridges along the way until they reached the Campo San Fantin. There was still a market in the campo, and Eurydice spied a man selling pistachios and oranges. She thought she might buy some of both after rehearsal to take back to the palazzo. Not only would Casanova enjoy them, but her mouth watered at the thought of having some herself. She missed the peaches she had while they were in Moscow and Kiev, but a nice, sweet orange might suffice.

The rehearsal went well, and Duchesi was in a cheerful mood. He would see her again the following morning, but he didn't think she and the orchestra *needed* it. After playing with so many musicians, Eurydice had learned to adapt herself, and provided the conductor didn't rearrange her music (as Herr Farkas had done in Pest), the orchestras had been given sufficient time prior to her arrival to familiarize themselves with the compositions well enough that being ready for performance only required minor changes.

Eurydice went to the stall in the market and bought a small jute sack of pistachios and a small basket of oranges. The man's prices were reasonable, and she only half-heartedly haggled with him to lower it by a few coins. Agniezka took her violin and reticule while Eurydice carried the basket. Casanova would enjoy removing the shells from the nuts, and it was going to leave a mess in his cage. She didn't mind; it would at least keep his mouth occupied with something other than issuing insults and propositions.

The way back to the palazzo was busy with people going in and out of the shops and businesses along the way, and Eurydice and Agniezka had to go single file to cross the bridge over the Rio dei Barcaroli. Eurydice felt her hip bump into the flimsy iron railing at the edge as she crossed, and she looked down at the dark blue-green water below. She couldn't see the bottom, and she couldn't tell how clean it was. She supposed the tides of the lagoon cleaned the canals, but it wouldn't be good to fall in, not any healthier than falling into the Thames or the Seine. The Ponte dei Fuseri that they would cross didn't have railing, but it was a slightly wider bridge.

They walked down the Frezzaria talking idly with one another about what they planned to do with the rest of their day. Eurydice was sure Ellsworth wouldn't be back before nightfall…probably not for several hours after. She and Agniezka would have supper alone again, but Eurydice hoped she would be awake when he came home. Several times as they walked, they had to get one behind the other to make room for someone carrying something in a pack or basket slung over his shoulder. The alley was wide enough for two people to walk side-by-side or to pass each other in opposite directions, but those who carried things made the passage very tight. The way would widen, at least for a brief while, when they turned onto the Ramo dei Fuseri, but it would narrow again once they crossed the bridge. Eurydice could understand why most everyone used boats—even walking was impossible at times.

Agniezka saw some interesting things in the shops along the way, and she thought she might like to come back to a few when she had the time and a free hand. She didn't know where she could put anything she bought, but she wanted to look. She still had a little room left in the trunk she had brought from Sergei's; she would just have to make sure she only bought things she *really* wanted. She was saying something to that effect over her shoulder to Eurydice as they crossed the bridge in single file when she heard a surprised squeak and a splash. When she turned to look, Eurydice was gone.

Eurydice had been walking along with a slight smile, listening to what Agniezka was saying when she was jostled particularly hard from behind and toppled over the edge of the bridge into the canal. The heavy basket of oranges and nuts on her arm made her sink below the surface quickly despite the air trapped beneath the skirt of her gown, and once the material became sodden, it only added more weight to hold her there. She quickly discovered the canal wasn't deep, less than six feet, but the bottom was soft and mucky. When her feet touched, she sank into it well past her ankles and further still, and she couldn't work her feet loose. The water was unbelievably cold, and the brine of it made her eyes sting as she tried to look around herself and toward the surface to get her bearings.

She tried to control her panic. It had happened so quickly she had been unable to fill her lungs with air, and she wasn't sure how long what she had would last. The first thing she did was work the basket off of her arm, but the increase in buoyancy wasn't very helpful because her legs had sunk into the silty bottom almost to her knees to hold her fast. She tried to swim toward the surface, trying to loosen her legs from the muck, but it held her tight. She unfastened the buttons on her pelisse to work the material off, but it became bound on her arms and only made the situation worse. She managed to get it back onto her shoulders where she could move her arms again and bent down to grab one of her legs to try to free it from the bottom. She had stopped sinking, but with it up to her knees, she couldn't generate the momentum to get them loose. She was too far away from either side of the canal to grab the wall and pull herself above the surface. Her lungs started to burn as she ran out of air, and she began to grow tired as her skin went numb from the cold. This wasn't supposed to happen.

She could hear the muffled sounds of shouting and yelling distantly from above the surface, made even vaguer as she began to lose consciousness. She didn't know how long she had been under, but she couldn't last much longer. Even if her lungs had been full of air, the water was so cold. She was still struggling, trying to get her legs free, but everything was beginning to feel so heavy. She could raise a hand above her head and almost touch the surface, but it was just beyond her reach, and grabbing nothing but air wouldn't help. It wasn't as if she could capture a handful and put it into her lungs.

Then powerful hands grab one of her arms, and she could feel them pulling on her. She tried to remain conscious because if she didn't her body's instincts would take over and try to get air into her lungs. With her head two feet below the surface, that would be a bad thing. She could slowly feel her legs rising out of the muck, and it gave her an extra burst of determination. She no longer had the strength to help, but she did have the strength not to die. She eventually felt her feet break free of the bottom, and whoever was saving her pulled her toward the surface. He (she assumed it could only be a he) put an arm around her to keep her head above the water, and then she felt even more hands lifting her from the canal. She was trying to work air into her lungs, and it was all she could manage. She dimly heard a voice shouting, and then she was lifted in a set of arms to be carried somewhere. Everything was so confusing. At that point she lost consciousness. Her body had the strength for her to breathe or to stay awake; it chose breathing.

The next time Eurydice awoke with full recollection of her surroundings, she was in bed at the palazzo under the blankets up to her chin. She could vaguely remember Agniezka bathing her in a tub of hot water and being examined by a doctor, but she couldn't remember any of it clearly. She was tired, but she was warm and she could breathe. It was dark outside and she could hear the sounds of a gentle thunderstorm, but she had no notion of the hour. She could only assume it was still the same day. Ellsworth was sitting on the edge of the bed watching her, and he reached out to brush a hand down her cheek when he saw her eyes open.

"Hallo," he said softly.

"Hi," replied Eurydice in a cracked whisper, giving him a slight smile.

"How are you feeling?" he asked as he moved closer and smoothed a hand across her forehead.

"Tired," she said with a frown, "and hungry," she added as an afterthought.

Ellsworth gave her a slight smile and leaned forward to kiss her gently on the forehead.

"Do you remember what happened?"

"I, um," she began, and she cleared her throat in an effort to add more volume to it. "I was walking back from rehearsal with Agniezka, and we were crossing the Ponte dei Fuseri when I got jostled by someone else crossing. I lost my footing on the bridge and went into the water. I couldn't get my feet loose from the bottom. Someone pulled me out. I'm fairly sure Agniezka gave me a bath, and I was seen by a physician, but I could have just imagined that."

"Schellen pulled you out," said Ellsworth quietly.

Eurydice's eyes widened slightly as she looked at him. "He saved my life," she said hoarsely. "I thought I was going to die."

"Shh," soothed Ellsworth, resting his forehead against hers. "If you were anyone else, …? Schellen said you were under for three minutes before he could pull you out, but the doctor said you should be fine. You didn't swallow any of the water or get it into your lungs, and Agniezka was able to get you washed quickly enough it shouldn't make you sick. The water in the canals is actually fairly clean, all things considered." He nuzzled her nose and sighed. "I was so worried."

"When did you…? How did you…? Did Schellen find you?" she asked with a slight frown.

"Once he got you back here, Agniezka got you into the tub, Montenegro went to find a doctor, and Schellen came to find me after he made sure you were going to be all right and put on dry clothes."

Eurydice shivered slightly. "The water was so cold," she whispered.

"Shh," he crooned, and he lay down on his side to pull her close. "You're fine," he sighed, and Eurydice huddled against him with a tired sigh. She drifted back to sleep after only a few minutes.

He couldn't tell her what Schellen had told him. She thought she had been accidentally jostled by someone and fell into the water, but Schellen had been following at an unobtrusive distance behind her and Agniezka when he saw a man between him and the two women quicken his pace when he reached the bridge and *shove* Eurydice off the side. Schellen had been unable to get a good look at him, and he had quickly faded into the tumult that followed Eurydice's going in. The crowd had been thick enough that it had taken Schellen awhile to get to the bridge and go in after her. He had honestly admitted to Ellsworth that he was surprised to find her still alive when he pulled her out; he had fully expected to see that she had drowned.

Ellsworth's concern now was that it seemed the man he was trying to find intended to kill Eurydice. Ellsworth wasn't entirely sure what the man's reasoning was behind it. He could get no information from her if he killed her outright. Killing her in a manner that seemed like an accident wouldn't send Ellsworth a message, if that was his intention, and it also couldn't put Ellsworth in jail as the murderer. He would be heartbroken if something happened to her, but it would only make him all the more determined to find the man, and instead of arranging for Cesaire Dubonnet to go to prison, Ellsworth would kill him…slowly.

Chapter Thirty Four

Eurydice woke up the next morning still feeling a little tired, but the main thing bothering her was nausea. She'd only had breakfast the day before, and she had left her stomach empty too long. Ellsworth had gotten up at some point to get undressed, and he was laying on his side with his arms around her, holding her close against him, his forehead resting against her temple. The sun was just barely up, and Eurydice wasn't surprised she woke up so early, considering how much sleep she'd had.

She carefully eased her way out of the bed, and then she hurried across the floor as quickly as she could to the water closet, where she threw up the nearly nonexistent contents of her stomach and dry heaved for a few minutes. She rested a hand on her stomach with her eyes closed as she waited for the nausea to subside. She was oddly relieved by the vomiting because it meant her baby was still there. She didn't *think* she would still be sick if she had miscarried. She didn't *feel* as if she had miscarried. She was sure she would know. It also seemed Ellsworth still didn't know she was pregnant, and that relieved her. She couldn't let him know.

Once her stomach had settled, she relieved herself, and then she went to wash her face and hands and brush her teeth. She noticed while she did it that her necklaces were missing, and she felt a panic that she might have lost them in the canal. She finished what she was doing, and then she went into the bedroom to her jewel box. Before she opened it, she found the koi lying on top of the table, looking none the worse for wear, along with the cuff bracelet. She opened her jewel box to look for the locket, but she couldn't find it. She felt a sinking feeling in her stomach. She would ask Agniezka when she saw her if she knew what had happened to it. She supposed she should consider herself lucky if her locket was all she had lost, but she hated that she had.

She glumly turned to go back to the bed and was almost there when the glint of something hanging from a hook near the fireplace caught her eye. She went to it and found her locket. When she opened it, the miniature seemed to be intact and undamaged, but the side with the lock of hair had a slight film of condensation inside it beneath the glass. Someone had hung it there to dry, but Eurydice was hopeful—and relieved—that she still had it. She could always get more of his hair if she needed to. He had lots. She smiled happily as she brushed her thumb over the miniature.

Ellsworth was still sleeping when she went back to the bed, and she carefully climbed onto it and snuggled under the covers beside him after she looked at the clock on the mantle for the time. She still had two or three more hours before she would have to go to the theater to rehearse. She had thought—for only a minute—about not going to rehearse that morning, possibly even not performing that night, but she did feel fine. The tiredness would be better once she had eaten some food and had some coffee. She honestly didn't feel any worse than she usually did every morning.

Her moving around woke Ellsworth, despite her trying to be quiet, and he opened his eyes and gave her a sleepy smile. Eurydice returned it and gave him a soft kiss on the lips.

"Good morning, Mr. Ellsworth," she said softly.

"Good morning, Mrs. Ellsworth," he said huskily, and he pulled her against him to give her a proper kiss. "How are you feeling?" he asked with a slight frown.

"Completely recovered," she said pertly.

"You're sure?"

She put her leg over his thighs and pressed herself against him with a soft smile. "All better," she purred.

"Hmm," said Ellsworth amusedly. "You wouldn't be trying to humor me, would you?"

Eurydice's smile widened, and she leaned toward him to begin nibbling his ear as one of her hands went between them for her to wrap her fingers around him. He had that same marvelous erection he seemed to have every morning when they woke up, and he moaned softly at the back of his throat as she gently stroked him. Ellsworth quirked his lips in a half-smile, and his heart began to beat a little faster.

"Do you really feel like it?" he sighed, his eyes closing pleasurably. Eurydice worked her shift higher, and she settled herself onto him as they remained lying on their sides facing each other. Ellsworth's eyes sprang open in surprise, and he gave her a grin. "Well, yes. Yes, you do," he drawled.

Eurydice kissed him hungrily, and Ellsworth slowly began to thrust into her. She ran her fingers down his cheek and nuzzled his chin as her breath came out in jagged gasps. She hadn't planned on making love when she woke up, but it was as if she couldn't help herself. She was happy to be alive and well and that he was there with her. If nothing else, her accident had given her the undivided attention of her husband. It wouldn't last, and she would take her moments however she came by them. She clutched at his shoulders as she began to orgasm, and it began to roll over her in slow, intense waves. Ellsworth smiled tenderly as he watched her face, holding her close against him as he kept to his languid pace. She kissed him heatedly as the spasms continued to grip her, and she heard his breath catch and he jerked slightly as he reached his own climax. She wrapped her arms around his neck as she felt him shudder, and she rested her forehead against his as he finally stilled.

"Yes," he panted, "you are definitely all better."

"Mm," sighed Eurydice with a soft smile.

They both heard the muffled sound of her watch chiming from somewhere in the room, looked around for it, and then looked at each other.

"I wonder what time it is," said Ellsworth thoughtfully.

"Eight," said Eurydice as she traced her fingers over his shoulder.

Ellsworth looked at her in amused speculation. "You sound very sure about that."

"I am sure, because I looked at the clock on the mantel before you woke up, and it was shortly after seven then."

"You've been out of bed?"

Eurydice quirked an eyebrow and gave him a wry smile. "I needed to go to the water closet, and I needed to find out the time so I wouldn't be late."

"Late? For what?" he asked confusedly.

"Rehearsal, of course," she said simply.

"I don't want you going to rehearsal," said Ellsworth firmly.

"Of course, I'm going to rehearsal," said Eurydice calmly. "I feel fine, and I want to be ready for the performance tonight."

"Eurydice, can't you cancel?"

"No, I cannot," she said, looking at him as if he had gone insane.

"You could have died. Don't you think you need to take a day to rest?"

"I *did* take a day to rest," she said mildly. "I slept all yesterday afternoon and last night." She gave him a smacking kiss on the lips. "I'm fine. I don't even have a cold."

"Dicy…," he sighed.

"It's not as if what I'll be doing is strenuous or physically taxing," she said with a self-deprecating smile.

Agniezka chose that moment to come out of her room, and she smiled happily when she saw that Eurydice was awake and seemed to be well.

"How are you feeling?" she asked on her way to the water closet.

"Wonderful," said Eurydice with a genuine smile. "I'll be ready to get dressed for rehearsal when you come out."

"Oh!" said Agniezka, her eyes widening in surprise, but she was happy nonetheless. "All right."

"Dicy, please, stay home," said Ellsworth after Agniezka left the room.

Eurydice put a hand to his cheek and kissed him soothingly. "I can't. This is *my* job," she said gently. "Right now, what I need is my music. It's the only thing keeping me sane."

Ellsworth gave her a thoughtful frown. She didn't know what he knew, that her accident had been nothing of the kind, and he wouldn't tell her. He didn't want to frighten her, and she would be if she knew. He needed to find Cesaire Dubonnet and put an end to this, but the man was proving very elusive. Ellsworth's usual sources for information were unable to provide him with much, so it had become necessary to begin looking elsewhere. It was taking far longer than he had thought it would. Considering what had happened, he felt sure the man was in Venice. It couldn't have been anyone else. It was unfortunate Schellen had been unable to get more than a brief look at him. The description was not very helpful: tall, muscular build, and with dark hair. That could be a lot of the men in the city.

And judging by what she said, something was troubling Eurydice. Ellsworth knew he was leaving her alone a lot, but he didn't think that was the only thing making her anxious. He didn't want to take her away from something that might help her.

"All right," he said finally, resting his forehead against hers. "If I can't stop you from going, I suppose I have things to do as well."

"I truly am fine," said Eurydice earnestly. She gave him a half-smile. "Besides, I have Schellen to rescue me."

Ellsworth gave her a slight grin. "He is most unhappy the watch you gave him for Christmas doesn't work now."

Eurydice's expression turned crestfallen. "Oh, that is unfortunate."

Agniezka came out of the water closet then and went to the wardrobe to get Eurydice's clothes. Eurydice gave Ellsworth a fond kiss, and then she got out of the bed to go to her maid to begin getting dressed. The air had turned cooler after the rain the previous night, and Agniezka dressed her warmly. She had turned Eurydice's clothes from the previous day over to the maids to be cleaned and mended, but she wasn't sure if anything could be done for them. Eurydice had lost her stockings and slippers in the mud. Those were easy enough to replace, and it wasn't as if she didn't have more clothes, either.

Ellsworth got out of bed to go to Schellen's room while Agniezka's attention was elsewhere, and Eurydice went to the dressing table to let Agniezka begin styling her hair. Eurydice's hair had become very unruly since she became pregnant, and the smoothly coiled braid Agniezka used to style it into was often difficult to achieve. It had required Agniezka to try different styles, and that morning, she put it into a loose knot at the back of her head with several of the strands escaping and refusing to go back. It was a very soft coiffure that gave Eurydice a romantic, disheveled appearance.

Once her hair was done, Eurydice put the koi pendant around her neck, and Agniezka helped her put uncomplicated black pearl drops in her ears. Eurydice went to the fireplace to look at her locket, and it was mostly defogged. She could see Ellsworth's hair beneath the glass, but it was still a bit moist. She contemplated for a moment whether she should wear it or leave it to dry longer, but then she shrugged and put it around her neck.

Ellsworth had still not come out of Schellen's room by the time she was dressed, but Eurydice couldn't wait for him. She was starving, and her stomach had a ball of queasiness in it that needed to be attended to. She would see him again before she left the palazzo for rehearsal. There was plenty of time. She went down with Agniezka for breakfast, and Signor Montenegro was there, coming up from the water floor.

"Lady Eurydice!" he said happily. "You are feeling better?"

"Much better. Thank you, Signor Montenegro," she said with a smile.

He gave her an assessing once-over and nodded satisfactorily. She did seem to be fine. "You eat," he said, gesturing toward the table. "Donatella has made lots of food."

Eurydice didn't need him to tell her twice. She went to the table and sat down. She helped herself to sausage and eggs, as well as pastries filled with lemon curd and raspberry preserves. Actually, she would be perfectly happy if all she had were the pastries, but she was so famished, she wanted to eat everything put in front of her. Agniezka was amused to watch Eurydice eat, but she could understand perfectly. There was regular coffee, but Eurydice loved the coffee flavored with lots of cream and chocolate.

She was getting more of everything when Ellsworth finally came down to join them. He looked at her with an amused smile as he took his own seat and got one of the lemon pastries and poured himself a cup of regular coffee. He was glad to see that at least her appetite hadn't suffered from the previous day. She looked luminous, even with the sad cast that had settled into her eyes since Laibach and wouldn't quite go away. He was beginning to wonder if he should look in her diary. He couldn't escape the feeling she had seen something.

The clock chimed the hour, and Eurydice tried to finish eating as quickly as she could. She would enjoy having another pastry, but she had eaten enough already. There was an errand she wanted to take care of before going to the theater, and she wanted to have the time to do it properly without being late. She popped the last of her pastry into her mouth and drank the remainder of the coffee in her cup and wiped her mouth with a napkin. Ellsworth looked at her with a raised eyebrow.

"You're off already? I thought rehearsal wasn't until ten," he said disappointedly.

"It's not, but I have something I want to do along the way, and I don't want to run if I don't have to."

"Run? You're not taking a boat?"

"No, I need the exercise."

"Dicy, I would feel better if you took a gondola," said Ellsworth levelly.

"I'm walking. I'll be careful," she said amusedly, bending to give him a kiss on the cheek.

Ellsworth grabbed her wrist to stay her awhile. "Dicy, take a boat."

"No," she said calmly.

"Eurydice, please, take a boat," he said more firmly.

"I will be fine," she assured him. "I'll take a boat to the performance tonight." Ellsworth exhaled exasperatedly, and Eurydice gave him a warm kiss on the lips and brushed a hand down his cheek. "I'll be fine," she said softly, and Ellsworth let go of her wrist, his jaw set firmly, so she could go back to her room for her violin and reticule.

She went to the sitting room for the Batov, still in its case from the previous day where Agniezka had left it, and her reticule sitting beside it. She started to leave the suite again when she paused at the door to the hallway for a moment and looked back. She went to the door of Schellen's room and knocked quietly. A light of surprise flickered in his eyes when he opened the door to find her standing there before it changed to impassive politeness.

"I'll be walking to the theater this morning, so be sure to wear comfortable shoes," she said diffidently.

Schellen bowed slightly at the waist and inclined his head. "I'll do that," he said evenly, but Eurydice could see a slight twitching of amusement at the corners of his mouth.

She nodded with a slight smile, and then she left the room. Ellsworth was still sitting at the table eating his breakfast when she returned to the great hall, a put-out expression on his face, but Agniezka had finished. She had already put on her hat and draped a woolen shawl over her shoulders in preparation for their departure. She helped Eurydice put on her own hat and a waist-length cashmere and velvet cloak over her pelisse. Eurydice gave her violin to Agniezka for a moment and went back to the table where Ellsworth still sat with a morose expression. She sat on his lap and wrapped her arms around his neck to give him a thorough kissing.

"I'll be fine, I promise," she whispered softly in his ear.

Ellsworth looked at her searchingly, and then he gave her a tight hug around the waist. He had to admire her willingness to walk to the theater again when another woman might have cowered at home, but then she didn't know someone had tried to kill her. He gave her a nod.

"You better be," he said gently, giving her a slight smile.

She gave him an affectionate grin and a peck on the cheek before getting out of his lap to take her violin from Agniezka.

"I love you," she called over her shoulder as the two women went down the hall to the back of the house.

Eurydice thought the temperature was easily twenty degrees colder than it had been the day before as she and Agniezka went to the exterior stairs to go to the rear courtyard. She was shocked to see icicles hanging in places, and there were some spots along the pavement that were slick with ice. She wouldn't have thought Venice would get that cold, but obviously it did.

As they turned right onto the Calle dei Fuseri, there was a particular shop she was looking for, and when she spied it, she went in. She told the jeweler what she was looking for, and he lifted out a tray with a selection of watches. She had a particular type in mind, something simple, but it had to have a cover.

She didn't find what she was looking for on the first tray, and the man put it away and displayed a second. She found what she was looking for there. Once she selected the watch, she asked the jeweler if she could have it inscribed. He told her that could be done, but it would take a few hours. Eurydice told him that would be fine and gave him a deposit after she wrote down what she wanted him to put in the watch. Agniezka gave her an amused smile as they left the store, but she didn't say anything.

Eurydice was a little nervous when she went over the Ponte dei Fuseri. It wasn't as crowded as the day before, and its surface was dry. She didn't breathe again until she reached the other side, and she exhaled in a sigh of relief when she safely made it across. Her anxiety was not as bad when they crossed the Ponte dei Barcaroli, but that was because it had railing (despite how fragile it seemed). She felt almost giddy when she made it across both bridges safely and went down the Calle dal Frutarol to Campo San Fantin.

Rehearsal went well, as Eurydice had expected. Duchesi had them go through each piece once. There would be the two concertos, and Eurydice would play the sonatas for violin and piano with a pianist. One of the nice things about playing the same pieces repeatedly was that the amount of practice she had to put into playing well was minor. There were a few times she had played when she was exhausted, dizzy, and barely able to control her stomach. Duchesi didn't know what had happened to her the previous day, and Eurydice didn't tell him. She didn't expect it was the type of accident that would surprise many people in Venice. She was sure she wasn't the first—or the last—to fall off one of the bridges into a canal. Signor Duchesi said he would see her back at nine that evening, and she assured him she would be there.

When they went out to the Campo San Fantin, Eurydice tempted fate and went to the vendor she had gone to the previous day and bought more oranges and pistachios. She was happy he was still there and that he still had the fruit and nuts. He remembered her, and he gave her an odd look when she bought exactly the same thing she had purchased the previous day, but he didn't ask her any questions. She wasn't able to get him to lower his price as much as he had the day before. She didn't mind; it was still a reasonable price.

She and Agniezka again crossed both bridges without mishap, and she went to the jeweler's to collect the watch. She looked at the inscription with a pleased smile and paid him the rest of what she owed. She put the box with the watch into her reticule. Agniezka wanted to do more shopping, but Eurydice said they could come back after dinner. She was hungry again, and they would still have several more hours before it was time to go back to the theater. She would like to work more on her symphony, but there would always be time for that on other days. Besides, she was almost finished.

Dinner was waiting when they returned to the palazzo, and much to Eurydice's delight, it was pizza, made with lots of cheese, ham, peppers, dried tomatoes, and mushrooms. She had not had any since they had traveled to Vienna, and she enjoyed it immensely. She would never have thought that something so simple could taste so good, and she would be perfectly happy if they had it for supper, too. It was so filling, it was unnecessary to serve anything else with it. She managed to eat three large slices before she wasn't able to fit in another bite. She wondered how hard it would be to get Cora's cook in Vienna to learn how to make it. On second thought, it would be easier to get Frau Kouts to learn how to make it.

Before she and Agniezka left to go shopping, Eurydice went upstairs to use the water closet. Once she was done with that, she washed her hands and brushed her teeth to get the smell of garlic off her breath. Then she removed the jeweler's box from her reticule and went to the door of Schellen's room. She knocked softly and waited for him to come open it. When he did, he looked at her with a raised eyebrow.

"Can I help you, my lady?" he said politely.

"I'm going shopping," she stated evenly.

"Lady Eurydice, it's not necessary for you to tell me when you are going somewhere," he said dryly.

"No, no, I know," she said hurriedly. "It's just...I thought it might be...polite to let you know."

His eyebrow went higher. "I'm a valet, mum. It's not necessary for you to be polite," he said evenly.

"Oh, but—" she began, but then she stopped. She could see he thought their entire conversation was improper. "All right," she said quietly, and she held the box out to him. "I wanted to give you this, and to say thank you. Ellsworth said your watch quit working, and I wanted to apologize."

He took the box. "Thank you," he said politely, "but there is no need for you to apologize to me, I'm a—"

"Valet, I know," said Eurydice dully. She gave him a brief smile. "Well, I'm going now, and thank you...again," she said hesitantly, and she turned to walk away.

Schellen watched her leave the room, and then he lifted the lid on the box. He opened the cover on the watch and saw the inscription, and then he looked up in surprise.

"You're welcome," he said softly.

≪ ≫

Eurydice had despaired that Ellsworth would return to the palazzo in time to go to the theater with her. It was already eight when he arrived, and Eurydice and Agniezka had already eaten a light meal and dressed. He had said he would never miss one of her performances, and she trusted that he wouldn't, but it was closer than she felt comfortable with. Agniezka had already gone down to arrange for the gondola to take them to the theater.

She sighed with relief when he came into their suite, and she watched as he quickly changed his coat and waistcoat for something more appropriate for evening. She looked him over for any signs of injury, remembering why he had been so late the last time it had happened, but she could see nothing obvious. He went to Schellen's room for a few minutes, and then he quickly came back out. He gave her a roguish smile as he tucked her hand into the crook of his elbow, and they went downstairs to join Agniezka in the great hall. Then, all three of them went to the water floor to the gondola.

Eurydice wasn't sure if walking or taking the gondola was faster. Taking the gondola did save them from going backward in order to go forward, but it didn't take them directly where they needed to go. The canal that was almost directly across from the front of the palazzo was very narrow, and it wound around to the front of the theater. But they didn't go in through the front. Instead, they took an alley that went down the side of the theater to the rear. Eurydice, luckily, remembered the way to the back of the stage from there, and Duchesi was waiting for her when she arrived.

She could hear the audience as she removed her violin from its case and tightened her bow. They were very loud, and it took her back to her performances at the larger theaters in Vienna. She had steadily grown more accustomed to performing in front of strangers, but there was still a knot of nervous tension in her stomach. There were more than twelve hundred people out there waiting to hear her play, almost twice as large as the largest audience she'd had while on tour so far. The only consolation she had was that none of the pieces she would be playing were to be performed by her alone. The piano was a Broadwood, a newer one that was even better for her music, and everything was prepared. Even though she was sure everything would go well, the performance anxiety was still there.

Eurydice still felt that shy hesitation when she walked onto the stage to see all the strange people looking at her. Most of the places she had performed since leaving Vienna had the audience ranged on a single level. La Fenice had the tiers of loges going up five levels as well as audience on the floor standing. Having the audience higher than her made her feel like a specimen being examined, very small and insignificant.

Once she immersed herself in her music, the anxiety began to wane, as it usually did, and she was able to give a happy smile and a graceful final curtsy when the performance was over. There were several people waiting backstage when she arrived there, reporters and members of the nobility who wished to meet her. Several invited her to dine with them, but she politely refused, as she always did. Donatella had prepared something delicious at the palazzo, and she didn't feel it was necessary to socialize with the audience. Some composers and musicians did it in an effort to obtain commissions and sponsors. Eurydice had no need of either.

It was well after midnight when they returned to the palazzo, but supper was waiting when they did, and that pleased Eurydice. She was famished. She had noticed since her pregnancy sickness had improved that her appetite had begun to increase. That had already started, actually, even before the nausea began to get better, but now that she didn't have the nausea to curb it, she constantly wanted something to eat. But there were certain foods that she liked more than others (like peaches) and some that her body absolutely refused to let her touch (like poached eggs). It was strange, but she was sure everything would return to normal after she had the baby.

She and Ellsworth shared a bath before going to bed, but he left at some point during the night. She awoke during the early hours of morning to find he wasn't there. He hadn't told her that he would be going out, but then he never did for the excursions he made after he thought she was asleep. He would be back when she woke up after sunrise, but whether he would be awake before she left for rehearsal would be doubtful.

Rehearsal the following morning was only a formality. After the first performance had gone so well, there wasn't any doubt they were prepared. There were more reporters at the theater to talk with Eurydice afterward, and she was never so ready to leave as when she managed to escape an hour later.

As she had expected, Ellsworth was home when she awoke, but he was soundly asleep. She had lain on her side watching him for several minutes before she got out of bed because she knew he would be gone when she returned after rehearsal. She tried to console herself by remembering she would have him to herself once they left Venice, at least for a week or two…until they reached Paris.

She and Agniezka spent the remainder of the day in the sitting room, and Eurydice finished her symphony. She was amazed she was done so quickly. She thought it was one of her more complicated pieces, especially with the exotic instruments, but she put the final notes onto the score sheet shortly after sunset. She could only imagine how it would sound, and she was somewhat disappointed that imagining it would probably be all she could ever do.

The performance on Friday night was again successful, and Eurydice was overwhelmed by people backstage when it was over. She didn't like that. She didn't like being overrun by strange people. She wanted to perform and have that be the end of it. If someone wanted an interview, they should come to call, to speak with her individually, rather than descending on her like a murder of crows.

At least Ellsworth was there to shield her from it somewhat. She clung to his arm nervously as the people crowded around her. It made it easier for her to understand why Arachne was so uncomfortable when she was surrounded by too many people. It was as if there were too many bodies sucking all the air from the room until she couldn't breathe. She had actually started to grow dizzy before she could politely make her escape. If it had continued for much longer, she might have done it rudely.

Ellsworth seemed preoccupied while they had supper, and Eurydice decided to ask him about it after they got into bed.

"Is something wrong?" she asked softly.

Ellsworth smoothed a hand over her hip and pulled her closer. "Nah," he said dismissively. "What makes you think that?"

Eurydice shrugged and ran her fingers over his chest before giving it a soft kiss. "You just seem to be very…contemplative."

"Contemplative?" he said amusedly. He kissed the top of her head. "Everything's fine."

"All right," said Eurydice agreeably, but she didn't believe him.

"Will you be going to rehearsal again tomorrow morning?"

"As far as I know," said Eurydice with a tired yawn, and she felt her jaw pop from the hugeness of it. "We don't need it, but it gives us a chance to warm up…make sure our instruments are still tuned. Why?"

"Just asking."

Saturday followed much the same pattern as Friday, the only difference being that Ellsworth was awake before Eurydice went to rehearsal. He still seemed preoccupied, but he wouldn't tell her what was bothering him. She could only assume it had something to do with his assignment. Eurydice was a bit at ends after dinner for something to do because she had finished her symphony, and she wasn't hearing anything new yet. She went to the inner courtyard to watch the koi for a while, and then she went to the library for a book and spent the afternoon reading while Agniezka embroidered.

Agniezka was looking more obviously pregnant every day. There was no way to disguise it now, not even with the loose, flowing, high-waisted skirts of her gowns. Her breasts had grown large enough that she had to add gussets to the bodices of her gowns to accommodate the expansion. It hadn't escaped the notice of the other maids and servants in the palazzo. Agniezka tried to make it seem inconsequential, but she mentioned to Eurydice that some of them had not been kind. Eurydice told her the simplest way to get them to stop would be to tell them she was married. That was only somewhat dishonest. She had been married to Sergei and was now widowed, and she *would* be married to Felton. The ceremony was only a formality. She had a ring on her finger, and she had nothing to be ashamed of. Eurydice also told her that if they persisted in being unkind to let her know. *She* would deal with them.

Ellsworth returned to the palazzo early enough before the performance that he was able to enjoy the light meal with Eurydice and Agniezka before they went. She thought he needed a shave when he came out of Schellen's room, and it was peculiar that he wasn't. She couldn't recall his valet ever letting him leave the house looking less than impeccable. It was too late to have one before they left anyhow, but he should have had one that morning.

The performance went well, but Eurydice was relieved she was done. Strangely, it wasn't the performing that had bothered her, either; it was the people who waylaid her when it was over. She was glad she would have a day of rest before they left for Milan. It was only unfortunate that Ellsworth would probably not be at the palazzo to enjoy it with her. They never did get to go to the Piazza San Marco the last time they were in Venice. She didn't imagine that just because tomorrow was Sunday that Ellsworth wouldn't be gone.

But she was surprised the next morning when she woke up to find that Ellsworth *was* there. He had gone out at some point during the night, but he had not been gone for long because he was awake before her. Not only that, but he was shaved. They took their time making love, and Eurydice felt utterly relaxed when they were through. She had missed that.

"What do you want to do today?" asked Ellsworth as he nuzzled her neck.

"Don't *you* have anything to do today?" she asked in surprise.

"Perhaps later, after dark. For now, I am all yours," he purred with a grin.

"Hmm," sighed Eurydice thoughtfully. "What can I do with you?" she asked with rhetorical humor.

"Anything you want," drawled Ellsworth with a seductive grin.

"I'd like to see the Doge's Palace and San Marco."

Ellsworth chuckled. "And I thought we'd get to spend the day in bed."

Eurydice rolled on top of him and propped herself up on her elbows. "That's very tempting, but we can do that after dinner."

"Hmm," said Ellsworth contemplatively. "All day tupping...or Doge's Palace. Hmm." He breathed in through his teeth and shook his head slightly. "I don't know. It doesn't seem like a fair trade."

Eurydice chuckled. "Yes, but we don't need daylight to do that."

"True," he agreed. He sighed with pretended long-suffering. "Fine. We'll be tourists." Eurydice lowered her head to give him a kiss. "You're going to make me change my mind." Eurydice giggled and wiggled against him. "Now you're *really* going to make me change my mind," he purred.

Eurydice rolled off of him and out of his reach with a laugh, and then she put on her dressing gown to go to the water closet. Ellsworth watched her go with an amused smile, and he lay back against the pillows with his hands behind his head. He could tell her health had improved. She didn't seem to be as tired, and she wasn't vomiting quite so often. It was a relief, especially after her accident. Doctor Herzen had been right, and Ellsworth was sure being in Venice was helping. Knowing she was feeling better, at least physically, let him focus his attention on other matters. For whatever was making her anxious...he couldn't help if she wouldn't tell him what was wrong.

Agniezka was just coming out of her room when Eurydice came out from using the water closet and brushing her teeth. She said good morning on her way to use the water closet herself, and Ellsworth thought that would be a good time to get out of bed and get dressed. She hadn't been bothered by seeing him naked in the *banya* in Moscow, but seeing him walk around naked in the room was a different matter.

"You should get dressed," said Eurydice as she hopped onto the bed.

"Yes, I was just going to do that," said Ellsworth with a wry grin as he grabbed her arm to pull her close and kiss her.

"You should scoot while you can," said Eurydice amusedly.

"Just a few more seconds," sighed Ellsworth as he began to nuzzle her neck, pulling her closer to grab her bottom and press her against him hungrily.

Eurydice chuckled and pushed at his shoulder. "Go!" she chortled.

Eurydice propped her cheek up on her palm as she watched him go to the chiffonier to get some clothes and go to Schellen's room. The door had just closed when Agniezka came out of the bathing room. She gave Eurydice an indulgent smile and went to get her some clothes from the wardrobe. Agniezka raised an eyebrow when Eurydice continued to lounge on the bed, and Eurydice stretched before she got up to dress. She was feeling entirely lazy and happy that she would have her husband to herself for the day.

Ellsworth came out of Schellen's room just as Agniezka finished with Eurydice's hair. The three of them went down to the great hall for breakfast, and Eurydice got one of the raspberry-filled pastries and a cup of the coffee with cream and chocolate before she got anything else. She would have something more eventually, but since becoming pregnant, she fancied sweets more than anything, fruit in particular and peaches especially. The raspberry filling with the coffee and chocolate was quite tasty.

Eurydice was trying to convince Agniezka that she should go to the piazza and palace with them, while Ellsworth was trying to convince Eurydice that they should walk. Agniezka's stomach was not quite so big yet to be getting in her way, but the extra weight was beginning to bother her back. She was sleeping with extra pillows tucked around her to make it more comfortable, and she became terribly stiff if she stood too long. Eurydice thought they would do enough walking once they got to the piazza, but Ellsworth didn't think it was that much farther to walk there than it had been to walk to the theater. The weather had warmed a little and the sun was shining; it would be perfect for walking. After all three of them bantering about it all through the meal, it was decided that Agniezka would stay at the palazzo, and Eurydice and Ellsworth would take a gondola.

Agniezka and Ellsworth finished eating before Eurydice, and Agniezka went upstairs to get Eurydice's things for going out while Ellsworth went down to the water floor to arrange for a gondola. Eurydice was almost done—she only needed to finish her last pastry and what was left of her coffee, but that was even after the other two were done and sat at the table several minutes waiting for her to finish.

She had just cleaned the last of the stickiness from her fingers when she heard the muffled sounds of a commotion at the front of the palazzo outside. Eurydice frowned. She could hear shouting, and then she heard repeated shrill bursts from a whistle. She remembered what had happened the last time she heard those sounds in Venice, and she got up from the table to quickly go to the doors of the loggia. When she opened them and walked onto the colonnade to look down at the water below, she didn't see anything, but it made the sounds much clearer. She didn't like what she was hearing. She turned her head to the right, and she could see where the noise was coming from. She closed the set of doors she had opened and went to a set that was closer to the activity with its own separate balcony.

There were several people standing on the small pier at the end of what used to be a *rio* but was now a street, as well as several more people in two gondolas. When she had been on the colonnade, she could see they were trying to remove something from the canal. When she got to the closer set, she could see what it was. One of her hands went to the balustrade and the other went to her throat as she felt the air constrict there until she couldn't breathe.

"Oh, no," she whispered in dismay. "Ellsworth," she gasped, and she couldn't get her voice to come out as more than a whisper. "Ellsworth!" she repeated, finally making it louder, and even she could hear the tinge of panic.

She turned from the balcony to go back to the great hall, and Agniezka looked at her in surprise as Eurydice almost ran across the room, heading for the stairs to the water floor.

"Ellsworth!" she called again, and he was coming to the top of the stairs just as she was preparing to go down.

"What's wrong?" he asked with a concerned frown.

"I...he...uh," she gasped as she fought the nausea she felt, and she pulled at his hand to lead him to the balcony as she took a deep breath in an effort to calm herself. "It's Schellen," she whispered weakly. "I think he's...dead."

Ellsworth went to the balcony to look down at the canal. They had just gotten the body into one of the gondolas, and he agreed with Eurydice: it was Schellen, and he was most assuredly dead. He was completely naked, and even from where he stood, Ellsworth could see his valet had been tortured and his throat cut. Ellsworth wasn't positive who was responsible, but he could make a fairly educated guess. He suspected it wasn't accidental that Schellen had been found at the Rio Tera degli Assassini. It was a sick joke at best.

"How could it have happened?" asked Eurydice brokenly. "Who would have done something so horrible to him?" She looked at Ellsworth sadly. "I didn't like him following me, but I wouldn't have wanted this for him. He didn't deserve this...not like this."

Ellsworth pulled Eurydice into his arms, and she buried her face in his chest. He watched as the police pulled something from Schellen's hand before covering him with a blanket. Ellsworth needed to go downstairs, but he didn't want Eurydice to be alone. He walked with her back into the great hall and looked at Agniezka.

"There's been a terrible accident," he said evenly. "Can you stay with Eurydice?"

"Of course," assured Agniezka.

She put her arm around Eurydice's shoulders and guided her toward the couch. She didn't know what had happened, but she could see from the behavior of both of them that it wasn't good. What concerned her even more was that she didn't think this was what Eurydice had seen in her dreams.

"What's happened?" asked Agniezka quietly after a few minutes. She wasn't sure she wanted to know.

"It's Schellen," said Eurydice sadly. "He's been murdered."

"What?" gasped Agniezka in dismay.

"I saw them pu-pull him from the canal."

"Are you certain he was murdered? Maybe he drowned," said Agniezka hopefully.

"No, he was murdered," sighed Eurydice, and she wiped at her cheeks to clear the tears from them.

Agniezka sat with her arms around Eurydice on the couch as they waited for Ellsworth. They wouldn't be going to San Marco that day after all, and they probably wouldn't be leaving Venice the next. Eurydice tried to get the image of Schellen's battered body out of her mind, but it was ingrained there. Death for him had not been swift and painless. She could only imagine how much he must have suffered before someone had cut his throat, only to toss him into the canal like garbage.

Looking at him, his ordeal had started before sunrise. Ellsworth had made no mention of Schellen not being there when he went to get dressed that morning. He hadn't even hinted by his behavior that anything was amiss. Yet she was sure he had to have wondered where his valet had gone. Eurydice could feel a knot forming in her stomach when she began to realize Schellen had been gone for quite a bit longer. *Days.* She recalled the night Ellsworth had gone to the theater without being shaved, and how he had seemed preoccupied, even the night before that. That had to be the day Schellen went missing. *Thursday.* Yet Ellsworth hadn't told her. Why not? Schellen wasn't her servant, but he had been following her at Ellsworth's request...for her protection. If Schellen had been gone as long as Eurydice believed he had been, Ellsworth wouldn't have let her leave the palazzo. She was confused, and she wanted to talk to her husband.

After about an hour, Ellsworth came up from the water floor, but he wasn't alone. Signor Montenegro was with him, as well as a man in a uniform, who Eurydice thought seemed vaguely familiar. When she saw Ellsworth, she got up from the couch and went to him, and she looked at the unknown man with polite uncertainty.

"Eurydice, this is Captain Vittorio Bustamente," said Ellsworth neutrally. "I don't know if you remember him or not, but he was here in September." Eurydice colored slightly when she understood why he had seemed familiar. She gave him a polite smile and a slight nod. "Captain Bustamente would like to ask you some questions."

Eurydice had her arms folded in front of her protectively, and Ellsworth pulled her closer to his side comfortingly. She frowned in confusion and scratched her forehead nervously, but she nodded her consent.

"Of course," she said quietly. "Do you mind if we sit down? I'm not feeling very well."

Bustamente nodded, and they went to the couch and chairs where Agniezka was already sitting. Eurydice introduced her to Captain Bustamente, and Agniezka nodded a greeting, but she looked at the captain suspiciously. Eurydice sat on the couch between her maid and husband, and Ellsworth put a soothing hand at the small of her back. Eurydice didn't know what questions the captain could have for her, but if it would find the person who murdered Schellen, she would do whatever she could to help. She had the feeling, though, that the captain would not find the man responsible.

"You are aware Erich Schellen was found murdered?" asked Bustamente evenly.

"Y-yes," said Eurydice with a slight nod. She had never known his first name.

"What was your relationship to him?"

Eurydice blinked in surprise. "My relationship? He was my husband's valet," she said simply.

"And that is all?"

"Of course," said Eurydice certainly.

"Can you explain why this was found in his hand?" asked Bustamente as he held the watch she had given Schellen on Thursday by the fob and chain she had given him at Christmas.

"No, I can't," she said quietly. Bustamente raised a doubtful eyebrow. "Well, I *did* give it to Schellen, but as for why that was the only thing he had when he…when everything else was…." She swallowed a lump in her throat and shrugged. "I don't know."

"It's an expensive gift for your husband's valet," he said suspiciously.

Eurydice shrugged. "Not so very. He has served as my husband's valet for many years with great aptitude and loyalty. He has no family, and I felt it would be a thoughtful Christmas gift."

"Christmas gift?"

"Yes," confirmed Eurydice with a nod.

"What about the inscription inside the watch…uh…'*To my Lohengrin. Many thanks for my rescue from the depths. Lady Eurydice*'?" He looked up at her from reading it. "It's dated the tenth of January."

Ellsworth looked at her in surprise. He hadn't realized she had bought Schellen another watch or that she'd had it inscribed. He did understand the meaning of it, and he thought it was a sweet gesture.

"That isn't the watch I gave him at Christmas. I gave him that watch on Thursday to replace the one from Christmas," said Eurydice simply.

"Lohengrin?" said Bustamente with a crisp smile. "Even your husband seems surprised."

"I imagine he is surprised as much by my giving his valet another watch as the inscription itself," said Eurydice dryly. "I didn't tell him."

"Signora Ellsworth, were you and Erich Schellen lovers?" asked Bustamente sternly.

"What?" gasped Eurydice in shock. "Don't be absurd! I love my husband very much, Captain Bustamente, and it would never—and I do mean *never*—enter my mind to be unfaithful." He looked at her doubtfully. "Perhaps you are confusing the name *Lohengrin* with *Lothario*—a horse of a completely different color." Bustamente still looked at her suspiciously, and Eurydice groaned frustratedly. "Schellen saved my life on Wednesday, Captain. I fell into the Rio dei Fuseri, and he rescued me from drowning. I'm sure there is any number of witnesses who would be able to verify that for you, my maid among them. His watch quit working when he did so, and to show him how grateful I was for his deed, I bought him another to replace it."

"It was very convenient for Signor Schellen to be there, don't you think?" queried Bustamente suspiciously.

"And fortuitous," concurred Eurydice wholeheartedly. "If he hadn't been there, I would have died." She rubbed her forehead with the back of her hand. "I don't know what you are trying to imply about his being there. There are several shops on the Fuseria and the Frezzaria. Perhaps he was shopping." She shrugged negligibly. "I am just very happy he was there."

"Humph," he scoffed. "Did you notice he had gone missing?"

"No."

"Did your husband mention *he* had noticed the disappearance of his valet?"

"No."

"Don't you find that suspicious?"

"No," said Eurydice evenly. She was beginning to see very clearly where the policeman was trying to go with his inquiry, and she didn't like it at all.

"Why not?"

"Because my husband was raised in a family who rarely even call their servants by their real names. Schellen was not in my employ; he didn't have any services he provided for me. In fact, even before he had *gone missing*—as you put it—it wasn't unusual for days to go by without my seeing him."

"Yes, but don't you think it just the least bit strange that Signor Schellen's being gone did not cause your husband any concern?"

Eurydice gave the captain a level stare. "Just because my husband didn't mention the absence of his valet to me doesn't mean he wasn't concerned. I have been unwell for several weeks now, not to mention that I have also been touring across Europe giving concerts in strange cities when performing in front of *any* audience besides family causes me anxiety. I'm sure my husband didn't want to add to the worries I already had."

"Mm-hmm," said Bustamente dismissively, "but don't you think—"

"Captain Bustamente," interrupted Eurydice patiently. "I can see what you are trying to imply, and I must tell you that you are mistaken."

"And what am I trying to imply?"

"You are trying to imply that my husband killed his valet. So, let me ask you: why would he want to do so?" Bustamente could not provide her with a motive. "My husband had no reason to commit such a heinous crime, Captain

Bustamente. Schellen was a loyal, trusted servant. My husband was always impeccably dressed and groomed; his needs were always tended to with the utmost respect and deference." She blinked and wiped at one of her cheeks. "He was a true gentleman's gentleman, and there is no one in this house who would have ever wished him harm." She inhaled with a shudder, and Ellsworth rubbed her back soothingly. "Schellen was a good man. He didn't deserve what happened to him, and if you insist on believing my husband did it, you will never find the monster truly responsible."

Bustamente looked at her consideringly and gave a slight shake of his head. "I don't know, Signora Ellsworth. You make a very strong point, but this is the second murder investigation to lead me to your husband." He shrugged. "I am finding it very hard to believe he is not somehow involved."

"Then you will have to believe me, Captain, when I tell you that my husband is innocent. He didn't know that man last year, and he was with me when the crime was committed. As for Schellen, I don't know why anyone would want to do anything like that to another human being, but I do know that my husband would not."

Bustamente looked at her speculatively. Whatever else, he believed she thought she was telling the truth, whether or not it actually was. He finally nodded and stood up with a gusty sigh. Eurydice and Ellsworth stood as well, and the captain looked from one to the other of them appraisingly.

"I trust you will be leaving Venice soon?"

"We had intended to leave tomorrow," said Eurydice evenly.

"As soon as you can would be good," said Bustamente firmly, "and I believe you not returning for quite some time would be in your best interests," he finished meaningfully.

"Thank you, Captain Bustamente," said Eurydice quietly.

He nodded, and Signor Montenegro left with him to walk him to the door. Ellsworth turned to look at Eurydice and smoothed a hand down her cheek before pulling her toward him in a comforting embrace.

"I'm sorry, Dicy," he sighed. "I didn't want to put you through that, but he insisted. I didn't know how to stop him."

"Why didn't you tell me Schellen had been gone since Thursday?"

"How did you…?" he began confusedly. "Like you said, I didn't want to worry you," he said softly.

"Was it the same man?" Eurydice didn't really have any doubt that it was. It made absolute sense.

"Yes, I think so."

Eurydice looked up at him sadly. "You're not going to find him," she whispered.

Ellsworth put his hands on her shoulders and looked at her determinedly. "Stop that!" he said firmly. "I *am* going to find him." Eurydice reached up to brush her fingers down his cheek with a wan smile, and then she turned away. "Where are you going?"

"To prepare Schellen to be buried. He has no family, so I will do it," she said quietly.

"Dicy, no. Let the maids do that," said Ellsworth, gently putting a hand on her arm.

Eurydice looked up at him and gave him a kiss on the cheek. "I'll be fine. It's the least I can do for him." She bent down to retrieve the watch from where Bustamente had left it on the low table in front of the couch. "Will you bring me some of his clothes?"

"Dicy," sighed Ellsworth softly. "Please, let the maids do it. You don't want to see him like that."

"No, I don't," she sighed tiredly, "but I owe him this." She gave Ellsworth a self-deprecating smile and a shrug. "It's not as if I haven't done this before."

"Dicy…."

"You need to get me some of his clothes, and then we'll need a coffin…a place for the funeral—our chapel is no longer consecrated for Catholic rites…a place to bury him." She looked at Ellsworth disappointedly. "I'm not going to be seeing much of you for the rest of the day."

Ellsworth went to her and gave her a kiss. "You don't have to do this," he whispered.

"Yes, I do," she said quietly. "You better scoot while you can," she said, giving him a reassuring smile.

She turned to walk down the stairs to the water floor, and Agniezka got up from the couch to follow her. She gave Ellsworth an assessing glance as she approached him. There was something going on that she didn't understand. Eurydice seemed positive that Ellsworth didn't kill Schellen, and Agniezka agreed. But, she also had to agree with Bustamente that he was somehow involved. She trusted Eurydice's judgment, but Agniezka was smart enough to realize that whatever had happened—was happening—it was a part of the dream Eurydice had.

"Stay with her, please," he said quietly. "Make sure she doesn't overtax herself."

"Of course," said Agniezka certainly.

"And if she decides to leave the palazzo, make sure Signor Montenegro knows she is going."

Chapter Thirty Five

Schellen was buried on the Isola di San Michele the following morning after his funeral at the church there. The cemetery had not been there long—there weren't many graves, considering it was the cemetery for the entire city, and Eurydice could see places where construction was ongoing. After the funeral, Ellsworth told her the cemetery had been there for about ten years. The people of Venice used to bury their dead in the city, but Napoleon told them they had to bury them elsewhere—San Michele. It was very strange there was an island just for burying, but Eurydice could understand the logic.

Schellen only had four mourners, and Eurydice thought it was sad that other than herself, Ellsworth, Agniezka, and Signor Montenegro, there was no one to miss him. He had no family, no loved ones. He had been young—a few months shy of thirty-five, and it only added to the tragedy. He should have lived many more years, long enough to have a wife and children, long enough to have more than his employers grieve for his passing. And to be buried so far from home, in a strange place. Eurydice could only assume he had spoken to Ellsworth about his wishes should anything happen to him, but she wondered if Schellen had ever considered it. She knew her brother, Gregory, had not.

As much as she hadn't wanted to, Eurydice had found herself examining the marks on his body as she had washed Schellen in preparation for his burial. Broken fingers—even the smallest ones on each hand missing. Several of his teeth were shattered and his jaw broken. He was covered in burns, the skin on his back flayed from whipping. Then there was the genital mutilation. None of the injuries by themselves would have been fatal—the cutting of his throat had been needed for the *coup de grâce*, but even if he had been found before that, it was likely he would have died from infection.

Eurydice tried not to think about what had been used to cause all the pain and misery he had endured, and she tried not to think about *why* someone might have wanted to do that to him. He had been abducted sometime on Thursday, in the afternoon or evening, and Eurydice tried not to think that it had happened when she and Agniezka had gone shopping. Would it not have happened if she had stayed at the palazzo? She couldn't help feeling in some part responsible. More than two days, he was tortured and abused, and whoever had done it had wanted Schellen to be found. As muddy as the bottoms of the canals were, the culprit could have weighted Schellen down, and he would have sunk into the depths and never been discovered.

They left from Venice on Tuesday morning, a day later than they had intended, and did not arrive in Milan until Wednesday afternoon. It was too far to make the journey in one day. It had seemed odd traveling in the coach without Schellen, and Eurydice found herself occasionally glancing to the place across from her expecting to see him there. Ellsworth had grown even more silent and introspective than usual, and Eurydice knew it was because of Schellen's death. It had been a very quiet journey.

Eurydice sent a message to Signor Simoneti as soon as they were settled into their hotel. She had thought to send him a message on Sunday as soon as she knew she would be delayed, but her letter wouldn't have reached him any faster than she would herself. She already knew she would be performing at the Teatro alla Scala, but she didn't know much about it. She had heard of it, she thought, but she couldn't claim to know any more about it than its name. She was relieved when she had a response back from Simoneti less than an hour later. The theater was not far from the hotel. He welcomed her to Milan and said he hoped to see her at the theater as soon as she had eaten dinner. By the time she received his response, she was almost finished.

Ellsworth had never been to Milan himself, so he wasn't familiar with the theater or its location. He agreed it was probably very close to the hotel, but just in case it wasn't, he arranged for a carriage. It would be just as well because they wouldn't return to the hotel until after dark; he wasn't sure of the safety of the area, so he didn't think it would be wise to walk. It did prove to be very close, less than half a mile from the hotel on the same street.

Eurydice became a bit alarmed when she got her first glimpse of the theater. It was quite large. It was at least as big as the Burgtheater, and she wouldn't have any trouble believing it was bigger. Signor Simoneti had given her no direction on where she should go once she got there, and she went to the doors under the portico at the front. Her eyes widened in shock when she saw her name displayed on a large placard announcing she would be performing— not once, but twice—the following day. She was as astonished by seeing her name publicly displayed as she was by seeing that she was giving an afternoon as well as evening performance. She didn't recall agreeing to that.

"Are you going to be prepared in time to give a matinée?" asked Ellsworth with a frown as he looked from the placard to her.

"I hope so," said Eurydice dryly.

Eurydice followed the faint sounds of an orchestra playing her music from somewhere to the left, and it led her to a set of stairs going to the next floor.

They were playing the symphony, her solitary published symphony, and she was pleased it sounded passable, as well it should after their having nearly two months to rehearse. She would have to hear it through in its entirety before she decided whether it would suit, but at least it didn't sound as if someone had rearranged anything. She found the orchestra and Simoneti in a rehearsal room, and she could only hope the acoustics of the auditorium were better.

Simoneti was pleased she had arrived so quickly. He wasn't expecting her for another hour. That was possibly because he had anticipated she would take a nap after dinner, as the Italians were wont to do. She might have considered it a week or two ago, but she was feeling much better. He introduced her to the first violinist, Alessandro Rolla, who was also the conductor and the orchestra director. He was an older man, with dark hair and eyes and a slender build. He reminded her of Salieri. He was very pleased to meet her, and he said he appreciated the style of her compositions—they kept him from falling asleep. She took that to be complimentary and thanked him.

On their way back to the hotel after what Eurydice thought was an excellent rehearsal, Ellsworth told her that he had heard of Rolla. He had been a teacher of Paganini, was a composer, and taught violin and viola at the Milanese Conservatory of Music. Eurydice raised an eyebrow, and Ellsworth told her Rolla was written about in the music journals in Austria. Eurydice had never heard of him, but he was very good at everything he did.

The only disconcerting thing about the day for Eurydice, and she was sure it would continue until the end of her performance the following night, was discovering that La Scala was capable of holding an audience of more than three thousand. She could only hope there wouldn't be that many attending, but even if only half were present, it would still be the largest audience for which she had ever performed. Simoneti and Rolla had shown her the auditorium after rehearsal, and it was one of the most beautiful she had ever seen but also by far the most cavernous. There was no separation on the floor between the orchestra and the audience who would be standing there, and there were six tiers of boxes. She was grateful her pregnancy sickness had mostly abated because the sight of it might have made her throw up otherwise.

One consolation was that she knew with a certainty her evening concert would be over before midnight. It wasn't allowed to go longer. She would perform two sonatas and the two concertos at the afternoon performance, and then at the evening performance, the symphony would be performed with an encore of the two concertos. She could only hope she would be able to eat at some point the following day besides at breakfast because she would be back to the theater in the morning for a final rehearsal, and then in the afternoon and evening to perform. She regretted she hadn't arrived in Milan a day earlier, as she had intended, but there had been no way to make it possible.

She had trouble falling asleep, and Ellsworth's solution was to make love to her until she was exhausted. She still couldn't fall asleep, but she felt more relaxed. It did the trick for Ellsworth. She didn't usually have trouble sleeping;

she was usually very tired at bedtime, but she couldn't get her brain to slow down. There were so many thoughts floating through her mind that even writing them down in her diary didn't quiet them.

She was nervous about her performances the following day. She was well-prepared, and the orchestra was splendid, but the thought of being in front of three thousand strangers caused a ball of tension to form in the pit of her stomach. It wouldn't be long before she would have to tell Ellsworth she was expecting. It had taken longer before it was noticeable on Agniezka, but then Ellsworth didn't see her maid naked. Eurydice's stomach wasn't quite as flat as it had been the week before. It could be due to all the sweets she was eating, but Eurydice had the sinking feeling it wasn't. Her breasts were also slightly larger. If things continued to enlarge at the rate they were, she would only have a week, two at most, before Ellsworth would realize it on his own without her having to tell him a thing.

Then there was Schellen's murder. That was what had made it difficult for Ellsworth to fall asleep. The man who had done it was the same one from her Dark Dream, but she couldn't see his face. Schellen had been following her when he was abducted, and she strongly suspected part of the reason for his murder was to make it easier for the man to get to her. She should have known from the things she had seen in her dreams that Schellen's death was inevitable, but she could have hoped his absence would have been brought about another way. Ellsworth didn't know about the dream, but he knew the same as she, that Schellen had been protecting her; he could only believe the man was after her. Ellsworth thought he could stop him. Eurydice knew he couldn't.

She did finally drift off to sleep by concentrating on Ellsworth's arm draped over her waist, his hand unknowingly resting on her stomach at just about the place where their baby was growing. She put her hand over his and snuggled against him with a soft sigh, pretending to herself that things weren't going to be what they would be.

After breakfast on Thursday, Eurydice spent little time at the hotel until that night. She went to the theater for rehearsal, which went well, and then she went back to the hotel for dinner and a quick bath before she was back to the theater for the afternoon performance. Her anxiety didn't quite dissipate the entire concert, but everything went smoothly. The theater wasn't full, but it was more than half. She had hoped the audience for the evening performance would be about the same, but when she returned after eating a light supper and changing her clothes, she was dismayed to find it was completely full. Even on the floor where there were no seats, the men standing there scarcely had any room between them. And while her concert was over before midnight, it was after midnight before she could leave the theater because of the people who wished to speak to her afterwards. It was almost one before she walked through the doors of their suite, and she was entirely relieved to be there and to be able to sit unmolested for a few minutes.

They would be leaving early the following morning, but she needed to eat. Her stomach was growling unhappily as she sat on the couch. Agniezka went down to see what could be arranged for her, and Eurydice knew her maid had to be exhausted as well. By the time they were through with their meal, it was after two, and Eurydice had no trouble falling asleep. She would sleep in the coach the next day to make up for what she missed.

They left for Geneva very early the next morning, earlier, in fact, than they normally did. Eurydice was extremely tired and didn't find it easy to motivate herself, but she wasn't nauseous. Well, she was, but barely, certainly not bad enough that she thought she was going to vomit. She didn't need to use her vinaigrette or her bracelet, and it was unnecessary for Agniezka to get the ginger tea. Other than being tired, she felt wonderful. Ellsworth had wanted to leave earlier because they were to go through the Swiss Alps...in winter. It was the only way to get to Geneva from Milan without going far out of their way, but it would be safer to travel as little as possible in the dark, and some of the passes were likely to be treacherous because of snow and ice.

They started into the mountains shortly before dinner, stopping in Omegna at the northern point of Lago d'Orta for the meal. The road they traveled from that point on wound through a river valley, but Eurydice could look in every direction from the windows of the coach and see nothing but mountains, tall mountains, taller than she had ever seen, all covered at their peaks with glistening white snow. Shortly after they went through Domodossola, the valley narrowed and climbed. The road was not heavily traveled. It might have been in the warmer months, but at this time of year, most people had better sense. There were several small villages along the way where they were able to exchange the horses and refill the coach stove with coals as they traveled through what was known as the Simplon Pass, but it was all very remote. Ellsworth had hoped they would reach the valley of the Rhone by the end of the day, but the terrain was too steep and snow-covered for it to be possible. They stopped at a small village called Schalbett for the night, not far from the border between Italy and Switzerland, and it was very cold. Eurydice was very glad to have her husband to cuddle with.

They did reach the Rhone the next day, and they would follow its valley all the way to Lac Leman. It was wide and well-populated, and the road was well-traveled. They had to travel almost the entire southern edge of the lake to reach Geneva, but it was better than traveling through more mountains. It was very late when they arrived, but it was a nice hotel, a pleasant change from the small inn they had stayed at the night before. Eurydice chuckled amusedly when she found out the hotel they were staying at was located near one of the towers in the city walls called *le Bastion de Chante Poulet*—the Bastion of the Crowing Chicken. She thought it sounded much better in French. Their hotel was, in fact, on the Terraux de Chantepoulet.

It was too late for Eurydice to send a message to Monsieur Badeau when they arrived, but she would do it first thing in the morning. They were back on schedule, and she wouldn't perform until Monday night. The problematic thing was that tomorrow would be Sunday. If Monsieur Badeau intended for her to perform with an orchestra, they wouldn't be able to rehearse on Sunday, and she didn't think rehearsal on just Monday morning would be enough. She would speak with Badeau tomorrow to see what he intended.

The next morning, Eurydice went to look out the doors onto the balcony of their suite and gasped in amazement. They had an unimpeded view of the lake and Mont Blanc in the distance. It was very beautiful. The rest of the city spread out on the other side of the Rhone, and Eurydice simply stood there watching as it steadily began to grow lighter. Ellsworth came behind her to put his arms around her waist and rest his chin on top of her head.

"It's very pretty," she said quietly, "but I still like Venice better…St. Petersburg…Moscow…Kiev."

"Wait until you see Paris," said Ellsworth amusedly.

Eurydice sighed deeply. "I can wait," she said dully.

"I'll be able to finish my assignment when we get there," said Ellsworth positively.

"Yes, I think you will," said Eurydice softly.

"Doesn't that make you happy?" asked Ellsworth confusedly.

Eurydice turned in his arms to look up at him with a slight smile. "Of course it does."

Ellsworth looked at her troubledly before he lowered his head to give her a soft kiss on the lips. "It will only be a couple more weeks, and I'll be done," he assured her.

Eurydice brushed her fingers down his cheek and gave him a smile. "I know."

When Eurydice met with Monseiur Badeau, she was disconcerted to learn the theater where she would be performing was not in regular use. When the French occupation ended three years before, the theater basically went with them. Since Badeau had spoken with her in Vienna, he had been making the theater ready for her performance. There was no orchestra. She would have to perform by herself. He told her that her concert would be a testing of the waters, to find out if the city was ready for regular performances. Judging from how well the tickets had sold, Badeau thought it seemed likely that it was. The theater would hold an audience of one thousand. Eurydice wasn't sure how she would be able to hold the interest of an audience that large playing only her sonatas. Even at the Theater an der Wien, she'd had Franz with her for two of the pieces. Solo sonatas weren't really intended for an audience that large.

Badeau was able to locate a decent Pleyel for her, and Eurydice spent the afternoon practicing after she had dinner. The only consolation to performing alone was that rehearsal wouldn't require hours and hours. The stage was very small, and there were only three tiers of boxes. It was almost as if someone had squeezed the Theater an der Wien into a space half its required size. It had an intimate feel to it like the smaller venues had given her while accommodating an audience comparable in size to the larger ones. The performance would be an interesting experiment for her as well.

Eurydice woke up early the following morning, before sunrise, just at the start of twilight. She didn't know if it was because of her conversation with Ellsworth about Paris the previous day, or if it was simply that she knew it was nearing, but she had the Dark Dream again. She still didn't see the beginning, but she saw the rest of it, all of it, to the very end. And still the Man was in the dream, but she couldn't remember his face when she was awake.

Eurydice carefully got out of bed so as not to wake Ellsworth and went to the desk where she had placed her diaries and stationery. She got a rush to light the lamp, turning the flame as low as she could, and then she sat down. She didn't know what she was doing, but she felt like she needed to do *something*. Maybe what she needed to do was try to *draw* his face rather than finding a description in words. She wasn't as capable at drawing and art as Arachne or Psyche, and she didn't know how she could draw something she couldn't recall.

She took a blank piece of composition paper and turned it to the side without lines. It was the largest she had, and in the absence of a sketchpad it was the best she could do. She picked up her pencil and looked down at the piece of paper in front of her. She couldn't see it. She closed her eyes and tried to clear her mind of every other thought. She focused instead on the feelings that thoughts of him evoked—fear, sadness, hatred, anger. Then she added the sensations she could recall—cold, pain, thirst, hunger. She didn't like going there, but she tried to remain calm, remembering that she was safe and warm in Geneva. She opened her eyes and began to draw.

As her hand moved across the paper, Eurydice tried not to consciously guide her actions. She continued to concentrate on the memories of the dream, and she let her hand do whatever it wanted. She tried not to even look at what was being put onto the paper. She felt herself moving in that place between dreaming and lucidity, the same place she went when she lived a forgotten vision. It was making her nauseous, but she had to stay there. Once she finished the drawing, she wouldn't have to go back.

When the pencil stopped moving, the sun had risen, and Eurydice could see its glimmer through the nearby window. It was light enough the lamp was no longer necessary, and she turned it off before she looked at what she drew. When she looked at it, her eyes widened and she gasped. She knew that face. She had seen that face before, and it wasn't in her dreams. It was the strange man from Kiev, the one who had known her name. She frowned as she looked at it. She thought she had drawn the man from the Dark Dream, but could it be possible she had drawn the man from Kiev by mistake? She sighed frustratedly and folded the piece of paper to fit it into her dream diary. Whether she had erred or not, it was a good likeness, and she was startled she had produced a drawing that accurate. She would need to think about it a little more before she decided to show it to Ellsworth.

She went back to bed and cuddled beside Ellsworth beneath the blankets, lying on her side to watch him sleep. She couldn't go back to sleep, despite waking early. She couldn't stop thinking about the drawing and the dream. She just couldn't be sure the man she drew and the one from the dream were the same. She didn't know what possible difference it could make one way or the other. She couldn't stop the inevitable.

"Was I muttering in Gaelic again?" asked Ellsworth sleepily.

Eurydice jumped slightly in surprise and blinked her eyes to focus on him. "No. Why?" she asked with a soft smile.

"You had a disgusted frown on your face just now."

"I was just thinking about something else." She snuggled against him and draped her leg over his thigh with a smile. "I like to hear you speak Gaelic."

"Do you now?" purred Ellsworth with a lazy grin.

"Mm-hmm," said Eurydice with a grin of her own. "It gets me hot."

"Thig an seo, m'eudail," he whispered as he pulled her closer. *"Tha feum agam ort."*

Eurydice chuckled. "I want more."

"Gu toilichte," sighed Ellsworth, nuzzling her neck.

"Mm, I like that," said Eurydice with a smile.

"Cha'n'eil ni nach deanainn duit," he whispered, *"ma tha e'm chomas."* Eurydice felt a lump forming in her throat, and she clutched her fingers in his hair as his lips traveled lower to one of her breasts. *"Cha'n urrainn domh t'àicheadh."* He rolled them over to place her beneath him and kissed her tenderly. *"Ni sam bith a th'agam is leat e."*

"Gareth," she sighed, and she blinked her eyes to keep herself from crying.

He slowly thrust into her, and Eurydice felt a tear slip from the corner of her eye. She had wanted to hear what he was telling her, but now that she was, she wished she hadn't. It was going to be so hard. He began to move in and out of her, and Eurydice's breath caught in her throat. She put a hand to his cheek and lifted her head to kiss him.

"Mo colunn...mo cridhe...m' anam. Fagaidh mi sin aca fein."

"Gareth," Eurydice choked out as she began to orgasm, and she felt dizzy, as much from the pleasure rolling through her body as from his words.

"Tha gràdh agam duit," he whispered.

"Oh, God!" she gasped, clutching at his arms. "I love you."

She felt Ellsworth begin to shudder as he reached his own climax, and she smoothed one of her hands up his shoulder to his cheek, giving him a soft smile. He had finally told her that he loved her, and she wished he hadn't. She could feel the tears pouring out of her eyes, and she tried to make them stop. She was happy, but she could feel her heart breaking at the same time. Ellsworth pulled her toward him after he moved off of her and whispered soothing noises.

"Shh, why are you crying?" he crooned.

"Because I'm s-so h-happy," said Eurydice brokenly.

"Really?" said Ellsworth doubtfully.

"I am," said Eurydice determinedly, and she wiped at her cheeks with a deep breath. She looked up at him to give him a kiss and a watery smile.

"If you say so," said Ellsworth slowly, still looking at her disbelievingly.

"Can I ask you something?"

"Ye-es," said Ellsworth charily.

"Why were you so different the first time I met you?" Ellsworth raised an eyebrow. "You were so quiet. You wouldn't talk. You wouldn't smile. You seemed very...wooden."

"Humph," scoffed Ellsworth.

"You *were*," swore Eurydice.

"That was probably because I was in a lot of pain and very drunk, and I didn't want anyone to know I was either."

"What?" blurted Eurydice, looking at him in surprise.

Ellsworth ran his finger over the long scar at the bottom of his ribs that she found so fascinating. "I'd just gotten this three hours before. It wasn't as if I could let anyone know about it."

She couldn't ask how it had happened. It was because of his job, and that was all she needed to know. He had pretended he was perfectly fine, even if the strain of it had made him seem cold and distant. He was *always* pretending everything was fine. She did wonder, though, what had happened to the person who was responsible. She could only hope he came out the worse for it.

"Then there was you, looking so prim and haughty...and so beautiful. I was so drunk, I was afraid if I opened my mouth to say anything I would sound like an idiot, so I thought it would be best to keep it shut." He ran his finger down her cheek. "You would never let yourself be wooed by an idiot."

"You wanted to woo me?" asked Eurydice with a half-smile.

"I thought I might want to...at some point, and then in Rotherhithe, you didn't even remember who I was. I was crushed."

Eurydice chuckled. "I doubt that."

"No, I was," averred Ellsworth with as straight a face as he could muster.

Eurydice's performance that evening went fairly well. She had been concerned the audience wouldn't appreciate hearing her alone, but they applauded as loudly for her as any other audience. Well, not as loudly as those in Russia, but they had enjoyed it. She wished Monsieur Badeau success in reviving the theater in Geneva after her performance, but she thought she might wait until he had actually done that before she returned.

It was surprising, but they were to Dijon by Tuesday night. Eurydice had thought it would take longer. Granted, it was very late at night, but it pleased her. She sent a message to Monsieur Fournier on Wednesday morning and rehearsed with the orchestra that afternoon.

Eurydice thought the entire performance was going to be strange. She was performing in what was little better than a gambling hall, and there were no seats for the audience. The city had started to build a real theater more than five years before, but they had stopped construction because of the war. They didn't know when they would start building again. If Eurydice had known how straitened the conditions for her concert would be, she might have declined. Even still, Fournier thought her audience would be around five hundred. She did not intend to play more than the concertos unless the audience requested an encore. She simply couldn't bear the thought of making them stand on their feet for that long.

Eurydice went to rehearsal again on Thursday morning, but in the afternoon before her performance, she and Ellsworth went for a brief walk through the town. It was too cold to walk for very long. It was pretty, with the old half-timber houses and cathedrals. There was an interesting clock tower on one that Eurydice thought was fascinating. If Pandora were there, she would try to climb up to have a closer look.

After a light meal, Eurydice went to the hall for her performance. It wasn't as bad as the one had been in Pest, but it wasn't spectacular. She didn't think it was all her doing, however. The venue was terrible, making the acoustics wrong. The audience still seemed to enjoy it, but Eurydice did notice they were all men. It was strange. She didn't think she wanted to perform in Dijon again unless it was at some nobleman's private theater or they finished work on the city theater.

There was a light snow falling the next morning when they left for Paris, and it didn't stop the entire day. The weather was bitingly cold, and Eurydice couldn't recall it being that cold since they had been in Russia. It was unusual for the weather to be that frigid. She couldn't recall hearing France ever got that cold, but she supposed it was possible, having never been there. But Ellsworth, who had been to France many times, thought it was strange as well.

They reached Paris before sunset, but the sky was overcast and the snow that had been with them the day before started again shortly after they stopped for dinner in Melun. Eurydice had been able to see ice on the margins of the Seine, but she didn't think it would freeze completely—that was even rarer than the Thames freezing. As they approached the city, Eurydice thought Paris seemed very bleak, with gray skies, swirling snow, and clouds of smoke billowing from the thousands of chimneys needed to warm it. She tried not to dwell on whether or not her premonition was coloring her perception. It was likely that if she came when it was warmer, she would think it was very pretty.

Their route into the city took them through a good portion of it on the Right Bank, as the hotel where they would be staying was on the far side of it. Eurydice didn't know where the theater was, but she would get that information from Monsieur Molyneux after she sent him a message letting him know she had arrived. Eurydice didn't imagine she would be rehearsing that day (she would refuse if he asked her to), and since the following day was Sunday, probably not then, either. She wasn't concerned. Her performance wasn't until Tuesday. It was their intention to stay in the city until next Saturday, and then they would continue across the country to Le Havre, where they would take a packet to Cardiff, provided they could find one. If not, they would travel to London and take a coach from there to Wilderland.

Ellsworth pointed things out to Eurydice and Agniezka as they traveled the streets, and there were lots of things to see, especially once they got closer to the *Île de la Cité*. They couldn't see the island itself except through occasional glimpses at cross streets, but Eurydice would look at things after she was done with her performance, perhaps even on Sunday. She would have to do something to occupy herself the four days afterward while Ellsworth attempted to finish his assignment.

When Ellsworth pointed out the Louvre, Eurydice decided perhaps the Russians did not have exclusive rights to building monstrous palaces after all. She especially thought that when he pointed out the other palace across the square from it…and the one behind it. The garden behind the Tuilleries would be better-appreciated in the spring. At the moment, it was mostly covered by snow and seemed very barren.

Their hotel was at the end of the rue de Rivoli, facing the Place de Louis Quinze, and when Eurydice first saw it, she wasn't sure it was a hotel. It looked like the building across the street from it with very little difference. Ellsworth assured her that it was indeed a hotel and had been for quite some time. He would know. Once the coach stopped, Eurydice reached over to unfasten Casanova's cage from its place on the seat opposite and draped it with its cloth. She would take it off again once they were settled into their room, but it would be best to keep it covered until then.

Within minutes of their arrival, servants came out to help with unloading their luggage…after one of them politely asked if the Ellsworths intended to stay as guests. Eurydice looked up at the building and wondered if it would have a bath. It didn't look very big from the front. When they walked into the lobby, Eurydice could see immediately that it was larger than it appeared. It apparently extended for quite some distance beyond. If their room was anything like the lobby, she would be able to have a bath.

There was a counter where guests could request a room and also retrieve messages or arrange for messages and letters to be sent. There were several fireplaces warming the large lobby, and halls led off of it in several directions. Eurydice occupied herself by looking at her surroundings while Ellsworth arranged for their lodgings, but she turned to look at him and the attendant at the desk curiously when Ellsworth raised his voice.

"There must be some mistake," said Ellsworth evenly, but Eurydice could detect the irritation in his voice.

"*Mais non, monsieur.* I am seeing that you were placed into a suite yesterday morning," the attendant said politely. "In fact, there are several messages waiting for you."

He turned to look at one of the slots on the wall behind him and retrieved the correspondence to give to Ellsworth.

"How is it possible we arrived yesterday morning?" argued Ellsworth flatly. "We've only just got here from Dijon."

He flipped through the letters to see they were indeed addressed to him and Eurydice, most of them for his wife, and he turned to give them to her with a distracted frown before turning back to the attendant. Eurydice recognized the handwriting on the top one as Psyche's, and she looked at it bemusedly.

"*Monsieur*, I apologize for the confusion. Perhaps there are more Ellsworths," he said disconcertedly with a slight shrug, "but I do not think it is likely there is more than one Monsieur Gareth and Lady Eurydice Ellsworth."

"No, there isn't," said Ellsworth darkly.

"I must also say that if this is not you who registered yesterday, we have no place to put you at the Hôtel de Crillon," said the attendant apologetically.

"What?" said Ellsworth arcticly.

"We have had several guests arrive since Thursday, and I am afraid we have no vacant rooms, not even of lesser quality."

Eurydice tugged at Ellsworth's sleeve to get his attention. She had frowned confusedly when she saw the address on the letter from Psyche. There wasn't one for her—just her name, but Psyche had her address as the hotel. That had made Eurydice open it, her eyes widening in surprise as she skimmed over the words quickly. And then she had looked at the addresses on the rest.

"It's our suite," she said breathlessly.

"But how can that—" began Ellsworth confusedly.

"They're here."

"*Who* is here?" asked Ellsworth with a frown.

"Everyone!" said Eurydice excitedly. "My family, your family, Leilah, and several more friends from Britain, it seems," she said as she thumbed through the messages again, looking at the names. She looked up at him with an amused smile, her cheeks pink and her eyes glowing. "Paris has been invaded again…by the Savages and their ilk, and the Hôtel de Crillon in particular."

"You're joking," said Ellsworth with a surprised expression. He had never heard a word about it.

"No, Psyche says they got a suite for us yesterday before they were all filled."

Ellsworth turned to look at the attendant. "I suppose we need to be shown to our suite, then," he said evenly.

"*Bien sûr,*" said the attendant with a relieved smile.

Eurydice started to pick up Casanova's cage to carry it to their rooms, but the attendant wouldn't let her. Instead, she sorted through all the messages in her hands as they walked, giving three of them to Ellsworth and one to Agniezka. The other eleven were for her, and they were all from family and friends. She would try to locate them once she was settled into her room, but she also wanted something to eat.

She was surprised and happy that her family was there. None of them had told her they were coming, and yet it seemed they were all there. Psyche had mentioned some of the people who were there from Britain, and Eurydice assumed they were all staying at the Hôtel de Crillon as well. It was no wonder there were no longer any rooms available if they were. She had at first wondered why they would have come to Paris when she would be in Britain in only a few weeks, but then she realized they had come to see her perform in a theater. The thought of it pleased her and made her nervous at the same time.

The attendant was about to open the door to their suite on the first floor when another door opened down the hall, and Eurydice saw Islington and Pandora coming out. Pandora squealed excitedly when she saw her sister and hurried down the hall toward her with a wide grin. Eurydice, for her part, was surprised to see her sister was expecting another child. It was true Alex and Myron were almost two, but her sister had made no mention of it. By her size, Eurydice expected Pandora would deliver before Agniezka. Pandora gave Eurydice a happy, affectionate hug and kissed her cheek.

"Dicy, where have you been? We expected you ages ago," scolded Pandora as she stood back from her sister and held her hands to look her up and down. Whatever else, marriage agreed with Eurydice physically. Pandora thought she looked absolutely beautiful, even after traveling all day, and she loved the fur-lined cloak Eurydice was wearing.

"So sorry. I didn't realize I was expected," said Eurydice dryly, "but it looks like I'm not the only thing you were expecting." She lifted an eyebrow, and gave her sister a wry smile as she looked at Pandora's belly.

Pandora's eyes widened. "Oh! I thought you knew. I thought I told you at Christmas."

"No, you didn't, but that's fine. Can I go into my room now?"

Islington and everyone else had already gone in, and the two of them were alone in the hall, having a conversation that would best be conducted in private.

Pandora linked her arm through Eurydice's and they went in. It was a lovely suite, with doors opening onto a small balcony in both the sitting room and the bed chamber. It seemed very similar in design to the one they had in Kiev, except this one didn't have its own dining room. There was even a piano. The sitting room was decorated in blues and gold, and the bathing room and water closet were finished in a warm, honey-colored marble. The tub would have to be filled by hand, but it had one, and there was also a bidet. The bed chamber was decorated in mostly greens and burgundy, and the large bed seemed like it was going to be comfortable. The suite would do nicely for the week they would be there. When Eurydice looked out one of the windows, she had a view of a lovely church not far away.

She asked the attendant to arrange for a tray of food and a pot of coffee to be brought up before he left, and then she turned her attention back to her sister. Islington and Ellsworth were talking quietly in front of the fireplace, and Agniezka had gone to her room.

"So, where might everyone else be?" asked Eurydice mildly.

"Mamá and Papá have the suite next to yours. You saw where we are, and Maiyin and Keung have a room in our suite. Psyche and Sheerness have the one up from that toward your room on the same side as ours, with Chrissoula and Stockbridge in a room in their suite, and Psyche brought her new lady's maid, Pelagia, also. Dorian and Selena have the one on the other side of Mamá and Papá. Um, Arachne and Persephone have rooms just around the corner when you turn at the end of the hall. We've somewhat put all of the children and nannies into one suite...well, two." Pandora rubbed the spot behind her ear. "I think if you knock on *any* door on this floor, it's unlikely you'll find someone you don't know."

"I expected as much," said Eurydice dryly.

"I have a surprise for you," said Pandora excitedly.

"What kind of surprise?" asked Eurydice with trepidation. As infrequent as they were, she wasn't fond of them, and she wasn't sure she could tolerate anything too surprising.

"I got you invited to perform for the king on Monday."

"What?" blurted Eurydice dumbly.

"It's not in a theater. You and Ellsworth are invited to dine with his highness and Monsieur on Monday, and then you will perform for them."

Eurydice blanched. She thought she had moved beyond being drawing room entertainment, but it seemed she had not. Only the class of audience had changed. She wasn't angry with Pandora, but she might have appreciated more advanced notice. Eurydice hoped Ellsworth would be able to be there. Paris was one of the cities he needed to go to for his assignment, the last city he needed to go to, and where he would finish it. That meant he would be very busy. At least if she weren't performing in a theater it would mean doing it alone and needing less time to rehearse.

"Hmm, well, I suppose since I've performed for the Emperor of Austria and the Tsar of Russia, I may as well perform for the King of France, too."

"That's what I thought," said Pandora with a chuckle. "I'm going to tell everyone you're here. Wait until you see Psyche. She's enormous!"

"That doesn't surprise me," said Eurydice dryly, "but I hope you haven't been telling her that."

"Oh, no, she knows it, and she's not happy about it, either. We're fairly sure she's having twins, which I think is her just reward for the bet she made about Alex and Myron. Actually, she's bigger than I was when I was that far along, which has her throwing seven fits." Eurydice had missed her sister's meandering conversations.

Eurydice started to say something but changed her mind. "I have no doubt," she said instead.

"So you've seen something?" asked Pandora curiously. "Psyche said you had, but you wouldn't tell her what."

"I'm not telling you either, so don't think you can winkle it out of me."

"I would never!" said Pandora with round-eyed innocence.

"Of course you wouldn't," said Eurydice with a dry smile.

Islington gave Eurydice a kiss on the cheek and a hug after telling her it was good to see her again, and then he and Pandora left. Agniezka was still in her room, and Ellsworth pulled Eurydice close to kiss her warmly. She put her arms around his waist and rested her ear against his chest, listening to his heartbeat. She loved to hear that sound. It made her feel safe.

"I need to speak to your father," said Ellsworth quietly after a few minutes.

Eurydice looked up at him with a frown. "Can't it wait until we've had something to eat?" she asked disappointedly.

"No, I'm afraid not," said Ellsworth with a sigh, smoothing a hand down her cheek. "Besides, I'm not hungry. We'll eat supper together later."

"Do you promise?"

Ellsworth smiled and gave her another kiss. "I promise."

"Fine, go see my father," said Eurydice with pretended long-suffering. "I'll just stay here and eat, be overrun by my sisters and various and sundry other females. But you go ahead."

Ellsworth smiled lazily and moved his hands to her bottom. "Hmm. To be the lone male in a room full of females," he said thoughtfully. "That could be a good thing...or a very bad thing."

"I'm fairly sure a lot of them are going to be round with child."

Ellsworth's eyes widened in surprise. "You're joking."

"No, I'm not. Psyche, Pandora, Chrissoula, Agniezka, Amalie—I believe you've met her; Selena said she was expecting another in August in her last letter, and Judith, the Stranraers' daughter, too. Those are the only ones I know about for certain."

"Good God!" blurted Ellsworth in shock. "Hmm, a lone man in a room full of *pregnant* women? I'll be viewed as one of the enemy," he chortled.

"I'd protect you," purred Eurydice warmly as she stood on her toes to kiss his neck.

"I believe a retreat from the field would be the wisest course, but I will be back by ten for supper, and I want a bath...with you for dessert."

Eurydice stepped out of his arms and bowed obeisantly. *"Hai, shu."*

Ellsworth laughed and pulled her toward him to kiss her soundly. "Just you remember that," he warned teasingly. His expression turned serious. "If you decide to go somewhere, make sure you tell someone, and don't go alone."

"I'll be—" began Eurydice evenly with a patient expression, and Ellsworth put a finger to her lips.

"Promise me," he said earnestly. "Schellen's not here to protect you anymore, and I can't always be with you. Until Cesaire Dubonnet is found, I don't want you going anywhere without someone being with you and someone else knowing where you've gone."

"Cesaire Dubonnet? That's the man? The one who killed Merletto...and Schellen?"

"I shouldn't have told you that, but yes, that's his name." He kissed her forehead and hugged her to him. "Promise me you'll do as I say, please?"

"It's not me you should be worried about, but I promise I will do what you say," said Eurydice quietly.

They both turned to look when there was a knock on the door.

"I'll take that as my cue to leave before the gaggle arrives," said Ellsworth, tweaking the end of her nose.

"Just be sure you're back by ten, or I'll set them on you," threatened Eurydice playfully, "and there will be no dessert for you, either."

Chapter Thirty Six

The knock at the door was a maid bringing food, which Eurydice wound up eating alone. Not long after Ellsworth left, Agniezka came out of her room to ask if it would be all right for her to go see Felton. Of course, Eurydice couldn't refuse. She was surprised the man hadn't been waiting at the door for Agniezka when they arrived. Eurydice was sure she would, but she wouldn't be surprised if Agniezka didn't return before morning. She told Agniezka to send Felton her regards, which Agniezka said she would do as she filched one of the croissants from the tray to take with her.

But, Eurydice didn't sit alone for long, which would have relieved Ellsworth. As she had expected, all the women in her family arrived *en masse*, bringing all the other women she knew from London and Vienna with them. Persephone was sent to ask that a tray with lots of tea and coffee be sent up, which she did after giving Eurydice a spine-cracking hug and a kiss on the cheek. Eurydice had needed to bite her lip because the pain it caused in her breasts was excruciating, even though the tenderness she had been feeling there had lessened. Her younger sister seemed to be doing well, despite being forced to wear a dress, but Eurydice would like to spend some time alone with her to be sure. Persephone was almost as good at pretending as Pandora when the situation called for it.

Eurydice was surprised her sitting room would hold so many women, but she was glad it was a large room with several couches and chairs. In addition to her sisters and mother, Annabelle, Selena, Cora and Leilah were there, as well as Chrissoula and Maiyin. They brought with them the Countesses of Stranraer and Lundey, Lady Sheerness, Lady Bardsey, Judith Cunningham (the Stranraers' daughter), and Penny Mordecai (the Lundeys' daughter). Of the eighteen women in the room, seven were pregnant, except none of them knew Eurydice was, and she wasn't going to tell them. She hadn't told her husband, so she wasn't going to tell anyone else. She wouldn't have chosen to have an impromptu tea party in her suite the first night she arrived in Paris—probably not any other night, either, but she was very happy to see them all.

Pandora had not been exaggerating about how big Psyche was. She was only halfway through her pregnancy, and she was already larger than Pandora, as large as Judith, who was due at the beginning of April. Psyche wasn't due until the end of May, but she wasn't going to make it that long. She simply could not. She had waddled into the suite, gave Eurydice a hug and a kiss, and promptly eased herself onto a couch to rest her feet on the low table in front of it. Eurydice wanted to tell her sister what she knew, but at this point it would cause Psyche to panic.

Selena wasn't even showing yet, which wasn't surprising to Eurydice, considering Selena was due after her. Chrissoula was about the same size as Agniezka, and she said her sister-in-law, Ioanna, was expecting another baby as well, due about the same time as hers. As for the other women in the room, other than Arachne, Persephone, and Annabelle, it wasn't likely the others could be pregnant. Well, their mother was still young enough, but Eurydice didn't think it was likely. That was too strange to even contemplate. Eurydice doubted that her unmarried sisters would be with child. Persephone liked children, as she occasionally behaved like one herself, but the thought of having one—or what was involved to create one—was something Persephone found distasteful. Arachne liked children and would like to have one of her own someday. But she couldn't have one without a husband, and Arachne was too particular to find one of *those* she wanted.

The women spent most of their time catching up on things that had happened since they had seen each other last, and all of them were interested in hearing about the places Eurydice had been and what it had been like performing for royalty. What her sisters and mother wanted to know in particular was how she was finding being married. Only Psyche had seen Eurydice and Ellsworth together, and she hadn't been positive all would be well. She hadn't mentioned (and neither had her father) the bruising on Eurydice's neck to anyone, especially not to the duchess. When Eurydice told them she was happy and that she loved her husband, nearly everyone doubted her. She didn't know what she could do to convince them it was the truth, but after they all continued to look at her, she decided it wasn't her responsibility to *make* them believe. Only Leilah didn't doubt it, and the duchess was doubtful but wanted to believe it was true.

When one of the hotel maids returned to begin clearing away the remnants of the tea party as ten approached, Eurydice made arrangements for supper and water for the bath to be brought in. The women had steadily started to depart to have their own supper and tend to their spouses and children. Before they did, the duchess told them that she was arranging for a private room at the hotel for all of them to have supper the following night…men included. The duchess was the last to leave, and she had purposely done that. She gave Eurydice a hug and a searching look.

"You're truly happy?" she asked hopefully.

"Yes, Mother, I am *truly* happy," assured Eurydice, giving her mother a smile. "I didn't think I would be, but I am more content than I have ever been."

"Then why do you look so sad?" asked her mother quietly, brushing a hand down her cheek.

"I'm not...," began Eurydice, and her mother raised an eyebrow. "It's not Gareth," said Eurydice softly. "I *do* love him, and he loves me. He does." She shrugged. "All the things I had worried would happen if I married haven't happened. In fact, it's been exactly the opposite."

Julia believed her, but there was still a sadness in her eyes. No one else might have noticed, but the duchess knew her daughter. It was as if she were trying to be happy, struggling to make everyone believe nothing was wrong. Julia had seen her do that before. She pulled Eurydice to her to give her a warm hug and smoothed a hand down her back comfortingly.

"I will be here for you," she soothed, "when you need me."

Eurydice blinked her eyes to hold back the tears and nodded her head. She wanted so much to tell her mother what was wrong, but she couldn't. She kept hoping that as long as she didn't say anything to anyone, it wouldn't happen, that she could pretend it had all been simply a bad dream. Somehow, it was very right her family should be there. It was good they were there.

"Now, I better get back to your father. I still have to tuck in your brothers before Xan and I have supper." She gave Eurydice an amused smile. "Supper tomorrow night, supper with the king on Monday, and performing for everyone else on Tuesday. Busy, busy, busy."

"Too right," chortled Eurydice. "Good night, Mother," she said as she kissed her mother's cheek.

"Good night, dearest," said Julia fondly before she left.

Ellsworth returned only a few minutes after ten, not long after her mother had left. The maids brought in their supper and steadily brought in buckets of water to fill the tub as they ate. It was strange to be sharing a meal alone with her husband. Usually, there was at least Agniezka, but Eurydice liked it. She enjoyed having her husband to herself. She mentioned her mother's plans for supper the following evening and performing for the king on Monday. He said he would do his best to make both engagements, but he couldn't promise. That disappointed Eurydice, but she understood...somewhat.

They were finished with their meal, and the maids were able to clear away the dishes. Agniezka had not returned from visiting with Felton, but Eurydice suspected it would be after midnight before she came back. She didn't think there was any way it could be arranged for them to be married before they returned to Britain. That they were of two different religions would have to be considered, but it was something Eurydice was sure they had discussed.

The tub was one of the larger ones they had used, almost as big as the one in Venice. Bath time was enjoyable and did not involve as much washing as it did playing. One of the soaps the hotel had provided was very foamy when agitated enough, and the two of them had fun playing with it, making fake beards and hair...clothing. The only drawback to the soap was that it didn't taste very good and it stung if it got in the eyes. Even still, there wasn't much of it left when the two of them were through.

Lovemaking afterward was just as playful, and for a time, Eurydice was able to forget all the things that were troubling her. She was learning more about her husband, things he liked, things he didn't, what his opinions were or whether he had them. The more she learned, the more she realized that she not only loved her husband, she *liked* him; they were not always the same thing. He was able to make her laugh, which wasn't very easy to accomplish.

At one point, they heard the door to the suite open, and Ellsworth stilled to listen closely. He started to get up from the bed, but Eurydice told him it was just Agniezka returning from seeing Felton. He still almost got out of bed to go see, but then they heard a sneeze that sounded entirely feminine followed by the door to Agniezka's room opening, and Ellsworth went back to worshiping Eurydice's body. He had become more skittish lately, since Schellen's death. She didn't think Ellsworth was afraid of Dubonnet, but he was concerned about what the man might do.

Eurydice snuggled against him tiredly when they were through making love, but she couldn't go to sleep. She couldn't stop thinking. She possibly had a week before she would have to tell Ellsworth she was pregnant. He had asked if he was imagining that her breasts were larger, and she was able to tease him into believing he was. He probably thought her stomach was a little bigger from all the sweets she had been eating, but it would soon be obvious that was not so when her body wasn't increasing anywhere *except* those two places. He was too observant for her to fool him for very much longer.

Then there was the picture she had drawn in Geneva. She was beginning to believe she *had* drawn Cesaire Dubonnet, and if she had, it would mean he was up to something far more sinister than just helping Napoleon escape from Saint Helena. The more she had thought about it, the more she knew it had to be him. So many things began to make sense when she did accept it was him, and it caused a nervous ball to form in her stomach. He was the strange man at the redoute in Vienna and at the hotel in Kiev and why she had felt so strange when she had met both of them; the noise she had thought she heard on the loggia at the palazzo in Venice; Schellen's murderer. It would explain all those things, and it meant the man might eventually intend to help Napoleon, but it wasn't the only thing he wanted to do. For whatever reason, his intention was something to do with Ellsworth, which would explain her dream. She would show Ellsworth the drawing when she had the chance, but she wasn't sure what she could accomplish by doing that.

For his part, Ellsworth also had trouble sleeping. He had told Aberdare about the things that had happened since they had seen each other in Venice...at least, the things he hadn't been able to tell Aberdare in the reports he had been sending. The duke wasn't happy to find out how much Eurydice knew about things. He was even more concerned when he learned what had happened to Eurydice in Venice and that Schellen had been murdered. His grace completely agreed that Eurydice needed to be protected, and he did concede perhaps her being aware of the danger might be more helpful than harmful. He had every confidence in her discretion.

When Ellsworth told him the name of the man he thought was responsible, Aberdare frowned in puzzlement. The name sounded familiar, but Dubonnet wasn't one of the people Aberdare thought was planning on or capable of freeing Napoleon. He suspected Dubonnet's plans had nothing to do with Napoleon and everything to do with Ellsworth. Schellen's torture and murder would have been unnecessary for anything else. His attempting to kill Eurydice would have been unnecessary for anything else. Aberdare agreed that finding and stopping Dubonnet was urgent, but not because of Napoleon. Aberdare felt confident the former French ruler was secure in his island prison for the time being. Dubonnet needed to be stopped because of the consequences his actions could bring to Aberdare's own family. Those worried him far more.

Aberdare and Ellsworth agreed that if Dubonnet was intent on doing something to Ellsworth, chances were very good he was in Paris. It was possible all Ellsworth would have to do was wait for the man to come to him, but Ellsworth wasn't the sort to sit and wait. Besides, Ellsworth knew about Eurydice's dream, which he hadn't mentioned to Aberdare, and the longer Dubonnet was free, the more likely it was that what she had seen would happen. Ellsworth didn't want it to.

Ellsworth waited until he thought Eurydice was asleep, and then he carefully, reluctantly eased out of the bed. He had to find someone who could tell him what Dubonnet looked like and where he might be found. He was more likely to find someone like that if he looked for them late at night. He hated leaving Eurydice alone, especially in a room so close to the ground with a balcony, but Aberdare said he would have his valet, Rafael, keep watch. The location of their room made it easy for Ellsworth to leave unobserved, but it also made it easy for someone to enter.

Ellsworth was sleeping soundly when Eurydice woke up the next morning. She knew he had gone out. He thought she had been sleeping, but it had taken her at least another hour after he had gone before she was simply too tired to stay awake any longer. After she gave him a soft kiss on the cheek and brushed the hair from his forehead, she got out of bed and went to write in her diaries. The dream she'd had was simply a bad one caused by the Dark Dream. She had accepted she would never see the beginning of it, and it was beyond the point it was any longer going to matter.

Her entry in her life diary was much longer because she wrote down her suspicions and concerns. When she saw the words on the page, it made her conclusions seem accurate. She wanted to show Ellsworth the drawing, but she didn't want to wake him. He had come back to their room barely before sunrise. Perhaps she could show him later.

She and Agniezka had breakfast together, and then Agniezka helped her dress, but she left to be with Felton not long after that. Eurydice sat on a chair near the fire in the sitting room watching the flames, her knees curled up to her chin and her arms wrapped around them. She occasionally felt a nervous fluttering in her stomach, and she finally got up to look out the windows at the street below. She felt imprisoned.

After watching several carriages and people go by, Eurydice sighed fitfully and went to the desk to write a message to Monsieur Molyneux. She fully anticipated he wouldn't want to rehearse until tomorrow morning. She waited to see if any of her sisters or other family would arrive, but none did. She finally decided the entire situation was ridiculous, and she put a shawl around her shoulders and went to the lobby to arrange for its delivery. She wasn't helpless, and it wasn't as if the man would try to do something to her in a hotel full of witnesses. The attendant at the desk was most kind and assured her the message would be delivered as quickly as possible, and Eurydice thanked him before going back up the stairs.

When she made it to the first landing, she had the oddest sensation that she was being watched, and she paused for a moment to look around. She looked up to the landing for her floor, but she didn't see anyone. When she turned to look back toward the lobby, however, she felt her heart lurch when she saw *him*. She did her best to pretend she hadn't noticed, and she began to walk up the rest of the stairs as calmly as she could. The dizziness she had felt on seeing him previously no longer affected her because she now knew who he was. If she'd had any doubt the man in Kiev was the one from her dream, seeing him in the lobby of her hotel in Paris rid her of it. She *knew* he hadn't been Russian.

Once she reached her floor, she quickened her pace. She didn't know if Dubonnet was following her, but she was almost to her room. She didn't think Ellsworth could have left in the short length of time she had been gone, and she hoped he was there. She needed to show him the drawing, and he needed to know the man was in the hotel. But after she got to her suite and closed and locked the door behind her, when she got to their room, she was disconcerted to see Ellsworth *had* gone. Without a word. Eurydice scratched her forehead nervously and went back to the sitting room to stand in the middle of it, trying to decide what to do. She jumped when there was a knock at the door and barely managed to keep herself from screaming. She hesitantly went closer.

"Who is it?" she called nervously.

"It's your sisters come to kidnap you!" called Persephone bluffly.

Eurydice sighed with relief and went to open the door. All four of them were there, with Annabelle and Selena, looking at her expectantly. Persephone grinned amusedly as she led them all into the room.

"What is that look on your face?" she chortled. "I was only joking."

"Oh, it's nothing," said Eurydice, waving a dismissive hand through the air. "I just wasn't expecting anyone."

While her sisters didn't actually kidnap her, they did insist on taking her out with them to see some of the city. She wrote a note and left it on the desk for Ellsworth, should he happen to return while she was gone, and she also made sure to tell her mother. Her father wasn't at the hotel. Her sisters looked at her strangely when she did it, but Eurydice was trying to keep her promise, especially after she had seen Dubonnet in the hotel. She would be safe with her sisters; Dubonnet would be in for a very unpleasant surprise if he were to try something, even if half of them were pregnant.

Persephone made sure to point out that the Place de Louis Quinze was where the guillotine had been during the Terror, luridly naming off all the famous and infamous who had lost their heads there. Eurydice tried not to think about it. Both Eurydice and Arachne had proposed they should get a carriage, at least for the comfort of Psyche and Pandora, but both of them insisted they were fine to walk and that the exercise would be good. All of them were warmly dressed, but Eurydice was probably more warmly dressed than all of them with a pelisse and gloves, her fox hat and fur-lined cloak as well as a fur muff, and her *valenki*. There was a light snow falling, but other than her face, Eurydice didn't feel that cold.

They went across the plaza to walk along the river on the quay. When Eurydice saw the river, that was when she felt a chill, but it wasn't because of the weather. The Seine was skinned over by a layer of ice except in the center, thicker at the edges. The banks of the river were built up with stone, making the natural course of it seem artificial, as if it were contained and somehow man-made. Any doubt she had that what she saw in her dream would happen in Paris disappeared when she saw it.

They followed the quay past the Jardin des Tuilleries, past the Louvre, to the Pont Neuf, which they crossed to the *Île de la Cité*. Psyche and Pandora wanted to see Notre Dame. When they reached the island, Eurydice could see that the narrower channel of the Seine that flowed past it to the south, on the Rive Gauche, was completely iced over. It wasn't thick enough to support a person or anything heavier...yet. She was ready to go back to the hotel.

But Eurydice went with her sisters to see the cathedral, and it was very beautiful and peaceful. She was fascinated by the acoustics, and she imagined a choir singing within its walls sounded heavenly. Psyche and Pandora needed to sit down and rest before they returned to the hotel, but they were enjoying themselves immensely. They crossed the Pont Neuf back to the Rive Droite, but rather than walking along the quay, they crossed over in front of the Louvre to the Rue de Rivoli to reach the hotel.

All of them were tired when they entered the lobby, but rather than going to their rooms, they went to the common room to have dinner. Eurydice had looked over the lobby and the common room for any sign of Dubonnet, but she didn't see him. He hadn't intended to be seen earlier, and if he was there now, he was being very careful not to let himself be seen again. They enjoyed their dinner together, and after they were done, they all went upstairs to their rooms for naps. It had been an entertaining morning for Eurydice, even with all of its upsets, simply because she had been with her sisters.

When she reached her suite, Ellsworth had not been back. She picked up the note she had left on the desk and put it into the waste basket. She didn't know why she had even bothered. Eurydice went to see if Agniezka had returned, and she wasn't surprised she was still gone. After going to the water closet, she went to her room to lie down. The walk with her sisters had tired her, and a nap would be the perfect thing. She wasn't hearing any new compositions, and with nothing else to do, sleeping seemed like a good idea.

It was dark when Eurydice woke from her nap, and she felt momentarily confused. She rubbed a hand across her forehead before sitting up and moving her legs over the edge of the bed. The maids had been in to refresh all the fires, but they hadn't lit the lamps, which led her to believe they had been in before sunset. She went to the fire to light a rush and used it to light some of the lamps in the room. A look at the clock on the mantel showed her it was just after seven. She had slept longer than she had intended, but she was alone. From the looks of it, other than the maids, no one had been in.

She went into the sitting room to light some of the lamps there, and Casanova sat in his cage on a table near the windows. He squawked in surprise at the light and scratched his head before giving her a look.

"*Bouna sera, bella mia,*" he crooned.

"*Bouna sera,* Casanova," said Eurydice dully, walking over to his cage. She put in her hand and clicked her tongue, and he walked onto her wrist to let her lift him out.

"*Siete solo?*" he asked.

"A little," said Eurydice absently, smoothing her hand across the feathers on his back.

"*Lascilo aiutare con quello,*" said Casanova silkily.

Eurydice pursed her lips. "It's only going to be momentary, I'm sure," she said dryly.

"*Bacilo, per favore,*" said Casanova.

Eurydice smiled and shook her head slightly in amusement, but she pursed her lips out. Casanova touched them lightly with his beak, and then he shook his head up and down.

"*Grazie,*" he said excitedly.

She perched him onto the top of his cage, and she went to get an apple to cut up and put into his dish. He still had plenty of water and nuts, but his fruit bowl was empty. She petted him and talked to him for several minutes more, and then she put him back into his cage. It was time for her to get ready for supper. Her mother said it would be at nine, and it was slightly after eight already with still no sign of Ellsworth or Agniezka.

She went to the bedroom to put on the gown she had selected with Agniezka's help that morning. She was able to fasten it, but it was a little tight in the bodice. She didn't imagine it had been made wrong; her breasts had simply grown larger since it had been purchased in Vienna. She adjusted her koi and locket, and then she went to look in the full-length mirror. She rearranged the sleeves and the edge of the bodice before she decided it was on properly. She wasn't used to getting dressed without help. Getting undressed wasn't a problem, but making sure it was on correctly in the first instance was different. She put on her slippers, and then she went to sit at the dressing table.

She sat for a few minutes looking at herself. She needed to do something with her hair after taking it down for her nap, but she wasn't sure what. She had picked up the brush to run through it when she thought she caught a flash of movement behind the curtain on the doors to the balcony as a reflection in the mirror. She turned to look at it with a frown, but she didn't see anything. She slowly got up from the bench and walked toward it. She had just put her hand on the knob to open it when Ellsworth came in from the sitting room.

"I'm sorry I'm late, and I'm afraid I'll have to leave again as soon as supper is over," he said hurriedly. He stopped when he saw her nervous expression and what she was doing. "What's wrong?"

"I thought I saw something on—" she began, and Ellsworth moved her away from the door to open it himself.

There was no one there. He walked out onto the balcony to look up the face of the building and then downward. He couldn't see anything. He started to turn back to the room when he noticed footprints in the snow on the balcony and a place on the balustrade where someone had went over the edge. Either he wasn't very professional, or Ellsworth had surprised him. Ellsworth went back inside and closed the door to look at Eurydice.

"Why didn't you get someone?" he demanded.

"What?" asked Eurydice with a confused frown.

"What are you doing in here alone?"

"But I've been alone most of the day, other than this morning when I went to see Notre Dame with my sisters," said Eurydice evenly. "Well, the maids came in at some point while I was taking a nap to put more wood on the fires," she amended with a shrug.

"You shouldn't be alone. Where is Agniezka?"

"With Felton." Eurydice was still frowning.

"You need to have someone with you," said Ellsworth firmly as he went to the chifforobe to change his coat and waistcoat.

"I can't deny Agniezka her time with Felton, and I can't stop you from doing your job. I can't tell my family someone has to stay with me simply because you say so, and they aren't going to believe I can't bear being alone. Yet I can't tell them the truth: that some lunatic has followed you across Europe from one end to the other." She shrugged and lifted her hands defeatedly. "So, what am I supposed to do?"

"How do you know he's been following us?" asked Ellsworth sharply.

"Because he has been," said Eurydice with a shrug. "He was in Vienna at the redoute, at the hotel in Kiev, in Venice at the palazzo, and now he's been here in the hotel."

"What?" said Ellsworth breathlessly.

Eurydice went to the sitting room to retrieve the drawing from her diary. Ellsworth had followed her, and she held it out to him.

"That man. That is Cesaire Dubonnet. He accosted me at the redoute in Vienna. He was wearing a mask, but I know it was him. I didn't know who he was then, and I didn't tell you what he had done because he disappeared and I didn't want you to do something foolish. Then he was the man in the hallway in Kiev. I thought it was my illness making me so dizzy and incapable of focusing when I was near him—why I didn't *like* him," she said with a frown, "but it was because I *knew*…him, and I didn't…*know* him."

Ellsworth looked from her to the picture and back again. He did recognize it was the man from Kiev, and it was a very good likeness of him. Ellsworth hadn't even realized Eurydice could draw.

"Then when we were in Venice, I thought I heard a noise on the loggia at the palazzo, but you came through the door to our room at about the same moment. I thought I had simply mistook where the sound came from, but then Schellen was tortured and murdered, and I knew…," she said with a slight shake of her head, "I knew someone had been there."

Eurydice scratched her forehead nervously. "Now he's here in Paris. I saw him in the lobby this morning. I thought you were still sleeping, and Agniezka had gone to see Felton. I went down to the lobby to send a message to Molyneux, and I saw him…*watching* me. You were already gone by the time I got back here, and it was only a few minutes after I returned that my sisters came to take me out with them. I didn't see him again, until just now, when I thought I saw something on the balcony."

She looked at Ellsworth anxiously. "I don't think he wants to help Napoleon. I think he wants to hurt *you*. I think that's what he's planned to do all along…starting with killing Signor Merletto."

Ellsworth's heart thudded in his chest. He hadn't known. He thought he had only met up with the man again in Venice. He had no doubt Eurydice was telling the truth, and what she told him dispelled any doubts Ellsworth had that Dubonnet might be after him specifically. Following him all over the continent would have been unnecessary otherwise. Torturing and killing Schellen would have been unnecessary. Wanting to harm Eurydice would be unnecessary. But *why* was Dubonnet after him? Ellsworth didn't recognize him. Aberdare thought his name sounded familiar, but Ellsworth had never heard of him before he was told his name in Venice. Maybe if he showed the drawing to Aberdare, the duke would remember why he recognized the name.

"I don't want you to be alone anymore," said Ellsworth finally. "Until he is found, I don't want you to be anywhere, not even this hotel suite, without someone being within the sound of your voice. Tell Agniezka she can have Felton stay with her in her room. Lie if you have to. Invent something clever. Just don't...be alone." He lifted the drawing in his hand slightly. "I'm going to keep this because it's a good likeness. It might help me find him quicker."

Eurydice nodded uncertainly. She couldn't tell him it wasn't going to matter. She couldn't tell him that no matter what he did, no matter if she had someone within the sound of her voice—even holding her hand, her dream was going to happen. She couldn't tell him that because he didn't know about her dream, and to tell him would break her heart.

Eurydice did her best to enjoy her mother's dinner party. Everyone else was happy, and there was lots of laughter and conversation. She almost felt as if she were in London with all the familiar faces. She tried to forget the conversation she had with Ellsworth, but she couldn't, and she had felt a nervous fluttering in her stomach occasionally throughout most of the night.

She had managed to fashion her hair into something presentable, and then Agniezka arrived just as she was preparing to go down and quickly made it better. Eurydice told her what Ellsworth said about Felton staying in her room without telling her why. She said she would do that without asking any questions, which relieved Eurydice.

She had hoped Ellsworth would come back to their suite, but he stayed behind to talk to her father. She was sure Ellsworth intended to tell her father about the drawing and that Dubonnet had been following them. She understood it was necessary, but she missed her husband. She hadn't been alone with him for more than ten minutes all day. She hoped he would come to their suite afterward, but he would go out directly in search of Dubonnet.

When she got back to the suite, she dressed for bed and climbed under the blankets after washing her face and brushing her teeth. She had only lain there for a few minutes when she felt the fluttering in her stomach again, just as she was drifting off to sleep. Her eyes flew open when she finally realized what it was, and she put her hand over the gentle swell that was beginning just below her navel. She had thought it was due to some nervousness, but every time she had felt it, she had been still and not particularly anxious. It was also very faint, which was why she only noticed it in those quiet moments. She blinked her eyes to hold back her tears and smiled happily. She was hopeful she could tell Ellsworth soon, but she didn't think she would ever get the chance.

Ellsworth was there, spooned behind her, when she woke up the following morning, but she didn't know when he had come in. He smelled of stale cigars, and she didn't think it was all from the men enjoying port and tobacco after their meal the previous night. He had gone to a tavern or two after speaking with her father, hoping to find Dubonnet or someone who could tell him how to find the man. She didn't think he was successful. She started to get up, and he tightened his arm around her waist and nuzzled her neck.

"Stay until I fall asleep," he said drowsily.

"You haven't been to sleep?" asked Eurydice in dismay, her eyes widening.

"No," he said with a yawn.

Eurydice turned over to look at him. Yes, looking at him, she could see he was exhausted. She smoothed a hand down his cheek and kissed him softly, and then she wrapped her arms around him to cradle his head against her chest. She couldn't tell him that he was making himself tired for nothing. The dream would happen no matter what, and it was going to happen soon. She would only have a matter of days because they only intended to be in Paris until Saturday. Six days at most. Six more days before everything changed.

"I love you," she whispered.

Ellsworth nestled his cheek against her skin, and after only a few minutes, she felt him settle more heavily against her as he drifted off to sleep. She didn't want to get out of bed, knowing he had only just gotten there and that she would not see him much more that day once she left. He would be gone by the time she got back from rehearsal. He said he would try to be at the dinner with the king and the comte d'Artois, but now that he had the picture of Dubonnet, she didn't hold much hope he would be there.

She lay for several minutes holding him, listening to the peaceful sound of him breathing, before she kissed the top of his head and carefully eased herself out of bed. She slipped on her dressing gown and went to the water closet, and then she washed her face and brushed her teeth. There had been a message from Molyneux when she went down for supper the previous night, and he would see her at the Salle de la rue de Richelieu, the city's opera theater, for rehearsal at ten. She would be there for most of the morning, and then she would come back to the hotel for dinner. She didn't know if Molyneux would want to see her back again that afternoon, but she would be going with most of her family to have supper with King Louis and the comte d'Artois at eight. She would be surprised if she was back to the hotel before midnight.

Agniezka came out of her room not long after Eurydice came out of the water closet, and her maid went down to arrange for a tray with breakfast to be brought up for them and Felton. Eurydice wondered if Felton had given up his room. It would be entirely logical and practical…and cheaper. Even a small room at the hotel was expensive. She didn't know how much Sheerness paid the doctor, but she didn't imagine, even if it were generous, that it comfortably allowed him to pay for a room at the Hôtel de Crillon. She and Ellsworth had no qualms about him staying in their suite, and there was an extra room, which would have been Schellen's, to give the situation a semblance of propriety should anyone ask.

When Agniezka came back from arranging the tray, she helped Eurydice dress. It was only a few minutes after that when a maid arrived with their breakfast. They sat at the small table near the windows, listening to Casanova squawk and twitter in his cage with occasional outbursts of rude language.

Felton would look at the bird with his eyes wide in shock when Casanova did so, but Eurydice and Agniezka had learned to ignore him. Eurydice had realized that trying to teach the parrot to say something else was pointless. His vocabulary was too ingrained, and he was too old to start over. Besides, after hearing it so long, it had become amusing occasionally.

By the time they finished breakfast, Eurydice needed to leave for the theater. She asked Agniezka and Felton if they would like to go with her, and she was relieved when they said they would. Even if Eurydice hadn't told Agniezka what was happening, she seemed to realize Eurydice did not want to go alone. They went downstairs and arranged for a carriage to take them to the theater. It wasn't any farther than going to the *Île de la Cité*, but Eurydice didn't want to arrive for rehearsal exhausted and then have the return walk to the hotel.

Monsieur Molyneux was just as nice as he had been in Vienna, and still enthusiastic about Eurydice performing, if not more so. He gave her a brief tour of the theater when she arrived, and she was surprised by how many rooms there were at the rear of the building. He showed her the entrance she could use to reach them without going to the main entrance, and he also showed her the room she could use to prepare before the performance. Eurydice had never had a room like that, but it would give her the perfect place to leave her belongings rather than giving them to Agniezka or someone else to hold. It was easy to find from the entrance he showed her, and she wouldn't have any problems locating it the following evening.

The auditorium itself was fairly large, and Molyneux told her it had a capacity of fifteen hundred audience members. It wouldn't be as large as La Scala, but larger than the Burgtheater. This was the theater used by the Royal Music Academy and one of several to be found within a very short distance of each other on nearby streets, including another on the very same block as the Salle de la rue de Richelieu. The acoustics would do nicely, but she imagined the stage was a bit cramped for operas.

Once he gave her the tour, Molyneux took her to the room where the orchestra was rehearsing. They would perform the two concertos and the symphony, and he asked that she be prepared to perform some of her sonatas should the audience call her back for encores. She always did, and his telling her was unnecessary. The orchestra seemed adequate, and she only had to make a few suggestions and minor adjustments before she felt it would be excellent. Molyneux didn't think she would need to return that afternoon, but he did think she should come back the following morning. She agreed.

As Eurydice expected when the three of them got back to the hotel, Ellsworth was gone. She didn't know if he was simply somewhere else in the hotel, but she imagined he was out looking for Dubonnet. If she were reckless, she might have suggested Ellsworth simply use her as bait since the man seemed to have formed an attachment for her. But she wasn't reckless, and Ellsworth wouldn't willingly do that in any event.

It was four in the afternoon by the time she finished dinner with Felton and Agniezka, and Persephone came to visit shortly after. Agniezka and Felton left to look at the church down the street, so Eurydice got to have the time alone with her sister that she had wanted. It was obvious Persephone's feelings about wearing a dress hadn't changed, but after six months, she had come to tolerate it. Something had changed about her, though. She wasn't as carefree as she had been the last time Eurydice saw her. She was still mischievous and lively, but she held something of herself in reserve. That was new, and Eurydice didn't think Persephone did it because of something about Eurydice herself, whether it was her being married or no longer living at home. It was as if Persephone had lost a bit of her trust in the world, and Eurydice was saddened to see that. She didn't know if it was because she had lost Myron and Gregory or because she was being forced to be something she wasn't, but Eurydice suspected it was because of what had happened at their parents' anniversary party.

The change was subtle, and Persephone did her best to hide it. Eurydice would not ask. Her sister wouldn't want to talk about it, and she would deny it. Eurydice enjoyed the time she spent with Persephone, and she hadn't realized how much she had missed it. It seemed they were both able to appreciate their time together more after being apart, and when Persephone had to leave for Oba to help her get ready for supper, Eurydice was sad to see her go.

Agniezka arrived just as Persephone was leaving, and she helped Eurydice get ready for the supper as well. She and Felton would not be going. Not that she had a court dress, but both Eurydice and Agniezka agreed it wouldn't be necessary for Eurydice to wear one. She had the impression from what Pandora had said that—for royalty—the event would be informal. Agniezka put her into a gown made of peach-colored velvet trimmed in cream lace and dark blue ribbon. The sleeves were long and gathered at intervals down their length, which would keep them from getting in her way while she was eating and performing, and it would be warmer.

Ellsworth arrived as Agniezka began to put up Eurydice's hair, and she was relieved he was there. She had not been looking forward to going alone. He went to the chifforobe to get his clothes after giving Eurydice a warm kiss, and then he left for the empty room to get dressed. He was ready by the time Agniezka was through, and Eurydice could see and smell that he had shaved.

Eurydice put her Stradivarius into its case to take with her. She and Ellsworth would be riding with her parents to the palace. The Tuilleries was very close, and Eurydice had walked past it when they went to and came back from Notre Dame, but it was cold and dark, and it was expected one would arrive for dinner with the king in a carriage rather than on foot.

To her surprise, when Eurydice arrived, she discovered the king would, in fact, *not* be there. She didn't feel slighted, and she wasn't disappointed. The entire event left her feeling as if she had been relegated to being a performing monkey again. She had never been to a supper with a table so large and so many people attending. She was seated next to Artois's younger son, Charles-Ferdinand, on one side. He was charming and intelligent, and somewhat resembled his father, but Eurydice was disappointed she wasn't seated by her husband. Ellsworth sat further down the table on the opposite side between two women Eurydice didn't know. On Eurydice's other side was Jules, comte de Polignac, who was attractive and intelligent but, again, not her husband. She occasionally looked to Ellsworth helplessly, wishing she could have avoided the entire affair and spent the time alone with him at the hotel, but if he wasn't at the supper, he wouldn't stay at the hotel. At least this way she could look at him, if nothing else.

Eurydice spent the time after supper when the women retired to the salon while the men had drinks and tobacco after supper to tune her violin. She didn't see a piano, even if there was a harpsichord. She did have one or two pieces she had composed for that instrument, but it had been so long since she played them, she wasn't sure she could remember them, and she wasn't fond of playing it. She also didn't know how many pieces she was expected to perform. She would play only one, unless she was requested to do more. The meal had lasted three hours. She didn't think she had ever sat at a table to eat for so long. She didn't consider this to be a legitimate public performance. She really did feel as if she was back to playing in a drawing room, and she was somewhat insulted. She didn't blame Pandora, and it wasn't as if she could refuse a royal command.

When the men joined the women thirty minutes later, Eurydice couldn't find Ellsworth among them. She saw her father, Sheerness, and Islington, but she couldn't find her husband. She didn't see Dorian either. She was sure they were there, but there were too many people. She waited for someone to tell her to begin playing, and no one did. Pandora came over to whisper in her ear.

"Why aren't you playing?"

"Because no one has told me I should!" Eurydice hissed back irritatedly.

"You look very silly just standing there with your violin," said Psyche amusedly, coming up on the other side of her.

"I can't read minds!" bit out Eurydice through her teeth.

Both of them laughed at her annoyance, and Eurydice narrowed her eyes and clenched her jaw in an effort to maintain her composure. All three of them straightened when Artois walked toward them to give them a charming smile. They all curtsied formally, which Psyche and Pandora had some difficulty doing with their large bellies.

"Lady Eurydice, would you do us the honor of playing something on your violin?" he asked graciously with a slight bow.

Eurydice refrained from heaving a sigh of relief and smiled in return.

"Of course, your highness, it would be my pleasure," said Eurydice evenly.

She chose one of her more lively sonatas, thinking that would be better appreciated rather than something slow. She decided she had chosen rightly when everyone applauded, and Artois signaled for her to play another, which she did. The audience again applauded, and Artois came over to directly ask her to play one more. If he had simply signaled with a hand motion, she might have pretended she hadn't seen it. She played the "Chase" sonata, and it was as well-received as the other two, but she was glad her performance was done. She was tired, and she wanted to be well-rested for the theater the following night. It was almost one in the morning.

She went to put her violin away, and several people came to tell her how much they enjoyed her performance and also that they looked forward to hearing her concert at the theater the following night. Some of them told her their names, and she was sure she should be impressed, but she would forget their names and most of their faces by the time she reached the hotel. She was glad they liked her music—that was the only reason she performed in public, but she simply couldn't remember them all.

She found her mother and told her she was ready to go back to the hotel. The duchess didn't argue. She was very tired herself. Eurydice was relieved to see Ellsworth standing with her father, and she was happy he intended to return with them to the hotel. She was preparing to leave with them when Artois approached her to press an envelope into her hand. Eurydice frowned. She suspected she was being paid, and that had not been her intention, but she couldn't refuse because it would be rude, especially in front of everyone else. She thanked him humbly, and then she left with her parents and husband.

Eurydice didn't open the envelope until she and Ellsworth were back to their suite at the hotel after telling her parents good night. She put her hand to her chest and felt herself go slightly dizzy when she looked at the amount of the bank note. It wasn't the largest number of zeroes she had ever seen, but she had a fair understanding of how much it would convert to in pounds. It was an unbelievable amount. It was actually shocking, and she couldn't believe for even one second that her performance had warranted it. She put the note in its envelope with the rest in the strong box. She would have to decide what to do with the money eventually, but she had one more performance. She got dressed for bed, washed her face, and brushed her teeth.

Ellsworth had changed from his evening clothes into the ones he usually wore when he went out after dark: everything black and loose-fitting, the pants with several pockets for tools and other odds and ends. He also had a black knit cap that he wore on his head. Eurydice was disappointed he had changed into those clothes. It meant he wasn't even going to stay until she fell asleep. She went to put her arms around him, resting her head against his chest.

"Can't you stay with me for just a little while?" she asked wistfully.

Ellsworth put a finger under her chin to lift her face and look at her. "I need to find Dubonnet," he said quietly. Eurydice pressed her lips together to keep herself from saying something. "What? What is it?"

"You *will* find him," said Eurydice dully.

"But I need to find him now…before something happens to you," said Ellsworth earnestly.

Eurydice narrowed her eyes suspiciously. "I'm not the one he's after," she finally said evenly. She put a hand to his cheek and stood on her toes to kiss him. "Stay with me, please?" she whispered.

"Dicy...," sighed Ellsworth patiently.

She tugged on his hand to coax him toward the bed, and he went reluctantly. She pulled the cap off his head and began to undo the fastenings on his clothes. She didn't want him to go yet. He *would* find Dubonnet, whether he stayed the hour or two with her or not.

"Stay with me until I fall asleep," she pleaded. "Just for a little while."

She began to kiss his chest, teasing one of his nipples with her teeth. Ellsworth gasped, and one of his hands went to the small of her back. His pants had fallen from the weight of the items in the pockets when she undid the drawstring, and she gently put her hands to his shoulders to make him sit on the bed. She pulled off his shoes and removed his pants, and then she straddled his lap on her knees on the edge of the bed and wrapped her arms around his neck to kiss him longingly. Ellsworth put his arms around her waist to pull her against him, and then he untied the sash on her dressing gown and slid it from her shoulders.

He didn't want to leave her alone, and he had seen so little of her since Saturday. He needed to go; he needed to put his feelings aside and take care of his responsibilities, but she looked so sad and forlorn. He could stay with her until she fell asleep. She had become so precious to him, and he sometimes found it difficult to remember what his life had been like before she was there.

He pulled her shift over her head and nuzzled the valley of her breasts before taking the tip of one into his mouth. She sighed his name and curled her fingers into his hair. He held her against him and turned with her to lay her back against the pillows, and he began to place kisses down her stomach, enjoying the softness of her skin, relishing the way she quivered with excitement. He slowly ran his lips over one of her hip bones before he began to play her with his mouth. She moaned softly and wrapped her legs around his back, and she trembled excitedly as her fingers dug into the blankets.

"I love you," she sighed as she began to orgasm, and her back arched slightly as she shuddered with pleasure.

Ellsworth moved back up her body slowly, pausing to tease her breasts before kissing her. He settled between her thighs and propped himself up on one of his forearms to run the fingers of his other hand gently over her features followed by soft kisses. Her feet were hooked behind his thighs, and her hands rested at his shoulders as she looked up at him thoughtfully. Then she trailed her fingers down his chest between them to take his erection in her hand, and she watched his jaw tighten as his eyes closed in enjoyment when she began to stroke him. She slowly guided him into her, and she lifted her head to kiss him tenderly before running her lips across his jaw to his ear to suck at the lobe.

Ellsworth began to move in and out of her slowly, and she put a hand to his cheek as she watched his face. His expression was so careful, and she could tell he wanted to go faster. She urged him to do so with a sigh, and he quickened his pace, plunging into her deeply. Her expression changed to one of surprise and rapture as she began to orgasm again, and she grabbed his shoulders spasmodically. Ellsworth began to go even faster, and he sucked in air through his teeth before letting it out again with a soft sigh as he reached his own climax. Eurydice loved the look of relief and gratification on his face as he quivered, and she lifted her head to place soft kisses over his features.

Ellsworth eased himself off of Eurydice and pulled her against him. She lifted her head to kiss him softly on the lips, and then she settled her head onto his chest, listening to his heart. She would never grow tired of hearing that sound, and it soon lulled her to sleep. She knew he would leave her once she did, but she was too tired to stay awake.

Ellsworth held her for several minutes after she fell asleep, cradling her against him. She seemed so small and defenseless, even though he knew it was somewhat deceptive. She still hadn't realized her accident in Venice was not, but Ellsworth knew from her dream that she at least understood Dubonnet intended to do her harm. Even if she hadn't mentioned it to him, she realized the Frenchman was the man from her dream.

Ellsworth had shown the drawing to Aberdare, and when he told the duke how he came by it, Aberdare was surprised Eurydice had drawn it, and yet he wasn't. That she had known the man's face, that she had felt compelled to draw it, was something Aberdare had found more disturbing than seeing it. It was obvious to Ellsworth that her family was aware of her gift. Aberdare had asked Ellsworth if Eurydice had told him what she had seen, but Ellsworth couldn't tell her father what he had read. He could only tell Aberdare that he believed her life was in danger. Aberdare had already suspected as much.

Ellsworth carefully eased his way out of bed. He couldn't escape the urgent feeling that Dubonnet needed to be found as soon as possible, and yet he also couldn't escape the feeling that he wouldn't be able to stop what Eurydice had seen. After he put his clothes back on and adjusted the blankets over her, he went to the sitting room and lit the lamp on the writing desk where Eurydice was keeping her diaries. He hadn't looked at them since they had been in Vienna, but he needed to. He had not missed that she removed the drawing from her dream diary, and he didn't think she had been keeping it there simply as a matter of convenience.

He sat for a moment trying to decide where he should start looking. It had been months, and he didn't have time to go through that many entries. He needed to know if she had finished the dream from Podpetsch. He smoothed his fingers over the space between his brows with his eyes closed before he decided where he needed to look. Laibach. The night she had first told him she loved him. Her entire demeanor had changed after that night. A haunted look that would never quite go away had settled into her eyes after that.

He went to that date in the diary, and he frowned when he saw there was no entry. The page wasn't missing; there was simply nothing there. He went backward a few days, and he found nothing. He flipped forward, closer to the present, and he finally found what he was looking for. He noticed she had still not seen the beginning, how it had gotten to the point where it always seemed to start, but the part she saw had even more detail. Now that he had a face to put with the man in the dream, it became even more vivid for Ellsworth while he read, and he could feel his stomach lurching occasionally. Then he got to the part that was new, and he looked to the door of the bedroom over his shoulder. He read it again, and then he slowly closed the diary and put it back where he had found it.

Ellsworth rose from the desk and turned off the lamp, and then he went back to the bedroom. He stood beside the bed watching Eurydice sleep for several minutes with a somber expression. Now he knew what she knew, and he could understand the change in her behavior. The entry was from several days after Laibach, while they were in Venice, but he didn't doubt the first time she had seen the end of it was the night she had seemed so desperate and frightened. He finally sighed fitfully, and then he leaned down to brush the hair from her face and placed a soft kiss on her cheek. Somehow, he was going to stop it from happening.

Chapter Thirty Seven

Eurydice sat in front of the mirror while Agniezka styled her hair in preparation for her concert. She was wearing a simple white gown of linen, trimmed at the bottom with rows of brown velvet ribbon and embroidery, the bodice made of a matching material. The sleeves were puffed at the shoulders, and the rest of their long length fit fairly close to the shape of her arm before flaring slightly at the cuff and being edged in fine crocheted lace. To offset the simplicity of the gown, Agniezka put her hair into an elaborate style, coiling most of it on top of her head and weaving a braided section through it, finishing it off with a brown silk bandeau. For jewelry, she wore her two necklaces, a simple pair of gold hoops in her ears with a single small pearl dangling from them, and her wedding ring—which she never removed…ever.

Ellsworth had been in the bed holding her when she woke that morning, but he was gone when she returned from rehearsal. He had not been back. Her performance was to begin at nine, and Agniezka had finished helping her dress. It was after eight, and Ellsworth was not back. Agniezka and Felton were dressed, and still there was no sign of Eurydice's husband. She waited as long as she dared, hoping he would come in, but he didn't. She disappointedly retrieved her Stradivarius after putting on her pelisse, cloak, and gloves.

She looked at the door expectantly when there was a knock, but it was only her mother and father coming for her, Felton, and Agniezka to ride with them to the theater. Her parents frowned when they discovered Ellsworth would not be coming, but for entirely different reasons. Eurydice wanted so much to ask her father if he knew where her husband was, but she couldn't in front of her mother and friends. She wouldn't have the opportunity to do so at any point before her concert. If Ellsworth didn't meet her at the theater beforehand or arrive there at some point, it would be the first time he had ever missed one of her performances. It frustrated Eurydice, but it also worried her because Ellsworth had promised he never would.

Rather than going to the main entrance of the theater, Eurydice wanted to be deposited near the door she would use to go to her dressing room. Her parents, Agniezka, and Felton got out with her and followed her in, and once they got to the small room, Agniezka helped her out of her pelisse and cloak. Eurydice explained how to go through the passages behind the stage to get to the front of the theater and their seats in the auditorium. Agniezka and Felton had been with her for both of her rehearsals, and they didn't think they would become lost. Molyneux came in while she was tuning her violin, and when there were only ten minutes left before it was time for her to go on stage, her parents gave her hugs and kisses and wished her luck, as did Agniezka and Felton, and all five of them left the room.

Eurydice scratched her forehead nervously after they left. She kept waiting and hoping that Ellsworth would come in. Of course, he wouldn't know where to find her in the labyrinth of rooms behind the stage. He hadn't been to the theater even once with her, but she was sure he knew how to find the building.

When she couldn't wait a minute longer, Eurydice left and walked through the corridors to the back of the stage. She could hear the audience applauding for the conductor as he took his place on the stand, and she quickened her pace to make her entrance. She put a hand to her stomach and breathed in and out slowly to calm her nerves, and then she walked out into the light.

The violin concerto was first, and Eurydice was glad she had become so familiar with the piece after playing it so many times because it was difficult to focus on what she was doing. All through the performance, she kept looking over the audience for her husband. She found the faces of her family and friends, all of them sitting—for the most part—in the same section of the theater, but she didn't see Ellsworth. There was a seat in the loge with her parents that had been intended for him, and he wasn't there. She couldn't help feeling something was wrong.

When the concerto was over, Eurydice curtsied and smiled pleasantly as the audience erupted with applause, and then she exited to the right of the stage. She could hear the orchestra beginning the symphony as she made her way back to her dressing room to put away her violin. She had hoped when she went behind the curtain that she would find Ellsworth waiting for her beside the stage as he often did, but there was no one. After she put away her violin, she wondered if she should keep it with her, just in case the audience requested an encore, but she decided if they did, she would play piano pieces. She had enough of those that it wouldn't be necessary to use the violin. Without someone there to hold it, she didn't feel comfortable leaving it at the edge of the stage.

Once she put away her violin, she went back to the curtain on the stage and took a seat in the chair she had requested Molyneux put there for that specific reason. The orchestra was nearing the end of the second movement by the time she returned, which meant she still had several more minutes to sit and think. The orchestra was doing well, and while Eurydice could have wished for better acoustics, she had played at venues with worse. Aside from that, she was willing to tolerate quite a bit because this would be her last public performance for quite some time. She would wait at least until after the baby was born.

Her foot began to tap impatiently as the symphony played on, and Eurydice had to forcibly make herself stop. She kept trying to tell herself that Ellsworth was fine and that he would have a perfectly reasonable and worthy explanation for why he wasn't there. He was capable of taking care of himself, and everything was going to be fine. If she didn't see him that night when she got back to the hotel, he would be there holding her in the morning, and she could ask him where he had been and give him a proper berating for scaring her. Then they would make love, perhaps have breakfast together, and she would feel entirely silly for being so worried.

She had to put a hand to her mouth to stifle a scream when the audience applauded at the end of the symphony. She had been so lost in her thoughts that she hadn't realized that time had arrived. She flexed her fingers and took a deep breath, and then she rose from the chair to walk back onto the stage to the piano for the final concerto. The audience applauded when they saw her again, and she nodded and smiled as she took her seat at the piano. She had to wonder how much of it was coming from the fifty or so people in the audience who knew her personally.

The concerto went smoothly, as she had anticipated, despite her lack of concentration. When she stood at the end to curtsy and thank the audience, they gave her a standing ovation and requested an encore. Eurydice had been hoping they wouldn't, but she wasn't surprised when they did. She played the "Anniversary" sonata, and when she was through, it was nearing midnight.

She received another ovation as she curtsied, and she began to leave the stage. She had actually gone behind the curtain with the intention of going to her dressing room, but when the cheering of the audience did not lessen and there were shouts for an encore, she sighed tiredly and walked back onto the stage. She waved and smiled as she went to the center of it, and she sat once again at the piano. By the end of the second sonata, she had decided she would not give another encore. She appreciated that the audience enjoyed her music, but she had personal concerns to attend to. She stood from the bench once again and curtsied several times, smiling and waving as she thanked the audience and they continued to applaud, but she was done.

She walked off the stage again, and while she could hear shouts for yet another encore, she could not bring herself to do it. It was after midnight, and that was her limit. She continued walking to the back of the stage and made her way to her dressing room. When she opened the door, she was startled to see someone standing there, but it wasn't anyone she might have expected.

"Thank God you're finally done!"

"Fraulein Rathmueller, what are you doing here?"

"You have to come!" said Anneliese, wringing her hands nervously.

Eurydice raised an eyebrow with a slight frown. "Why?"

Anneliese had recuperated from the beating Eurydice had given her on Halloween, but her nose was slightly crooked. She wore a bright red coat trimmed in ermine with a matching hat, and even at the distance she was from Anneliese to the door, Eurydice could smell that she still wore the same noxious perfume. Her features were anxious, and she seemed very agitated.

"Because your husband has been hurt," said Anneliese hurriedly, "and he sent me to find you."

"I don't believe you," said Eurydice flatly, but she could feel her heart lurch regardless.

"I know we didn't get off on the right foot, and I perfectly understand why you don't trust me," pleaded Anneliese, "but you have to believe me. Gareth sent me a letter from Venice asking me to come here to help him find Dubonnet." Eurydice still looked at her doubtfully. "Please, we have to hurry! He's been very badly hurt!"

Eurydice was still hesitant. She knew Anneliese worked for whoever paid her the most, but she seemed entirely sincere. His being injured would explain why Eurydice hadn't seen him all day, why he had broken his promise.

"I need to tell my family I'm going," said Eurydice evenly.

"No, no! He said you're to come alone! What can you be thinking? He's a spy! Do you want everyone to know?" said Anneliese testily.

Eurydice didn't trust the woman, but Anneliese was no match for her physically. If it did prove to be a lie, Eurydice would have no trouble getting away from Anneliese. But if it was the truth, then her husband could be lying somewhere calling for her.

"Let me get my things," Eurydice said finally, going to retrieve her pelisse and cloak.

She was putting on her pelisse when Anneliese grabbed her by the arm and began to pull her toward the door.

"There's no time! We have to go now!" hissed Anneliese.

Eurydice looked at Anneliese questioningly, but she let the woman lead her out. She put her other arm into her pelisse just as they went out the side door of the theater into the cold night air, and she buttoned it as she hurried along behind Anneliese. She led Eurydice south at a very fast pace, almost at a trot, and whatever else, Eurydice did believe Anneliese was anxious. Eurydice wondered how far they would have to walk. The air was frigid, and there was a light snow falling. Her pelisse was warm, but she had on no gloves or hat, and Anneliese hadn't given her time to take her cloak. If they had to go very far, Eurydice would prefer a carriage.

"Where is he?" asked Eurydice as she tried to match her pace to that of Anneliese.

"He's just on the other side of the river," said Anneliese breathlessly.

"Perhaps we should get a carriage," suggested Eurydice calmly.

She wasn't tired or winded, but she could see Anneliese wasn't used to physical exercise. For her part, Eurydice wanted a carriage because she would be freezing by the time she walked that far in only her pelisse. Eurydice didn't imagine Anneliese had walked that far to find her. The woman should have told the hack to wait.

"Don't be silly, we're almost there," puffed Anneliese.

It was true they were already to the rue de Rivoli, but they couldn't get to the river without either turning to the right to go to the Place de Louis Quinze or going to the left to cross at the Pont Neuf, which would add almost a half-mile to the distance. There were bridges between those two on the river, but it would still require them to go around the Tuilleries and Louvre to reach them. Anneliese turned to the left.

Several carriages passed as they walked along the sidewalk, but there weren't many other pedestrians. There were guards standing at the entrances to the palaces, and while they may have noticed the two women hurrying along, they made no comment. Eurydice could tell Anneliese was tired, and while she was beginning to feel a bit of a strain to the muscles in her calves from maintaining her balance on the snow, which continued to fall and coat the ground, Eurydice was really beginning to feel the cold.

Eurydice wished she had been able to leave a message for her family. She was sure they had gone to her dressing room by now and found she wasn't there. She didn't intend this to take long. One way or the other. If Anneliese was telling the truth about Ellsworth being injured, she would arrange to get her husband back to the hotel as quickly as possible to be tended by Felton and Keung. If Anneliese was lying, Eurydice would break her nose again and find a hack to take her back to the hotel as quickly as possible. Her family would be worried, but she would be with them soon enough.

They reached the rue du Pont Neuf, and Eurydice was relieved as they went south again. The pace they maintained was keeping her body warm, but her extremities were growing numb, particularly her nose and her ears. Her toes and fingers were stinging, and even her bottom was beginning to feel stiff. Eurydice looked down at the water as they crossed the bridge, and the ice at the edges had grown thicker. There was only a narrow swath down the middle that wasn't coated with ice, and once they reached the *Île de la Cité* and started to the Rive Gauche, the southern channel was completely frozen.

Anneliese continued south once they crossed the bridge, and Eurydice looked at her expectantly. Eurydice wasn't familiar with Paris at all, so she had to wonder where Ellsworth might be. If he had been looking for Dubonnet on this side, was this the seedy side? As they went further down the street, Eurydice didn't think that was the case because she could see several buildings and homes that appeared to be completely respectable.

"Where is my husband?" demanded Eurydice when they continued to walk on without any sign of stopping. She was sure they had already walked over a mile, and if reaching Ellsworth meant they would have to go much farther, she wanted a carriage.

"We're…almost…there," panted Anneliese tiredly.

Eurydice stopped. "No, we *are* there. Until you tell me where Gareth is and how badly he is injured, I'm not taking one more step," she said firmly.

She shouldn't have even left the theater until she had that information. Anneliese wouldn't answer her, and Eurydice threw her hands up in the air and shook her head disbelievingly.

"It was a lie, wasn't it? My husband doesn't even know you're here," said Eurydice angrily. She couldn't believe she had been so stupid. "The best thing you can do is go back to Vienna before I break your nose again."

Eurydice turned to begin walking back the way she'd come. She was hopeful she would be able to find a hack before she had to walk all the way to the Hôtel de Crillon. She began to quicken her step as she approached a fairly busy intersection, confident she could find a carriage. She was almost to the corner when she felt two powerful arms wrap around her and grip her tightly as a cloth was placed over her mouth and nose. She struggled to get loose, but there was something on the cloth. She felt herself going dizzy, losing consciousness, and it seemed the more she breathed, the worse it became. As the world began to turn black, Eurydice realized Anneliese had led her into a trap, and everything she had feared in her darkest dream was about to happen.

Ellsworth and the Aberdares reached the dressing room before anyone else, but the rest of the family wasn't far behind. Ellsworth wanted to be there before anyone else to apologize. He had arrived just as she began the second encore, and he had needed to pay a large bribe to be let in by that point. He had thought for a time about waiting at the hotel for Eurydice to return, but he wanted her to know he had at least made an effort to be there.

He felt terrible that he had missed her performance chasing what proved to be a false lead. He wouldn't have done it if he had known that's what it would be, but he had thought he was close to finding Dubonnet. He had wanted to prove that not all her visions had to happen the way she saw them. He still intended to do that; it just wasn't going to be accomplished that night.

The three of them frowned when they reached the room and saw Eurydice wasn't there. Her things were still there, letting them know they had found the right room, but she was nowhere to be seen. They weren't immediately concerned. They had left their box to make their way back stage when the audience was still applauding and shouting in an attempt to get her to return for a third encore. Ellsworth had known she wouldn't. She didn't perform past midnight. She would think a third encore was avoidable. They suspected they had simply reached the room before her and she would arrive any second.

But when the door opened only a moment later, it wasn't Eurydice. It was the twins and their husbands with Maiyin, Keung, Chrissoula, and Stockbridge. And when the door opened not long after that, it was the rest of Eurydice's siblings, Annabelle and Selena, as well as Felton and Agniezka. That was when everyone began to grow concerned. It was unlikely Eurydice would have gotten lost. Molyneux shortly arrived to give Eurydice her bank note, but Ellsworth took it on her behalf after asking the director if he knew were the garderobe could be found. Ellsworth suspected it was unlikely she was there, but it was possible. He didn't want to dismiss any possibility yet, because to do so would mean something incredibly bad had happened, the something he had been trying so hard to prevent.

Ellsworth followed Molyneux to the garderobe, and he cautiously went in. It was empty. When he got back to the now very crowded dressing room, he found that his mother and Leilah had arrived, along with most of the people from London who had come to see her, but Eurydice hadn't made her own entrance. It was a large room, but it wouldn't hold many more people. Ellsworth asked Westerkirk if he would stand at the door to prevent anyone else from entering, especially if it wasn't someone who actually knew Eurydice. Ellsworth made his way through all the people in the room toward Agniezka, and it was obvious she was worried.

"Did you come in with her tonight?" he asked evenly. Agniezka nodded waveringly. "Can you tell if anything is missing?"

Agniezka went to look at Eurydice's things. Her violin was there in its case. Her reticule was there, and so were her gloves, hat, and cloak, but the cloak wasn't where Agniezka had hung it, and her pelisse was missing.

"H-her pelisse," said Agniezka nervously.

"Anything else?"

"No, but her cloak isn't where I put it after I helped her remove it."

Ellsworth rubbed at his forehead as he thought. There were too many voices. None of them were talking loudly, but he couldn't think, and time was essential. He wanted to believe she had just gone back to the hotel. He wanted to believe she might have gone for a short walk, but believing either of those things would be a waste of time. He had to accept, whether he liked it or not, that Dubonnet had taken her. It couldn't have been long ago—only minutes; he could possibly find them before they got very far.

Something about it wasn't right to him, though. Eurydice knew Dubonnet was a bad man, and she knew what he looked like. She wouldn't have gone with him willingly, let alone bothered to take a pelisse. There would have been some sign of a struggle, and there was none. Dubonnet wouldn't have bothered to get the coat for her himself, especially considering what he intended to do to her. That led Ellsworth to believe Dubonnet had an accomplice. It could possibly be someone she knew, but even a stranger might have gotten her to go with him (or her) if what he (or she) told Eurydice seemed plausible. As he thought about it, Ellsworth realized it would be more likely whoever was helping Dubonnet was a woman. His wife wouldn't have been foolish enough to go somewhere alone with a strange man. Whether or not Dubonnet had been waiting outside when the woman got Eurydice to leave the building was the question. He went to Aberdare.

"I'm going to look for her; they haven't been gone long," he said quietly.

"Do you think—" began Aberdare gravely.

"Yes, I do think," cut in Ellsworth. "I'm hoping I can catch them before they get to where they're going…provided they didn't take a coach."

"Do you know where he would have taken her?"

"Not specifically, but I have a general idea." Ellsworth hesitated for a moment, but then he made up his mind. "You need to read her dream diary, particularly the entry from the tenth. She also has another diary she's been writing in Arabic, but I can't read it. You may find something in there to help as well. I'll meet you all back at the hotel…I hope."

Aberdare looked at him with a frown. He didn't know why his daughter was writing a diary in Arabic, but he could make an educated guess. He had to agree it might hold something useful. He was displeased with Ellsworth for not telling him the details of the dream that had led Eurydice to make a drawing of Dubonnet. It was obvious Ellsworth didn't understand Eurydice's gift, had never asked her to explain it. Either that or he didn't *want* to understand it.

The duchess looked from one man to the other worriedly. Something terrible had happened to her daughter, and it was because of them. She knew a little about what her husband did for an *occupation*, and if Eurydice's disappearance was related to it, Julia wouldn't be able to breathe properly until her daughter was found. She could only imagine why anyone would want to take her daughter, and she didn't even want to think about it.

Ellsworth left shortly to go find Eurydice. He hadn't bothered to check his coat and hat at the cloak room, and he put them on hurriedly as he went through the crowd of people to the door.

Eurydice's family looked from Ellsworth leaving to the duke, and he tented his fingers under his chin thoughtfully before he said anything because he couldn't be sure of the details. He couldn't tell them what was happening— even of what he knew, but he was good at thinking on his feet. He would just have to make sure he told his wife as much of the truth when he learned what that was as he could because he would never hear the end of it if he didn't.

"Where's my sister?" demanded Persephone hotly.

"I don't want to alarm anyone, and be assured we are going to get her back," began Aberdare evenly.

"Too right, but where's she gone?" repeated Persephone flatly.

"Only moments ago, Eurydice was abducted by a man of questionable mental faculty, who appears to be suffering from the delusion that he is in love with her."

"What?" was the collective shocked reply.

"He has stalked her like prey all across the continent, waiting for the opportunity to take her, and tonight, he finally got it. Ellsworth has just left to see if he can find the man before he disappears with her or causes her harm. We're going back to the hotel, and once I'm able to glean a few more details, we'll join the search ourselves. Be aware this man is most likely armed and should be considered extremely dangerous even if he isn't. He has already committed two known murders in his pursuit of Eurydice, and now that he has her, I can only guess what lengths he will go to to keep her."

"Shouldn't we notify the authorities?" asked Alex Nichols, Sheerness's younger brother.

"Let's see what the situation is first," said Aberdare evenly.

≪ ≫

Eurydice began to wake slowly. Everything was very disjointed and dreamlike. She felt nauseous and dizzy, and above all, cold. But not as cold as she might have thought she would. For a moment, she didn't know where she was, but then she remembered Anneliese and that she had been ambushed. Eurydice had worried how it would begin, and now she knew. She couldn't believe she had been foolish enough to go anywhere with Anneliese. She should have known from the woman's demeanor that something was wrong, something that didn't involve Ellsworth.

Eurydice could feel that her hands and feet were bound to a frame of some type, spread-eagled. She was too cold to know for certain whether she was naked, but she could feel that her shoes had been removed and she was at least no longer wearing her pelisse. She could hear voices, but she couldn't see anything or open her eyes. That was when she realized she was blindfolded. Her jaw ached, and she discovered her mouth was gaping open, forced that way by something lodged there. She tried to move her tongue to determine what the object was by touch, but her mouth was spread so widely, the thing so large, she couldn't move her tongue. It made her jaw hurt even worse when she tried and nearly made her choke. The only thing she knew for certain was that the thing was made of metal, and it tasted horrible.

And yet she knew what it was. Nothing about what she was feeling and discovering on waking was surprising her. She was frightened—terrified, but it was because she knew the worst was yet to come. She had still not reached the point where her dream began, so she *knew* there was far worse to come. If being blindfolded and gagged with a *poire d'angoisse*, tied naked to a rack, was all she would have to endure, it would be bearable, but it was only beginning.

"You gave her too much ether," Eurydice could hear a man saying stiffly, and she could recognize that it was the voice of the man from the redoute in Vienna who spoke German, the man from Kiev who spoke Russian, and who now spoke French. Cesaire Dubonnet.

"Oh, calm down! She'll be fine," said a woman testily, and Eurydice recognized Anneliese.

"She will be useless if she's dead. You could have killed her!"

"Considering what she did to me the last time, I didn't want to take any chances," said Anneliese airily. "What makes you so sure she can tell you what you want to know?"

"She knows," said Dubonnet flatly.

Eurydice flinched when she felt cold water splash against the front of her body, no doubt thrown from a bucket, and she knew Anneliese had done it.

"See! She's awake!" said Anneliese gleefully, and Eurydice could hear her clapping her hands.

Eurydice blinked confusedly when the blindfold was removed from her eyes, and she once again gazed on the face of Cesaire Dubonnet very close to her own. He was looking at her assessingly, and Eurydice gave him a dull stare back. Her eyes were still adjusting to the sudden light, such as it was. There were several torches in sconces on the walls and a large brazier, explaining why she wasn't as cold as she might have thought she would be. There were no windows, but there wouldn't be any in the catacombs.

Dubonnet had brought her to a large chamber in the tunnels burrowed beneath the city. She didn't know where, exactly. It was almost square in shape, about twenty feet on a side, with a tall ceiling. Most of the walls had been reinforced with prepared stone, but there was one wall that still bore the marks of having been mined for its limestone about halfway across its length. She could see two entrances going in different directions, and the floor was bare dirt and bits of rock. There was also a well and a shelf along the wall that remained unfinished, as if the quarriers had just decided to stop when they reached that point. She didn't think Dubonnet was the first to use this chamber, but she was sure its location had long been forgotten.

Dubonnet moved out of Eurydice's sight behind her, and Anneliese came to look at her with malevolent glee.

"Hallo, *liebling*," she purred. "I think we are going to see how careless you are with your words now," she taunted.

Eurydice could feel that her wrists and ankles were held by iron shackles attached to the wooden rack through holes, which allowed them to be adjusted to different positions for people of different heights. The frame was square, and her feet were positioned so that she could just support her weight on the balls of her feet and relieve the pressure on her ankles. She had been hanging by her wrists and ankles until she regained consciousness, and she could barely feel her fingers and toes from the lack of circulation. Eurydice didn't think this rack was in the chamber when Dubonnet decided to use it, and she tried not to think about the fact that Schellen had probably been the last one to be bound to it. It was unlike anything she had ever seen or read about before. She could see from its construction that it would be easy to dismantle and transport to another location in preparation for the next victim.

Anneliese moved to the side of the rack, her gaze almost manic. Eurydice could barely see her from the corner of her eye, and she watched as Anneliese removed a metal pin from the frame before walking to the other side and removing the matching one there. Eurydice could feel the frame rock on its base, and then Anneliese grinned evilly as she placed both hands on it to give it a forceful shove. The frame began to spin in a circle, sending Eurydice upside down and back again. She managed to maintain her balance on the balls of her feet and flexed her arms to reduce the pull of the motions on her wrists and ankles, but the spinning made the nausea she had felt on waking grow even worse. Eurydice felt like she was going to vomit, but if she did it with the pear in her mouth, she could choke to death.

"Whoop, whoop! Isn't that fun?" giggled Anneliese.

The spinning began to slow, but Eurydice needed to get the pear out of her mouth soon. She felt herself come to a jolting halt rightside up, and Cesaire took the pins away from Anneliese with an irritated glare to put them back in the frame and secure it in place once again. When he had walked behind Eurydice, he had apparently gone out of the chamber through an entrance she couldn't see, and he had only just returned to see Anneliese taunting her.

"Behave," he said coldly to Anneliese, and she stuck out her tongue.

He wiggled the key on the choke pear in Eurydice's mouth to get her attention, and it made her jaw throb and her teeth ache to their roots. Eurydice inhaled sharply at the pain, and she looked at him hatefully. She knew he was no better than Anneliese.

"I'm going to remove this, but if you scream, I'll cut out your tongue. Do you understand?" he said quietly.

Eurydice nodded waveringly. He began to turn the key to slowly reduce the instrument in size until it was finally small enough to remove from her mouth. The relief of pressure on her jaw was agonizing, and Eurydice couldn't close her mouth. It was just as well, because within seconds of Cesaire's removing it, she leaned her head forward to throw up, trying to avoid getting it on herself and barely managing. Cesaire looked at her in surprise before glaring at his comrade, and Anneliese cackled amusedly.

"Do you know why you're here?" Cesaire asked Eurydice mildly, folding his arms across his chest.

Eurydice shook her head negatively. She tried to say 'no,' but she couldn't make her mouth work properly yet.

"We're going to have a conversation, you and I," said Cesaire with a friendly smile.

He went to stand behind Anneliese and put his arm over her shoulder to place his hand tightly around her throat. Anneliese's expression was momentarily alarmed, but she began to smile saucily when it turned into a caress that moved toward her bosom. He grabbed one of her breasts and began to firmly knead it through her bodice, and Anneliese gave Eurydice a licentious grin as he freed it from the fabric to begin tweaking her nipple.

"If you tell me the things I want to hear, you will find I'm a very nice man," continued Cesaire silkily.

Eurydice colored with embarrassment and wanted to look away, but it was as if she were too stunned to move. She watched as he lifted the back of Anneliese's dress and roughly begin to thrust into her, slightly bending her forward at the waist and holding her in place by keeping a firm grip on her breast. The whore was enjoying it, her expression lustful as she made noises of pleasure that made Eurydice's stomach begin to churn. Anneliese was doing it purposely, because she knew it would disturb Eurydice to see and hear it.

"If you don't tell me what I want to hear," said Cesaire as he began to bugger Anneliese, both of them never losing their enthusiasm, "you will find that I can be very…disagreeable."

Eurydice watched as Anneliese began to climax, panting and moaning loudly with an ecstatic expression, and then she watched as Cesaire took the knife from the sheath Anneliese kept on her thigh to cut her throat with it as he reached his own climax. Eurydice watched in horror as the blood began to spray from the severed veins and arteries in her neck, some of it reaching Eurydice quite some distance away to splash warmly against her skin and making her flinch. She could feel her heart thudding in her chest anxiously, and she blinked her eyes quickly to keep herself from crying as she began to breathe in and out quickly through her nose to keep herself from screaming. The euphoric expression on Anneliese's face changed to surprise, and Eurydice could hear her gurgling and hissing. She would never forget that sound.

Cesaire let Anneliese's lifeless body drop to the floor of the chamber, and he bent down to wipe the blade of the knife and his hands on her dress before he adjusted his clothes and walked closer to Eurydice. All the while, he had never lost the pleasant smile he had started with. In that instant, if someone had told Eurydice that the man was crazy, she would have had no trouble believing it. He had to be completely insane.

"So, you be nice to me, and I'll be nice to you, *oui*?" he said cheerfully.

"You just killed her," said Eurydice disbelievingly.

Her speech was slurred because her jaw still ached, and she had a hard time making it work. Anneliese hadn't been in her vision. Now she knew why.

"I did," agreed Cesaire mildly.

"But she was your…friend," said Eurydice dumbly.

Cesaire laughed and shook his head. "Oh, no, no, no," he said blithely. "She was vain and foolish, and she let her decisions be controlled by her…*chat.* Once she got you here, she had served her purpose. But I did let her come one last time, and she died with a smile on her face," he said with a wide grin. "You saw, eh? She did have a big smile on her face." Eurydice looked at him in shock, and Cesaire clapped his hands together once loudly. "But enough about her," he said with a wave of his hand. "I want to talk about *you.*"

"Why are you doing this to me?" asked Eurydice evenly.

"Don't you know?" asked Cesaire in surprise. "I *know* you know," he said mockingly.

"You were in Kiev…in the hall, but I don't know why you've done this," said Eurydice slowly.

Cesaire clicked his tongue and shook his head chidingly as he walked closer. "Now, that is the attitude that will put me into a very bad mood."

"What?" gasped Eurydice confusedly. "I don't even know who you are!"

"Don't you?" he said softly, and Eurydice inhaled sharply and jerked as he lifted the knife to run it along her neck to the tip of one of her breasts. He didn't bear down, but Eurydice could feel an occasional sting as it skipped over her skin and left nicks. "I am Cesaire Dubonnet, in service to his majesty, the Emperor Napoleon, and you are going to tell me everything you know about your husband."

"My husband will come for me, and then he is going to kill you," said Eurydice evenly. "That is what I know."

"Lady Eurydice, I can already see you intend to be difficult, but before I am through, you will *beg* to tell me what you know."

Chapter Thirty Eight

Ellsworth left the theater going south on rue de Richelieu. Knowing what he did, it was obvious he needed to go toward the river. He ran to the end of the street where it met rue de Rivoli, and he stood for a moment as he tried to decide which way he should go. There were catacombs on this side of the river, beyond the Champs Elysées and even more further to the north, but neither of those felt like the directions he needed to go. There weren't as many tunnels and quarries on this side of the river. But he didn't know which direction they might have gone on rue de Rivoli—left or right. The Pont Neuf would be the closer bridge, so he chose left.

He did take the time to ask the guards at the entrances to the palaces along the way if they had seen two women walk by. He was able to give a good description of Eurydice, but he wasn't sure who might have taken her, other than that it was a woman. Ellsworth was heartened when his questioning yielded results. A guard at the Palais Royal was able to tell him that he saw a woman matching Eurydice's description go hurriedly by with another woman only ten to fifteen minutes before. Ellsworth was furious when the guard gave him a description of the woman with Eurydice. Anneliese. It had to be. He could only assume Anneliese had told Eurydice something incredibly disturbing to make his wife go anywhere with her willingly, and it made perfect sense to Ellsworth that the whore would be helping Dubonnet. He thought Eurydice would have realized that as well. Ellsworth could only decide that Anneliese had better hope he never saw her again.

With it confirmed the two women were on foot and going across the river not far ahead of him, Ellsworth began to run. A light snow was falling and traffic was scarce. If he could get close enough, he might be able to find their footprints and track them. If Anneliese got Eurydice below ground without his finding the entrance, it would be difficult—if not impossible—to find them. He tried not to think about that. He was going to find her.

He stopped again when he reached the Rive Gauche. He paced back and forth for a few minutes as he tried to decide which way he should go. The area was so vast, both above ground and below. They could have gone anywhere. He looked around for anyone who might have been in one place for an extended length of time, someone who might have seen the two women and where they had gone. As the snow continued to fall, chances of finding their footprints began to disappear. He pulled out his watch to look at the time. It was nearing one in the morning. One hour. She had been gone for an hour, and he was sure she had been taken below ground by that point.

He decided to continue down rue Dauphine. It was all he could think to do. Eurydice had described the place where she could be found underground, but nothing to tell him the path she had taken to get there or how he would find it. All he knew was that he *would* find it. It was too late for most people to be out, so the chance of finding a witness was unlikely. He had nothing. No clues, and yet he couldn't just stand in one place and wait.

≪ ≫

When Aberdare arrived at the hotel, he went directly to Eurydice and Ellsworth's suite. He asked Dorian to oversee gathering up all the men who wanted to help look for Eurydice and tell them to wait in Aberdare's suite. The duke had Agniezka show him where Eurydice kept her diaries, and then he sat down at the desk, put on his spectacles, and went to the entry in the dream diary Ellsworth had told him that he should see.

He could feel the blood draining from his face as he read, and he rubbed a hand at the back of his neck where the skin had become suddenly tight. When he got to the end, he went back to read it again, trying to ignore the worrisome parts and concentrating on those that might have clues. It was worse than he had thought it would be, and he was furious Ellsworth hadn't told him. He suspected Eurydice was unaware her husband had even known about it.

He left the dream diary open to that entry and set it aside. Then he picked up the diary in Arabic and went to the same date to begin reading. The more he read, the more he realized it wasn't going to help on where he should look for his daughter, but it made him believe it was all the more urgent he find her quickly. He felt as if he had aged ten years, but at least now he did have a better idea of what needed to be done.

He looked back at the section from the dream diary, and then he closed them both and stood to go to his room. He was surprised to find Persephone with the men, dressed in breeches and boots with an impatient look on her face.

"I tried to stop her," said Dorian dryly.

"Psyche and Pandora said I had to help since they can't, and Mum said I could," said Persephone determinedly.

Aberdare sighed. It would be useless to tell her no, and he didn't have time to argue. Aside from that, they were going to need all the help they could get.

"Are any of you familiar with the quarries and catacombs beneath the city?" he asked evenly. He was unsurprised to find no one was. "I have been able to discover that's where Eurydice's been taken, but there are miles of tunnels, *hundreds* of miles of tunnels. So, this is what we're going to do: first, we are going to contact the Inspector General of Quarries for maps. Then, we need to make sure we have lanterns, torches, candles—whatever it takes, and we are going to look for her until we find her."

"But that could take days!" said Persephone in alarm, her eyes round.

"Then we better get started," said Aberdare dryly. "We'll divide into pairs, mark them when we've looked through them so we don't repeat ourselves, and I think it's safe to assume we can ignore the ones frequented by tourists."

"I'll go find the Inspector General," volunteered Dorian.

"I'll see what the hotel can supply for us in the way of light," said Islington. "Hopefully, we won't have to look elsewhere."

"Something else that needs to be kept in mind is that your daughter has become a bit famous, Aberdare," said Lord Stranraer evenly. "I don't know how you would feel about it, but letting the public know might smoke him out."

"It might do that, or it might make him decide to kill her," said Sheerness levelly.

"I'll have to agree with Sheerness," said Aberdare. "We want this to be as discreet as possible." He pulled a piece of paper from his pocket to unfold it and held it up for the rest of the men in the room to see. "This is what the man looks like—dark brown hair, brown eyes, about six feet tall, weighing about fourteen stone. He is French, but he is able to speak many other languages. That's all I know."

≪ ≫

"Tell me what I want to know!" said Cesaire angrily.

Eurydice was tremoring from the pain. Cesaire had put the choke pear into her mouth to stifle her screams when he first began to torture her, but he had eventually removed it and not bothered to put it back yet. He would, though. He had started with a hot poker, burning her along the insides of her thighs in three or four places on each leg, but it had only yielded her genealogical history. He then moved on to a whip, flaying the skin on her back. Eurydice had fainted from the pain, and when he revived her by throwing a bucket of cold water in her face, she would only tell Cesaire that her husband liked cigars and Islay whisky. He had adjusted the position of the frame and sodomized her. She had no more tears after that, and when he put her back upright and went to stand in front of her to see if she would finally give him some useful information, she spat in his face. He ripped the earrings from her ears.

"My husband will come for me, and then he's going to kill you."

Cesaire laughed evilly. "No, he won't! How do you think he's going to find you?" He folded his arms across his chest and smiled amusedly with a shake of his head. "There was a man who came to the catacombs once…alone, not so long ago. It took eleven *years* before he was found! Nothing but cloth and bones, gnawed on by rats, mere feet from a way out. No one heard his cries. Alone in the dark and silence. Your husband will *never* find you."

"My husband will come for me, and then he's going to kill you."

Cesaire put his hand around Eurydice's throat to begin choking her, his expression furious, but he released her suddenly and gave her a pleasant smile that didn't reach his eyes. He pulled out his watch to look at the time, and then he picked up the pear of anguish to force it back into her mouth.

"I think what you need is some time alone to consider things," he said mildly as he turned the key to widen out the leaves of the instrument until Eurydice thought her teeth were going to break. "Some people think better when they're alone."

He put a heavy iron collar around her neck with a bell attached that chimed whenever she moved. He then walked around the chamber, extinguishing the torches in a bucket of water he carried until only one was left. Then he used the water to put out the fire in the brazier. He walked back in front of her with the single torch in his hand.

"I may be back. Then again, maybe I won't. Enjoy your solitude, *ma chere. Au revoir.*"

Eurydice watched him leave, and then she was alone in the dark. She could hear the sound of his gradually fading footsteps on the sand and gravel in the tunnel, and then she was left to the silence. But it wasn't completely silent. She could hear the faint sound of water dripping not far away, but it was oddly muffled, and it was impossible to judge its direction. She found the stillness peaceful and soothing. It meant she was still alive and that Dubonnet was no longer torturing her.

She could feel a slight tickle on her neck where the blood dripped from the jagged tears in her ears to trickle down the sides of it slowly until it reached the collar. Her calves ached from balancing her weight on the balls of her feet, and there was a cramp forming in the left one. Her necklaces were gone, and she didn't know if Cesaire and Anneliese had taken them or if she had lost them. Her back and inner thighs throbbed in time to the beat of her heart from where she had been whipped and burned. Her bottom hurt from his raping her, and something had run down her thigh, but she didn't know if it was blood or semen or both. Her fingers had gone numb from their hanging above her head reducing the circulation to them, but she had noticed at one point that she still wore her wedding ring. She didn't know how long she had been there. It felt like an eternity, and there was still more yet to come.

She had to keep her head upright. Drooping it forward made her jaw hurt. Tilting it backward made it difficult to breathe because of the collar and the pear in her mouth. She was exhausted and wanted to sleep, but her position was too uncomfortable. She closed her eyes and tried to relax, but she couldn't. She didn't know how long Dubonnet would leave her like this, and she shivered as the cold began to seep in. Without the torches and the brazier, the temperature began to drop even further.

Eurydice felt the soft fluttering in her stomach, and she sobbed and whimpered with relief. She had been so frightened. Through everything Cesaire had done to her, she had been afraid she might miscarry. Her vision had not shown her…not even that she was pregnant. She was overjoyed that, for now, her baby was safe, but there was still so much left to endure. Eurydice could bear it all, just as long as her baby survived.

Then she heard a noise that caused the hairs to rise on the back of her neck, a squeaking and scuffling that could only mean one thing. Rats. As with the water dripping, Eurydice was unable to tell what direction the sound came from, but it was loud enough she knew there was more than one, far more. She hoped she would be safe from them on the rack, but it was the smell of her blood and Anneliese's that had attracted them. They had simply been waiting for the light to disappear. The noise came closer, and when she felt something brush against one of her feet, Eurydice screamed.

The snow had stopped an hour or two before, and the sun was rising. Ellsworth had searched all night without any progress. He had gone far away from the Seine, going even further south, without finding any clues. He had even walked through some of the catacombs, but he found nothing but the bones of people long since dead. He was exhausted, but he wasn't going to stop until he found her, even if it meant he went days without sleep.

He made his way back to the Pont Neuf and rue Dauphine. He would look again starting at the beginning. He was hopeful he might find something now that the sun was coming up, something he may have missed in the dark, but he knew any clues that might have been left behind could be lost with people waking and coming out to start their day's business to trample them underfoot. The chimney sweeps and wood sellers were already out, and it would only be a matter of time before the charwomen joined them.

Ellsworth walked slowly, his eyes sweeping the ground as he thought over the things he knew. Eurydice had left the theater with Anneliese on foot, and they were still that way and alone at least until they reached the Left Bank. His wife had been foolish enough to go with Anneliese, but Eurydice didn't trust her. She had probably gone thinking she could get away from the bawd if she needed to, not realizing Anneliese was helping Cesaire, who had meanwhile found a way to keep Ellsworth distracted long enough for Cesaire to get to the Left Bank to abduct Eurydice. Eurydice would have been cold with just her pelisse, and she was not fond of walking long distances, even under the best of conditions. She would have eventually decided they needed a carriage, and at about the same moment, she would have realized that Anneliese had tricked her.

He stopped and looked around himself. He had crossed the Boulevard Saint Germain, at the place where the rue de l'Ancienne Comédie became three—Condé, l'Odéon, and Monsieur le Prince. Then he saw something gold glinting in the early morning sunlight, almost buried in the snow. He picked it up to look at it, and his heart skipped a beat. It was Eurydice's koi necklace. It was the first real thing he had to confirm she had been on this side of the river, in this particular place. He looked around in the snow for anything else that might give him a hint about which direction he needed to go. He had three to choose from. There was nothing else; any signs of a struggle that might have happened and any footprints were covered by the snow. He decided to follow the street to the right—rue de Condé.

He examined the chain on the necklace as he walked. It was intact, the clasp undamaged. That let him know it had not been broken in a struggle, but Eurydice wouldn't have removed it unless it was necessary. He slipped it into the pocket of his coat where he still carried her bank note from the previous night's concert as he continued to look at the ground and think while he walked. She *might* have taken it off, hoping he would find it, but he didn't think she would have been able to without it being noticed unless she broke the chain and let it fall. That hadn't happened. It seemed reasonable to assume she had been incapacitated and was being carried, slung over Dubonnet's shoulder perhaps, with her head hanging upside down. That would have allowed the necklace to fall off and land in the snow unnoticed.

He found himself hoping she had lost the locket as well and that he hadn't missed it, because finding it would give him another clue on which direction they had gone. Knowing the point when she was no longer moving under her own power made it possible to narrow down how far away from the river he needn't bother searching. It might have been late, but not so late there wouldn't have been a few other people out, returning from a play or the opera, possibly a ball or dinner party. If Dubonnet had to carry her too far, it would have risked attracting attention. He wouldn't have wanted that. Ellsworth had to be very close, and finding the locket could possibly put him within a hundred feet or less of the entrance to the catacombs he needed to use to find her.

Of course, that was based on the assumption Dubonnet hadn't carried her only a short distance to a coach in order to take her further away. Ellsworth believed he hadn't, though. If he were going to take her somewhere in a coach, why bother having Anneliese lure her away from the theater and across the river? Why not simply take her in the coach from the very beginning? No, Ellsworth was almost positive it was all done on foot, and he was very close to finding Eurydice. He needed to find the locket.

≪ ≫

Aberdare and his family and friends had been searching the catacombs for much of the day with only brief rests for breakfast and dinner, and there was always someone out looking. They had been joined by a company of fifty gendarmes, sent by order of the comte d'Artois shortly after sunrise. Apparently, the Inspector General of Quarries, vicomte de Thury, was on close terms with Artois, and when the prince learned of what had happened to Eurydice, he wasted no time in providing assistance. With the soldiers helping them search, it was going much quicker, but Thury warned them not all the quarries had been mapped. He also warned them some of the tunnels were unstable and dangerous. Aberdare didn't doubt that, but the maps were better than nothing, and he greatly appreciated the help Artois had sent.

Rather than having everyone return to the Hôtel de Crillon to give a report of what they were finding, Aberdare located a tavern on the Left Bank and commandeered it after paying the owner large sum. Psyche, Pandora, and the duchess were there, keeping a record of the places already searched. By late afternoon, the area covered was growing, starting from the outer reaches and moving inward.

There was still no sign of Eurydice, and Aberdare grew more concerned as the day progressed. She had been gone for nearly eighteen hours as the sun began to set, and he tried not to think about all the things she had endured by that point, understanding as he did how her dreams worked and what he had read. How much more would she have to bear before they found her? Aberdare tried not to think about the fact that in her vision, they didn't find her.

When he went back to the tavern with Stranraer to mark off the section of tunnels they had explored, he asked his wife and daughters if anyone had seen Ellsworth. No one had. He hadn't been seen since he left the theater the previous night. Aberdare knew his son-in-law worked best on his own, but he was concerned. There were still people at the hotel who would be able to tell Ellsworth where to find Aberdare and everyone else should he go there, but no one at the hotel had seen him, either.

The duchess tried to keep her spirits up. All that was humanly possible was being done to find her daughter, but Julia was frantic for her to be found. At one point, Aberdare had taken her aside and told her what he knew, leaving out the worst parts. Luckily, they had been in a room alone, so no one saw her slap him. Then she had told him if Eurydice died, she would never forgive him. She knew she couldn't put all the blame for what was happening on her husband, but she was full of anger and fear, and he was available. Aberdare swore he would find Eurydice.

When Cesaire returned, he splashed Eurydice with a bucket of water to rouse her after he lit the torches and brazier again. He came back with a renewed determination to have her tell him what he wanted to know. He could see the rats had been to visit. Looking at Anneliese's body where it still lay as he had let it fall, she had been obviously gnawed on. Eurydice was for the most part untouched, except for her feet and the lower parts of her legs, which he could see had been bitten and scratched quite a bit. He grinned wickedly when he thought how painful and terrifying that must have been, and he was regretful he hadn't been there to see or hear it. He would have to make sure he left the rack at an angle to make it easier for the rats to get to her if she didn't tell him what he wanted to know before he left.

Before he did anything else, he sodomized her again. It hadn't yielded any results the day before, but it was fun. He could tell no one else had been there, and even if it didn't make her tell him anything, it was demoralizing and degrading...not to mention it hurt like hell. She looked at him dimly when he went to stand in front of her, but she still had a bit of spirit left in her eyes. He would have to see what he could do about changing that. Breaking the spirit was key to getting answers. He wiggled the key on the choke pear before he went to check the fire in the brazier, and he smiled satisfactorily when she moaned at the throbbing it caused in her jaw and teeth. The flames were just about right, and he put the poker in the coals to begin heating.

"Did you have a pleasant night?" he asked blithely as he started to remove the pear from her mouth. "I see you had some guests. I hope they didn't keep you awake too long."

He set the instrument aside on a nearby small table where he kept other tools, including two more pears. All of the items looked far more gruesome than what he had used so far, and Eurydice dreaded he might decide to use them on her. He removed the collar with the bell and put it on the table as well. Then he looked at her with his arms folded across his chest.

"Do you feel like talking now?" he asked evenly.

"My husband will come for me, and he will kill you," she said carefully.

Eurydice was thirsty and hungry, and her mouth didn't want to work properly anymore because of the pear. She had to concentrate to make her jaw move. She had finally fainted from the pain and terror caused by the rats, and she didn't wake until Cesaire had splashed her with the water. She tried not to look at Anneliese on the floor because the sight of her eaten corpse made Eurydice's stomach churn with revulsion. She was thankful she couldn't see her own legs because she was sure they looked no less horrific.

"Why do you persist in saying that when we both know it isn't true?" asked Cesaire tightly.

"He *will* come for me, and he *will* kill you," said Eurydice dully.

"Stop saying that!" barked Cesaire, and he went to the brazier to remove the poker and pressed it against her hip.

Eurydice cried out at the pain, and she thought her heart was going to stop beating. Cesaire put the poker back in the fire, and then he went to stand in front of her again with his fingers tented in front of him.

"Let us establish what we know," he said with a reasoning smile. "We both know your husband is an unprincipled cur and an immoral blackguard. He's also a spy and an assassin. I think you are, too."

"No, I'm not," panted Eurydice weakly. "I am Lady Eurydice Ellsworth, daughter of Alexander Savage, the ninth Duke of Aberdare, and Lady Julia Sanders. My grandparents were Samuel Savage, the eighth Duke of Aberdare, and the Countess Alexa Feodorovna Goydanova, and Rupert Sanders, the third Viscount Glamorgan, and the Contessa Genoveffa Contarini. My great grandparents were—"

Cesaire removed the poker from the fire to burn her other hip, and Eurydice bit at her lower lip until it bled to keep herself from screaming.

"We heard all that yesterday, and I...don't...care!" bit out Cesaire. "Who does your husband work for?"

"My husband doesn't work!" said Eurydice breathlessly. "He is a gentleman, and gentlemen do not *work*."

Cesaire burned the back of her left thigh just above the bend of her knee. "Who does he answer to?" shouted Cesaire.

"My husband answers to no man!" whimpered Eurydice, and she tried to twist away as Cesaire moved the poker toward the back of her other leg, but there was nowhere for her to go. She released a low wail as she heard and felt the hot metal sizzle as it seared her skin.

Cesaire roared with frustration, and he removed the pins from the frame to begin spinning it. Eurydice closed her eyes and gasped at the pain it caused in her wrists and ankles. She no longer had the strength to brace herself and keep it from pulling against the joints, and she whimpered when she felt the bones snap in her right wrist. The pain and vertigo made her vomit the nonexistent contents of her stomach, and she continued to dry heave as she spun end over end. Cesaire brought her to a jolting stop, hanging upside down. Eurydice could feel the blood rushing to her head as she continued to gasp and retch, and her ankles hurt as the weight of her body hung from them.

"How would you like to spend the night like that, eh? In the dark, with the rats?" asked Cesaire evilly. He spun her rightside up and put the pins back in. "That is something to keep in mind, isn't it? I think they would find your eyes to be a very tasty treat. They certainly enjoyed Anneliese's," he chortled.

Eurydice looked at him dully. She was finding it difficult to focus, and she was going to faint soon. Cesaire realized that. He would wait before he did anything else, to give her a brief amount of time to recover, and then it would start again.

≪ ≫

"I'm telling you we've already gone this way," said Persephone irritatedly to Lambeth. "See? There's the mark."

She couldn't understand why her father had paired her with such an imbecile. She loathed Baron Lambeth, and she had pleaded to be put with someone else—repeatedly—throughout the day. Her father wouldn't let her. She was stuck with him, and she had needed to refrain several times from maiming him. He was arrogant and cocksure and would listen to nothing she told him. Not only that, but he had a feeble memory because he couldn't understand why she obviously hated him.

"My apologies, Lady Persephone," he said sarcastically, "but perhaps if you made them larger, I might be able to see them."

"It shouldn't be necessary to draw a mural," she said tartly. "Perhaps you need spectacles."

"You shouldn't even be here," he said as they turned to retrace their steps.

"Don't you dare try to lecture me," warned Persephone.

"What are you going to do? Scream at me some more?" he asked sarcastically.

"You're an idiot," said Persephone flatly as she stopped to wave her torch around the end of a tunnel that wasn't marked yet. It was short with no branches, and she placed a mark to the right of the entrance.

"And you're a spoiled, selfish bitch," said Lambeth in a matching tone.

Persephone swung the torch around and narrowly missed scorching his face with the flames.

"A man like you—who has his nose stuck so far up his own arse—is in no position to make judgments about me," she said arcticly. "And if you call me a bitch one more time, you'll find yourself piled in one of the ossuaries with the rest of the bones down here. Count yourself lucky I haven't done it already."

"Ooh, stop. You're scaring me," mocked Lambeth.

Persephone groaned and walked on, muttering under her breath.

"What have I ever done to make you dislike me so much?" asked Lambeth finally.

Persephone stopped and turned to look at him with shocked disbelief. "You honestly don't remember, do you?"

"Should I?" he asked archly. "I don't even know you really."

Persephone shook her head once slowly, incredulously, and she turned to continue walking. She blinked her eyes several times to fight back her tears, and she rubbed at her nose with the back of her hand. She needed to find her sister, and she needed to get away from Lambeth before she killed him. She thought she could see something ahead of her in the tunnel, and she quickened her step slightly as it began to curve.

"Perhaps if you—" began Lambeth.

Persephone held up her hand and stopped. "Shh!"

"Would you just—"

"Shut up!" hissed Persephone irritatedly.

She couldn't hear anything, but she thought she could see light ahead that wasn't coming from their torches. She pulled her pistol from the holster at her hip and cocked it as she slowly began to walk up the tunnel toward it. Lambeth raised a doubtful eyebrow. They had yet to see anyone else in the tunnels, not even other people searching for Eurydice, because of the way they were going about it. He thought Persephone was a spoiled brat who needed to grow up, and she certainly shouldn't have been allowed to help look for her sister. When the tunnel straightened, Persephone saw someone turn onto it from an off-shooting branch some thirty feet away with a lantern. Lambeth's eyes widened in surprise. Maybe he did need spectacles.

"Friend or foe?" called Persephone firmly.

"Depends on who's asking," said Ellsworth evenly.

Persephone grinned and uncocked her pistol to put it back in the holster. She hurried up the tunnel to meet him.

"Ellsworth! Where have you been?"

"What are you doing down here, Persephone?" asked Ellsworth confusedly. He nodded to Lambeth.

"Well, Dad told us about the crazy man who thinks he's in love with Dicy and how he took her down here, so we're looking for her."

"Oh," said Ellsworth dully. It was as plausible a story as any. "Any luck?"

"Nah. You?"

What kind of luck was he having? Terrible. He had found Eurydice's locket—finally, after spending several hours looking in the wrong places. It had been on one of the narrow streets that passed the side of the Odeon Theater to rue de Vaugirard. That had led him to this set of tunnels near the Palais de Luxembourg, but he hadn't seen or heard anything until he met Persephone and Lambeth.

"Obviously not much at all," he said dryly.

He pulled out his watch to look at it. It was just after nine. In three hours, his wife would have been missing for twenty-four, and he had gone longer than that without food or sleep. He was exhausted and disheartened because he knew when he did find her all the things she had seen, that she had feared, would have happened. He had been unable to stop it.

"We've been that way," said Persephone, pointing over her shoulder with her thumb. "We didn't see anything." Her brother-in-law looked like he was about to collapse. "You should go to the tavern on rue Danton," she said gently. "There's food and a place to rest. You look like you could use it."

"Thank you, but I'm fine," said Ellsworth evenly.

"We're all looking for her," said Persephone softly, "and we're going to find her. Artois even sent fifty gendarmes to help."

That surprised Ellsworth and gave him some hope she would be found soon, but he knew *he* was the one who was going to find her. He also knew he needed to move on, but he had no idea where to go now. When he had found the stairway leading down to this set of tunnels, he had been so sure it would be the ones where he would find Eurydice, and it wasn't.

"If you're already looking here, I think I'll go back topside and see if I can find some others," he said finally.

"We've got to be getting close," said Persephone encouragingly. "There aren't many more. We've been looking since three this morning, and we've covered almost all of them."

"At least the ones we know about," put in Lambeth. Persephone looked at him darkly. She was trying to give Ellsworth some hope.

"Right," said Ellsworth noncommittally. "Well, I'm off," he said finally, and he turned to go.

"We'll find her," called Persephone to his departing back.

"Are we even sure she's down here?" asked Lambeth after the light from Ellsworth's lantern disappeared.

Persephone turned to look at him levelly, and then she gave Lambeth an abrupt blow to his jaw with her right fist.

"You're not just an idiot; you're an arse," she said disgustedly.

≪ ≫

"Are you sure you don't want to tell me? You still have two left," coaxed Cesaire.

"My husband will come for me, and then he's going to kill you," said Eurydice tonelessly.

She had no more strength left. After raping her again, he had placed one of the pears into her anus and widened out the leaves. It was still there. Then he had begun to break her fingers and toes. He had gone through all her toes, and now he was on her right hand. Despite how numb her fingers felt from the cold and lack of circulation, she still felt the pain, and after her answer, he broke another, using his bare hands. Eurydice whimpered and released a low moan.

"Wrong answer," said Cesaire flatly with a dark glare. "Who...does...your husband...work for?" he asked, and he grabbed her by the hair at the back of her head and jerked at it painfully.

"My husband will come for me," she whispered, "and then he's going to kill you."

Cesaire roared angrily and backhanded her. Eurydice heard a ringing in her ear, but what caused her the most pain was when her jaw popped and came out of its socket on that side. Having the pear in her mouth, stretching it so widely for so long, had loosened the ligaments. That one forceful blow was all it had taken to dislocate it. Eurydice could feel that her face was crooked, and she couldn't close her mouth. Not only did it cause her agony when she tried, but it simply wouldn't close. She could feel blood trickling from the corner of her mouth, and she couldn't focus. Cesaire realized what he had done.

"I think I'll go have some supper," he said with a slight smile. "Then, when I return, we'll put that back where it belongs, and you can tell me what I want to know." Eurydice could only imagine how painful that was going to be.

Cesaire didn't put out the torches or the brazier before he left, so she knew he wasn't done and wouldn't be gone long. She didn't know how much longer she could last. She would never tell Cesaire what he wanted to know, and he would continue to torture her until she died unless she did. She didn't know how long she had been there. He said he was going to have supper, but she couldn't be sure he was telling the truth. It could be morning above ground for all she knew. She had completely lost track of time.

Eurydice lifted her head to look at her fingers, and she quickly turned her eyes away when the sight of it made her stomach churn. They were all bent at unnatural angles, except for her index finger and thumb. She imagined when he came back he would break them and move on to her left hand. And then he would do God knew what else. She couldn't remember what was going to happen anymore.

She began to hear the faint sound of music and thought she must surely be hallucinating. It was so quiet, it was easy to believe she was imagining it. But it wasn't a new composition. It wasn't hers. She lifted her head to look at the ceiling of the chamber. Then she could hear voices singing. An opera. That confirmed it wasn't a new composition. She had never heard an opera. When she recognized what it was, she softly began to laugh at the irony, and she knew she had to be hallucinating. It was Gluck's *Orphée et Eurydice.*

≪　≫

Ellsworth climbed the stairs from the catacombs where he had met Persephone and Lambeth and made his way to the street. He adjusted the collar of his coat and his hat against the cold. It was warmer in the tunnels. It had begun to snow again, much heavier than it had the night before, and it fell in large, wet flakes.

He walked up the rue de Vaugirard, going back to the theater where he had found the locket. As he neared it, he could hear the night's performance had begun. When he reached the front of the Odeon, he stopped, listening to the music while he thought of what to do next. Eurydice had to be near. He had found the koi some distance from here, and the locket mere feet around the corner. Eurydice didn't weigh much, but enough that a man wouldn't be able to carry her far, especially if he didn't want to attract attention. There had to be more tunnels somewhere nearby…or at least an entrance to them.

He looked up at the front of the theater, and his eyes widened. He knew that music. He knew that opera, and when he realized what it was, he *knew* he had to be close. The one clue he had almost ignored was ringing in his ears. He looked down at the ground beneath his feet. His wife could be right below him. He just needed to find the way in. He looked around himself, up and down the surface of the street. Other than the tracks of vehicles and footprints, it was undisturbed. He would find it surprising that the stairs would be in the middle of the street.

There were two footmen standing at the top of the steps to the theater, and he went to speak to them. Both of them looked at him hesitantly and shook their heads, but Ellsworth could tell they knew what he was asking after. One of them began to give him directions back to the tunnels he had just left, and he explained he had already been there. Ellsworth offered them each fifty livres, if they would simply tell him where to find the entrance. That got the desired result, and they pointed to the edge of a park across the open space in front of the theater, a mere seventy feet from where Ellsworth had found the locket, telling him that he would find an old, crumbling stone building hidden there just into the trees. The door was locked, but there was a set of stairs inside. Ellsworth thanked them, and he made his way across the street at a fast walk.

When he stepped beneath the trees, it was overgrown with underbrush, but as he lifted the lantern higher, it highlighted slate roof tiles on a very low, small, square building. As he made his way toward it, he spotted footprints, and he knew he had found the right place. The squat building looked like a wellhouse, and the people in the area had probably forgotten what it really was, assuming the well inside was no longer any good.

Unlike Dubonnet, Ellsworth was careful not to leave any prints of his own, stepping into those that were already made, just in case Dubonnet wasn't there and was smart enough to notice such things. Ellsworth had the impression he would be. He found the door, and he was unsurprised to discover it was no longer locked. Cesaire didn't have as much finesse as Ellsworth, because it had simply been broken rather than unlocked. Ellsworth carefully opened the door and looked in.

He didn't know how old the small building was, but it seemed ancient. It was only large enough to contain the stairs, but it might have been bigger a long time ago. He needed to crouch once he was inside because the roof was so low. He closed the door behind him and carefully went down the spiraling stone stairway. When he got to the bottom, there was a path leading forward and one that went to the left. He chose forward. He wasn't sure what direction from the theater the bottom of the stairs placed him, but he was going to start with the assumption he was facing it.

After going only about forty feet, he came to the end of the tunnel, and it continued either left or right. It went on interminably in either direction. He chose right. He could still faintly hear the opera playing, so he believed his assumption about heading toward the building had been correct. A tunnel branched off to the left after about fifty feet, but Ellsworth continued forward. The walls were unfinished, and the ceiling was very low, requiring him to walk stooped to avoid hitting his head. He looked at the sand and gravel on the floor of the tunnel, but he didn't see any footprints. When he had gone another hundred feet or so, the tunnel ended abruptly.

He turned back the way he came and went down the tunnel that branched off. When he looked at the floor, he could see two sets of footprints, one male and one female. The male footprints had come and gone a few times, but those of the female went in and never came out. That could either mean they were Eurydice's, or they belonged to Anneliese, and she could still be there, guarding Eurydice. Ellsworth quickened his pace. The tunnel seemed to go on forever, with no branches. He stopped at one point to shine his lantern back the way he had come, trying to determine how far he had gone. He couldn't.

The tunnel eventually began to curve slightly to the right and straightened, the music from the opera still faintly playing. After about fifty feet, the tunnel ended and split. He followed it to the right, and it curved around sharply before opening into a wide chamber and split again. Ellsworth took the one to the right, since he seemed to be having luck with it, but after the tunnel meandered and turned for a distance, it ended where the ceiling had collapsed…obviously not recently. He made his way back the way he had come and took the other branch, only to find that it, too, ended after only a short distance. He went back to the original split and took the left one.

This part of the tunnel was wider, with little niches carved out here and there where the stone had been quarried. There were also unstable-looking pillars made of remnant stone, unmortared and unfinished. The tunnel curved to the left before opening into a small chamber and then continued on the other side of it. After he went around a place where the tunnel jogged sharply to the right, he could see light coming from somewhere not far ahead.

He slowed his steps as he approached. In this place, the walls were finished stone, if unmortared, and he could see ahead of him where the tunnel continued on, but a chamber had been walled and separated from it. He could see two doorways on one wall, and there might be another a little further down the tunnel. He cautiously approached one of the doorways to look in, and what he saw made his blood run cold.

He set the lantern down once he reached the rack and beheld his wife. She looked wretched, covered in blood and wounds, bones obviously broken. Her head hung forward limply, and Ellsworth couldn't tell if she was breathing or not. He put a gentle hand against her neck, and he jumped when she lifted her head weakly. He felt tears sting his eyes as he looked at her.

"Jesus, Dicy!" he whispered brokenly. "Why didn't you tell him what he wanted to know?" She tried to speak, but all she could do was whimper and mewl. "Oh, God!" he gasped. "Where has he gone?"

Eurydice tried to answer, and the only thing he could determine was that Cesaire wasn't there. Ellsworth rubbed at his nose with the back of his hand and gave her a slight shake of his head.

"It doesn't matter. Let's get you down from there," he said huskily.

He started to unfasten the cuffs at her ankles, and Eurydice began to make sounds of protest and shake her head, her eyes wide. He looked at her with a frown, and she tried to motion with her head and point with the unbroken fingers on her left hand behind her back. What he saw when he went there made him gasp and sob, and his face crumpled with anguish. He could hear Eurydice trying to speak, trying to soothe him, and Ellsworth pushed the heels of his palms against his eyes and inhaled deeply in an effort to regain his composure. He reached out with a shaking hand to turn the screw on the pear and remove it as gently as he could, and then he went back around to look at Eurydice sadly.

"I am so sorry…*so* sorry he did this to you," he whispered.

Eurydice tried to smile, and a tear slipped from the corner of one of her eyes to run down her cheek. Ellsworth was there, and it was over. That was all that mattered. He gently put a hand to her neck and kissed her forehead, and then he cleared his throat and bent down to remove the shackles on her ankles. He carefully helped her move her feet inward so that her weight rested on the frame on her heels to lessen the pressure on her toes, and he could see where the skin on her ankles had been rubbed raw and blistered. He removed his sealskin coat to have it ready to put around her, and then he unfastened her left wrist. When it was free, Eurydice weakly moved her hand to his cheek and rested her forehead against his lovingly, trying to speak.

"I know, I know," he whispered softly. "Can you stand on your own for just a little bit?"

Eurydice nodded waveringly, and Ellsworth reached up to unfasten her right wrist. She moaned at the pain it caused to the broken bones, and she carefully cradled it with her left hand to relieve the agony caused by it simply hanging. Ellsworth quickly wrapped her in his coat and gently lifted her in his arms. Eurydice rested her head against his shoulder and sighed tiredly. Her body was still aching, but she could bear it now that he was there. She managed to work her arm into the left sleeve and put it around his neck.

Ellsworth was faced with a dilemma. He couldn't find his way out of the catacombs without the lantern, but he couldn't carry both it and Eurydice. Her carrying it with her right hand was out of the question. He would have to turn her around. Eurydice caught his attention while he was thinking and pointed to the well.

"You want water?" he asked.

Eurydice nodded. She was so thirsty. She would feel a little better if she could just have some water. She didn't know if she would be able to swallow because of her jaw, but she would try. Ellsworth set her down on the low stone shelf not far from the well and cupped some of the water into his hands for her to drink. He carefully dribbled it into her mouth, and she managed to swallow it with a bit of choking and coughing. Once she decided how to compensate for her dislocated jaw, it was painful, but she was able to swallow a few handfuls. She was willing to suffer a little more because she did feel better once she had some water.

"I'm going to pick you up with your right side against me," said Ellsworth gently. "You'll have to carry the lantern with your left hand so we can see where we're going. Can you manage?" Eurydice nodded, and Ellsworth gave her a slight smile. "That's my girl."

Ellsworth was getting ready to pick her back up in his arms after going to get the lantern when Eurydice's eyes widened in terror at something behind him. He turned to see Dubonnet had returned, coming toward him from one of the entrances.

"I was hoping you'd come back before I left," said Ellsworth with a vicious smile as he began to remove his evening coat and waistcoat.

"That's good, because I was hoping you'd come," said Cesaire with a look that was no less dark, and he removed his coat and waistcoat as well.

Eurydice could feel her heart pounding in her chest anxiously as the two men began to fight. Cesaire wasn't going to be a match for Ellsworth, but he was better prepared than most. She was incapable of stopping it or going for help. As much as she wanted to see Cesaire dead, she wanted this to stop. She needed this to stop.

She watched as they circled each other, neither one of them managing to land a punch. Then Ellsworth drew first blood with a fist to Cesaire's nose. Cesaire wiped at the blood dripping from his nose and spat, and then he grinned evilly as he moved toward Ellsworth.

"Oh, I'm going to enjoy this," said Cesaire silkily.

"Not as much as I am," grated Ellsworth blackly.

He moved in toward Cesaire and landed several punches to the man's midsection before bringing the heel of his hand up powerfully against Cesaire's chin. Cesaire stumbled backward dazedly and spat, revealing that several of his front teeth had been shattered. Cesaire lunged toward Ellsworth, feinting one direction before coming at him from another, and Eurydice stifled a scream when Ellsworth stumbled backward, the left side of his shirt blossoming red with blood from a wound there. Cesaire had pulled a knife at the last moment.

Ellsworth was only momentarily stunned by the attack, and he moved toward Cesaire as if he took no notice of the wound. Cesaire still held the knife in his right hand, and he pulled another to place in his left. That made the fight a little one-sided, but Ellsworth wasn't going to stop. He looked around for something to use, and then he removed the poker from the brazier. It was a little over three feet long, and he put his hands close to the center of it, using it almost like a short staff. When Cesaire came at him again with the knives, Ellsworth was easily able to deflect them, burning Cesaire's right wrist with the hot end, and he used the poker to first hit Cesaire on the side of the head before bringing it downward and using the hot end to burn Cesaire's right leg. The Frenchman yelled with pain from the two burns, blood streaming from the blow to his head, but he was just as determined as Ellsworth to win.

The two men continued to circle each other for several minutes, looking for an opening, and Eurydice watched worriedly as the bloodstain on Ellsworth's shirt grew larger. Cesaire managed to get under his guard and cut Ellsworth's arm, but Ellsworth brought up the hot end of the poker to burn Cesaire's face and part of his scalp. The room was filled with the smell of singed hair and burned flesh, and Cesaire was no longer able to use his right eye. Ellsworth swung the other end of the poker to slam it into Cesaire's side, and he staggered backward when it broke several of his ribs.

Cesaire came at Ellsworth again with a roar of anger, and Ellsworth easily managed to avoid the attack. He brought up the poker and burned the other side of Cesaire's face. He was now blind, but he continued to swing around with his knives, determined not to admit defeat. Ellsworth circled him slowly, and it reminded Eurydice of a cat stalking its prey. He casually reached out with the hot end of the poker occasionally to burn different parts of Cesaire's body as the mood took him, and Eurydice could see the malevolent smile on her husband's face. He was enjoying this. Once Ellsworth had blinded Cesaire, he could have killed him immediately, but he was taking his time, slowly torturing Cesaire in revenge.

Once Ellsworth had burned Cesaire with the poker as many times as he could remember marks on Eurydice, he decided it was time. Cesaire was panting and groaning, still on his feet and swinging his knives, but even he knew it was over. Ellsworth circled behind the blind man and thrust the poker upward through Cesaire's body with all his strength, forcing it up through Cesaire's rectum to his intestines and vital organs. Cesaire collapsed to his knees, making the protruding portion of the poker go even further into his body. Ellsworth grabbed Cesaire's hands from behind, keeping the knives clamped in them, and he forced them upward to make Cesaire cross them over his neck and cut his own throat. As Cesaire gasped and gurgled, Ellsworth put a booted foot to his shoulder and shoved him to the ground.

With Cesaire dead, Eurydice watched worriedly as Ellsworth staggered and stumbled on his feet when he turned to go to her on the shelf. She whimpered and frowned as she put a hand to his cheek when he sat down, and Ellsworth covered it with one of his own and gave her a reassuring smile.

"I'm fine," he panted. "Just…a little…winded." He closed his eyes for a moment, and Eurydice could tell he was having trouble breathing. "I can't carry you now, and we can't stay here," he said softly. "I have to leave you for a few minutes to go get help."

Eurydice's eyes rounded in alarm, and she shook her head vigorously. "No!" she gasped. "Don't go!"

"Shh, don't try to talk," soothed Ellsworth, kissing her forehead. "You'll be safe, and I won't be gone long. The Odeon is just across the street from the stairs. I can get help there."

"No," whimpered Eurydice, shaking her head.

"Dicy, I have to go," said Ellsworth somberly. "We're both going to die if I don't."

He stood up to put his coat and waistcoat on again, and he was very unsteady on his feet. He walked back to her and bent down to carefully kiss her on the lips and smooth a hand over her hair, and then he picked up the lantern after he made sure she was covered with his coat and put his hat on her head.

"I'll be back in a jiffy," he said softly, giving her a reassuring smile.

Eurydice watched him leave, tears streaming down her cheeks, trying to tell him to come back. She carefully lifted her feet from the floor and curled up in a ball on the shelf beneath the coat. Then she began to weep, and despite how much it hurt her jaw, she began to choke out heart-rending sobs because there was nothing else she could do.

≪ ≫

"Dad, do you hear that?" asked Persephone softly as she stopped in the middle of the tunnel.

Persephone and Lambeth had met up with their fathers, along with Islington and Keung, all of them starting from different entrances but apparently exploring the same group of tunnels. Persephone, at least, had a compass among the things she had brought with her, and she looked at it to get her bearings. They were heading almost due east through a large complex of chambers and tunnels when she heard sound coming from somewhere. It seemed familiar, yet somehow not, and it certainly wasn't a sound Persephone would expect to hear in the tunnels beneath Paris. She didn't believe in ghosts.

"Yes, I do," said Aberdare as he tilted his head to listen. "Straight ahead, it sounds like."

The six of them picked up their pace, and while they passed a few off-shooting tunnels and chambers, they all appeared to be full of water. There was a bend in the tunnel they followed, and it eventually ended at a wider tunnel, braced with columns of finished stone.

"Where are we?" asked Islington.

Keung looked at the piece of paper in his hand in the light of the lantern he held in the other hand. "Don't know. Not on the map."

Stranraer looked at his, and so did Lambeth. This section wasn't on their maps either. The six of them stood listening; the sound had become louder. Weeping. A woman weeping, and none of them could ever recall hearing it sound so haunting and mournful.

"I have an idea," said Persephone. She gave her torch to her father. "Wait here. I'll see if I can find any light without ours to obscure it. I shouldn't have to go far, I don't think."

She went to the left for a short distance, but she only went about thirty feet before she turned to go the other way. She went around a sharp curve in the tunnel, nearly running headlong into it, but when the tunnel straightened out, she could see light coming from not too far ahead of her. She drew her pistol and shouted over her shoulder.

"This way!"

Persephone only paused briefly at the entrance to make sure it was safe before she rushed in. She saw the empty rack and the two nearly unidentifiable dead bodies on the floor. While the woman had red hair, it was too red to be Eurydice's, and while the man had dark brown hair, the style of it was wrong (what little of it remained) for it to be Ellsworth. She almost turned around to leave when she saw movement on the shelf on the other side of the chamber.

"Eurydice!" she gasped, and she put her gun away to run to her sister. "Oh, Lord, Dicy, what have they done to you?" she asked sadly. She looked at the doorway. "In here! Hurry!" she yelled. "Dad's here, and Islington, Keung,

Lambeth, and Stranraer. Dad read your diary so we would know how to find you. We'll have you out of here soon," reassured Persephone.

Eurydice tried to speak, but she couldn't form the words. She grabbed at Persephone's arm to get her attention. She quickly began to sign as best she could with her left hand. Persephone frowned.

"Ellsworth was here, but now he's gone. He was injured and went to find help," said Persephone slowly. Eurydice nodded urgently. Aberdare and everyone else arrived. Persephone looked at Eurydice concernedly. "How badly was he injured?" Eurydice signed frantically and sobbed. "Do you know which way he went?"

Eurydice pointed at the doorway everyone else had come through, which was opposite from the one Ellsworth had come in originally. He had gone the wrong way, and Eurydice couldn't tell him. Persephone looked at her father, and then she looked back at Eurydice.

"I'll go look for him," said Persephone soothingly.

She stood up and jerked her head in a nod to Lambeth to let him know he needed to come with her. She would have rathered take someone else, but Keung and Islington needed to stay to take care of Eurydice, and her father would need to be there to translate when Eurydice signed because no one else could understand it. That left Lord Stranraer, and the older man looked as if he could use the rest.

Keung and Islington both went to Eurydice to begin looking at her injuries. Keung didn't have his box of medicines. She needed to be taken back to the hotel. Aberdare had told them she was pregnant, and even with just a cursory glance at her injuries they knew she needed to be tended to immediately. Islington examined her jaw, and he and Keung agreed it was dislocated and not broken, but the longer it was left out of place, the more it would swell, and the harder it would be to put back. It would be very painful, and Islington wanted to ask her a few questions before they attempted it because he was sure it was going to make her faint, and the answers were something he needed.

"Have you had any bleeding or cramping?" he asked her gently. Eurydice thought for a moment and looked to her father to sign something.

"She doesn't think so, but she doesn't know," translated Aberdare. He blanched as Eurydice continued. "There was so much other pain and blood, she can't be sure."

"Are you far enough along yet that you've felt the baby move?" Eurydice nodded. "When was the last time that happened?"

Eurydice signed something again. Aberdare looked at his watch, and then he looked at her. "It's nearly eleven at night...on Wednesday." Eurydice nodded and signed something else. Aberdare looked at Islington. "Not since yesterday," said Aberdare quietly.

Islington and Keung shared a glance. It didn't necessarily mean the worst. Just looking at her, Islington was able to tell she wasn't that far along. She was barely showing. It was unusual to feel the baby move that early, and he was sure it was extremely faint. It was possible she hadn't felt it because of the trauma and stress she had been suffering. He wouldn't know for sure until he got her back to the hotel and examined her properly. He looked at Eurydice seriously and put a gentle hand on her shoulder.

"We need to put your jaw back in its place," he said evenly. "We could wait until we get back to the hotel, but the longer we wait, the worse it will be." Eurydice's eyes widened. "We don't have anything to give you for pain, and I'm not going to lie and tell you that it isn't going to hurt." Eurydice began to sign again.

"She wants to wait until Persephone and Lambeth come back," said Aberdare.

They had been gone for almost twenty minutes. Depending on whether or not they found branching tunnels and how far they had to go before they found Ellsworth, it could be at least that much longer or more before they returned. Neither Keung or Islington thought setting her jaw could wait, not to mention all her other injuries. The longer they waited to tend to them, the more risk increased for infection and having them become something worse.

"This really needs to be done now," said Islington gently. "The swelling has already started."

Eurydice shook her head vigorously and began signing again.

"Just a few more minutes," said Aberdare. He frowned as Eurydice continued to sign, her eyes filling with tears. "It won't be long before she's sure it's finished." He looked at her concernedly. "What do you mean?"

"You'll see," she managed to whisper.

The men shared a glance with each other. Aberdare thought he knew what she meant, but he didn't want to think about it. Seeing her in the condition she was, only being able to imagine what she had been through and finding even that disturbing, Aberdare didn't want her to suffer anymore. Seeing her so battered broke his heart. He was proud of her bravery and strength, but he didn't know how much more she could bear before she broke.

"Surely, we can wait just a few more minutes," he reasoned.

Islington tightened his jaw, but he nodded. "Not long," he said tersely.

Persephone and Lambeth had been gone a little over thirty minutes when they returned. Persephone's eyes sparkled with unshed tears as she looked from her father to her sister, and her mouth worked silently for a moment before she could speak.

"We followed the tunnel all the way to the end—a little over a quarter of a mile," she said dully. "I...he...it...uh," she stammered, and she rubbed a hand over her mouth and cleared her throat. She looked down because she couldn't bear to see the misery in her sister's face. "It ended at a hidden doorway on the quay at the Seine...well, below the quay. We found traces of blood here and there in the tunnel, so we know he went that way. He didn't know where he was...we think." She looked up at Eurydice then, her face crumbling. "He fell through the ice!" gasped Persephone. "We could see where he had been on the embankment and a hole where he went in, but we couldn't find where he came out!" Her shoulders began to shake with silent sobs. "I'm so sorry, Dicy! I tried to find him."

All the color had drained from Eurydice's face, and she felt as if she couldn't breathe. The one thing from the vision she had most hoped wouldn't happen had happened. It had never been fear of what was going to happen to her; it had terrified her because she knew she was going to lose Ellsworth when all was said and done. The reason she had made sure to tell him often that she loved him was because she knew she wouldn't be able to in the end, and she hadn't wanted him to die not knowing. Eurydice took Islington's hand and put it on her jaw to let him know he could set it now. There was nothing more she wanted to hear. There was nothing more that could be said.

Chapter Thirty Nine

It took three days before Islington, Felton, and Keung agreed Eurydice was well enough to travel. It would be much longer than that before she was completely healed, but it took at least that long before they felt confident her going somewhere wouldn't make her worse. Felton had set the bones in her fingers, toes and wrist. Her right hand was wrapped in bandages and splints to keep it immobilized, and she slept with a makeshift frame over her feet to keep the blankets from putting pressure on her toes that might prevent them from mending properly. Agniezka had quickly knitted her a pair of very large woolen socks to wear that didn't cover her toes; otherwise, she would have been completely barefoot, which wouldn't have been good in the middle of winter. Eurydice kept her jaw immobilized with a strap tied around her head, except when she was eating, and for the time being she was only able to drink or to eat foods that were soft and didn't require much chewing. She could speak, but not for long periods or very loudly or emotionally.

They did what they could for the places where she had been branded by the poker, but other than bandaging them and doing what they could to prevent infection and minimize the scarring, there was nothing to be done. Where she had been whipped, Islington stitched closed the deeper wounds with very fine sutures to help them heal. Her back would be permanently scarred, but the careful stitching would hopefully make the scars less disfiguring. Islington had stitched her ears as well, but it would be quite some time before she would be able to wear earrings, and it would require a new set of holes to be pierced. Her bottom would heal from the damage Cesaire had done, and it seemed she was safe from any lasting harm to her bowel or the risk of peritonitis.

The biggest concern had been the state of her pregnancy. Islington had been able to confirm she hadn't miscarried...yet, but there would be no way of determining whether the baby had survived, not until Eurydice felt the little one move. That didn't happen until late Thursday night. Maiyin had plied her with strengthening teas from the moment she had returned to the hotel and been able to drink. Until Eurydice felt that small fluttering, like butterflies brushing against her stomach from inside, she had been despondent to think she had lost both her husband and her baby. She had started crying when it happened, and her mother, who had been sleeping in a chair by Eurydice's bed keeping watch over her, had been concerned something might be wrong.

Agniezka had found Eurydice's necklaces and bank note in the pocket of Ellsworth's coat when she was putting it away with his things. She had put the envelope in the strongbox, but she had taken the jewelry to Eurydice, who insisted on wearing them. She spent hours looking at the miniature, often with silent tears running down her cheeks. Seeing his face only made her miss him more, but she couldn't stop looking.

Someone had removed her wedding ring and placed it on the night table while she was unconscious. When she had realized it was there and she was no longer wearing it, Eurydice had promptly reached for it to put it where it belonged. That was when she saw the inscription inside the simple gold band. She had never taken off her ring once it had been put on during their wedding ceremony, not for bathing, not for performing, and she had never realized the words were there. It read, "I like my choice," in Gaelic. Because of the language, Eurydice knew it had to be something Ellsworth had had inscribed there. Because of the words, she knew he had loved her from the very beginning. It made her weep all over again.

Physically, Eurydice would heal, but emotionally, no one could say for certain. She was suffering from melancholia, understandably, and no one had seen her smile yet. Part of that could be explained by the injury to her jaw, but the sadness in her eyes couldn't be excused by any wound except that to her heart. Annabelle went to visit her a few times, offering Eurydice what comfort she could, having been faced with a somewhat similar situation—minus the trauma, but whenever she left, Annabelle wasn't even sure Eurydice had been listening. Everyone began to grow concerned she had lost the will to live.

It didn't seem anything could help until Cora and Leilah went to visit Eurydice on Friday. Both women were sympathetic, but Cora's compassion was delivered with a bit of compunction. Eurydice had gotten permission from her father to tell Cora what her son had really been doing with the last thirteen years of his life. Eurydice never would have believed she would see it, but Cora had wept. Eurydice hadn't told her to make her feel bad, but the woman deserved to know the truth about Ellsworth. She had wanted to let the woman know she had a son who she could be proud of.

Cora had felt Eurydice deserved to have a bit of the truth returned in kind. On Friday, Cora told her daughter-in-law that she wasn't going to tolerate seeing her mope. Eurydice would have the rest of her life to mourn the loss of her husband; it would be best to spread her grief evenly over the remaining time she had because she would have lots of it. Life wasn't fair, but no one had promised it would be. Cora told Eurydice that one of the reasons she had been so angry with Ellsworth was that she thought he had surrendered to the misery and guilt he felt over William's death, letting life lead him rather than the other way around, and she wasn't going to let Eurydice take that path. She had long ago forgiven him for any imaginary responsibility he bore for William's death, and she had told him so. She thought Gareth had never forgiven himself.

Eurydice spent several hours after their visit lying in bed thinking, staring at the locket and her ring. She didn't know what she wanted to do with the rest of her life, to fill herself with a new purpose for being. Since she was small, she had wanted to go to Vienna. She did that. She had wanted to have her music appreciated, to have her talent seen as something more than a curiosity for the drawing room. She had definitely accomplished that. Once she married Ellsworth, she had wanted to spend the rest of her life with him (after she realized she loved him), to share and do things together, to help him fulfill his dreams the way he had helped her satisfy hers. Now he was gone, and she couldn't. Or could she? Eurydice's expression cleared, and she realized where she needed to go and what she needed to do.

Her parents tried to discourage Eurydice from going, but she wouldn't listen, and a determination settled on her they had never seen before. It wasn't only that she wanted to leave Paris before she was fully healed that worried them. It was where she wanted to go. They didn't want to tell her not to go outright because it seemed to have at least put some spirit back into her, but it was going to be a gargantuan task. Then they found out Psyche and Pandora planned to go with her to help. The Aberdares couldn't decide which was more alarming: that their three pregnant daughters were going to take on the project or that Eurydice had willingly entrusted it to the twins. But what could they do? All three of them were grown women with their own lives, and if their husbands were willing to let Psyche and Pandora under take the journey and the chore, there was little the Aberdares could say. Despite their misgiving, they were actually curious to see what happened.

What the Aberdares found even more shocking was that Eurydice's decision had prompted Cora and Leilah to do something the duke and duchess had never thought they would see. Both of them were moving back to Great Britain...permanently. Neither woman had sworn she would never return, but after twenty-five years for Leilah and fourteen for Cora, the Aberdares had thought it was an unspoken oath. They would both return to Vienna to put their affairs in order and pack their belongings, and they would be to Britain before the beginning of the Season. The Aberdares were beginning to wonder if the insanity were contagious.

Eurydice sat with her back propped against several cushions on the bench in the gazebo, her feet stretched out in front of her with a warm, knitted blanket over her legs. She was a little cool, but the noise of construction was barely discernible in her place of solitude. She was craving the peace, and she was willing to tolerate being cold to have it. She could watch the waterfowl swimming across the surface of the lake or walking along its bank a little further down the hill from the gazebo, and she could look over her shoulder through the ogeed window in the lattice up the hill to the castle and see what was happening there. Besides, it wasn't as if anyone or anything needed her immediate attention. After all this time, things were moving along quite well without her input.

Eurydice and her sisters and their families had arrived at Ellsworth Park in Scotland almost two months before. They had begun making plans on the *Medea* from the moment it had set sail from Rouen. Some things had needed to wait until they arrived and saw the full extent of the damage done to the castle, but Eurydice had given her sisters a list of items she definitely wanted to have and those she didn't. As long as those things were done, they could do whatever they wanted. Her sisters thought Christmas had come again, and Sheerness and Islington had looked at Eurydice as if she were crazy to willingly give their wives free rein.

The destruction of the castle caused by the fire had been almost complete. Other than one wing, most of it was little more than the stone walls, but the stone and masonry were sound despite nearly a decade of neglect. Psyche and Pandora felt that would only make restoration easier. There would be no walls or floors in the way to interfere with the laying of pipes for running water and sewage. The furnishings that hadn't been destroyed in the fire had been taken to a warehouse in nearby Neilston, and Psyche and Sheerness had both went through the things to decide which items would still be useful and what would need to be purchased. Maiyin and Keung had both accompanied Pandora, and Eurydice had enlisted Keung's assistance in restoring and planning the gardens and fountains around the castle. She again gave him a few specific things she wanted, but otherwise left him to his own devices.

In addition to restoring the castle, Eurydice arranged to have three small houses built at different places on the estate—one for Cora, one for Leilah, and one for Agniezka's father. Leilah and Cora had both requested their houses be located with a view of the water, while Gennadiy had wanted his with a surrounding of forest, if possible. There wasn't much woodland on the estate anymore, but a place was located not far from the castle. They were all completed, and the occupants had settled in only a week or two before.

Construction on the castle was ongoing, but it would be finished before the end of April. The undamaged wing had been habitable (if uncomfortable) when they arrived, and that was where the family had stayed until enough construction had been completed to increase the amount of livable space. All that remained was the refurbishment of the undamaged wing. Eurydice had wanted the project to be finished before the beginning of the Season to allow for everyone to go to London. It wouldn't be done quite on time, but remarkably close. Eurydice had told her sisters to hire as many workers as necessary to make it possible. They had employed four hundred men at the height of construction. The current number was one hundred.

The expense of all the construction was paid for with some of the money Eurydice had made from touring Europe. It had been an astounding amount. Her family was flabbergasted, but not nearly as much as Eurydice herself. She had entrusted the task of overseeing the funds to Dorian and her father. When they told her how much it amounted to, Eurydice had felt nauseous. She wondered if Ellsworth had known how much she had been carrying in her little strongbox. She would have had trouble sleeping at night if she had known.

Agniezka and Felton were married at the beginning of March, shortly after her father arrived from Russia. They had two ceremonies—one Anglican, one Orthodox. They wanted to make sure there was no question about the validity of their marital state. It hadn't been easy to find a Russian Orthodox priest, but they were able to locate one at the Russian embassy in London. He had been shocked by Agniezka's obviously pregnant belly, but he had no misgivings about seeing them wed and thought it was happening not a moment too soon. Gennadiy liked his new son-in-law, appreciating the doctor's kindness and intelligence, but especially the gentleness and respect he showed to Agniezka.

As Agniezka had gotten further along in her pregnancy, Eurydice had arranged for another lady's maid. She had asked Cora to find out if Ottilie, one of the upstairs Annas, would be interested in the position. Eurydice had been pleased to find out she was. The maid had always been friendly and helpful, and Eurydice had suspected the girl would be good as a lady's maid. As a matter of fact, Eurydice was startled when Cora brought several of her servants with her from Vienna—Edith, Frau Geiger, and Etzel all came with her, as well as her cook, who Eurydice learned was named Frau Stentzel. Nanny Rigsby, of course, came as well to care for the Windhams. What also pleased Eurydice was that Leilah had brought Frau Kouts.

The hiring of servants to care for the castle and grounds had been a difficult chore for Eurydice. For that task, she had enlisted the help of her parents. She hadn't realized how many she would need. The only thing she knew for certain was that she wanted to manage them the way her parents managed the servants at Wilderland. Once she hired them, she didn't want them leaving her employment every few months for other positions because of some dissatisfaction over their position with her. It was going to be hard enough to learn all their names the first time around; Eurydice didn't want to constantly be doing that. She had steadily filled all the positions and learned all their names (with help from Psyche), and the arrangement was going to work quite well for them and Eurydice.

Her parents had arranged to import a cook from Venice for Eurydice after Psyche mentioned how much she had enjoyed the food while they stayed at the palazzo. Her name was Francesca Vidal, and she happened to be Donatella's sister. She was very accomplished in the kitchen, just like her sibling, and she was quickly learning to make all of Eurydice's favorite dishes, whether they were Italian or not. Eurydice was overjoyed. She had pizza at least once a week, and there were always fruit-stuffed pastries at breakfast.

Eurydice read the book balanced on top of her stomach, held in place with her left hand while she absently twirled a set of small metal balls, about the size of plums, in her right. Keung had told her they were *baoding* balls, and as they spun around each other on her palm, propeled by her fingers, they made a soothing chiming noise. Keung had given them to her to help her restore the dexterity of her fingers after the bones had healed. When she had first started using them, it had been painful and difficult. Now she used them as much for the exercise as she did for the meditative, relaxing sounds they made. Besides that, the baby seemed to like it.

Her belly was steadily growing. She had no difficulty telling when the baby was moving anymore. Just the day before, she had watched in amazement as one body part or another had moved in a steady arc across her stomach beneath the skin, just below her navel. It had been an odd sensation, and fascinating to watch, and she had found herself wondering whether she would have a boy or a girl. She hoped, for Ellsworth, that she would have a boy—the son he had wished for, but she would love their baby regardless of its sex.

Despite how hard her family had tried to keep what had happened to Eurydice from becoming public knowledge, there were too many people who had known about it over whom they had no control. The tale had been repeated everywhere that Dubonnet had been insane and had abducted her because of some delusional love for her. The "popular" theory was that Schellen had been murdered as a rival for her affections, Anneliese because of her resemblance. The reason for Merletto's death was still uncertain, but it was thought Dubonnet had murdered him because the Venetian had discovered what he intended to do and tried to stop him. In the end, Ellsworth had died saving her from a madman. That was the only part of the story that had been accurate.

The truth was that Dubonnet had wanted revenge against Ellsworth because Ellsworth had assassinated Dubonnet's half-brother, Captain Charles Marie LeMaire of the French Imperial Army. That was why Cesaire's name had sounded familiar to Aberdare; it had been in the information gathered about LeMaire. It was true Dubonnet had worked as a spy for Napoleon, but his plan of retribution for Ellsworth had been purely personal. His intention had been to get rid of Ellsworth and the man responsible for giving him the order to assassinate LeMaire, as well as anyone else who had been involved in the decision. That he had murdered several innocent people in the process meant nothing to him. That Ellsworth had died a servant of the Crown was something very few people knew.

The false story had circulated across the continent, and even to Britain, only increasing Eurydice's notoriety. It had cast her as a romantic, tragic figure, giving her a history that seemed only entirely suitable to a beautiful, talented, female composer of noble birth. Eurydice had never wanted to be famous, and now it seemed she had become infamous. She had found it necessary to hire guards to patrol the boundaries of the estate to keep out the curious and downright intrusive. Even after two months, there were at least one or two every week. That she had lost her husband and was in mourning meant nothing to them. That she had only recently recovered from nearly being killed was inconsequential. It was frustrating and infuriating.

Eurydice marked her place in the book and set it aside with a yawn. She smoothed her hand over her stomach with a slight smile, and then she put the *baoding* balls into their small storage box. She adjusted the cushions on the bench and settled herself into them comfortably before pulling the blanket up around her. She would take a short nap before she went back to the castle for dinner. Perhaps she would go to Leilah's instead. Frau Kouts made the best dishes with bratwurst and pasta, and Eurydice thought that would be just wonderful for dinner…unless Francesca had made pizza.

≪ ≫

"Sir, I'll have ta ask ye ta leave now," said Haimish Padgorny evenly.

"No, I'm afraid not."

"Sir, if ye don't leave, I'll have ta use this," said Padgorny, removing his pistol from its holster and cocking it before aiming it at the stranger mounted on the bay gelding at the gate to Ellsworth Park with a steady hand.

"I have traveled more miles than you can possibly imagine to get here, and this is my home. I'm telling you, I am *not* leaving."

"Sir, I know everyone who lives here. This is *not* yer home. Move along," said Padgorny firmly.

"The hell this isn't my home! I was born here!" he shouted furiously.

The volume of his voice made his horse sidle skittishly, and he reached down to pat its neck as he continued to look at the man in front of him darkly.

"Do ye have no pity? Th' woman just lost her husband, an' ye sick people canna gie her a moment ta grieve in peace."

"*I* am her husband," said Ellsworth tightly.

Padgorny shook his head and looked at Ellsworth disgustedly. "I sud shoot ye where ye sit for that."

"If you won't let me go to my wife, then take me to someone else," said Ellsworth patiently, taking a deep, calming breath. "Who's here? Bardsey? Sheerness? Felton? Any of them will tell you exactly who I am." Padgorny didn't budge. "What about my mother or Leilah Mahone?"

The guards who normally stood at the gate looked at Padgorny with awe. They knew he had been hired away from Holyrood, and they found his resolve impressive. That was why one of them had gone to the castle to get Padgorny when the man had shown up. Padgorny normally stayed within the sound of Lady Eurydice's voice at all times, but when the man came to the gate claiming to be her husband, they thought Padgorny should come see. No one had ever tried to gain entrance to the estate with that tale before.

"I don't have anything to prove who I am," said Ellsworth tiredly, "absolutely nothing." He lifted his left hand and wiggled his ring finger. "I have my wedding ring." He pulled it off to look inside the band. "I don't imagine you've seen it, but hers is inscribed the same as mine with ' *'S toigh leam mo roghainn.*'" He put the ring back on his finger, and then he removed his cravat and unfastened the top of his shirt. "She gave me this for Christmas," he said as he lifted the jade pendant on its leather thong. "I gave her one made of gold that actually moves. She was always wearing it…would never take it off unless she was in the tub. We both loved those damned fish." The slight smile he had faded. "It's how I found her. She lost it, and I found it lying in the snow."

Padgorny looked at him suspiciously. He had seen the necklace the stranger was talking about. She still always wore it. Padgorny had never seen her without it since he had been hired by the marquess and his wife to protect her at the middle of February. Padgorny still wasn't sure the man was who he claimed to be. To his knowledge, Lady Eurydice's husband was dead, and if this was he, where had he been for the last two months? Padgorny decided he would let someone who had actually met her husband make the decision because he couldn't decide if the man was telling the truth or not. There had been several odd folk who had tried to get onto the grounds, some of them with some very interesting, outlandish tales, but none of them had been quite as believable as this man. He holstered his pistol and went to mount his horse.

"Ye're ta stay wi' me at all times. Ye leave th' drive, I'll shoot ye. Do ye ken?" he asked firmly.

"Absolutely," said Ellsworth evenly.

Islington could stand it no longer. There were entirely too many pregnant women surrounding him, their emotions growing proportionally to the size of their bellies. He needed some peace. He would go to the lake for a spot of fishing. He asked Sheerness, Stockbridge, and Felton if they would like to come. The three men positively fell over themselves for the opportunity. He wasn't the only man craving the relaxation of manly company and manly pursuits. Pandora told him to take Alex and Myron with him, and Islington willingly said he would without hesitation. They were men, too, and it was his duty as their father to rescue them.

Sheerness had never thought it would happen, but he was looking forward to the opening of Parliament. He adored his wife, and she had never looked lovelier, but the emotional swings she was having were positively nerve-racking. He didn't know what to say, so he tried not to say anything at all. Lately, no matter the question, he always seemed to give the wrong answer. He wasn't sure how much longer he could bear it. Everything would go back to normal once Psyche had the baby, if he could just survive a little longer.

They located a sufficient amount of fishing tackle, and the four men and two toddlers went across the courtyard to the gate. They had only gone a few steps down the gravel drive, preparing to leave it and walk across the lawn to the lake, when they saw Padgorny approaching with another man on a horse. Islington frowned, knowing it was the Scotsman's job to stay with Eurydice. As they came even closer, when he recognized who the other man was, his eyes widened in shock.

"Bloody hell!" he gasped.

"Da said bad word," giggled Alex. "Bloody, bloody," he repeated.

"This'un's been tellin' me he's a dead man," said Padgorny mildly after he dismounted in front of Islington.

"He'd be telling the truth, then," said Islington as he looked at Ellsworth.

His brother-in-law looked tired and roadworn but far from dead. Ellsworth dismounted, and a stablehand soon came to take the reins from both horses to lead them to the stables.

"I am going to be interested in hearing what happened," said Islington wonderingly as he shook Ellsworth's hand, "but I think there's someone else who might be even more interested."

"Is she inside?" asked Ellsworth, preparing to make his way to the courtyard.

"Oh, no," said Islington dully. "You don't want to go in there. I would advise you to turn around and leave while you still had the chance, but Dicy would kill me." Ellsworth frowned, and Islington waved a dismissive hand through the air and gave a slight shake of his head. "She's probably down at the gazebo. Haimish can show you. We're going fishing. We might be back."

Islington took his sons' hands and began to lead them across the lawn toward the lake with the other three men following behind after they all shook hands with Ellsworth and welcomed him back. Ellsworth frowned as it looked like they were *fleeing* from the castle. He could see the courtyard from where he stood with Padgorny, and he frowned even more. It looked nothing like he remembered it, but he liked it. Padgorny was looking at him expectantly and held out his hand.

"I'm Haimish Padgorny, by the way," he said good-naturedly.

Ellsworth took his hand. "Gareth Ellsworth," he said calmly.

Padgorny waved his hand in another direction across the lawn that would take them to another part of the lake where it went around the back side of the castle, curving around the knoll where it was situated in the shape of a horseshoe. Ellsworth began to walk with Padgorny, but he kept looking back occasionally over his shoulder at the castle and around himself with a puzzled frown. If he hadn't seen the castle burned mostly to the ground after his brother died, he wouldn't have believed it was the same place. All of the windows gleamed with glass. The lawn was mowed, if brown from the coldness of the weather, and he could see where the flowerbeds were planted. There were even a few new ones, and he was fairly sure he was looking at a greenhouse or something of that nature not far away. The castle had been completely rebuilt...and enhanced, it seemed.

"I'm sorry I didn't believe ye," said Padgorny evenly as they walked.

"No harm done," said Ellsworth. "You're very dedicated."

"Oh, aye," said Padgorny with a nod. "I was a constable at Holyrood before th' marquess an' his leddy asked me ta come here ta keep an eye on their sister. Too many people arriving from nowhere, not giving her a moment's peace. It's disgraceful." He stopped a short way down the hill and pointed to the gazebo, which was also new. "Ye'll find her there," said Padgorny calmly.

"Thank you," said Ellsworth, and he held out his hand to shake Padgorny's again. "And thank you for protecting her."

"My pleasure," said Padgorny with an amused smile.

Ellsworth walked down the hill to the gazebo. It had been planted around with climbing roses that would eventually cover it, but the weather was unseasonably cold, and the plants remained dormant. It gave a picturesque view of the lake, and when he paused to look up the hill to the castle before he went around the side of it to the doorway, he could see it gave a nice view in that direction as well. Its location had been perfectly chosen. He would have several questions for his wife before the day was over.

When he stepped into the gazebo, he could see her curled up on one of the benches sound asleep. She looked as beautiful as ever, just as fragile as ever, and he had missed her so much. There had been a time or two when he had thought he would never see her again. Ellsworth squatted on the floor in front of her and watched her sleep for several minutes. Then he reached out to brush a gentle finger down her cheek and kissed her forehead. When he settled back on his haunches to look at her again, her eyes were open.

"I miss you so much," she whispered sadly.

"I'm here," he said softly.

"But you went away," said Eurydice brokenly. "You're not real."

Ellsworth reached out to put a hand on her cheek. "Yes, I am."

Eurydice's expression changed to one of terror, and she screamed loudly and punched him in the nose before she tried to scrabble away from him on the bench. Ellsworth wiped at the blood coming from his nose, and he tried to put his arms around her to calm her.

"Get away from me! You demon!" she wailed.

"Dicy, Dicy, it's me," said Ellsworth patiently.

He managed to get a grip on the upper part of her arms to keep her from hitting him again, and he sat down beside her on the bench. Perhaps he hadn't gone about that the right way. He did suppose after he had been gone for two months, after being told he was dead, seeing him there alive and well would be a terrible shock. He turned his head to look over his shoulder when he heard footsteps approaching quickly. It was Padgorny.

"Is everything all right?" he asked, looking from one to the other of them.

Padgorny could see Eurydice's panicked expression and the way Ellsworth was holding her, and even if the man was her husband, Padgorny would have no trouble taking care of him if necessary. He was hired to protect her.

"You see him, too?" asked Eurydice breathlessly.

"O' course I do," said Padgorny with a slight smile. "Are ye all right?"

"What? Yes, yes, I'm fine," said Eurydice distractedly, looking at her husband with a stunned expression.

Padgorny nodded, and he turned to leave them alone. Ellsworth turned to look at Eurydice again when he'd gone, and Eurydice lifted shaking hands to run them over Ellsworth's face.

"It's you," she gasped in astonishment. "It's really you!"

"Yes, it's me," said Ellsworth with gentle amusement, and he leaned forward to give her a soft kiss on the lips.

"I thought you were dead! You fell through the ice, and Persy couldn't find you." Eurydice looked at him sternly. "Where have you been?" she demanded.

"Obviously, I went the wrong way and fell through the ice, but I *did* get out. Not long after, I suppose, a priest was walking along the quay, looking for people without shelter to offer them a place out of the weather. He found me and took me to the Hôtel Dieu on the *Île de la Cité*. I was in no condition to tell them who I was, where you were, or that I don't react well to opium. I developed an infection in my lungs from my wound and my swim in the Seine, and they gave me laudanum. That started a coma vigil…before they gave me even more laudanum, which put me into a full-blown coma. They would have killed me with kindness if Dr. Dupuytren, the head surgeon, hadn't intervened.

"I was in a coma for two weeks, and it took another three before I was well enough to leave the hospital. I went to the hotel to find, of course, that no one was there. Then I went to Vienna, thinking that was where I would find you. Imagine my surprise when I got to Palais Crantzdorf to find that not only were *you* not there, but my entire family was gone. Even Leilah had fled to parts unknown. The only place I could think to go after that was Wilderland, and your father told me where I could find you." He looked at Eurydice dimly. "Your mother is pregnant."

"Yes, I know. Islington went to confirm it for her at the end of last month. I had thought that was just a dream, seeing her with a belly." She grimaced. "It's very strange."

She looked at him uncertainly, and then she put her hands to his cheeks and leaned forward to kiss him softly before resting her forehead against his. She had wondered why she kept having the Dark Dream, even after it had happened. She had thought it was just a nightmare. Now she realized it was because she hadn't seen the end of it. She had never seen the end of it.

"So, you've been busy," said Ellsworth evenly, his lips twitching.

Eurydice colored and gave a slight shrug. "After I thought you had died, I couldn't decide what to do. You had been there to help me realize my dreams, and rebuilding this place was the one thing I knew you had wanted."

"I like the courtyard."

"There are koi in the fountain, did you see?"

"No, I didn't make it that far. Islington was fleeing from the castle with the rest of the men and advised me not to go in."

"My sisters have become a bit...*emotional* as they've gotten bigger, what with overseeing the construction...and getting bigger. Then Agniezka and Chrissoula are that way, too." Eurydice shrugged with raised eyebrows. "Even I need to escape from them occasionally."

Ellsworth pulled her toward him to kiss her warmly. "I missed you," he sighed. He looked at her searchingly. "And you're well now?"

"I'm well," assured Eurydice. "Now that you're here, I am even better." She smiled and brushed her fingers across his cheek. "I have a surprise."

"Another one?" he blurted with raised eyebrows.

Eurydice smiled amusedly and took one of his hands to place it on her stomach. It hadn't been obvious when she was sitting, and Ellsworth had been distracted by other things. His eyes widened in realization, and he looked at his hand in amazement when he felt the baby push against it, almost as if trying to shove it away. Then he looked at Eurydice with a frown.

"It happened at Halloween," she said softly. "My illness? Pregnancy sickness. I didn't know until Dr. Herzen examined me in Kiev."

"Why didn't you tell me?"

"You already had Schellen following me everywhere I went. I knew you would never let me go anywhere if you knew, or you would try to make me go back to Vienna. Then there was so much you were already dealing with, I didn't want to add to that." She shrugged. "I was trying to be as undemanding as possible. When I saw what I thought was the end of my dream, I didn't want to tell you because of what would happen to you."

"But I didn't die," said Ellsworth gently.

"I never saw you come out of the water," said Eurydice sadly. "Everything happened exactly as I saw that it would."

"Yes, it did," agreed Ellsworth.

Eurydice looked at him suspiciously. "You read my dream diary, didn't you?" she asked knowingly.

"A few times," he said with a slight nod and a sheepish grin. "The first time was on the *Medea.*" Eurydice's eyes widened in surprise. "I thought you were carrying on with Felton—or someone else—when we were on the ship. When I saw the diary, I thought it would tell me with whom, and then I read the entry about your brother and realized it wasn't that kind of diary. Then I read it once in Vienna and once in Paris because I wanted to know what you had seen that had frightened you and why you didn't want to tell me. I didn't have Schellen begin to follow you until I read it in Vienna."

"It was never about me," she said quietly. "I didn't like what I would have to go through, but knowing I would lose you was the worst part of it."

"I'm sorry you had to go through that, and I'm sorry you had to see that. I'm sorry you have to see things like that at all," said Ellsworth sympathetically. "When...will you...?"

"July…late July," said Eurydice as she put her hand over his on her stomach.

Ellsworth wrapped his arms around her and pulled her against him with her back resting against his chest. He kept his hands on her belly and cuddled against her, resting his cheek against hers contentedly.

"I don't suppose you know what you're having," he said softly after a few minutes.

"No, but I'm hoping it will be a boy."

Ellsworth kissed her neck and rubbed her stomach. "I'm hoping it will be a girl just like her mother."

Eurydice leaned her head sideways to look at him in surprise. "I thought you wanted an heir."

Ellsworth shrugged and smiled. "Eventually."

"Hmm," said Eurydice thoughtfully. She turned in his arms and kissed him soundly. "I suppose we'll have to go to London for the Season now that you're alive."

"I can pretend to be dead for a little while longer if you'd like," said Ellsworth amusedly.

"Don't you dare," warned Eurydice.

Author's Afterword

As with the previous two novels, there are lots of unusual things that happen. I suppose there is nothing stranger than Eurydice's presentient dreaming. Before you say there is no such thing, let me say that—no disrespect to you—I believe there is. For several years, I teetered on the edge between believing in psychic ability and thinking it was just a lot of hooey. There's nothing like a firsthand experience to alter one's perspective. No, I'm not going to tell you what happened. Do I believe everyone who claims to be psychic is? Not for a minute. Call me kooky if you like—you wouldn't be the first. If you don't want to believe in it, that's your prerogative. Anyway....

There were lots of actual, historic figures making appearances in this novel—some well-known, some not. I tried to portray them in a manner I felt was true to things I had read about them. Some had "cameo" roles, while others had pivotal importance to the plot. I could have made up every character, but I felt using real people when possible lended itself better to the story. I hope you agree.

This time period in European history was not a very good one for a musician wanting to take a tour. The Napoleonic Wars had just ended, and there was a dearth of public theaters and performance halls. Many of the theaters familiar today hadn't been built yet. If this novel had been set about ten years later.... It would have made things easier for me if they had been there, but I think their absence made things more interesting in the long run.

What else is there? The catacombs of Paris? The section I mention is no longer accessible. It is shown on earlier survey maps, but by the beginning of the twentieth century, it does not appear. I should say there was not a portion that led all the way to the river, as far as I know. I'm sure most people already know there are indeed hundreds of miles of tunnels beneath Paris, and it would be very easy to become lost without a map. That's why most of them are blocked off from public access, and there is a police force tasked specifically with keeping people out.

I am sure there is more that has you scratching your head, but I think I'll leave things where they stand. Regardless, I hope you enjoyed it, and I hope you will join me for the next one.

Emyll O'Bryan
September 9, 2009

About the Author

Emyll O'Bryan lives in a small, gray box on the edge of nowhere with an onion and a cat (there used to be more...so many more). She would say the middle of nowhere, but she knows someone who lives there. It's close but not quite within rock-throwing distance. She had dreams of becoming a member of a big-hair 80s band in her teens; started on an anthropology degree with ambitions of becoming an archeologist in her twenties; and decided in her thirties that she should just stick with what she knew: telling stories. She enjoys history (although anything after 1865 is current events to her), languages (both real and imaginary), cooking (mostly Italian and Greek...with a soupçon of Oriental and TexMex), watching movies (a *good* sci-fi horror adventure), singing in the shower (it provides its own special auto-tune), and sleeping (*lots* of sleeping). Not necessarily in that order. She also finds it very peculiar to be referring to herself in the third person as she writes this but feels it would be bucking the system and just the least bit vain to do otherwise.